I0785113

Emma Orczy

The Scarlet Pimpernel & The First Sir Percy

OK Publishing 2021

Emma Orczy

The Scarlet Pimpernel & The First Sir Percy

Historical Action-Adventure Novels

Published by

MUSAICUM
Books

- Advanced Digital Solutions & High-Quality book Formatting -

musaicumbooks@okpublishing.info

2021 OK Publishing

ISBN 978-80-272-7869-5

Contents

The First Sir Percy

Chapter I – A Night on the Veluwe

1

A MOONLESS night upon the sandy waste – the sky a canopy of stars, twinkling with super-radiance through the frosty atmosphere; the gently undulating ground like a billowy sea of silence and desolation, with scarce a stain upon the smooth surface of the snow; the mantle of night enveloping every landmark upon the horizon beyond the hills in folds of deep, dark indigo, levelling every chance hillock and clump of rough shrub or grass, obliterating road and wayside ditch, which in the broad light of day would have marred the perfect evenness of the wintry pall.

It was a bitterly cold night of mid-March in that cruel winter of 1624, which lent so efficient a hand to the ghouls of war and of disease in taking toll of human lives.

Not a sound broke the hushed majesty of this forgotten corner of God's earth, save perhaps at intervals the distant, melancholy call of the curlew, or from time to time the sigh of a straying breeze, which came lingering and plaintive from across the Zuyder Zee. Then for awhile countless particles of snow, fanned by unseen breaths, would arise from their rest, whirl and dance a mad fandango in the air, gyrate and skip in a glistening whirlpool lit by mysterious rays of steel-blue light, and then sink back again, like tired butterflies, to sleep once more upon the illimitable bosom of the wild. After which Silence and Lifelessness would resume their ghostlike sway.

To right and left, and north and south, not half a dozen leagues away, humanity teemed and fought, toiled and suffered, unfurled the banner of Liberty, laid down life and wealth in the cause of Freedom, conquered and was down-trodden and conquered again; men died that their children might live, women wept and lovers sighed. But here, beneath that canopy dotted with myriads of glittering worlds, intransmutable and sempiternal, the cries of battle and quarrels of men, the wail of widows and the laughter of children appeared futile and remote.

2

But to an eye trained to the dreary monotony of winter upon the Veluwe, there were a few faint indications of the tracks, which here and there intersect the arid waste and link up the hamlets and cities which lie along its boundaries. There were lines – mere shadows upon the even sheet of snow – and tiny white hillocks that suggested a bordering of rough scrub along the edges of the roads.

That same trained eye could then proceed to trace those shadowy lines along their erratic way 'twixt Amersfoort and the Neder Rhyn, or else from Barneveld as far as Apeldoorn, or yet again 'twixt Utrecht and Ede, and thence as far as the Ijssel, from the further shores of which the armies of the Archduchess, under the command of Count Henri de Berg, were even then threatening Gelderland.

It was upon this last, scarcely visible track that a horse and rider came slowly ambling along in the small hours of the morning, on this bitterly cold night in March. The rider had much ado to keep a tight hold on the reins with one hand, whilst striving to keep his mantle closely fastened round his shoulders with the other.

The horse, only half-trusting his master, suspicious and with nerves a-quiver, ready to shy and swerve at every shadow that loomed out of the darkness, or at every unexpected sound that disturbed the silence of the night, would more than once have thrown his rider but for the latter's firm hand upon the curb.

The rider's keen eyes were searching the gloom around him. From time to time a forcible ejaculation, indicative of impatience or anxiety, escaped his lips, numb with cold, and with unconsidered vehemence he would dig his spurs into his horse's flanks, with the result that a fierce and prolonged struggle 'twixt man and beast would ensue, and, until the quivering animal was brought back to comparative quietude again, much time was spent in curses and recriminations.

Anon the rider pulled up sharply at the top of the rising ground, looked round and about him, muttered a few more emphatic 'Dondersteens' and 'verdommts.'

Then he veered his mount right round and started to go back down hill again – still at foot-pace – spied a side-track on his right, turned to follow it for a while, came to a halt again, and flung his head back in a futile endeavor to study the stars, about which he knew nothing.

Then he shook his head dolefully; the time had gone by for cursing – praying would have been more useful, had he known how to set about it – for in truth he had lost his way upon this arid waste, and the only prospect before him was that of spending the night in the saddle, vainly trying by persistent movement to keep the frost out of his limbs.

For the nonce, he had no idea in which direction lay Amersfoort, which happened to be his objective. Apparently he had taken the wrong road when first he came out of Ede, and might now be tending toward the Rhyn, or have left both Barneveld and even Assel considerably behind.

The unfortunate wayfarer did not of a surety know which to rail most bitterly against: his want of accurate knowledge as to the disposal of the stars upon a moonless firmament, so that he could not have told you, gaze on them how he might, which way lay the Zuyder Zee, the Ijssel, or the Rhyn; or that last mug of steaming ale of which he had partaken ere he finally turned his back on the hospitable doors of the "Crow's Nest" at Ede.

It was that very mug of the delicious spiced liquor – and even in this hour of acute misery, the poor man contrived to smack his half-frozen lips in retrospective enjoyment – which had somehow obscured his vision when first he found himself outside the city gates, confronted by the verfloekte waste, through which even a cat could not have picked its way on a night like this.

And now, here he was, hopelessly stranded, without drink or shelter, upon the most desolate portion of the Veluwe. In no direction could the lights of any habitation be seen.

"Dondersteen!" he muttered to himself finally, in despair. "But I must get somewhere in time, if I keep following my nose long enough!"

3

In truth, no more lonely spot could be imagined in a civilized land than that wherein the stranded traveler now found himself. Even by day the horizon seems limitless, with neither tower nor city nor homestead in sight. By night the silence is so absolute that imagination will conjure up strange and impossible sounds, such as that of the earth whistling through space, or of ceaseless rolls of drums and trampings of myriads of feet thousands of leagues away.

Strangely enough, however, once upon a time, in the far long ago and the early days of windmills, a hermit-miller – he must have been a hermit in very truth – did build one here upon the highest point of the Veluwe, close to the junction of the road which runs eastward from Amersfoort and Barneveld, with the one which tends southward from Assel, and distant from each a quarter of a league or so. Why that windmill was erected just there, far from the home of any peasant or farmer who might desire to have his corn ground, or who that hermit-miller was who dwelt in it before flocks of wild geese alone made it their trysting-place, it were impossible to say.

No trace of it remains these days, nor were there any traces of it left a year after the events which this veracious chronicle will presently unfold, for reasons which will soon appear obvious to anyone who reads. But there it stood in this year of grace 1624, on that cold night in March, when a solitary horseman lost his way upon the Veluwe, with serious consequences, not only to himself, but to no less a person than Maurice, Prince of Nassau, Stadtholder of the United Provinces of the Netherlands, and mayhap to the entire future history of that sorely tried country.

On a winter's night such as this, the mill looked peculiarly weird and ghost-like looming out of the darkness against the background of a star-studded firmament, and rising, sombre and dense, from out the carpet of glabrous snow, majestic in its isolation, towering above the immensity of the waste, its domed roof decked in virgin white like the mother-bosom of the wild. Built of weather-worn timber throughout, it had a fenced-in platform supported by heavy rafters all around it, like a girdle, at a height of twenty feet and more from the ground: and the gaunt, skeleton wings were stretched out to the skies, scarred, broken, and motionless, as if in piteous appeal for protection against the disfiguring ravages of time.

There were two small windows close under the roof on the south side of the building, and a large, narrow one midway up the same side. The disposal of these windows, taken in conjunction with the door down below, was so quaint that, viewed from a certain angle, they looked for all the world like the eyes, nose, and pursed-up mouth of a gargantuan, grinning face.

4

If a stranger travelling through Gelderland these days had thought it fit to inquire from a native whether that particular molen upon the Veluwe was doing work or was inhabited, he would of a certainty have been told that the only possible inhabitants of the molen were gnomes and sprites, and that if any corn was ground there it could only be in order to bake bread for the devil's dinner.

The mill was disused and uninhabited, had been for many years – a quarter of a century or more probably – so any and every native of Gelderland and Utrecht would have emphatically averred. Nevertheless, on this same memorable night in March, 1624, there were evident signs of life – human life – about that solitary and archaic molen on the Veluwe. Tiny slits of light showed clearly from certain angles through the chinks of the wooden structure; there were vague sounds of life and movement in and about the place; the weather-worn boards creaked and the timber groaned under more tangible pressure than that of the winds. Nay, what's more two horses were tethered down below, under the shelter afforded by the overhanging platform. These horses were saddled; they had nosebags attached to their bridles, and blankets thrown across their withers; all of which signs denoted clearly, methinks, that for once the mill was inhabited by something more material than ghosts.

More ponderous, too, than ghoulish footsteps were the sounds of slow pacing up and down the floor of the millhouse, and of two voices, now raised to loud argument, now sunk to a mere cautious whisper.

Two men were, in effect, inside the millhouse at this hour. One of them – tall, lean, dark in well-worn, almost ragged, black doublet and cloak, his feet and legs encased in huge boots of untanned leather which reached midway up his long thighs, his black bonnet pushed back from his tall, narrow forehead and grizzled hair – was sitting upon the steps of the steep, ladder-like stairs which led to the floor above; the other – shorter, substantially, even richly clad, and wearing a plumed hat and fur-lined cloak, was the one who paced up and down the dust-covered floor. He was younger than his friend, had fair, curly hair, and a silken, fair moustache, which hid the somewhat weak lines of his mouth.

An old, battered lanthorn, hanging to a nail in the wall, threw a weird, flickering light upon the scene, vaguely illumined the gaunt figure of the man upon the steps, his large hooked nose and ill-shaven chin, and long thin hands that looked like the talons of some bird of prey.

"You cannot stay on here forever, my good Stoutenburg, "the younger of the two men said, with some impatience. "Sooner or later you will be discovered, and —"

He paused, and the other gave a grim laugh.

"And there is a price of two thousand guilders upon my head, you mean, my dear Heemskerk?" he said dryly.

"Well, I did mean that," rejoined Heemskerk, with a shrug of the shoulders. "The people round about here are very poor. They might hold your father's memory in veneration, but there is not one who would not sell you to the Stadtholder if he found you out."

Again Stoutenburg laughed. He seemed addicted to the habit of this mirthless, almost impish laugh.

"I was not under the impression, believe me, my friend," he said, "that Christian charity or loyalty to my father's memory would actuate a worthy Dutch peasant into respecting my sanctuary. But I am not satisfied with what I have learned. I must know more. I have promised De Berg," he concluded firmly.

"And De Berg counts on you," Heemskerk rejoined. "But," he added, with a shrug of the shoulders, "you know what he is. One of those men who, so long as they gain their ambitious ends, count every life cheap but their own."

"Well," answered Stoutenburg, " 'tis not I, in truth, who would place a high price on mine."

"Easy, easy, my good man," quoth the other, with a smile. "Hath it, perchance, not occurred to you that your obstinacy in leading this owl-like life here is putting a severe strain on the devotion of your friends?"

I make no appeal to the devotion of my friends," answered Stoutenburg curtly. "They had best leave me alone."

"We cannot leave you to suffer cold and hunger, mayhap to perish of want in this God-forsaken eyrie."

"I'm not starving," was Stoutenburg's ungracious answer to the young man's kindly solicitude; "and have plenty of inner fire to keep me warm."

He paused, and a dark scowl contracted his gaunt features, gave him an expression that in the dim and flickering light appeared almost diabolical.

"I know," said Heemskerk, with a comprehending not. "Still those thoughts of revenge?"

"Always!" replied the other, with sombre calm.

"Twice you have failed."

"The third time I shall succeed," Stoutenburg affirmed with fierce emphasis. "Maurice of Nassau sent my father to the scaffold – my father, to whom he owed everything: money, power, success. The day that Olden Barneveldt died at the hands of that accursed ingrate I, his son, swore that the Stadtholder should perish by mine. As you say, I have twice failed in my attempt.

"My brother Groeneveld has gone the way of my father. I am an outlaw with a price upon my head, and my poor mother has three of us to weep for now, instead of one. But I have not forgotten mine oath, nor yet my revenge. I'll be even with Maurice of Nassau yet. All this fighting is but foolery. He is firmly established as Stadtholder of the United Provinces – the sort of man who sees others die for him. He may lose a town here, gain a city there, but he is the sovereign lord of an independent State, and his sacred person is better guarded than was that of his worthier father.

"But it is his life that I want," Stoutenburg went on fiercely, and his thin, claw-like hand clutched in imaginary dagger and struck out through the air as if against the breast of the hated foe. "For this I'll scheme and strive. Nay, I'll never rest until I have him at my mercy as Gerard in his day held William the Silent at his."

"Bah!" exclaimed Heemskerk hotly. "You would not emulate that abominable assassin!"

"Why not call me a justiciary?" Stoutenburg retorted dryly. "The Archduchess would load me with gifts. Spain would proclaim me a hero. Assassin or executioner – it only depends on the political point of view. But doubt me not for a single instant, Heemskerk. Maurice of Nassau will die by my hand."

"That is why you intend to remain here?"

"Yes. Until I have found out his every future plan."

"But how can you do it? You dare not show yourself abroad."

"That is my business," replied Stoutenburg quietly, "and my secret."

"I respect your secret," answered Heemskerk, with a shrug of the shoulders. "It was only my anxiety for your personal safety and for your comfort that brought me hither to-night."

"And De Berg's desire to learn what I have spied," Stoutenburg retorted, with a sneer.

"De Berg is ready to cross the Ijssel, and Isembourg to start from Kleve. De Berg proposes to attack Arnheim. He wishes to know what forces are inside the city and how they are disposed, and if the Stadtholder hath an army wherewith to come to their relief or to offer us battle, with any chance of success."

"You can tell De Berg to send you or another back to me here when the crescent moon is forty-eight hours older. I shall have all the information then that he wants."

"That will be good news for him and for Isembourg. There has been too much time wasted as it is."

"Time has not been wasted. The frosts have in the meanwhile made the Veluwe a perfect track for men and cannon."

"For Nassau's men and Nassau's cannon, as well as for our own," Heemskerk rejoined dryly.

"A week hence, if all's well, Maurice of Nassau will be too sick to lead his armies across the Veluwe or elsewhere," said Stoutenburg quietly, and looked up with such a strange, fanatical glitter in his deep-sunk eyes that the younger man gave an involuntary gasp of horror.

"You mean —" he ejaculated under his breath; and instinctively drawing back some paces away from his friend, stared at him with wide, uncomprehending eyes.

"I mean," Stoutenburg went on slowly and deliberately, "that De Berg had best wait patiently a little while longer. Maurice of Nassau will be a dying man ere long."

His harsh voice, sunk to a strange, impressive whisper, died away in a long-drawn-out sigh, half of impatience, wholly of satisfaction. Heemskerk remained for a moment or two absolutely motionless, still staring at the man before him as if the latter were some kind of malevolent and fiend-like wraith, conjured up by devilish magic to scare the souls of men. Nor did Stoutenburg add anything to his last cold-blooded pronouncement. He seemed to be deriving a grim satisfaction in watching the play of horror and of fear upon Heemskerk's usually placid features.

Thus for a space of a few moments the old molen appeared to sink back to its habitual ghost-haunted silence, whilst the hovering spirits of Revenge and Hate called up by the sorcery of a man's evil passions held undisputed sway.

"You mean —" reiterated Heemskerk after awhile, vaguely, stupidly, babbling like a child.

"I mean," Stoutenburg gave impatient answer, "that you should know me well enough by now, my good Heemskerk, to realize that I am no swearer of futile oaths. Last year, when I was over in Madrid, I cultivated the friendship of one Francis Borgia. You have heard of him, no doubt; they call him the Prince of Poets over there. He is a direct descendant of the illustrious Cesare, and I soon discovered that most of the secrets possessed by his far-famed ancestor were known to my friend the poet."

"Poisons!" Heemskerk murmured, under his breath.

"Poisons!" the other assented dryly. "And other things."

With finger and thumb of his right hand, he extracted a couple of tiny packets from a secret pocket of his doublet, toyed with them for awhile, undid the packets and gazed meditatively on their contents. Then he called to his friend. "They'll not hurt you," he said sardonically. "Look at this powder, now. Is it not innocent in appearance? Yet it is of incalculable value to the man who doth not happen to possess a straight eye or a steady hand with firearms. For add but a pinch of it to the charge in your pistol, them aim at your enemy's head, and if you miss killing him, or if he hold you at his mercy, you very soon have him at yours. The fumes from the detonation will cause instant and total blindness."

Despite his horror of the whole thing, Heemskerk had instinctively drawn nearer to his friend. Now, at these words, he stepped back again quickly, as if he had trodden upon an adder. Stoutenburg, with his wonted cynicism, only shrugged his shoulders.

"Have I not said that it would not hurt you?" he said, with a sneer. "In itself it is harmless enough, and only attains its useful properties when fired in connection with gunpowder. But when used as I have explained it to you, it is deadly and unerring. I saw it at work once or twice in Spain. The Prince of Poets prides himself on its invention. He gave me some of the precious powder, and I was glad of it. It may prove useful one day."

He carefully closed the first packet and slipped it back into the secret receptacle of his doublet; then he fell to contemplating the contents of the second packet – half a dozen tiny pillules, which he kept rolling about in the palm of his hand.

"These," he mused, "are of more proved value for my purpose. Have not De Berg," he added, with a sardonic grin, as he looked once more on his friend, "and the Archduchess, too, heard it noised abroad that Maurice of Nassau hath of late suffered from a mysterious complaint which already threatens to cut him off in his prime, and which up to now hath baffled those learned leeches who were brought over specially from England to look after the health of the exalted patient? Have not you and your friends, my good Heemskerk, heard the rumour too?"

The young man nodded in reply. His parched tongue seemed to cleave to the roof of his mouth; he could not utter a word. Stoutenburg laughed.

"Ah!" he said, with a nod of understanding. "I see that the tale did reach your ears. You understand, therefore, that I must remain here for awhile longer."

And with absolute calm and a perfectly steady hand, he folded up the pillules in the paper screw and put them back in his pocket.

"I could not leave my work unfinished," he said simply.

"But how —" Heemskerk contrived to stammer at last; and his voice to his own ears sounded hoarse and toneless, like a voice out of the grave.

"How do I contrive to convey these pillules into the Stadtholder's stomach?" retorted Stoutenburg, with a coarse chuckle. "Well, my friend, that is still my secret. But De Berg and the others must trust me a while longer – trust me and then thank me when the time comes. The Stadtholder once out of the way, the resistance of the United Provinces must of itself collapse like a house of cards. There need be no more bloodshed after that – no more sanguinary conflicts. Indeed, I shall be acclaimed as a public benefactor – when I succeed."

"Then – then you are determined to – to remain here?" Heemskerk murmured, feeling all the while that anything he said was futile and irrelevant.

But how can a man speak when he is confronted with a hideous spectre that mocks him, even whilst it terrifies?

"I shall remain here for the present," Stoutenburg replied, with perfect coolness.

"I – I'd best go, then," the other suggested vaguely.

"You had best wait until the daylight. 'Tis easy to lose one's way on the Veluwe."

The young man waited for a moment, irresolute. Clearly he was longing to get away, to put behind him this ghoul-infested molen, with its presiding genii of hatred and of crime. Nay, men like Heemskerk, cultivated and gently nurtured, understood the former easily enough. Men and women knew how to hate fiercely these days, and there were few sensations more thoroughly satisfying than that of holding an enemy at the sword's point.

But poison! The slow, insidious weapon that worked like a reptile, stealthily and in the dark! Bah! Heemskerk felt a dizziness overcome him; sheer physical nausea threatened to rob him of his faculties.

But there was undoubted danger in venturing out on the arid wild, in the darkness and with nought but instinct and a few half-obliterated footmarks to guide one along the track. The young man went to the door and pulled it open. A gust of ice-laden air blew into the great, empty place, and almost knocked the old lanthorn off its peg. Heemskerk stepped out into the night. He felt literally frightened, and, like a nervous child, had the sensation of someone or something standing close behind him and on the point of putting a spectral hand upon his shoulder.

But Stoutenburg had remained sitting on the steps, apparently quite unmoved. No doubt he was accustomed to look his abominable project straight in the face. He even shrugged his shoulders in derision when he caught sight of Heemskerk's white face and horror-filled eyes.

"You cannot start while this blind man's holiday lasts," he said lightly. "Can I induce you to partake of some of the refreshment you were good enough to bring for me?"

But Heemskerk gave him no answer. He was trying to make up his mind what to do; and Stoutenburg, with another careless laugh, rose from his seat and strode across the great barn-like space. There, in a remote corner, where sacks of uncrushed grain were wont to be stacked, stood a basket containing a few simple provisions; a hunk of stale bread, a piece of cheese and two or three bottles of wine. Stoutenburg stooped and picked one of these up. He was whistling a careless tune. Then suddenly he paused, his long back still bent, his arm with the hand that held the bottle resting across his knee, his face, alert and hawk-like, turned in an instant toward the door.

"What was that?" he queried hurriedly.

Heemskerk, just as swiftly, had already stepped back into the barn and closed the door again noiselessly.

"Useless!" commented Stoutenburg curtly. "The horses are outside."

"Where is Jan?" he added after an imperceptible pause, during which Heemskerk felt as if his very heart-beats had become audible.

"On the watch, outside," replied the young man.

Even whilst he spoke the door was cautiously opened from the outside, and a grizzled head wrapped in a fur bonnet was thrust in through the orifice.

"What is it, Jan?" the two men queried simultaneously.

"A man and horse," Jan replied in a rapid whisper.

"Coming from over Amersfoort way. He must have caught sight of the molen, for he has left the track and is heading straight for us."

"Some wretched traveler lost on this God-forsaken waste," Stoutenburg said, with a careless shrug of the shoulders. "I have seen them come this way before."

"But not at this hour of the night?" murmured Heemskerk.

"Mostly at night. It is easier to follow the track by day."

"What shall we do?"

"Nothing. Let the man come. We'll soon see if he is dangerous. Are we not three to one?"

The taunt struck home. Heemskerk looked abashed. Jan remained standing in the doorway, waiting for further orders. Stoutenburg went on quietly collecting the scanty provisions. He found a couple of mugs, and with a perfectly steady hand filled the first one and then the other with the wine.

"Drink this Heemskerk," he said lightly; and held out the two mugs at arm's length. "It will calm your nerves. You too, Jan."

Jan took the mug and drank with avidity, but Heemskerk appeared to hesitate.

"Afraid of the poison?" Stoutenburg queried with a sneer. Then, as the other, half-ashamed, took the mug and drank at a draught, he added coolly: "You need not be afraid. I could not afford to waste such precious stuff on you."

Then he turned to Jan.

"Remain outside," he commanded; "well wrapped in your blanket, and when the traveler hails you pretend to be wakened from pleasant dreams. Then leave the rest to chance."

Jan at once obeyed. He went out of the molen, closing the door carefully behind him.

Five minutes later, the hapless traveler had put his horse to a trot. He had perceived the molen looming at the top of the rising ground, dense and dark against the sky, and looking upon it as a veritable God-sent haven of refuge for wearied tramps, was making good haste to reach it, fearing lest he himself dropped from sheer exhaustion out of his saddle ere he came to his happy goal.

That terrible contingency, however, did not occur, and presently he was able to draw rein and to drop gently if somewhat painfully to the ground without further mishap. Then he looked about him. The mill in truth appeared to be uninhabited, which was a vast pity, seeing that a glass of spiced ale would – but no matter, 'twas best not to dwell on such blissful thoughts! A roof over one's head for the night was the most urgent need.

He led his horse by the bridle, and tethered him to a heavy, supporting rafter under the overhanging platform; was on the point of ministering to the poor, half-frozen beast, when his ear caught a sound which caused him instantly to pause first and then start on a tour around the molen. He had not far to go. The very next moment he came upon a couple of horses tethered like his own, and upon Jan, who was snoring lustily, curled up in a horse-blanket in the angle of the porch.

To hail the sleeper with lusty shouts at first, and then with a vigorous kick, was but the work of a few seconds; after which Jan's snores were merged in a series of comprehensive curses against the disturber of his happy dreams.

"Dondersteen!" he murmured, still apparently half asleep. "And who is this verfloekte plepshurk who ventures a weary traveler from his sleep?"

"Another weary traveler, verfloekte plepshurk yourself," the other cried aloud. Nor were it possible to render with any degree of accuracy the language which he subsequently used when Jan persistently refused to move.

"Then, dondersteen," retorted Jan thickly, "do as I do – wrap yourself up in a blanket and go to sleep."

"Not until I have discovered how it comes that one wearied traveler happens to be abroad with two equally wearied and saddled horses. And I am not mistaken, plepshurk, thou are but a varlet left on guard outside, whilst thy master feasts and sleeps within."

Whereupon, without further parley, he strode across Jan's outstretched body and, with a vigorous kick of his heavy boot, thrust open the door which gave on the interior of the mill.

Here he paused, just beneath the lintel, took off his hat, and stood at respectful attention; for he had realized at once that he was in the presence of his betters – of two gentlemen, in fact, one of whom had a mug of wine in his hand and the other a bottle. These were the two points which, as it were, jumped most directly to the eye of the weary, frozen, and thirsty traveler: two gentlemen who haply were now satiated, and would spare a drop even to a humble varlet if he stood before them in his full, pitiable plight.

"Who are you man? And what do you want?" one of these gentlemen queried peremptorily. It was the one who had a bottle of wine – a whole bottle – in his hand; but he looked peculiarly stern and forbidding, with his close-cropped, grizzled head and hard, bird-like features.

"Only a poor tramp, my lord," replied the unfortunate wayfarer, in high-pitched, flute-like tones, "who hath lost his way, and has been wandering on this verdommte plain since midnight."

"What do you want?" reiterated Stoutenburg sternly.

"Only shelter for the rest of the night, my lord, and – and – a little drink – a very little drink – for I am mightily weary, and my throat is dry as tinder."

"What is your name?"

At this very simple question the man's round, florid face with the tiny, upturned nose, slightly tinged with pink, and the small, round eyes, bright and shiny like new crowns, took on an expression of comical puzzlement. He scratched his head, pursed up his lips, emitted a prolonged and dubious whistle.

"I haven't a name, so please your lordship," he said, after a while. "That is, not a name such as other people have. I have a name, in truth, a name by which I am known to my friends; a name —"

"Thy name, plepshurk," command Stoutenburg roughly, "ere I throw thee out again into the night."

" 'So please your lordship." replied the man, "I am called Pythagoras – a name which I believe belongs by right to a philosopher of ancient times, but to which I will always answer, so please your High and Mightiness."

But this time his High and Mightiness did not break in upon the worthy philosopher's volubility. Indeed, at the sound of that highly ludicrous name – ludicrous, that is, when applied to its present bearer – he had deliberately put mug and bottle down, and then become strangely self-absorbed, even whilst his friend had given an involuntary start.

"H'm! Pythagoras!" his lordship resumed, after a while. "Have I ever seen thine ugly face before?"

"Not to my knowledge, my lord," replied the other, marvelling when it would please these noble gentlemen to give him something wherewith to moisten his gullet.

"Ah! Methought I had once met another who bore an equally strange name. Was it Demosthenes, or Euripides, or —"

"Diogenes, no doubt, my lord," replied the thirsty philosopher glibly. "The most gallant gentleman in the whole wide world, one who honours me with his friendship, was pleased at one time to answer to that name."

Now, when Pythagoras made his announcement he felt quite sure that lavish hospitality would promptly follow. These gentlemen had no doubt heard of Diogenes, his comrade in arms, the faithful and gallant friend for whom he – Pythagoras – would go through fire and water and the driest of deserts. They would immediately accord a welcome to one who had declared himself honoured by the friendship of so noble a cavalier. Great was the unfortunate man's disappointment, therefore, when his glib speech was received in absolute silence; and he himself was still left standing upon the lintel of the door, with an icy cold draught playing upon him from behind.

It was only after a considerable time that my lord deigned to resume his questionings again.

"Where dost come from, fellow?" he asked.

"From Ede, so please your lordship," Pythagoras replied dolefully, "where I partook —"

"And whither art going?" Stoutenburg broke in curtly.

"I was going to Amersfoort, my lord, when I lost my way."

"To Amersfoort?"

" 'Yes, my lord."

"Mynheer Beresteyn hath a house at Amersfoort," Stoutenburg said, as if to himself.

"It was to Mynheer Beresteyn's house that I was bound, my lord, when I unfortunately lost my way."

"Ah!" commented my lord dryly. "Thou was on thy way to the house of Mynheer Beresteyn in Amersfoort?"

"Yes, my lord."

"With a message?"

"No, my lord. Not with a message; I was just going there for the wedding."

"The wedding?" ejaculated Stoutenburg, and it seemed to Pythagoras as if my lord's haggard face took on suddenly an almost cadaverous hue. "Whose wedding fellow?" he added more calmly.

"That of my friend Diogenes, so please your lordship, with the Jongejuffrouw Beresteyn, he —"

"Take care, man, take care!" came with an involuntary call of alarm from Heemskerk; for Stoutenburg, uttering a hoarse cry like that of a wounded beast, had raised his arm and now strode on the unfortunate philosopher with clenched fist and a look in his hollow eyes which boded no good to the harbinger of those simple tidings.

At sound of his friend's voice, Stoutenburg dropped his arm. He turned on his heel, ashamed no doubt that this stranger-varlet should see his face distorted as it was with passion.

This paroxysm of uncontrolled fury did not, however, last longer than a moment or two; the next instant the lord of Stoutenburg, outwardly calm and cynical as before had resumed his haughty questionings, looked the awe-struck philosopher up and down; and he, somewhat scared by the danger which he only appeared to have escaped through the timely intervention of the other gentleman, was marvelling indeed if he had better not take to his heels at once and run, and trust his safety and his life to the inhospitable wild, rather than in the company of this irascible noble lord.

I think, if fact, that he would have fled the very next moment, but that my lord with one word kept him rooted to the spot.

"So," resumed Stoutenburg coolly after awhile, "thou, fellow, art a bidden guest at the marriage feast, which it seems is to be solemnized 'twixt the Jongejuffrouw Beresteyn and another plepshurk as low as thyself. Truly doth democracy tread hard on the heels of such tyranny as the United Provinces have witnessed of late. Dost owe allegiance, sirrah, to the Stadtholder?"

"Where Diogenes leads, my lord," replied Pythagoras, with a degree of earnestness which sat whimsically upon his rotund person, "there do Socrates and I follow unquestioningly."

"Which means that ye are three rascals, ready to sell your skins to the highest bidder. Were ye not in the pay of the lord of Stoutenburg during the last conspiracy against the Stadtholder's life?"

"We may have been, your honour," the man replied naively; "although, to my knowledge, I have never set eyes on the lord of Stoutenburg."

" 'Twere lucky for thee knave, if thou didst," rejoined Stoutenburg with a harsh laugh, "for there's a price of two thousand guilders upon his head, and I doubt not but thy scurrilous friend Diogenes would add another two thousand to that guerdon."

Then, as Pythagoras, almost dropping with fatigue, was swaying upon his short, fat legs, he jerked his thumb in the direction where the tantalizing bottles and mugs were faintly discernible in the gloom. My lord continued curtly:

"There! Drink thy fill! Amersfoort is not far. My man will put thee on thy way when thou hast quenched thy thirst!"

Quench his thirst! Where was that cellar which could have worked this magic trick? In the corner to which my lord was pointing so casually there was but one bottle, which my lord had put down a while ago, and that, after all, was only half full.

Still, half a bottle of wine was better than no wine at all, and my lord, having granted his gracious leave, took no more notice of the philosopher and his unquenchable thirst, turned to his friend, and together the two gentlemen retired to a distant corner of the place and there whispered eagerly with one another.

Pythagoras tiptoed up to the spot where unexpected bliss awaited him. There was another bottle of wine there beside the half-empty one – a bottle that was full up to the neck, and the shape of which proclaimed that it came from Spain. Good, strong, heady Spanish wine!

And my lord had said "Drink thy fill!" Pythagoras did not hesitate, save for one brief second, while he marvelled whether he had accidentally wandered into Elysian fields, or whether he was only dreaming. Then he poured out for himself a mugful of wine.

Twenty minutes later, the last drop of the second bottle of strong, heady Spanish wine had trickled down the worthy Pythagoras' throat. He was in a state of perfect bliss, babbling words of supreme contentment, and seeing pleasing visions of gorgeous feasts in the murky angles of the old millhouse.

" 'Tis time the plepshurk got to horse," Stoutenburg said at last.

He strode across to where Pythagoras, leaning against the raftered wall, his round head on one side, his sugar-loaf hat set at the back of his head, was gazing dreamily into his empty mug.

"To horse, fellow!" he commanded curtly. " 'Tis but a league to Amersfoort, and thy friend will be waiting thee."

The old instinct of deference and good behaviour before a noble lord lent some semblance of steadiness to Pythagoras' legs. He struggled to his feet, vainly endeavored to keep an upright and dignified position – an attempt which, however, proved utterly futile.

Whereupon my lord called peremptorily to Jan, who appeared so suddenly in the doorway that, to Pythagoras' blurred vision, it seemed as if he had been put there by some kind of witchery. He approached his master, and there ensued a brief, whispered colloquy between those two – a colloquy in which Heemskerk took no part. After which, the lord of Stoutenburg said aloud:

"Set this worthy fellow on his horse, my good Jan, and put him on the track which leads to Amersfoort. He has had a rest and a good warm drink. He is not like to lose his way again."

Vaguely Pythagoras felt that he wished to protest. He did not want to be set on his horse, nor yet to go to Amersfoort just yet. The wedding was not until the morrow-- no, the day after the morrow – and for the nonce he wanted to sleep. Yes, sleep! Curled up in a blanket in any corner big enough and warm enough to shelter a dog.

Sleep! That was what he wanted; for he was so confoundedly sleepy, and this verfloekte darkness interfered with his eyes so that he could not see very clearly in front of him. All this he explained with grave deliberation to Jan, who had him tightly by the elbow and was leading him with absolutely irresistible firmness out through the door into the white, inhospitable open.

"I don't want to get to horse," the philosopher babbled thickly. "I want to curl up in a blanket and I want to go to sleep."

But, despite his protestations, he found himself presently in the saddle. How he got up there, he certainly could not have told you. Instinct, however, kept him there. Never could it be said that Pythagoras had tumbled off a horse. Anon he felt that the horse was moving, and that the air around him was bitterly cold.

The dull, even carpet of snow dazzled him, though it was pitch dark now both overhead and down below; of darkness that enveloped one like a mantle, and which felt as if it could have been cut through with a knife.

The horse went on at a steady trot, and another was trotting by its side, bearing a cavalier who wore a fur bonnet. Pythagoras vaguely imagined that this must be Jan. He owed Jan a grudge for taking him away from that hospitable molen, where half-bottles of wine were magically transformed into large ones, filled to overflowing with delicious liquor.

Presently Pythagoras began to feel cold again after the blissful warmth produced by that super-excellent Spanish wine.

"Is it far to Amersfoort?" he queried drowsily from time to time.

But he never seemed to get a reply. It appeared to him as if he had been hours in the saddle since last he felt comfortable and warm over in that hospitable molen. And he was very sleepy. His head felt heavy and his eyes would not keep open as hours and hours went by and the cold grew more and more intense.

"Is it far to Amersfoort?" he questioned whenever his head rolled forward with a jerk that roused him to momentary consciousness.

"Less than half a league now," Jan replied presently, and brought his own horse to a halt. "Follow the track before you and it will lead you straight to the city gates."

Pythagoras opened his eyes very wide. Straightway in front of him he perceived one or two tiny lights, which were too low down on the horizon for stars. The road, too, on which he found himself appeared straighter and more defined than those upon that verfloekte waste.

"Are those the lights of Amersfoort?" he murmured vaguely, and pointed in as straight a direction as his numbed arm would allow.

He expected an answer from Jan but there came none. The darkness appeared to have swallowed up horse and rider. Anyway, they had disappeared. Good old Jan! Pythagoras would have liked to thank him for his company, even though he did owe him a grudge for taking him away from the molen where there had been such wonderful —

The horse followed the track for a minute or two longer Pythagoras, left to his own devices, tried to keep awake. Suddenly the sharp report of a pistol rent the silence of the night. It was immediately followed by another.

Pythagoras felt a strange, sinking sensation in his stomach, a dizzy feeling in his head, a feeling which was no longer blissful like the one he had experienced after the third mugful of Spanish wine. A moment later, he fell forward on his horse's neck, then rolled out of the saddle down upon the bed of snow.

And at this spot, where the poor philosopher lay, the white pall which covered the Veluwe was dyed with a dark crimson stain.

5

A grey, dull light suffused the sky in the East when Jan once more knocked at the door of the old molen.

Stoutenburg's voice bade him enter.

"All well?" my lord queried, at sight of his faithful servant.

"All quiet, my lord," replied Jan. "That windbag, I'll warrant, will tell no tales."

"How far did you take him?"

"Nearly as far as Lang Soeren. I had to keep a track for fear of losing my way. But he lies eight leagues from Amersfoort now and six from Ede. His friends, I imagine, won't look for him thus far."

"And his horse?"

"It did not follow me. No doubt it will get picked up by some one in the morning."

Heemskerk shivered. It was certainly very cold inside this great, barn-like place at this hour just before sunrise; and the passing wayfarer had consumed the last measure of wine. The young man looked grimy, too, and untidy, covered with dust from the floor, where he had lain stretched out for the past three hours, trying to get a wink of sleep; whilst Stoutenburg, restless and alert, had kept his ears open and his nerves on the stretch for the first sound of Jan's return.

"You have been a long time getting to Lang Soeren and back," the latter remarked further to Jan.

I was guiding a drunken man on a wearied horse," the man replied curtly. "And I myself had been in the saddle all day."

"Then get another hour's rest now," Stoutenburg rejoined. "You will accompany my lord of Heemskerk back to Doesburg as soon as the sun is up."

Jan made no reply. He was accustomed to curt commands and to unquestioning obedience. Tired, saddle-sore and wearied, he would be ready to ride again, go anywhere until he dropped. So he turned on his heel and went out into the cold once more, in order to snatch that brief hour's rest which had been graciously accorded him.

Heemskerk gave an impatient sigh.

"I would the dawn were quicker in coming!" he murmured under his breath.

"The atmosphere of the Veluwe is getting oppressive for your fastidious taste," Stoutenburg retorted with a sneer. Then, as his friend made no other comment, he continued lightly: "Dead men tell no tales. I could not risk that blabbering fool going back to Amersfoort and speaking of what he saw. Even your unwonted squeamishness, my good Heemskerk, would grant me that."

"Or, rather," rejoined the other, almost involuntarily, "did not the unfortunate man suffer for being the messenger of evil tidings?"

Stoutenburg shrugged his shoulders with an assumption of indifference. "Perhaps," he said. "Though I doubt if the news was wholly unexpected. Yet I would have deemed Gilda Beresteyn too proud to wed that plepshurk."

"A man with a future," Heemskerk rejoined. "He is credited with having saved the Stadtholder's life, when the lord of Stoutenburg planned to blow up the bridge under his passage."

"And Beresteyn is grateful to him too," added Stoutenburg with a sarcastic curl of his thin lips, "for having rescued the fair Gilda from the lord of Stoutenburg's fierce clutches. But Nicolaes might have told me that his sister was getting married."

"Nicolaes?" ejaculated Heemskerk, with obvious surprise. "You have seen Nicolaes Beresteyn, then of late?"

For the space of a few seconds – less perhaps – Stoutenburg appeared confused, and the look which he cast on his friend was both furtive and searching. The next moment, however, he had recovered his usual cool placidity.

"You mistook, me, my friend," he said blandly. "I did not say that I had seen Nicolaes Beresteyn of late. I have not seen him, in fact, since the day of our unfortunate aborted conspiracy. Rumor reached me that he himself was about to wed the worthy daughter of some prosperous burgher. I merely wondered how the same rumor made no mention of the other prospective bride."

Once again the conversation flagged. Heemskerk regarded his friend with an anxious expression in his pale wearied face. He knew how passionately, if somewhat intermittently, Stoutenburg had loved Gilda Beresteyn. He knew of the original girl and boy affection between them, and of the man's base betrayal of the girl's trust. Stoutenburg had thrown over the humbler burgher's daughter in order to wed Walburg de Marnix, whom he promptly neglected, and who had since set him legally free. Heemskerk knew, too, how Stoutenburg's passion for the beautiful Gilda Beresteyn had since then burst into a consuming flame, and how the obscure soldier of fortune who went by the nick-name of Diogenes had indeed snatched the fair prize from his grasp.

Nigh on three months had gone by since then. Stoutenburg was still nurturing thoughts of vengeance and of crime, not only against the Stadtholder, but also against the girl who had scorned him. Well, this in truth was none of his friend's business. Hideous as was the premeditated coup against Maurice of Nassau, it would undoubtedly, if successful, help the cause of Spain in the Netherlands, and Heemskerk himself was that unnatural monster – a man who would rather see his country ruled by a stranger than by those of her sons whose political or religious views differed from his own.

Thus, when an hour later he took leave of Stoutenburg, he did so almost with cordiality, did not hesitate to grasp the had of a man whom he knew to be a scheming and relentless murderer.

"One of us will come out to wait on you in two days' time," he said at the last. "I go back to camp satisfied that you are not so lonely as you seem, and that there is some one who sees to it that you do not fare so ill even in this desolation. May I say this to De Berg?"

"If you like," Stoutenburg replied. "Anyway, you may assure him, and through him the Archduchess, that Maurice of Nassau will be in his grave before I, his judge and executioner, perish of hunger or of cold."

He accompanied his friend to the door, and stood there while the latter and Jan were getting to horse. Then, as they went out into the open, he waved them a last adieu. On the far distant east, the pale, wintry sun had tinged the mist with a delicate lemon gold. The vast immensity of the waste lay stretched out as if limitless before him. As far as the eye could see not a tower or column of smoke broke the even monotony of the undulating ground. The shadow of the great molen with its gaunt, mained wings lay, like patches of vivid blue upon the vast and glistening pall of snow.

The two riders put their horses to a trot. Soon they appeared like mere black specks upon a background of golden haze, whilst in their wake, upon the scarce visible track, the traces of their horses' hoofs, in stains of darker blue upon the virgin white, were infinitely multiplied.

Stoutenburg watched them until the mist-laden distance had completely hidden them from his view. Then, with a sigh of relief, he went within.

Chapter II – The Double Wedding

1

IT was one of those days when earth and heaven alike appear to smile. A day almost warm, certainly genial; for the wind had dropped, the sky was of a vivid blue, and the sun had a genuine feeling of warmth in its kiss. From the overhanging eaves the snow dropped down in soft, moist lumps, stained by the thaw, and the quay, where a goodly crowd had collected, was quickly transformed under foot into a sea of mud.

It almost seemed as if the little town was out on a holiday. People came and went, dressed in gay attire, stood about all along the bank of the river, staring up at the stately gabled house which looked so wonderfully gay with its decorations of flags and valuable tapestries and stuffs hanging from the numerous windows.

That house on the quay – and it was the finest house in the town – was indeed the centre of attraction. It was from there that the air of holiday-making emanated, and certainly from there that the gay sounds of music and revelry came wafted on the crisp, wintry air.

Mynheer Beresteyn had come to his house in Amersfoort, of which city he was chief civic magistrate, in order to celebrate the double wedding. No wonder such an event was made an excuse for a holiday. Burgomaster Beresteyn never did things by halves, and his hospitality was certain to be lavish. Already doles and largesse had been poured out at the porch of St. Maria Kerk; a crowd of beggars more or less indigent, crippled, sick, or merely greedy, had assembled there very early in the morning. Whoever was there was sure to get something. And there was plenty to see besides: the brides and bridegrooms and the wedding party; and of course His Highness the Stadtholder was a sight in himself. He did not often go abroad these days, for his health was no longer as good as it was. He had aged considerably, looked moody and ailing for the most part. There had been sinister rumours, too. The widowed Archduchess Isabella, Mistress of Flanders and Brabant, hated him because he held the United Provinces of the Netherlands free from the bondage of Spain. And in Spain the arts of poison and of secret assassination were carried on with as much perfection as they had ever been in Italy in the days of the Borgias.

However, all such dark thoughts must be put away for the day. This is a festive occasion for Amersfoort, when every anxiety for the fate of the poor fatherland – ever threatened and ever sore-pressed – must be laid to rest. Let the brides and bridegrooms see naught but merry faces – happy auguries of the auspicious days to come.

Here they come –the entire wedding party – walking down the narrow streets from the quay to the St. Maria Kerk. Every one is walking, even the Stadtholder. He is conspicuous by his great height, and the richness of his attire: embroidered doublet, slashed sleeves, priceless lace. His face looks thin and drawn, but he has lost nothing of his martial bearing, nor have his eyes lost their eagle glance. He had come over the previous afternoon from Utrecht, where he was in camp, and had deigned to grace Mynheer Beresteyn's house by sleeping under its roof. It was understood that he would return to Utrecht after the banquet which was to follow the religious ceremony, and he, too, for this one day was obviously making a valiant attempt to cast off the load of anxiety attendant upon ceaseless campaigning. In truth, the Archduchess Isabella, not content with the fairest provinces of Belgium, with Flanders, Brabant, and the Hainault, which her father, King Philip of Spain, had ceded to her absolutely, was even now striving to force some of the United Provinces back under the domination of Spain.

Small wonder then that the Stadtholder, wearied and sick, the shadow of his former self, was no longer sure of a whole-hearted welcome when he showed himself abroad. Nor had the people forgiven him the judicial murder of Olden Barneveldt – the trusted councillor in the past, afterwards the bitter opponent of his master's ambitions – of his severity towards Barneveldt's sons. His relentless severity toward those who offended him, his reckless ambition and stern disciplinarianism, had made him an object of terror rather than of affection. Nevertheless, he still stood for the upholder of the liberties of the United Provinces, the finest captain of his age, who by his endurance, his military skill, and his unswerving patriotism, kept his country's frontiers free from the incursions of the most powerful armies of the time. He still stood as the man who had swept the sacred soil of the Netherlands free from Spanish foes and Spanish tyranny, who had amplified and consolidated the work of his father and firmly established the independence of the Republic. Because of what he had done in the past, men like Mynheer Beresteyn and those of his kind still looked upon him with grave respect, as the chosen of God, the prophet sent to them from Heaven to keep the horrors of a new Spanish invasion away from their land.

And when Maurice of Nassau came to a small city like Amersfoort, as he had done today, he was received with veneration, if not with the old cheers and acclamations. His arbitrary temper was momentarily forgotten, his restless ambition condoned, in the joy of beholding the man who had fought for them, never spared himself until he had won for them all those civil and religious liberties which they prized above all the treasures of the earth.

All heads, then, were bowed in respectful silence as he walked by, with the brides one on each side of him. But the loving glances of the crowd, the jokes and whispered words of cheer and greeting, were reserved for Mynheer Beresteyn and for his family.

2

Two brides, and both comely! Jongejuffrouw Katharina van den Poele, the only child of the wealthy shipowner, member of the Dutch East India Company, a solid burgher both physically and financially, and one of the props of his country's overseas commerce. His daughter, in rich brocade, with stiff stomacher that vainly strove to compress her ample proportions, splashed through the mud on her high pattens beside the Stadtholder, her heavily be-ringed hands clinging to the folds of her gown, so as to save them from being soiled. Stolid and complacent, she heard with a satisfied smile the many compliments that rose from out the crowd on her dazzling complexion, her smoothly brushed hair and magnificent jewelry. The fair Katharina beamed with good-nature and looked the picture of happiness, despite the fact that her bridegroom, who walked immediately behind her, appeared somewhat moody, considering the occasion.

Nicolaes Beresteyn, the Burgomaster's only son, had in truth, no reason for surliness. His bride excited universal admiration, his own private fortune would be more than doubled by the dowry which the good Kaatje brought him along with her plump person, and all the disagreements between himself and his father, all the treachery and the deceit of the past three months, had been amply forgiven. It was all the more strange, therefore, that on this day his face alone should appear as a reflection of the Stadtholder's silent mood, and more than one comment was made thereon as he passed.

Of the other bride and bridegroom it is perhaps more difficult to speak. We all know the beautiful picture of Gilda Beresteyn which Frans Hals made of her some three months previously. That incomparable master of portraiture has rendered that indescribable air of force, coupled with extreme youthfulness, which was her greatest charm. Often she hath been called etherial, yet I do not see how that description could apply to one who was so essentially alive as Gilda Beresteyn. Her blue eyes always sparkled with vitality, and whenever she was moved – which was often enough – they became as dark as sloes. Probably the word came to be applied to her because there was always a little something mysterious about her – an enigmatic little smile, which suggested merriment that came from within rather than in response to an outside joke. Many have remarked that her smile was the gentle reflex of her lover's sparkling gaiety.

Him – that ardent lover, sobered bridegroom now – you cannot forget, not whilst Frans Hals' immortal work, whom he hath called "The Laughing Cavalier," depicts him in all is irrepressible joyousness, and gladdens the eye with its exhilaration and its magnificent gaite de coeur – a veritable nepenthe for jaded seek-sorrows.

For once in his life, as he walks gravely behind his bride, there is a look of seriousness not unmixed with impatience in his laughing eyes. A frown, too, between his brows. The crowd have at once taken him to its heart – especially the women. Those who have no sons wish for one at once, who would grow up just like him: tall and stately as a young sapling, with an air of breeding seldom seen in the sons of the Low Countries, and wearing his magnificent bridal attire as if he had never worn leather jerkin or worsted doublet in his life. The women admire the richly wrought doublet, the priceless lace at neck and wrists, the plumed hat that frames a face alike youthful and determined. But everyone marvels why a bridegroom should go to church in high riding-boots and spurred at this hour. Many whispered comments are exchanged as he goes by.

"A stranger, so they say."

"Though he has fought in the Netherlands."

"Ah, but he really comes from England."

"A romantic story. Never knew his father until recently."

Some said the bridegroom's name was really Blakeney, and that his father was a very rich and very great gentleman over in England. But there were others who remembered him well when he was just a penniless soldier of fortune who went by the name of Diogenes. No one knew him then by any other, and no one but Frans Hals, the painter over in Haarlem, knew whence he had come and what was his parentage. In those days his merry laughter would rouse the echoes of the old city where he and his two boon companions – such a quaint pair of loons! – were wont to dwell in the intervals of selling their swords to the highest bidders.

Ay, Jongejuffrouw Beresteyn's stranger bridegroom had fought in France and in Flanders, in Groningen and Brabant and 'twas said that recently he had saved the life of the Stadtholder at great risk of his own. Many more tales were whispered about him, which would take too long to relate, while the crowd stood agape all down the quay and up the Korte Gracht as far as the St. Maria Kerk.

3

Indeed, Mynheer Beresteyn had not done things by halves. He had chosen that the happy double event should take place at the old house at Amersfoort, where his children had been born, and where he had spent the few happy years of his married life, rather than at Haarlem, which was his business and official residence. He wished, for the occasion, to be just a happy father rather than the distinguished functionary, the head of the Guild of Armourers, one of the most important burghers of the Province, and second only in the council chamber to the Stadtholder.

The religious ceremony was over by noon. It was now mid-afternoon, and the wedding guests had assembled in the stately home on the quay for a gargantuan feast. The Stadtholder sat at a magnificently decked-out table at the far end of the panelled room, on a raised dais surmounted by a canopy of Flemish tapestry, all specially erected for the occasion. Around this privileged board sat the wedding party; Mynheer Beresteyn, grave and sedate, a man who had seen much of life, had suffered a great deal, and even now scarcely dared to give his sense of joy full play. He gazed from time to time on his daughter with something of anxiety as well as of pride. Then the worthy shipowner, member of the Dutch East India Company, and mejuroffluw, his wife – the father and mother of Nicolaes Beresteyn's bride, pompous and fleshy, and with an air of prosperous complacence about their persons which contrasted strangely with Mynheer Beresteyn's anxious earnestness. Finally, the two bridal couples, of whom more anon.

In the body of the nobly proportioned banqueting-hall, a vast concourse of guests had assembled around two huge tables, which were decked out with costly linen and plate, and literally groaned under the succulent dishes which serving-men repeatedly placed there for the delectation of the merry party. Roast capons and geese, fish from the Rhyn and from the sea, pasties made up of oysters and quails, and, above all, a constant supply of delicious Rhine or Spanish wines, according as the guests desired light or heady liquor.

A perpetual buzz of talk, intermingled with many an outburst of hilarity and an occasional song, filled the somewhat stuffy air of the room to the exclusion of any individual sound.

The ladies plied their fans vigorously, and some of the men, warmed by good cheer, had thrown their padded doublets open and loosened their leather belts. The brides-elect sat one on each side of the Stadtholder; a strange contrast, in truth. Kaatje van den Poele, just a young edition of her mother, her well-rounded figure already showing signs of the inevitable coming stoutness, comely to look at, with succulent cheeks shining like rosy apples, her face with the wide-open, prominent eyes, beaming with good-nature and the vigorous application of cold water. Well-mannered, too, for she never spoke unless spoken to, but sat munching her food with naive delight, and whenever her somewhat moody bridegroom hazarded a laboured compliment or joke, she broke into a pleasant giggle, jerked her elbow at him, and muttered a "Fie, Klaas!" which put and end to further conversation.

Gilda Beresteyn, who sat at the Stadtholder's right hand, was silent, too; demure, not a little prim, but with her, even the most casual observer became conscious that beneath the formal demeanor there ran an undercurrent of emotional and pulsating life. The terrible experience which she had gone through a few brief months ago had given to her deep blue eyes a glance that was vividly passionate, yet withal resposeful, and with a curiously childlike expression of trust within its depth.

The stiff bridal robes which convention decreed that she should wear gave her an air of dignity, even whilst it enhanced the youthfulness of her personality. There was all the roundness in her figure which is the attribute of her race; yet, despite her plump shoulders and full throat, her little round face and firm bosom, there remained something ethereal about her, a spirituality and a strength which inspired reverence, even whilst her beauty provoked admiring glances.

"Your Highness is not eating," she remarked timidly.

"My head aches," Maurice of Nassau replied moodily. "I cannot eat. I think I must be over-tired," he went on more pleasantly as he met the girl's kind blue eyes fixed searchingly upon him. "A little fresh air will do me good. Don't disturb any one," he continued hastily, as he rose to his feet and turned to go to the nearest open window.

Beresteyn quickly followed him. The prince looked faint and ill, and had to lean on his host's arm as he tottered towards the window. The little incident was noticed by a few. It caused consternation and the exchange of portentful glances.

A grave-looking man in sober black velvet doublet and sable hose quickly rose from the table and joined the Stadtholder and Mynheer Beresteyn at the window. He was the English physician especially brought across to watch over the health of the illustrious sufferer.

Gilda turned to her neighbour. Her eyes had suddenly filled with tears, but when she met his glance the ghost of a smile immediately crept around her mouth.

"It seems almost wicked," she said simply "to be so happy now."

Unseen by the rest of the company, the man next to her took her tiny hand and raised it to his lips.

"At times, even to-day," she went on softly, "it all seems like a dream. Your wooing, my dear lord, hath been so tempestuous. Less than three months ago I did not know of your existence —"

"My wooing hath been over-slow for my taste!" he broke in with a short, impatient sigh. "Three months, you say? And for me you are still a shadow, an exquisite sprite that eludes me behind an impenetrable, a damnable wall of conventions, even though my very sinews ache with longing to hold you in mine arms for ever and for aye!"

He looked her straight between the eyes, so straight and with such a tantalizing glance that a hot blush rose swiftly to her cheeks; whereupon he laughed again – a merry, a careless, infectious laugh it was – and squeezed her hand so tightly that he made her gasp.

"You are always ready to laugh, my lord," she murmured reproachfully.

"Always," he riposted. "And now, how can I help it? I must laugh, or else curse with impatience. It is scarce three o'clock now, and not before many hours can we be free of this chattering throng."

Then, as she remained silent, with eyes cast down now and the warm flush still lingering in her cheeks, he went on, with brusque impatience, his voice sunk to a quick, penetrating whisper:

"If anything should part me from you now, ma donna, I verily believe that I should kill someone or myself!"

He paused, almost disconcerted. It had never been his wont to talk of his feelings. The transient sentiments that in the past had grazed his senses, without touching his heart, had only led him to careless protestations, forgotten as soon as made. He himself marvelled at the depth of his love for this exquisite creature who had so suddenly come into his life, bringing with her a fragrance of youth and of purity, and withal of fervid passion, such as he had never dreamed of through the many vicissitudes of his adventurous life.

Still she did not speak, and he was content to look on her, satisfied that she was in truth too completely happy at this hour to give vent to her feelings in so many words. He loved to watch the play of emotions in her tell-tale face, the pursed-up little mouth, so ready to smile, and those violet-tinted eyes, now and then raised to him in perfect trust and abandonment of self, then veiled once more demurely under his provoking glance.

He loved to tease her, for then she blushed, and her long lashes drew a delicately pencilled shadow upon her cheeks. He loved to say things that frightened her, for then she would look up with a quick, inquiring glance, search his own with a palpitating expression that quickly melted again into one of bliss.

"You look so demure, ma donna," he exclaimed whimsically, "that I vow I'll create a scandal – leap across the table and kiss Kaatje, for instance – just to see if it would make you laugh!"

"Do not make fun of Kaatje, my lord," Gilda admonished. "She hath more depth of feeling than you give her credit for."

"I do not doubt her depth of feeling, dear heart," he retorted with mock earnestness. "But, oh, good St. Bavon help me! Have you ever seen so solid a yokemate, or," he added, and pointed to Nicolaes Beresteyn, who sat moody and sullen, toying with his food, beside his equally silent bride, "so ardent a bridegroom? Verily, the dear lady reminds me of those succulent fish pasties they make over in England, white and stodgy, and rather heavy on the stomach, but, oh, so splendidly nourishing!"

"Fie! Now you are mocking again."

"How can I help it, dear heart, when you persist in looking so solemn – so solemn, that, in the midst of all this hilarity, I am forcibly reminded of all the rude things you said to me that night at the inn in Leyden, and I am left to marvel how you ever came to change your opinion of me?"

"I changed my opinion of you," she rejoined earnestly, "when I learned how you were ready to give your life to save the Stadtholder from those abominable murderers; and almost lost it," she added under her breath, "to save my brother Nicolaes from the consequence of his own treachery."

"Hush! That is all over and done with now, ma donna," he retorted lightly. "Nicolaes has become a sober burgher, devoted to his solid Kaatje and to the cause of the Netherlands; and I have sold my liberty to the fairest tyrant that ever enslaved a man's soul."

"Do you regret it," she queried shyly, "already?"

"Already!" he assented gravely. "I am kicking against my bonds, longing for that freedom which in the past kept my stomach empty and my head erect."

"Will you never be serious?" she retorted.

"Never, while I live. My journey to England killed my only attempt at sobriety, for there I found that the stock to which I belonged was both irreproachable and grave, had been so all the while that I, the most recent scion of so noble a race, was roaming about the world, the most shiftless and thriftless vagabond it had ever seen. But in England" – he sighed and raised his eyes and hands in mock solemnity – "in England the climate is so atrocious that the people become grim-visaged and square-toed through constantly watching the rain coming down. Or else," he added, with another suppressed ripple of that infectious laugh of his, "the climate in England has become so atrocious because there are so many square-toed folk about. I was such a very little while in England," he concluded with utmost gravity, "I had not time to make up my mind which way it went."

"Methinks you told me," she rejoined, "that your home in England is beautiful and stately."

"It is both, dear heart," he replied more seriously; "and I shall learn to love it when you have dwelt therein. I should love it even now if it had ever been hallowed by the presence of my mother."

"She never went there?"

"No, never. My father came to Holland in Leicester's train. He married my mother in Haarlem, then deserted her and left her there to starve. My friend Frans Hals cared for me after she died. That is the whole of her history. It does not make for deep, filial affection, does it?"

"But you have seen your father now. Affection will come in time."

"Yes; I have seen him, thanks to your father, who brought us together. I have seen my home in Sussex, where one day, please God, you'll reign as its mistress."

"I, the wife of an English lord!" she sighed. "I can scarcely credit it."

"Nor can I, dear heart," he answered lightly; "for that you'll never be. Let me try and explain to you just how it all is, for, in truth, English honours are hard to understand. My father is an English gentleman with no handle to his name. Blake of Blakeney they call him over there; and I am his only son. It seems that he rendered signal services to his king of late, who thereupon desired to confer upon him one of those honours which we over here find it so difficult to apprise. My father, however, either because he is advanced in years or because he desired to show me some singular mark of favour, petitioned King James to bestow the proposed honour upon his only son. Thus am I Sir Percy Blakeney, it seems, without any merit on my part. Funny is it not? And I who, for years, was known by no name save Diogenes, one of three vagabonds, with perhaps more wits, but certainly no more worth, than my two compeers!"

"Then I should call you Sir Percy?" she concluded. "Yet I cannot get used to the name."

"You might even call me Percy," he suggested; "for thus was I baptized at my dear mother's wish. Though, in truth, I had forgotten it until my father insisted on it that I could not be called Diogenes by mine own servants, and that he himself could not present me to his Majesty the King of England under so fanciful a name."

"I like best to think of you as Diogenes," she murmured softly. "Thus I knew you first, and your brother philosophers, Socrates and Pythagoras – such a quaint trio, and all of you so unsuited to your names! I wish," she added with a sigh, "that they were here now."

"And they should be here," he assented. "I am deeply anxious. But Pythagoras —"

He broke off abruptly. Mynheer Beresteyn's voice called to him from the recess by the open window.

"A goblet of wine!" Mynheer commanded; "for his Highness."

Diogenes was about to comply with the order, but Nicolaes forestalled him. Already he had poured out the wine.

"Let me take it," he said curtly, took up the goblet and went with it to the window. He offered it to the Stadtholder, who drank greedily.

It was but a brief incident. Nicolaes had remained beside the prince while the latter drank; then he returned, with the empty goblet in his hand, to take his place once more beside his stolid and solid bride.

"You were speaking of Pythagoras, sir," Gilda rejoined, as soon as Diogenes was once more seated beside her. "I never know which is which of the two dear souls. Is Pythagoras the lean one with the deep, bass voice?"

"No. He is the fat one, with the round, red nose," Diogenes replied gravely. "He was at Ede the night before last, and was seen there, at the tavern of the Crow's Nest, somewhere after midnight, imbibing copious draughts of hot, spiced ale. After that all traces of him have vanished. But he must have started to join me here, as this had been pre-arranged, and I fear me that he lost his way on that verfloekte waste. I have sent Socrates, my lean comrade – to look for poor Pythagoras upon the Veluwe. They should be here, in truth, and —"

But the next word died in his throat. He jumped to his feet.

"The Stadtholder!" he exclaimed. "He hath fainted."

4

Indeed, there was quite a commotion now in the window recess, where Prince Maurice had remained all this while by the open casement, inhaling the fresh, keen air. The English physician stood beside him, and Mynheer Beresteyn was gazing with anxious eyes on the master to whom, in spite of all, he had remained so splendidly loyal. The dizziness had apparently come on quite suddenly, while the Stadtholder was acknowledging the acclamations of the crowd who had seen and cheered him. He tottered and would have fallen but for the physician's supporting arm.

Not many of the guests had noticed the incident. They were for the most part too much absorbed in their enjoyment of the feast to pay attention to what went on in other parts of the room. But Diogenes had seen it and was already over by the window; and Nicolaes Beresteyn, too, had jumped to his feet. He looked wide-eyed and scared, even whilst the stolid Kaatje, flushed with good cheer, remained perfectly unconcerned, munching some sweetmeats which seemed to delight her palate.

The Stadtholder, however, had quickly recovered. The faintness passed off as suddenly as it came, but it left the illustrious guest more silent and moody than before. His face had become of a yellowish pallor, and his eyes looked sunken as if consumed with fever. But he chose to return to his seat under the dais, and this time he called to Diogenes to give him the support of his arm.

"'Twas scarce worth while, eh, my friend," he said bitterly, "to risk your precious young life in order to save this precarious one. Had Stoutenburg's bomb done the assassin's work, it would only have anticipated events by less than three months."

"Your Highness is over-tired," Diogenes rejoined simply. "Complete rest in the midst of your friends would fight this insidious sickness far better than the wisest of physicians."

"What do you mean?" the Stadtholder immediately retorted, his keen, hawk-like glance searching the soldier's smiling face. "Why should you say 'in the midst of your friends?" he went on huskily. "You don't mean —?"

"What, your Highness?"

"I mean – you said it so strangely – as if —"

"I, your Highness?" Diogenes queried, not a little surprised at the Stadtholder's febrile agitation.

"I myself have oft wondered —"

Maurice of Nassau paused abruptly, rested his elbows on the table, and for a moment or two remained quite still, his forehead buried in his hands. Gilda gazed on him wide-eyed and tearful; even Kaatje ceased to munch. It seemed terrible to be so great a man, wielding such power, commanding such obedience, and to be reduced to a mere babbling sufferer, fearing phantoms and eagerly gleaning any words of comfort that might come from loyal lips.

Diogenes had remained silent, too; his eyes, usually so full of light-heartedness and merriment, had a strange, searching glitter in them now. A minute or two later the prince had pulled himself together, tried to look unconcerned, and assumed a geniality which obviously he was far from feeling. But it was to Diogenes that he spoke once more.

"Anyhow, I could not rest yet awhile, my friend," he said with a sigh; "whilst the Archduchess threatens Gelderland, the De Berg is making ready to cross the Ijssel."

"Your Highness's armies under your Highness's command," rejoined the soldier firmly, "can drive the Archduchess's hosts out of Gelderland, and send Henri de Berg back across the Ijssel. Maurice of Nassau is still the finest commander in Europe, even —"

He paused, and the Stadtholder broke in bitterly:

"Even though he is a dying man, you mean."

"No!" here broke in Gilda, with glowing fervour. "I swear that nothing was further from my lord's thoughts. Sir," she added, and turned boldly to her lover, "you spoke with such confidence just now. A toast, I pray you, so that we may all join in expressions of loyalty to our guest and sovereign lord, the Stadtholder!"

She poured a goblet full of wine. Diogenes gave her a quick glance of approval. Then he picked up the goblet, stood upon his seat, and placed one foot on the table.

"Long life to your Highness!" he cried aloud. "May it please God to punish your enemies and to give victory unto your cause!"

Then, holding the goblet aloft, he called at the top of his voice:

"Maurice of Nassau and the cause of Liberty!"

Every one rose, and a rousing cheer went echoing round the room. It was heard and taken up lustily by the crowd outside, until the very walls of the ancient city echoed the loyal toast, from the grim towers of Koppel Poort to the Vrouwetoren of St. Maria Kerk; from gateway to gateway, and rampart to rampart. And the bells of St. Joris and St. Maria took up the joyful call and sent peal after peal of bells resounding gleefully through the keen, wintry air.

"Maurice of Nassau!" rang the chimes. "Nassau and liberty!"

5

But after this manifestation of joy and enthusiasm, comparative silence fell upon the wedding assembly. None but those who had partaken over freely of Mynheer Beresteyn's good cheer could fail to see that the Stadtholder felt ill, and only kept up a semblance of gaiety by a mighty effort of his iron will. Thereafter, conversation became subdued. People talked in whispers, an atmosphere of constraint born of anxiety reigned there where light-hearted gaiety had a while ago held undisputed sway. The host himself did his best to revive the temper of his guests. Serving-men and maids were ordered to go around more briskly with the wine. One or two of the younger men hazarded the traditional jokes which usually obtained at wedding feasts; but those who laughed did so shamefacedly. It seemed as if a vague terror held erstwhile chattering tongues in check.

The Stadtholder, leaning back against the cushions of his chair, spoke very little. His long, nervy fingers played incessantly with crumbs and pellets of bread. He looked impatient and ill at ease, like a man who wants to get away yet fears to offend his host. He had kept Diogenes by his side this time, and Beresteyn was able to snatch a few last words with his daughter. Once she was married, her husband would take her to his home in England one day, and the thought of parting from the child he loved was weighing the father's spirit down.

" 'Tis the first time," he said sadly, "that you will pass out of my keeping. You were the precious heritage bequeathed to me your dead mother. Now 'tis to a stranger that I am entrusting my priceless treasure."

"A stranger, father," riposted Gilda quietly, "who hath proved himself worthy of the truth. And when we do go to England," she went on gaily, "there will only be a narrow strip of water between us, and that is easily crossed."

Beresteyn gave a quickly smothered sigh. He looked across at the stranger to whom, as he said, he was about to hand over the most precious gift he possessed. Handsome he was, that erstwhile penniless soldier of fortune; handsome and brave, frank and loyal, and with that saving grace of light-hearted gaiety in him which had helped him through the past terrible crisis in his life, and brought him to the safe haven of a stately home in England and wealthy father, eager to make amends for the wrongs committed long ago.

But still a stranger for all that, a man who had seen more of the seamy side of the world, who had struggled more, suffered more – ay, perhaps sinned more – than those of his rank in life usually did at his age. Something of that rough-and-tumble life of the soldier of fortune, without home or kindred, who sells his sword to the highest bidder, and knows no master save his own will, must have left its mark upon the temperament of the man. Despite the humorous twinkle in the eyes, the bantering curl on the lip, the man's face bore the impress of the devil-may-care existence that takes no heed of the morrow. And at times, when it was in repose, there was a strangely grim look in it of determination as well as of turbulent passions, not always held in check.

Beresteyn sighed with inward apprehension. His well-ordered mind, the mind of a Dutch middle-class burgher, precise and unemotional, could not quite fathom that of the Anglo-Saxon – the most romantic and the most calculating, and the most impulsive and the most studied, the most sensuous and most self-repressed temperament that ever set the rest of the world wondering. He could see the reckless scapegrace, the thoughtless adventurer, fuming and fretting under the restraint put upon him by the cut-and-dried conventions attendant upon these wedding ceremonies could watch him literally writhing under the knowing looks and time-honoured innuendos which custom deemed allowable on these occasions. His hands indeed must be itching to come in contact with the checks of mocking friends and smug relatives, all eager to give advice or to chaff the young bride, until the hot blood rushed to her cheeks and tears of annoyance gather in her eyes.

The whole atmosphere of noise and drinking – ay, of good-humour and complacency – did, in truth, grate upon Diogenes' nerves. He had not lied to Gilda nor yet exaggerated his sentiments when he said that his sinews ached with longing to seize her and carry her away into solitude and quiet, where nought would come to disturb their love-dream; away upon his horse, her soft arms encircling his neck her head resting on his shoulder, her dear face turned up to his gaze, with those heavenly eyes closed in rapture; the delicate mouth slightly parted, showing a vision of tiny teeth, a tear mayhap trembling on her lashes, a soft blush mantling on her cheek. Away! Across the ocean to that stately home in England, where the spring air was soft with the scent of violets and of fruit blossom, and where beside the river the reeds murmured a soft accompaniment to songs of passion and hymns of love. Away from all save the shrine which he had set up for her in his heart; from all save the haven of his arms.

To feel that, and then be forced to sit and discuss plans for the undoing of the Spanish commander or for the relief of Arnheim, was, in fact, more than Diogenes' restive temperament could stand. His attention began to wander, his answers became evasive; so much so that, after a while, the Stadtholder, eyeing him closely, remarked with the pale ghost of a smile:

" 'Tis no use fretting and fuming, my friend. Your English blood is too mutinous for this sober country and its multitude of stodgy conventions. One of these demands that your bride shall sit here till the last of the guests has departed, and only a few fussy and interfering old tantes are left to unrobe her and commiserate with her over her future lot – a slave to a bullying husband, a handmaid to her exacting lord. Every middle-aged frump in the Netherlands hath some story to tell that will bring tears to a young bride's eyes or a blush to her cheeks."

"Please God," Diogenes ejaculated fervently. "Gilda will be spared that."

"Impossible, you rogue!" the Stadtholder retorted, amused despite his moodiness by the soldier's fretful temper. "The conventions--"

"Verfloekt will be the conventions as far as we are concerned," Diogenes rejoined hotly. "And if your Highness would but help —" he added impulsively.

"I? What can I do?"

"Give the signal for dispersal," Diogenes entreated; "and graciously promise to forgive me if, for the first time in my life, I act with disrespect toward your Highness."

"But, man, how will that help you?" the Stadtholder demurred.

"I must get away from all this wearying bombast, this jabbering and scraping and all these puppy-tricks!" Diogenes exclaimed with comical fierceness. "I must get away ere my wife becomes a doll and a puppet, tossed into my arms by a lot of irresponsible monkeys! If I have to stay here much longer, your Highness," he added earnestly "I vow that I shall flee from it all, leave an angel to weep for my abominable desertion of what I hold more priceless than all the world, and an outraged father to curse the day when so reckless and adventurer crossed his daughter's path. But stand this any longer I cannot!" he concluded, and, with a quick sweep of the arm, he pointed to the chattering, buzzing crowd below. "And if your Highness will not help me —"

"Who said I would not help you, you hotheaded rashling?" the Stadtholder broke in composedly. "You know very well that I can refuse you nothing, not even the furtherance of one of your madcap schemes. And as for disrespect – why, as you say, in the midst of so much bowing and scraping some of us are eager for disrespect as an aging spinster for amorous overtures. By way of a change, you know."

He spoke quite simply and with an undercurrent of genuine sympathy in his tone, as a man towards his friend. Something of the old Maurice of Nassau seemed for the moment to have swept aside the arbitrary tyrant whom men had learned to hate as well as to obey. Diogenes' irascible mood melted suddenly in the sunshine of the Stadtholder's indulgent smile, the mocking glance faded out of his eyes, and he said with unwonted earnestness:

"No wonder that men have gone to death or to glory under your leadership."

"Would you follow me again if I called?" the prince retorted.

"Your Highness hath no need of me. The United Provinces are free, her burghers are free men. 'Tis time to sheathe the sword, and a man might be allowed, methinks, to dream of happiness."

"Is your happiness bound up with the mad scheme for which you want my help?"

"Ay, my dear lord!" Diogenes replied. "And, secure in your gracious promise, I swear that naught can keep me from the scheme now save mine own demise."

"There are more arbitrary things than death, my friend," the Stadtholder mused.

"Possibly, your Highness," the soldier answered lightly; "but not for me to-night."

6

More than one chronicler of the time hath averred that Maurice of Nassau had in truth a soft corner in his heart for the man who had saved him from the bomb prepared by the Lord of Stoutenburg, and would yield to the "Laughing Cavalier" when others, less privileged, were made to feel the weight of his arbitrary temper. Be that as it may, he certainly on this occasion was as good as his word. Wearied with all these endless ceremonials, he was no doubt glad enough to take his departure, and anon he gave the signal for a general breaking up of the party by rising, and, in a loud voice, thanking Mynheer Beresteyn for his lavish hospitality.

"An you will pardon this abrupt departure," he concluded with unwonted graciousness, "I would fain get to horse. By starting within the hour, I could reach Utrecht before dark."

All the guests had risen, too, and there was the usual hubbub and noise attendant on the dispersal of so large a party. That Stadtholder stepped down from the dais, Mynheer Beresteyn and the English physician remaining by his side, while the bridal party brought up the rear. Room was made for his Highness to walk down the room, the men standing bareheaded and the women curtseying as he passed. But he did not speak to any one, only nodded perfunctorily to those whom he knew personally. Obviously he felt ill and tired, and his moodiness was, for the most part, commented on with sympathy.

The brides and bridegrooms, on the other hand, had to withstand a veritable fusillade of banter, which Nicolaes Beresteyn received sulkily, and the solid Kaatje with much complacence. Indeed, this bride was willing enough to be chaffed, had even a saucy reply handy when she was teased, and ogled her friends slily as she went by. But Gilda remained silent and demure. I don't think that she heard a word that was said. She literally seemed to glide across the room like the veritable sprite her ardent lover had called her. Her tiny hand, white and slightly fluttering, rested on his arm, lost in the richly embroidered folds of his magnificent doublet. She was not fully conscious of her actions, moved along as in a dream, without the exertion of her will. She was wont to speak afterwards of this brief progress of hers through the crowded room with the chattering throng of friends all around, as a walk through air. Nothing seemed to her to exist. There was no room, , no crowd, no noise. She alone existed, and ethereally. Her lover was there, however, and she was fully conscious of his will. She knew that anon she would be a captive in his arms, to be dealt with my him as he liked; and this caused her to feel that fearful and yet wholly content.

He, Diogenes, on the other hand, was the picture of fretful impatience, squeezing his soft felt hat in his hand as if it were the throat of some deadly enemy. He never once looked at his bride; probably if he had he would have lost the last shred of self-control, would have seized her in his arms and carried her away then and there, regardless of the respect due to the Stadtholder and to his host.

But the trial, though severe to any ebullient temper, was not of long duration. Anon the Stadtholder was in the hall, booted once more and spurred, and surrounded by his equerries and by the bridal party.

His bodyguard encumbered the hall, their steel bonnets and short breastplates reflecting the wintry light which came, many-hued, through the tall, stained glass windows. In the rear the wedding guests were crowding forward to catch a last glimpse of the Stadtholder, and of the pageant of his departure. The great hall door had been thrown open, and through it, framed in the richness of the heavy oaken jambs, a picture appeared, gay, animated, brilliant, such as the small city had never before seen.

There was the holiday throng, moving ceaselessly in an ever flowing and glittering stream. The women in huge, winged hoods and short kirtles, the men in fur bonnets and sleeved coats, were strolling up and down the quay. There were the inevitable musicians with pipes, viols, and sackbuts, pushing their way through the dense mass of people, with a retinue behind them of young people and old, and of children, all stepping it to the measure of the tune. There was the swarthy foreigner with his monkey dressed out in gaily coloured rags, and the hawker with his tray full of bright handkerchiefs, of glass beads, chains, and amulets, crying out his wares. It was, in fact, a holiday crowd, drawn thither by Mynheer Beresteyn's largesse; the shopkeepers with their wives, who had been induced to shut down shop for the afternoon, as if some official function had been in progress; the apprentices getting in everybody's way, hilarious and full of mischief, trying to steal the hawkers' wares, or to play impish pranks on their employers; servant maids and sober apothecaries, out-at-elbow scriveners and stolid rustics, to-gether with the rag and tag of soldiery, the paid mercenaries of Maurice of Nassau's army, in their showy doublets and plumed bonnets, elbowing their way through with the air of masters.

And all this brilliant gathering was lit by a pale, wintry sun: and with the sleepy waters of the Eem, and the frowning towers of the Koppel-poort forming just the right natural-tinted background to the scene.

"Make way there!" the prince's herald shouted, whilst another rang a fanfare upon the trumpet. "Make way for his High and Mightiness, Maurice of Nassau, Prince of Orange, Stadtholder of the United Provinces of Holland, Friesland, Utrecht, Gelderland, Over Yssel, and Groningen! Make way!"

The equerries were bringing the prince's charger, the pikemen followed in gorgeous padded trunks and slashed hose. To the noise of the moving throng, the chatter and the laughter, the scraping of viols and piping of sackbuts, was now added the din of champing horses, rattle of bits and chains, the shouts of the men who were bringing the horses along. The crowd receded, leaving an open space in front of the house, where mounted men assembled so quickly that they seemed as if they had risen out of the ground.

The Stadtholder was taking final leave of his host listening with what patience he could master to lengthy, loyal speeches from the more important guests, and from the other bride and bridegroom. He had – deliberately methinks – turned his back on Diogenes, who, strangely enough, was booted and spurred too, had his sword buckled to his belt, and carried a dark cloak on his arm, presenting not at all the picture of a bridegroom in holiday attire.

And it all happened so quickly that neither the guests within, nor the soldiers, nor the crowd outside, had time to realize it or to take it in. No one understood, in fact, what was happening, save perhaps the Stadtholder, who guessed; and he engaged the sober fathers near him in earnest conversation.

A mounted equerry, dressed in rough leather jerkin and leading another horse by the bridle, had taken up his stand in the forefront of the crowd. Now at a signal unheard by all save him, he jumped out of the saddle and stood beside the stirrup leathers of the second charger. At that same instant Diogenes, with movements quick as lightning, had thrown the cloak, which he was carrying round Gilda's shoulders, and before she could utter a scream or even a gasp, he had stooped and picked her up in his arms as if she were a weightless doll.

Another second and he was outside the door, at the top of the steps which led down to the quay. For an instant he stood there, his keen eyes sweeping over the picture before him. Like a young lion that hath been caged and now scents liberty once more, he inhaled the biting air; a superb figure, with head tossed back, eyes and lips laughing with the joy of deliverance, the inert figure of the girl lying in his arms.

He felt her clinging more closely to him, and revelled in that intoxicating sense of power when the one woman yields who holds a world of happiness in her tiny hand. He felt the tightening of her hold, watched the look of contentment stealing over her face, saw her eyes close, her lips smile, and knew that they were ready for a kiss.

Then he caught sight of his horse, and of the man in the leather jerkin. He signalled to him to bring the horses near. The crowd understood his meaning and set up a ringing cheer. Many things had been seen in Dutch cities before, but never so romantic an abduction as this. The bridegroom carrying off his bride in the face of scandalized and protesting wedding guests! The Stadtholder even was seen to laugh. He could be seen in the background, reassuring the horrified guests, and trying by kind words and pressure of hand to appease Mynheer Beresteyn's agonized surprise.

"I knew of his mad project, and I must say I approved," the prince whispered to the agitated father. "He is taking her to Rotterdam to-night. Let the child be, Mynheer; she is safe enough in his arms."

Beresteyn was one of those men who throughout his life had always known how to accept the inevitable. Perhaps in his heart he knew that the Stadtholder was right.

"Give them your blessing, Mynheer," Maurice of Nassau urged. "English gentleman or soldier of fortune, the man is a man and deserves it. Your daughter loves him. Let them be."

Diogenes had encountered Beresteyn's reproachful glance. He did not move from where he stood, only his arms closed tighter still around Gilda's motionless form. It was an instinctive challenge to the father – almost a defiance. What he had would hold, in spite of all.

Beresteyn hesitated for the mere fraction of a second longer; then he, too, stepped out through the door and approached the man and his burden. He said nothing, but, in the face of the crowd, he stooped and pressed his lips against his daughter's forehead. Then Mynheer Beresteyn murmured something which sounded like a blessing, and added solemnly:

"May God's wrath descend upon you, my lord, if you ever cause her unhappiness."

"Amen to that!" responded Diogenes lightly. "She and I, Mynheer, will dream together for awhile in England, but I'll bring her back to you when our orchards are gay with apple-blossom and there is a taste of summer in the air."

He bowed his head to receive the father's blessing. The crowd cheered again; sackbuts and viols set up a lively tune. At every window of the house, along the quay eager faces were peering out, gazing on the moving spectacle. In the doorway of Mynheer Beresteyn's house the

Stadtholder remained to watch. For the moment he seemed better and brighter, more like his former self. The rest of the bridal party was still in the hall, but the wedding guests had gone back into the banqueting-room, whence they could see through the open windows what was going on.

7

Then it was that suddenly a curious spectacle presented itself to view. It was, in truth, so curious an one that those of the crowd who were in the rear withdrew their consideration from the romantic scene before them in order to concentrate it on those two strange-looking cavaliers who had just emerged from under the Koppel-port, and were slowly forging their way through the throng.

It was the ringing shout, reiterated twice in succession by one of these cavaliers, that had at first arrested the attention of the crowd, and had even caused Diogenes to pause in the very act of starting for his sentimental adventure. To him the voice that uttered such peremptory clamour was familiar enough, but what in St. Bavon's name did it all mean?

"Hola! you verdommte plepshurk!" came for the third time from the strange cavalier. "Make way there! We are for the house of Mynheer Beresteyn, where we are bidden as his guests."

A loud burst of hilarity greeted this announcement, and a mocking voice retorted lustily:

"Hey! Make way there for the honoured guests of Mynheer Beresteyn!"

In truth, it was small wonder that the aspect of these two cavaliers caused such wild jollity amongst the people, who at this precise moment were overready for laughter. One of them, as lean as a gatepost, sat high on his horse with long shanks covered in high leathern boots. A tall sugar-loaf hat sat precariously upon his head, and his hatchet face, with the hooked, prominent nose and sharp, unshaved chin, looked blue with the cold.

Behind him on a pillion rode – or rather clung – his companion, a short man as rotund as the other was lean, with round face which no doubt had once been of a healthy ruddy tint, but was now streaked and blotched with pallor. He, too, , wore a sugar-loaf hat, but it had slid down to the back of his head, and was held in place by a piece of black tape, which he had in his mouth like a horse has its bit. He was holding on very tightly with his short, fat arms to his companion's body, and his feet were tied together with thick cord beneath the horse's belly. His doublet and hose were smeared with mud and stained with blood, and altogether he presented a pitiable spectacle, more especially when he rolled his small, beady eyes and looked with a scared expression on the hilarious apprentices who were dancing and screaming around him.

But the other appeared quite indifferent to the jeers and mockeries of the crowd. He passed majestically through the gateway of the Koppel-poort that spans the river, not unlike the figure of that legendary knight of the rueful countenance of whom the SeÒor Cervantes had been writing of late.

Diogenes had remained on the top of the steps, perfectly still. His keen eyes, frowning now under the straight, square brow, watched the slow progress of those two quaint figures. Who will ever attempt to explain the subtle workings of that mysterious force which men term Intuition? Whence does it come? Where does it dwell? How doth it come knocking at a man's heart with cold, hard knuckles that bruise and freeze? Diogenes felt that sudden call. Gilda was still lying snugly in his arms; she had seen nothing. But he had become suspicious now, mistrustful of that Fate which had but a moment ago smiled so encourageingly upon him. All his exhilaration fell away from him like a discarded mantle, leaving him chilled to the soul and inert, and with the premonition of something evil looming from afar on the horizon of his Destiny.

The two quaint companions came nearer. Soon Diogenes could read every line upon the familiar countenances. He and those men had fought side by side, shoulder to shoulder, had bled together, suffered together, starved and triumphed together. There was but little the one thought that the others could not know. Even now, on Socrates; lean, lantern-jawed face Diogenes read plainly the message of some tragedy as yet uncomprehended by the other, but which Pythagoras' sorry plight had more that suggested. It was a deeper thing than Intuition; it was Knowledge. Knowledge that the hour of happiness had gone by, the hour of security and of repose, and that the relentless finger of Fate pointed once more to paths beset with sorrow and with thorns, to the path of an adventurer and of a soldier of fortune, rather than to the easy existence of a wealthy gentleman.

As Socrates swung himself wearily out of the saddle, Diogenes' piercing glance darted a mute, quick query toward his friend. The other replied by a mere nod of the head. They knew; they understood one another. Put into plain language, question and answer might have been put thus:

"Are we to go on the warpath again, old compeer?"

"So it seems. There's fighting to be done. Will you be in it, too?"

And Diogenes gave that quick impatient sigh which was so characteristic of him, and very slowly, very gently, as if she were a sheaf of flowers, he allowed his beloved to glide out of his arms.

1

THE next moment Diogenes was down on the quay, in time to help Socrates to lift his brother philosopher off the pillion.

Gilda, a little scared at first, not understanding, looked wonderingly around her, blinking in the glare, until she encountered her father's troubled glance.

"What is it?" she murmured, half-stupidly.

He tried to explain, pointed to the group down below, the funny, fat man in obvious pain and distress, being lifted off the horse and received in those same strong arms which had sheltered her – Gilda – but a moment ago.

The Stadtholder, too, was curious, asked many questions, and had to be waited on deferentially with replies and explanations, which were still of necessity very vague.

"Attend to his Highness, father," Gilda said more firmly. "I can look to myself now."

She felt a little strange, a little humiliated perhaps, standing here alone, as if abandoned by the very man who but a moment ago had seemed ready to defy every convention for her sake. Just now she had been the centre of attraction, the pivot round which revolved excitement, curiosity, interest. Even the Stadtholder had, for the space of those few minutes, forgotten his cares and his responsibilities in order to think of her and to plead with her father for her freedom and her happiness. Now she was all alone, seemed so for the moment, while her father and Mynheer van den Poele and the older men crowded around his Highness, and every one had their eyes fixed on the curious spectacle below.

But that sense of isolation and of disappointment was only transient. Gilda Beresteyn had recently gone through experiences far more bitter than this – experiences that had taught her to think and to act quickly and on her own initiative. She saw her lover remounting the steps now. He was carrying his friend in his arms as if the latter had been a child, his other compeer following ruefully. The rowdy 'prentices had been silenced; two or three kindly pairs of hands had proved ready to assist and to care for the horse, which looked spent. The holiday crowd was silent and sympathetic. Every one felt that in this sudden interruption of the gay and romantic adventure there lurked a something mysterious which might very well prove to be a tragedy.

It was Gilda who led the way into the house, calling Maria to open a guest-chamber forthwith, one where the bed was spread with freshly-aired linen. The English physician, at a word from the Stadtholder, was ready to minister to the sick man, and Mynheer Beresteyn himself showed the young soldier and his burden up the stairs, while the crowd of wedding guests and of the prince's bodyguard made way for them to pass through the hall.

What had been such a merry and excited throng earlier in the day was now more than ever subdued. The happenings in the house of Mynheer Beresteyn, which should have been at this hour solely centred around the Stadtholder and the wedding party, were strange enough indeed to call forth whispered comments and subdued murmurings in secluded corners. To begin with, the Stadtholder had put off his departure for an hour and more, and this apparently at the instance of Diogenes, who had begged for the assistance of the prince's English physician to minister to his friend.

People marvelled why the town leech should not have been called in. Why should a strange plepshurk's sickness interfere with his Highness's movements? Also the Stadtholder appeared agitated and fretful since Diogenes had had a word with him. Maurice of Nassau, acquiescing with unwonted readiness both in his physician remaining to look after the sick man and in the postponement of his own departure, had since then retired to a small private room on a floor above, in the company of Mynheer Beresteyn and several of the more important guests. The others were left to conjecture and to gossip, which they did freely, whilst Gilda was no longer to be seen, and the worthy Kaatje was left pouting and desolate beside her morose bridegroom.

Nicolaes Beresteyn, indeed, appeared more moody than any one, although the interruption could not in itself have interfered with his new domestic arrangements. At first he had thought of following his father and Stadtholder into the private chamber upstairs, but to this Mynheer Beresteyn had demurred.

"Your place, my son," he said, with a gently mocking smile, "is beside your Kaatje. His Highness will understand."

And when Nicolaes, trying to insist, followed his father up the stairs to the very threshold of the council room, Mynheer quite firmly and unceremoniously closed the door in his face.

2

Up in the guest-chamber, Diogenes was watching over his sick friend. The first moment that he was alone with his two old compeers, he had turned to Socrates and queried anxiously:

"What is it? What hath happened?"

"He'll tell you when he can speak," the other replied. "We found him lying in the snow outside Lang Soeren with two bullet-wounds in his back, after we had searched the whole verfloekte Veluwe for him all day. We took him into Lang Soeren, where there was a leech, who extracted the one bullet that had lodged under his shoulder blade; the other had only passed through the flesh along his ribs, where it made a clean hole but could not otherwise be found."

"Well, yes – and —" Diogenes went on impatiently, for the other was somewhat slow of speech.

"The leech," Socrates rejoined unperturbed, "said that the patient must lie still for a few days because of the fever; but what must this fool do but shout and rave the moment he is conscious that he must to Amersfoort to see you at once. And so loudly did he shout and so wildly did he rave, that the leech himself got scared and ran away. Whereupon I set the bladder-bellied loon upon the pillion behind me and brought him hither, thinking the ride would do him less harm than all that wild screeching and waving of arms. And here we are!" Socrates concluded blandly, and threw himself into the nearest chair; for he, too, apparently was exhausted with the fatigue of his perilous journey across the waste.

Just then the leech returned, and nothing more could be said. The sick man groaned a good deal under the physician's hands, and Socrates presently dropped off to sleep.

The noise in the street below had somewhat abated, but there was still the monotonous hubbub attendant on a huge crowd on the move. Diogenes went to the window and gazed out upon the throng. Even now the wintry sun was sinking slowly down in the west in a haze of purple and rose, licking the towers of St. Maria and Joris with glistening tongues of fire, and tinting the snow-covered roofs and gables with a rosy hue. The sluggish waters of the Eem appeared like liquid flame.

For a few minutes the Koppel-poort, the bridges, the bastions, the helmets and breastplates of the prince's guard threw back a thousand rays of multi-coloured lights. For a brief instant the earth glowed and blushed under this last kiss of her setting lord. Then all became sombre and dreary, as if a veil had been drawn over the light that illuminated the little city, leaving but the grey shadows visible, and the sadness of evening and the expectance of a long winter's night.

Diogenes gave a moody sigh. His fiery temper chafed under this delay. Not for a moment would he have thought of leaving his sick comrade until he had been reassured as to his fate; but if everything had happened as he had planned and wished, he would be half-way to Utrecht by now, galloping adown the lonely roads with a delicious burden upon his saddle-bow, and feeling the cold wintry wind whistling past his ears as he put the leagues behind him.

He turned away from the window, and tiptoed out of the room. The groans of the sick man, the measured movements of the leech, the snoring of Socrates, were grating on his nerves. Closing the door softly behind him, he strode down the gallery which ran in front of him along the entire width of the house. Up and down once or twice. The movement did him good, and he liked the solitude. The house was still full of a chattering throng; he could hear the murmur of conversation rising from below. Once he peeped over the carved balustrade of the gallery and down into the hall. The prince's bodyguard was still there, and two or three equerries. The clank of their spurs resounded up the stairs as they moved about on the flag-covered floor.

3

When Diogenes resumed his pacing up and down, he suddenly became aware of the soft and distant sound of a woman's voice, singing to the accompaniment of a quaint-toned virginal. He paused and listened. The voice was Gilda's, and the sentimental ditty which she sang had just that melancholy strain in it which is to be found in the songs of all nations that are foredoomed to suffer and to fight. Chiding himself for a fool, Diogenes, nevertheless, felt for a moment or two quite unable to move. It seemed as if Gilda's song – he could not catch the words – was tearing at his heart even whilst it reduced him to a state of silent ecstasy. Much against his will he felt the hot tears welling to his eyes. With his wonted impatience he swept them away with the back of his hand.

"Curse me for a snivelling blockhead!" he muttered; and strode resolutely in the direction whence had come the sweet sad sound.

Then it was that he noticed that one of the doors which gave on the gallery was ajar. It was through this that the intoxicating sound had come to his ears. After an instant's hesitation he pushed the door open. It gave on a small panelled room with deep-embrasured window, through which the grey evening light came in, shyly peeping. On the window-ledge a couple of pots of early tulips flaunted their crude colours against the neutral-tinted background, whilst on the shelves in a corner of the room gleamed the vivid blue of bright-patterned china plates. But the flowers and the china and the grey evening light were but momentary impressions, which did not fix themselves upon the man's consciousness. All that he retained clearly was the vision of Gilda sitting at the instrument, her delicate hands resting upon the keys. She had ceased to play, and was looking straight out before her, and Diogenes could see her piquant profile silhouetted against the pale, slivery light. She had changed her stiff bridal robes for a plain gown of dark-coloured worsted, relieved only by dainty cuffs and collar of filmy Flemish lace.

At the sound of her husband's footsteps she turned to look on him, and her whole face became wreathed in smiles. He was still booted and spurred, ready for the journey, with his long, heavy sword buckled to his belt; but he had put hat and mantle aside. The moment he came in Gilda put a finger to her lips.

"Sh-sh-sh!" she whispered. "If you make no noise they'll not know you are here."

She pointed across the room to where a heavy tapestry apparently masked another door.

"The Stadtholder is in there," she added naively, "with father and Mynheer van den Poele and a number of other grave seigneurs. Kaatje is weeping and complaining somewhere down in mejuffrouw van den Poele's arms. So I sat down to the virginal and left the door open, so that you might hear me sing; for if you heard I thought you would surely come. I was lonely," she added simply, "and waiting for you."

Quite enough in truth to make a man who is dizzy with love ten thousand times more dizzy still. And Diogenes was desperately in love, more so indeed than he had ever thought himself capable of being. He quietly unbuckled his sword, which clanged against the floor when he moved, and deposited in cautiously and noiselessly in an angle of the room. Then he tiptoed across to the virginal and knelt beside his beloved.

For a moment or two he rested his head against her cool white hands.

"To think," he murmured, with a sigh of infinite longing, "that we might be half-way to Rotterdam by now! But I could not leave my old Pythagoras till I knew that he was in no danger."

"What saith the physician, my lord?" she asked.

"I am waiting now for his final verdict. But he gives me every hope. In an hour I shall know."

He paused, trying to read the varying play of emotions upon her face. From the other side of the tapestry came the low sound of subdued murmurings.

"It would not be too late," he went on, slightly hesitating, taking her hands in his and forcing her glance to meet his. "You knew I meant to take you to England – to carry you away – to-night?"

She nodded.

"Yes, I knew," she replied. "And I was glad to go."

"Will you be afraid to come presently?" he urged, his voice quivering with excitement. "In the dark – I know the road well. We could make Rotterdam by midnight – and set sail for England To-morrow as I had prearranged —"

"Just as you wish, my dear lord," she assented simply.

"I could not wait, ma donna! I had planned it all – to ride with you Rotterdam to-night – and then to-morrow on the seas – with you – and England in sight, I could not wait!" he reiterated, almost pathetically, so great was his impatience.

"I am ready to start when you will, my lord," she said again, with a smile.

"And you'll not be afraid?" he insisted. "It will be dark – and cold. We could not reach Rotterdam before midnight."

"How should I be afraid of the darkness or of anything," she retorted, "when I am with you. And how should I be cold, when I am nestling in your arms?"

He had his arms round her in an instant. He would have kissed her if he dared. But with the kiss all restraint would of a surety have vanished, as doth the snow in the warm embrace of the sun. He would have seized her then and there once more and carried her away. And this time no consideration on earth would have stayed him. With a muttered exclamation, he jumped to his feet and passed his slender hand across his forehead.

"Good St. Bavon!" he murmured whimsically. "Why are you so unkind to me to-night?"

And she, a little disappointed because, in truth, she had been ready for the kiss, rejoined with a quaint little pout:

"You are always appealing to St. Bavon, my dear lord! Why is that?"

"Because," he replied very seriously, "St. Bavon is the patron saint of all men that are weak."

She fixed great, wondering eyes on him. The reply was ambiguous; she did not quite understand the drift of it.

"But you, my lord, are so strong," she objected.

It was perhaps too dark for her to see the expression in his face; but even so she felt herself unaccountably blushing under that gaze which she could not clearly see. Whereupon he uttered an ejaculation which sounded almost as if he were angered, and abruptly, without any warning, he turned on his heel and went out of the room, leaving Gilda alone once more beside the virginal.

But she no longer felt the desire to sing. The happiness which filled her entire soul was too complete even for song.

4

One of the equerries had awhile ago found his way to the guest-chamber where the sick man was lying, and had informed Diogenes that the Stadtholder was now ready to start on his way, but desired his presence that he might take his leave. Then it was that Diogenes sent an urgent message to his Highness, entreating him to remain but a little while longer. The sick man was better, would soon wake out of a refreshing sleep. Diogenes would then question him. Poor old Pythagoras had something to say, something that the Stadtholder himself must hear. Of this Diogenes was absolutely convinced.

"I know it," the young soldier asserted earnestly. "I seem to feel it in my bones."

Whereupon the Stadtholder had decided to wait, and Diogenes, after his brief glimpse of Gilda, felt easier in his mind, less impatient. Already he chided himself for his gloomy forebodings. Since his beloved was ready to entrust herself to him, the journey to England would only be put off by a few hours. What need to repine? Joy would be none the less sweet for this brief delay.

A quarter of an hour later Pythagoras was awake the physician out of the room, and Diogenes was sitting on the edge of the bed holding his faithful comrade's hand, and trying to disentangle some measure of coherence out of the other's tangled narrative, whilst Socrates stood by making an occasional comment or just giving an expressive grunt from time to time. It took both time and patience, neither of which commodities did Diogenes possess in super-abundance; but after the first few moments of listening to the rambling of the sick man, he became very still and attentive. The busy house, the noisy guests, the waiting Stadtholder down below, all slipped out from his ken. Holding his comrade's hand, he was with him on the snow-clad Veluwe, and had found his way with him into the lonely mill.

"It was the Lord of Stoutenburg," Pythagoras averred, with as much strength as he could command. "I'd stake my life on't! I knew him at once. How could I ever forget his ugly countenance, after all he made you suffer?"

"Well – and?" queried Diogenes eagerly.

"I knew the other man too, but could not be sure of his name. He was one of those who was with Stoutenburg that day at Ryswick, when you so cleverly put a spoke in their abominable wheel. I knew them both, I tell you!" the sick man insisted feverishly; "but I had the good sense not to betray what I knew."

"But Stoutenburg did not know you?" Diogenes insisted.

"Yes, he did," the other replied, sagely nodding his head. "That is why he ordered his menial to put a bullet into my back. The two noble gentlemen questioned me first," he went on more coherently; "then they plied me with wine. They wanted to make me drunk so as to murder me at their leisure."

"They little know they, eh, thou bottomless barrel?" Diogenes broke in with a laugh. "The cask hath not been fashioned yet that would contain enough liquor even to quench thy thirst, what?"

"They plied me with wine," Pythagoras reiterated gravely; "and then I pretended to get very drunk. For I soon remarked that the more drunk they thought I was, the more freely they talked."

"Well, and what did they say?"

"They talked of De Berg crossing the Ijssel with ten thousand men between Doesburg and Bronchorst; and of Isembourg coming up from Kleve at the same time. I make no doubt that the design is to seize Arnheim and Nijmegen. They talked a deal about Arnheim, which they thought was scantily garrisoned and could easily be taken by surprise and made to surrender. Having got these two cities, the plan is to march across the Veluwe and offer battle to the Stadtholder with a force vastly superior to his, if in the meanwhile —"

He paused. It seemed as if his voice, hoarse with fatigue, was refusing him service. Diogenes reached for the potion which stood on a small table beside the bed. The sick man made a wry face.

"Physic?" he ejaculated reproachfully. "From you, old compeer? Times were when—"

"There will be a time now," retorted the other gruffly, "when you'll sink back into a raging fever, and will be babbling bibulous nonsense if you don't do as you are told."

"I'll sink into a raging fever now," the sick man retorted fretfully, "if I have not something potable to drink ere long."

"You'll drink this physic now, old compeer," Diogenes insisted, and held the mug to his friend's parched lips, forcing him to drink. "Then I'll see what can be done for you later on."

He schooled himself to patience and gentleness. At all costs Pythagoras must complete his narrative. There was just something more that he wished to say, apparently – something fateful and of deadly import, but which for some obscure reason he found difficult to put into words.

"Now then, old friend, make an effort!" Diogenes urged insistently. "There is still something on your mind. What is it?"

Pythagoras' round, beady eyes were rolling in their sockets. He looked scared, like one who has gazed on what is preternatural and weird.

"Stoutenburg has a project," he resumed after a while, and sank his spent voice to the merest whisper. "Listen, my compeer; for the very walls have ears. Bend yours to me. There! That's better," he added, as Diogenes bent his long back until his ear was almost on a level with the sick man's lips. "Stoutenburg hath a project, I tell you. A damnable project, akin to the one which you caused to abort three months ago."

"Assassination?" Diogenes queried curtly.

The sick man nodded.

"Do you know the details?"

"Alas, no! But it is aimed at the Stadtholder. What form it is to take I know not, and they had evidently talked it all over before. It seemed almost as if the other man – Stoutenburg's friend – was horrified at the project. He tried to argue once or twice, and once I heard him say quite distinctly: 'Not that, Stoutenburg! Let us fight him like men; even kill him, like men kill one another. But not like that.' But my Lord Stoutenburg only laughed."

Diogenes was silent. He was deep in thought.

"You had no other indication?" he asked reflectively.

"No," Pythagoras replied. All I saw was that my lord kept the finger and thumb of his right hand in a hidden pocket of his doublet, and once he said: 'The Prince of Poets taught me to manufacture them; and I supply them to him you know of, wherever he can find an opportunity to come out here to me. He uses them at his discretion. But we can judge by results! And then he laughed because his friend appeared to shudder. I was puzzled," the sick man went on wearily, "because of it all; and I marvelled who the Prince of Poets might be, for I am no scholar and I thought that perhaps —"

"You are quite sure Stoutenburg said 'Prince of Poets'?" Diogenes insisted, frowning. "Your ears must have been buzzing by then."

"I am quite sure," Pythagoras asserted. "But I could not see what he had in his hand."

Diogenes said nothing more, and silence fell upon the stately chamber, the sombre panelling and heavy tapestries of which effectually deadened every sound that came from the outside. Only the monumental clock up against the wall ticked in a loud monotone. The sick man, wearied with so much talking, fell back against the pillows. The shades of evening were quickly gathering in now; the corners of the room were indistinguishable in the gloom. Only the bed-clothes still gleamed white in the uncertain light. From the distant tower of St. Maria Kerk a bell chimed the hour of seven. A few minutes went by. Anon there came a scratching at the door.

In response to Diogenes' loud "Enter!" the physician came in, preceded by a serving-man carrying two lighted candles in massive silver sconces.

"His Highness cannot wait any longer," the physician said, as soon as he had perceived Diogenes, still sitting pensive on the edge of the bed. "And as I have no anxiety about the patient now, I will, by your leave, place him in your hands."

Diogenes appeared to wake as if out of a dream. He rose and looked about him somewhat vaguely. The physician thought he must have been asleep.

"Will you pay your respects to his Highness?" the latter said. "I think he desires to see you."

Just for a moment Diogenes remained quite still. The physician had approached the sick man, and was surveying him with critical but obviously reassured attention. Socrates was again snoring somewhere in a far corner of the room, and the serving-man, having placed the candles on the table, stood waiting at the door.

"Yes. I'll to his Highness," Diogenes said abruptly; and , beckoning to the serving-man to precede him, he strode out of the room.

Outside on the landing he paused. Then, with a characteristic, impulsive gesture, he suddenly beat his forehead with the palm of his hand.

"The Prince of Poets, of course!" he murmured under his breath. "Francis Borgia, the true descendant of his infamous ancestors! Poison! And a slow one at that! Oh, the miserable assassins! Please God, this knowledge hath not come too late!" he added with earnest fervor.

5

A quarter of an hour later the Stadtholder was in possession of all the facts as they had been revealed to Diogenes by his comrade in arms.

"I seem fated," he said to Diogenes kindly, yet not without a measure of bitterness, "to owe my safety to you and your brother philosophers."

He was discussing De Berg's surprise plans on Arnheim and Nijmegen. Of that abominable crime, hatched with the chance aid of a poison-mongering Borgia, Diogenes had not as yet spoken one word. Accustomed to swift decisions and prompt action, he had already made up his mind that he would speak of it first to the English physician, whose business it would be to see to it that the insidious poison no longer reached the prince's lips, at the same time enjoining the strictest secrecy in the matter; for it would only be by rigid circumspection and ceaseless watching that the assisin's accomplice could be brought to justice.

Mynheer Beresteyn and some of his older friends were in the room with his Highness. They all put their grave heads together, for there was no doubt that the Archduchess's advisers had planned an invasion of the United Provinces on a grand scale.

"Arnheim is insufficiently defended, of that there's no doubt," the Stadtholder said. "It was my intention to reinforce all the frontier cities, and to keep their garrisons up to the requisite numbers. If I only had the strength--"

He paused. The feeling of physical weakness consequent on disease caused him endless and acute bitterness.

"It is not too late to send troops to Arnheim and to Nijmegen," Diogenes broke in, in his usual abrupt manner. "Three thousand in one city, four thousand in the other would be sufficient, if your Highness can act quickly."

"I cannot detach seven or eight thousand troops from my forces at the present moment," the prince rejoined. "If Spinola were to attack from the south I am only just strong enough to defend myself as it is."

"Marquet is in Overijssel, I believe," urged the soldier. "He hath three or four thousand troops. Let him push on to Arnheim to reinforce the garrison."

"And De Keysere is at Wageningen," the prince broke in, fired, despite himself, by the other's enthusiasm. "He hath three thousand mercenaries from Switzerland and Germany."

"Excellent fighters and well-seasoned," Diogenes asserted. "And trained under Maurice of Nassau, the first captain of this or any epoch!"

"Ay!" sighed Maurice wearily. "But time is against us. Marquet is at Vorden —"

"But Arnheim and Nijmegen can hold out for awhile," Diogenes argued forcefully.

"And would hold out to the last man," Mynheer Beresteyn added, "if they knew that succor would come in due course."

" 'Tis only uncertainty that paralyses the endurance of a garrison," Diogenes went on with firm emphasis. "Send to Arnheim and to Nijmegen, your Highness! Bid them hold out against any attack until you come with ten thousand troops to their aid. In the meanwhile, send orders to Marquet and to De Keysere to advance forthwith with reinforcements for these two garrisons. Then raise your standard once more in Friesland, Drenthe, and Groningen. I'll warrant you will have twenty thousand men there ready to fight once more for liberty and for you!"

His sonorous voice rang clear and metallic in the small, panelled room. His enthusiasm appeared almost like a living thing, a tangible force that touched the hearts and minds of all the solemn burghers here, causing their eyes to glow and their fists, not yet wholly unskilled in the use of the sword, to clench with inward excitement. The Stadtholder looked up at him with undisguised admiration.

"Is it the English blood in you, man," he said with a smile, "that makes you valorous in war and wise in counsel?"

Diogenes shrugged his broad shoulders.

"I fought for your Highness before now," he rejoined, with a quaint, self-deprecating laugh, "when I had nothing to lose save my skin, and still less to gain. The English blood in me dearly loves a fight, and all doth hate the Spaniard and all his tyrannies."

"Then I can reckon on you?" the prince riposted quickly.

"On me, your Highness?" the other exclaimed.

"On you, of course. With your mother's blood in your veins, the United Provinces have a double claim on you. You have fought for us before, as you say, unknown to us then, an obscure soldier of fortune with nothing to lose and but little to gain. Join us now, man, in the field and under the council tent. Get to horse to-night. You will find Marquet at Vorden, on his way south from Overijssel. Tell him to push on at once to Arnheim with all the troops he hath at his command. From thence I would bid you go straightway to De Keysere, who is at Wageningen, and order him to reinforce Nijmegen forthwith with three thousand men, if we have them. Tell both Marquet and De Keysere to fight and hold the towns. I'll to their aid as soon as may be. Then, man, join my brother Frederick, and help him to raise my standard in Gelderland and in Overijssel, and rally ten thousand men to our cause. I feel that success will attend our arms if we keep you by our side."

Maurice of Nassau had spoken with more vigor and verve than he had shown for the past three months. Indeed, his deeply anxious friends could not help but feel that the old fighting spirit of this peerless commander had not wholly been undermined by disease. Five pairs of eager eyes had scanned his features while he spoke; five hearts beat in response to his enthusiasm. Now, when he had finished speaking, Mynheer Beresteyn and the others turned their expectant gaze upon the stranger who had been so signally honoured; but he looked uncertain, gravely perturbed. In the flickering light of the wax candles his face appeared haggard and drawn, and a set line had crept around his ever-laughing lips.

"You seem to hesitate, my friend," the Stadtholder remarked, with that tone of bitterness which had become habitual to him. "Methought you said that the English blood in you dearly loved a fight. But in truth, I had forgotten! You have other claims upon you now – one, at least, which is paramount. An easy, untroubled life awaits you. No wonder you hesitate to embark on so perilous an adventure!" Then, as if loth to give up the thought that was foremost in his mind, he added, with persuasive insistence; "If you followed me, you'd have everything to gain – nothing to lose save a sentimental pastime."

Just then Diogenes caught Mynheer Beresteyn's eyes fixed steadily upon him. The old man who knew well enough what was going on in that wayward, turbulent mind – the doubts, the fears, the hideous, horrible disappointment.

Nothing to lose! Ye gods, at the hour when a whole life's happiness not only beckoned insistently, but was actually there to hand, like a bunch of ripe and luscious fruit, ready to drop into a yearning hand! Here was the end of a vagabond life, here was love and home and peace, and all to be given up as soon as found to the equally insistent call of honour and of duty!

The others did not speak; perhaps they, too, understood. Men in those days were used to stern sacrifices. They and there forebears had given up their all so that their children's children might live in freedom and security. They only marvelled if this stranger, with the combative English blood in him, would give up what was so infinitely dear to him – the exquisite wife to whom he had plighted his troth but a few hours ago – and if he would fight for them again as he had done in the past.

The Stadtholder remained moody and silent, and the close atmosphere of the heavily curtained room seemed to become suddenly still, hushed, as if expectant of the grave decision to come. The wax candles burned quite steadily, with just a tiny fillet of smoke rising up towards the low-raftered ceiling, almost like the incense of silent prayer rising unwaveringly to God.

To many the silence appeared absolute, but not to the man who stood in the midst of them all beside a table littered with papers and documents, his slender hand – the hand of an idealist, rendered firm and hard by action – resting lightly upon the board. A tense look in his eyes. Through the silence he could hear his beloved in the little room behind the heavy tapestry. He could hear the soft, insidious sound of the quaint-toned virginal, and her voice, tender and melancholy as the call of the bird to its mate, humming the sweet refrain gently under her breath. with every note she seemed to tear at his heart with an unendurable regret for what might have been.

Oh, it had been such a perfect dream! Gilda and that stately home over in England, and the ride through the night in pursuit of happiness which had proved as elusive as Fata Morgana, as unreal as the phantoms born in the mind of a rhapsodist.

Then the silence did, indeed, become absolute, even to him. Gilda had ceased her song. Only his straining ears caught the sound of her footsteps as she rose from the virginal, then moved swiftly about the room.

"Well," the Stadtholder reiterated, after awhile, "which is it to me, my friend? I start for Utrecht within the hour and if we are to save Arnheim and Nijmegen, you should be on your way to Vorden with the necessary moneys and my written orders to-night. Of course, I cannot compel you," he added simply "The decision rests with you, and if you —"

The words died on his lips, and in an instant all eyes were turned to that end of the room where a heavy portiere divided it from the room beyond. A faint rustling sound had come from there, then the grating of metal rings upon the cornice-pole that held the tapestry. The next moment Gilda appeared in the doorway, shadowy, wraith-like in her sombre gown that melted into the gloom. Just her small, white face and delicate hands stood out against the murky background, and the gossamer lace at her throat and wrists.

For a moment she stood there, one hand still holding back the heavy portiere, quite still, taking in the company at a glance. A sigh of longing and of renunciation came from an over-burdened heart, and was wafted up to the foot of Him who knows all and understands all. Then Gilda allowed the tapestry to fall together behind her, and she came quickly forward. In the other hand she was holding, firmly clasped, her husband's heavy sword.

She came close to him, and then said simply, with an ingenuous smile: "I thought you might wonder where you had left it. It was in the other room. You will be wanting it, my dear lord, if you start for Vorden within the hour."

With deft fingers she buckled the sword to his belt. This, in truth, was her decision, and she had acted with scarce a moment's hesitation, even whilst he marvelled how he could set to work to break her heart by leaving her this night.

Now, when their glances met, they understood one another. The power that lay within both their souls had met and, as it were, clasped hands. They accepted one another's sacrifice. Hers, mayhap, was the more complete of the two, because for her his absence would mean weary waiting, the dull heartache so terrible to bear.

For the man, the wrench would be eased by action, danger and hard fighting; for her there would be nothing to do but wait. But she acquiesced. No one had seen the struggle which it had cost her, over there in the little room, all alone with only the dumb virginal and the dying light to see the tears of rebellion and of agony which for one brief moment – for her an eternity – had seared her eyes. By the time the full meaning of what she had overheard from the other side of the portiere had entered into her brain, she had recovered full outward calm, and had brought him his sword in token of her resolve.

Gilda Beresteyn came of a race that had learned to fight even from its infancy. She had handled her father's sword at an age when little maids are content with playthings. Now, when she made the buckles of her husband's sword secure, she met his glance with perfect serenity, and said simply and calmly:

"You will find me, as before, in the other room. I will be waiting there to bid you farewell."

Then she glided out of the room, wraith-like, ethereal, as she had come. And Diogenes woke as if out of a trance.

The Stadtholder jumped to his feet. "Then you're with us?" he exclaimed.

"If your Highness hath need of me," the soldier replied.

"Have I not said so?" the prince retorted. "Henceforth, Sir Percy Blakeney – for that is your name, is it not? – accompanies us as our Master of the Camp wherever we go!"

"Nay, " the other replied quite firmly and without even a sigh of regret this time, "my name is Diogenes, as it hath always been. It is the nameless and homeless adventurer, the son of the poor Dutch tramp, who once again places his sword at your Highness's disposal. Sir Percy Blakeney was only a myth, a shade that hath already been exorcized by the magic of your Highness's call, in the name of our faith and of liberty."

"Frankly, man," the Stadtholder retorted with a smile, "I could not picture you in the character of a placid and uxorious country gentleman, watching with unruffled complacence the life and death struggles of your friends."

"I should have waxed obese, your Highness," Diogenes assented whimsically; "and the horror of it would have sent me to my grave."

"Then, you inveterate mocker, are you ready to start?"

"Booted and spurred, your Highness, and a sword on my hip," replied the other lightly. "And my horse hath been waiting for me these two hours past."

Already Maurice of Nassau was on his feet. He took the sacrifice, the self-denial, as a matter of course; was unaware of it, probably. Every other thought was completely merged in that of the coming struggle – De Berg crossing the Ijssel, Spinola threatening from the south, and victory beckoning once more.

The burghers crowded round him, speaking words of loyalty and of encouragement. He responded with somewhat curt farewells. His thoughts were no longer here; they were across the Veluwe with Marquet and De Keysere; inside Arnheim and Nijmegen.

He kept Diogenes by his side, wrote out his orders in sign-manual, discussed plans, possibilities with the man in whose luck and resource he had unbounded belief.

It took time to get everything ready. There was the financial question, too, for some of the troops were mercenaries, who would be demanding their pay ere they engaged to start on a fresh expedition. For this the aid of the loyal burghers had again to be requisitioned. Arrangements had to be made for credits at Zutphen and Arnheim.

This part of the great adventure the Stadtholder was willing to leave in the hands of Mynheer Beresteyn and his friends. Money to him was dross, save as a means of gaining his great ends. For the nonce he was in a hurry to get away, to get back to his camp at Utrecht, and to make ready for the coming fight.

Then at last there came a moment when everything appeared settled. The messenger had his sealed orders, and the credit notes and the read money upon his person. The Stadtholder was back in the hall with his equerries around him, ready for departure, giving brief, decisive orders such as soldiers love to hear.

But Diogenes did not follow him immediately, and Mynheer Beresteyn remained behind with him. He was the only one who really understood what the once careless and thoughtless adventurer felt at this moment, in face of the inevitable farewell. It was an understanding born in a staunch heart that had known both love and sorrow.

Beresteyn had idolized his young wife, who had died leaving her baby-girl in his arms. That deep affection the lonely widower had thereupon transferred to his motherless daughter, had cherished and guarded her as his most precious treasure, and had only consented to relinquish her into the guardianship of another because he knew that the other was worthy of the trust.

He knew also what hungering passion means; he knew the bitterness of parting and of a burning disappointment with the prospect of loneliness through the vista of years. But, with that infinite tact which is the attribute of a self-less heart, he offered no words of consolation or even of comment.

"I will leave you to bid farewell to Gilda alone," was all that he said.

Diogenes nodded in assent. The most terrible moment of this terrible hour was yet to come, for Gilda, having precipitated his decision, was now waiting for the last kiss.

6

She was, in truth, waiting for him, submissive and composed. What she had done, when she with her own act had mutely bidden him to go, that she did not regret. She had done it not so much perhaps from a sense of duty or of patriotism, but rather because she knew that this course was the only one that he would never rue.

Hers was that perfect love that dwells on the other's happiness, and not on its own. She knew that, though for the time being he would find bliss and oblivion in her arms, he would soon repine in inactivity whilst others fought for that which he held sublime.

So now, when he pushed aside the tapestry and once more stood before her, with the lovelight in his eyes obscured by the shadow of this coming parting, she met him without a tear. The next moment he had her in his arms, and his hand rested lightly across her eyes, lest they should perceived that his were full of tears.

For a long while he could not speak; then he drew her closer to him and pressed his lips against hers, drinking in all the joy and rapture which he might never taste again.

"What is it that hath happened, my lord?" she murmured. " I could not hear everything, and did not wish to be caught prying. All that I heard was that the Stadtholder needed you, and that in your heart you knew that your place, whilst there was danger to our land, was by his side, and not by mine."

"Your father will explain more fully, my beloved," he replied. You are right. The Stadtholder hath need of every willing sword. This unfortunate land is gravely threatened. The Archduchess is throwing the full force of her armies against the Netherlands. His Highness thinks that I might help to save the United Provinces from becoming once more the vassals of Spain. As you say, my place is on this soil where I and my mother were born. I should be a coward indeed were I to turn my back now on this land when danger is so grave. So I am going, my beloved," he continued simply.

"To-night I go to Vorden on his Highness's business, thence on to Wageningen. I shall go, taking your dear image in my heart, and with your exquisite face before me always. For I love you with every fibre of my being, every bone in my body and with every beat of my heart. Try not to weep, my dear. I shall return one day soon to take you in my arms, as I shall clasp your spirit only until then. I shall return, doubt it not. Such love as ours was not created to remain unfulfilled. Whatever may happen, believe and trust in me, as I shall believe in you, and keep the remembrance of me in your heart without sadness and without regret."

He spoke chiefly because he dared not trust to the insidiousness of silence. He knew that she wept for the first time because of him. Yet how could it be otherwise? And sorrow made her sacred. When, overcome with grief, she lay half-swooning in his arms, he picked her up quite tenderly and laid her back against the cushions of the chair. Then, as she sat there, pale and wan-looking in the uncertain light of the wax candles, with those exquisite hands of hers lying motionless in her lap, he knelt down before her.

For a second or two he rested his head against those soft white palms, fragrant as the petals of a lily. Then he rose, and, without looking at her again, he walked firmly out of the room.

1

NCOLAES Beresteyn accompanied his brother-in-law during the first part of the journey. He had insisted on this, despite Diogenes' preference for solitude. There was not much comrade-ship lost between the two men. Though the events of that memorable New Years Day, distant less than three months, were ostensibly consigned to oblivion, nevertheless, the bitter humiliation which Nicolaes had suffered at the hands of the then nameless soldier of fortune still rankled in his heart. Since then so many things had come to light which, to an impartial observer, more than explained Gilda Beresteyn's love for the stranger, and Mynheer her father's acquiescence in an union based on respect for so brave a man.

But Nicolaes had held aloof from the intimacy, and soon his own courtship of the wealthy Kaatje gave him every reason for withdrawing more and more from his own family circle. But to-night, after the tempestuous close of what should have been a merely conventional day, he sought Diogenes' company in a way he had never done before.

"Like you," he said, "I am wearied and sick with all this mummery. A couple of hours on the Veluwe will set me more in tune with life."

Diogenes chaffed him not a little.

"The lovely Kaatje will pout," he suggested, "and rightly, too. You have no excuse for absenting yourself from her side at this hour."

"I'll come with you as far as Barneveld," Nicolaes insisted. "A matter of less than a couple of hours' ride. It will do me good. And Kaatje is still closeted with her garrulous mother."

"You think it will do her good to be kept waiting," Diogenes retorted with good-natured sarcasm. "well, come, if you have a mind. But I'll not have your company further than Barneveld. I am used to the Veluwe, and intend taking a short cut over the upland, through which I would not care to take a companion less well acquainted with the waste than I."

Thus it was decided. Already the Stadtholder had gone with his numerous retinue, with his bodyguard and his pike-men and with his equerries, and those of the wedding-party who had come in his train from Utrecht, friends of Mynheer Beresteyn, who had ridden over for the most part with wife or daughter pillioned behind them, and all glad to avail themselves of the protection of his Highness's escort against highway marauders, none too scarce in these parts. Torch-bearers and linkmen completed the imposing cavalcade, for the night would be moonless, and the tracks across the moorland none too clearly defined.

Diogenes had waited with what patience he could muster until the last of the numerous train had defiled under the Koppel-poort. Then he, too, got to horse. Despite Socrates' many protestations, he was not allowed to accompany him.

"You must look after Pythagoras," was Diogenes' final word on the subject.

" 'Tis the first time," the other answered moodily, "that you go on such an adventure without us. Take care, comrade! The Veluwe is wide and lonely. That swag-bellied oaf up there hath cause to rue his solitary wanderings on that verfloekte waste."

"I'll be careful, old compeer," Diogenes retorted with a smile. "But mine errand is not one on which I desire to draw unnecessary attention, and I can remain best unperceived if I am alone. 'Tis no adventure I am embarking on this night. Only a simple errand as far as Vorden, a matter of ten leagues at most.

"And the whole of the verdommte Veluwe to traverse at dead of night!" the other muttered sullenly.

"I know every corner of it," Diogenes rejoined impatiently. "And it will not be the first time that I travel on it alone."

Thus Socrates was left grumbling, and anon Diogenes, accompanied by Nicolaes Beresteyn, started on his way.

At first the two men spoke little. The air was still cold and very humid, and the thaw was persisting. The horses stepped out briskly on the soft, sandy earth.

The distance between Amersfoort and Barneveld is but a couple of leagues. Within the hour the lights of the little city could be seen gleaming ahead. After a while Nicolaes Beresteyn became more loquacious, talked quite freely of the past.

"My father no longer trusts me," he said, with ill-concealed bitterness. "Did you see how he shut me out of the council-chamber?"

"Yet the Stadtholder himself told you everything that occurred subsequently," Diogenes retorted kindly, "including his own plans and mine errand at this hour. I think that your conscience troubles you unnecessarily, and you see a deliberate intention in every simple act."

"And if he did, you could scarce blame him. 'Tis only in the future you can prove your true worth. And methinks," he added, more seriously than he was usually wont to speak, "that you will have occasion to do this very soon."

"In the meanwhile, here's Barneveld ahead of us," Nicolaes rejoined, with a quick, indefinable sigh, and giving a sudden turn to the conversation. "I'll see you across the city, then return to the bosom of my family, there to live in uxorious idleness, whilst you, a stranger, are entrusted with the destinies of our land. A poor outlook for a man who is young and a patriot, you'll own."

To this Diogenes thought it best to make no reply. He knew well enough that the mistrust of which Nicolaes accused his father was a very real thing, and that it was indeed only time that would soften the proud burgher's heart toward his only son. It was not likely that one who but a brief while ago had conspired against the Stadtholder's life with that abominable Stoutenburg could be admitted readily into the councils of the very man whom he had plotted to assassinate. With every desire to forgive, it was but natural that Mynheer Beresteyn should fail entirely to forget.

No more, however, was said upon the subject now, and Nicolaes soon relapsed into that sullen mood which had of late become habitual to him. Thus Diogenes was glad enough to be rid of his company. At Barneveld he obtained a fresh horse, left his own in charge of a man known to him, with orders to ride it quietly on the morrow as far as Wageningen, where he himself would pick it up a couple of days later. His journey would now lie due east to Zutphen. There he meant to make a halt of a few hours, and thence proceed to Vorden, where Marquet was in camp, with four thousand seasoned troops, trained under Mansfeld, and rested now since the campaign in Groningen.

The Stadtholder's orders were that the general proceed, at once to Arnheim, ere the forces of the Archduchess had time to cross the Ijssel, and to cut off all access to so important a city.

From Vorden to Wageningen, which lies due south form Barneveld, the journey would be a long one, and, with De Berg's army so near, might even prove perilous. But De Keysere was at Wageningen, with three thousand troops and some artillery. His help would be of immense service to Nijmegen if the latter city, too, were to be attacked.

"How will you journey from Vorden to Wageningen?" Nicolaes asked Diogenes in the end. "You will have to avoid the Ijssel."

"I'll cut across to Lang Soeren," the other replied; "and thence go to Ede."

"There's scarce a track on the Veluwe just there," the other urged.

"Such as there is, I know," Diogenes retorted curtly. "And I must trust to luck."

They had brought their horses to a halt about a quarter of a league outside Barneveld, where the two men decided to part. The stretch of the great waste, with its undulating, barren hills, and narrow, scarce visible tracks, lay straight out before them. Diogenes was sniffing the frosty air out toward the east, where lay Vorden, and whence there came to his nostrils the sharp tang of the breeze, that cut like a knife. The thaw which had held sway in the cities and on the low-lying lands had been vanquished ere it reached the arid upland. The snow upon the Veluwe lay as even and as pure as before. Above, a canopy of stars seemed but a diamond-studded veil of mysterious indigo, stretched over a world of light, which it failed altogether to dim. The silence and desolation were absolute; but not so the darkness. To the keen eye of the adventurer, accustomed to loneliness, the vast stretches of open country and limitless horizons, there was no such thing as absolute darkness. He could perceive the slightest accidental upon the smooth carpet of snow, noted every tiny mound that marked a clump of rough shrub or grass, and every footmark of beast or bird, mere flecks of blue upon the virgin pall.

"Such track as there is, I know," he had carelessly asserted awhile ago, in response to a warning from Nicolaes. And now, without an instant's hesitation, and tossing to the other a last curt word of farewell, he gave his horse a slight taste of the spur, and soon became a mere speck upon the illimitable waste.

3

It was close on midnight when, weary, saddle-sore, his boots covered in half-melted snow, Mynheer Nicolaes Beresteyn demanded admittance into his native city.

At first the guard at the Koppel-poort, roused from his slumbers, refused to recognize in the belated traveler the bridegroom of a few hours ago. Had anyone ever heard, I ask you, of a bridegroom absenting himself on the very night of his nuptial until so late an hour? And then returning in a mood that was so irascible and inconsequent that the sergeant in command of the gate was on the point of ordering his detention in the guard-room, pending investigation and the orders of the burgomaster, whose decision on such points was final? But since the burgomaster, whose decision on such points was final? But since the burgomaster happened to be Mynheer Beresteyn, and as the weary and pugnacious traveler did, in truth, appear to be his only son – why, it was perhaps best on the whole to take the matter as a joke, and not to say too much about it. The sergeant did, indeed, as Nicolaes was finally allowed to ride over the bridge, essay one or two of the most time-honoured witticisms at the expense of the belated bridegroom; but Mynheer Nicolaes was clearly in no mood for chaff, and when he had passed by, the sergeant and one or two of the men, who had witnessed his strangely sullen mood, shook their heads in ominous prognostication of sundry matrimonial difficulties to come.

The house on the quay, plainly visible from the Koppel-poort, was dark enough to suggest that every one of its inmates was already abed. Nicolaes, however, did not ride up to the front door; but, after he had crossed the bridge, he went straight on through one or two narrow streets which lay at the back of his home until he reached the corner of the Korte Gracht, which, again, abuts on the quay. Thus he had gone round in a semicircle, in obvious avoidance of the paternal house, and now he brought his horse to a halt outside a tall and narrow door which was surmounted by a lanthorn let into the wall. A painted sign which hung from an iron bracket above the door indicated to the passing wayfarer that the place was one where rider and horse could find food and shelter.

Nicolaes dismounted, and going up to the door, he knocked against it with the point of his foot. This he had to do several times before the welcome sound of someone moving inside the house came to his ear. A moment or two later the door was opened cautiously. A man appeared on the threshold, wrapped in a night-robe and still wearing a night-bonnet on his head.

"Is that you, mynheer?" he queried drowsily.

"Who else should it be, you loon?" Nicolaes replied irritably. "here's your horse," he added, and without waiting for further commend or protest from the unfortunate landlord thus roused from his slumbers, he proceeded to tether the animal by the reins to one of the iron rings in the wall.

"It is so late, mynheer," the man protested dolefully; and so cold. Will you not take the horse round to the stable yourself? It is but a step to the right, and there's the gate —"

"It is late, as you say, and cold," Nicolaes retorted curtly. "And when I paid you so liberally for the horse, I did not bargain to take service with you as ostler in the middle of the night."

"But, mynheer —" urged the landlord, still protesting.

But Nicolaes did not listen. In faith, he had ceased to hear, for already he was striding rapidly down the Korte Gracht, and the next moment was back on the quay. A few steps brought him to the door of his father's house. Here he paused for a moment ere he mounted the stone steps that led up to the massive front door, stamped his feet so as to shake the melted snow from his boots, and with a few quick touches tried to re-establish some semblance of order in his clothes. Indeed, when presently he rapped vigorously with the iron knocker against the door, he looked no longer like a wearied and querulous traveler, but rather like a man just returned from a short and pleasant ride.

To his astonishment it was Maria, his sister Gilda's faithful tire-woman, who opened the door for him. She anticipated his very first query by a curt:

"Everyone is abed. The jongejuffrouw alone chose to wait for you, and I could not let her wait alone."

Nicolaes uttered an angry exclamation.

"Tell my sister to go to bed, too," he commanded briefly. "I'll go to my rooms at once, as it is so late."

Maria made no audible reply. She mumbled something about "Shameful conduct!" and "Wedding-night!" But Nicolaes paid no heed, strode quickly across the hall, and ran swiftly up the stairs.

But on the landing he came abruptly to a halt. He had almost fallen against his sister Gilda, who stood there waiting for him.

Behind her, a little way down the passage, a door stood ajar, and through it there came a narrow fillet of light. At sight of him, and before he could utter a sound, she put a finger to her lip, then let the way along the passage. The door which stood ajar was the one which gave on her own room. She went in, and he followed her, his heart beating with something like shame or fear.

"Hush!" she whispered, and gently closed the door behind him. "Make no noise!" Kaatje has at last sobbed herself to sleep. She hath been put to bed in her mother's room. 'Twere a shame to disturb her." Then, as Nicolaes muttered something that sounded very like a curse, the girl added reproachfully: "Poor Kaatje! You have shown very little ardour toward her, Klaas."

"I lost my way in the dark," he answered. "I had no thought it could be so late."

Just then the tower clock of St. Maria Kerk chimed the midnight hour.

Gilda hazarded timidly: "You should not have thought of accompanying my lord. He was ready to start out alone; and your place, Klaas, was beside your wife!"

"Are you going to lecture me about my duty, Gilda?" he said irritably. "You must not think that because —"

"I think nothing," she broke in simply, "save that Kaatje wept when the evening wore on and you did not return; and that the more she wept the greater was our father's anger against you."

"He knew that I meant to accompany your husband a part of the way," Nicolaes retorted. "In truth, had he done me the justice to read my thoughts, he himself would have bade me go."

"It was kind of you," she rejoined somewhat coolly, to be concerned as to my lord's safety. But I can assure you —"

" 'Twas not concern for his safety," he broke in gruffly, "that caused me to accompany him to-night."

"What then?"

But he gave no reply, but his lip and turned away from her, with the air of one who fears that he hath said too much and cares not to be questioned again.

"I'd best go now," he said abruptly.

He looked around for his gloves, which he had thrown down upon the table. His manner seemed so strange that Gilda was suddenly conscious of a nameless kind of fear; the sort of premonition that comes to highly sensitive natures, at times when hitherto unsuspected danger suddenly looms upon the cloudless sky of life. She forced him to return her searching glance.

"You are hiding something from me, Klaas," she said determinedly. "What is it?"

"I?" he riposted, feigning surprise. "Hiding something? Why should I have something to hide?"

"That I know not," she replied. "But there was some hidden meaning in your words just now when you said that 'twas not concern for my lord's safety that caused you to accompany him this night. What, then, was it?" she insisted, seeing that he remained silent, even though he met her gaze with a look that appeared both fearful and pitying.

She had her back to the door now, looked like some timid creature brought to bay by a cruel and hitherto unsuspected enemy.

"You must not ask me for my meaning, Gilda," Nicolaes said at last. "There are things which concern men only, and with which women should have no part."

His tone of ill-concealed compassion stung her like a cut from a whip across the face.

"There is nothing that concerns my lord," she retorted proudly, "in which he would not desire me to bear my part."

"Then let him tell you himself."

"What?"

She threw the question at him like a challenge, stepped up to him and seized him by the wrist – no longer a timid creature at bay. But a strong, determined woman, who feels in some mysterious way that the man whom she loves is being attacked, and who is prepared, with every known and unknown weapon almighty love can suggest, to defend him, his life or his honour, or both.

"You are not going out of this room, Klaas, until you have explained!" she said with unquestionable determination. "What is it that my lord should tell me himself?"

"Why he, newly wed and a stranger, was so determined on this, his wedding night, to carry the Stadtholder's message across the Veluwe."

Nicolaes spoke abruptly, almost fiercely now, as if wearied of this wrangling, and burdened with a secret he could no longer hold. But she did not at first understand his meaning.

"I do not understand what you mean," she murmured vaguely, a perplexed frown between her eyes.

"There were plenty there eager and willing to go," Nicolaes went on roughly. "Nay, the errand was not in itself perilous. Speed was required, yes; and a sound knowledge of the country. But a dozen men at least who were in this house to-day know the Veluwe as well as this stranger, and any good horse would cover the ground fast enough. But he wanted to go – he, this man whom none of us know, who was married this day, and whose bride had the first call on his attention. He insisted with the Stadtholder, and he went — And I went with him; would have gone all the way if he had not forced me to go back. Why did he wish to go, Gilda? Why did he leave you deliberately this night? Think! Think! And why did he insist on going alone, with not even one of those besotted boon companions of his to share in his adventure? A message to Marquet – my God!" he added with a sneer. "A message to the Archduchess, more like, to cross the Ijssel ere it be too late!"

"You devil!"

She hissed out the words through set lips and teeth clenched in an access of fierce and overwhelming passion. And before he could recover himself, before he could guess her purpose, she had seized his heavy, leathern gloves, which were lying on the table, and struck him with them full in the face. He staggered, and put his hand up to his eyes.

"Go!" she commanded briefly.

He tried to laugh the situation off, said almost flippantly:

"I'll punish you for this, you young vixen!"

But she did not move, and her glance seemed to freeze the words upon his lips.

"Go!" she commanded once more.

He shrugged his shoulders.

"I understand your indignation, Gilda. Nay, I honour it. But remember my warning! Your stranger lord," he went on with slow and deliberate emphasis, "will be returning anon to the

Stadtholder's camp, a courted and honoured man; but 'tis the armies of the Archduchess who will have crossed the Ijssel by then, whilst the orders to Marquet will have reached that commander too late."

Then he turned on his heel and went out of the room, and anon Gilda heard his footstep resounding along the passage. She listened until she heard the opening and closing of a distant door, after which she sighed and murmured, "Poor Kaatje!" That was all; but there was a world of meaning in the sorrowful compassion wherewith she said those words.

Then she raised her left hand, round the third finger of which glittered a plain gold ring. The ring she pressed long and lingeringly against her lips, and in her heart she prayed, "God guard you, my dear lord!"

Chapter V – A Race for Life

1

AS for Diogenes, he reached Zutphen in the small hours of the morning, and after a few hours' rest pushed on to Vorden at dawn. He himself would have deprecated any suggestion of making of this journey across the Veluwe a romantic adventure. The upland, under its covering of snow, held neither terrors nor secrets for him. The wind, the stars, an unerring instinct and sound knowledge of the scarce visible tracks, guided him across the arid waste. A real child of the open, he had less difficulty in finding his way across such a God-forsaken wild than he would through the intricate streets of a city.

Messire Marquet, encamped outside Vorden, welcomed the Stadtholder's messenger effusively. His troops, for the most part composed of mercenaries from Germany, were getting restive in idleness; once or twice they had used threats when demanding their pay. Diogenes, bringing both money and the prospect of a fight, was doubly welcome. His stay at the camp was brief. By late morning he was once more on his way, with the intention of re-crossing the Ijssel at Dieren and of reaching Wageningen before dark. He had but half a dozen leagues to cover, and eight hours of daylight wherein to do it. Weather, too, and circumstances favored him. The thaw, which had been so completely vanquished upon the upland, had remained sole monarch in the plain. The air was mild and intensely humid. A dense sea-fog lay over the river and the surrounding marshes. The numerous little tributaries of the Ijssel and the intervening canals and ditches were already free from ice, and as Diogenes put his horse to an easy gallop in the direction of the river, the animal sank fetlock deep in mud.

The road was solitary, and, as far as the eye could reach through the mist, seemed entirely deserted. The countryside here had the desolate appearance peculiar to districts that have been fought over. The few thatched cottages, which from time to time loomed out of the mist, still bore the marks of passing fire and sword; the trees were truncated and sparse, the marshland was riddled with the scars of ceaseless tramping of men, of wagons, and of beasts. The inevitable windmills, gaunt-looking and ghost-like through the humid atmosphere, appeared neglected and forlorn.

But the solitary rider had no eyes for landscape just now. He could have wished for a clearer day, for it was impossible even for his keen eyes to see what was going on behind that impenetrable wall of fog. If Pythagoras' ears had not played him false, De Berg was there, not very far away, waiting to cross the Ijssel when opportunity arose.

Thanks to that faithful hypertrophied loon, the ambitious designs of the Archduchess could still be frustrated. De Berg's armies were still on the right bank of the Ijssel, and if Marquet got his men on the move by midday, as he had promised he would do, the crossing of the enemy troops would become difficult, mayhap impossible.

These were pleasing thoughts for the man on whose speed and resource these important plans depended. All that he chafed against was the imperative slowness of his progress, as the mist enveloped him more closely the nearer he got to the river. But withal it protected him, too, hid him mayhap from the prying eyes of vedettes on the watch. Already, judging by certain landmarks that met him on the way, Brummen was half a league behind him on his right, Hengles far away on the left, and Dieren not more than another league on ahead. For the last quarter of an hour he had heard from time to time the heavy booming sound, akin to the reverberation of distant cannonade, which came from the breaking and cracking of the ice as it drifted downstream. He put his horse to slow trot, as he pried through the mist for the first indication of a short cut he knew of, which would take him to the river bank in less than half an hour.

The next moment he had spied the narrow track and set his horse to follow it; when suddenly, out of the mist, there came a loud report, and Diogenes heard the whistle of a bullet close to his ear. It almost grazed his shoulder. Without an instant's pause, without turning to look whence had come this unexpected greeting, he set spurs to his horse and galloped at breakneck speed toward the river. Over fields and ditches; no thought of prudence now, only of speed! Mud and water flew out in all directions under the horse's frantic gallopade, the plucky beast sinking at times almost to his knees in the marshy ground. A few minutes later – five, perhaps – Diogenes heard the sound of many hoofs behind him, obviously in pursuit. He turned to look this time, and through the mist vaguely discerned some three or four cavaliers, who were distant from him then less than two hundred yards. So far, so good! The Ijssel was close by now, and if, when he reached the banks, he turned off in the direction of the stream, he could easily reach the ford on this side of Brummen and get across – on foot, if need be, if his horse proved an obstacle to rapid progress.

A few more minutes now and the river was in sight, with, far away on the opposite bank, Brummen, nestling at the foot of the rising ground, the gate of the Veluwe. With renewed vigor the rider sped along, his blood whipped up by the chase, his whole body exhilarated by this sensation of danger and of one of those sportive races for life for which three months of idleness and luxury had given him a hitherto unsuspected longing.

Ah, there was the shore at last, the group of three windmills close to the bank, an unmistakable landmark. Here, too, within two hundred paces on ahead, was the ford, which no amount of drifting ice would cause the daring adventurer to miss. Already he was within a few yards of the low-lying bank, searching the approach to the ford with eyes now doubly keen, when, with staggering suddenness, another cavalier appeared, straight in front of him this time, and barring the way to the river-brink.

No time to note his face; just a second wherein to decide what had best be done, not only to save his own life, but also the message which he must carry to Wageningen, at whatever cost. Then the cavalier turned for one brief second in his saddle, to call to some companions as yet unseen. A brief second, did I say? 'Twas but a fraction. The next moment Diogenes had whipped out a pistol from his saddlebow, and with a steady hand fired at his foe. The cavalier reeled in his saddle and fell, just as half a dozen others issued with a shout from out the mist, and those in pursuit put fresh spurs to their mounts.

It had been madness to attempt the ford now. The young soldier, sore-pressed, might in truth have sold his life dearly, but with it, too, he would have sold Nijmegen and the possible success of the Stadtholder's plans. Ofttimes before, in the course of his adventurous life, he had been in as tight a place, where life and death hung quite evenly in the scales of Fate; but never before had he been quite so anxious to flee. He could not trust the valor of his sword, his own well-nigh unexampled skill in a fight against odds that would have made the bravest pause. No! It meant running away, away as fast as his horse would take him, and faster if the poor brute gave out. A short gallop along the bank, the cavalier behind him warming to the pursuit; keeping closer and closer to the low-lying bank, till the horse began to flounder in what was sheer morass.

The ford now lay well behind him. The waters of the Ijssel, tossed for awhile upon the shallows, flowed with increased swiftness here. Huge ice-blocks floated seaward upon the heaving bosom of the stream. The foremost of the pursuing cavaliers was then less than fifty yards behind, and more than one bullet had whizzed past the fleeing rider, one of them piercing his hat, the other grazing his thigh, but none doing him serious injury. Already the rallying cry of the pursuers had turned to one of triumph as the distance lessened between them and their quarry, when, with a sudden jerk of the reins, Diogenes plunged headlong into the river.

The Ijssel at this point is close on a quarter of a mile wide, her current is no longer sluggish, whilst the drifting ice-blocks constitute a peril which had to be boldly faced. But the mist, which hung thickly over the river, was the daring adventurer's most faithful ally.

Strangely enough, Diogenes' first thought, when his horse, finally losing its foothold upon the rapidly shelving bank, started to swim, was of Gilda, and of that ride which he had promised himself, with her dear arms clinging around him, her fair hair, tossed by the wind, brushing against his face. It was one of those sweet, sad visions which some mocking sprite seems to conjure up at moments such as this when life – ay, and honour too! – are trembling in the balance. Sad and swift! It vanished almost as quickly as it came, giving place to thoughts of De Keysere, still unsuspecting at Wageningen, and of Marquet, who haply had already started. Was there a trap waiting for him, too? Was this just an outpost of De Berg's armies; and had they indeed been mysteriously warned by traitor or spy, as Diogenes more than half suspected?

But what was the use of speculating? Indeed, every conjecture was futile, for this now was a supreme struggle – a tussle with Death, who was watching, uncertain whence and how he would strike. For the moment the adventurer was at grips with the flood and with the ice, guiding his horse as best he could toward mid-stream, where the current kept the threatening floes at bay. His pursuers had come to a halt upon the bank. Indeed, not one of them had the mind to follow his quarry on this perilous adventure. They stood there, some half-dozen of them, holding council, their eyes peering through the mist in search of the one black speck – horse and rider – now appearing clearly silhouetted against the silvery water, now vanishing again under cover of the floes. Then one of them raised his musket and took steady aim at the valiant swimmer, who had succeeded at last in reaching mid-stream.

The bullet whizzed through the mist. Diogenes' horse, hit through the neck, plunged and reared, pawed the waters wildly for a moment, then gave that heart-rending scream which is so harrowing to the ears of all animal-lovers. But already the rider had his feet clear of the stirrups, and as the waters finally swept over the head of the stricken beast, he slid out of the saddle and struck out for the opposite shore.

Chapter VI – A Nest of Scorpions

1

OF the extraordinary events which threatened to make March 21, 1624, one of the most momentous dates in the history of the Netherlands we have not much in the way of detail. The broad facts we know chiefly through Van Aitzema's ponderous and minute "Saken v. Staet," whilst De Voocht was, of course, a friend of the Beresteyn family, and, as I understand it, was present in the house at Amersfoort when the terrible catastrophe was so auspiciously and mysteriously averted.

The one thing, however, which neither he nor Van Aitzema have made quite clear is the motive which prompted the Stadtholder to go to Amersfoort in person. He had quite a number of knights and gentlemen around him whom he could have fully trusted to take even so portentous a message and such explicit orders as he desired to send. De Voocht, indeed, suggests that it was Nicolaes Beresteyn who persuaded him, urging the obstinacy of his father, the burgomaster, and of the burghers of the city, who had steadily opposed the Stadtholder's wishes when he – Nicolaes – had been sent to convey them.

Nicolaes Beresteyn had joined his sovereign lord at the camp at Utrecht a couple of days after his wedding. Wearied of sentimental dalliance with the stolid Kaatje, he was glad enough that his duty demanded his presence in camp rather than in the vicinity of his young wife's apron-strings.

It was but natural that, when the Stadtholder desired to send orders to Amersfoort, he should do so through the intermediary of Nicolaes. But on that day, which was March 20, the young man returned, vowing that these were not being obeyed; not a matter of disloyalty, of course, just of tenacity. Civic dignitaries, conscious of their worth and of the sacrifices they had made in the common cause, were wont to wax obstinate where the affairs of their own cities were concerned. But, on the other hand, resistance to his will had invariably the effect of rousing the Stadtholder's arbitrary temper to a point of unreasoning anger. Olden Barneveldt had expiated his contumacy on the scaffold, and I doubt not that, when Nicolaes returned from Amersfoort that evening and delivered his report, the fate of even so trusted a councillor as Mynheer Beresteyn hung for awhile in the balance.

That the matter was one of supreme importance it were impossible to doubt. Maurice of Nassau would not lightly have left his camp at Utrecht that day. The forces of the Archduchess Isabella, who, under the leadership of De Berg and of Isembourg, were threatening Gelderland from two sides, had succeeded on the one part in crossing the Ijssel. His own army was threatened by that of Spinola from the south. On the other hand, the messenger whom he had sent across the Veluwe to urge Marquet and De Keysere to concentrate inside Arnheim and Nijmegen had not yet returned. Nevertheless, he chose, by this suddenly planned excursion to Amersfoort, to expose his valuable person to serious danger; a fact which subsequent events proved only too conclusively.

Nicolaes Beresteyn was sent back at dawn the following morning to warn the burgomaster of the Stadtholder's coming, and enjoining the strictest secrecy. The young man was under orders to say nothing beyond that fact. When closely questioned, however, by his father and also by others, he did admit that fugitives from Ede had succeeded in reaching the camp.

Fugitives from Ede? What did that mean? Why should there be fugitives from Ede, when the armies of the Archduchess were so many leagues away?

Nicolaes Beresteyn shrugged his shoulders. "The Stadtholder will explain," was all that he said.

He appeared impatient and consequential, made them all feel that he could say more if he cared. He had been kept out of the prince's councils while he was under the paternal room, but now he had gained a place in the camp which had always been his by right. These solemn burghers – important enough within the purlieus of their own city – had become insignificant, mere civilians, now that the fate of the country rested upon those who were young enough to bear arms.

Nicolaes tried to meet his sister's glance.

Her indifference toward him galled his sense of importance, and he wished her to know that he neither repented nor was ashamed of what he had said the other night. Anon, when he had succeeded in forcing her eyes to meet his, he gave her a look charged with a mocking challenge. Up to this hour, she had said nothing to her father; now Nicolaes appeared to dare her to speak. But his sneers had not the power to disturb her sublime trust in the man she loved. That some mystery did cling to his journey across the Veluwe she could no longer doubt; but her fears upon the subject dwelt solely on any personal danger that might have overtaken him.

As for her father and his friends, they had apparently decided to possess their souls in patience. There was, indeed, nothing to do but to wait the Stadtholder's arrival, and in the meanwhile to try and hold those fears in check which had been aroused by the ominous words, "Fugitives from Ede."

2

The Stadtholder arrived in the course of the morning. Mynheer Beresteyn did not receive him on the doorstep, as he would have done had the visit been an open one. As it was, the passers-by on the busy quay did not bestow more than a passing glance on the plainly clad cavalier who swung himself out of the saddle outside the burgomaster's house. A message from the camp, probably, they thought. Mynheer Nicolaes had been backward and forward from Utrecht several times these past two or three days. The burgomaster awaited his exalted guest in the hall. His attitude and the expression of his face were alike pregnant with eager questionings. The Stadtholder gave curt acknowledgement to the greetings of Mynheer Beresteyn, of his family, and of his friends, and then strode deliberately into the banqueting-hall.

It looked vast and deserted at this early hour of a winter's morning. Nothing of the animation, the riotous gaiety of that day, less that a week ago, seemed to linger in its sombre, panelled walls. The dais upon which the brides and bridegrooms and the wedding party had sat, and which had crowned so brilliant a spectacle, had been removed, and the magnificent gold and silver plate, the fine linens and priceless crystals been carefully stowed away. Serving-men and sweepers were busy airing and dusting the room when the door was thrown open, and His Highness came in, ushered in by his host. They fled at sight of these great gentlemen, like so many rabbits into carefully hidden burrows.

The Stadtholder went up to the long centre table and faced Mynheer Beresteyn and those who had come in with him – the members of his family and half a dozen burghers, men of importance in the little city. Every one could see that His Highness's anger was bitter against them all. "And so, mynheer," he began curtly, and in tones of marked irritation, and addressing himself more particularly to the burgomaster, "you have thought fit to defy my orders."

"Your Highness!" protested Mynheer Beresteyn.

"Yet they were clear enough," the Stadtholder went on, not heeding the interruption. "Or did your son Nicolaes fail to explain?"

"He told us, your Highness, that it was feared the armies of the Archduchess had crossed the Ijssel —"

"The armies of the Archduchess crossed the Ijssel three days ago," Maurice of Nassau broke in impatiently. "Since then they have overrun Gelderland and occupied Ede, putting that city to fire and sword."

There came a sound like the catching of breath, the rise of a gasp of horror and anguish in every one's throat. But it was quickly suppressed, and His Highness was listened to in silence until the end. Even now, when he paused, no one spoke. All eyes were cast to the ground in self-centered meditation. The whole thing had come as a thunderbolt out of a cloudless sky. Ede had always seemed so safe, so remote. A little city which led nowhere save to the Zuyder Zee, and in the very heart of the United Provinces. What could be the motive of the Archduchess's commanders to adventure thus far into a country which was so universally hostile to them, even to the most miserable peasant, who would pollute every well and stream rather than see the enemy overrun the land?

But all these men – ay, and the women, too – had seen so much, suffered so much; fire and sword were such familiar dangers before their eyes, that for them the time had gone when sighs and lamentations would ease their overburdened hearts. They had learned to receive every fresh blow from God's hands in silence, but with determination to fight on, to fight again and to the death once more, if need be, for their liberties, their rights, and the welfare of their children. It was indeed Mynheer Beresteyn who took the next words out of the Stadtholder's mouth.

"Then Amersfoort, too, is threatened?" he said simply.

The prince nodded.

"Think you," he retorted, "that I would have ordered the evacuation of the town had there not been imperative necessity for such a course? Now, you may pray God that your wilful disobedience hath not placed your city in jeopardy."

" 'Twas but yesterday we had the order," one of the burghers urged. "And —"

" 'Twas yesterday it should have been obeyed," the Stadtholder broke in roughly. "You would then have saved me a perilous journey, for the country already is infested with spies and vedettes, outposts of the Spanish armies."

"We are all ready to guard your Highness with our lives," the burgomaster said quietly.

" 'Tis your wits I want, mynheer," the prince riposted dryly, "not your blood. Indeed, I do fear that Amersfoort is threatened, though I know not if De Berg will spend his forces on you, or, rather, concentrate them on Arnheim. But you must be prepared," he added with stern emphasis.

"You are not in a position to defend yourselves, and I cannot detach any of my troops to come to your assistance if you are attacked. Therefore, my orders were: 'Evacuate the town.' You, mynheer burgomaster, must issue your proclamation at once. Let every one go who can, taking women and children with them. Those who remain do so at their risk. Some of you can go north to Amsterdam, others west to Utrecht. Let De Berg find an empty shell when he comes."

3

Only those who had ever had the sorry task of abandoning a home in the face of an advancing enemy can have any conception of what this peremptory order meant to these burghers – fathers of families for the most part, who after the terrible privations which they had suffered for over half a century, had begun but a few years ago to reconstitute their country and their homes, to resume their interrupted industries, their commerce, their splendid art, to re-establish the wealth and power which had been their birthright, and which the tyranny of a bigoted and jealous overlord had wilfully wrested from them.

Now it meant laying aside spindles and looms once again, lathes, chisels, or books, in order to buckle on swords which threatened to rust in their scabbards, and to don steel helmets. It meant leaving the women to weep, the children fatherless.

Anxious eyes searched the Stadtholder's drawn, moody face; more than one mind reverted to memories of this peerless and fearless commander, the hero of Turnhout and Ostend. Would he have spoken in those days of "evacuation" and of "helplessness"? Would he have dreaded Spinola or the hosts of the Archduchess?

Ah, that subtle, insidious disease had indeed done its work! What mysterious poison was it that had shaken this great man's nerve, made him gloomy and fretful, weakened that indomitable will which had once made the tyrant of Madrid quake for the future of his kingdom?

"De Berg would not dare —" one of the burghers hazarded timidly.

"He may not," His Highness answered. "In which case it might be safe for you all to return to your homes a few days hence. But some of those who fled from Ede believe that De Berg intends to detach some of his troops and with them push on as far as the Zuyder Zee, leaving it to others to join Isembourg, who is coming up from Kleve, and with his help capture Nijmegen first and then Arnheim."

"Marquet by now," observed Beresteyn, "must be well on the way to Arnheim, and De Keysere close to Nijmegen. They can intercept Isembourg and cut him off from Ede and De Berg. Your Highness's messenger —"

"Our messenger," the prince broke in curtly, "failed to deliver our messages. Marquet is not on his way to Arnheim, and De Keysere was still at Wageningen when the first fugitives from Ede ran terror-stricken into our camp."

The words were scarce out of his mouth when the sound of a low, quickly suppressed cry came from the rear of the little group that had gathered around His Highness. Few heard it, or guessed whence it had come. Only Mynheer Beresteyn, turning swiftly, caught his daughter's eyes fixed with a set expression upon him. With an almost imperceptible glance he beckoned to her, and she pushed her way through to his side, and slid her cold little hand into his firm grasp. Encouraged by her father's nearness, it was Gilda who uttered the word of protest which had risen to more than one pair of lips.

"Impossible, your Highness!" she said resolutely.

"Impossible!" Maurice of Nassau retorted curtly. "Why impossible, mejuffrouw?"

"Because my lord is a brave man, as full of resource as he is of courage. He undertook to deliver your Highness's commands to Messire Marquet and Mynheer de Keysere. He is not a man to fail."

She looked brave and determined, without a trace of self-consciousness, even though the rigid education meted out to girls in these times forbade their raising a voice in the councils of their lords. But in this case she had been voicing what was in more than one mind, and when she looked around her with a kind of timid defiance, she only encountered kindly glances.

Her father pressed her hand in tender encouragement. The Stadtholder himself appeared gracious and indulgent. It was only her brother's gaze that was unendurable, for it was charged with sarcasm, not unmixed with malevolence. Did Nicolaes hate her, then? A sickening sense of horror filled the poor girl's soul at the thought. Klaas, her little brother, whom she had loved and mothered, though he was her elder.

Ofttimes had she stood between his childish peccadillos and his father's wrath. And now—she could not even bear to meet his glance. She knew that he triumphed, and that he rejoiced in his triumph, even though he must know that she was wounded to the quick. His warning was ringing in her ear, his warning which had, in truth, proved prophetic: "The orders to Marquet will reach that commander too late!"

As in a dream, she listened to the Stadtholder's words. The whole situation appeared unreal—impossible.

"Your defense of your husband," the prince was saying, "does you honour, mejuffrouw. But this is not a time for sentiment, but for facts. And these it is our duty to face. We placed our every hope on Marquet's co-operation, but Arnheim and Nijmegen are in peril at this hour because certain messages which I sent failed to reach their destination. We have not the leisure to discuss the causes of this failure; rather must we take immediate measures for the safety of our subjects here."

Gilda perforce had to remain silent. To the others, in fact, the matter was only important, in so far that the messenger's failure to arrive had placed Arnheim and Nijmegen in jeopardy. What cared they for her heart-breaking anxiety on account of her beloved?

She looked up at her father, because from him she could always expect sympathy. But he, too, was over-preoccupied just now; patted her hand gently, then let it go, absorbed as he was in listening to the Stadtholder's orders for the speedy evacuation of Amersfoort.

She turned away with a bitter sigh, all the more resolutely suppressed as her brother's mocking glance followed her every movement. The men now were in close conference, the Stadtholder sitting at the table, the burgomaster beside him, with pen and ink, drafting the necessary proclamation, the others grouped around, discussing and tendering advice. Every one was busy, every one had something to think about.

Gilda, heavy-hearted, took the opportunity of slipping unseen out of the room.

4

What prompted her to run up to the very top of the house, like some stricken bird seeking an eyrie, she could not herself have told you. There is such a thing as instinct, and instinct takes innumerable forms according to the most pressing needs of the heart. For the moment, Gilda's most pressing need was a sight of her beloved. Quite apart from the importance of his presence now with news from the threatened cities, she longed to see him, to feel his arms round her, to warm her starved soul in the sunshine of his love and his never absent smile. This longing it was that drove her up to the attic chambers, under the apex of the roof; for these chambers had tiny dormer windows which commanded extensive views of the countryside far beyond the ramparts and beyond the Eem.

Gilda wandered into one of the attic chambers and threw open the narrow casements that gave on the back of the house. Leaning against the window frame, she looked out over the river and beyond it into the mist-laden distance. The sharp, humid air did her good, with its savour of the sea and the tang of spring already lurking in the atmosphere. The sea-fog which had hung over the country for some days still made a dense white veil that enveloped all the life that lay beyond the ramparts, and gave to the little city a strange air of isolation, as if the very world ended on the other side of its walls. From where Gilda stood, high above a forest of roofs and gables, she could see the picturesque fortifications, the monumental gates and turrets, and the Joris Poort and Nieuwpoort, which spanned the Eem on this side. Far away on her right was Utrecht; on her left Barneveld, beyond which stretched the arid upland which held in its cruel breast the secret of her husband's fate.

The girl felt inexpressibly alone, weighted with that sense of forlornness from which only the young are wont to suffer. With the years there comes a more complete self-sufficiency, a greater desire for solitude. Gregariousness is essentially the attribute of youth. And Gilda had no one in whom she could confide. Her father, in truth, had been all to her that a mother might have been; but just now the girl was pining for one of her own sex, for some one who would not be busy with many things, with politics and wars and dissensions, but whose breast would be warm and soft to pillow a head that was weary.

The tears gathered in Gilda's eyes and fell unheeded down her cheeks. It seemed to her as if every moment now she must see a rider galloping swiftly toward her as if she must hear that merry laugh ringing right across the marshland. But all that she saw was the sleepy little city, stretching out before her until it seemed to melt and merge in the arms of the mist; the network of narrow streets, the crow's foot gables, the dormer windows and ornamental corbellings; and, above everything, the tower of St. Maria and St. Joris, with quaint market-place alive with people that looked like ants, fussy and minute.

Even as she gazed, wide-eyed and tearful, the bell of St. Maria began to toll. The slow monotonous reverberation seemed in itself a presage of evil. From the height, Gilda could see the human ants pause awhile in their activities. Their very attitude, the grouping of individual figures, a kind of arrested action in the entire life of the town, proclaiming brooding terror. A moment or two later the sharp clang of the town-crier's bell mingled with the majestic booming, and people started to run toward the market-place from every direction.

Gilda watched this gathering, could see the narrow streets waxing dark with moving forms. She saw the casements thrown open one by one, heads and shoulders filling the dark squares of the window frames. And down below, the arrival of the town-crier, with his halberd and his bell, a crowd of diminutive ant-like forms pressed round his heels. A grey picture, yet all alive with movement, like unto one over which an impatient artist has hastily passed an obliterating brush; the outlines blurred, the colours dull and hazy in the humid atmosphere. It all seemed so dreamlike, so remote. Only a week ago life had appeared so exquisitely gay and so easy! An ardent lover, a happy future, home, adventure! Everything was tumbling out fulsomely from the Cornucopia of Fate. And now all the tragedy represented by those running people below; the enemy at the gates; the abandoned homes; the devastated city; crying children and starving women – a whole herd of fugitives wandering over the desolate marshland, seeking shelters in cities already over-filled, asking for food where so little was to be had.

It was cruel! Oh, horribly cruel! And aweful to see the children dancing around the town-crier, teasing by pulling at his doublet or trying to steal his bell. The crowd in the market-place had become very dense, and still people came running out of the side streets. The steps of St. Maria Kerk were black with the moving throng, and Gilda thought with added heartache of that same crowd, five short days ago, rallying for a holiday, cheering her and her handsome lover, wishing her joy and prosperity in the endless days to come.

Soon the city appeared weltering in confusion. The town-crier continued to ply his bell, and to call the proclamation ordered by the burgomaster. He went on so that every citizen in turn might hear, and now the crowd no longer tended all one way. Some had heard and were hurrying home to consult with their families, to make arrangements either for speedy departure or for weathering the terrible alternative of an invading army. Others lingered in groups on the market-place or at street corners, discussing or lamenting, according to their temperament, pausing to ask friends what they would do or what they thought of the terrible situation.

Gilda, up at the attic casement, could almost guess by the attitude, the gestures of the scared human ants, just how unsteady had become their mental balance. It was all so unexpected, and there was nothing that anyone could do to help in this terrible emergency. The Stadtholder was going back to camp. He had declared that he could not help. Threatened from every side, he could not spare his forces to come to the aid of so small a place as Amersfoort. And he – the stranger with the happy smile and the gay, inconsequent temper – who had been sent across the Veluwe to obtain succour – had failed to return. There was no garrison at Amersfoort, so there was nothing for it but to flee.

5

At what precise moment Gilda became aware of the solitary rider galloping tete baissee toward the city, it were impossible to say. He came out of the mist from the direction of Utrecht, and Gilda saw him long before the sentry at the Joris Poort challenged him. Apparently he had papers and all necessaries in order, for he was admitted without demur; and at the sight Gilda turned away from her point of vantage, ran across the attic chamber and down the stairs. It was such a very short distance between the Joris Poort and the front door of the burgomaster's house, and she wanted so much to be the first to welcome him.

It was then half an hour before noon. The city by this time was in the throes of a complete upheaval. The noise in the streets had become incessant and deafening. Church bells tolling, town-criers bawling, the clang of the halberds of the city guards mingling with the rattle of cart-wheels upon the cobble-stones, with the tramping of hundreds of feet and stamping of innumerable horses' hoofs. The air was resonant with shrieks and cries, with the grating and jarring of metal, with peal of bells and the hubbub of a throng on the move. Gilda, when she reached the foot of the stairs, found herself facing the wide-open doorway, and through it saw the quay alive with people running, with horses and driven cattle, with crowds scrambling into the boats down below, with carts and dogs and children and barrows piled up with furniture and luggage hastily tied together.

The confusion bewildered her. Determined not to allow futile terror to overmaster her, she, nevertheless, felt within her whole being the sense of an impending catastrophe. She could not approach the door, because the crowd was swarming up the stone steps, and her father's serving-men, armed with stout sticks and cudgels, had much ado to keep some of the more venturesome or more terrified among that throng from invading the house.

How that solitary rider whom she had spied in the distance would succeed in forging his way through the dense mass of surging humanity, she could not imagine; and yet through all the turmoil, the din, the terror she was more conscious of his nearness than of any other sensation. The longing to see him was, in a certain sort of way, appeased. She knew that he lived and that time alone stood between her present and past longing and the bliss of nestling once more in his arms.

Oh, the crowd! It was rapidly becoming unmanageable. The serving-men plied their cudgels in vain. There were men and women there stronger and bolder than others who were determined to have a word with the burgomaster.

"I am Mynheer Beresteyn's friend!" was shouted authoritatively to the helpless guardians of their master's privacy. Or, "You know me, Anton? Make way for me there. I must speak with the burgomaster!"

"The burgomaster is busy!" the serving-men bawled out until they were hoarse. "No one can be admitted!"

But it was difficult for any man to raise a stick against well-known burghers of the city, friends and acquaintances who had supped here in the house at Mynheer's own table; and the pressure became more and more difficult to withstand every moment. Some of the people had actually pushed their way into the hall, making it impossible for Gilda to get near the door; and the longing was irresistible to be close at hand when he dismounted, so that her smile might be the first to greet him as he ran up the steps. She pictured it all – his coming, his appearance, the way he would look about him, knowing that she must be near.

Then all at once something awful happened. Gilda, from where she stood, could neither see nor hear what it was; and yet she knew, just from looking at the crowd, that something more immediately terrifying had turned this seething mass of humanity into a horde of scared beasts. Their movements suddenly became more swift; it seemed as if some fearsome goad had been applied to the entire population of the city, and the desire, to get away, to run, to flee had become more insistent.

Those who had swarmed up the steps of the burgomaster's house ran down again. They had no longer the desire to speak with anyone, or to appeal to the servants to let them pass. They only wanted to run like the others, the few more grave ones gathering their scattered families around them like a mother hen does her chicks.

And, oh, the awful din! It had intensified a thousand-fold, and seemed all of a sudden like hell let loose. So many people shrieked, the women and the children for the most part. And the boatmen down on the water, plying for hire their small craft, already dangerously overloaded with fugitives and their goods. But now everyone on the quay appeared obsessed with the desire to get into the boats. There was scrambling and fighting upon the quay, shrieks of terror followed by ominous splashes in the murky waters. Gilda closed her eyes, not daring to look.

And still the clang of the church bells tolling and the hideous cacophony of a whole population stampeding in a mad panic.

The hall, the doorway, the outside steps were now deserted. Life and movement and din were all out on the quay and in the streets around. The serving-men even had thrown down their sticks and cudgels. Some of them had disappeared altogether, others stood in groups, skulking and wide-eyed. Gilda tried to frame a query. Her pale, anxious face no doubt expressed the words which her lips could not utter, for one of the men in the hall replied in a husky whisper:

"The Spaniards! They are on us!"

She wanted to ask more, for at first it did not seem as if this were fresh news. The Spaniards were at Ede, the town was being evacuated because of them. What had occurred to turn an ordered evacuation into so redoubtable a stampede?

And still no sign of my lord.

Then suddenly the doors of the banqueting-hall were thrown open, and the burgomaster appeared. Had Gilda doubted for a moment that something catastrophic had actually happened, she would have felt her doubts swept aside by the mere aspect of her father. He, usually so grave, so dignified, was trembling like a reed, his hair was dishevelled, his cheeks of a grey, ashen colour. The word "Gilda" was actually on his lips when he stepped across the threshold, and quite a change came over him the moment he caught sight of his daughter. Before he could call to her she was already by his side, and in an instant he had her by the hand and dragged her with him back into the banqueting-hall.

"What has happened?" she asked, in truth more bewildered than frightened.

"The Spaniards!" her father replied briefly. "They are on us."

"Yes," she ventured, frowning; "but —"

"Not three leagues away," he broke in curtly. "Their vanguard will be here by nightfall."

She looked round her, puzzled to see them all so calm in contrast to the uproar and the confusion without. The Stadtholder was sitting beside the table, his head resting on his hand. He looked woefully ill. Nicolaes Beresteyn was beside him, whispering earnestly.

"What are you going to do, father dear?" Gilda asked in a hurried whisper.

"My fellow-burghers and I are remaining at our posts," Beresteyn replied quietly. "We must do what we can to save our city, and our presence may do some good."

"And Nicolaes?" she asked again.

"Nicolaes has his horse ready. He will take you to Utrecht in His Highness's train." Then, as Gilda made no comment on this, only gave his hand a closer pressure, he added tentatively: "Unless you would prefer to go with Mynheer van den Poele and his family. He is taking Kaatje and her mother to Amsterdam."

"I would prefer to remain with you," she said simply.

"Impossible, my dear child!" he retorted.

"My place is here," she continued firmly, "and I'll not go. Oh, can't you understand?" she pleaded, with a break in her voice. "If you sent me away, I should go mad or die!"

"But, Gilda —" the poor man protested.

"My lord is here," Gilda suddenly broke in more calmly.

"My lord? What do you mean?"

"I saw him awhile ago. I was up in the attic-chamber, he came through the Joris Poort."

"Your eyes deceived you. He would be here by now."

"He should be here," she asserted. "I cannot understand what has happened. Perhaps the crowd —"

"Your eyes deceived you," he reiterated, but more doubtfully this time. Then, as just at that moment the Stadtholder and caught his eye, Beresteyn called to him, "My daughter says that my lord has returned."

"Impossible!" burst forth impulsively from Nicolaes.

"Why should it be impossible?" Gilda retorted quickly, and fixed coldly challenging eyes upon her brother. "Why should you say that it is impossible?" she insisted, seeing that Nicolaes now looked shamefaced and confused. "What do you know about my lord?"

"Nothing, nothing!" Nicolaes stammered. "I did not mean that, of course; it only seems so strange —" And he added roughly, "Then why is he not here?"

"The crowd is very dense about the streets," one of the burghers suggested. "My lord, mayhap hath found it difficult to push his way through."

"Why should he be coming to Amersfoort?" mused Mynheer Beresteyn.

"He came from the direction of Utrecht," Gilda replied. "Some one at the camp must have told him that His Highness was here."

"No one knew I was coming hither," the Stadtholder broke in impatiently.

"My sister more like hath been troubled with visions," Nicolaes rejoined with a sneer. "Nor have we the time," he added, "to wait on my lord's pleasure. If your Highness is ready, we should be getting to horse."

"But surely," Gilda protested with pitiful earnestness, "your Highness will wait to see your messenger. He must be bringing news from Messire Marquet. He —"

"Yes," the Stadtholder broke in decisively, "I'll see him. Let some one go out into the streets at once and find the man. Tell him that we are waiting —"

"He knows his way about the town," Nicolaes interposed, with an ill-concealed note of spite in his voice. "Why should he need a pilot.?"

There was a moment's silence. Every one looked nervy and worried. Then the Stadtholder turned once more to the burgomaster, and queried abruptly:

"Are those two companions of my lord's still in your house, mynheer? Can you not send one of them?"

The suggestion met with universal approval. And Mynheer Beresteyn himself urged the advisability of finding my lord's friends immediately. He took his daughter's hand. It was cold as ice, and quivered like a wounded bird in his warm grasp. He patted it gently, reassuringly. Her wild eyes frightened him. He knew what she suffered, and in his heart condemned his son for those insinuations against the absent. But this was not a moment for delicacy or for scruples. The hour was a portentous one, and fraught with peril for a nation and its chief. The individual matters so little at such times. The feelings, the sufferings, the broken heart of one women or one man – how futile do they seem when a whole country is writhing in the throes of her death agony?

"Go, my dear child," Beresteyn admonished firmly. "Obey His Highness's commands. Find my lord's friends and tell them to go at once, and return hither with my lord. Go," he added; and whispered gently in Gilda's ear, as he led her, reluctant yet obedient, to the door, "Leave your husband's honour in my hands."

She gave him a grateful look, and he gave her hand a last reassuring pressure. Then he let her go from him, only urging her to hurry back.

It must not be supposed for a moment that he did not feel for her in her anxiety and her misery. But the man in question was a stranger – an Englishman, what? – and Mynheer Beresteyn was above all a patriot, a man who had suffered acutely for his country, had sacrificed his all for her, and was ready to do it again whenever she called to him. The Stadtholder stood for the safety and the integrity of the United Provinces; he was the champion and upholder of her civil and religious liberties. His personal safety stood, in the minds of Beresteyn and his fellow burghers, above every consideration on earth.

Gilda knew this, and though she trusted her father implicitly, she knew that her beloved would be ruthlessly sacrificed, even by him, if, through misadventure or any other simple circumstance entirely beyond his control, he happened to have failed in the enterprise which had been entrusted to him. Nicolaes, of course, was an avowed enemy. Why? Gilda could not conjecture. Was it jealousy, or petty spite only? If so, what advantage could he reap from the humiliation of one who already was a member of his own family? But she felt herself encompassed with enemies. No one had attempted to defend my lord's honour when it was so ruthlessly impugned save her father, and he was too absorbed, too much centered in thoughts of his country's peril, to do real battle for the absent.

It was with a heavy heart that she turned to go up the stairs in search of the two men who alone were ready to go through fire in the defense of their friend. A melancholy smile hovered round Gilda's lips. She felt that with those two quaint creatures she had more in common at this hour than with her father, whom she idolized. In those too poor caitiffs she had all that her heart had been hungering for: simple hearts that understood her sorrow, loyal souls that never wavered. For evil or for good, through death-peril or through seeming dishonour, their friend whom they reverenced could count upon their devotion. And as Gilda went wearily up the stairs, her mind conjured up the picture of those two ludicrous vagabonds, with their whimsical saws and rough codes of honour, and she suddenly felt less lonely and less sad.

7

Great was her disappointment, therefore, when she reached the guest-chamber, which they still occupied, to find that it was empty. The whole house was by this time in a hopeless state of turmoil and confusion. Serving-men and maids rushed aimlessly hither and thither, up and down the stairs, along the passages, in and out of the rooms; or stood about in groups, whispering or cowering in corners. Some of them had already fled; the few who remained looked like so many scared chickens, fussy and inconsequent, – the maids, with kirtles awry and hair unkempt, the men striving to look brave and determined, putting on the air of masters, and adding to the maids' distress by their aimless, hectoring ways.

There was nothing in the house now left of that orderly management which is the pride of every self-respecting housewife. Doors stood open, displaying the untidiness of the rooms; there was noise and bustle everywhere, calls of distress and loud admonitions. From no one could Gilda learn what she desired to know. She was forced to seek out Maria, her special tiring-woman, who, it was to be hoped, had some semblance of reason left in her. Maria, however, had no love for the two rapscallions, who were treated in the house as if they were princes, and knew nothing of the respect due to their betters. She replied to her young mistress's inquiries by shrugging her shoulders and calling heaven to witness her ignorance of the whereabouts of those abominable louts.

"Spoilt, they have been," the old woman asserted sententiously. "Shamefully spoilt. They have neither order nor decency, nor the slightest regard for the wishes of their betters —"

"But, Maria, whither have the two good fellows gone?" Gilda broke in impatiently.

"Gone? Whither have they gone? Maria ejaculated, in pious ignorance of such probable wickedness. "Nay, that ye cannot expect any self-respecting woman to know. They have gone, the miserable roysterers! Went but an hour ago, without saying by your leave. This much I do know. And my firm belief is that they were naught but a pair of Spanish spies, come to hand us all, body and soul, to —"

"Maria, I forbid thee to talk such rubbish!" Gilda exclaimed wrathfully.

And, indeed, her anger and her white and worried look did effectually silence the garrulous woman's tongue.

Even the waiting-maids! Even these ignorant fools! Gilda could have screamed with the horror of it all, as if she had suddenly landed in a nest of scorpions and their poison encompassed her everywhere. This story of spies! God in Heaven, how had it come about? Whose was the insidious tongue that had perverted her brother Nicolaes first, and then every trimmer and rogue in the house? Gilda felt as if it might ease her heart to run around with a whip, and lash all these base detractors into acknowledgment of their infamy. But she forced herself to patience.

A vague instinct had already whispered to her that she must not go back to the banqueting-hall with the news that my lord's friends had gone, and that no one had any knowledge of their whereabouts. She felt that if she did that, her brother's sneers would become unendurable, and that she might then be led to retort with accusations against her only brother which she would afterwards forever regret.

So she waited for awhile, curtly bade Maria to be gone, and to leave her in peace. She wanted to think, to put a curb on her fears and her just wrath against this unseen army of calumniators; for wrath and fear are both evil counsellors. And above all, she wanted to see her beloved.

He was in the town. She knew it as absolutely as that she was alive. Were her eyes likely to be deceived? Even now, when she closed her eyes, she could see him, as she had done but a few minutes ago, walking his horse through the Joris Poort, his plumed hat shading the upper part of his face. She could see him, with just that slight stoop of his broad shoulders which denoted almost unendurable fatigue. She had noted this at the moment, with a pang of anxiety, and then forgotten it all in the joy of seeing him again. She remembered it all now. Oh, how could they think that she could be deceived?

Just for a second or two she had the mind to run back to the casement in the attic-chamber and see if she could not from thence spy him again. But surely this would be futile. He must have reached the quay by now, would be at the front door, with no one to welcome him. In truth, the longing to see him had become sheer physical pain.

So Gilda once more made her way down into the hall.

1

DOWN below, in the banqueting-hall, Gilda's departure had at first been followed by a general feeling of obsession, which caused the grave men here assembled to remain silent for awhile and pondering. There was no lack of sympathy, I repeat; not even on the part of the Stadtholder, whose heart and feelings were never wholly atrophied. But there had sprung up in the minds of these grave burghers an unreasoning feeling of suspicion toward the man whom they had trusted implicitly such a brief while ago.

Terror at the imminence of their danger, the appearance of the dreaded foe almost at their very gates, had in a measure – as terror always will – blurred the clearness of their vision, and to a certain extent warped their judgements. The man now appeared before them as a stranger, therefore a person to be feared, even despised to the extent of attributing the blackest possible treachery to him. They forgot that the closest possible ties of blood and of tradition bound the English gentleman to the service of the Prince of Orange. Sir Percy Blakeney now, and Diogenes the soldier of fortune of awhile ago, were one and the same. But no longer so to them. The adder's fork had bitten into their soul and left its insidious poison of suspicion and of misbelief.

So none of them spoke, hardly dared to look on Mynheer Beresteyn, who, they felt, was not altogether with them in their distrust. The Stadtholder had lapsed into one of his surly moods. His lean, brown hands were drumming a devil's tattoo upon the table.

Then suddenly Nicolaes broke into a harsh and mirthless laugh.

"It would all be a farce," he exclaimed with bitter malice, "if it did not threaten to become so tragic." Then he turned to the Stadtholder, and his manner became once more grave and earnest. "Your Highness, I entreat," he said soberly, "deign to come away with me at once, ere you fall into some trap set by those abominable spies —"

"Nicolaes," his father broke in sternly, "I forbid you to make these base insinuations against your sister's husband."

"I'll be silent if you command me," Nicolaes rejoined quietly. "But methinks that his Highness's life is too precious for sentimental quibbles. Nay," he went on vehemently, and like one who is forced into speech against his will, "I have warned Gilda of this before. While were all waiting here calmly, trusting to that stranger who came, God knows whence, he was warning De Berg to effect a quick crossing"

"It is false!" protested the burgomaster hotly.

"Then, I pray you," Nicolaes insisted hotly, "tell me how it is that De Berg did forestall his Highness's plans? Who was in the council-chamber when the plans were formulated save yourselves? Who knew of the orders to Marquet? Marquet hath not gone to relieve Arnheim, and the armies of the Archduchess are at our gates!"

He paused, and a murmur of assent went round the room, and when Mynheer Beresteyn once more raised his voice in protest, saying firmly: "I'll not believe it! Let us wait at least until we've heard what news my lord hath brought!" No one spoke in response, and even the Stadtholder shrugged his shoulders, as if the matter of a man's honour or dishonour had no interest for him.

"Your Highness," Nicolaes went on with passionate earnestness, "let me beg of you on my knees to think of your noble father, of the trap into which he fell, and of his assassin, Gerard – a stranger, too —"

"But this man saved my life once!" the Stadtholder said, with an outburst of generous feeling in favour of the man to whom, in truth, he owed so much.

"He hated Stoutenburg then, your Highness," Nicolaes retorted, and boldly looked his father in the face – his father who knew his own share in that hideous conspiracy three months ago. "He loved my sister Gilda. It suited his purpose then to use his sword in your Highness's service.

But remember, he is only a soldier of fortune after all. Have we not all of us heard him say a hundred times that he had lived hitherto by selling his sword to the highest bidder?"

This time his tirade was greeted by a distinct murmur of approval. Only the burgomaster raised his voice admonishingly once more.

"Take care, Nicolaes!" he exclaimed. "Take care!"

"Take care of what?" the young man retorted with all his wonted arrogance, and challenged his father with a look.

"Would you give your only son away," that look appeared to say, "in order to justify a stranger?"

Then, as indeed Mynheer Beresteyn remained silent, not exactly giving up the contention, but forced into passive acquiescence by the weight of public opinion and that inalienable feeling of family and kindred which makes most men or women defend their own against any stranger, Nicolaes continued, with magnificent assumption of patriotic fervor:

"Have we the right hazard so precious a thing as his Highness's life for the sake of sparing my sister's feelings?"

In this sentiment every one was ready to concur. They did not actually condemn the stranger; they were not prepared to call him a traitor and a potential assassin, or to believe one half of Nicolaes Beresteyn's insinuations. They merely put him aside, out of their minds, as not entering into their present schemes. And even the burgomaster could not gainsay the fact that his son was right.

The most urgent thing at the present juncture was to get the Stadtholder safely back to his camp at Utrecht. Every minute spent in this garrisonless city was fraught with danger for the most precious life in the United Provinces.

"Where is his Highness's horse?" he asked.

"Just outside," Nicolaes replied glibly; "in charge of a man I know. Mine is ready too. Indeed, we should get to horse at once."

The Stadtholder did not demur.

"Have the horses brought to," he said quickly. "I'll be with you in a trice."

2

Nicolaes hurried out of the room, his Highness remaining behind for a moment or two, in order to give his final instructions, a last admonition or two to the burghers.

"Do not resist," he said earnestly. "You have not the means to do aught but to resign your-selves to the inevitable. As soon as I can, I will come to your relief. In the meanwhile, conciliate De Berg by every means in your power. He is not a harsh man, and the Archduchess has learnt a salutary lesson from the discomfiture of Alva. She knows by now that we are a stiff-necked race, whom it is easier to cajole than to coerce. If only you will be patient! Can you reckon on your citizens not to do anything rash or foolish that might bring reprisals upon your heads?"

"Yes," the burgomaster replied. "I think we can rely on them for that. When your Highness has gone we'll assemble on the market place, and I will speak to them. We'll do our best to stay the present panic and bring some semblance of order into the town."

Their hearts were heavy. 'Twas no use trying to minimize the deadly peril which confronted them. There was a century of oppression, of ravage, and pillage, and bloodshed to the credit of the Spanish armies. It was difficult to imagine that the spirit of an entire nation should have changed suddenly into something more tolerant and less cruel.

However, for the moment, there was nothing more to be said, and alas! it was not as if the whole terrible situation was a novel one. They had all been through it before, at Leyden and Bergen-op-Zoom, at Haarlem and Delft, when they were weeping their land free from the foreign tyrant; and it was useless at this hour to add to the Stadtholder's difficulties by futile lamentations. All the more as Nicolaes had now returned with the welcome news that the horses were there, and everything ready for his Highness's departure. He appeared more excited than before, anxious to get away as quickly as may be.

"There is a rumour in the town," he said, "that Spanish vedettes have been spied less than a league away."

"And have you heard any rumour as to the arrival of our Diogenes?" the Stadtholder asked casually.

Nicolaes hesitated a moment ere he replied: "I have heard nothing definite."

3

A minute later the Stadtholder was in the hall. The doors were open and the horses down below in the charge of an equerry.

Nicolaes, half way down the outside stone steps, looked the picture of fretful impatience. With a dark frown upon his brow, he was scanning the crowd, and now and again a curse broke through his set lips when he saw the Stadtholder still delayed by futile leave-takings.

"In the name of heaven, let us to horse!" he exclaimed almost savagely.

Just at that moment his Highness was taking a kindly farewell of Gilda.

"I wish, mejuffrouw," he was saying, "that you had thought of taking shelter in our camp."

Gilda forced herself to listen to him, her lips tried to frame the respectful words which convention demanded. But her eyes she could not control, nor yet her thoughts, and they were fixed upon the crowd down below, just as were those of her brother Nicolaes. She thought that every moment she must catch sight of that plumed hat, towering above the throng, of those sturdy shoulders, forging their way to her. But all that she saw was the surging mass of people. A medley of colour. Horses, carts, the masts of ships. People running. And children. Numberless children, in arms or on their tiny feet; the sweet, heavy burdens that made the present disaster more utterly catastrophic.

Then suddenly she gave a loud cry.

"My lord!" she called, at the top of her voice. Then something appeared to break in her throat, and it was with a heart-rending sob that she murmured almost inaudibly: "Thank God! It is my lord!"

The Stadtholder turned, was across the hall and out in the open in a trice.

"Where?" he demanded.

She ran after him, seized his surcoat with a trembling hand, and with the other pointed in the direction of the Koppel-poort.

"A plumed hat!" she murmured vaguely, for her teeth were chattering so that she could scarcely speak. "All broken and battered with wind and weather – a torn jerkin – a mud-stained cloak. He is leading his horse. He has a three days' growth of beard on his chin, and looks spent with fatigue. There! Do you not see him?"

But Nicolaes already had interposed.

"To horse, your Highness!" he cried.

He would have given worlds for the privilege to seize the Stadtholder then and there by the arm, and to drag him down the steps and set him on his horse before the meeting which he dreaded could take place. But Maurice of Nassau, torn between his desire to get out of the threatened city as quickly as possible and his wish to speak with the messenger whom an inalienable instinct assured him that he could trust, was lingering on the steps trying in his turn to catch sight of Diogenes.

"Beware of the assassin's dagger, your Highness!" Nicolaes whispered hoarsely in his ear. "In this crowd who can tell? Who knows what deathly trap is being laid for you?"

"Not by that man, I'll swear!" the Stadtholder affirmed.

"Nay, if he is loyal he can follow you to the camp and report to you there. But for God's sake remember your father and the miscreant Gerard. There too, a crowd; the hustling, the hurry! In the name of your country, come away!"

There was no denying the prudence of this advice. Another instant's hesitation, the obstinacy of an arbitrary temperament that abhors being dictated to, the Stadtholder was ready to go. Gilda, on the top of the steps, was more like a stone statue of expectancy than like a living woman. Nay, all that she had alive in her were just her eyes, and they had spied her beloved. He was then by the Koppel-poort, some hundred yards or more on the other side of the quay, with a seething mass of panic-stricken humanity between him and the steps of Mynheer Beresteyn's house.

He had dismounted and was leading his horse. The poor beast, spent with fatigue, looked ready to drop, and, indeed, appeared too dazed to pick his own way through the crowd. As it was, he was more than a handful for his equally wearied master, whose difficulties were increased a hundredfold by the number of small children who were for ever getting in the way of the horse's legs, and were in constant danger of being kicked or trampled on.

But Gilda never lost sight of him now that she had seen him. With every beat of her heart she was measuring the footsteps that separated him from the Stadtholder. And the more Nicolaes fretted to hurry his Highness away, the more she longed and yearned for the quick approach of her beloved.

4

Amongst all those here present, Gilda was the only one who scented some unseen danger for them all in Nicolaes' strangely feverish haste. What the others took for zeal, she knew by instinct was naught but treachery. What form this would take she could not guess; but this she knew, that for some motive as sinister as it was unexplainable, Nicolaes did not wish the Stadtholder and his messenger to meet. That same motive had caused him to utter all those venomous accusations against her husband, and was even now wearing him into a state of fretfulness which bordered on dementia.

"My lord!" she cried out to her beloved at one time; and felt that even through all the din and clatter her voice had reached his ear, for he raised his head, and it even seemed to her as if his eyes met hers above the intervening crowd and as if the supernal longing for him which was in her heart had drawn him with its mystic power over every obtruding obstacle.

For, indeed, the next moment he was right at the foot of the steps, not five paces from the Stadtholder.

Nicolaes spied him in a moment, and a loud curse broke from his lips.

"That skulking assassin!" he cried; and with a magnificent gesture covered the Stadtholder with his body. "To horse, your Highness, and leave me to deal with him!"

Maurice of Nassau, indeed was one of the bravest men of his time, but the word "assassin" was bound to ring unpleasantly in the ears of a man whose father had met his death at a murderer's hand. Half-ashamed of his fears, he nevertheless did take advantage of Nicolaes' theatrical attitude to slip behind him and mount his horse as quickly as he could. But with his foot already in the stirrup compunction appeared to seize him. Wishing to palliate the gross insult which was being hurled at the man who had once saved his life at imminent peril of his own, he now turned and called to him in gracious, matter-of-fact tones:

"Why, man, what made you tarry so long? Come with us to Utrecht now. We can no longer wait."

With this he swung himself in the saddle.

"Not another step man, at your peril!"

This came from Nicolaes Beresteyn, who was still standing in a dramatic pose between Diogenes and the Stadtholder, with his cloak wrapped around his arm.

"Stand back, you fool!!" retorted the other loudly, and would have pushed past him, when suddenly Nicolaes disengaged his arm from his cloak wrapped around his arm.

For one fraction of a second the gleam of steel flashed in the humid air; then, without a word of warning, swift as a hawk descending on his prey, he struck at Diogenes with all his might.

It had all happened in a very few brief seconds. Diogenes, spent with fatigue, or actually struck, staggered and half fell against the bottom step. But Gilda, with a loud cry, was already by his side, and as Nicolaes raised his arm to strike once again, she was on him like some lithe pantheress.

She seized his wrist, and gave it such a violent twist that he uttered a cry of pain, and the dagger fell with a clatter to the ground. After which everything became a blur. She heard her brother's loudly triumphant shout:

"His Highness's life was threatened. Mine was but an act of justice!" even as he in his turn swung himself into the saddle.

5

The Stadtholder looked dazed. It had all happened so quickly that he had not the time to visualize it all. De Voocht, who was in the hall of the burgomaster's house from the moment when the Stadtholder bade farewell to Gilda until that when he dug his spurs into his horse and scattered the crowd in every direction, tells us in his "Brieven" – the one which is dated March 21, 1626 – that the incidents followed on one another with such astounding rapidity that it was impossible for any one to interfere.

All that he remembers very clearly is seeing his Highness getting to horse, then the flash of steel in the air and Nicolaes Beresteyn's arm upraised ready to strike. He could not see if any one had fallen. The next moment he heard Gilda's heart-piercing shriek, and saw her running down the stone steps – almost flying, like a bird.

Mynheer Beresteyn followed his daughter as rapidly as he could. He reached the foot of the steps just as his son put his horse to a walk in the wake of his Highness. He was wont to say afterwards that at the moment his mind was an absolute blank. He had heard his daughter's cry and seen Nicolaes strike; but he had not actually seen Diogenes. Now he was just in time to see his son's final dramatic gesture and to hear his parting words:

"There, father," Nicolaes shouted to him, and pointed to the ground, "is the pistol which the miscreant pointed at the Stadtholder when I struck him down like a dog!"

The people down on the quay had hardly perceived anything. They were too deeply engrossed in their own troubles and deadly peril.

When the horses reared under the spur they scattered like so many hens out of the way of immediate danger; but a second or two later they were once more surging everywhere, intent only on the business of getting away.

Gilda, at the foot of the steps, saw and heard nothing more. The sudden access of almost manlike strength wherewith she had fallen on her brother and wrenched the murderous dagger from his grasp had as suddenly fallen from her again. Her knees were shaking; she was almost ready to swoon.

She put out her arms and encountered those of her father, which gave her support. Her brother's voice, exultant and cruel, reached her ears as through a veil.

"My lord!" she murmured, in a pitiful appeal.

She did not know how severely he had been struck; indeed, she had not seen him fall. Her instinct had been to rush on Nicolaes first and to disarm him. In this she succeeded. Then only did she turn to her beloved.

But the crowd, cruelly indifferent, was all around like a surging sea. They pushed and they jostled; they shouted and filled the air with a medley of sounds. Some actually laughed. She saw some comely faces and ugly ones; some that wept and others that grinned. It seemed to her even for a moment that she caught sight of a round red face and of lean and lanky Socrates. She tried to call to him, to beg him to explain. She turned to her father, asking him if in truth she was going mad.

For she called in vain to her beloved. He was no longer here.

Chapter VIII – Devil's-Writ

1

WHEN Diogenes, taken wholly unawares by Nicolaes' treacherous blow, had momentarily lost his balance, he would have been in a precarious position indeed had not his faithful friends been close at hand at the moment.

It is difficult to surmise how terribly anxious the two philosophers had been these past few days. Indeed, their anxiety had proved more than a counterpart to that felt by Gilda, and had, with its simple-hearted sympathy, expressed in language more whimsical than choice, been intensely comforting to her.

Both these worthies had been inured to blows and hurts from the time when as mere lads, they first learned to handle a sword, and Pythagoras' wound, which would have laid an ordinary man low for a fortnight, was, after four days, already on the mend. To keep a man of that type in bed, or even within four walls, when he began to feel better was more than any one could do. And when he understood that Diogenes had been absent four days on an errand for the Stadtholder, that the jongejuffrouw was devoured with anxiety on his behalf, and that that spindle-legged gossoon Socrates was spending most of the day and one half of the night on horseback, patrolling the ramparts watching for the comrade's return; when he understood all that, I say, it was not likely that he – Pythagoras – an able-bodied man and a doughty horseman at that, would be content to lie abed and be physicked by any grovelling leech.

Thus the pair of them were providentially on the watch on that memorable March 21, and they both saw their comrade-in-arms enter the city by the Joris Poort. They followed him as best they could through the crowd, cursing and pushing their way, knowing well that Diogenes' objective could be none other than a certain house they wot of on the quay, where a lovely jongejuffrouw was waiting in tears for her beloved.

Remember that to these two caitiffs the fact that the Spaniards were said to be at the very gates of Amersfoort was but a mere incident. With their comrade within the city, they feared nothing, were prepared for anything. They had been in far worse plights than this many a time in their career, the three of them, and had been none the worse for it in the end.

Of course, now matters had become more complicated through the jongejuffrouw. She had become the first consideration, and though it was impossible not to swear at Diogenes for thus having laid this burden on them all, it was equally impossible to shirk its responsibilities.

The jongejuffrouw above all. That had become the moral code of these two philosophers, and with those confounded Spaniards likely to descend on this town – why, the jongejuffrouw must be got out of it as soon as may be! No wonder that Diogenes had turned up just in the nick of time! Something evidently was in the wind, and it behooved for comrades-in-arms to be there, ready to help as occasion arose.

A simple code enough, you'll admit; worthy of simple, unsophisticated hearts. Socrates, being the more able-bodied of the two, then took command, dismounted, and left his lubberly compeer in charge of the horses at a comparatively secluded corner of the market-place.

"If you can get hold of one more horse," he said airily, "one that is well-saddled and looks sprightly and fresh, do not let your super-sensitive honesty stand in your way. Diogenes' mount looked absolutely spent, and I'm sure he'll need another.

With which parting admonition he turned on his heel and made his way toward the quay.

2

Thus it was that Socrates happened to be on the spot, or very near it, when Diogenes was struck by the hand of a traitor, and, wearied, sick, and faint, lost his footing and fell for a moment helpless against the steps, whilst Nicolaes Beresteyn dug his spurs into his horse's sides and urged the Stadtholder to immediate haste.

A second or two later these two were lost to sight in the crowd. It was Socrates who received his half-swooning friend in his arms, and who dragged him incontinently into the recess formed by the side of the stone steps and the wall of the burgomaster's house.

By great good fortune, the dagger-thrust aimed by the abominable miscreant had lost most of its virulence in the thick folds of Diogenes' cloak. The result was just a flesh wound in the neck, nothing that would cause so hardened a soldier more than slight discomfort. His scarf, tied tightly around his shoulders by Socrates' rough, but experienced hands, was all that was needed for the moment. It had only been fatigue, and perhaps the unexpectedness of the onslaught, that had brought him to his knees for that brief second, and rendered him momentarily helpless. Time enough, by mischance for Nicolaes to drag the Stadtholder finally out of sight.

But by the time Diogenes' faithful comrade had found shelter for him in the angle of the wall the feeling of sickness had passed away.

"The Stadtholder," he queried abruptly, "where is he?"

"Gone!" Socrates grunted through clenched teeth. "Gone, together with that spawn of the devil who —"

"After him!" Diogenes commanded, speaking once more with that perfect quietude which is the attribute of men of action at moments of acute peril. "Get me a horse, man! Mine is spent."

"In the market-place," Socrates responded laconically. "Pythagoras is in charge. You can have the beast, and we'll follow." Then he added, under his breath: "And the jongejuffrouw? She was so anxious--"

Diogenes made no reply, gave one look up at the house which contained all that for him was dearest on God's earth. But he did not sigh. I think the longing and the disappointment were too keen even for that. The next moment he had already started to push his way through the throng along the quay, and thence into Vriese Straat in the direction of the market-place, closely followed by his long-legged familiar.

As soon as the Groote Market lay open before him, his sharp eyes searched the crowd for a sight of the Stadtholder's plumed bonnet. Soon he spied his Highness right across the place, with Nicolaes riding close to his stirrup.

The two horsemen were then tending toward Joris Laan, which leads straight to the poort.

At that end of the markt the crowd was much less dense, and Joris Laan beyond appeared practically deserted. It was, you must remember, from that side that the enemy would descend upon the city when he came, and the moving throng, if viewed from a height, would now have looked like a column of smoke when it is all blown one way by the wind. Already the Stadtholder and Nicolaes had been free to put their horses to a trot. Another moment and they would be galloping down Joris Laan, which is but three hundred yards from the poort.

"Oh, God, grant me wings!" Diogenes muttered, between his teeth.

"What are you going to do?" Socrates asked.

"Prevent the Stadtholder from falling into an abominable trap, if I can," the other replied briefly.

Socrates pointed to the distant corner of the markt, where Pythagoras could be dimly perceived waiting patiently beside three horses.

"I see the ruffian has stolen a horse," he said. "So long as it is a fresh one —"

"I shall need it." Diogenes remarked simply.

"I told him only to get the best, but you can't trust that loon since good fortune hath made him honest."

The next few seconds brought them to the spot. Pythagoras hailed them with delight. He was getting tired of waiting. Three horses, obviously fresh and furnished with excellent saddlery, were here ready. Even Socrates had a word of praise for his fat compeer's choice.

"Where did you get him from?" he queried, indicating the mount which Diogenes had without demur selected for himself.

Pythagoras shrugged his shoulder. What did it matter who had been made the poorer by a good horse? Enough that it was here now, ready to do service to the finest horseman in the Netherlands. Already Diogenes had swung himself into the saddle, and now he turned his horse toward Nieuwpoort.

"Where do we go?" the others cried.

"After me!" he shouted in reply.

3

Nose to heels, the three riders thundered through the city. It was deserted at this end of it, remember. Thank God for that! And now for a host of guardian angels to the rescue! Down the Oude Straat they galloped, their horses' hoofs raising myriads of sparks from the uneven cobblestones. "God grant me wings!" the leader had cried ere he set spurs to his horse, and the others followed without an instant's thought as to the whither or the wherefore. "After me!" he had called; and they who had fought beside him so often, who had bled with him, suffered with him, triumphed at times, been merry always, were well content to follow him now and forget everything in the exhilaration of this chase.

A chase it was! They could not doubt it, even though they seemed at this moment to be speeding in the opposite direction to that pursued by the Stadtholder and Nicolaes Beresteyn. But they well knew their friend's way, when he let his mount have free rein and threw up his head with that air of intense vitality which in him was at its height when life and death were having a tussle somewhere at the end of a ride.

Down the Oude Straat, which presently abuts on the ramparts. Then another two hundred yards to Nieuwpoort. No one in sight now. This part of the city looks like one of the dead. Doors open wide, litter of every sort encumbering the road. The din from afar, even the ceaseless tolling of St. Maria bell, seem like dream-sounds, ghost-like and unreal. Now the poort. Still no one insight. No guard. No sentry. The gate left open. Here two or three halberds hastily thrown down in some hurried flight. There a culverin, forlorn looking, gaping wide-mouthed, like some huge toad yawning, as if astonished or wearied to find itself deserted. Then again, a pile of muskets. It must have been a sudden panic that drove the guard from their post. But, thank God, the gate!

Diogenes is already through; after him his two compeers. A quarter of a league further on they suddenly draw rein. The horses rear, snorting and tossing, panting with the excitement and fretted with the curb. The riders blink for a second or two in the glare. The white mist is positively blinding here, where its sovereignty is unfettered. Just a clump of trees, way out on the right, here and there a hut with thatched roof and a piece of low fencing, or the gaunt arms of a windmill stretched with eerie stillness to the silvery sky. And above it all the mist – a pale shroud that envelopes everything.

To the east and the south the arid upland plunges head-long through it into infinity, cloaks within its stern bosom the secrets of the lurking enemy – the armies of De Berg, the Spanish outposts, the ambuscades. To the west Utrecht, unseen – and just now two tiny specks speeding along its road – the Stadtholder and Nicolaes Beresteyn. They came out into the open through Joris Poort, and are now some four hundred yards or less from the spot where three panting but exhilarated philosophers were now filling their lungs with the crisp, humid air.

They looked neither to right nor left. The Stadtholder, easily recognizable by his plumed bonnet, rides a length or less in advance of his companion. The fog has not yet swallowed them up. Diogenes takes all this in. A simple enough picture – the sea-fog and two riders speeding towards Utrecht. But a swift intaking of his breath, a tight closing of his firm lips, indicate to the others that all is not as simple as it seems.

Then a very curious thing happened. At first it seemed nothing. But to the watchers outside Nieuwpoort it had the same effect as a flash of lightning would have in an apparently cloudless sky. It began with Nicolaes Beresteyn drawing his horse close up to the Stadtholder, on his Highness's right. Then for another few seconds the two riders went along side by side, like one black speck now, still quite distinguishable through the fog. Socrates and Pythagoras had their eyes on Diogenes. But Diogenes did not move. He was frowning, and his face had a set and tense expression. He had his horse tightly on the curb, and appeared almost wilfully to fret the animal, who was pawing the wet, sandy ground and covering itself with lather – a picture of tearing impatience.

"What do we do now?" Pythagoras exclaimed at last, unable, just like the horse, to contain his excitement.

"Wait," Diogenes replied curtly. "All may be well after all."

"In which case?" queried Socrates.

"Nothing!"

A groan of disappointment rose to a couple of parched throats; but it was never uttered. What went on in the mist on the road to Utrecht, four hundred yards away, had stifled it at birth.

The Stadtholder's horse had become restive. A simple matter enough; but in this case unexplainable, because Maurice of Nassau was a splendid horseman. He could easily have quietened the animal if there had not been something abnormal in its sudden antics. It reared and tossed for no apparent reason, would have thrown a less experienced rider.

"The brute is being teased with a goad," Pythagoras remarked sententiously.

That was clear enough. Even in the distance, and experienced eye could have perceived that the horse became more and more unmanageable every moment, and the Stadtholder's seat more and more precarious. Then suddenly there came the sharp report of a pistol. The horse, goaded to madness, took the bit between its teeth, and with a final plunge bolted across country, away from that strident noise, which, twice repeated at intervals, had turned its fretfulness into blind panic.

It was at the first report that Socrates and Pythagoras again glanced at their leader. A gurgle of delight escaped them when they caught his eye. They had received their orders. The next moment all three had dug their spurs in their horses' flanks and were galloping over sand and ditch.

Diogenes' horse, given free rein at last, after the maddening curb of awhile ago, was soon half a dozen lengths ahead of the others, tearing along with all its might at right angles to the direction in which the Stadtholder's panic-stricken animal was rushing like one possessed. That direction was Ede.

5

In truth, the low-lying land veiled in sea-fog must at that moment have presented a very curious spectacle. Maurice of Nassau, Prince of Orange, the hope and pride of the Netherlands, helpless upon a horse that was running away with him straight in the direction of the nearest Spanish outposts.

Three soldiers of fortune, strangers, in the land hastening to intercept him, and a couple of hundred yards or so behind the Stadtholder, Nicolaes Beresteyn, puzzled and terror-filled at this unexpected check to his manoeuvre, pushing along for dear life.

It had been such a splendid scheme, evolved over there in the lonely mill on the Veluwe, between a reprobate and a traitor. The Spaniards on the watch. The Stadtholder helpless, whilst his mount carried him headlong into their hands. What a triumph for Stoutenburg, who had planned it all, and for Nicolaes Beresteyn, the worker of the infamous plot! The

Stadtholder prisoner in the hands of the Archduchess! His life the price of the subjection of the Netherlands!

And all to be frustrated by a foolish mischance! Three riders intent upon intercepting that runaway horse! Who in thunder were they? The mist, remember, would have blurred Nicolaes' vision. His thoughts were not just then on the man whom he hated. They were fixed upon the possibility – remote, alas! – of convincing the Stadtholder after this that the goaded horse had been the victim of a series of accidents.

Even at this moment the foremost of the three riders had overtaken the runaway. He galloped for a length or two beside it, then, with a dexterous and unerring grip, he seized the panic-stricken animal by the bridle. A few seconds of desperate struggle 'twixt man and beast. Then man remained the conqueror. The horse, panting, quivering in every limb, covered in sweat and foam, was finally brought to a standstill, and the Stadtholder in an instant had his feet clear of the stirrups and swung himself out of the saddle.

6

Then, and then only, did Nicolaes Beresteyn recognize the man who for the second time had frustrated his nefarious plans – the man whom, because of his easy triumphs, the humiliation which he had inflicted upon him, because of his careless gaiety and his very joy of life, he hated with a curious, sinister intensity.

A ferocious imprecation rose to his lips. For awhile everything became a blank. The present, the future, even the past. Everything became chaos in his mind, he could no longer think. All that he had planned became a blur, as if the sea-fog had enveloped his senses as well as the entire landscape.

But this confused mental state only lasted a very little while – a few seconds perhaps. Slowly, while he gazed on that distant group of men and horses, his perceptions became clearer once more. And even before the imprecation had died on his lips it gave place to a smile of triumph. Nicolaes Beresteyn had remembered that his Majesty the devil might well be trusted to care for his own. Had he not served the hell-born liege lord well?

For the nonce he brought his horse to a halt. It would be worse than folly to go on. With recognition of those three horsemen over there had also come the certainty that he was now irretrievably unmasked. The Stadtholder, his father, his sister, even his young wife, would turn from him in horror, as from a traitor and an outcast – a pariah, marked with the brand of Cain.

No! Henceforth, for good or for evil, his fortunes must be linked openly with Stoutenburg – with the man who wielded such a strange cabalistic power over him that he (Nicolaes) – rich, newly wed, in a highly enviable worldly position – had been ready to sacrifice his all in his cause, and to throw in the last shred of his honour into the bargain. In Stoutenburg's cause – ay, and in order to be revenged on the man who had never wronged him save in his conceit – that most vulnerable spot in the moral armour of such contemptible rogues as was Nicolaes Beresteyn.

The spot where he had brought his horse to a halt was immediately behind a low, deserted hut, which concealed him from view. Here he dismounted and, throwing the reins over his arm, advanced cautiously to a point of vantage at the angle of the little building, whence he could see what those four men were doing over there but himself remain unseen.

They, too, had dismounted, and were obviously intent on examining the Stadtholder's horse. A sinister scowl spread over Nicolaes Beresteyn's face. There was still a chance, then, of putting a bullet in one or other of those two men – the hated enemy or the Stadtholder. Nicolaes pondered; the scowl on his face became almost satanic in its expression of cruelty. Awhile ago, he had replaced his pistol in the holster, after it had served its nefarious purpose. Now he took it out again and examined it thoroughly.

It had one more charge in it, the devilish charge invented by the Borgias, the secret of which one of that infamous race had confided to Stoutenburg. The fumes from the powder when it struck the eyes must cause irretrievable blindness. Indeed, it had proved its worth already.

Nicolaes, from his hiding-place, could see those four men quite clearly. The Stadtholder, Diogenes, the two caitiffs, all standing round the one horse. Then Diogenes took something out of his belt. He raised his arm, and the next moment a sharp report rang through the mistladen air. The poor animal rolled over instantly into the mud.

The scowl on Nicolaes' face now gave place once more to a smile of triumph – more sinister than the frown. With the gesture of a conqueror, he clutched the pistol more firmly. The potent fumes had, in truth, wrought their fiendish work on the innocent beast. Diogenes had just put it out of its misery, and his two familiars were preparing to mount one of the horses, whilst he and the Stadtholder had the other two by the reins.

Why not?

The miscreant was sure enough of his aim, and the others would be unprepared. He was sure, too, of the swiftness of his horse, and the Spanish outposts were less than a quarter of a league away, whilst within half that distance Stoutenburg was on the watch with a vedette, waiting to capture the Stadtholder on his runaway horse as it had been prearranged.

Once there he – Nicolaes – would be amongst friends.

Then, why not?

Already the riders had put their horses to a trot. Diogenes and the Stadtholder on ahead, the two loons some few lengths in their rear. In less than three minutes they would be within range of Nicolaes' pistol and its blinding fumes. And Diogenes was riding on the side nearest to his enemy.

Nicolaes Beresteyn grasped his weapon more firmly. He realized with infinite satisfaction that his arm was perfectly steady. Indeed, he had never felt so absolutely calm. The measured tramp of the horses keyed him up to a point of unswerving determination. He raised his arm. The horses were galloping now. They would pass like a flash within twenty paces of him.

The next moment the sharp report of the pistol rang stridently through the mist. There was a burst, a flash, a column of smoke. Nicolaes jumped into the saddle and set spurs to his horse. The other riders went galloping on for a few seconds – not more. Then one of them swayed in his saddle. Nicolaes then was a couple of hundred yards away.

"You are hit, man!" the Stadtholder exclaimed. "That abominable assassin —"

But the words died in his throat. The reins had slipped out of Diogenes' grasp, and he rolled down into the mud.

7

A sudden jerk brought the Stadtholder's horse to a halt. He swung himself out of the saddle, ran quickly to his companion.

"You are hit, man!" he reiterated; this time with an unexplainable feeling of dread.

The other seemed so still, and yet his clothes and the soft earth around him showed no stains of blood.

Pythagoras now was also on the spot. He had slid off the horse as soon as the infamous assassin had started to ride away. Socrates was trying to give chase. Even now two pistol-shots rang out in quick succession right across the moorland. But the hell-hound was well mounted, and the avenging bullets failed to reach their mark. All this the Stadtholder took in with a rapid glance, even whilst Pythagoras, round-eyed and scared, was striving with gentle means to raise the strangely inert figure.

"He hath swooned," the Stadtholder suggested.

The stricken man had one arm across his face. His had had fallen from his head, leaving the fine, square brow free and the crisp hair weighted by the sweat of some secret agony. The mouth, too, was visible, and the chin, with its four days' growth of beard, the mouth that was always ready with a smile. It was set now in an awesome contraction of pain, and, withal, that terrible immobility.

Now Socrates was arriving. A moment or two later he, too, had dismounted, cursing lustily that he had failed to hit the hell-hound. A mute query, an equally mute reply, was all that passed between him and Pythagoras.

Then the stricken man stirred as if suddenly roused to consciousness.

"Are you hit, man?" the Stadtholder queried again.

"No – no!" he replied quickly. "Only a little dazed. That is all."

He raised himself to a sitting posture, helping himself up with his hands, which sank squelching into the mud; whereat he gave a short laugh, which somehow went a cold shiver down the listener's spines.

"Where is my hat?" he asked. "Pythagoras, you lazy loon, get me my hat."

He must indeed have been still dazed, for when his friend picked up the hat and gave it to him, his hand shot out for it quite wide of the mark. He gave another laugh, short and toneless as before, and set the hat on his head, pulling down well over his eyes.

"I had a mugful of hot ale at Amersfoort before starting," he said. "It must have got into my head."

He made no attempt to get to his feet, but just sat there, with his two slender hands all covered with mud, tightly clasped between his knees.

"Can you get to horse?" his Highness queried at last.

"No," Diogenes replied, "not just yet, an' it please you, I verily think that I would roll out of my saddle again, which would, in truth, be a disgusting spectacle."

"But we cannot leave you here, man," the Stadtholder rejoined, with a slight tone of impatience.

"And why not, I pray you?" he retorted. "Your Highness must get to Utrecht as quickly as may be. A half-drunken lout like me would only be a hindrance."

His voice was thick now and halting, in very truth like that of a man who had been drinking heavily. He rested his elbows on his knees and held his chin between his mud-stained hands.

"Socrates, you lumpish vagabond," he exclaimed all of a sudden, "don't stand gaping at me like that! Bring forth his Highness's horse at once, and see that you accompany him to Utrecht without further mishap, or 'tis with us you'll have to deal on your return!"

"But you, man!" the Stadtholder exclaimed once more.

He felt helpless and strangely disturbed in his mind, not understanding what all this meant; why this man, usually so alert, so keen, so full of vigour, appeared for the moment akin to a babbling imbecile.

"I'll have a good sleep inside that hut, so please you," the other replied more glibly. "These two ruffians will find me here after they have seen your gracious Highness safely inside your camp."

Then, as the Stadtholder still appeared to hesitate, and neither of the others seemed to move, Diogenes added, with an almost desperate note of entreaty:

"To horse, your Highness, I beg! Every second is precious. Heaven knows what further devilry lies in wait for you, if you linger here."

"Or for you, man," the Stadtholder murmured involuntarily.

"Nay, not for me!" the other retorted quickly. "The Archduchess and her gang of vultures fly after higher game than a drunken wayfarer lost on the flats. To horse, I entreat!"

And once more he pressed his hands together, and so tightly that the knuckles shone like polished ivory, even through their covering of mud.

The Stadtholder then gave a sign to the two men. It was obviously futile to continue arguing here with a man who refused to move. He himself had very rightly said that every second was precious. And every second, too, was fraught with danger. Already his Highness had well-nigh been the victim of a diabolical ambuscade, might even at this hour have been a prisoner in the hands of the enemy, a hostage of incalculable value, even if his life had been spared, but for the audacious and timely interference of this man, who now appeared almost like one partially bereft of reason.

"We'll see you safely inside the hut, at any rate," was his Highness's last word.

"And I'll not move," Diogenes retorted with a kind of savage obstinacy, "until the mist has swallowed up your gracious Highness on the road to Utrecht."

After that there was nothing more to be said. And we may take it that the Stadtholder got to horse with unaccountable reluctance. Something in that solitary figure sitting there, with the plumed hat tilted over his eyes and the slender, mud-stained hands tightly locked together, gave him a strange feeling of nameless dismay, like a premonition of some obscure catastrophic tragedy.

But his time and his safety did not belong to himself alone. They were the inalienable property of a threatened country, that would be grasping in her death-throes if she were deprived of him at this hour of renewed and deadly danger. So he gathered the reins in his hands and set spurs to his horse, and once he had started he did not look behind him, lest his emotion got the better of his judgement.

The two gossoons immediately followed in his wake. This they did because the friend they had always been wont to obey had thus commanded, and his seeming helplessness rendered his orders doubly imperative at this hour. They rode a length or two behind the Stadtholder, who presently put his horse to a gallop. Utrecht now was only a couple of leagues away.

The three horsemen galloped on for a quarter of a league or less at the same even, rapid pace. Then Pythagoras slackened speed. The others did not even turn to look at him, he seemed to have done it by tacit unspoken consent. The Stadtholder and Socrates sped on in the direction of Utrecht and Pythagoras turned his horse's head round toward the direction whence he had come.

8

The afternoon lay heavy and silent upon the plain. There was as yet no sign of the approach of the enemy from the south, and the low-lying land appeared momentarily hushed under its veil of mist, as if conscious of the guilty secret enshrined within its bosom. The fog, indeed, had thickened perceptibly. It lay like a wall around that lonely figure, still sitting there on the soft earth, with its head buried in its hands.

Far away, the gaunt-looking carcase of the dead horse appeared as the only witness of a hideous deed as yet un-recorded. Each a blurred and uncertain mass – the dead horse and the lonely figure, equally motionless, equally pathetic – were now the sole occupants of the vast and silent immensity.

Not far away, in the little town of Amersfoort, humanity, panic-stricken and terrorized, filled the air with clamour and with wails. Here, beneath the ghostly shroud of humid atmosphere, everything was stilled as if in ghoulish expectancy of something mysterious, indiscernible which was still to come. It was like the arrested breath before the tearing cry, the hush which precedes a storm.

Overhead, a flight of rooks sent their melancholy cawing through the air.

When Pythagoras was within fifty yards of his friend he dismounted, and, leading his horse by the bridle, he walked toward him. When he was quite near Diogenes put out a hand to him.

"I knew you would come back, you fat-witted nonny," he said simply.

"Socrates had to go on with the Stadtholder," the other remarked, "or he'd be here, too." Then he added tentatively: "Will you lean on my arm?"

"Yes, I'll have to do that now, old crony, shall I not?" Diogenes replied. "That devil," he murmured under his breath, "has blinded me!"

Chapter IX – Mala Fides

1

NICOLAES Beresteyn, riding like one possessed had reached Stoutenburg's encampment one hour before nightfall. He brought the news of the failure of his plan for the capture of the Stadtholder, spoke with many a muttered oath of the Englishman and his two familiars, and of how they had interposed just in the nick of time to stop the runaway horse.

"But for that cursed rogue!" he exclaimed savagely, "Maurice of Nassau would now be a prisoner in our hands. We would be holding him to ransom, earning gratitude, honours, wealth at the hands of the Archduchess. Whereas – now —"

But there was solace to the bitterness of this disappointment. The blinding powder, invented by the infamous Borgia, had done its work. The abominable rogue, the nameless adventurer, who had twice succeeded in thwarting the best-laid schemes of his lordship of Stoutenburg, had paid the full penalty for his audacity and his arrogant interference.

Blind, helpless, broken, an object now of contemptuous pity rather than of hate, he was henceforth powerless to wreak further mischief.

"Just before I put my horse to a swift gallop," Nicolaes Beresteyn had concluded, "I saw him sway in the saddle and roll down into the mud. One of the vagabonds tried to chase me; but my horse bore me well and I was soon out of his reach."

That news did, indeed compensate Stoutenburg for all the humiliation which he had endured at the hands of his successful rival in the past. A rival no longer; for the Laughing Cavalier, blind and helpless, was not like ever to return to claim his young wealthy wife and to burden her with his misery. This last tribute to the man's pluck and virility Stoutenburg paid him unconsciously. He could not visualize that splendid creature, so full of life and gaiety, and conscious of might strength, groping his way back to the side of the woman whom he had dazzled by his power.

"He would sooner die in a ditch," he muttered to himself, under his breath, "than excite her pity!"

"Then the field is clear for me!" he added exultantly; and fell to discussing with Nicolaes his chances of regaining Gilda's affections. "Do you think she ever cared for the rogue?" he queried, with a strange quiver of emotion in his harsh voice.

Nicolaes was doubtful. He himself had never been in love. He liked his young wife well enough; she was comely and rich. But love? No, he could not say.

"She'll not know what has become of him," Stoutenburg said, striving to allay his own doubts. "And women very quickly forget."

He sighed, proud of his own manly passion that had survived so many vicissitudes, and was linked to such a tenacious memory.

"We must not let her know," Nicolaes insisted.

Stoutenburg gave a short, sardonic laugh. "Are you afraid she might kill you if she did?" he queried.

Then, as the other made no reply, but stood there brooding, his soul a prey to a sudden horror, which was not unlike a vague pang of remorse, Stoutenburg concluded cynically:

"I'll give the order that every blind beggar found wandering around the city be forthwith hanged on the nearest tree. Will that allay your fears?"

Thereafter he paid no further heed to Nicolaes, whom, in his heart, he despised for a waverer and a weakling; but he gave orders to his master of the camp to make an immediate start for Amersfoort.

Amersfoort had, in the meanwhile, so De Voocht avers, become wonderfully calm. Those whose nerves would not stand the strain of seeing the hated tyrants once more within the gates of their peace-loving little city, those who had no responsibilities, and those who had families, fled at the first rumour of the enemy's approach. Indeed, for many hours the streets and open places, the quays and the sleepy, sluggish river, had on the first day been nothing short of a pandemonium. Then everything gradually became hushed and tranquil. Those who were panic-stricken had all gone by nightfall; those who remained knew the risk they were taking, and sat in their homes, waiting and pondering. Amersfoort that evening might have been a city of the dead.

Darkness set in early, and the sea-fog thickened at sundown. Some wiseacres said that the Spaniards would not come until the next day. They proved to be right. The dawn had hardly spread o'er the whole of the eastern sky on the morning of the twenty-second, when the master of the enemy's camp was heard outside the ramparts, demanding the surrender of the city.

The summons was received in absolute silence. The gates were open, and the mercenaries marched in. In battle array, with banners flying, with pikemen, halberdiers and arquebusiers; with fifes and drums and a trainload of wagons and horses, and the usual rabble of beggarly camp followers, they descended on the city like locusts; and soon every tavern was filled to overflowing with loud-voiced, swarthy, ill-mannered soldiery, and all the streets and places encumbered with their carts and their horses and their trappings.

They built a bonfire in the middle of the market-place, and all around it a crowd of out-at-elbows ruffians, men, women, and children, filled the air with their shrieks and their bibulous songs. Some four thousand troops altogether, so De Voocht states, spread themselves out over the orderly, prosperous town, invaded the houses, broke open the cellars and storehouses, made the day hideous with their noise and their roistering.

As many as could found shelter in the deserted homes of the burghers; others used the stately kerks as stabling for their horses and camping ground for themselves. The inhabitants offered no resistance. A century of unspeakable tyranny ere they had gained their freedom had taught them the stern lesson of submitting to the inevitable. The Stadtholder had ordered them to submit. Until he could come to their rescue they must swallow the bitter cup of resignation to the dregs. It could not be for long. He who before now had swept the Spanish hordes off the sacred soil of the United Provinces could do so again. It was only a case for a little patience. And patience was a virtue which these grave sons of a fighting race knew how to practise to its utmost limit.

And so the burghers of Amersfoort who had remained in the city in order to watch over its fate and over their property submitted without murmur to the arrogant demands of the invaders. Their wives ministered in proud silence to the wants of the insolent rabble. The saw their dower-chests ransacked, their effects destroyed or stolen, their provisions wasted and consumed. They waited hand and foot, like serving wenches, upon their tyrants; for, indeed, it had been the proletariat who had been the first to flee.

They even succeeded in keeping back their tears when they saw their husbands – the more noted burghers of the town – dragged as hostages before the commander of the invading troops, who had taken up his quarters in the burgomaster's house.

That commander was the Lord of Stoutenburg. In high favour with the Archduchess now, he had desired leave to carry through this expedition to Amersfoort. Private grudge against the man who had robbed him of Gilda, or lust for revenge against the Stadtholder for the execution of Olden Barneveldt, who can tell? Who can read the inner workings of a tortuous brain, or appraise the passions of an embittered heart?

Attended by all the sinister paraphernalia which he now affected, the Lord of Stoutenburg entered Amersfoort in the late afternoon as a conqueror, his eyes glowing with the sense of triumph over a successful rival and of power over a disdainful woman. The worthy citizens of the little town gazed with astonishment and dread upon his sable banner, broidered in silver with a skull and crossbones – the emblem of his relentlessness, now that the day of reckoning had come.

He rode through the city, hardly noticing its silent death-like appearance. Not one glance did he bestow on the closed shutters to the right or left of him. His eyes were fixed upon the tall pinnacled roof of the burgomaster's house, silhouetted against the western sky, the stately abode on the quay where, in the days long since gone by, he had been received as an honoured guest. Since then what a world of sorrow, of passion, of endless misery had been his lot! It seemed as if, on the day when he became false to Gilda Beresteyn in order to wed the rich and influential daughter of Marnix de St. Aldegonde, fickle fortune had finally turned her back on him. His father and brother ended their days of the scaffold; his wife, abandoned by him and broken-hearted; he himself a fugitive with a price upon his head, a potential assassin, and that vilest thing on earth, a man who sells his country to her enemies.

No wonder that, at a comparatively early age, the Lord of Stoutenburg looked a careworn and wearied man. The lines on his face were deep and harsh, his hair was turning grey at the temples. Only the fire in his deepset eyes was fierce and strong, for it was fed with the fire of an ever-enduring passion – hatred. Hatred of the Stadtholder; hatred of the nameless adventurer who had thwarted him at every turn; hatred of the woman who had shut him out wholly from her heart.

But now the hour of triumph had come. For it had schemed and lied and striven and never once given way to despair. It had come, crowned with immeasurable success. The Stadtholder – thanks to the subtle poison of an infamous Borgia, administered by a black-hearted assassin – was nothing but a physical wreck; whilst those who had brought him – Stoutenburg – to his knees three short months ago were at his mercy at last. A longing as cruel as it was vengeful had possession of his soul whenever he thought of these two facts.

His schemes were not yet mature, and he had not yet arrived at any definite conclusion as to how he would reach the ultimate goal of his desires; but this he did know – that the Stadtholder was too sick to put up a fight for Amersfoort, and that Gilda and her stranger lover were definitely parted, and both of them entirely in his power. Their fate was as absolutely in his hands as his had once been in theirs. And the Lord of Stoutenburg, with his eyes raised to the pinnacled roof of the house that sheltered the woman whom he still loved with such passionate ardour, felt that for the first time for this man a year he might count himself as almost happy.

3

Nicolaes Beresteyn was among the last to enter his native city. He did so as a shameless traitor, a dishonoured gambler who had staked his all upon a hellish die. Indeed now he seemed like a man possessed, careless of his crime, exulting in it even. The vague fear of meeting his father and Gilda eye to eye seemed somehow to add zest to his adventure. He did not know how much they knew, or what they guessed, but felt a strange thrill within his tortuous soul at the thought of standing up before them as their master, of defying them and deriding their reproaches.

His young wife he knew to be away. Her father had started off for Amsterdam with his family and his servants at the first rumour of the enemy's approach. In any case she was his. She and her wealth and Mynheer van den Poele's influence and business connexions. He – Nicolaes – who had always been second in his father's affections always subservient to Gilda and to Gilda's interests, and who since that affair in January had been treated like a skulking schoolboy in the paternal home, would now rule there as a conqueror, a protector on whose magnanimity the comfort of the entire household would depend.

These and other thoughts – memories, self-pity, rage, too, and hatred, and imputations against fate – coursed through his mind as he rode into his native city at the head of the rearguard of Stoutenburg's troops. He drew rein outside his father's house. Not the slightest stirring of his dormant conscience troubled him as he ran swiftly up the familiar stone steps.

With the heavy basket-hilt of his rapier he rapped vigorously against the stout oak panels of the door, demanding admittance in the name of the Archduchess Isabella, Sovereign Liege Lady of the Netherlands. At once the doors flew open, as if moved by a spring. Two elderly serving-men stood alone in the hall, silent and respectful.

At the sight of their young master they both made a movement as if to run to him, deluded for the moment into hopes of salvation, relief from this awful horror of imminent invasion. But he paid no heed to them. His very look chilled them and froze the words of welcome upon their lips, as he strode quickly past them into the hall.

The shades of evening were now rapidly drawing in. Except for the two serving-men, the house appeared deserted. In perfect order, but strangely still and absolutely dark. As he looked about him, Nicolaes felt as if he were in a vault. A cold shiver ran down his spine. Curtly he bade the men bring lighted candles into the banqueting-hall.

Here, too, silence and darkness reigned. In the huge monumental hearth a few dying embers were still smouldering, casting a warm glow upon the red tiles, and flicking the knobs and excrescences of the brass tools with minute crimson sparks.

Nicolaes felt his nerves tingling. He groped his way to one of the windows, and with an impatient hand tore at the casement. Stoutenburg's troops were now swarming everywhere. The quay was alive with movement. Some of the soldiers were bivouacking against the house, had build up a fire, the ruddy glow of which, together with the flicker of resin torches, thew a weird and uncertain light into the room. Nicolaes felt his teeth chattering with cold. His hands were like fire. Could it be that he was afraid – afraid that in a moment or two he would hear familiar footsteps coming down the stairs, that in a moment or two he would have to face the outraged father, come to curse his traitor son?

Bah! This was sheer cowardice! But a brief while ago he had exulted in his treachery, gloried in his callous disregard of his monstrous crime. How it seemed to him that a pair of sightless yet still mocking eyes glared at him from out the gloom. With a shudder and a quickly smothered cry of horror, Nicolaes buried his face in his hands.

The next moment the two serving-men came in, carrying lighted candles in heavy silver candelabra. These they set upon the table; and one of them, kneeling beside the hearth, plied the huge bellows, coaxing the dying embers into flame. After which they stood respectfully by, awaiting further commands. Obviously they had had their orders – absolute obedience and all those outward forms of respect which they were able to accord. Nicolaes looked at them with a fierce, defying glance. He knew them both well. Greybeards in the service of his father, they had seen the young master grow up from cradle to this hour when he stood, a rebel and a skunk, on the paternal hearth.

But they did not flinch under his glance. They knew that they had been specially chosen for the unpleasant task of waiting upon the enemy commanders because their tempers had no longer the ebullience of youth, and they might be trusted to remain calm in the face of arrogance or even of savagery – even in the face of Mynheer Nicolaes, the child they had loved, the youth they had admired, now a branded traitor, who had come like a thief in the night to barter his honour for a crown of shame.

4

A certain commotion outside on the quay proclaimed the fact that the commander of the troops, the Lord of Stoutenburg, had entered the town at the head of his bodyguard, and followed by his master of the camp and his equerries.

He, too, made straight for the burgomaster's house, brought his horse to a halt at the foot of the stone steps. With a curt nod, Nicolaes bade the old crones to run to the front door and receive his Magnificence. In this, as in everything else, the men obeyed at once and in silence.

But already Stoutenburg, preceded by his equerries and his torchbearers, had stepped across the threshold. He knew his way well about the house. As boys, he and his brother Groeneveld had played their games in and around the intricate passages and stairs. As a young man he had sat in the deep window embrasures, holding Gilda's hand, taking delight in terrifying her with his impetuous love, and forcing her consent to his suit by his masterful wooing. A world of memories, grave and gay, swept over him as he entered the banqueting-hall, where, but for his many misfortunes – as he callously called h is crimes – he would one day have sat at the bridegroom's table beside Gilda, his plighted wife.

Both he and Nicolaes felt unaccountably relieved at meeting one another here. For both of them, no doubt, the silence and gloom of this memory-haunted house would in the long run have proved unendurable.

"I did not know that I should meet you here," Stoutenburg exclaimed, as he grasped his friend by the hand.

"I thought it would be best," Nicolaes replied curtly.

But this warm greeting from the infamous arch-traitor, in the presence of the two loyal old servants, brought a hot flush to the young man's brow. The last faint warning from his drugged conscience, mayhap. But the feeling of shame faded away as swiftly as it had come, and the next moment he was standing by, impassive and seemingly unconcerned, while the Lord of Stoutenburg gave his orders to the men.

These orders were to prepare the necessary beds for my lord and for Mynheer Nicolaes Beresteyn, also for the equerries, and proper accommodation for my lord's bodyguard, which consisted of twenty musketeers with their captain. Moreover, to provide supper for his Magnificence and mynheer in the banqueting-hall, and for the rest of the company in some other suitable room, without delay.

The two old crones took the orders in silence, bowed, and prepared to leave the room.

"Stay," my lord commanded. "Where is the burgomaster?"

"In his private apartments, so please you," one of the men replied.

"And his daughter?"

"The jongejuffrouw is with Mynheer the Burgomaster."

"Tell them both I want them to sup here with me and Mynheer Nicolaes."

Again the men bowed with the same silent dignity. It was impossible to gather from their stolid, mask-like faces what their thoughts might be at this hour. When they had gone, Stoutenburg peremptorily dismissed his equerries.

"If you have anything to complain of in this house," he said curtly, "come and report to me at once. To-morrow we leave at dawn."

Both the equerries gave a gasp of astonishment.

"To-morrow?" one of them murmured, apparently quite taken aback by this order.

"At dawn," Stoutenburg reiterated briefly.

This was enough. Neither did the equerries venture on further remarks. They had served for some time now under his Magnificence, knew his obstinacy and the irrevocableness of his decisions when once he had spoken.

"No further commands until then, my lord?" was all that the spokesman said.

"None for you," Stoutenburg replied curtly. "But tell Jan that the moment – the moment, you understand – that the burgomaster enters this room, he is to be prevented from doing any mischief. If he carries a weapon, he must at once be disarmed; if he resists, there should be a length of rope handy wherewith to tie his hands behind his back. But otherwise I'll not have him hurt. Understand?"

"Perfectly, my lord," the equerry gave answer. " 'Tis simple enough."

5

Now the two friends – brothers in crime – were alone in the vast, panelled hall.

Nicolaes had said nothing, made no movement of indignation or protest, when the other delivered his monstrous and treacherous commands against the personal liberty of the burgomaster. He had sat sullen and glowering, his head resting against his hand.

Stoutenburg looked down on him for a moment or two, his deep-set eyes full of that contempt which he felt for this weak-kneed and conscience-plagued waverer. Then he curtly advised him to leave the room.

"You might not think it seemly," he remarked with a sneer, "to be present when I take certain preventive measures against your father. These measures are necessary, else I would not take them. You would not have him spitting some of our men, or mayhap do himself or Gilda some injury, would you?"

"I was not complaining," Nicolaes retorted dryly.

Indeed, he obeyed readily enough. Now that the time had come to meet his father, he shrank from the ordeal with horror. It would have come, of course; but, like all weak natures, Nicolaes was always on the side of procrastination. He rose without another word, and, avoiding the main door of the banqueting-hall, he went out by the back one, which gave on a narrow antechamber and thence on the service staircase.

"I'll remain in the ante-chamber," he said. "Call me when you wish."

Stoutenburg shrugged his shoulders. He was glad to remain alone for awhile – alone with that wealth of memories which would not be chased away. Memories of childhood, of adolescence, of youth untainted with crime; of love, before greed and ambition had caused him to betray so basely the girl who had believed in him.

"If Gilda had remained true to me," he sighed, with almost cynical inconsequence, exacting fidelity where he had given none. "If she had stuck to me that night in Haarlem everything would have been different."

He went up to the open window, and, leaning his arm against the mullion, he gazed upon the busy scene below. The current of cold, humid air appeared to do him good. His arquebusiers and pikemen, bivouacking round the spluttering fires, striving to keep the damp air out of their stiffening limbs; the shouts, the songs, the peremptory calls; the shrieks of frightened women and children; the loud Spanish oaths; the medley of curses in every tongue – all this confused din pertaining to strife seemed to work like a tonic upon his brooding spirit. A blind beggar soliciting alms among the soldiery chased all softer thoughts away.

"Hey, there!" he shouted fiercely, to one of the soldiers who happened just then to have caught his eye, "Have I not given orders that every blind beggar lurking around the city be hung to the nearest tree?"

The men laughed. A monstrously tyrannical order such as that suited their present mood.

"But this one was inside the city, so please your Magnificence," one of them protested with a cynical laugh, "when we arrived."

"All the more reason why he should be hung forthwith!" Stoutenburg riposted savagely in reply.

A loud guffaw greeted this inhuman order. His Magnificence was loudly cheered, his health drunk in deep goblets of stolen wine. Then a search was made for the blind beggar. But he, luckily for himself, had in the meanwhile taken to his heels.

6

The next moment a slight noise behind him caused the Lord of Stoutenburg to turn on his heel. The door had been thrown open, and the burgomaster, having his daughter on his arm, stood upon the threshold. He was dressed in his robes of office, with black cloak and velvet bonnet; but he wore a steel gorget round his neck and rapier by his side.

At the sight of his arch enemy, he had paused under the lintel, and the ashen pallor of his cheeks became more marked. But he had no time to move, for in an instant Jan and three or four men were all around him.

At this treacherous onslaught a fierce oath escaped Beresteyn's lips. In an instant his sword was out of its scabbard, he himself at bay, covering Gilda with his body, and facing the men who had thus scurrilously rushed on him out of the gloom.

But obviously resistance was futile. Already he was surrounded and disarmed, Gilda torn forcibly away from him, thrust into a corner, whilst he himself was rendered helpless, even though he fought and struggled magnificently. The whole unequal combat had only lasted a few seconds; and now the grand old man stood like a fettered lion, glowering and defiant, his hands tied behind his back with a length of rope, against which he was straining with all his might.

One of the most disloyal pitfalls ever devised against an unsuspecting civilian – and he the chief dignitary of a peace-loving city. Stoutenburg watched the scene with an evil glitter in his restless eyes. Shame and compunction did, in truth, bear no part in his emotions at this moment. He was exulting in the thought of his vile stratagem, pleased that he had thought of enticing Gilda hither by summoning her father at the same time. It was amusing to watch them both – the burgomaster still dignified, despite his helplessness, and Gilda beautiful in her indignation. By St. Bavon, the girl was lovely, and still desirable. And thank Beelzebub and all the powers of darkness who lent their aid in placing so exquisite a prize in the hands of the conqueror.

Stoutenburg could have laughed aloud with glee. As it was, he made an effort to appear both masterful and indifferent. He knew that he could take his time, that any scheme which he might formulate for his own advancement and the satisfaction of his every ambition was now certain of success. The future was entirely his, to plan and mould at will.

So now he deliberately turned back to the window, closed it with a hand that had not the slightest tremor in it. Then he returned to the centre of the room, sat down beside the table, and took on a cool and judicial air. All his movements were consciously slow. He looked at the burgomaster and at Gilda with ostentatious irony, remained silent for awhile as if in pleasant contemplation of their helplessness. "You are in suspense," his silence seemed to express. "You know that your fate is in my hands. But I can afford to wait, to take mine ease. I am lord of the future, and you are little better than my slaves."

"Was it not foolishness to resist, mynheer?" he said at last, in a tone of gentle mockery. "Bloodshed, eh? In truth, the role of fire-eater ill becomes your dignity and your years."

"Spare me your insults, my lord," Beresteyn retorted, with calm dignity. "What is your pleasure with my daughter and with me?"

"I will tell you anon," Stoutenburg replied coolly, "when you are more composed."

"I am ready now to hear your commands."

"Quite submissive, eh?" the other retorted with a sneer.

"No; only helpless, and justly indignant at this abominable outrage."

"Also surprised – what? – at seeing me here to-night?"

"In truth, my lord, I had not expected to see the son of Olden Barneveldt at the head of enemy troops."

"Or your son in his train, eh?"

The burgomaster winced at the taunt. But he rejoined quite simply:

"If what rumour says is true, my lord, then I have no son."

"If," Stoutenburg retorted dryly, "rumour told you that Nicolaes Beresteyn hath returned to his allegiance, then the jade did not lie. Your son, mynheer, hath shown you which way loyalty lies. Not in the service of a rebel prince, but in that of Archduchess Isabella, our Sovereign Liege."

He paused, as if expecting some word of reply from the burgomaster; but as the latter remained silent, he went on more lightly:

"But enough of this. Whether you, Mynheer Beresteyn, and your son do make up your differences presently is no concern of mine. You will see him anon, no doubt, and can then discuss your family affairs at your leisure. For the nonce, I do desire to know whether your city intends to be submissive. I have exercised great leniency up to this hour; but you must remember that I am equally ready to punish at the slightest sign of contumely or of resistance to my commands."

"For the leniency to which the Lord of Stoutenburg lays claim," Beresteyn rejoined with perfect dignity, "in that, up to this hour he has not murdered our peaceful citizens, burned down our houses, or violated our homes, we tender him our thanks. As for the future, the treacherous pitfall into which I have fallen, and the unwarrantable treatment that is meted out to me, will mayhap prove to my unfortunate fellow-citizens that resistance to overwhelming force is worse than useless."

"Excellent sentiments, mynheer!" Stoutenburg retorted. "Dictated, I make no doubt, by one who knows the usages of war."

"We do all of us," the burgomaster gave quiet answer, "obey the behests of our Stadtholder, our Sovereign Liege."

"The rebel prince, mynheer, who, by commanding you to submit, hath for once gauged rightly the temper of the Sovereign whom he hath outraged. Will you tell me, I pray you," Stoutenburg added, with a sardonic grin, "whether the jongejuffrouw your daughter is equally prepared to obey Maurice of Nassau's behests and submit to my commands?"

At this cruel thrust an almost imperceptible change came over the burgomaster's calm, dignified countenance; and even this change was scarce noticeable in the uncertain, flickering light of the wax candles. Perhaps he had realized, for the first time, the full horror of his position, the full treachery of the snare which had been laid for him, and which left him, pinioned and helpless, at the mercy of an unscrupulous and cowardly enemy. Not only him, but also his daughter.

A groan like that of a wounded beast escaped his lips, and his powerful arms and shoulders strained at the cords that fettered him. Nevertheless, after a very brief moment of silence he rejoined with perfect outward calm:

"My daughter, my lord, was under my protection until vile treachery rendered me helpless. Now that her father can no longer watch over her, she is under the protection of every man of honour."

"That is excellently said, mynheer," Stoutenburg replied. "And in a few words you have put the whole situation tersely and clearly. You have orders from the Stadtholder to obey my commands; therefore I do but make matters easier for you by having you removed to your apartments, instead of merely commanding you to return thither – an order which, if you were free, you might have been inclined to disobey."

"A truce on your taunts, my lord!" broke in the burgomaster firmly. "What is your pleasure with us?"

"Just what I have had the honour to tell you," Stoutenburg replied coolly. "That you return forthwith to your apartments."

"But my daughter, my lord?"

"She sups here, with her brother Nicolaes and with me."

" 'Tis only my dead body you'll drag away from here," the burgomaster rejoined quietly.

Once more Stoutenburg broke into that harsh, mirthless laugh which had become habitual to him and which seemed to find its well-spring in the bitterness of his soul.

"Fine heroics, mynheer!" he said derisively. "But useless, I fear me, and quite unnecessary. Were I to assure you that your daughter hath ceased to rouse the slightest passion in my heart or to stir my senses in any way, you would mayhap not credit me. Yet such is the case. The jongejuffrouw, I'll have you believe, will be as safe with me as would the ugliest old hag out of the street."

"Nevertheless, my lord," Beresteyn rejoined with calm dignity, "whilst I live I remain by my daughter's side."

Stoutenburg shrugged his shoulders.

"Jan," he called, "take mynheer the burgomaster back to his apartments. I have no further use for him."

Mynheer Beresteyn was still a comparatively young and vigorous man. In his day, he had been counted one of the finest soldiers in the armies of the Prince of Orange, and had accomplished prodigies of skill and valour at Turnhout and Ostend. The feeling that at this moment, when he would have given his life to protect his daughter, he was absolutely helpless, was undoubtedly the most cruel blow he had ever had to endure at the hands of Fate. His eyes, pathetic in their mute appeal for forgiveness, sought those of Gilda. She had remained perfectly still all this while, silent in the dark corner whither Jan and the soldiers had thrust her at their first onslaught on the burgomaster. But she had watched the whole scene with ever-increasing horror, not at thought of herself, of her own danger, only of her father and all that he must be suffering. Now her one idea was to reassure him, to ease the burden of sorrow and of wrath which his own impotence must have laid upon his brave soul.

Before any of the men could stop her, she had evaded them. Swift and furtive as a tiny lizard, she had wormed her way between them to her father's side. Now she had her arms round his neck, her head against his breast.

"Do not be anxious because of me, father dear," she whispered under her breath. "God hath us all in His keeping. Have no fear for me."

A deep groan escaped the old man's breast. His eyes, fierce and indignant, rested with an expression of withering contempt upon his enemy.

"Jan," Stoutenburg broke in harshly, "didst not hear my commands?"

Four pairs of hands immediately closed upon the burgomaster. He, like a creature at bay, started to struggle.

"Some one knock that old fool on the head!" his lordship shouted with a fierce oath.

And Jan raised his fist, overwilling to obey. But, with a loud cry of indignation, Gilda had already interposed. She seized the man's wrist with her own small hands and turned flaming eyes upon Stoutenburg.

"Violence is unnecessary, my lord," she said, vainly striving to speak coolly and firmly. "My father will go quietly, and I will remain here to listen to what you have to say."

"Bravely spoken!" Stoutenburg rejoined with a sneer. "And you, Mynheer Beresteyn, would do well to learn wisdom at so fair a source. You and your precious daughter will come to no harm if you behave like reasonable beings. There is such a thing," he added cynically, "as submitting to the inevitable."

"Do not trust him, Gilda," the old man cried. "False to his country, false to his wife and kindred, every word which he utters is a lie or a blasphemy."

"Enough of this wrangle," Stoutenburg exclaimed, wrathful and hoarse. "Jan, take that ranting dotard away!"

Then it was that, just before the men had time to close in all round the burgomaster, Gilda, placing one small, white hand upon her father's arm, pointed with the other to the door at the far end of the room. Instinctively the old man's glance turned in that direction. The door was open, and Nicolaes stood upon the threshold. He had heard his father's voice, Stoutenburg's brutal commands, his sister's cry of indignation.

"Nicolaes is here, father dear," Gilda said simply. "God knows that he is naught but an abominable traitor, yet methinks that even he hath not fallen so low as to see his own sister harmed before his eyes."

At sight of his son an indefinable look had spread over the burgomaster's face. It seemed as if an invisible and ghostly hand had drawn a filmy grey veil all over it. And a strange hissing sound – the intaking of a laboured sigh – burst through his tightly set lips.

"Go!" he cried to his son, in a dull, toneless voice, which nevertheless could be heard, clear and distinct as a bell, from end to end of the vast hall. "A father's curse is potent yet, remember!"

Nicolaes broke into a forced and defiant laugh, tried to assume a jaunty, careless air, which ill agreed with his pallid face and wild, scared eyes. But, before he could speak, Jan and the soldiers had finally seized the burgomaster and forcefully dragged him out of the room.

Chapter X – A Prince of Darkness

1

GILDA had seen her father dragged away from her side without a tear. Whatever tremor of apprehension made her heart quiver after she had seen the last of him, she would not allow these two men to see.

She was not afraid. When a woman has suffered as Gilda had suffered during these past two days, there is no longer in her any room for fear. Not for physical fear, at any rate. All her thoughts, her hopes, her anxieties were concentrated on the probable fate of her beloved. That unerring instinct which comes to human beings when they are within measurable distance of some acute, unknown danger amounts at times to second sight. This was the case with Gilda. With the eyes of her soul she could see and read something of what went on in her enemy's tortuous brain. She could see that he knew something about her beloved, and that he meant to use that knowledge for his own abominable ends. What these were she could not divine. Prescience did not go quite so far. But it had served her in this, that when her father was taken away she had just sufficient time and strength of will to brace herself up for the ordeal which was to come.

It is always remarkable when a woman, young and brought up in comparative seclusion and ignorance, is able to face moral danger with perfect calm and cool understanding. It was doubly remarkable in the case of a young girl like Gilda. She was only just twenty, had been the idol of her father; motherless, she had no counsels from those of her own sex, and there are always certain receptacles in a woman's soul which she will never reveal to the most loving, most indulgent father.

Three months ago, this same absolutely innocent, unsophisticated girl had suddenly been confronted with the vehement, turbulent passions of men. She had seen them in turmoil all round her – love, hatred, vengeance, treachery – she herself practically the pivot around which they raged. Out of the deadly strife she had emerged pure, happy in the arms of the man whom her wondrous adventures as much as his brilliant personality had taught her to love.

Since then her life had been peaceful and happy. She had allowed herself to be worshipped by that strangely captivating lover of hers, whose passionately wilful temperament, tempered by that persistent, sunny gaiety she had up to now only half understood. He made her laugh always made her taste a strange and exquisite bliss when he held her in his arms. But withal she had up till now kept an indulgent smile in reserve for his outbursts of vehemence, for his wayward, ofttimes irascible moods, his tearing impatience when she was away from him. Her love for him in the past had been almost motherly in its tenderness.

Somehow, with his absence, with the danger which threatened him, all that had become changed, intensified. The tenderness was still in her heart for him, an exquisite tenderness which caused her sheer physical ache now, when her mind conjured up that brief vision which she had had of him yesterday morning, wearied, with shoulders bent, his face haggard above a three-day's growth of beard, his eyes red-rimmed and sunken. But with that tenderness there was mingled at this hour a feeling which was akin to fierceness – the primeval desire of the woman to defend and protect her beloved – that same tearing impatience with Fate, of which he had been wont to suffer, for keeping him away from her sheltering arms.

Oh, she understood his vehemence now! No longer could she smile at his fretfulness. She, too, was a prey at this hour to a wildly emotional mood, tempest-tossed and spirit-stirring; her very soul crying out for him. And she hated – ay, hated with an intensity which she herself scarcely could apprise – this man whom she knew to be his deadly enemy.

"Sit down, sister; you are overwrought."

Nicolaes' cool, casual words brought her straightway back to reality. Quietly, mechanically she took the seat which he was offering – a high-backed, velvet-covered chair – the one in which the Stadtholder had sat at her wedding feast. She closed her eyes, and sat for a moment or two quite still. Visions of joy and of happiness must not obtrude their softly insidious presence beside the stern demands of the moment. Stoutenburg brought a footstool, and placed it to her feet. She felt him near her, but would not look on him, and he remained for awhile on his knees close beside her, she unable to move away from him.

"How beautiful you are!" he murmured, under his breath.

Her hand was resting on the arm of her chair. She felt his lips upon it, and quickly drew it back, wiping it against her gown as if a slimy worm had left its trail upon her fingers Seeing which, he broke into a savage curse and jumped to his feet.

"I thank you for the reminder, mejuffrouw," he said coldly.

After which he sat down once more beside the long centre table, at some little distance from her, but so that the light from the candles fell upon her dainty figure, graceful and dignified against the background of the velvet-covered chair, the while his own face remained in shadow. Nicolaes, nervous and restless, was pacing up and down the room.

"Allow me, mejuffrouw," Stoutenburg began coolly after awhile, "to tender you my sincere regrets for the violence to which necessity alone compelled me to subject the burgomaster; a worthy man, for whom, believe me, I entertain naught but sincere regard."

"I pray you, my lord," she retorted with complete self-possession, "to spare me this mockery. Had you not determined to put an insult on me, an insult which, apparently, you dared not formulate in the presence of my father. You had not, of a certainty subjected him to such an outrage."

"You misunderstand my motives, mejuffrouw. There was, and is, no intention on my part to insult you. Surely, as you yourself very rightly said just now, your brother's presence is sufficient guarantee for that."

"I said that, in order to quieten my father's fears. The treacherous snare which you laid for him, my lord, is proof enough of your cowardly intentions."

"You do yourself no good, mejuffrouw," rejoined the lord of Stoutenburg harshly, "by acrimony or defiance. I had to lure your father hither, else he would not have allowed you to come. Violence to you – though you may not believe it – would be repellent to me. But, having got you both here, I had to rid myself of him, using what violence was necessary."

"And why, I pray you, had you, as you say, to rid yourself of my father? Were you afraid of him?"

"No," he replied; "but I am compelled to put certain matters before you for your consideration, and did not desire that you should be influenced by him."

A quick sigh of satisfaction – or was it excitement? – escaped her breast. Fretful of all these preliminaries, which she felt were but the opening gambits of his dangerous game, she was thankful that, at last, he was coming to the point.

"Let us begin, mejuffrouw," Stoutenburg resumed, after a moment's deliberation, "by assuring you that the whereabouts of that gallant stranger who goes by the name of Diogenes are known to me and to your brother Nicolaes. To no one else."

He watched her keenly while he spoke. Shading his eyes with his hand, he took in every transient line of her face, noted the pallor of her cheeks, the pathetic droop of the mouth. But he was forced to own that at that curt announcement, wherewith he had intended to startle and to hurt, not the slightest change came over her. She still sat there, cool and impassive, her head resting against the velvet cushion of the chair, the flickering light of the candle playing with the loose tendrils of her golden hair. Her eyes he could not see, for they were downcast, veiled by the delicate, blue-veined lids; but of a surety, not the slightest quiver marred the perfect stillness of her lips.

In truth, she had expected some such statement from that execrable traitor. Her intuition had not erred when it told her that, in some subtle, devilish way, he would use the absence of her beloved as a tool wherewith to gain what he had in view. Now what she realized most vividly was that she must not let him see that she was afraid. Not even let him guess if she were hurt. She must keep up a semblance of callousness before her enemy for as long as she could. With her self-control, she would lose her most efficacious weapon. Therefore, for the next minute or two, she dared not trust herself to speak, lest her voice, that one uncontrollable thing, betrayed her.

"I await your answer, mejuffrouw," Stoutenburg resumed impatiently, after awhile.

"You have asked me no question, my lord," she rejoined simply. "Only stated a fact. I but wait to hear your further pleasure."

"My pleasure, fair one," he went on lightly, "is only to prove to you that I, as ever before, am not only your humble slave but also your sincere friend."

"A difficult task, my lord. But let me see, without further preamble, I pray you, how you intend to set about it."

"By trying to temper your sorrow with my heartfelt sympathy," he murmured softly.

"My sorrow?"

"I am forced to impart sad news to you, alas!"

"My husband is dead?" The cry broke from her heart, and this time she was unable to check it. Will and pride had been easy enough at first. Oh, how easy! But not now. Not in the face of this! She would have given worlds to appear calm, incredulous. But how could she? How could she, when such a torturing vision had been conjured up before her eyes?

For a moment it seemed as if reason itself began to totter. She looked on the man before her, and he appeared like a ghoulish fiend, with grinning jaws and sinister eyes, the play of light behind him making his face appear black and hideous. She put her hands up to her face, closed her eyes, and, oh, Heaven, how she prayed for strength!

None indeed but an implacable enemy, a jealous suitor, could have seen such soul-agony without relenting. But Stoutenburg was one of those hard natures which found grim pleasure in wounding and torturing. His love for Gilda, intensely passionate but never tender, was nothing now but fierce desire for mastership of her and vengeance upon his successful rival. The girl's involuntary cry of misery had been as balm to his evil soul. Now her hands dropped once more on her lap. She looked at him straight between the eyes, her own still a little wild, lit by a feverish brightness.

"You have killed him," she said huskily. "Is that it? Answer me! You have killed him?"

He put up his hand, smiling, as if to soothe a crying child.

"Nay! On my honour!" he replied quietly. "I have not seen that gallant adventurer these three months past."

"Well, then?"

"Ask your brother Nicolaes, fair one. He saw him but a few hours ago."

"Ay, yesterday," she retorted. "When he tried to assassinate him. I saw the murderous hand uplifted; I saw it all I tell you! And in my heart I cursed my only brother for the vile traitor that he is. But, thank Heaven, my lord was only hurt. I believe —"

She paused, put her hand up to her throat. The glance in Stoutenburg's eyes gave her a feeling as if she were about to choke.

"You are quite right, mejuffrouw," he broke in drily, "in believing that the intrepid Englishman who, for reasons best known to himself, hath chosen to meddle in the affairs of this country – that he, I say, was only hurt when your brother interposed yesterday betwixt him and the Stadtholder. The two ragamuffins who usually hang around him did probably save him from further punishment at the moment. But not altogether. Nicolaes will tell you that, half an hour later, that same intrepid and meddlesome English gentleman did once more try to interfere in the affairs of our Sovereign Liege the Archduchess Isabella. This time with serious consequences to himself."

"My brother Nicolaes," she murmured, more quietly this time, "hath killed my husband?"

"No, no!" here broke in Nicolaes at last. "The whole thing, I vow, was the result of an accident."

"What whole thing?" she reiterated slowly. "I pray you to be more explicit. What hath happened to my husband?"

"The explosion of a pistol," Nicolaes stammered, shamed out of his defiance at seeing his sister's misery, yet angered with himself for this weakness. "He is not dead, I swear!"

"Maimed?" she asked.

"Blind," Nicolaes replied, "but otherwise well. I swear it!" he protested, shutting his ears to Stoutenburg's scornful laugh, his eyes to the other's sardonic grin, his miserably weak nature swaying like a pendulum 'twixt his ambition, his hatred of the once brilliant soldier of fortune, and his dormant tenderness for the sweet and innocent sister to whom his treacherous hand had dealt such a devilish blow.

There was silence in the room now. Gilda had uttered no cry when that same blow fell on her like a crash. It had seemed to snap the very threads that held her to life. One sigh, and one only, came through her lips, like the dying call of a wounded bird. All feeling, all emotion, seemed suddenly to have died out of her, leaving her absolutely numb, scarcely conscious, with wide, unseeing eyes staring straight out before her, striving to visualize that splendid creature, that embodiment of gaiety, of laughter, of careless insouciance, stricken with impotence; those merry, twinkling eyes sightless. The horror of it was so appalling that it placed her for the moment beyond the power of suffering. She was not a human being now at all; she had no soul, no body, no life. Her senses had ceased to be. She neither saw nor heard nor felt. She was just a thing, a block of insentient stone into which life would presently begin to trickle slowly, bringing with it a misery such as could not be endured even by lost souls in hell.

How the time went by she did not know.

Just before this awful thing had happened she had chanced to look at the clock. It was then five minutes to eight. But all this was in the past. She no longer heard the ticking of the clock, nor her enemy's laboured breathing, nor Nicolaes' shuffling footsteps at the far end of the room. Fortunately, she could not see the triumph, the ominous sparkle, which glittered in Stoutenburg's eyes. He knew well enough what she suffered, or would be suffering anon when consciousness would return. Knew and revelled in it. He was like those inquisitors, the unclean spirits that waited on Spanish tyranny, who found their delight in watching the agony of their victims on the rack; who treasured every groan, exulted over every cry, wrung by unendurable bodily pain. Only with him it was the moral agony of those whom he desired to master that caused him infinite bliss. His stygian nature attained a demoniacal satisfaction out of the mental torture which he was able to inflict.

It is an undoubted fact that even the closest scrutiny of contemporary chronicles has failed to bring to light a single redeeming feature in this man's character, and all that the most staunch supporters of the Barneveldt family can bring forward in mitigation of Stoutenburg's crimes is the fact that his whole soul had been warped by the judicial murder of his father and of his elder brother, by his own consequent sufferings and those of his unfortunate mother.

4

"You will, I hope, mejuffrouw, give me the credit of having tried to break this sad news to you as gently as I could."

The words, spoken in smooth, silky tones were the first sounds that reached Gilda's returning perceptions. What had occurred in between she had not the vaguest idea. She certainly was still sitting in the same chair, with that sinister creature facing her, and her brother Nicolaes skulking somewhere in the gloom. The fire was still cracking in the hearth, the clock still ticking with insentient monotony. A tiny fillet of air caused the candle-light to flicker, and sent a thin streak of smoke upwards in an ever-widening spiral.

That streak of smoke was the first thing that Gilda saw. It arrested her eyes, brought her back slowly to consciousness. Then came Stoutenburg's hypocritical tirade. Her senses were returning one by one. She even glanced up at the clock. It marked three minutes before eight. Only two minutes had gone by. One hundred and twenty seconds. And they appeared longer than the most phantasmagoric conception of eternity. Two minutes! And she realized that she was alive, that she could feel, and that her beloved was sightless. Was it at all strange that, with return to pulsating life, there should arise within her that indestructible attribute of every human heart – a faint germ of hope?

When first the awful truth was put before her by her bitterest foe, she had not been conscious of the slightest feeling of doubt. Nicolaes' stammering protests, his obvious desire to minimise his own share of responsibility, had all helped to confirm the revelation of a hideous crime.

"He is not dead, I swear!" and "He is not otherwise hurt!" which broke from the dastard's quaking lips at the moment, had left no room for doubt or hope. At least, so she thought. And even now that faint ray of light in the utter blackness of her misery was too elusive to be of any comfort. But it helped her to collect herself, to look those two craven miscreants in the face. Nicolaes obviously dared not meet her glance, but Stoutenburg kept his eyes fixed upon her, and the look of triumph in them whipped up her dormant pride.

And now, when his double-tongued Pharisaism reached her ear, she swallowed her dread, bade horror be stilled. She knew that he was about to place an "either--or" before her which would demand her full understanding, and all the strength of mind and body that she could command. The fate of her beloved was about to be dangled before her, and she would be made to choose – what?

"You began, my lord," she said, with something of her former assurance – and God alone knew what it cost her to speak – "by saying that you desired to place certain matters before me for my consideration. I have not yet heard, remember, what those matters are."

"True – true!" he rejoined, with hypocritical unction. "But I felt it my duty – my sad duty, I may say —"

"A truce on this hollow mockery!" she riposted. "I pray you, come to the point."

"The point is, fair one, that both Nicolaes and I desire to compass your welfare," he retorted blandly.

"This you can do best at this hour, my lord, by allowing me to return to the privacy of mine apartments."

"So you shall, myn engel – so you shall," he rejoined suavely. "You will need time to prepare for departure."

She frowned, puzzled this time.

"For departure?" she asked, a little bewildered.

"I leave this town to-morrow at the head of my troops."

"Thank God for that!" she rejoined earnestly.

"And you, mejuffrouw," he added curtly, "will accompany us."

"I?" she asked, not altogether understanding, the frown more deeply marked between her brows.

"Methought I spoke clearly," he went on, in his habitual harsh, peremptory tone. "I only came to this town in order to fetch you, myn engel. To-morrow we go away together."

"The folly of human grandeur hath clouded your brain, my lord!" she said coldly.

"In what way?" he queried, still perfectly bland and mild.

"You know well that I would sooner die than follow you."

"I know well that most women are over-ready with heroics. But," he added, with a shrug of the shoulders, "these tantrums usually leave me cold. You are an intelligent woman, mejuffrouw, and you have seen your valiant father resign himself to the inevitable."

"I pray you waste no words, my lord," she rejoined coolly. "Three months ago, when at Ryswick, your crimes found you out, and you strove to involve me in your own disgrace and ruin, I gave you mine answer – the same that I do now. My dead body you can take with you, but I, alive, will never follow you!"

" 'Twas different then," he retorted, with a cynical smile. "You had a fortune-hunting adventurer to hand who was determined to see that your father's shekels did not lightly escape his grasp. To-day––"

"To-day," she retorted, and rose to her feet, fronted him now, superb with indignation, "he is sightless, absent, impotent, you would say, to protect me against your villainy! You miserable, slinking cur!"

Stoutenburg's harsh, forced laugh broke in upon her wrath.

"Ah!" he exclaimed lightly. "You little spit-fire! In very truth, I like you better in that mood. Heroics do not become you, myn schat, and they are so unnecessary. Did you perchance imagine that it was love for you that hath influenced my decision to take you away from here?"

"I pray God, my lord, that I be not polluted by as much as a thought from you!"

"Your prayers have been granted, fair one," he retorted with a sneer. " 'Tis but seldom I think of you now, save as an exquisite little termagant whom it will amuse me to tame. But this is by the way. That pleasure will lose nothing by procrastination. You know me well enough by now to realise that I am not likely to be lenient with you after your vixenish treatment of me. For the nonce, I pray you to keep a civil tongue in your head," he added roughly. "On your conduct at this hour will depend your future comfort. Nicolaes will not always be skulking in dark corners, ready to interfere if my manner become too rough."

"He is here now," she said boldly, "and if there is a spark of honour left in him he will conduct me to my rooms!"

With this she turned and walked steadily across the room. Even so his harsh laugh accompanied her as far as the door. When her hand was upon the knob, he called lightly after her:

"The moment you step cross the threshold, myn schat, Jan will bring you back here – in his arms!"

5

Instinctively she paused, realizing that the warning had come just in time – that the next moment, in very truth, she would be in the hands of those vile traitors who were there ready to obey their master's every command. She paused, too, in order to murmur a quick prayer for Divine guidance, seeing that human protection was denied her at this hour. What could she do? She was like a bird caught in a snare from which there seemed to be no issue. Stoutenburg's sneering laugh rang in her ear. He was beside her now, took her hand from the knob and held it for a moment forcibly in his. His glance, charged with cruel mockery, took in every line of her pallid face.

"Heroics again, fair one!" he said, with an impish grin. "Must I assure you once more that you are perfectly safe with me? See, if you were in danger from me, would not your brother interfere? Bah! Nicolaes knows well enough that passion doth not enter into my schemes at this hour. My plans are too vast to be swayed by your frowns or your smiles. I have entered this city as a conqueror. As a conqueror I shall go out of it to-morrow, and you will come with me. I shall go hence because I choose, and for reasons which I will presently make clear to you.

"But you shall come with me. When you are with me in my camp, I may honour you as my future wife, or cast you from me as I would a beggar. That will depend on my mood, and upon your temper. Nicolaes will not be there to run counter to my will. Therefore, understand me, my pretty fire-eater, that from this hour forth you are as absolutely my property as my dogs are, my horse, or the boots which I wear. I am the master here," he concluded with strangely sinister calm, "And my will alone is law."

"A law unto yourself," she retorted, faced him with absolute composure, neither defiant nor afraid, her nerves quiescent, her voice perfectly steady, "and mayhap unto your cringing sycophants. But above your will, my lord, is that of God; and neither death nor life are your slaves."

"Ay! But methinks they are, myn engel," he answered drily. "Yours in any case."

"No human being, my lord, can lose the freedom to die."

"You think not?" he sneered. "Well, we shall see."

He let go her hand, then quietly turned and walked to the window, threw open the casement once more, then beckoned to her. Strangely stirred, she followed, moved almost mechanically by something she could not resist.

At a sign from him she looked out upon the busy scene on the quay below – the enemy soldiers in possession, their bivouac fires, their comings and goings, the unfortunate citizens running hither and thither at their bidding, fetching and carrying, hustled, pushed, beaten, ordered about with rough words or the persuasive prod of pike or musket. A scene, alas, which already as a child had been familiar to her. A peaceable town in the hands of ruthless soldiery; the women fleeing from threatened insults, children clinging to their mother's skirts, men standing by, grim and silent, not daring to protest lest mere resentment brought horrible reprisals upon the city.

Gilda looked out for awhile in silence, her heart aching with the misery which she beheld, yet could not palliate. Then she turned coldly inquiring eyes on the prime mover of it all.

"I have seen a reign of terror such as this before, my lord," she said. "I was at Leyden, as you well know, and I have not forgotten."

"A reign of terror, you call it, mejuffrouw?" he retorted coolly. "Nay, you exaggerate. What is this brief occupation? To-morrow we go, remember. Is there a single house demolished at this hour, a single citizen murdered? You are too young to recollect Malines of Ghent, the reign of Alva over these recalcitrant countries. I have been lenient so far. I have spared fire and sword. Amersfoort still stands. It will stand to-morrow, even after my soldiers have gone," he went on speaking very slowly, "if —"

"If what, my Lord?" she asked, for he had paused.

The moment had come, then, the supreme hour when that dreaded "either--or" would be put before her. Even now he went on with that same sinister quietude which seemed like the voice of some relentless judge, sent by the King of Darkness to sway her destiny.

"If," Stoutenburg concluded drily, "you mejuffrouw, will accompany me. Oh," he added quickly, seeing that at once she had resumed that air of defiance which irritated even whilst it amused him. "I do not mean as an unwilling slave, pinioned to my chariot-wheel or strapped into a saddle, nor yet as a picturesque corpse, with flowing hair and lilies 'twixt your lifeless hands. No, no, fair one! I offer you the safety of your native city, the immunity of your fellow-citizens, in exchange for a perfectly willing surrender of your live person into my charge."

She looked on him for awhile, mute with horror, then murmured slowly:

"Are you a devil, that you should propose such an execrable bargain?"

He laughed and shrugged his shoulders.

"I am what you and my native land have made me," he replied. "As to that, the Stadtholder never offered to bargain with me for my father's life."

"Who but a prince of darkness would dream of doing so?" she retorted.

"Call me that, an you wish, fair one," he put in lightly; "and come back to the point."

"And the point is, my Lord?"

"That I will respect this city if you come to-morrow, willing and submissive, with me,"

"That, never!" she affirmed hotly.

"In that case," he riposted coldly, "my soldiers will have a free hand ere they quit the town, to sack it at their pleasure. Pillage, arson, will be rewarded; looting will be deemed a virtue, as will murder and outrage. Even your father —"

"Enough, my lord!" she exclaimed, with passionate indignation. "Tell me, I pray, which of the unclean spirits of Avernus did suggest this infamy to you?" Then, as he met her burning glance with another careless shrug and a mocking laugh, she turned to Nicolaes, and cried out to him, almost with entreaty: "Klaas! You at least are not a party to such hideous villainy!"

But he, sullen and shamefaced, only threw her an angry look.

"You make it very difficult for us, Gilda," he said moodily, "by your stupid obstinacy."

"Obstinacy?" she retorted, puzzled at the word. Then reiterated it once or twice. "Obstinacy – obstinacy? My God, hath the boy gone mad?"

"What else is it but obstinacy?" he rejoined vehemently. "You know that, despite all he says, Stoutenburg hath never ceased to love you. And now that he is master here you are lucky indeed to have him as a suitor. He means well by you, by us all, else I were not here. Think what it would mean to me, to father, to everyone of us, if you were Stoutenburg's wife. But you jeopardize my future and the welfare of us all by those foolish tantrums."

She gazed on him in utter horror – on this brother whom she loved; could scarcely believe her ears that it was he – really he – who was uttering such odious words. She felt her gorge rising at this callous avowal of a wanton and insulting treachery. And he, feeling the contempt which flashed on him from her glowing eyes, avoided her glance, tried to shift his ground, to argue his point with the sophistry peculiar to a traitor, and sank more deeply every moment into the mire of dishonour.

"It is time you realized, Gilda," he said, "that our unfortunate country must sooner or later return to her true allegiance. The Stadtholder is sick. His arbitrary temper hath alienated some of his staunchest friends. The Netherlands are the unalienable property of Spain; though two rebel princes have striven to wrest them from their rightful master, the might of Spain was sure to be felt in the end. 'Twas folly ever to imagine that this so-called Dutch Republic would ever abide; and the hour, though tardy, has struck at last when such senseless dreams must come to an end."

"Well spoken, friend Nicolaes!" Stoutenburg put in lustily. "In verity, our Liege Lady the Archduchess Isabella, whom may God protect, could with difficulty find a more eloquent champion."

"Or our noble land so vile a traitor!" Gilda murmured, burning now with shame. "Thank Heaven, Nicolaes, that our poor father is not here, for the disgrace of it all would have struck him dead at your feet. Would to God," she murmured under her breath, "that it killed me now!"

"An undutiful prayer, myn engel," Stoutenburg rejoined, "seeing that its fulfilment would mean that Amersfoort and her citizens would be wiped off the face of the earth."

This time he spoke quite quietly, without any apparent threat, only with determination, like one who knows that he is master and hath full powers to see his will obeyed. She looked at him keenly for a moment or two, wondering if she could make him flinch, if she could by word or prayer shake him in that devilish purpose which in truth must have found birth through the whisperings of uncanny fiends.

Gilda gazed critically at his lean, hard face with the sunken, restless eyes that spoke so eloquently of disappointed hopes and frustrated ambitions; the mouth, thin-lipped and set; the unshaven chin; the hollow temples and grizzled hair. She took in every line of his tall, gaunt figure; the shoulders already bent, the hands fidgety and claw-like; the torn doublet and shabby boots, all proclaiming the down-at-heel adventurer who has staked his all – honour, happiness, eternity – for ambition; has staked all he possessed and played a losing game.

But for pity or compunction Gilda sought in vain. The glance which after awhile was raised to hers revealed nothing but unholy triumph and a cruel, callous mockery. In truth, that glance had told her that she could expect neither justice nor mercy from him, and had spared her the humiliation of a desperate and futile appeal.

A low moan escaped her lips. She tottered slightly, and felt her knees giving way under her.

Vaguely she put out her hand, fearing that she might fall. Even so, she swayed backwards, feeling giddy and sick. But the dread of losing consciousness before this man whom she loathed and despised kept up both her courage and her endurance. She felt the panelling of the window-embrasure behind her, and leaned against it for support.

6

Stoutenburg had made no effort to come to her assistance, neither had Nicolaes. Probably both of them knew that she would never allow either of them to touch her. But Stoutenburg's mocking glance had pursued her all through her valiant fight against threatening unconsciousness. Now that she leaned against the framework of the window, pale and wraith-like, only her delicate profile vaguely distinguishable in the semi-gloom, her lips parted as if to drink in the cold evening air, she looked so exquisite, so desirable, that he allowed his admiration of her to override every other thought.

"You are lovely, myn schat," he said quietly. "Exquisite and worthy to be a queen. And, by Heaven," he exclaimed with sudden passion, "you'll yet live to bless this hour when I broke your obstinacy. Hand in hand, myn engel, you and I, we'll be masters of this beautiful land. I feel that I could do great things if I had you by my side. Listen, Gilda," he went on eagerly, thinking that because she remained silent and motionless she had given up the fight, and was at last resigned to the inevitable – "listen, my beautiful little vixen! The Archduchess will wish to reward me for this; the capture of Amersfoort is no small matter, and I have further projects in mind. In the meanwhile, De Berg hath already hinted that she might re-establish the republic under the suzerainty of Spain, and appoint me as her Stadtholder. Think, myn Geliefde: think what a vista of glorious, satisfied ambition lies before us both! Nay, before us all. Your father, chief pensionary; Nicolaes, general of our armies; your family raised above every one in the land. You'll thank me, I say; thank me on your knees for my constancy and for my unwavering loyalty to you. And even to-night, presently, when you are quite calm and at rest, you'll pray to your God, I vow, for His blessing upon your humble and devoted slave."

He bent the knee when he said this, still scornful even in this affectation of humility, and raised the hem of her gown to his lips. She did not look down on him, nor did she snatch her skirts out of his hand. She just stared straight out before her, and said slowly, with great deliberation:

"To-night – presently – when I am at rest – I will pray God to kill you ere you put your monstrous threat into execution."

With a light laugh he jumped to his feet.

"Still the shrewish little vixen, what?" he said carelessly. "Yet, see what a good dog I am. I'll not bear resentment, and you shall have the comfort of your father's company at the little supper party which I have prepared. Only the four of us, you and the burgomaster, and Nicolaes and I; and we can discuss the arrangements for our forthcoming wedding, which shall be magnificent, I promise you. But be sure of this, fair one," he went on harshly, drew up his gaunt figure to its full height, "that what I've said I've said. To-morrow at sunrise I go hence, and you come with me, able-bodied and willing, to a place which I have in mind. But this city will be the hostage for your good behaviour. My soldiers remain here under the command of one Jan, who obeys all my behests implicitly and without question, because he hates the Stadtholder as much as I do, and hath a father's murder to avenge against that tyrant, just as I have. Jan will stay in Amersfoort until I bid him go. But at one word from me, this city will be reduced to ashes, and not one man, woman or child shall live to tell the tale of how the jongejuffrouw Gilda Beresteyn set her senseless obstinacy above the lives of thousands.

"Think not that I'll relent," he concluded, and once more turned to the open window, gazed down upon the unfortunate city which he had marked as the means to his fiendish ends. His restless eyes roamed over the busy scene; his soldiers, his – the executioners who would carry out his will! Never had he been so powerful; never had his ambition been so near its goal! It had all come together – the humiliation of the Stadtholder, his own success in this daring enterprise, Gilda entirely at his mercy! Success had crowned all his nefarious schemes at last.

"Nothing will change me from my purpose," he said, with all the harsh determination which characterized his every action – "nothing! Neither your tears nor your frowns nor your prayers. There is no one, understand me, no one who can stand between me and my resolve."

"No one but God," she murmured under her breath. "Oh, God, protect me now! My God, save me from this!"

Dizzy, moving like a sleep-walker, she tried to hold herself erect, tried to move from the window, and from the propinquity of that execrable miscreant.

"Have I your permission to go now?" she murmured faintly.

"Yes," he replied; "to your father. I'll order Jan to release our worthy burgomaster, and you and he can pray for my demise at your leisure. Whether you confide in him or not is no concern of mine. I would have you remember that my promise to respect this city and her inhabitants only holds good if you, of your own free will, come with me to-morrow. Amersfoort shall live if you come willingly. You are the best judge whether your father would be the happier for this knowledge. Methinks it would be kinder to let him think that you come to-morrow as my willing bride. But that is for you to decide. I want him here anon to give his blessing upon our future union in the presence of your brother Nicolaes. I wish the bond to be made irrevocable as soon as may be. If you or your father break it afterwards, it will be the worse for Amersfoort. Try and believe that the alternative is one of complete indifference to me. I have everything in the world now that I could possibly wish for. My ambition is completely satisfied. To have you as my wife would only be the pandering to a caprice. And now you may go, myn schat," he concluded. "The destinies of your native city are in your dainty hands."

He watched her progress across the room with a sarcastic grin. But in his heart he was conscious of a bitter disappointment. Unheard by her, he muttered under his breath:

"If only she would care, how different everything might be!"

Aloud he called to Nicolaes: "Escort your sister, man, into the presence of the burgomaster! And see that Jan and a chosen few form a guard of honour on the passage of the future Lady of Stoutenburg."

Nicolaes hastened to obey. Gilda tried to check him with a brief. "I thank you; I would prefer to go alone!"

But already he had thrown open the door, and anon his husky voice could be heard giving orders to Jan.

Gilda, at the last, turned once more to look on her enemy. He caught her eye, bowed very low, his hand almost touching the ground ere he brought it with a sweeping flourish back to his breast, in the most approved fashion lately brought in from France.

"In half an hour supper will be served," he said. "I await the honour of the burgomaster's company and of your own!"

And he remained in an attitude of perfect deference whilst she passed silently out of the room.

1

GILDA had refused her brother's escort, preferring to follow Jan; and Nicolaes, half indifferent, half ashamed, watched her progress up the stairs, and when she had disappeared in the gloom of the corridor above, he went back to his friend.

The two old serving-men were now busy in the banqueting-hall, bringing in the supper. They set the table with silver and crystal goblets, with jugs of Spanish and Rhenish wines, and dishes of cooked meats. They came and went about their business expeditiously and silently, brought in two more heavy candelabra with a dozen or more lighted candles in their sconces, so that the vast room was brilliantly lit. They threw fresh logs upon the fire, so that the whole place looked cosy and inviting.

Stoutenburg had once more taken up his stand beside the open window. Leaning his arm against the mullion, he rested his head upon it. Bitterness and rage had brought hot tears to his eyes. Somehow it seemed to him as if in the overflowing cup of his triumph something had turned to gall. Gilda eluded him. He could not understand her. The experience which he had of women had taught him that these beautiful and shallow creatures, soulless for the most part and heartless, were easily to be cajoled with soft words and bribed with wealth and promises. Yet he had dangled before Gilda's eyes such a vision of glory and exalted position as should have captured, quite unconditionally, the citadel of her affections, and she had remained indifferent to it all.

He had owned himself still in love with her, and she had remained quite callous to his ardour. He had tried indifference, and had only been paid back in his own coin. To a man of Stoutenburg's intensely egotistical temperament, there could only be one explanation to this seeming coldness. The wench's senses – it could be nothing more – were still under the thrall of that miserable adventurer who, thank Beelzebub and his horde, had at last been rendered powerless to wreak further mischief. There could be, he argued to himself, no aversion in her heart for one who was so ready to share prosperity, power, and honour with her, to forgive and forget all that was past, to raise her from comparative obscurity to the most exalted state that had ever dazzled a woman's fancy and stormed the inmost recesses of her soul.

She was still infatuated with the varlet, and that was all. A wholly ununderstandable fact. Stoutenburg never could imagine how she had ever looked with favour on such an adventurer, whose English parentage and reputed wealth were, to say the least, problematical. Beresteyn had been a fool to allow his only daughter to bestow her beauty and her riches on a stranger, about whom in truth he knew less than nothing. The girl, bewitched by the rascallion, had cajoled her father and obtained his consent. Now she was still under the spell of a handsome presence, a resonant voice, a provoking eye. It was, it could be, nothing more than that. When once she understood what she had gained, how utterly inglorious that once brilliant soldier of fortune had become, she would descend from her high attitude of disdain and kiss the hand which she now spurned.

But, in anticipation of that happy hour, the Lord of Stoutenburg felt moody and discontented.

2

Nicolaes' voice, close to his elbow, roused him from his gloomy meditations.

"You must be indulgent, my friend," he was saying in a smooth conciliatory voice. "Gilda had always a wilful temper."

"And a tenacious one," Stoutenburg retorted. "She is still in love with that rogue."

"Bah!" the other rejoined, with a note of spite in his tone. "It is mere infatuation! A woman's whimsey for a good-looking face and a pair of broad shoulders! She should have seen the scrubby rascal as I last caught sight of him – grimy, unshaven, broken. No woman's fancy would survive such a spectacle!"

Then, as Stoutenburg, still unconsoled, continued to stare through the open window, muttering disjointed phrases through obstinately set lips, he went on quite gaily:

"You are not the first by any means, my friend, whose tempestuous wooing hath brought a woman, loving and repentant, to heel. When I was over in England with my father, half a dozen years ago, we saw there a play upon the stage. It had been writ by some low-born mountebank, one William Shakespeare. The name of the play was 'The Taming of the Shrew.' Therein, too, a woman of choleric temper did during several scenes defy the man who wooed her. In the end he conquered; she became his wife, and as tender and submissive an one as e'er you'd wish to see. But, by St. Bavon, how she stormed at first! How she professed to hate him! I was forcibly reminded of that play when I saw Gilda defying you awhile ago; and I could have wished that you had displayed the same good-humour over the wrangle as did the gallant Petruchio – the hero of the piece."

Stoutenburg was interested.

"How did he succeed in the end?" he queried. "Your Petruchio, I mean."

"He starved the ranting virago into submission," Nicolaes replied, with an easy laugh. "Gave her nothing to eat for a day and a night; swore at her lackeys; beat her waiting-maids. She was disdainful at first, then terrified. Finally, she admired him, because he had mastered her."

"A good moral, friend Nicolaes!"

"Ay! One you would do well to follow. Women reserve their disdain for weaklings, and their love for their masters."

"And think you that Gilda —"

"Gilda, my friend, is but a woman after all. Have no fear, she'll be your willing slave in a week."

Stoutenburg's eyes glittered at the thought.

"A week is a long time to wait," he murmured. "I wish that now--"

He paused. Something that was happening down below on the quay had attracted his attention – unusual merriment, loud laughter, the strains of a bibulous song. For a minute or two his keen eyes searched the gloom for the cause of all this hilarity. He leaned far out the window, called peremptorily to a group of soldiers who were squatting around their bivouac fire.

"Hey!" he shouted. "Peter! Willem! – whatever your confounded names may be! What is that rascallion doing over there?"

"Making us all laugh, so please your lordship," one of the soldiers gave reply; "by the drollest stories and quips any of us have ever heard."

"Where does he come from?"

"From nowhere, apparently," the man averred. "He just fell among us. The man is blind, so please you," he added after a moment's hesitation.

Stoutenburg swore.

"How many times must I give orders," he demanded roughly, "that every blind beggar who comes prowling round the camps be hanged to the nearest post?"

"We did intend to hang him," the soldier replied coolly; "but when first he came along he was so nimble that, ere we could capture him, he gave us the slip."

"Well," Stoutenburg rejoined harshly, "it is not too late. You have him now."

"So we have, Magnificence," the man replied, hesitated for a second or two, then added: "But he is so amusing, and he seems a gentleman of quality, too proud for the hangman's rope."

"Too proud is he?" his lordship retorted with a sneer. "A gentleman of quality, and amusing to boot? Well, let us see how his humour will accommodate itself to the gallows. Here, let me have a look at the loon.

There was much hustling down below after this; shouting and prolonged laughter; a confused din, through which it was impossible to distinguish individual sounds. Stoutenburg's nerves were tingling. He was quite sure by now that he had recognised that irrepressible merry voice. A gentleman of quality! Blind! Amusing! But, if Nicolaes' report of yesterday's events were true, the man was hopelessly stricken. And what could induce him to put his head in the jackal's mouth, to affront his triumphing enemy, when he himself was so utterly helpless and abject?

Not long was the Lord of Stoutenburg left in suspense. Even whilst he gazed down upon the merry, excited throng, he was able to distinguish in the midst of them all a pair of broad shoulders that could only belong to one man. The soldiers, laughing, thoroughly enjoying the frolic, were jostling him not a little for the sheer pleasure of measuring their valour against so hefty a fellow. And he, despite his blindness, gave as good as he got; fought valiantly with fist and boot and gave his tormentors many a hard knock, until, with a loud shout of glee, some of the men succeeded in seizing hold of him, and hoisted him up on their shoulders and brought him into the circle of light formed by the resin torches.

A double cry came in response – one of amazement from Stoutenburg and one of horror from Nicolaes. But neither of them spoke. Stoutenburg's lips were tightly set; a puzzled frown appeared between his brows. In truth, for once in the course of his devilish career, he was completely taken aback and uncertain what to do. The man whom he saw there before him, in ragged clothes, unshaved and grimy, blinking with sightless eyes, was the man whom he detested above every other thing or creature on earth – the reckless soldier of fortune of the past, for awhile the proud and successful rival; now just a wreck of humanity, broken, ay, and degraded, and henceforth an object of pity rather than a menace to his rival's plans. His doublet was in rags, his plumed hat battered, his toes shone through the holes in his boots. The upper part of his face was swathed in a soiled linen bandage. This had, no doubt, been originally intended to shield the stricken eyes; but it had slipped, and those same eyes, with their horrible fixed look, glittered with unearthly weirdness in the flickering light.

"Salute his Magnificence, the lord and master of Amersfoort and of all that in it lies!" one of the soldiers shouted gaily.

And the blind man forthwith made a gesture of obeisance swept with a wide flourish his battered plumed hat from off his head.

"To his Magnificence!" he called out in response. "Though mine eyes cannot see him, my voice is raised in praise of his nobility and his valour. May the recording angels give him his full deserts."

3

The feeling of sheer horror which had caused Nicolaes to utter a sudden cry was, in truth, fully justified.

"It can't be!" he murmured, appalled at what he saw.

Stoutenburg answered with a hoarse laugh. "Nay, by Satan and all his myrmidons it is!"

Already he was leaning out of the window, giving quick orders to the men down below to bring that drunken vagabond forthwith into his presence. After which he turned once more to his friend.

"We'll soon see," he said, "if it is true, or if our eyes have played us both an elusive trick. Yet, methinks," he added thoughtfully, "that the pigwidgeon who of late hath taken my destiny in hand is apparently intent on doing me a good turn."

"In what way?" the other asked.

"By throwing my enemy across my path," Stoutenburg replied drily.

"You'll hang him of course?" Nicolaes rejoined.

"Yes; I'll hang him!" Stoutenburg retorted, with a snarl. "But I must make use of him first."

"Make use of him? How?"

"That I do not know as yet. But inspiration will come, never you fear, my friend. All that I want is a leverage for bringing the Stadtholder to his knees and for winning Gilda's love."

"Then, in Heaven's name, man," Nicolaes rejoined earnestly, "begin by ridding yourself of the only danger-spoke in your wheel!"

"Danger-spoke?" Stoutenburg exclaimed, threw back his head and laughed. "Would you really call that miserable oaf a serious bar to mine ambition or a possible rival in your sister's regard?"

And, with outstretched hand he pointed to the door.

There, under the lintel – pushed on by Jan and two or three men who, powerfully built though they were, looked like pigmies beside the stricken giant, drunk as an owl, his hat awry above that hideous bandage, dirty, unkempt, and ragged – appeared the man who had once been the brilliant inspiration of Franz Hals' immortal "Laughing Cavalier."

At sight of him Nicolaes Beresteyn gave a loud groan and collapsed into a chair; burying his face in his hand. He was ever a coward, even in villainy; and when the man whom he had once hated so bitterly, and whom his craven hand had struck in such a dastardly manner, lurched into the room, and as he fell against the table uttered an inane and bibulous laugh, his nerve completely forsook him.

At a peremptory sign from Stoutenburg, Jan closed the doors which gave on the hall; but he and two of the men remained at attention inside the room.

The blind man groped with his hands till they found a chair, into which he sank, with powerful limbs outstretched, snorting like a dog just come out of the water. With an awkward gesture he pushed his hat from off his head, and in so doing he dislodged the grimy bandage so that it sat like a scullion's cap across his white forehead.

Stoutenburg watched him with an expression of cruel satisfaction. It is not often given to a man to have an enemy and a rival so completely in his power, and the exultation in Stoutenburg's heart was so great that he was content to savour it in silence for awhile. Nicolaes was beyond the power of speech, and so the silence for a moment or two remained absolute.

Then the blind man suddenly sat up, craning his neck and rolling his sightless eyes.

"I wonder where the devil I am!" he murmured through set lips. He appeared to listen intently; no doubt caught the sound of life around him, for he added quickly: "Is anybody here?"

"I am here," Stoutenburg replied curtly. "Do you know whom I am, sirrah?"

"In truth, I do not," Diogenes replied. "But by your accent I would judge you to be a man who at this moment is mightily afraid."

"Afraid?" Stoutenburg retorted, with a loud laugh. I, afraid of a helpless vagabond who has been fool enough to run his head into a noose which I had not even thought of preparing for him?"

"Yet you are afraid my lord," the other rejoined quietly, "else you would not have ordered your bodyguard to watch over your precious person whilst you parleyed with a blind man."

"My bodyguard is only waiting for final orders to take you to the gallows," Stoutenburg rejoined roughly. "You may as well know now as later that it is my intention to hang you."

"As well now as later," the blind man assented, with easy philosophy. "I understand that for the nonce, whoever you Magnificence may be, you are master in Amersfoort. As such, you have a right to hang anyone you choose. Me or another. What matters? I was very nearly hung once, you must know, by the Lord of Stoutenburg. I did not mind much then; I'd mind it still less now. People talk of a hereafter. Well, whatever it is, it must be a better world that this, so I would just as soon as not, go and find out for myself."

He struggled to his feet, still groping with his hands for support, found the edge of the table and leaned up against it.

"Let's to the hangman, my lord," he said thickly. "If I'm to hang, I prefer it to be done at once. And if we tarry too long I might get sober ere I embark on the last adventure. But," he added, and once more appeared to search the room with eyes that could not see, "there's someone else here besides your lordship. Who is it?"

"My friend and yours," Stoutenburg replied. "Mynheer Nicolaes Beresteyn."

There was a second or two of silence. Nicolaes made as if he would speak, but Stoutenburg quickly put a finger up to his lips, enjoining him to remain still. The blind man passed his trembling hand once or twice in front of his eyes as if to draw aside an unseen veil that hid the outer world from his gaze.

"Ah!" he murmured contentedly. "My friend Klaas! He is here too, is he? That is indeed good news. For Nicolaes was ever my friend. That time three months ago – or was it three years, or three centuries? I really have lost count – that time that the Lord of Stoutenburg was on the point of hanging me, Klaas would have interposed on my behalf, only something went wrong with his heart at the moment, or his nerves, I forget which."

" 'Twere no use to rely on mynheer's interference this time," Stoutenburg put in drily. "There is but one person in the world now who can save you from the gallows."

"You mean the Lord of Stoutenburg himself?" the blind man queried blandly.

"Nay! He is determined to hang you. But there is another."

"Then I pray your lordship to tell me who that other is," Diogenes replied.

"You might find one, sirrah, in the jongejuffrouw Gilda Beresteyn, the Lord of Stoutenburg's promised wife."

Diogenes made no reply to this. He was facing the table now, still clinging to it with one hand, whilst the other wandered over the objects on the table. Suddenly they encountered a crystal jug which was full of wine. An expression of serene beatitude overspread his face. He raised the goblet to his lips, but ere he drank he said carelessly:

"Ah, the jongejuffrouw Beresteyn is the promised wife of the Lord of Stoutenburg?"

"My promised wife!" Stoutenburg put in roughly. "Methought you would ere this have recognized the man whom you tried to rob of all that he held most precious."

"Your lordship must forgive me," the blind man rejoined drily. "But some unknown miscreant – whom may the gods punish – interfered with me yesterday forenoon, when I was trying to render assistance to my friend Klaas. In the scuffle that ensued, I received a cloud of stinking fumes in the face, which has totally robbed me of sight."

As he spoke he raised his eyes, blinking in that pathetic and inconsequent manner peculiar to the blind. Nicolaes gave an audible groan. He could not bear to look on those sightless orbs, which in the flickering light of the wax candles appeared weird and unearthly.

"Oh," Stoutenburg put in carelessly, "is that how the – er – accident occurred?"

"So, please your lordship, yes," Diogenes replied. "And I was left stranded on the moor, since those two unreclaimed varlets, Pythagoras and Socrates by name, did effectually ride off in the wake of the Stadtholder, leaving me in the lurch. A pitiable plight, your lordship will admit."

"So pitiable," the other retorted with a sneer, "that you thought to improve your condition by bearding the Lord of Stoutenburg in his lair."

"I did not know your lordship was in Amersfoort," Diogenes replied imperturbably. "I thought – I hoped —"

He paused, and Stoutenburg tried in vain to read what went on behind that seemingly unclouded brow. The blind man appeared serene, detached, perfectly good-humoured. His slender hand, which looked hard beneath its coating of grime, was closed lovingly around the crystal jug. Stoutenburg vaguely wondered how far the man was really drunk, or whether his misfortune had slightly addled his brain. So much unconcern in the face of an imminent and shameful death gave an uncanny air to the whole appearance of the man. Even now, with a gently apologetic smile, he raised the jug once more to his lips. Stoutenburg placed a peremptory hand upon his arm.

"Put that down, man," he said harshly. "You are drunk enough as it is, and you'll have need of all your wits to-night."

"There you are wrong my lord," Diogenes retorted, and quietly transferred the jug to his other hand. "A man, meseems, needs no wits to hang gracefully. And I feel that I could do that best if I might quench my thirst ere I met my friend the hangman."

"You may not meet him at all."

"But just now you said —"

"That it was my intention to hang you," Stoutenburg assented. "So it is. But I am in rare good humour to-night, and —"

"So it seems, my lord," the blind man put in carelessly. "So it seems."

He appeared to be swaying on his feet, and to have some difficulty in retaining his balance. He still clung to the edge of the table with one hand. In the other he had the jug fill of wine.

"The jongejuffrouw Gilda Beresteyn," Stoutenburg went on, "will sup with me this night to celebrate our betrothal. The fulfillment of this, my great desire, hath caused me to feel lenient toward mine enemies."

"Have I not always asserted," Diogenes broke in with comical solemnity – "always ass-asserted that your lordship was a noble and true gentleman?"

"Women, we know," his lordship continued, ignoring the interruption, "are wont to be tenderhearted where their – their former swains are concerned. And I feel that if the jongejuffrouw herself did make appeal to me on your behalf, I would relent towards you."

"B-b-but would that not be an awkward – a very awkward decision for your lordship?" Diogenes riposted, turning round vacant eyes on Stoutenburg.

"Awkward? How so?

"If I do not hang, the jongejuffrouw, 'stead of being my widow, would still be my wife. And the laws of this country —"

"I have no concern with the laws of this country" Stoutenburg rejoined drily, "in which, anyhow, you are an alien. As soon as the Archduchess our Liege Lady is once more mistress here, we shall again be at war with England."

"Poor England!"

Diogenes sighed, and solemnly wiped a tear from his blinking eyes.

"And every English plepshurk will be kicked out of the country. But that is neither here nor there."

"Neither here nor there," the other assented, with owlish gravity. "But before England is s-sh-s-swept off the map, my lordship, what will happen?"

"My marriage to the jongejuffrouw," Stoutenburg replied curtly. "She hath consented to be my wife, and my wife she will be as soon as I have mind to take her. So you may drink to our union, sirrah. I'll e'en pledge you in a cup."

He poured himself out a goblet of wine, laughing to himself at his own ingenuity. That was the way to treat the smeerlap. Make him feel what a pitiable, abject knave he was! Then show him up before Gilda, just as he was – drunk, ragged, unkempt, an object of derision in his misfortune rather than of pity.

"Nay," the rascal objected, his speech waxing thicker and his hand more unsteady, "I cannot pledge you, my lord, in drinking to your union with my own wife, unless – unless my friend Klaas will drink to that union, too. Mine own brother by the law, you see, my lord, and —"

"Mynheer Nicolaes will indeed drink to his sister's happy union with me," Stoutenburg retorted, with a sneer. "His presence here is a witness to my good intentions toward the wench. So you may drink, sirrah. The jongejuffrouw herself is overwilling to submit to my pleasure —"

But the imperious words were smothered in his throat, giving place to a fierce exclamation of choler. The blind man had at his invitation raised the jug of wine to his lips, but in the act his feet apparently slipped away from under him. The jug flew out of his hand, would have caught the Lord of Stoutenburg on the head had he not ducked just in time. But even so his Magnificence was hit on the shoulder by the heavy crystal vessel, and splashed from head to foot with the wine, whilst Diogenes collapsed on the floor with a shamed and bibulous laugh.

A string of savage oaths and tempestuous abuse poured from Stoutenburg's lips, which were in truth livid with rage. Already Jan had rushed to his assistance, snatched up a serviette from the table, and soon contrived to wipe his lordship's doublet clean.

The blind man in the meanwhile did his best to hoist himself up on his feet once more, clung to the edge of the table; but the sight of him released the last floodgate of Stoutenburg's tempestuous wrath. He turned with a vicious snarl upon the unfortunate man, and it would indeed have fared ill with the defenceless creature, for the Lord of Stoutenburg was not wont to measure his blows by the helplessness of his victims, had not a sudden exclamation from Nicolaes stayed the hand that was raised to strike.

"Gilda!" the young man cried impulsively.

Stoutenburg's arm dropped to his side. He turned toward the door. Gilda had just entered with her father, and was coming slowly down the room.

Chapter XII – Tears, Sighs, Hearts

1

GILDA caught sight of her beloved the moment she entered. To say that their eyes met would indeed be folly. Certain it is, however, that the blind man turned his sightless gaze in her direction. She only gave a gasp, pressed her hands to her heart as if the pain there was unendurable, and at the moment even the beauty of her face was marred by the look of soul-racking misery in her eyes and the quivering lines around her mouth.

The next moment, even while Jan and the soldiers retired, closing the doors behind them, she was in her husband's arms. Ay, even though Stoutenburg tried to intercept her. She did not hear his mocking laugh, or her brother's vigorous protest, nor yet her father's cry of horror. She just clung to him who, blind, fallen, degraded an you will, was still the beloved of her heart, the man to whom she had dedicated her soul.

She swallowed her tears, too proud to allow those who had wrought his ruin to see how mortally she was hurt.

She passed her delicate hands, fragrant as the petals of flowers, over his grimy face, those poor, stricken eyes, the noble brow so deeply furrowed with pain. She murmured words of endearment and of tenderness such as a mother might find to soothe the trouble of a suffering child. All in a moment. Stoutenburg had not even the time to interfere, to utter the savage oaths which rose from his vengeful heart at sight of the loving pity which this beautiful woman lavished on so contemptible an object.

Nor had the blind man time to encircle that exquisite form in his trembling arms. He had put them out at first, with a pathetic gesture of infinite longing. It was just a flash, a vision of his past self, an oblivion of the hideous, appalling present. Her arms at that moment were round his neck, her head against his breast, her soft, fair hair against his lips.

2

Then something happened. A magnetic current seemed to pass through the air. Diogenes freed himself with a sudden jerk from Gilda's clinging arms, staggered back against the table, swaying on his feet and uttering an inane laugh; whilst she, left standing alone, turned wide, bewildered eyes on her brother Nicolaes, who happened to be close to her at the moment. I think that she was near to unconsciousness then, and that she would have fallen, but that the burgomaster stepped quickly to her side and put his arms round her.

"May God punish you," he muttered between his teeth, and turned to Stoutenburg, who had watched the whole scene with a sinister scowl, "for this wanton and unnecessary cruelty!"

"You wrong me, mynheer," Stoutenburg retorted, with a shrug "I but tried to make your daughter's decision easier for her."

Then, as the burgomaster made no reply, but, with grim, set look on his face, drew his daughter gently down to the nearest chair, Stoutenburg went on lightly, speaking directly to Gilda:

"In the course of my travels, mejuffrouw, I came across a wise philosopher in Italy. He was a man whom an adverse fate had robbed of most things that he held precious; but he told me that he had quite succeeded in conquering adversity by the following means. He would gaze dispassionately on the objects of his past desires, see their defects, appraise them at their just value, and in every case he found that their loss was not so irreparable as he had originally believed."

"A fine moral lesson, my lord," the burgomaster interposed, seeing that Gilda either would not or could not speak as yet. "But I do not see its point."

" 'Tis a simple one, mynheer," Stoutenburg retorted coldly. "I pray you, look on the man to whom, an you had your way, you would even now link your daughter."

Instinctively Beresteyn turned his lowering gaze in the direction to which his lordship now pointed with a persuasive gesture. Diogenes was standing beside the table, his powerful frame drawn up to its full height, his sightless eyes blinking and gleaming with weird inconsequence in the flickering light of the candles. His hands were clasped behind his back, and on his face there was a curious expression which the burgomaster was not shrewd enough to define – one of self-deprecation, yet withal of introspection and of detachment, as if the helpless body alone were present and the mind had gone a-roaming in the land of dreams. The burgomaster tried manfully to conceal the look of half-contemptuous pity which, much against his will, had crept into his eyes.

"The man," he rejoined calmly, "is what Fate and a dastard's hand have made him, my lord. Many a fine work of God hath been marred by an evildoer's action."

"That is as may be mynheer," Stoutenburg riposted coolly. "But 'tis of the present and of the future you have to think now – not of the past."

"Even so, my lord, I would sooner see my daughter in the arms of the stricken lion than in those of a wily jackal."

"Am I the wily jackal?" Stoutenburg put in, with a sneer. Then, as the burgomaster made no reply, he added tersely: "I see that the jongejuffrouw hath told you —"

"Everything," Beresteyn assented calmly.

"And that I await your blessing on our union?"

"My blessing you cannot have, my lord, as you well know," the burgomaster retorted firmly. " 'Twas blasphemy to invoke the name of God on such an unholy alliance. My daughter is the lawfully wedded wife of an English gentleman, Sir Percy Blakeney by name, and until the law of this country doth sever those bonds she cannot wed another."

Stoutenburg gave a strident laugh.

"That is, indeed, unfortunate for the English gentleman with the high-sounding name," he said, with a sneer, "whom I gravely suspect of being naught but the common varlet whom we all know so well in Haarlem. But, gentleman or churl," he added, with a cynical shrug, " ' tis all one to me. He hangs to-morrow, unless —"

A loud cry of burning indignation escaped the burgomaster's lips.

"You would not further provoke the wrath of God," he exclaimed, "by this foul and cowardly crime!"

"And why not, I pray you?" the other coolly retorted. "Nor do I think that the Almighty would greatly care what happened to this drunken knave. The refuse of human kind, the halt, the lame, and the blind, are best out of the way."

"A man, my lord," the burgomaster protested, "Who when he had you in his power, generously spared your life!"

"The more fool he!" Stoutenburg riposted drily. " 'Tis my turn now. He hangs to-morrow, unless, indeed —"

"Unless, what, my lord?"

"Unless," Stoutenburg went on, with an evil leer, "my future wife will deign to plead with me for him – with a kiss."

A groan like that of a wounded beast broke from the burgomaster's heavy heart. For a moment a light that was almost murderous gleamed in his eyes. His fists were clenched; he murmured a dark threat against the man who goaded him wellnigh to madness. Then, suddenly, he met Stoutenburg's mocking glance fixed upon him, and a huge sob rose in his throat, almost choking him. Gilda, with a pitiful moan, had hidden her face against her father's sleeve.

" 'Tis but anticipating the happy time by a few hours," Stoutenburg went on, with calm cynicism. "But I have a fancy to hold my future wife in my arms now – at this moment – and to grant her in exchange for her first willing kiss the life of a miserable wretch whose life or death are, in truth, of no account to me."

He took a step or two forward in the direction where Gilda sat, clinging with desperate misery to her father. Then, as the burgomaster, superb with indignation, grand in his dignity,

Instinctively interposed his burly figure between his daughter and the man whom she loathed, Stoutenburg added, with well-assumed carelessness:

"If the jongejuffrouw prefers to put off the happy moment until we are alone in my camp to-morrow, we'll say no more about it. Let the rogue hang; I care not!"

"My lord," – the burgomaster spoke once more in a vigorous protest, which, alas, he knew to be futile – "what you suggest is monstrous, inhuman! God will never permit —"

"I pray you, mynheer," Stoutenburg broke in fiercely, "let us leave the Almighty out of our affairs. I have read my Bible as assiduously as you when I was younger, and in it I learned that God hath enjoined all wives to submit themselves to their husbands. A kiss from my betrothed, a word or gentle pleading, are little enough to ask in exchange for an act of clemency. And you, Heer Burgomaster, do but stiffen my will by your interference. Will you, at least, let the jongejuffrouw decide on the matter for herself, and, in her interests and your own, give to all that she does your unqualified consent!"

"My consent you'll never wring from me, as you well know, my lord. I and my daughter are powerless to withstand your might, but if we bend to the yoke it is because it hath pleased God that we should wear it, not because we submit with a free will. By exulting in such a monstrous crime you do but add to the loathing which we both feel for you —"

"Silence!" Stoutenburg broke in fiercely. "Silence, you dolt! What good, think you, you do yourself or your daughter by provoking me beyond endurance? She knows my decision, and so, methinks, do you. If the jongejuffrouw feels such unqualified hatred for me, let her return to your protecting arms and leave Amersfoort to its fate. As for that sightless varlet, let him hang, I say! I am a fool, indeed to listen to your gibberish! Jan!" he called, and strode to the door with a great show of determination, staking his all now on this card which he had decided to play.

But the card was a winning one, as well he knew. Already Gilda, as if moved by an unseen voice, had jumped to her feet and intercepted him ere he reached the door. Her whole appearance had changed – the expression of her eyes, her tone, her gestures.

"My father is overwrought, my lord," she said firmly. "He hath already promised me that he would offer no opposition to my wishes."

She looked him straight in the eyes, and he returned her gaze, his restless eyes seeming to search her very soul. she had, in truth, changed most markedly. She was, of course, afraid – afraid for that miserable plepshurk's life. But the change was something more than that – at least, Stoutenburg chose to think so. There was something in her glance at this moment that he did not quite understand, that he did not dare understand. A wavering – almost he would have called it a softness, had he dared. He came nearer to her, and, though at first she drew back from him, she presently held her ground, still gazing on him like a bird when it is fascinated and cannot move.

Now he was quite sure that her blue eyes looked less hard, and certainly her mouth was less tightly set. Her lips were slightly parted, and her breath came quick and panting. Ah, women were queer creatures! Had Nicolaes been right when he quoted the English play? Gilda had certainly begun by falling against that contemptible rascal's breast, but since then? Had her wayward fancy been repelled by that whole air of physical degradation which emanated from the once brilliant cavalier, or had it been merely dazzled by visions of power and of wealth, which had their embodiment in him who was her future lord?

He himself could not say. All that he knew, all that he felt of a certainty now, was that he held more than one winning card in this gamble for possession of an exquisite and desirable woman. Still holding her gaze, he took her hands. She did not resist, did not attempt to draw away from him, and he murmured softly:

"What are your wishes, myn engel?"

"To submit to your will, my lord," she replied firmly.

"At last!" he exclaimed, on a note of triumph, drew her still closer to him. "A kiss, fair one, to clinch this bargain, which hath made me the happiest of men!"

He had lost his head for the moment. Satisfaction, and an almost feverish sense of exultation, had turned his blood to liquid fire. All that he saw was this lovely woman, whom he had nearly conquered. Nearly, but not quite. At his desire for a kiss he felt that she stiffened. She closed her eyes, and even her lips became bloodless. She appeared on the verge of a swoon. Bah! Even this phase would pass away. Nicolaes was right. Women reserved their contempt for weaklings. In the end 'twas the master whom they adored.

"A kiss, fair one!" he called again. "And the rogue shall live or hang according as your lips are sweet or bitter!"

He was on the point of snatching that kiss at last, when suddenly there came so violent a crash that the whole room shook with the concussion, and even the windows rattled in their frames. The blind man, more unsteady than ever on his feet, had tried to get hold of a chair, lost his balance in the act, and, in the endeavour to save himself from falling, had lurched so clumsily against the table that it overturned, and all the objects upon it – silver, crystal, china dishes, and candelabra – fell with a deafening clatter on the floor.

Stoutenburg, uttering one of his favourite oaths, had instinctively turned to see whence had come this terrific noise. In turning, his hold on Gilda's wrists had slightly relaxed; sufficiently, at any rate, to enable her to free herself from his grasp and to seek shelter once more beside her father. Diogenes alone had remained unruffled through the commotion. Indeed, he appeared wholly unconscious that he had brought it about. He had collapsed amidst the litter, and now sprawled on the floor, surrounded by a medley of broken glass, guttering candles, hot food and liquor, convulsed with laughter, whist his huge, dark eyes, with the dilated pupils and pale, narrow circles of blue light, looked strangely ghostlike in the gloom.

"Who in thunder," he muttered inarticulately, "is making this confounded din?"

3

At the noise, too, the men had come running in from the hall. The sound had been akin to the detonation of a dozen pistols, and they had rushed along, prepared for a fight. With the fall of the candelabra, the vast banqueting hall had suddenly been plunged into semi-darkness. Only a couple of wax candles in tall sconces, which had originally set on the sideboard, vaguely illumined the disorderly scene.

Diogenes, with his infectious laugh, did in truth succeed in warding off the punishment which his Magnificence already held in preparation for him. As it was, Stoutenburg caught sight of Gilda's look of anxiety, and this at once put him into a rare good humour. He had had his wish. Gilda had been almost kind, had practically yielded to him in the presence of the man whom he desired to humiliate and to wound, as he himself had been humiliated and wounded in the past.

Whether the blind man's keen sense of hearing had taken in every detail of the scene, it was of course impossible to say. But one thing he must have heard – the brief soliloquy at the door, when Gilda, in response to his ardent query. "What are your wishes, myn engel?" had replied quite firmly: "To submit to your will, my lord!" That moment must, in truth, have been more galling and more bitter to the once gallant Laughing Cavalier than the rattle of the rope upon the gallows, or the first consciousness that he was irremediably blind.

Indeed, Stoutenburg had had something more than his wish. To make a martyr of the rogue, he would have told you, was not part of his desire. All that he wanted was to obliterated the man's former brilliant personality from Gilda's mind; that he should henceforth dwell in her memory as she last saw him, abject in his obvious impotence, owing his life to the woman whom he had wooed and conquered in the past with the high hand of a reckless adventurer. After that, the rogue might hang or perish in a ditch: his lordship did not care. What happened to blind men in these days of fighting when none but the best men had a chance to live at all, he had never troubled his head to inquire. At any rate, he knew that a sightless lion was less harmful than a keen-eyed mouse. Ah, in truth he had had more than his wish and satisfied now as to the present and the future, the thought that the moment had come to let well alone, and to remove from Gilda's sight the spectacle which, by some subtle reaction, might turn her heart back to pity for the knave. He gave Jan a significant nod.

But Gilda, whose glowing eyes had watched his every movement, was quick to interpose.

"My lord," she cried in protest, "I hold you to your bargain!"

"Have no fear, myn chat," he answered suavely. I will not repudiate it. The fellow's life is safe enough whilst you and the Heer Burgomaster honour me by supping with me. After that, the decision rests with you. As I said just now, he shall live or hang according as your lips are sweet or bitter. For the nonce, I am wearied and hungry. We'll sup first, so please you."

And Gilda had to stand by whilst she saw her husband dragged away from her presence. He offered no resistance; indeed, accepted the situation with that good-humoured philosophy which was so characteristic of him. But, oh, if she could have conveyed to him by a look all the tenderness, the sorrow, the despair, that was torturing her heart! If she could have run to him just once more, to whisper into his ear those burning words of love which would have eased his pain and hers!

If she could have defied that abominable tyrant who gloated over her misery, and, hand in hand with her beloved, have met death by his side, with his arms around her, her spirit wedded to his, ere they appeared together before the judgement seat of God!

But, as that arrogant despot had reminded her, she had even lost the freedom to die. The destinies of her native city were in her hands. Unless she bowed her willing neck to his will, Amersfoort and all its citizens would be wiped off the face of the earth. And as she watched the chosen of her heart led like a captive lion to humiliation if not to death those monstrous words rang in her ears, that surely must provoke the wrath of God.

Therefore, she watched his departure dry-eyed and motionless. Ay! envying him in her heart, that he, at least, was not called upon to make such an appalling sacrifice as lay now before her. She had indeed come to that sublimity of human suffering that she almost wished to see those dear, sightless eyes closed in their last long sleep, rather than that he should be forced to endure what to him would be ten thousand times worse than death – her submission to that miscreant – her willing union; and he, ignorant of how the tyrant had wrung this submission from her.

Chapter XIII – The Stygian Creek

1

THE Lord or Stoutenburg was conscious of a great feeling of relief when the blind man was finally removed from his presence. While the latter stood there, even in the abjectness of his plight, Stoutenburg felt that he was a living menace to the success of all his well-thought-out schemes. He kept his eyes fixed on Gilda with a warning look, that should be a reminder to her of the immutability of his resolve. He tried, in a manner, to surround her with a compelling fluid that would engulf her resistance and leave her weak and passive to his will.

There was of necessity a vast amount of confusion and din ere order was restored among the debris; and conversation was impossible in the midst of the clatter that was going on – men coming and going, the rattle of silver and glass. Gilda, the while, sat quite still, her blue eyes fixed with strange intensity on the door through which her beloved had disappeared. Her father stood beside her, holding her hand, and she rested her cheek against his.

The burgomaster, throughout the last scene, had not once looked at Diogenes. A dark, puzzled frown lingered between his brows whilst he stared moodily into the fire. He absolutely ignored the presence of his son, putting into practice his stern dictum that henceforth he had no son, whilst Nicolaes, who was becoming inured to his shameful position, put on a careless and jaunty air, spoke with easy familiarity to Stoutenburg, and peremptorily to the men.

Then at last the table was once more set, the candles relit, and the board again spread for supper. Stoutenburg, with an elegant flourish, invited his guests to sit, offered his arm to Gilda to lead her to the table. She, moved by a pathetic desire to conciliate him, a forlorn hope that a great show of submission on her part would soften his cruel heart and lighten the fate of her beloved, placed her hand upon his sleeve, and when she met his admiring glance a slight flush drove the pallor from her cheeks.

"You are adorable, myn geloof!" he murmured.

He appeared highly elated, sat at the head of the table, with Gilda on his right and the burgomaster on his left, whilst Nicolaes sat beside his sister.

The two old crones served the supper, coming and going with a noiselessness and precision acquired in long service in the well-conducted house of the burgomaster. They knew the use of the two pronged silver utensils which Mynheer Beresteyn had acquired of late direct from France, where they were used at the table of gentlemen of quality for conveying food to the mouth. They knew how to remove each service from the centre of the table without unduly disturbing the guests, and how to replace one cloth with another the moment it became soiled with sauce or wine.

Jan stood at the Lord of Stoutenburg's elbow and served him personally and with his own hands. Every dish, before it was handed to his lordship, was placed in front of the burgomaster, who was curtly bidden to taste of it. His Magnificence, adept in the poisoner's art, was taking no risks himself.

The cook had done his best, and the supper was, I believe, excellent. The Oille, the most succulent of dishes, made up of quails, capons, and ducks and other tasty meats, was a marvel of gastronomic art, and so were the tureens of beef with cucumber and the breast of veal larded and garnished with hard-boiled eggs. In truth it was all a terrible waste, and sad to see such excellent fare laid before guests who hardly would touch a morsel. Gilda could not eat, her throat seemed to close up every time she tried to swallow. Indeed, she had to appeal to the very last shred of her pride to keep up a semblance of dignity before her enemy. The burgomaster, too, flushed with shame at the indignity put upon him, did no more than taste of the dishes as they were put before him by the surly Jan.

The Lord of Stoutenburg, on the other hand, put up a great show of hilarity, talked much and drank deeply, discussed in a loud, arrogant voice with Nicolaes the Archduchess's plans for the subduing of the Netherlands. And Nicolaes, after he had imbibed two or three bumpers of heady Spanish wine, felt more assured, returned Gilda's reproachful glances with indifference, and his father's contempt with defiance.

2

What Gilda suffered it were a vain attempt to describe. How she contrived to remain at the table; to appear indifferent almost gay; to glance up now and again at a persuasive challenge from Stoutenburg, will for ever remain her secret. She never spoke of that hour, of that hateful, harrowing supper, like an odious nightmare, which was wont in after years to sent a shudder of horror right through her whenever she recalled it.

The burgomaster remained at first obstinately silent, whilst the Lord of Stoutenburg talked with studied insolence of the future of the Netherlands. The happy times would now come back, the traitor vowed, when the United Provinces, dissolved into feeble and separate entities, without form or governance, would once more return to their allegiance and bow the knee before the might of Spain; when the wholesome rule of another Alva would teach these stiffnecked and presumptuous burghers that comfort and a measure of welfare could only be obtained by unconditional surrender and submission to a high, unconquerable Power.

"Freedom!" Liberty!" he sneered. "Ancient Charters! Bah! Empty, swaggering words, I say, which their masters will soon force them to swallow. Then will follow an era more suited to all this beggarly Dutch rabble, one that will teach them a lesson which will at last stick in their memories. The hangman, that's what they want! The stake! The rack! Our glorious Inquisition, and the relentlessness which, alas, for the nonce hath lain buried with our immortal Alva!"

He drank a loyal toast to the coming new era, to the Archduchess, to King Philip IV, who in his glorious reign would see Spain once more unconquered, the Netherlands subdued, England punished at last. Nicolaes joined him with many a lustful shout, whilst the burgomaster sat with set lips, his eyes glowing with suppressed indignation. Once or twice it seemed as if his stern self-control would give way, as if his burning wrath would betray him into words and deeds that might cause abysmal misery to hundreds of innocent people whilst not serving in any way the cause which he would have given his life to uphold.

Indeed, in the book of heroic deeds of which God's angel hath a record, none stand out more brilliantly than the endurance of the Burgomaster of Amersfoort and of his daughter on this memorable occasion. Nor is there in the whole valorous history of the Netherlands a more glorious page than that which tells of the sacrifice made by father and daughter in order to save the city which they loved from threatened annihilation.

3

But like all things, good and evil, the trial came to an end at last. The Lord of Stoutenburg gave the signal, and the burgomaster and Gilda rose from the table both, in truth, with a deep sigh of thankfulness.

Stoutenburg remained deferential until the end – deferential, that is, with an undercurrent of mockery, which he took no pains to conceal, His bow, as he finally took leave of his guests, bidding the burgomaster a simple farewell and Gilda au revoir until the dawn on the morrow, was so obviously ironical that Beresteyn was goaded into an indignant tirade, which he regretted almost as soon as he had uttered it.

"Let him who stands," he said firmly, and with all of his wonted dignity, "take heed lest he fall. The Netherlands are not conquered yet, my lord, because your mercenary troops have succeeded, for the time being, in overrunning one of her provinces. Ede may have fallen. Amersfoort may for the moment, be under your heel –"

"Arnheim and Nijmegen may have capitulated by now," Stoutenburg broke in derisively. "Sold to De Berg, like Amersfoort and Ede, by the craven smeerlap to whom you have given your daughter."

"Even that may have happened," the burgomaster riposted hotly, "if so be the will of God. But we are a race of fighters. We have beaten and humiliated the Spaniard and driven him from off our land before now. And Maurice of Nassau, the finest captain of the age, is unconquered still!"

"Mightily sick, so I'm told," the other put in carelessly. "He was over-ready, methinks, to abandon Amersfoort to its fate."

"Only to punish you more effectually in the end. Take heed, my lord, take heed! The multiplicity of your crimes will find you out soon enough."

" 'Sblood!" retorted Stoutenburg, unperturbed; "but you forget, mynheer burgomaster, that, whate'er betide me, your daughter's fate is henceforth linked to mine own."

Then it was that Beresteyn repented of his outburst, for indeed he had gained nothing by it, and Stoutenburg had used the one argument which was bound to silence him. What, in truth, was the use of wrangling? Dignity was sure to suffer, and that mocking recreant would only feel that his triumph was more complete.

Even now he only laughed, pointed with an ironical flourish of his arm to the widely open doors, through which in the dimly lighted hall, a group of men could be perceived, sitting or standing around the centre table, with Diogenes standing in their midst, his fair head crowned by the hideous bandage, and his broad shoulders towering above the puny, swarthy Spanish soldiery. He had a mug of ale in his hand, and holding it aloft he was singing a ribald song, the refrain of which was taken up by the men. In the vague and flickering light of resin torches, his sightless orbs looked spectral, like those of a wraith.

"You should be grateful to me, mynheer," Stoutenburg added with a sneer, "for freeing your daughter from such a yoke."

He returned to Gilda, took her unresisting hand and raised it to his lips. Above it, he was watching her face. She was looking beyond him, straight at the blind man; and though Stoutenburg at that moment would have bartered much for the knowledge of what was in her thoughts, he could not define the expression of her eyes. At one time he thought that they had softened, that the fulfilment of all his hopes was hanging once more in the balance. It seemed for the moment as if she would snatch away her hand and seek shelter, as she had done before, against the heart of her beloved; that right through that outer husk of misery and degradation she saw something that puzzled her rather than repelled. A question seemed to be hovering on her lips. A question of a protest. Or was it a mute appeal for forgiveness?

Stoutenburg could not tell. But he felt that for a space of a few seconds the whole edifice of his desires was tottering, that Fate might, after all, still be holding a thunderbolt in store for him, which would hurl him down from the pinnacle of this momentary triumph. Gilda – as a woman – was still unconquered. Neither her heart nor her soul would ever be his. Somehow it was the glance wherewith she regarded the blind man that told the Lord of Stoutenburg this one unalterable fact.

The sortilege which he had tried to evoke, by letting her look on the pitiful wreck who had once been her lover, had fallen short in its potent charm. His own brilliant prospects, his masterful personality, ay, his well-assumed indifference, had all failed to cast their spells over her. Unlike the valiant Petruchio of the English play, he had not yet succeeded in taming this beautiful shrew. In the past she had resisted his blandishments; if she succumbed at all, it would be beneath the weight of his tyranny.

Well, so be it! Nicolaes, no doubt, had been right when he said that women reserved their disdain for weaklings. It was the man of iron who won a woman's love. The thought sent a fierce glow of hatred coursing through his blood. Mythical and fatalistic as he was, he believed that his lucky star would only begin to rise when he had succeeded in winning Gilda for his own. He had deemed women an easy conquest in the past. This one could not resist him for long. Even men were wont to come readily under his way – witness Nicolaes Beresteyn, who was as wax in his hands. In the past, he had delighted in wielding a kind of cabalistic power, which he undoubtedly possessed, over many a weak or shifty character. His mother even was wont to call him a magician, and stood not a little in awe of the dark-visaged, headstrong child, and later on of the despotic, lawless youth, who had set the crown on her manifold sorrows by his callousness and his crimes.

That power had been on the wane of late. But it was not – could not – be gone from him forever. Nicolaes was still his sycophant. Jan and his kind were willing to go to death for him. His own brain had devised a means for bringing that obstinate burgomaster and the beautiful Gilda to their knees. Then, of a surety, in the Cornucopia of Fate there was something more comforting, more desirable, than a thunderbolt!

Was he not a man the master of his destiny?

Bah! What was a woman's love, after all? Why not let her go – be content with worldly triumphs? The sacking of Amersfoort, which would yield him wealth and treasure; the gratitude of the Archduchess: a high – if not the highest – position in the reconquered provinces! Why not be content with those? And Stoutenburg groaned like a baffled tiger, because in his heart of hearts he knew these things would not content him in the end. He wanted Gilda! Gilda, of the blue eyes and the golden hair, the demure glance and fragrant hands. His desire for her was in his bones, and he felt that he would indeed go raving mad if he lost her after this – if that beggarly drunkard, unwashed, dishonoured, and stricken with blindness, triumphed through his very abasement and the magnitude of his misfortune.

"This, at any rate, I can avert!" he murmured under his breath. And somehow the thought eased the racking jealousy that was torturing him – jealousy of such an abject thing. He waited until Gilda had passed out of the room, and when she was standing in the hall, so obviously bidding a last farewell in her heart to the man she loved so well, he called peremptorily to Jan:

"Take the varlet," he commanded roughly, "and hang him on the Koppel-poort!"

At the word Gilda turned on him like an infuriated tigress. Pushing past her father, past the men, who recoiled from her as if from a madwoman, she was back beside the execrable despot who thus put the crown on his hideous cruelties.

"Your bargain, my lord!" she cried hoarsely. "You dare not – you dare not —"

"My bargain, fair one?" Stoutenburg retorted coolly. "Nay, you were so averse to fulfilling your share of it, that I have repented me of proposing it. The varlet hangs. That is my last word."

His last word! And Jan so ready to obey! The men were already closing in around her beloved; less than a minute later they had his hands securely pinioned behind his back. Can you wonder that she lost her head, that she fought to free herself from her father's arms, and, throwing reserve, dignity to the winds, threw herself at the feet of that inhuman monster and pleaded with him as no woman on earth had, mayhap, ever pleaded before?

We do not like to think of that exquisite, refined woman kneeling before such an abominable dastard. Yet she did it! Words of appeal, of entreaty, poured from her quivering lips. She raised her tear-stained face to his, embraced his knees with her arms. She forgot the men that stood by, puzzled and vaguely awed – Jan resolute, her father torn to the heart. She forgot everything save that there was a chance – a remote chance – of softening a cruel heart, and she could not – no, could not! – see the man she loved dragged to shameful death before her eyes.

She promised – oh, she promised all that she had to give!

"I'll be your willing slave, my lord, in all things," she pleaded, her voice broken and hoarse. "Your loving wife, as you desire. A kiss from me? Take it, an you will. I'll not resist! Nay, I'll return it from my heart, in exchange for your clemency."

Then it was that the burgomaster succeeded at last in tearing her away from her humiliating position. He dragged her to her feet, drew her to his breast, tried by words and admonition to revive in her her sense of dignity and her self-control. Only with one word did he, in his turn, condescend to plead.

"An you have a spark of humanity left in you, my lord," he said loudly, "order your executioners to be quick about their business."

For the Lord of Stoutenburg had, with a refinement of cruelty almost unbelievable, were it not a matter of history, stayed Jan from executing his inhuman order.

"Wait!" his glittering eyes appeared to say to the sycophant henchman who hung upon his looks. "Let me enjoy this feast until I am satiated."

Then, when Gilda lay at last, half-swooning in the shelter of her father's arms, he said coolly:

"Have I not said, fair one, that if you deigned to plead the rascal should not hang? See! The potency of your charm upon my sensitive heart! The man who hath always been my most bitter enemy, and whom at last I have within my power, shall live because your fair arms did encircle my knees, and because of your free will you offered me a kiss. Mynheer Burgomaster," he added, with easy condescension, "I pray you lead your daughter to her room. She is over-wrought and hath need of rest. Go in peace, I pray you. That drunken varlet is safe now in my hands."

The burgomaster could not trust himself to reply. Only his loving hands wandered with a gentle, soothing gesture over his beloved daughter's hair, whilst he murmured soft, endearing words in her ear. Gradually she became more calm, was able to gather her wits together, to realize what she had done and all that she had sacrificed, probably in vain. Stoutenburg had spoken soft words, but how could she trust him, who had ever proved himself a liar and a cheat? She was indeed like a miserable, captive bird, held, maimed and bruised, in a cruel trap set by vengeful and cunning hands. It seemed almost incredible why she should be made to suffer so.

What had she done? In what horrible way had she sinned before God, that His hand should lie so heavily upon her? Even her sacrifice – sublime and selfless – failed to give her the consolation of duty nobly accomplished. Everything before her was dreary and dark. Life itself was nought but torture. The few days – hours – that must intervene until she knew that Amersfoort was safe confronted her like the dark passage into Gehenna. Beyond them lay death at last, and she, a young girl scarce out of adolescence, hitherto rich, beautiful, adulated, was left to long for that happy release from misery with an intensity of longing akin to the sighing of souls in torment.

Chapter XIV – Treachery

1

Throughout this harrowing scene the blind man had stood by, pinioned, helpless, almost lifeless in his immobility. The only sign of life in him seemed to be in those weird, sightless orbs, in which the flickering light of the resin torches appeared to draw shafts of an unearthly glow. He was pinioned and could not move. Half a dozen soldiers had closed in around him. Whether he heard all that went on, many who were there at the time declared it to be doubtful. But, even if he heard, what could he have done? He could not even put his hands up to his ears to shut out that awful sound of his beloved wife's hoarse, spent voice pleading desperately for him.

One of the men who was on guard over him told De Voocht afterwards that he could hear the tough sinews cracking against the bonds that held the giant captive, and that great drops of sweat appeared upon the fine, wide brow. When Gilda, leaning heavily upon her father's arm, finally mounted the stairs which led up to her room, the blind man turned his head in that direction. But the jongejuffrouw went on with head bent and did not glance down in response.

All this we know from De Voocht, who speaks of it in his "Brieven." But he was not himself present on the scene and hath it only from hearsay. He questioned several of the men subsequently as he came in contact with them, and, of course, the burgomaster's testimony was the most clear and the most detailed. Mynheer Beresteyn admitted that, throughout that awful, ne'er-to-be-forgotten evening, he could not understand the blind man's attitude, was literally tortured with doubts of him. Was he, in truth, the craven wretch which he appeared to be – the miserable traitor who had sold the Stadtholder's original plans to De Berg, betrayed Marquet and De Keysere, and hopelessly jeopardized the whole of Gelderland, if not the entire future of the Netherlands? If so, he was well-deserving of the gallows, which would not fail to be his lot.

But was he? Was he?

The face, of course, out of which the light of the eyes had vanished, was inscrutable. The mouth, remember, was partially hidden by the three days' growth of beard, and grime and fatigue had further obliterated all other marks of expression. Of course, the man must have suffered tortures of humiliation and rage, which would effectually deaden all physical pain. But at the time he seemed not to suffer. Indeed, at one moment it almost seemed if he were asleep, with sightless eyes wide open, and standing on his feet.

2

After Gilda and her father had disappeared on the floor above, the Lord of Stoutenburg, like a wild and caged beast awaiting satisfaction, began pacing up and down the long banqueting-hall. The doors leading into it from the hall had been left wide open, and the men could see his lordship in his restless wanderings, his heavy boots ringing against the reed-covered floor. He held his arms folded across his chest, and was gnawing – yes, gnawing – his knuckles in the excess of his excitement and his choler.

Then he called Jan, and parleyed with him for awhile, consulted Mynheer Nicolaes, who was more taciturn and gloomy than ever before.

The soldiers knew what was coming. They had witnessed the scene between the jongejuffrouw and his Magnificence and some of them who had wives and sweethearts of their own, had felt uncomfortable lumps, at the time, in their throats. Others, who had sons, fell to wishing that their offsprings might be as finely built, as powerful as that poor, blind, intoxicated wretch who, in truth, now had no use for his magnificent muscles.

But what would you? These were troublous times. Life was cheap – counted for nothing in sight of such great gentlemen as was the Lord of Stoutenburg. The varlet, it seems, had offended his lordship awhile ago. Jan knew the story, and was very bitter about it, too. Well, no man could expected to be treated with gentleness by a great lord whom he had been fool enough to offend. The blind rascallion would hang, of that there could be no doubt. The jongejuffrouw had been pacified with soft words and vague promises, but the rascal would hang. Any man there would have bet his shirt on the issue. You had only to look at his lordship. A more determined, more terrifying look it were impossible to meet. Even Jan looked a little scared. When his Magnificence looked like that it boded no good to any one. All the rancour, the gall, that had accumulated in his heart against everything that pertained to the United Provinces and to their Stadtholder would effectively smother the slightest stirring of conscience or pity. Perhaps, when the jongejuffrouw knelt at his feet, he had thought of his mother, who, equally distraught and equally humiliated, had knelt in vain at the Stadtholder's feet, pleading for the life of her sons. Oh, yes, all that had made the Lord of Stoutenburg terribly hard and callous.

But the men were sorry for the blind vagabond, for all that. He had had nothing to do with the feuds between the Stadtholder and the sons of Olden Barneveldt. He had done nothing, seemingly, save to win the love of the beautiful lady whom his Magnificence had marked for his own. He was brave, too. You could not help admiring him as he stood between you and your comrades, his head thrown back, a splendid type of virility and manhood. Half-seas over he may have been. His misfortunes were, in truth, enough to make any man take a drink; but you could not help but see that there was an air of spirituality about the forehead and the sensitive nostrils which redeemed the face from any suggestion of sensuality. And now and again a quaint smile would play round the corners of his mouth, and the whole wan face would light up as if with a sudden whimsical thought.

Then all at once he threw back his head and yawned.

Such a droll fellow! Yawning on the brink of eternity! It was, in truth, a pity he should hang!

3

Yes, the blind man yawned, loudly and long, like one who is ready for bed. And the harmless sound completed Stoutenburg's exasperation. He once more gave the harsh word of command:

"Take the varlet out and hang him!"

Obviously this time it would be irrevocable. There was no one here to plead, and there was Jan, stolid and grim as was his wont, already at attention under the lintel – a veritable tower of strength in support of his chief's decisions.

Jan was not in the habit of arguing with his lordship. This, or any other order, was as one to him. As for the blind vagabond – well, Jan was as eager as his Magnificence to get the noose around the rascal's throat. There were plenty of old scores to settle between them – the humiliation of three months ago, which had sent Stoutenburg, disgraced and a fugitive, out of the land, had hit Jan severely, too.

And that never-to-be-forgotten discomfiture was entirely due to this miserable caitiff, who, indeed would get naught but his deserts.

The task, in truth, was a congenial one to Jan. A blind man was easy enough to deal with, and this one offered but little resistance. He had been half-asleep, it seems, and only woke to find himself on the brink of eternity. Even so, his good-humour did not forsake him.

"Odd's fish!" he exclaimed when, roughly shaken from his somnolence, he found himself in the hands of the soldiery. "I had forgotten this hanging business. You might have left a man to finish his dreams in peace."

He appeared dazed, and his speech was thick. He had been drinking heavily all the evening, and, save for an odd moment or so of lucid interval, he had been hopelessly fuddled all along. And he was merry in his cups; laughter came readily to his lips; he was full of quips and sallies, too, which kept the men in rare good-humour. In truth, the fellow would joke and sing apparently until the hangman's rope smothered all laughter in his throat.

But he had an unquenchable thirst; entreated the men to bring him a jug of wine.

"Spanish wine," he pleaded. "I dote on Spanish wine, but had so little of it to drink in my day. That villainous rascal Pythagoras – some of you must have known the pot-bellied loon – would always seize all there was to get. He and Socrates. Two scurvy runagates who should hang 'stead o' me. Give me a mug of wine, for mercy's sake!"

The men had none to give, and the matter was referred to Jan.

"Not another drop!" Jan declared with unanswerable finality. "The knave is quite drunk enough as it is."

"Ah!" the blind man protested with ludicrous vehemence. "But there thou'rt wrong, worthy Jan. No man is ever – is ever drunk enough. He may be top-heavy, he may be as drunk as a lord, or as fuddled as David's sow. He may be fuzzy, fou, or merely sottish; but sufficiently drunk? No!"

A shout of laughter from the men greeted this solemn pronouncement. Jan shrugged his shoulders impatiently.

"Well, that is as may be!" he rejoined gruffly. "But not another drop to drink wilt thou get from me."

"Oh, Jan," the poor man protested, with a pitiable note of appeal, "my good Jan, think on it! I am about to hang! Wouldst refuse the last request of a dying man?"

"Thou'rt about to hang," Jan assented, unmoved. "Therefore, 'twere a pity to waste good liquor on thee."

"I'll pay the well, my good Jan," Diogenes put in, with a knowing wink of his sightless eyes.

"Pay me?" Jan retorted, with a grim laugh. " 'Tis not much there's left in thy pockets, I'm thinking."

"No," the blind man agreed, nodding gravely. "These good men here did, in truth – empty my pockets effectually awhile ago. 'Twas not with coin I meant to repay thee, good Jan —"

"With what, then?"

"Information, Jan!" the blind man replied, sinking his voice to a hoarse whisper. "Information for the like of which his Lordship of Stoutenburg would give his ears."

Jan laughed derisively. The men laughed openly. They thought this but another excellent joke on the part of the droll fellow.

"Bah! Jan said, with a shrug of the shoulder. "How should a varlet like thee know aught of which his lordship hath not full cognisance already?"

"His lordship," the other riposted quickly, even whilst a look of impish cunning overspread his face – "his lordship never was in the confidence of the Stadtholder. I was!"

"What hath the Stadtholder to do with the matter?"

"Oh, nothing, nothing!" the blind man replied airily. "Thou art obstinate, my good Jan, and 'tis not I who would force thee to share a secret for the possession of which, let me assure thee, his lordship would repay me not only with a tankard of his best wine, but with my life! Ay, and with a yearly pension of one thousand guilders to boot."

These last few words he had spoken quite slowly and with grave deliberation, his head nodding sagely while he spoke. The look of cunning in those spectral orbs had lent to his pale, wan face an air of elfin ghoulishness. He was swaying on his feet, and now and again the men had to hold him up, for he was on the very point of measuring his length on the hall floor.

Jan did not know what to make of it all. Obviously the man was drunk. But not so drunk that he did not know what he was talking about. And the air of cunning suggested that there was something alive in the fuddled brain. Jan looked across the hall in the direction of the banqueting-room.

The doors were wide open, and he could see that his lordship, who at first had paced up and down the long room like a caged beast, had paused quite close to the door, then advanced on tip-toe out into the hall, where he had remained for the last minute or two, intent and still, with eager, probing glance fixed upon the blind man. Now, when Jan questioned him with a look, he gave his faithful henchman a scarce perceptible sign, which the latter was quick enough to interpret correctly.

"Thou dost set my mouth to water," he said to the blind man, with well-assumed carelessness, "By all this talk of yearly pensions and of guilders. I am a poor man, and not so young as I was. A thousand guilders a year would keep me in comfort for the rest of my life."

"Yet art so obstinate," Diogenes riposted with a quaint, inane laugh, "as to deny me a tankard of Spanish wine, which might put thee in possession of my secret – a secret, good Jan, worth yearly pensions and more to his lordship."

"How do I know thou'rt not a consummate liar?" Jan protested gruffly.

"I am!" the other riposted, wholly unruffled. "I am! Lying hath been my chief trade ever since I was breeched. Had I not lied to the Stadtholder he would not have entrusted his secrets to me, and I could not have bartered those secrets for a tankard of good Spanish wine."

"Thy vaunted secrets may not be worth a tankard of wine."

"They are, friend Jan, they are! Try them and see."

"Well, let's hear them and, if they are worth it, I'll pay thee with a tankard of his lordship's best Oporto."

But the blind man shook his head with owlish solemnity.

"And then sell them to his lordship," he retorted, "for pensions and what not, whilst thine own hand, mayhap, puts the rope around my neck. No, no, my good Jan, say no more about it. I'd as lief see his lordship and thee falling into the Stadtholder's carefully laid trap, and getting murdered in your beds, even while I am on my journey to kingdom come."

"Who is going to murder us?" Jan queried, frowning and puzzled, trying to get his cue once more from his master. "And how?"

"I'll not tell thee," the blind man replied, with a quick turn to that obstinacy which so oft pertains to the drunkard, "not if thou wert to plunge me in a bath of best Oporto."

Some of the men began to murmur.

"We might all share?" one or two of them suggested.

"Let's hear what it is," others declared.

"I'll tell thee, knave, what I'll do," Jan rejoined decisively. "I'll bring thee a tankard of Oporto to loosen thy tongue. Then, if thy secret is indeed as important as thou dost pretend, I'll see that the hangman is cheated of thy carcass."

For awhile the blind man pondered.

"Loosen my hands then, friend Jan," he said, "for, in truth, I am trussed like a fowl; then let's feel the handle of that tankard. After that we'll talk."

4

The soldiers sat around the table, watching the blind man with grave attention. At a sign from Jan they soon loosened his bonds. There was something magnetic in the air just then, something that sent sensitive nerves aquiver, and of which these rough fellow were only vaguely conscious. They could not look on that drunken loon without laughing. He was more comical than ever now, with that air of bland beatitude upon his face as his slender fingers closed around the handle of the tankard which Jan had just placed in his hand.

"I would sell my soul for a butt of this nectar," he said; and drank in the odour of the wine with every sign of delight, even before he raised the tankard to his lips.

The Lord of Stoutenburg watched the blind man, too. A deep furrow between his brows testified to the earnest concentration of his thoughts. The man knew something, or thought he knew, of that his lordship could not be in doubt. The question was, was that knowledge of such importance as the miserable wretch averred, or was he merely, like any rogue who sees the rope dangling before his eyes, trying to gain a respite, by proposing vain bargains or selling secrets that had only found birth in his own fuddled brain. Stoutenburg, remember, was no psychologist. Indeed, psychology did not exist as a science in these days when men were over-busy with fighting, and had no time or desire to probe into the inner workings of one another's soul.

On the other hand, here was a man, thus his lordship argued to himself, who might know something of the Stadtholder's plans. He was wont, before he rolled so rapidly down the hill of manhood and repute, to be an inimate of Maurice of Nassau. He might, as lately as yesterday, have been initiated into the great soldier's plans for repelling this sudden invasion of the land which he had thought secure. The Stadtholder, in truth, was not the man to abandon all efforts at resistance just because his original plans had failed.

True, the attempt to rescue Arnheim and Nijmegen had ended in smoke. Marquet and De Keysere were, thanks to timely warning, being held up somewhere by the armies of Isembourg and De Berg. But Maurice of Nassau would not of a certainty, thus lightly abandon all hopes of saving Gelderland. He must have formulated a project, and Stoutenburg, who was no fool, was far from underestimating the infinite brain power and resourcefulness of that peerless commander. Whether he had communicated that project to this besotted oaf was another matter.

Stoutenburg searched the blind man's face with an intent glance that seemed to probe the innermost thoughts behind that fine, wide brow. For the moment, the face told him nothing. It was just vacant, the sightless eyes shone with delight, and the tankard raised to the lips effectually hid all expression around the mouth.

Well, there was not much harm done, the waste of a few moments, if the information proved futile. Jan was ready with the rope, if the whole thing proved to be a mere trick for putting off the fateful hour. As the Lord of Stoutenburg gazed on the blind man, trying vainly to curb his burning impatience, he instinctively thought of Gilda. Gilda, and his hopeless wooing of her, her coldness toward him and her passionate adherence to this miserable caitiff, who, in truth, had thrown dust in her eyes by an outward show of physical courage and a mock display of spurious chivalry.

What if the varlet had been initiated in the Stadtholder's projects? What if he betrayed them now – sold them in exchange for his own worthless life, and stood revealed, before all the world, as an abject coward, as base as any Judas who would sell his master for thirty pieces of silver? The thought turned the miscreant giddy, so dazzling did this issue appear before his mental vision. What a revelation for a fond and loyal woman, who had placed so worthless an object on a pinnacle of valour! What a disillusionment! She had staunchly believed in his integrity up to now. But after this?

In truth, what more can a man desire than to see the honour of a rival smirched in the eyes of a woman who spurns him? That was the main thought that coursed through Stoutenburg's brain, driving before it all obstinacy and choler, ay, even soothing his exacerbated nerves.

He gave a sign to Jan.

"Bring that varlet here to me," he commanded. "I'll speak to him myself."

The sound of his voice chased the look of beatitude from the blind man's face, which took on an expression of bewildered surprise.

"I had no thought his lordship was here," he said, with a self-conscious, inane laugh.

The men were murmuring audibly. Some of them had seen visions of good reward, shared amongst them all, after the blind man had been made to speak. But Jan paid no heed to their discontent. In a trice he had seen the blind man secure once more, with arms tied as before behind his back. Diogenes had uttered a loud cry of protest when the empty tankard was torn out of his hand.

"Jan," he shouted, in a thick, hoarse voice, "if thou'rt a knave and dost not keep faith with me, the devil himself will run away with thee."

"His Magnificence will hear what thou hast to say," Jan retorted gruffly. "After that, we'll see."

He led the prisoner through into the banqueting-hall, and despite the men's murmurings, he closed the door upon them. He sat the blind man down in a chair, opposite his lordship. The poor loon had begun to whimper softly, just like a child, and continued to appeal pitiably to Jan.

"If his lordship is satisfied," he murmured confidingly, "you'll see to it, Jan, that I do not hang."

"Jan has his orders!" his lordship put in roughly. "But take heed, sirrah! If your information is worth having, you may go to hell your own way; I care nought! But remember," he added, with slow and stern emphasis, "if you trick me in this, 'twil not be the rope for you at dawn – but the stake!

Diogenes gave a quick shudder.

"By the lord," he said blandly, "how very unpleasant! But I am a man of my word. Jan put good wine into me. He shall be paid for it. And I'll tell you what the Stadtholder hath planned for the defeat of the Lord of Stoutenburg."

"Well," his lordship retorted curtly. "I wait!"

There was silence for a moment whilst the blind man apparently collected his thoughts. He sat, trussed and helpless in the chair, with his head thrown back, and the full light of the candles playing upon his pale face – the latter still vacant and with a childish expression of excitement about those weird, dark orbs. The Lord of Stoutenburg, master of the situation, sat in a high-backed chair opposite him, his chin resting in his hand, his eyes, glowering and fierce, searching that strange, mysterious face before him. Strange and mysterious, in truth, with those sightless eyes, that glittered uncannily whenever the flickering candle-light caught the abnormally dilated pupils, and those quavering lips which every moment broke into a whimsical and inane smile.

"Jan, my friend," the blind man asked after a while, "art here?"

"Ay!" Jan replied gruffly. "I'm here right enough to see that thou'rt up to no mischief."

"How can I be that, worthy Jan?" the other retorted blandly, "since thou hast again trussed me like a capon?"

"Well, the sooner thou hast satisfied his lordship," Jan rejoined with stolid indifference, "the sooner thou wilt be free —"

"To go to hell mine own way!" Diogenes put in with a hiccough. "So his lordship hath pledged his word. Let all those who are my friends bear witness that his lordship did pledge his word."

He paused, and once again a look of impish cunning over-spread his face. He seemed to be preparing for a fateful moment which literally would mean life or death for him. An exclamation of angry impatience from Stoutenburg recalled him to himself.

"I am ready," he protested with eager servility, "to do his lordship's pleasure."

"Then speak, man!" Stoutenburg retorted savagely, "ere I wring the words from thee with torture!"

"I was only thinking how to put the matter clearly," Diogenes protested blandly. "The Stadtholder only outlined his plan to me. There was so little time. My friend Klaas will remember that after his Highness's horse bolted across the moor I was able to stop it —"

"Yes – curse your interference!" Stoutenburg muttered between his teeth.

"Amen to that!" the blind man assented. "But for it, I should still have the privilege of beholding your lordship's pleasing countenance. But at the moment I had no thought save to stop a runaway horse. The Stadtholder was mightily excited, scented that a trap had been laid for him. My friend Klaas again will remember that, after his Highness dismounted he stopped to parley with me upon the moor."

Nicolaes nodded.

"Then it was," Diogenes went on, "that he told what he meant to do. I was, of course, to bear my part in the new project, which was to make a feint upon Ede —"

"A feint upon Ede?"

"Ay! A surprise attack, which would keep De Berg, who is in Ede, busy whilst the Stadtholder —"

"Bah!" Stoutenburg broke in contemptuously, "De Berg is too wary to be caught by a feint."

"So he is, my lord, so he is!" Diogenes rejoined with solemn gravity. "But if I were to tell you that the surprise attack is to be made in full force, and that the weight will fall on the south side of the town, what then?"

"I do not see with what object."

"Yet you, my lord, would know the Stadtholder's tactics of old. You fought under his banner – once."

"Before he murdered my father, yes!" Stoutenburg broke in impatiently. He did not relish this allusion to his former fighting days, before black treachery had made him betray the ruler he once served. "But what of that?"

"For then your lordship would remember," the blind man went on placidly, "that the Stadtholder's favorite plan was always to draw the enemy away by a ruse from his own chief point of attack."

"But where would the chief point of attack be in this case?" Stoutenburg queried with a frown.

"At a certain molen your lordship wot of on the Veluwe."

"Impossible!"

"Oh, impossible? Your lordship is pleased to jest. Some days ago, spies came into Utrecht with the information that the Lord of Stoutenburg had his camp at an old molen, which stands disused and isolated on the highest point of the Veluwe, somewhere between Apeldoorn and Barneveld."

"My camp? Bah! The mill was only a halting place —"

"The spies averred, my lord," the blind man broke in blandly, "that vast stores of arms and ammunition are accumulated in that halting-place. And that the attack on Amersfoort was planned within its rickety walls."

Then, as the Lord of Stoutenburg made no comment on this – indeed, he had cast a rapid, significant glance on Nicolaes, who throughout this colloquy had appeared as keen, as interested, as his friend – the blind man went on slowly:

"The Stadtholder's objective is the molen on the Veluwe."

"What? From Ede!" Nicolaes exclaimed.

"No, no! Have I not said that the attack on Ede would be a feint? It will be the Stadtholder himself who, with a comparatively small force, will push on toward Barneveld and the molen, and at once cut off all communication between Ede and Amersfoort."

"I understand," Stoutenburg rejoined, with a grave nod. "But if it is a small force we can easily —"

"You can now," Diogenes assented coolly, "since you are warned."

"Quite right! Eh, friend Nicolaes?" his lordship retorted, and strove to let his harsh voice express a world of withering contempt. "If all this is not a trick you varlet hath served us well. What say you? Shall we let him go to hell his own way, and save the hangman a deal of pother?"

"If it all prove true," Nicolaes put in cautiously. "But what proof have we?"

"None, in truth. Nor would I let this craven vagabond out of Jan's sight until we do make sure that he hath not lied. But there'll be no harm in being prepared. Here, sirrah!" his lordship continued, once more addressing the blind man. "With how strong a force doth the Stadtholder propose to cut us off from Ede?"

But, during this brief colloquy between the two friends, the blind man had begun to nod. His head fell forward on his chest, the heavy lids veiled the stricken eyes, and anon a peaceable snore came through the partially open mouth. Stoutenburg swore, as was his wont, the moment his choler was roused, and Jan shook the prisoner roughly by the shoulder.

"Eh? Eh? What?" the latter queried, blinked his sightless eyes, and turned a pale and startled face vaguely from side to side. "What is it? Where's that confounded —?

"Answer his lordship's question!" Jan commanded briefly.

"Question? What question? Your lordship must forgive me. I am so fatigued, and that tankard of—"

"I asked thee, knave," Stoutenburg broke in impatiently, "with how strong a force the Stadtholder proposed to cut us off from Ede?"

"Call it four thousand, my lord," the blind man babbled, "and let me go to sleep"

"You shall sleep till Judgement Day when I've done with you, sirrah! Will the Stadtholder lead that force in person?"

The blind man winked and blinked, tried to collect his thoughts, which apparently had all wandered off toward the Land of Nod. Then he said:

"The plan was to leave the bulk of that force to menace Amersfoort. But the Stadtholder himself meant to push on as far as the molen, with but a few hundred of his picked men. He thought to seize the stores of arms and ammunition there and then to await the coming of the Lord of Stoutenburg, who, driven out of Amersfoort and cut off from Ede, would make of necessity for his headquarters."

"Ah!"

The exclamation, deep and prolonged, came from three pairs of lips. Stoutenburg, Nicolaes and Jan looked at one another, and there was triumph and satisfaction depicted in their glance. The same thought had occurred simultaneously to these three traitors; the Stadtholder, with a comparatively small force, pushing on to the lonely molen on the Veluwe, not knowing that some of De Berg's troops were holding the Ijssel beyond.

He would be caught like a rat in a trap; and the question was whether it would not be better to allow him to carry out his plan, not to oppose him on his way, to let him reach the molen and then close in behind him, so that he would have but two alternatives before him – to surrender in the molen or to turn his small force in the direction of the Zuider Zee, and therein seek a watery grave.

5

"I must have a little time to think," Stoutenburg muttered to himself, after a while.

The blind man had apparently dropped off to sleep again. His head had once more fallen forward on his chest. Jan was prepared to give him another rude awakening, but his lordship stopped him with a sign.

"Let the muckworm sleep," he said. "I must think out the whole position. If what the knave says is true-

"I am inclined to believe it true," Nicolaes interposed. "The man is too fuddled to have invented so circumstantial a story. And I have it in my mind," he added reflectively, "that when the Stadtholder visited Amersfoort yesterday he said something to my father about devising a plan later on if the city were seriously threatened."

"Then, by Satan! all would be well indeed!" And Stoutenburg drew up his gaunt figure to its full height, looked every inch a conqueror, with heel set upon the neck of his foes. Jan alone looked dubious.

"I wouldn't trust the rogue," he said grimly.

"Would you hang him now?" Stoutenburg retorted.

"No; I would wait to make sure. Let him sleep awhile now. When he wakes out of his booze, he might be able to give us further details."

"In the meanwhile," his lordship rejoined, "keep the men under arms, Jan. I have not yet thought the matter over; but this I know – that I'll start for the molen with a few hundred musketeers and pikemen as soon as I am sure that this rascallion hath not spun a tissue of lies. Do you send out spies at once in every direction, with orders to bring back information immediately. We must hear if an attack hath indeed been made on Ede, and if the Stadtholder is moving out of Utrecht. Have you some men you can trust?"

"Oh, yes, so please your lordship," Jan replied. "I can send Piet Walleren in the direction of Ede, and I myself will push on toward Utrecht. We'd both be back long before dawn."

"And 'tis not you who could be nousled, eh, good Jan?" his lordship was pleased to say.

"If we have been tricked by this tosspot," Jan riposted gruffly, "I'll see him burnt alive, and 'tis mine own hand will set the brand to the stake."

He paused, and drew in his breath with a shudder; for he had turned to look on the blind man whom he was threatening with so dire a fate and whom he had thought asleep, and encountered those sightless orbs fixed upon him as if they could see something through and beyond him, some ghoul or spectre lurking in a distant corner of the room. So uncanny and terrifying did the rascal look, indeed, that instinctively Jan, who believed neither in God nor the devil, remembered his mother's early teachings, and made sundry and vague signs of the Cross upon his breast, with a view to exorcising those evil spirits which must be somewhere lurking about, unseen by all save by the man who had lost his sight.

"What is it now?" Stoutenburg queried with a scowl.

The blind man indeed appeared to be listening – listening so intently, with head now craned forward and eyes fixed into vacancy – that instinctively the three recreants listened too. To what, they could not have told. Through the open casement the sound of life – camp life, of sentries' challenging call, of bivouac fires, and rowdy soldiery – came in as before. A little less roisterous, perhaps, seeing that most of the men, tired after long days of marching and hours of carousing, had settled themselves down to sleep.

Inside the room, the monumental clock up against the wall ticked off each succeeding second with tranquil monotony. It was now close upon midnight. Nothing had happened. Nothing could have happened, to disturb the wonted tenor of the life of an army in temporary occupation of an unresisting city. Nothing, in fact, unless that blind tatter-demalion over there had indeed spoken the truth.

And still he listened. A vague anxiety seemed to have completely banished sleep, even momentarily to have dissipated the potent effect of that excellent Oporto; and on his face there was that strained look peculiar to those who have been robbed of one sense and are at pains to exert the others to their utmost power. It seemed as if his sightless orbs must pierce some hidden veil which kept vital secrets hidden from ordinary human gaze. And these three men – traitors all – whose craven hearts, weighted with crime, were sensitive to every uncanny spell, felt their own senses unaccountably thrilled by that motionless, stony image of a man whose very soul appeared on the alert, and in whom life itself, was as it were, momentarily arrested.

The spell continued for a moment or two. A minute, perhaps, went by; then, with an impatient curse, Stoutenburg jumped to his feet, strode rapidly to the window, and, leaning out far over the sill, he listened.

Indeed, at first it was naught but the habitual confused sounds that reach his ear. But as he, in his turn, strained every sense to hear, something unusual seemed to mingle with the other sounds. A murmuring. Strange voices. A few isolated words that rose above the others, louder than the sentries' call; also a patter of feet, like men running and a clang of arms that at this hour should have been stilled.

The Lord of Stoutenburg could not have told you then why those sounds should have suddenly filled his mind with foreboding – why, indeed, he heard them at all. Beneath the window, ranged against the wall, the men of his picked company were sleeping peacefully. Their bivouac fire fed by those on guard, shed a pleasant glow over the familiar scene. Beyond its ruddy gleam everything looked by contrast impenetrably dark. The river beyond it, nothing; only blackness – a blackness that could be felt. The lights of the city had long since been extinguished, only one tiny glimmer, which came from a small oil-lamp, showed above the Koppel-poort.

But that confused sound, that murmuring, came from the rear of the burgomaster's house, from the direction of the Market Place, where the bulk of his lordship's army was encamped.

"What in thunder does it mean?" Stoutenburg muttered.

Nicolaes came and joined him by the window. He, too, strained his ears to hear, feeling his nerves vaguely stirred by a kind of superstitious dread. But Stoutenburg turned to the blind man, and tried to read an answer in the latter's white, set face.

Jan shook Diogenes fiercely by the shoulder.

"Dost hear, knave?" he said harshly. "What does it all mean?"

"What does what mean, worthy Jan?" the blind man queried blandly.

"Thou are listening for something. What is it? His lordship desires to know."

"Canst thou hear anything, friend Jan?" the other riposted serenely.

"Only the usual sounds. What should I hear?"

"The armies of the Stadtholder on the move."

An exclamation of incredulity broke from Stoutenburg's lips. Nevertheless, he turned imperatively to Jan.

"Go or send at once into the town," he commanded. "Let us hear if anything has happened."

In a moment Jan was out of the room; and soon his gruff voice could be heard from outside, questioning and giving orders. He had gone himself to see what was amiss.

And Stoutenburg, half incredulous, yet labouring under strong excitement, once more approached the window and, leaning far out into the night, set his ears to listen.

His senses, too, were keyed up now, detached as they were from everything else except just what went on outside. The subdued murmurings reached his perceptions independently of every other sound. A hum of voices, and through it that of Jan, questioning and commanding; and others that talked agitatedly, with many interruptions.

After awhile he felt that he could stand the strain no longer. Very obviously something had happened, something was being discussed out on the Market Place, and there was a kind of buzzing in the air, as if around the hive of bees that have been disturbed by a company of robber-wasps. And to him – Stoutenburg – for whom that buzzing might mean the first step toward the pinnacle of his desires, the turning point of his destiny, beyond which lay power, dominion, ambition satisfied, and passion satiated, every moment of suspense and silence became positive torture. A primeval, savage instinct would, but for the presence of Nicolaes, have driven him to seizing the helpless prisoner by the throat, and thus to ease the tension on his nerves and still the wild hammering of blood on his temples.

But Nicolaes did, as it happened, exercise in this instance a restraining influence on his friend; quite unknowingly, of course, as his was the weaker nature. But the last half hour had wrought a marked change in Stoutenburg – a subtle one, which he himself could not have defined. Before then, he had been striving for great things – for revenge, for power, for the satisfaction of his passions. But now he felt that he had attained all that, and more. Obviously his stricken enemy had not lied. The Stadtholder was about to fall into a trap which was easy enough to set. The once brilliant Laughing Cavalier had sunk to a state of moral and physical degradation from which he could never now recover. And Gilda! Gilda had but to realize the slough of turpitude into which her former lover had sunk to turn gratefully and with a sigh of infinite relief to the man who had freed her from such a yoke.

In truth, Stoutenburg felt that he no longer needed to climb. He had reached the summit. The summit of ambition, of power, of sentimental satisfaction. He was a conqueror now; master in the land of his birth; the future Stadtholder of the United Province, wedded to the richest heiress in the Netherlands; happy, feared, and obeyed.

That was his position now, and that was the cause of the subtle change in him – a change which forced him to keep his savage instincts in check before his servile friend; forced to try and appear before others as above petty passions; a justiciary and not a terrorist.

6

The minutes sped by, leaden-footed for the impatience of these two men. Nicolaes and Stoutenburg, each trying to appear calm, hardly dared to speak with one another lest their speech betrayed the exacerbation of their nerves.

It was Nicolaes' turn now to pace up and down the room, to halt beside the window and peer out into the darkness in search of Jan's familiar figure. Stoutenburg had once more taken a seat on the highbacked chair, striving to look dignified and detached. His arm was thrown over the table, and with his sharply pointed nails he was drumming a devil's tatoo on the board.

Alone, the blind man appeared perfectly serene. After that brief moment of comparative lucidity, he had relapsed into somnolence. Occasional loud snores testified that he was once more wandering in the Elysian fields of unconsciousness.

Half an hour after midnight Jan returned.

"There is no doubt about it," were the first words he spoke. "An attack on Ede appears to be in progress, and the Stadtholder left his camp at Utrecht a couple of hours ago with a force of four thousand men."

He was out of breath, having run, he said, all the way from the Joris Poort, where he had gleaned the latest information.

"Who brought the news?" his lordship asked.

"No one seems to know, my lord," Jan replied. "But every one in the town has it. The rumour hath spread like wildfire. It started at opposite quarters of the city. The Nieuw Poort had it that a surprise attack had been delivered on Ede earlier in the evening, and the Joris Poort that the Stadtholder and his force are on the move. The captains at the gates had heard the news from runners who had come direct from Utrecht and from Ede."

"Where are those runners now?"

"In both cases the captains sent them back for further information. The fellows were willing enough to go, for a consideration; but the business has become a dangerous one, for the roads to Utrecht and Ede, they averred are already full of the Stadtholder's vedettes."

"Bah!" Stoutenburg ejaculated contemptuously. "A device for extorting money!"

"Probably," Jan riposted dryly. "But the money will be well spent if we get the information. The men are not to be paid until they return. And if they do not return —" Jan shrugged his shoulders. If the spies did not return, it would go to prove that the Stadtholder's vedettes were not asleep.

"I sent Piet Wallerin and one or two others out, too," he added, "with orders to push on both roads as far as possible, and bring back any information they can obtain – the sooner the better.

"They have not yet returned?" Stoutenburg asked.

"Oh, no! They have only been gone half an hour."

"Is the night very dark?"

"Very dark, my lord."

"Piet may never get back."

"In that case we shall know that the Stadtholder's vanguard has sighted him," Jan rejoined coolly. "Nothing else would keep Piet from getting back."

Stoutenburg nodded approval.

"You think, then, that this varlet here spoke the truth?"

"I have no longer any doubt of it, my lord," Jan gave reply. "Though I did not actually speak with the men who seem originally to have brought the news, the captains at the Poorts had no doubt whatever as to its authenticity. But we shall know for certain before dawn. Piet and the others will have returned by then – or not, as the case may be. But we shall know."

"And, of course, we are prepared?"

"To do just what your lordship commands. The men will be under arms within the next two hours, and I can seek the Master of the Camp, and send him at once to your lordship for instructions."

"Mine instructions are simple enough, good Jan; and thou canst convey them to the Master of the Camp thyself. They are, to remain quiescent, under arms but asleep. To surrender the town if it be attacked —"

"To surrender?" Jan protested with a frown.

"We must throw dust in the Stadtholder's eyes," Stoutenburg riposted. "Give the idea that we are feeble and unprepared, and that I have fled out of Amersfoort. The surrender of the city and its occupation will keep the main force busy, whilst Maurice of Nassau, anxious to possess himself of our person, will push on as far as the molen, where I, in the meanwhile, will be waiting for him."

His voice rang with a note of excitement and of triumph.

"With the Stadtholder a prisoner in my hands," he exclaimed, "I can command the surrender of all his forces. And then the whole of the Netherlands will be at my feet!"

Never, in his wildest dreams had he hoped for this. Fate, in very truth, had tired of smiting him, had an overfull cornucopia for him now and was showering down treasures upon him, one by one.

7

It was Nicolaes who first remembered the blind man.

During the last momentous half-hour he had been totally forgotten. Stoutenburg during that time had been in close confabulation with Jan, discussing plans, making arrangements for the morrow's momentous expedition. Neither of them seemed to feel the slightest fatigue. They were men of iron, whom their passions kept alive. But Nicolaes was a man of straw. He had been racked by one emotion after the other all day, and now he was so tired that he could hardly stand. He envied the blind man every time that a lusty snore escaped the latter's lips, and tried to keep himself awake by going to the fire from time to time and throwing a log or two upon it. But he stood in too great an awe of his friend to dare own to fatigue when the future of his native land was under discussion.

It was really in order to divert Stoutenburg's attention from these interminable discussions on what to do and what not to do on the morrow, that presently, during a pause, he pointed to Diogenes.

"What is to happen to this drunken loon?" he asked abruptly.

Stoutenburg grinned maliciously.

"Have no fear, friend Nicolaes," he said. "The fate of our valued informer will be my special care. I have not forgotten him. Jan knows. While you were nodding, he and I arranged it all. You did not hear?"

Nicolaes shook his head.

"No," he said. "What did you decide?"

"You shall see, my good Klaas," Stoutenburg replied with grim satisfaction. "I doubt not but what you'll be pleased. And since we have now finished the discussion of our plans, Jan will at once go and bid the Heer Burgomaster rise from his bed and attend upon our pleasure."

"My father?" Nicolaes exclaimed in surprise. "Why? What hath he —"

"You will see, my good Klaas," the other broke in quietly. "You will see. I think that you will be satisfied."

Jan, at his word, had already gone. Nicolaes, really puzzled, tried to ask questions, but Stoutenburg was obviously determined to keep the secret of his intentions awhile longer to himself.

It was long past one o'clock now, and bitterly cold. Even the huge blazing logs in the monumental hearth failed to keep the large room at a pleasing temperature. Nicolaes, shivering and yawning, crouched beside the blaze, knocked his half-frozen hands one against the other. He would at this moment have bartered most of his ambitions for the immediate prospect of a good bed. But Stoutenburg was as wide awake as ever, and evidently some kind of inward fever kept the cold out of his bones.

After Jan's departure he resumed that restless pacing of his up and down the long room. Up and down, until Nicolaes, exasperated beyond endurance, could have screamed with choler.

Less than a quarter of an hour later, the burgomaster arrived, ushered in by Jan. He had apparently not taken off his clothes since he had been upstairs. It was indeed more that likely that he had spent the time in prayer, for Mynheer Beresteyn was a pious man, and the will of God in fortune or adversity was a very real thing to him. With the same dignified submission which he had displayed throughout, he had immediately followed Jan when curtly ordered to do so. But he came down to face the arrogant tyrant for the third time to-night with as heavy a heart as before, not knowing what fresh indignity, what new cruel measure, would be put upon him. Grace or clemency he knew that he could not expect.

The look of malignant triumph wherewith Stoutenburg greeted him appeared to justify his worst forebodings. The presence, too, of Diogenes, fettered and asleep, filled his anxious heart with additional dread. As he stepped out into the room he took no notice of his son, but only strove to face his arch-enemy with as serene a countenance as he could command.

"Your lordship desired that I should come," he said quietly. "What is your lordship's pleasure?"

But Stoutenburg was all suavity. A kind of feline gentleness was in his tone as he replied:

"Firstly, to beg your forgiveness, mynheer, for having disturbed you again – and at this hour. But will you not sit? Jan," he commanded, "draw a chair nearer to the hearth for the Heer Burgomaster."

"I was not asleep, my lord," Beresteyn rejoined coldly. "And by your leave, will take your commands standing."

"Oh, commands, mynheer!" Stoutenburg rejoined blandly. " 'Tis no commands I would venture to give you. It was my duty – my painful duty – not to keep you in ignorance of certain matters which have just come to my knowledge, and which will have a momentous bearing upon all my future plans. Will you not sit?" he added, with insidious urbanity. "No? Ah, well, just as you wish. But you will forgive me if I —"

He sat down in his favourite chair, with his back to the table and the candle-light and facing the fire, which threw ruddy gleams on his gaunt face and grizzled hair. His deepset eyes were inscrutable in the shadow, but they were fixed upon the burgomaster who stood before him dignified and calm, half-turned away from the pitiful spectacle which the blind man presented in somnolent helplessness.

"Since last I had the pleasure of addressing you, mynheer," Stoutenburg began slowly, after awhile, "it hath come to my knowledge that the Stadtholder, far from abandoning all hope of reconquering Gelderland from our advancing forces, did in truth not only devise a plan whereby he intended to deliver Ede and Amersfoort from our hands, but his far-reaching project also embraced the possibility of seizing my person, and once for all ridding himself of an enemy – a justiciary, shall we say? – who is becoming might inconvenient."

"A project, my lord," the burgomaster riposted earnestly, "which I pray God may fully succeed."

Stoutenburg gave a derisive laugh.

"So it would have done, mynheer," he said with a sardonic grin. "It would have succeeded admirably, and by this hour to-morrow I should no doubt be dangling on a gibbet, for Maurice of Nassau hath sworn that he would treat me as a knave and as a traitor unworthy of the scaffold."

"And the world would have been rid of a murderous miscreant," the burgomaster put in coldly, "had God so willed it."

"Ah, but God – your God, mynheer," Stoutenburg retorted with a sneer, "did not will it, it seems. And forewarned is forearmed, you know."

Instinctively, as the full meaning of Stoutenburg's words reached his perceptions the Burgomaster's eyes had sought those of his son, whilst a ghastly pallor overspread his face even to his lips.

"The Stadtholder's schemes have been revealed to you," he murmured slowly. "By whom?"

Then, as Stoutenburg made no reply, only regarded him with a mocking and quizzical gaze, he added more vehemently:

"Who is the craven informer who hath sold his master to you?"

"What would you do to him if you knew?" Stoutenburg retorted coolly.

"Slay him with mine own hand," the burgomaster replied calmly, "were he my only son!"

" 'Twas not I!" Nicolaes cried involuntarily.

Stoutenburg appeared vastly amused.

"No," he said. "It was not your son Klaas, whose merits, by the way, you have not yet learned to appreciate. Nicolaes hath rendered me and the Archduchess immense services, which I hope soon to repay adequately. But," he added with mocking emphasis, "the most signal service of all, which will deliver the Stadtholder into my hands and re-establish thereby the dominion of Spain over the Netherlands, was rendered to me by the varlet whom, but for me, you would have acclaimed as your son."

And with a wide flourish of the arm, Stoutenburg turned in his chair and pointed to Diogenes, who, sublimely unconscious of what went on around him, was even in the act of emitting a loud and prolonged snore. Instinctively the burgomaster looked at him. his glance, vague and puzzled, wandered over the powerful figure of the blind man, the nodding head, the pinioned shoulders, and from him back to Stoutenburg, who continued to regard him – Beresteyn – with a malicious leer.

"I fear me," the latter murmured after awhile, "That your lordship will think me over-dull; but – I don't quite understand —"

"Yet, 'tis simple enough," Stoutenburg rejoined; rose from his chair, and approached the burgomaster, as he spoke with a sudden fierce tone of triumph. "This miserable cur on whom Gilda once bestowed her love, seeing the gallows dangling before his bleary eyes, hath sold me the secrets which the Stadtholder did entrust him – sold the to me in exchange for his worthless life! I entered into a bargain with him, and I will keep my pledge. In very truth, he hath saved my life by his revelations, and jeopardized that of the Stadtholder – my most bitter enemy. Maurice of Nassau had thought to trap me in the lonely molen on the Veluwe which is my secret camp. Now 'tis I who will close the trap on him there, and hold his life, his honour, these provinces, at my mercy. And all," he concluded with a ringing shout, "thanks to the brilliant adventurer, the chosen of Gilda's heart, her English milor, mynheer! – the gay and dashing Laughing Cavalier!"

He had the satisfaction of seeing that the blow had gone home. The burgomaster literally staggered under it, as if he had actually been struck in the face with a whip. Certain it is that he stepped back and clutched the table for support with one hand, whilst he passed the other once or twice across his brow.

"My God!" he murmured under his breath.

Stoutenburg laughed as a demon might, when gazing on a tortured soul. Then he shrugged his shoulders and went on airily:

"You are surprised, mynheer Burgomaster?" Frankly, I was not. You believed this fortune-hunter's tales of noble parentage and English ancestry. I did not. You doubted his treachery when he went on a message to Marquet, and sold that message to de Berg. I knew it to be a fact. My love for Gilda made me clear-sighted, whilst yours left you blind. Now you see him at last in his true colours – base, servile, without honour and without faith. You are bewildered, incredulous, mayhap? Ask Jan. He was here and heard him. Ask my captains at the gate, my master of the camp. The Stadtholder is heading straight for the trap which he had set up for me, because the cullion who sits there did sell his one-time master to me."

The burgomaster, overcome with horror and with shame, had sunk into a chair and buried his face in his hands. The echo of Stoutenburg's rasping voice seemed to linger in the noble panelled hall, its mocking accents to be still tearing at the stricken father's aching heart, still deriding his overwhelming sorrow. Gilda! His proud, loving, loyal Gilda! If she were to know! A great sob, manfully repressed, broke from his throat and threatened to choke him.

And for the first time in this day of crime and of treachery, Nicolaes felt a twinge of remorse knocking at the gates of his heart. He could not bear to look on his father's grief, and not feel the vague stirrings of an affection which had once been genuine, even though it was dormant now. His father had been perhaps more just toward him than indulgent. Gilda had been the apple of his eyes, and he – Nicolaes – had been brought up in that stern school of self-sacrifice and self-repression which had made heroes of those of his race in their stubborn and glorious fight for liberty.

No doubt it was that rigid bringing-up which had primarily driven an ambitious and discontented youth like Nicolaes into the insidious net spread out for him by the wily Stoutenburg. Smarting under the discipline imposed upon his self-indulgence by the burgomaster, he had lent a willing ear to the treacherous promises of his masterful friend, who held out dazzling visions before him of independence and of aggrandisement. Even at this moment Nicolaes felt no remorse for his treachery to his country and kindred. He was only sentimentally sorry to see his father so utterly broken down by sorrow.

And then there was Gilda. Already, when Stoutenburg had placed that cruel "either – or" before her, Nicolaes had felt an uncomfortable pain in his heart at the sight of her misery. Stoutenburg would have called it weakness, and despised him for it. But Stoutenburg's was an entirely warped and evil nature, which revelled in crime and cruelty as a solace to past humiliation and disappointment, whereas Nicolaes was just a craven time-server, who had not altogether succeeded in freeing himself from past teachings and past sentiments.

And Gilda's pale, tear-stained face seemed to stare at him through the gloom, reproachful and threatening, whilst his father's heartrending sob tore at his vitals and shook him to the soul with a kind of superstitious awe. The commandment of Heaven, not wholly forgotten, not absolutely ignored, seemed to ring the death-knell of all that he had striven for, as if the Great Judge of All had already weighed his deeds in the balance, and decreed that his punishment be swift and sure.

But Stoutenburg, in this the hour of his greatest triumph, had none of these weaknesses. Nor indeed did he care whether the burgomaster was stricken with sorrow or no. What he did do now was to go up to Jan, and from the latter's belt take out a pistol. This he examined carefully, then he put it down upon the table close to where the burgomaster was sitting.

8

A quarter of an hour later the stately house on the quay appeared wrapped in the mantle of sleep. The soldiers, wearied and discontented, had after a good deal of murmuring, finally settled down to rest. They had collected what clothes, blankets, curtains even that they could lay their hands on, and wrapped up in these, they had curled themselves up upon the floor.

We may take it, however, as a certainty that Jan remained wide awake, with one ear on that door which gave on the banqueting hall, and which he, at the command of his master, had carefully closed behind him.

Upstairs, Nicolaes had thrown himself like an insentient and wearied mass upon his own bed in the room wherein he had slept as a child, as an adolescent, as a youth, now as a black-hearted traitor, haunted by memories and the ghoulish shadows, of his crime. He could not endure the darkness, so left a couple of wax candles burning in their sconces. Whether he actually fell asleep or no, he could not afterward have told you. Certain it is that he was not fully awake, but rather on that threshold of dreams which for those that are happy is akin to the very gate of paradise, but unto souls that are laden with crime is like the antechamber of hell. Half consciously Nicolaes could hear Stoutenburg pacing up and down an adjoining room, restless and fretful, like some untamed beast on the prowl.

Then suddenly the sharp report of a pistol rang through the silence of the night. Nicolaes jumped from his bed, with a feeling of sheer physical nausea, which turned him dizzy and faint. Stoutenburg had paused abruptly in his febrile wanderings. To the listener it almost seemed as if he could hear his friend's laboured breathing, the indrawing of a sigh that spoke of torturing suspense.

A few minutes went by, and then a heavy step was heard ascending the stairs, after that, the closing and shutting of a door. Then nothing more.

In that heavy step, Nicolaes had recognized his father's. Even now he could hear the burgomaster moving about in his room close by, which had always been his. Gilda's was further along, down the passage. Everything now seemed so still. Just for awhile, after the burgomaster had gone upstairs, Nicolaes had heard the soldiers moving down below. Rudely awakened from their sleep, they had done a good deal of muttering. Voices could be heard, and then a rattle, like the shaking of a door. But apparently the men had been quickly reassured by Jan.

The silence acted as a further irritant on Nicolaes' nerves. Taking up a candle, he went out of the room in search of Stoutenburg. Outside on the landing he came upon Jan, who was on the same errand bent.

"What has happened?" the young man queried hoarsely.

Jan shook his head. "Which is His Lordship's room?" was all that he said.

Nicolaes led the way, and Jan followed. They found Stoutenburg standing in the middle of the room which he had selected for his own use. He was still fully dressed, had not even taken off his boots. Apparently he was waiting for news, but otherwise he seemed quite calm.

"Well?" he queried curtly, as soon as he caught sight of Jan.

"We cannot get into the room," Jan replied. "After we heard the shot fired, we saw the burgomaster come out of it; but he locked the door and, with the key in his hand he walked steadily up the stairs."

"How did he look?"

"Like a man who had seen a ghost."

"Well?" Stoutenburg queried again, impatiently. "What did you do after that?"

"I tried the door, of course. It is a stout piece of oak, and I had no orders to break it down. It would take a heavy joist, and the men are already grumbling —"

"Yes!" Stoutenburg put in curtly. "But the windows?"

"I thought of them, and myself went round to look. Of course we could climb up to them, but they appeared to be barred and shuttered."

"So much the better!" his lordship retorted with a note of grim spite in his rasping voice. "Let the varlet's carcase rot where it is. Why should we trouble? Go back to bed, Nicolaes," he added after a slight pause. "And you too, Jan. As for me, I feel that I could sleep peacefully at last!"

He threw himself on the bed with a long sigh of satisfaction, and when spoken to again by one of the others, he curtly ordered them to leave him in peace. So Jan did leave him, and went back to his men. But Nicolaes, terrified of solitude, which he felt would for him be peopled with ghouls, elected to find what rest he could in an armchair beside his friend. And a few minutes later the house was once more wrapped in the mantle of sleep.

Chapter XV – The Molen on the Veluwe

1

AGAIN it is to de Voocht's highly interesting and reliable "Brieven" that we like to turn for an account of the Lord of Stoutenburg's departure out of Amersfoort. It occurred at dawn of a raw, dull March morning, and was effected with all the furtiveness, the silence, usually pertaining to a surprise attack.

The soldiers bivouacking inside that part of the city knew nothing of the whole affair. But few of them did as much as turn in their sleep when his lordship rode through the Koppel-poort, together with four companies of cavaliers. Jan was an adept at arranging these expeditions, and the Lord of Stoutenburg had made a specialty of marauding excursions ever since he had started on his career of treachery against his own country.

His standard-bearer preceded the companies, carrying the sable standard embroidered in silver, with the skull and cross-bones, which his lordship had permanently adopted as his device. But they went without drums or pipes, and with as little clatter as may be, choosing the unpaved streets whereon the mud lay thick and effectually deadened the sound of horses' hoofs.

A litter taken from the burgomaster's coach-house and borne by two strong Flemish horses, bore the jongejuffrouw Gilda Beresteyn in the train of her future lord. She had offered no resistance, no protest of any kind, when finally ordered by her brother to make herself ready. She had spent the greater part of the night in meditation and in prayer. Her father, hearing her move about in her room, had come to her in the small hours of the morning and had sat with her for some time. Nicolaes, wakeful and restless, had wandered out into the corridor on which gave most of the sleeping rooms, and had heard the subdued murmurings of the burgomaster's voice, and occasionally that of his sister. What they said he could not hear, but he was able subsequently to assure Stoutenburg that the burgomaster's tone was distinctly one of admonition, and Gilda's one of patience and resignation.

Just before dawn, one of the old serving men, who had remained on watch in the house all through the night, brought her some warm milk and bread, which she swallowed eagerly. The burgomaster was with her then. But later on, when the Lord of Stoutenburg desired her presence in the living room, she went to him alone.

That room was the one where, a little more than a week ago, the Stadtholder had held council with the burgomaster and his friends, on the day of her wedding, Her wedding! And she had sat in the little room next to it and played on the virginal so as to attract her beloved to her side. Then had come the hour of parting, and she had with her own hands taken his sword to him and buckled it to his side, and bade him go wither honour and duty beckoned.

My God, what memories!

But she met Stoutenburg's mocking glance with truly remarkable serenity. She felt neither faint nor weak. He communion with God, her interview with her father had given her all the strength she needed, not to let her enemies see what she suffered or if she were afraid. And when Stoutenburg with callous irony reminded her of his decision, she answered quite calmly:

"I am ready to do your wish, my lord."

"And you'll not regret it, Gilda," he vowed with sudden earnestness; and his sunken eyes lighted up with a kind of fierce ardour which sent a cold shudder coursing down her spine. "By Heaven! you'll not regret it! You shall be the greatest lady in Europe, the most admired, the most beloved. Aye! With you beside me, I feel that I shall have the power to create a throne, a kingdom, for us both. Queen of the Netherlands, myn engel! What say you to this goal? And I your king —"

He paused and closely scrutinized her face, marvelled what she knew of that drunken oaf, once her lover, who now lay dead in the room below, slain by the avenging hand of an outraged father and an indignant patriot. But she looked so serene that he came to the conclusion that she knew nothing. The burgomaster had apparently desired to spare her for the moment this additional horror and shame.

Well no doubt it was all for the best. She was ready to come with him, and that, after all, was the principal thing. In any event she knew the alternative.

"Jan remains here," he said, "in command of the troops. He will not leave until I send him word."

Until then, Amersfoort and the lives of all its citizens were in jeopardy. The quick, scared look in her eyes, when he reminded her of this, was sufficient to assure him that she fully grasped the position. Of the Stadtholder's plans, as betrayed by the informer, she knew, of course, nothing. Better so, he thought. The whole thing, when accomplished, when he – Stoutenburg – was made master of Gelderland, the Stadtholder a prisoner in his hands, the United Provinces ready to submit to him, would be a revelation to her – a revelation which would make her, he doubted not, a proud and happy woman, rather than a mere obedient slave.

2

In the meanwhile, he had strictly enjoined Jan to leave the banqueting hall undisturbed.

"Let the locked door and close shutters guard the grim secret within," he said decisively. "Apparently the Heer Burgomaster intends for the nonce to hold his tongue."

In the hurry and excitement of the departure, the soldiers, who in the night had been roused by the pistol shot, forgot that unimportant event. Certain it is that not one of them did more than cursorily wonder what it had been about. Then, as no one gave reply, the matter was soon allowed to fall into oblivion. At one moment, Stoutenburg who was standing in the hall waiting for Gilda, felt tempted to go and have a last look on his dead enemy; but the key was not in the lock and he would not send to the burgomaster for it.

It was better so.

Just then Gilda came down the stairs. She was accompanied by her old waiting woman, Maria, and was wrapped in fur cloak and hood ready for the journey. Apparently she had taken final leave of her father, and had quite resigned herself to parting from him.

"The burgomaster is well, I trust, this morning?" Stoutenburg asked with great urbanity, as soon as he had formally greeted her.

"I thank you, my lord," she replied coolly. "My father is as well as I can desire."

The litter was her own. Oft had she travelled in it between Haarlem and Amersfoort, when the weather was too rough for riding. Those had been happy journeys to and fro, for both homes were dear to her. Both now had become hallowed through the presence in them of her beloved. To Stoutenburg, who watched her keenly while she crossed the hall, it seemed as if once she glanced round in the direction of the banqueting room, and craned her neck as if trying to catch whatever faint sound might be coming from there. She appeared to shiver, and drew her fur cloak closer round her shoulders, her lips moved slightly as if murmuring. Stoutenburg thought that she was bidding a last farewell to the man who she could not bring herself to forget or to despise and an acute feeling of unbridled jealousy shot through him like a poisoned dart – jealousy even of the dead.

3

A mounted scout led the way, to clear the road of encumbrance that might retard progress. After him came the standard-bearer. Twelve Spanish halberdiers followed, the shafts of their halberts swathed in black velvet, behind them one hundred cavaliers, who were armed with muskets, and a hundred more carrying lances. Then came the litter, which was covered in leather with richly stamped leather curtains, at the sides, the shafts, front and back, supported by heavy Flemish horses, which were sumptuously caparisoned and plumed. The Lord of Stoutenburg rode on one side of the litter and Nicolaes on the other, and behind it came two more companies of musketeers and lancers.

The way lay through the Koppel-poort and then straight across the Veluwe, on the road which runs to the north of Amersfoort, thus avoiding any possible encounter with the Stadtholder's vedettes. Stoutenburg's intention was to await Maurice of Nassau's coming at the molen, not to offer him battle in the open.

The road was lonely at this early hour, and a cutting wind blew across from the Zuider Zee, chasing the morning mist before it. Already on the horizon above the undulating tableland, the pale wintry sun tinged that mist with gold. Stoutenburg's keen hawklike eyes searched the distance before him as he rode.

A little after seven o'clock, Barneveld was reached, and a brief halt called outside the city whilst the scouts went in, in search of provisions. The inhabitants, scared by the advent of these strangers, submitted to being fleeced of their goods, not daring to resist. Though closely questioned, they had but little information to impart. They had, in truth, heard that Ede was in the hands of the Spaniards and that Amersfoort had shared the like fate. Runners had brought the news, which was authentic, together with many wild rumours that had terrorized the credulous and paved the way for Stoutenburg's arrival. His sable standard, with its grim device, completed the subjugation of the worthy burghers of Barneveld, who, with no garrison to protect them, thought it wisest to obey the behests of His Magnificence with a show of goodwill, rather than see their little city pillaged or their citizens dragged as captives in the train of the conqueror.

Gilda did not leave her litter during the halt. Maria, who had been riding on a pillion behind one of the equerries, who she roundly trounced and anathematized all the way, came and waited on her mistress. But Stoutenburg and Nicolaes kept with unwonted discretion, or mayhap indifference, out of her way.

The halt, in truth, lasted less than a couple of hours. By nine o'clock the troop was once more on the way, and an hour later on the high upland, out toward the east, the lonely molen loomed, portentous and weird, out of the mist.

4

The spies of the Stadtholder, who had, according to Diogenes' statement, spoken of the molen as Stoutenburg's camp, where he had secreted great stores of arms and ammunition, had in truth been either deceived or deceivers.

The molen was lonely and uninhabited, as it had always been. No sign of life appeared around it, or sign of the recent breaking of a camp. True, here and there upon the scrub in the open, the scorched rough grass or a heap of ashes, indicated that a fire had been lit there at one time; whilst under the overhanging platform, the trampled earth converted into mud, and certain debris of straw and fodder, accused the recent presence of horses and of men.

But only a few. As to whether the stores of arms and ammunition were indeed concealed inside the mill-house itself, it was impossible to say from the mere aspect of the tumble-down building. Whatever secret the molen contained, it had succeeded in guarding inviolate up to this hour.

Standing as it did upon a high point of the arid upland, the molen dominated the Veluwe. Toward the west, whence the Stadtholder would come, a gentle, undulating slope led down to Barneveld and Ede, Amersfoort and Utrecht; but in the rear of the building toward the east, the ground fell away more abruptly, down to a narrow gorge below.

It was in this gorge, secluded from the prying eyes of possible vedettes, that Stoutenburg had put up his camp ere he embarked upon his fateful expedition to Amersfoort, and it was here that he disposed the bulk of his troop: horses, men and baggage, under the command of Nicolaes Beresteyn; whilst he himself, with a bodyguard of fifty picked men, took up his quarters in the molen.

The plan of action was simple enough. The fifty men would remain concealed in and about the building, until the Stadtholder thinking the place deserted, walked straight into the trap that had been laid for him. Then, at the first musket shot, the men from the camp below were to rush up the sloping ground with a great clatter and much shouting and battle cry.

The Stadtholder's troops wholly unprepared for the attack would be thrown into dire confusion, and in the panic that would inevitably ensue, the rout would be complete. Stoutenburg himself would see to it that the Stadtholder did not escape.

"Welcome home, myn engel!" had been his semi-ironical, wholly triumphant greeting to Gilda when her litter came to a halt and he dismounted in order to conduct her into the molen.

She gave him no answer, but allowed her hand to rest in his and walked beside him with a firm step through the narrow door which gave on the interior of the mill-house. She looked about her with inquiring eyes that had not a vestige of terror in them. Almost, it seemed, at one moment as if she smiled.

Did her memory conjure back just then the vision of that other molen, the one at Ryswick, where so much had happened three short months ago, and where this arrogant tyrant had played such a sorry role? Perhaps. Certain it is that she turned to him without any defiance, almost with a gentle air of appeal.

"I am very tired," she said, with a weary little sigh, "and would be grateful for a little privacy, if your lordship would allow my tire-woman to attend on me."

"Your wishes are my laws, myn schat," he replied airily. "I entreat you to look on this somewhat dilapidated building only as a temporary halt, where nothing, alas! can be done for your comfort. I trust you will not suffer from the cold, but absolute privacy you shall have. The loft up those narrow steps is entirely at your disposal, and your woman shall come to you immediately."

Indeed, he called at once through the door, and a moment or two later Maria appeared, reduced to silence for the nonce by a wholesome fear. Stoutenburg, in the meanwhile, still with that same ironical gallantry, had conducted Gilda to the narrow, ladder-like steps which led up to the loft. He stood at the foot, watching her serene and leisurely progress.

"How wise you are, mejuffrouw," he said, with a sigh of satisfaction. "And withal how desirable!"

She turned for a second, then, and looked down on him. But her eyes were quite inscrutable. Never had he desired her so much as now. With the gloomy background of those rickety walls behind her, she looked like an exquisite fairy; her dainty head wrapped in a hood, through which her small, oval face appeared, slightly rose-tinted, like a piece of delicate china.

The huge fur coat concealed the lines of her graceful figure, but one perfect hand rested upon the rail, and the other peeped out like a flower between the folds of her cloak. He all but lost his head when he gazed on her, and met those blue eyes that still held a mystery for him. But, with Stoutenburg, ambition and selfishness always waged successful warfare even against passion, and at this hour his entire destiny was hanging in the balance.

The look wherewith he regarded her was that of a conqueror rather than a lover. The title of the English play had come swiftly through his mind: "The Taming of the Shrew." In truth, Nicolaes had been right. Women have no use for weaklings. It is their master whom they worship.

Just one word of warning did he give her ere she finally passed out of his sight.

"There will be noise of fighting anon, myn engel," he said carelessly. "Nothing that need alarm you. An encounter with vedettes probably. A few musket shots. You will not be afraid?"

"No," she replied simply. "I will not be afraid."

"You will be safe here with me until we can continue our journey east or south. It will depend on what progress de Berg has been able to make."

She gave a slight nod of understanding.

"I shall be ready," she said.

Encouraged by her gentleness, he went on more warmly:

"And at the hour when we leave here together, myn schat, a runner will speed to Amersfoort with order to Jan to evacuate the city. The burgomaster will be in a position to announce to his fellow-citizens that they have nothing to fear from a chivalrous enemy, who will respect person and property, and who will go out of the gates of Amersfoort as empty-handed as he came.

Whereupon he made her a low and respectful bow, stood aside to allow the serving woman to follow her mistress. Gilda had acknowledge his last pompous tirade with a faintly murmured, "I thank you, my lord." Then she went quickly up the steps and finally passed out of his sight on the floor above.

Just for a little while he remained quite still, listening to her footsteps overhead. His lean, sharp-featured face expressed nothing but contentment now. Success – complete, absolute – was his at last! Less than a fortnight ago, he was nothing but a disappointed vagrant, without home, kindred, or prospects; scorned by the woman he loved; despised by a successful rival; an outcast from the land of his birth.

To-day, his rival was dead – an object of contempt, not even of pity, for every honest man; while Gilda, like a ripe and luscious fruit, was ready to fall into his arms. And he had his foot firmly planted on the steps of a throne.

5

And now the midday hour had gone by, and silence, absolute, reigned in and around the molen. Stoutenburg had spend some time talking to the captain in command of his guard, had himself seen to it that the men were well concealed in the rear of the molen. The horses had been sent down to the camp so as to preclude any possibility of an alarm being given before the apportioned time. Two men were stationed on the platform to keep a look-out upon the distance, where anon the Stadtholder and his troop would appear.

Indeed, everything was ordained and arranged with perfect precision in anticipation of the great coup which was destined to deliver Maurice of Nassau into the hands of his enemy. Everything! – provided that blind informer who lay dead in the banqueting hall of the stately house at Amersfoort had not lied from first to last.

But even if he had lied, even if the Stadtholder had not planned this expedition, or, having planned it, had abandoned it or given up the thought of leading it in person – even so, Stoutenburg was prepared to be satisfied. Already his busy brain was full of plans, which he would put into execution if the present one did not yield him the supreme prize. Gilda was his now, whatever happened. Gilda, and her wealth, and the influence of the Burgomaster Beresteyn, henceforth irrevocably tied to the chariot wheel of his son-in-law. A vista of riches, of honours, of power, was stretched out before the longing gaze of this restless and ambitious self-seeker.

For the nonce, he could afford to wait, even though the hours crept by leaden-footed, and the look-out men up on the platform had nothing as yet to report. The soldiers outside, wrapped up in horse-blankets, squatted against the walls of the dilapidated building, trying to get shelter from the cutting north wind. They had their provisions for the day requisitioned at Barneveld; but these they soon consumed for want of something better to do. The cold was bitter, and anon an icy drizzle began to fall.

6

Stoutenburg, inside the mill-house, had started on that restless pacing up and down which was so characteristic of him. He had ordered the best of the provisions to be taken up to the jongejuffrouw and her maid. He himself had eaten and had drunk, and now he had nothing to do but wait. And think. Anon he got tired of both, and when he heard the women moving about overhead, he suddenly paused in his fretful wanderings, pondered for a moment or two, and then went resolutely up the stairs.

Gilda was sitting on a pile of sacking; her hands lay idly in her lap. With a curt word of command, Stoutenburg ordered the waiting woman to go below.

Then he approached Gilda, and half-kneeling, half-reclining by her side, he tried to take her hand. But she evaded him, hid her hands underneath her cloak. This apparently vastly amused his lordship, for he laughed good-humouredly, and said, with an ardent look of passionate admiration:

"That is where you are so desirable, myn engel. Never twice the same. Awhile ago you seemed as yielding as a dove; now once more I see the young vixen peeping at me through those wonderful blue eyes. Well!" he added with a sigh of contentment, "I will not complain. Life by your side, myn geliefde, will never be dull. The zest of taming a beautiful shrew must ever be a manly sport."

Then, as she made no sign either of defiance or comprehension, but sat with eyes strained and neck craned forward, almost as if she were listening, he raised himself and sat down upon the sacking close beside her. She puzzled him now, as she always did; and that puzzlement added zest to his wooing.

"I was waxing so dejected down below," he said, and leaned forward, his lips almost touching the hood that kept her ears concealed. "Little did I guess that so much delight lay ready to my hand. Time is a hard task-master to me just now, and I have not the leisure to make as ardent love to you as I would wish. But I have the time to gratify a fancy, and this I will do. My fancy is to have three kisses from your sweet lips on mine. Three, and no more, and on the lips, myn schat."

In an instant his arms were round her. But equally suddenly she had evaded him. She jumped up and ran, as swift as a hare, to the farther end of the loft, where she remained ensconced behind a transverse beam, her arms round it for support, her face, white and set, only vaguely discernible in the gloom.

The dim afternoon light which came but shyly peeping in through two small windows high up in the walls, failed to reach this angle of the loft where Gilda had found shelter. With this dim background behind her, she appeared like some elusive spectre, an apparition, without form or substance, her face and hands alone visible.

When she escaped him, Stoutenburg had cursed, as was his wont, then struggled to his feet and tried to carry off the situation with an affected laugh. But somehow the girls' face, there in the semi-darkness, gave him an unpleasant, eerie sensation. He did not follow her, but paused in the centre of the loft, laughter dying upon his lips.

"Am I to remind you again, you little termagant," he said, with a great show of bluster, "that Jan is still at Amersfoort, and that I may yet send a runner to him if I have a mind, ordering that by nightfall that accursed city be ablaze?"

He was looking straight at her while he spoke. And she returned his glance, but gave him no reply. Just for the space of a few seconds an extraordinary stillness appeared to have descended upon the molen. Up here, in the loft, nothing stirred, nothing was heard above that silence save the patter of the rain upon the roof overhead against the tiny window panes. For a few seconds, whilst Stoutenburg stood like a beast of prey about to spring, and Gilda, still and silent, like a bird on the alert.

And suddenly, even as he gazed, the man's expression slowly underwent a change. First the arrogance died out of it, the forced irony. Every line became set, then rigid, and more and more ashen in hue, until the whole face appeared like a death-mask, colourless and transparent as wax, the jaw dropping, the lips parted as for a cry that would not come. And the sunken eyes opened wider and wider, and wider still as they gazed, not on Gilda any longer, but into the darkness behind her, whilst the whole aspect of the man was like a living statute of horror and of a nameless fear.

Then suddenly, right through the silence and above the weird patter of the rain, there rang a sound which roused the very echoes that lay dormant among the ancient rafters. So strange a sound was it that when it reached his ear, Stoutenburg lost his balance and swayed on his feet like a drunken man; so strange that Gilda, her nerves giving way for the first time under the terrible strain which she had undergone, buried her face against her arms, whilst a loud sob broke from her throat. Yet the sound in itself was neither a terrifying nor a tragic one. It was just the sound of a prolonged and loud peal of laughter.

"By my halidame!" a merry voice swore lustily. "But meseems that your lordship had no thought of seeing me here!"

Just for a few seconds, superstitious fear held the miscreant gripped by the throat. A few seconds? To him to Gilda, they seemed an eternity. Then a hoarse whisper escaped him.

"Spectre or demon, which are you?"

"Both, you devil!" the mocking voice gave reply. "And I would send you down to hell and shoot you like a dog where you stand, but for the noise which would bring your men about mine ears."

"To hell yourself, you infamous plepshurk!" Stoutenburg cried, strove to shake off with a mighty effort the superstitious dread that made a weakling of him. He fumbled for his sword, succeeded in drawing it from its scabbard, and cursed himself for being without a pistol in his belt.

"Where you came from, I know not," he went on in a husky whisper. "But be you wraith or demon, you ——"

He seemed to speak involuntarily, as if sheer terror was forcing the words through his blood-less lips. Suddenly he uttered a hoarse cry:

"A moi! Somebody there! A moi!"

But the walls of the old molen were thick, and his voice, spent and still half-choked with the horror of that spectral apparition, refused him effective service. It failed to carry far enough. The tiny windows were impracticable; the soldiers were outside at the rear of the building, out of earshot; and down below there was only the old waiting woman.

"That smeerlap!" he cried, half to himself. "Either a wraith or blind. In either case —"

And, sword in hand, he rushed upon his mocking enemy. A blind man! Bah! What had he to fear? The rogue had in truth thrust Guild behind him. He stood there, with one of those short English daggers in his hand, which had of late put the fine Toledo blades to shame. But a blind man, for all that! How he had escaped out of Amersfoort, and by whose connivance Stoutenburg had not time to think. But the man was blind. Every phase of last evening's interview with him – the vacant eyes, the awkward movements – stood out clearly before his lordship's mental vision, and testified to that one fact; the man was blind and helpless.

Crouching like a feline creature upon his haunches, Stoutenburg was ready for a spring. His every movement became lithe and silent as that of a snake. He had marked out to himself just how and where he would strike. He only waited until those eyes – those awful eyes – ceased to look on him. But their glance never wavered. They followed his ever step. They mocked and derided and threatened withal! By Satan and all his hordes! those stricken orbs could see!

At what precise moment that conviction entered Stoutenburg's tortured brain, he could not himself have told you. But suddenly it was there. And in an instant his nerve completely forsook him. An icy sweat broke all over his body. His head swam, his knees gave way under him, the sword dropped out of his nerveless hand. Then, with a quick hoarse cry, he turned to flee. His foot was on the top step of the ladder which led to the room below. A prolonged, mocking laugh behind him seemed to lend him wings. But freedom – aye, and more! – beckoned from below. There was only an old woman there, and his soldiers were outside. Ye gods! He was a fool to fear!

He flew down the few steps, nearly fell headlong in the act, for his nerves were playing him an unpleasant trick, and the afternoon light was growing dim. At first, when he reached the place below, he saw nothing. Nothing save the welcome door, straight before him which led straight to freedom from this paralysing obsession. With one bound he had covered half the intervening space, when suddenly he paused, and an awful curse rose to his lips. There, in the recess of the doorway, two men were squatting on their heels, intent upon a game of hazard. One of these men was long and lean, the other round as a curled-up hedge-hog. They did no more than glance over their shoulder when His Magnificence the Lord of Stoutenburg came staggering down the steps.

"Five and four," the lean vagabond was saying. "How many does that make?"

"Eight, you loon!" the other replied. "My turn now."

They continued their game, regardless of his lordship who stood there rooted to the spot, trembling in every limb, his body covered with sweat, feeling like an animal that sees a trap slowly closing in upon him.

The situation was indeed one to send a man out of his senses. Stoutenburg, for one brief instant, felt that he was going mad. He looked from the door to the steps, and back again to the door, marvelling which way lay his one chance of escape. If he shouted, would he be heard? Could his men get to him before those two ruffians fell to and murdered him? Dared he make a dash for the door? Or — It was unthinkable that he – Stoutenburg – should be standing here, at the mercy of three villains, utterly powerless, when outside, not fifty paces away, the other side of those walls, fifty men at arms were there, set to guard his person.

And suddenly fear fell away from him. The trembling of his limbs ceased, his vision became clear, his mind alert. Even around his quaking lips there came the ghost of a smile.

His senses, keyed up by the imminence of his danger, had seized upon a sound which came from outside, faint as yet, but very obviously drawing nearer. In the semi-darkness and with his head buzzing and his nerves tingling, he could not distinguish either the quality of the sound nor yet the exact direction whence it came. But whatever it was – even if it was not all that he hoped – the sound was bound to set his soldiers on the alert; and if he could only temporize with those ruffians for a minute or two, the very next would see the captain of his guard rushing in to report what was happening: That Stadtholder sighted, the signal given, Nicolaes Beresteyn coming swiftly to the rescue.

Therefore, in the face of his own imminent peril, the Lord of Stoutenburg no longer felt afraid, only tensely vitally expectant. The two caitiffs, on the other hand appeared to have heard nothing. At any rate, they went on with their game, and the flute-like, high-pitched tones of the fat loon alternated with the deep base of his companion:

"Three and two make five!"

"No, four, you varlet!"

"Six!"

"Blank, by Beelzebub! My luck is dead out to-day."

And the sound drew nearer. There was no mistaking it. Men running. The clatter of arms. Horses, too. A pawing, and a champing, and a general hubbub, which those two ruffians could not fail to hear. Nor did any sound come down from the loft. Yet Gilda was there with the miserable plepshurk who, whatever else happened, would inevitably stand before her now as an informer and a cheat. This, at any rate, was a fact. The man had betrayed his master in order to save his miserable life, and the burgomaster had connived at his escape through an access of doltish weakness. But the fact remained. The Stadtholder was approaching. The next few minutes – seconds, perhaps – would see the final triumphant issue of this terrible adventure.

Stoutenburg, like a feline at bay, waited.

Then, all at once, a musket shot rang through the air, then another, and yet another; and all at once the whole air around was alive with sounds. The clang of arms; the lusty battle cries. Men out there had come to grips. In the drenching rain they were at one another's throats.

The two caitiffs quietly put aside their dice and rose to their feet. They stood with their backs to the door, their eyes fixed upon his lordship.

"Stand aside, you dolts!" Stoutenburg cried aloud; for he thought that he read murder in those two pairs of eyes, and he had need of all his nerves to assure himself that all was well, that, though his captain had not come to him for a reason which no doubt was sound, his soldiers were at grips with the Stadtholder's vanguard, and Nicolaes was already half-way up the slope.

But he, Stoutenburg, was unarmed, and could not push past those two assassins who were guarding the door. He bethought himself of his sword, which lay on the floor of the loft. He turned with a sudden impulse to get hold of it at all costs, and was met at the very foot of the steps by the man who had baffled him at every turn.

Diogenes, sword in hand, did not even pause to look on his impotent enemy. With one spring, he was across the floor and out by the door, which one of the ruffians immediately closed behind him.

It had all happened swifter even than thought. Stoutenburg, trapped, helpless, more bewildered in truth than terrified, still believed in a happy issue to his present desperate position. The thought came to him that he might purchase his safety from those potential murderers.

"Ten thousand guilders," he called out wildly, "if you will let me pass!"

But the fat runnion merely turned to the lean one, and the look of understanding which passed between them sent an icy shudder down his lordship's spine. He knew that from these two he could expect no mercy. A hoarse cry of horror escaped his lips as he saw that each held a dagger in one hand.

Then began that awful chase when man becomes a hunted beast – that grim game of hide-and-seek, with the last issue never once in doubt. The Lord of Stoutenburg trapped between these narrow walls, ran round and round like a mouse in a cage; now seeking refuge behind a girder, now leaping over an intervening obstacle, now crouching, panting and bathed in sweat, under cover of the gloom. And no one spoke; no one called. Neither the hunted nor the hunters. It seemed as if a conspiracy of silence existed between them; or else that the nearness of death had put a seal on all their lips.

Out there the clang of battle appeared more remote. Nothing seemed to occur in the immediate approach of the molen. It all came from afar, resounding across the Veluwe, above the patter of the rain and the soughing of the wind, through the rafters of the old mill. Drumming and thumping, the angle of armour, the clang of pike and lance, of metal; the loud report of musket shot, the strident grating of chains and wheels. But all far away, not here. Not outside the molen, but down there in the gorge, where Nicolaes had been encamped. My heavens, what did it mean?

Already the trapped creature was getting exhausted. Once or twice he had come down on his knees. His eyes were growing dim. His breath came and went with a wheezing sound from his breast. It was not just two murderous brigands who were pursuing him, but Nemesis herself, with sword of retribution drawn, in her hand an hour-glass, the sands of which were running low.

All at once the miscreant found himself at the foot of the steps, and, blindly stumbling, he ran up to the loft – instinctively, without set purpose save that of warding off, if only for a minute, the inevitable end.

7

Gilda was standing at the top of the steps with neck craned forward, her hands held tightly to her breast, her whole attitude one of nameless horror. She had been listening to the multifarious sounds which came from outside, and the natural, womanly fear for the safety of her beloved had been her one dominant emotion.

She had heard nothing else for a time, until suddenly she caught one or two stray sounds of that grim and furtive fight for life which was going on down below. She had reached the top of the steps, and tried to peer through the gloom to ascertain whose were those stealthy, swift footfalls so like those of a hunted beast, and whose the heavy, lumbering tread that spoke of stern and unwavering pursuit. At first she could see nothing, and the very silence which lay like a pall upon the grim scene below struck her with a sense of paralysing dread.

Then she caught sight first of one figure, then of another, as they crossed her line of vision. She could distinguish nothing very clearly – just those slowly moving figures – and for a moment or two felt herself unable to move. Then she heard the laboured breathing of a man, a groan as of a soul tortured with fear, and the next instant the Lord of Stoutenburg appeared, stumbling up the narrow steps.

At sight of her he fell like an inert thing with a husky cry at her feet. His arms encircled her knees; his head fell against her gown.

"Gilda, save me!" he whispered hoarsely. "For the love of Heaven! They'll murder me! Save me, for pity's sake! Gilda!"

He sobbed and cried like a child, abject in his terror, loathsome in his craven cowardice. Gilda could not stir. He held her with his arms as in a vise. She would have given worlds for the physical strength to wrench her gown out of his clutch, to flee from the hated sight of him who had planned to do her beloved such an irreparable injury. Oh, she hated him! She hated him worse, perhaps, than she had ever done before, now that he clung like a miserable dastard to her for mercy.

"Leave the poltroon to us, mejuffrouw," a gentle, flute-like tone broke in on the miscreant's ravings.

"Now then, take your punishment like a man!" a gruff voice added sternly.

And two familiar faces emerged out of the gloom, immediately below where Gilda was standing, imprisoned by those cringing arms. The man, in truth, had not even the primeval pluck of a savage. He was beaten, and he knew it. What had happened out there on the Veluwe, how completely he had been tricked by the Englishman he did not know as yet. But he was afraid to die, and shrank neither from humiliation nor contempt in order to save his own worthless life from the wreck of all his ambitions.

At the sound of those two voices, which in truth were like a death-knell in his ears, he jumped to his feet; but he did not loosen his hold on Gilda. Swift as thought he had found refuge behind her, and held her by the arms in front of him like a shield.

Historians have always spoken of the Lord of Stoutenburg as extraordinarily nimble in mind and body. That nimbleness in truth, stood him in good stead now; or whilst Socrates and Pythagoras, clumsy in their movements, lumbering and hampered by their respect for the person of the jongejuffrouw, reached the loft, and then for one instant hesitated how best to proceed in their grim task without offending the ears and eyes of the great lady, Stoutenburg had with one bound slipped from behind her down the steps and was across the floor of the molen and out the door before the two worthies had had time to utter the comprehensive curse which, at this unexpected manoeuvre on the part of their quarry, had risen to their lips.

"We had promised Diogenes not to allow the blackguard to escape!" Pythagoras exclaimed ruefully.

And both started in hot pursuit, whilst Gilda, seeking shelter in a dark angle of the loft, fell, sobbing with excitement and only half-conscious, upon a pile of sacking.

Chapter XVI – The Final Issue

1

PYTHAGORAS and Socrates failed to find the trail of the miscreant, who had vanished under cover of the night. We know that Stoutenburg did succeed, in fact, in reaching de Berg's encampment, half-starved and wearied, but safe. How he did it, no one will ever know. His career of crime had received a mighty check and the marauding expeditions which he undertook subsequently against his own country were of a futile and desultory nature. History ceases to trouble herself about him after that abortive incursion into Gelderland.

How that incursion was frustrated by the gallant Englishman, known to fame as the first Sir Percy Blakeney, but to his intimates as Diogenes, the erstwhile penniless soldier of fortune, we know chiefly through van Aitzema's Saken von Staet. The worthy chronicler enlarges upon the Englishman's adventure - he always calls him "the Englishman" – from the time when a week and more ago, he took leave of Nicolaes Beresteyn outside Barneveld to that when he reached Amersfoort, just in time to avert a terrible catastrophe.

The author of Saken v. Staet tells of the ambuscade on the shores of the Ijssel, "the Englishman's swim for life through the drifting floes." On reaching the opposite bank, it seems that he was so spent and more than half frozen, that he lay half unconscious on the bank for awhile. Presently, however, alive to the danger of possible further ambuscades, he re-started on his way, found a deserted hut close by, and crawled in there for shelter. As soon as darkness had set in he started back for Zutphen, there to warn Marquet not to proceed. The whole of the Stadtholder's plans had obviously been revealed to de Berg by some traitor – whose identity Diogenes then could not fail but guess – and it would have been sheer madness to attempt to cross the Ijssel now at any of the points originally intended.

To reach Zutphen at this juncture meant for the undaunted adventurer two leagues and more to traverse, and with clothes frozen hard to the skin. But he did reach Zutphen in time, and with the assistance of Marquet, then evolved the plan of an advance into Gelderland by effecting the crossing of the Ijssel as far north as Apeldoorn, and then striking across the Veluwe either to Amersfoort or to Ede, threatening de Berg's advance, and possibly effecting a junction with the Stadtholder's main army.

After this understanding with Marquet, Diogenes then proceeded to Arnheim, where the garrison could now only be warned to hold the city at all costs until assistance could be sent.

In the meantime, de Berg's troops were swarming everywhere. The Englishman could only proceed by night, had to hide by day on the Veluwe as best he could. Hence much delay. More than once he was on the point of capture, but succeeded eventually in reaching Arnheim.

Here he saw Coorne, who was in command of the small garrison, assured him of coming relief, and made him swear not to surrender the city, since the Stadtholder would soon be on his way with strong reinforcements. Thence to Nijmegen on the same errand. A more easy journey this, seeing that Isembourg ad not begun his advance from Kleve. After that, De Keysere and Wageningen.

Van Aitzema says that it was between Nijmegen and Wageningen that "the Englishman," lurking in a thicket of scrub, overheard some talk of how the Stadtholder was to be waylaid and captured on his return to camp from Amersfoort. This fact the chronicler must have learned at first hand. By this time the forces of de Berg were spreading over Gelderland. "The Englishman" gathered that the Archduchess's plans were to leave Isembourg's army to deal with Arnheim and Nijmegen for the present, whilst de Berg was to march on Ede, and, if possible, push on as far as Amersfoort. But as to how the coup against the Stadtholder was to be effected, he could not ascertain. At the time he did not know that his Highness intended to visit Amersfoort again. But for him, that little city where Gilda dwelt was just now the hub of the universe, and thank Heaven his errand was now accomplished, all his Highness's orders executed, and he was free to go to his young wife as fast as his own endurance and Spanish vedettes would allow.

This meant another tramp across open country, which by this time was overrun with enemy troops. Fugitives from Ede were everywhere to be seen. "The Spaniards. They are on us!" rang from end to end of the invaded province, and the echo of that dismal cry must by now have been rolling even as far as Utrecht.

It meant also seeking cover against enemy surprise parties, who threw the daring adventurer more than once out of his course, so that we hear of him once as far south as Rhenen, and then as far east as Doorn. It meant hiding amongst the reeds in the half-frozen marshes, swimming the Rhyn at one point, the Eem at another; it meant days without food and nights without rest. It meant all that, and more in pluck and endurance and determination, to which three qualities in "the Englishman" the worthy chronicler, though ever chary of words, pays ungrudging tribute.

He reached Amersfoort, as we know, just in time to see the Stadtholder leave the city in the company of the traitor, Nicolaes Beresteyn, and, struck by that same treacherous hand, fell, helpless for a moment, at the very threshold of the burgomaster's house.

After which began the martyrdom which had ended in such perfect triumph and happiness.

The daring adventurer, left lonely and stricken upon the moorland, did in truth go through an agony of misery and humiliation such as seldom falls to the lot of any man. Indeed, what he did suffer throughout that terrible day, whilst he believed himself to irretrievable blinded, was never known to any one save to the two faithful friends who watched lovingly over him. Socrates, after he had accompanied the Stadtholder, returned to sit and watch with Pythagoras beside the man to whom they both clung with such whole-hearted devotion.

2

It was not until late in the night that a faint glimmer of light, coming from the fire which the two caitiffs had managed to kindle as the night was bitterly cold, reached the young soldier's aching limbs, and seemed to him like a tiny beacon of hope in the blackness of his misery. By the time that the grey dawn broke over the moorland, he had realized that the injury which he had thought irremediable, had only been transient, and that every hour now brought an improvement in his power of vision.

Whereupon, three heads were put together to devise a means for using the Englishman's supposed blindness to the best advantage. One wise head and two loyal ones, not one of them even remotely acquainted with fear, what finer combination could be found for the eventful undoing of a pack of traitors?

Ede was in the hands of the Spaniards, Amersfoort on the point of sharing the like fate. These facts were sufficiently confirmed by the stray fugitives who wandered homeless and distracted across the moorland, and were in turn interrogated by the three conspirators.

With the woman he loved inside the invaded city, and with that recreant Stoutenburg in command of the enemy troops there, Diogenes' first thought was to get into Amersfoort himself at all risks and costs. As for the plan for freeing the town and punishing the miscreants, it was simple enough. To collect a small troop of ruffians from amongst the fugitives on the moorlands and place these under the command of Socrates, was the first move. The second was to send Pythagoras with an urgent message to Marquet to hurry eastward with his army from Apeldoorn, to the relief of Amersfoort, taking on his way the lonely molen on the Veluwe, where an important detachment of enemy troops might be expected to encamp.

The one thing with which Diogenes was, most fortunately amply provided, was money; money which he had by him when first he started out of Amersfoort on the Stadtholder's errand; money which was needful now to enable Socrates to recruit his small army of ne'er-do-wells and to assist Pythagoras on his embassy to Marquet.

Thereafter Diogenes, feigning blindness and worse, made his way into the presence of the Lord of Stoutenburg, who held Gilda at his mercy and the whole city to ransom for her obedience.

To dangle before the miscreant's eyes the prospect of capturing the Stadtholder's person, and thus make himself master of the Netherlands, was the pivot around which the whole plan revolved. The bait could not fail to attract the ambitious cupidity of the traitor, and verisimilitude was given to the story by Socrates' band of ruffians, whose orders were to spread the news of the Stadtholder's advance both on Ede and Amersfoort, and to silence effectually any emissaries of Stoutenburg's who might be sent out to ascertain the truth of these rumours.

We may take it that Socrates and his little troop saw to it that none of these emissaries did return to Amersfoort for the Lord of Stoutenburg marched out of the city at dawn, with his sinister banner flying, with his musketeers, pikemen and lancers, and with Gilda Beresteyn a virtual prisoner in his train.

That the daring adventurer risked an ignominious death by this carefully laid plan cannot be denied; but he was one of those men who had gambled with life and death since he was a child, who was accustomed to stake his all upon the spin of a coin; and, anyhow, if he failed, death would have been thrice welcome, as the only escape out of untold misery and sorrow.

Chance favoured him in this, that at the last he was left face to face with the burgomaster, to whom he immediately confided everything, and who enabled him to escape out of the house by the service staircase, and thence into the streets, where no one knew him and where he remained all night, effectually concealed as a unit in the midst of the crowd. He actually went out of Amersfoort in the train of Stoutenburg; and whilst his lordship's troops made a long halt at Barneveld, "the Englishman" continued his way unmolested across the Veluwe to the lonely molen, which was to witness his success and happiness, or the final annihilation of all that made life possible.

3

All this and more, in the matter of detail, hath the meticulous chronicler of the time put conscientiously on record. We must assume that he was able to verify all his facts at source, chiefly through the garrulous offices of "the Englishman's" two well-known familiars.

What, however, will for ever remain unrecorded, save in the book of heroic deeds, is a woman's perfect loyalty. During those hours and days, full of horror and of dread, Gilda never once wavered in her belief in the man she loved. From the moment when Nicolaes tried to poison her mind against him, and through all the vicissitudes which placed her face to face with what was a mere semblance of her beloved, she had never doubted him, when even the Stadtholder seemed to doubt.

She knew him to be playing a dangerous game – but a game for all that – when first she beheld him, sightless and abject, in the presence of their mutual enemy, and had rested for one brief second against his breast. That his eyes, still dazed by the poisonous fumes, could vaguely discern her face, even though they could not read the expression thereon, she did not know. The fear that he was irremediably blind was the most cruel of all the tortures which she had undergone that night.

When her father came to her in the small hours of the morning to tell her that all was well with the beloved of her heart, but that he would have all the need of all her courage and of all her determination to help him to complete his self-imposed task, she realized for the first time how near to actual death the torturing fear had brought her. But from that time forth, she never lost her presence of mind. With marvellous courage she gripped the whole situation and played her role unswervingly until the end.

Everything depended on whether Marquet reached the molen before the Lord of Stoutenburg, or his captains suspected that anything was wrong. True, Pythagoras had brought back the news that he had met the loyal commander at Apeldoorn, and that the latter, despite the fact that he and his troops intend to take there a well-earned rest, had immediately given the order to march. But, even so, the future of the Netherlands and of her Stadtholder, as well as the fate of the gallant Englishman and his beloved wife, lay in the hands of God.

One hour before dusk Marquet's vedettes first came in contact with the outposts of Beresteyn's encampment in the gorge below the molen. There was a brief struggle, fierce on both sides, until the main body of Marquet's army, four thousand strong, appeared on the eastern heights above the gorge.

Whilst the Lord of Stoutenburg ran round and round the narrow space wherein he was a hunted prisoner, trying to escape that shameful death which threatened him at the hand of two humble justiciaries, his few hundred men were falling like butchered beasts beneath the pike-thrusts and musket shots of Marquet's trained troops.

Nicolaes Beresteyn was the first to fall.

It was better so. Dishonour so complete could be only wiped out by death.

When, a day or two later, after Marquet had driven the Spaniards out of Amersfoort, the burgomaster heard the news of the death of his only son. He murmured an humble and broken-hearted: "Thank God!"

Chapter XVII – The Only Word

1

OUT there, in the lonely molen on the Veluwe, Gilda had remained for a while, half numb with nerve strain, suffering from the reaction after the terrible excitement of the past few hours. Presently her old serving-woman came to her, still raging with choler at the outrage committed against her person by those two abominable rascallions.

With great volubility, she explained to her mistress that they had fallen on her unawares when first she had been sent down-stairs by his lordship – whom may God punish! – The had bound and gagged her, and then told her quite cheerfully that this was an act of friendship on their part, to save her from a worse fate and from the temptation of talking when she should remain silent.

She had been thrust into a dark angle of the mill-house, from whence she could see absolutely nothing, and where she had lain all this while, entirely helpless, hearing that awful din which had been going on outside, expecting to be murdered in cold blood at any moment, and tortured with fear as to what was happening to her mistress. Only a few moments ago, the two ruffians had reappeared, running helter-skelter down the steps and thence out through the door into the open. Fortunately, one of them, conscience-stricken no doubt, had thought, before fleeing, to release her from her bonds.

Maria was stupid, uncomprehending and garrulous; but she was loyal, and had a warm and ample bosom, whereon a tired and aching head could find a little rest.

Gilda, her body still shaken by hysterical sobs, her teeth chattering, her senses reeling with the horror of all that she had gone through, found some measure of comfort in the old woman's ministrations. A mugful of wine, left over from the midday meal, helped her to regain command over her nerves. Holding her young mistress in her arms, Maria, crooning like a mother over her baby, rocked the half-inert young form into some semblance of sleep.

2

And here Diogenes found her a couple of hours later, curled up like a tired child in the arms of the old woman.

He came up on tiptoe, carrying a lanthorn, for now it was quite dark. This he placed on the floor, and then, with infinite caution, he slid into Maria's place and took the beloved form into his own strong arms.

She scarcely moved, just opened her eyes for a second or two, and then nestled closer against his shoulder, with a little sigh, half of weariness, but wholly of content.

She was just dead-tired after all she had gone through, and now she slept just like a baby in his arms; whilst he was as happy as it is possible for any human being to be, for she was safe and well, and nothing could part her from him now. He was satisfied to watch her as she slept, her dear face against his breast, her soft breath coming and going with perfect evenness through her parted lips.

Once he stooped and kissed her, and then she woke, put her arms around his neck, and both forgot for the time being that there was another world save that of Love.

THE END

The Scarlet Pimpernel

CHAPTER I
PARIS: SEPTEMBER, 1792

A surging, seething, murmuring crowd of beings that are human only in name, for to the eye and ear they seem naught but savage creatures, animated by vile passions and by the lust of vengeance and of hate. The hour, some little time before sunset, and the place, the West Barricade, at the very spot where, a decade later, a proud tyrant raised an undying monument to the nation's glory and his own vanity.

During the greater part of the day the guillotine had been kept busy at its ghastly work: all that France had boasted of in the past centuries, of ancient names, and blue blood, had paid toll to her desire for liberty and for fraternity. The carnage had only ceased at this late hour of the day because there were other more interesting sights for the people to witness, a little while before the final closing of the barricades for the night.

And so the crowd rushed away from the Place de la Greve and made for the various barricades in order to watch this interesting and amusing sight.

It was to be seen every day, for those aristos were such fools! They were traitors to the people of course, all of them, men, women, and children, who happened to be descendants of the great men who since the Crusades had made the glory of France: her old NOBLESSE. Their ancestors had oppressed the people, had crushed them under the scarlet heels of their dainty buckled shoes, and now the people had become the rulers of France and crushed their former masters — not beneath their heel, for they went shoeless mostly in these days — but a more effectual weight, the knife of the guillotine.

And daily, hourly, the hideous instrument of torture claimed its many victims — old men, young women, tiny children until the day when it would finally demand the head of a King and of a beautiful young Queen.

But this was as it should be: were not the people now the rulers of France? Every aristocrat was a traitor, as his ancestors had been before him: for two hundred years now the people had sweated, and toiled, and starved, to keep a lustful court in lavish extravagance; now the descendants of those who had helped to make those courts brilliant had to hide for their lives — to fly, if they wished to avoid the tardy vengeance of the people.

And they did try to hide, and tried to fly: that was just the fun of the whole thing. Every afternoon before the gates closed and the market carts went out in procession by the various barricades, some fool of an aristo endeavoured to evade the clutches of the Committee of Public Safety. In various disguises, under various pretexts, they tried to slip through the barriers, which were so well guarded by citizen soldiers of the Republic. Men in women's clothes, women in male attire, children disguised in beggars' rags: there were some of all sorts: CI-DEVANT counts, marquises, even dukes, who wanted to fly from France, reach England or some other equally accursed country, and there try to rouse foreign feelings against the glorious Revolution, or to raise an army in order to liberate the wretched prisoners in the Temple, who had once called themselves sovereigns of France.

But they were nearly always caught at the barricades, Sergeant Bibot especially at the West Gate had a wonderful nose for scenting an aristo in the most perfect disguise. Then, of course, the fun began. Bibot would look at his prey as a cat looks upon the mouse, play with him, sometimes for quite a quarter of an hour, pretend to be hoodwinked by the disguise, by the wigs and other bits of theatrical make-up which hid the identity of a CI-DEVANT noble marquise or count.

Oh! Bibot had a keen sense of humour, and it was well worth hanging round that West Barricade, in order to see him catch an aristo in the very act of trying to flee from the vengeance of the people.

Sometimes Bibot would let his prey actually out by the gates, allowing him to think for the space of two minutes at least that he really had escaped out of Paris, and might even manage to reach the coast of England in safety, but Bibot would let the unfortunate wretch walk about ten metres towards the open country, then he would send two men after him and bring him back, stripped of his disguise.

Oh! that was extremely funny, for as often as not the fugitive would prove to be a woman, some proud marchioness, who looked terribly comical when she found herself in Bibot's clutches after all, and knew that a summary trial would await her the next day and after that, the fond embrace of Madame la Guillotine.

No wonder that on this fine afternoon in September the crowd round Bibot's gate was eager and excited. The lust of blood grows with its satisfaction, there is no satiety: the crowd had seen a hundred noble heads fall beneath the guillotine to-day, it wanted to make sure that it would see another hundred fall on the morrow.

Bibot was sitting on an overturned and empty cask close by the gate of the barricade; a small detachment of citoyen soldiers was under his command. The work had been very hot lately. Those cursed aristos were becoming terrified and tried their hardest to slip out of Paris: men, women and children, whose ancestors, even in remote ages, had served those traitorous Bourbons, were all traitors themselves and right food for the guillotine. Every day Bibot had had the satisfaction of unmasking some fugitive royalists and sending them back to be tried by the Committee of Public Safety, presided over by that good patriot, Citoyen Foucquier-Tinville.

Robespierre and Danton both had commended Bibot for his zeal and Bibot was proud of the fact that he on his own initiative had sent at least fifty aristos to the guillotine.

But to-day all the sergeants in command at the various barricades had had special orders. Recently a very great number of aristos had succeeded in escaping out of France and in reaching England safely. There were curious rumours about these escapes; they had become very frequent and singularly daring; the people's minds were becoming strangely excited about it all. Sergeant Grospierre had been sent to the guillotine for allowing a whole family of aristos to slip out of the North Gate under his very nose.

It was asserted that these escapes were organised by a band of Englishmen, whose daring seemed to be unparalleled, and who, from sheer desire to meddle in what did not concern them, spent their spare time in snatching away lawful victims destined for Madame la Guillotine. These rumours soon grew in extravagance; there was no doubt that this band of meddlesome Englishmen did exist; moreover, they seemed to be under the leadership of a man whose pluck and audacity were almost fabulous. Strange stories were afloat of how he and those aristos whom he rescued became suddenly invisible as they reached the barricades and escaped out of the gates by sheer supernatural agency.

No one had seen these mysterious Englishmen; as for their leader, he was never spoken of, save with a superstitious shudder. Citoyen Foucquier-Tinville would in the course of the day receive a scrap of paper from some mysterious source; sometimes he would find it in the pocket of his coat, at others it would be handed to him by someone in the crowd, whilst he was on his way to the sitting of the Committee of Public Safety. The paper always contained a brief notice that the band of meddlesome Englishmen were at work, and it was always signed with a device drawn in red — a little star-shaped flower, which we in England call the Scarlet Pimpernel. Within a few hours of the receipt of this impudent notice, the citoyens of the Committee of Public Safety would hear that so many royalists and aristocrats had succeeded in reaching the coast, and were on their way to England and safety.

The guards at the gates had been doubled, the sergeants in command had been threatened with death, whilst liberal rewards were offered for the capture of these daring and impudent Englishmen. There was a sum of five thousand francs promised to the man who laid hands on the mysterious and elusive Scarlet Pimpernel.

Everyone felt that Bibot would be that man, and Bibot allowed that belief to take firm root in everybody's mind; and so, day after day, people came to watch him at the West Gate, so as to be present when he laid hands on any fugitive aristo who perhaps might be accompanied by that mysterious Englishman.

"Bah!" he said to his trusted corporal, "Citoyen Grospierre was a fool! Had it been me now, at that North Gate last week . . ."

Citoyen Bibot spat on the ground to express his contempt for his comrade's stupidity.

"How did it happen, citoyen?" asked the corporal.

"Grospierre was at the gate, keeping good watch," began Bibot, pompously, as the crowd closed in round him, listening eagerly to his narrative. "We've all heard of this meddlesome Englishman, this accursed Scarlet Pimpernel. He won't get through MY gate, MORBLEU! unless he be the devil himself. But Grospierre was a fool. The market carts were going through the gates; there was one laden with casks, and driven by an old man, with a boy beside him. Grospierre was a bit drunk, but he thought himself very clever; he looked into the casks — most of them, at least — and saw they were empty, and let the cart go through."

A murmur of wrath and contempt went round the group of ill-clad wretches, who crowded round Citoyen Bibot.

"Half an hour later," continued the sergeant, "up comes a captain of the guard with a squad of some dozen soldiers with him. 'Has a cart gone through?' he asks of Grospierre, breathlessly. 'Yes,' says Grospierre, 'not half an hour ago.' 'And you have let them escape,' shouts the captain furiously. 'You'll go to the guillotine for this, citoyen sergeant! that cart held concealed the CI-DEVANT Duc de Chalis and all his family!' 'What!' thunders Grospierre, aghast. 'Aye! and the driver was none other than that cursed Englishman, the Scarlet Pimpernel.'"

A howl of execration greeted this tale. Citoyen Grospierre had paid for his blunder on the guillotine, but what a fool! oh! what a fool!

Bibot was laughing so much at his own tale that it was some time before he could continue.

"'After them, my men,' shouts the captain," he said after a while, "'remember the reward; after them, they cannot have gone far!' And with that he rushes through the gate followed by his dozen soldiers."

"But it was too late!" shouted the crowd, excitedly.

"They never got them!"

"Curse that Grospierre for his folly!"

"He deserved his fate!"

"Fancy not examining those casks properly!"

But these sallies seemed to amuse Citoyen Bibot exceedingly; he laughed until his sides ached, and the tears streamed down his cheeks.

"Nay, nay!" he said at last, "those aristos weren't in the cart; the driver was not the Scarlet Pimpernel!"

"What?"

"No! The captain of the guard was that damned Englishman in disguise, and everyone of his soldiers aristos!"

The crowd this time said nothing: the story certainly savoured of the supernatural, and though the Republic had abolished God, it had not quite succeeded in killing the fear of the supernatural in the hearts of the people. Truly that Englishman must be the devil himself.

The sun was sinking low down in the west. Bibot prepared himself to close the gates.

"EN AVANT the carts," he said.

Some dozen covered carts were drawn up in a row, ready to leave town, in order to fetch the produce from the country close by, for market the next morning. They were mostly well known to Bibot, as they went through his gate twice every day on their way to and from the town. He spoke to one or two of their drivers — mostly women — and was at great pains to examine the inside of the carts.

"You never know," he would say, "and I'm not going to be caught like that fool Grospierre."

The women who drove the carts usually spent their day on the Place de la Greve, beneath the platform of the guillotine, knitting and gossiping, whilst they watched the rows of tumbrils arriving with the victims the Reign of Terror claimed every day. It was great fun to see the aristos arriving for the reception of Madame la Guillotine, and the places close by the platform were very much sought after. Bibot, during the day, had been on duty on the Place. He recognized most of the old hats, "tricotteuses," as they were called, who sat there and knitted, whilst head after head fell beneath the knife, and they themselves got quite bespattered with the blood of those cursed aristos.

"He! la mere!" said Bibot to one of these horrible hags, "what have you got there?"

He had seen her earlier in the day, with her knitting and the whip of her cart close beside her. Now she had fastened a row of curly locks to the whip handle, all colours, from gold to silver, fair to dark, and she stroked them with her huge, bony fingers as she laughed at Bibot.

"I made friends with Madame Guillotine's lover," she said with a coarse laugh, "he cut these off for me from the heads as they rolled down. He has promised me some more to-morrow, but I don't know if I shall be at my usual place."

"Ah! how is that, la mere?" asked Bibot, who, hardened soldier that he was, could not help shuddering at the awful loathsomeness of this semblance of a woman, with her ghastly trophy on the handle of her whip.

"My grandson has got the small-pox," she said with a jerk of her thumb towards the inside of her cart, "some say it's the plague! If it is, I sha'n't be allowed to come into Paris to-morrow." At the first mention of the word small-pox, Bibot had stepped hastily backwards, and when the old hag spoke of the plague, he retreated from her as fast as he could.

"Curse you!" he muttered, whilst the whole crowd hastily avoided the cart, leaving it standing all alone in the midst of the place.

The old hag laughed.

"Curse you, citoyen, for being a coward," she said. "Bah! what a man to be afraid of sickness."

"MORBLEU! the plague!"

Everyone was awe-struck and silent, filled with horror for the loathsome malady, the one thing which still had the power to arouse terror and disgust in these savage, brutalised creatures.

"Get out with you and with your plague-stricken brood!" shouted Bibot, hoarsely.

And with another rough laugh and coarse jest, the old hag whipped up her lean nag and drove her cart out of the gate.

This incident had spoilt the afternoon. The people were terrified of these two horrible curses, the two maladies which nothing could cure, and which were the precursors of an awful and lonely death. They hung about the barricades, silent and sullen for a while, eyeing one another suspiciously, avoiding each other as if by instinct, lest the plague lurked already in their midst. Presently, as in the case of Grospierre, a captain of the guard appeared suddenly. But he was known to Bibot, and there was no fear of his turning out to be a sly Englishman in disguise.

"A cart, . . ." he shouted breathlessly, even before he had reached the gates.

"What cart?" asked Bibot, roughly.

"Driven by an old hag. . . . A covered cart . . ."

"There were a dozen . . ."

"An old hag who said her son had the plague?"

"Yes . . ."

"You have not let them go?"

"MORBLEU!" said Bibot, whose purple cheeks had suddenly become white with fear.

"The cart contained the CI-DEVANT Comtesse de Tourney and her two children, all of them traitors and condemned to death."

"And their driver?" muttered Bibot, as a superstitious shudder ran down his spine.

"SACRE TONNERRE," said the captain, "but it is feared that it was that accursed Englishman himself — the Scarlet Pimpernel."

In the kitchen Sally was extremely busy — saucepans and frying-pans were standing in rows on the gigantic hearth, the huge stock-pot stood in a corner, and the jack turned with slow deliberation, and presented alternately to the glow every side of a noble sirloin of beef. The two little kitchen-maids bustled around, eager to help, hot and panting, with cotton sleeves well tucked up above the dimpled elbows, and giggling over some private jokes of their own, whenever Miss Sally's back was turned for a moment. And old Jemima, stolid in temper and solid in bulk, kept up a long and subdued grumble, while she stirred the stock-pot methodically over the fire.

"What ho! Sally!" came in cheerful if none too melodious accents from the coffee-room close by.

"Lud bless my soul!" exclaimed Sally, with a good-humoured laugh, "what be they all wanting now, I wonder!"

"Beer, of course," grumbled Jemima, "you don't 'xpect Jimmy Pitkin to 'ave done with one tankard, do ye?"

"Mr. 'Arry, 'e looked uncommon thirsty too," simpered Martha, one of the little kitchen-maids; and her beady black eyes twinkled as they met those of her companion, whereupon both started on a round of short and suppressed giggles.

Sally looked cross for a moment, and thoughtfully rubbed her hands against her shapely hips; her palms were itching, evidently, to come in contact with Martha's rosy cheeks — but inherent good-humour prevailed, and with a pout and a shrug of the shoulders, she turned her attention to the fried potatoes.

"What ho, Sally! hey, Sally!"

And a chorus of pewter mugs, tapped with impatient hands against the oak tables of the coffee-room, accompanied the shouts for mine host's buxom daughter.

"Sally!" shouted a more persistent voice, "are ye goin' to be all night with that there beer?"

"I do think father might get the beer for them," muttered Sally, as Jemima, stolidly and without further comment, took a couple of foam-crowned jugs from the shelf, and began filling a number of pewter tankards with some of that home-brewed ale for which "The Fisherman's Rest" had been famous since that days of King Charles. "'E knows 'ow busy we are in 'ere."

"Your father is too busy discussing politics with Mr. 'Empseed to worry 'isself about you and the kitchen," grumbled Jemima under her breath.

Sally had gone to the small mirror which hung in a corner of the kitchen, and was hastily smoothing her hair and setting her frilled cap at its most becoming angle over her dark curls; then she took up the tankards by their handles, three in each strong, brown hand, and laughing, grumbling, blushing, carried them through into the coffee room.

There, there was certainly no sign of that bustle and activity which kept four women busy and hot in the glowing kitchen beyond.

The coffee-room of "The Fisherman's Rest" is a show place now at the beginning of the twentieth century. At the end of the eighteenth, in the year of grace 1792, it had not yet gained the notoriety and importance which a hundred additional years and the craze of the age have since bestowed upon it. Yet it was an old place, even then, for the oak rafters and beams were already black with age — as were the panelled seats, with their tall backs, and the long polished tables between, on which innumerable pewter tankards had left fantastic patterns of many-sized rings. In the leaded window, high up, a row of pots of scarlet geraniums and blue larkspur gave the bright note of colour against the dull background of the oak.

That Mr. Jellyband, landlord of "The Fisherman's Rest" at Dover, was a prosperous man, was of course clear to the most casual observer. The pewter on the fine old dressers, the brass above the gigantic hearth, shone like silver and gold — the red-tiled floor was as brilliant as the scarlet geranium on the window sill — this meant that his servants were good and plentiful, that the custom was constant, and of that order which necessitated the keeping up of the coffee-room to a high standard of elegance and order.

As Sally came in, laughing through her frowns, and displaying a row of dazzling white teeth, she was greeted with shouts and chorus of applause.

"Why, here's Sally! What ho, Sally! Hurrah for pretty Sally!"

"I thought you'd grown deaf in that kitchen of yours," muttered Jimmy Pitkin, as he passed the back of his hand across his very dry lips.

"All ri'! all ri'!" laughed Sally, as she deposited the freshly-filled tankards upon the tables, "why, what a 'urry to be sure! And is your gran'mother a-dyin' an' you wantin' to see the pore soul afore she'm gone! I never see'd such a mighty rushin'" A chorus of good-humoured laughter greeted this witticism, which gave the company there present food for many jokes, for some considerable time. Sally now seemed in less of a hurry to get back to her pots and pans. A young man with fair curly hair, and eager, bright blue eyes, was engaging most of her attention and the whole of her time, whilst broad witticisms anent Jimmy Pitkin's fictitious grandmother flew from mouth to mouth, mixed with heavy puffs of pungent tobacco smoke.

Facing the hearth, his legs wide apart, a long clay pipe in his mouth, stood mine host himself, worthy Mr. Jellyband, landlord of "The Fisherman's Rest," as his father had before him, aye, and his grandfather and great-grandfather too, for that matter. Portly in build, jovial in countenance and somewhat bald of pate, Mr. Jellyband was indeed a typical rural John Bull of those days — the days when our prejudiced insularity was at its height, when to an Englishman, be he lord, yeoman, or peasant, the whole of the continent of Europe was a den of immorality and the rest of the world an unexploited land of savages and cannibals.

There he stood, mine worthy host, firm and well set up on his limbs, smoking his long churchwarden and caring nothing for nobody at home, and despising everybody abroad. He wore the typical scarlet waistcoat, with shiny brass buttons, the corduroy breeches, and grey worsted stockings and smart buckled shoes, that characterised every self-respecting innkeeper in Great Britain in these days — and while pretty, motherless Sally had need of four pairs of brown hands to do all the work that fell on her shapely shoulders, worthy Jellyband discussed the affairs of nations with his most privileged guests.

The coffee-room indeed, lighted by two well-polished lamps, which hung from the raftered ceiling, looked cheerful and cosy in the extreme. Through the dense clouds of tobacco smoke that hung about in every corner, the faces of Mr. Jellyband's customers appeared red and pleasant to look at, and on good terms with themselves, their host and all the world; from every side of the room loud guffaws accompanied pleasant, if not highly intellectual, conversation — while Sally's repeated giggles testified to the good use Mr. Harry Waite was making of the short time she seemed inclined to spare him.

They were mostly fisher-folk who patronised Mr. Jellyband's coffee-room, but fishermen are known to be very thirsty people; the salt which they breathe in, when they are on the sea, accounts for their parched throats when on shore, but "The Fisherman's Rest" was something more than a rendezvous for these humble folk. The London and Dover coach started from the hostel daily, and passengers who had come across the Channel, and those who started for the "grand tour," all became acquainted with Mr. Jellyband, his French wines and his home-brewed ales.

It was towards the close of September, 1792, and the weather which had been brilliant and hot throughout the month had suddenly broken up; for two days torrents of rain had deluged the south of England, doing its level best to ruin what chances the apples and pears and late plums had of becoming really fine, self-respecting fruit. Even now it was beating against the leaded windows, and tumbling down the chimney, making the cheerful wood fire sizzle in the hearth.

"Lud! did you ever see such a wet September, Mr. Jellyband?" asked Mr. Hempseed.

He sat in one of the seats inside the hearth, did Mr. Hempseed, for he was an authority and important personage not only at "The Fisherman's Rest," where Mr. Jellyband always made a special selection of him as a foil for political arguments, but throughout the neighborhood, where his learning and notably his knowledge of the Scriptures was held in the most profound awe and respect. With one hand buried in the capacious pockets of his corduroys underneath his elaborately-worked, well-worn smock, the other holding his long clay pipe, Mr. Hempseed sat there looking dejectedly across the room at the rivulets of moisture which trickled down the window panes.

"No," replied Mr. Jellyband, sententiously, "I dunno, Mr. 'Empseed, as I ever did. An' I've been in these parts nigh on sixty years."

"Aye! you wouldn't rec'llect the first three years of them sixty, Mr. Jellyband," quietly interposed Mr. Hempseed. "I dunno as I ever see'd an infant take much note of the weather, leastways not in these parts, an' I've lived 'ere nigh on seventy-five years, Mr. Jellyband."

The superiority of this wisdom was so incontestable that for the moment Mr. Jellyband was not ready with his usual flow of argument.

"It do seem more like April than September, don't it?" continued Mr. Hempseed, dolefully, as a shower of raindrops fell with a sizzle upon the fire.

"Aye! that it do," assented the worthy host, "but then what can you 'xpect, Mr. 'Empseed, I says, with sich a government as we've got?"

Mr. Hempseed shook his head with an infinity of wisdom, tempered by deeply-rooted mistrust of the British climate and the British Government.

"I don't 'xpect nothing, Mr. Jellyband," he said. "Pore folks like us is of no account up there in Lunnon, I knows that, and it's not often as I do complain. But when it comes to sich wet weather in September, and all me fruit a-rottin' and a-dying' like the 'Guptian mother's first born, and doin' no more good than they did, pore dears, save a lot more Jews, pedlars and sich, with their oranges and sich like foreign ungodly fruit, which nobody'd buy if English apples and pears was nicely swelled. As the Scriptures say — "

"That's quite right, Mr. 'Empseed," retorted Jellyband, "and as I says, what can you 'xpect? There's all them Frenchy devils over the Channel yonder a-murderin' their king and nobility, and Mr. Pitt and Mr. Fox and Mr. Burke a-fightin' and a-wranglin' between them, if we Englishmen should 'low them to go on in their ungodly way. 'Let 'em murder!' says Mr. Pitt. 'Stop 'em!' says Mr. Burke."

"And let 'em murder, says I, and be demmed to 'em." said Mr. Hempseed, emphatically, for he had but little liking for his friend Jellyband's political arguments, wherein he always got out of his depth, and had but little chance for displaying those pearls of wisdom which had earned for him so high a reputation in the neighbourhood and so many free tankards of ale at "The Fisherman's Rest."

"Let 'em murder," he repeated again, "but don't lets 'ave sich rain in September, for that is agin the law and the Scriptures which says — "

"Lud! Mr. 'Arry, 'ow you made me jump!"

It was unfortunate for Sally and her flirtation that this remark of hers should have occurred at the precise moment when Mr. Hempseed was collecting his breath, in order to deliver himself one of those Scriptural utterances which made him famous, for it brought down upon her pretty head the full flood of her father's wrath.

"Now then, Sally, me girl, now then!" he said, trying to force a frown upon his good-humoured face, "stop that fooling with them young jackanapes and get on with the work."

"The work's gettin' on all ri', father."

But Mr. Jellyband was peremptory. He had other views for his buxom daughter, his only child, who would in God's good time become the owner of "The Fisherman's Rest," than to see her married to one of these young fellows who earned but a precarious livelihood with their net.

"Did ye hear me speak, me girl?" he said in that quiet tone, which no one inside the inn dared to disobey. "Get on with my Lord Tony's supper, for, if it ain't the best we can do, and 'e not satisfied, see what you'll get, that's all."

Reluctantly Sally obeyed.

"Is you 'xpecting special guests then to-night, Mr. Jellyband?" asked Jimmy Pitkin, in a loyal attempt to divert his host's attention from the circumstances connected with Sally's exit from the room.

"Aye! that I be," replied Jellyband, "friends of my Lord Tony hisself. Dukes and duchesses from over the water yonder, whom the young lord and his friend, Sir Andrew Ffoulkes, and other young noblemen have helped out of the clutches of them murderin' devils."

But this was too much for Mr. Hempseed's querulous philosophy.

"Lud!" he said, "what do they do that for, I wonder? I don't 'old not with interferin' in other folks' ways. As the Scriptures say — "

"Maybe, Mr. 'Empseed," interrupted Jellyband, with biting sarcasm, "as you're a personal friend of Mr. Pitt, and as you says along with Mr. Fox: 'Let 'em murder!' says you."

"Pardon me, Mr. Jellyband," feebly protested Mr. Hempseed, "I dunno as I ever did."

But Mr. Jellyband had at last succeeded in getting upon his favourite hobby-horse, and had no intention of dismounting in any hurry.

"Or maybe you've made friends with some of them French chaps 'oo they do say have come over here o' purpose to make us Englishmen agree with their murderin' ways."

"I dunno what you mean, Mr. Jellyband," suggested Mr. Hempseed, "all I know is — "

"All *I* know is," loudly asserted mine host, "that there was my friend Peppercorn, 'oo owns the 'Blue-Faced Boar,' an' as true and loyal an Englishman as you'd see in the land. And now look at 'im! — 'E made friends with some o' them frog-eaters, 'obnobbed with them just as if they was Englishmen, and not just a lot of immoral, Godforsaking furrin' spies. Well! and what happened? Peppercorn 'e now ups and talks of revolutions, and liberty, and down with the aristocrats, just like Mr. 'Empseed over 'ere!"

"Pardon me, Mr. Jellyband," again interposed Mr. Hempseed feebly, "I dunno as I ever did — "

Mr. Jellyband had appealed to the company in general, who were listening awe-struck and open-mouthed at the recital of Mr. Peppercorn's defalcations. At one table two customers — gentlemen apparently by their clothes — had pushed aside their half-finished game of dominoes, and had been listening for some time, and evidently with much amusement at Mr. Jellyband's international opinions. One of them now, with a quiet, sarcastic smile still lurking round the corners of his mobile mouth, turned towards the centre of the room where Mr. Jellyband was standing.

"You seem to think, mine honest friend," he said quietly, "that these Frenchmen, — spies I think you called them — are mighty clever fellows to have made mincemeat so to speak of your friend Mr. Peppercorn's opinions. How did they accomplish that now, think you?"

"Lud! sir, I suppose they talked 'im over. Those Frenchies, I've 'eard it said, 'ave got the gift of gab — and Mr. 'Empseed 'ere will tell you 'ow it is that they just twist some people round their little finger like."

"Indeed, and is that so, Mr. Hempseed?" inquired the stranger politely.

"Nay, sir!" replied Mr. Hempseed, much irritated, "I dunno as I can give you the information you require."

"Faith, then," said the stranger, "let us hope, my worthy host, that these clever spies will not succeed in upsetting your extremely loyal opinions."

But this was too much for Mr. Jellyband's pleasant equanimity. He burst into an uproarious fit of laughter, which was soon echoed by those who happened to be in his debt.

"Hahaha! hohoho! hehehe!" He laughed in every key, did my worthy host, and laughed until his sided ached, and his eyes streamed. "At me! hark at that! Did ye 'ear 'im say that they'd be upsettin' my opinions? — Eh? — Lud love you, sir, but you do say some queer things."

"Well, Mr. Jellyband," said Mr. Hempseed, sententiously, "you know what the Scriptures say: 'Let 'im 'oo stands take 'eed lest 'e fall.'"

"But then hark'ee Mr. 'Empseed," retorted Jellyband, still holding his sides with laughter, "the Scriptures didn't know me. Why, I wouldn't so much as drink a glass of ale with one o' them murderin' Frenchmen, and nothin' 'd make me change my opinions. Why! I've 'eard it said that them frog-eaters can't even speak the King's English, so, of course, if any of 'em tried to speak their God-forsaken lingo to me, why, I should spot them directly, see! — and forewarned is forearmed, as the saying goes."

"Aye! my honest friend," assented the stranger cheerfully, "I see that you are much too sharp, and a match for any twenty Frenchmen, and here's to your very good health, my worthy host, if you'll do me the honour to finish this bottle of mine with me."

"I am sure you're very polite, sir," said Mr. Jellyband, wiping his eyes which were still streaming with the abundance of his laughter, "and I don't mind if I do."

The stranger poured out a couple of tankards full of wine, and having offered one to mine host, he took the other himself.

"Loyal Englishmen as we all are," he said, whilst the same humorous smile played round the corners of his thin lips — "loyal as we are, we must admit that this at least is one good thing which comes to us from France."

"Aye! we'll none of us deny that, sir," assented mine host.

"And here's to the best landlord in England, our worthy host, Mr. Jellyband," said the stranger in a loud tone of voice.

"Hi, hip, hurrah!" retorted the whole company present. Then there was a loud clapping of hands, and mugs and tankards made a rattling music upon the tables to the accompaniment of loud laughter at nothing in particular, and of Mr. Jellyband's muttered exclamations:

"Just fancy ME bein' talked over by any God-forsaken furriner! — What? — Lud love you, sir, but you do say some queer things."

To which obvious fact the stranger heartily assented. It was certainly a preposterous suggestion that anyone could ever upset Mr. Jellyband's firmly-rooted opinions anent the utter worthlessness of the inhabitants of the whole continent of Europe.

CHAPTER III
THE REFUGEES

Feeling in every part of England certainly ran very high at this time against the French and their doings. Smugglers and legitimate traders between the French and the English coasts brought snatches of news from over the water, which made every honest Englishman's blood boil, and made him long to have "a good go" at those murderers, who had imprisoned their king and all his family, subjected the queen and the royal children to every species of indignity, and were even now loudly demanding the blood of the whole Bourbon family and of every one of its adherents.

The execution of the Princesse de Lamballe, Marie Antoinette's young and charming friend, had filled every one in England with unspeakable horror, the daily execution of scores of royalists of good family, whose only sin was their aristocratic name, seemed to cry for vengeance to the whole of civilised Europe.

Yet, with all that, no one dared to interfere. Burke had exhausted all his eloquence in trying to induce the British Government to fight the revolutionary government of France, but Mr. Pitt, with characteristic prudence, did not feel that this country was fit yet to embark on another arduous and costly war. It was for Austria to take the initiative; Austria, whose fairest daughter was even now a dethroned queen, imprisoned and insulted by a howling mob; surely 'twas not — so argued Mr. Fox — for the whole of England to take up arms, because one set of Frenchmen chose to murder another.

As for Mr. Jellyband and his fellow John Bulls, though they looked upon all foreigners with withering contempt, they were royalist and anti-revolutionists to a man, and at this present moment were furious with Pitt for his caution and moderation, although they naturally understood nothing of the diplomatic reasons which guided that great man's policy.

By now Sally came running back, very excited and very eager. The joyous company in the coffee-room had heard nothing of the noise outside, but she had spied a dripping horse and rider who had stopped at the door of "The Fisherman's Rest," and while the stable boy ran forward to take charge of the horse, pretty Miss Sally went to the front door to greet the welcome visitor. "I think I see'd my Lord Antony's horse out in the yard, father," she said, as she ran across the coffee-room.

But already the door had been thrown open from outside, and the next moment an arm, covered in drab cloth and dripping with the heavy rain, was round pretty Sally's waist, while a hearty voice echoed along the polished rafters of the coffee-room.

"Aye, and bless your brown eyes for being so sharp, my pretty Sally," said the man who had just entered, whilst worthy Mr. Jellyband came bustling forward, eager, alert and fussy, as became the advent of one of the most favoured guests of his hostel.

"Lud, I protest, Sally," added Lord Antony, as he deposited a kiss on Miss Sally's blooming cheeks, "but you are growing prettier and prettier every time I see you — and my honest friend, Jellyband here, have hard work to keep the fellows off that slim waist of yours. What say you, Mr. Waite?"

Mr. Waite — torn between his respect for my lord and his dislike of that particular type of joke — only replied with a doubtful grunt.

Lord Antony Dewhurst, one of the sons of the Duke of Exeter, was in those days a very perfect type of a young English gentlemen — tall, well set-up, broad of shoulders and merry of face, his laughter rang loudly wherever he went. A good sportsman, a lively companion, a courteous, well-bred man of the world, with not too much brains to spoil his temper, he was a universal favourite in London drawing-rooms or in the coffee-rooms of village inns. At "The Fisherman's Rest" everyone knew him — for he was fond of a trip across to France, and always spent a night under worthy Mr. Jellyband's roof on his way there or back.

He nodded to Waite, Pitkin and the others as he at last released Sally's waist, and crossed over to the hearth to warm and dry himself: as he did so, he cast a quick, somewhat suspicious glance at the two strangers, who had quietly resumed their game of dominoes, and for a moment a look of deep earnestness, even of anxiety, clouded his jovial young face.

But only for a moment; the next he turned to Mr. Hempseed, who was respectfully touching his forelock.

"Well, Mr. Hempseed, and how is the fruit?"

"Badly, my lord, badly," replied Mr. Hempseed, dolefully, "but what can you 'xpect with this 'ere government favourin' them rascals over in France, who would murder their king and all their nobility."

"Odd's life!" retorted Lord Antony; "so they would, honest Hempseed, — at least those they can get hold of, worse luck! But we have got some friends coming here to-night, who at any rate have evaded their clutches."

It almost seemed, when the young man said these words, as if he threw a defiant look towards the quiet strangers in the corner.

"Thanks to you, my lord, and to your friends, so I've heard it said," said Mr. Jellyband.

But in a moment Lord Antony's hand fell warningly on mine host's arm.

"Hush!" he said peremptorily, and instinctively once again looked towards the strangers.

"Oh! Lud love you, they are all right, my lord," retorted Jellyband; "don't you be afraid. I wouldn't have spoken, only I knew we were among friends. That gentleman over there is as true and loyal a subject of King George as you are yourself, my lord saving your presence. He is but lately arrived in Dover, and is setting down in business in these parts."

"In business? Faith, then, it must be as an undertaker, for I vow I never beheld a more rueful countenance."

"Nay, my lord, I believe that the gentleman is a widower, which no doubt would account for the melancholy of his bearing — but he is a friend, nevertheless, I'll vouch for that — and you will own, my lord, that who should judge of a face better than the landlord of a popular inn — "

"Oh, that's all right, then, if we are among friends," said Lord Antony, who evidently did not care to discuss the subject with his host. "But, tell me, you have no one else staying here, have you?"

"No one, my lord, and no one coming, either, leastways — "

"Leastways?"

"No one your lordship would object to, I know."

"Who is it?"

"Well, my lord, Sir Percy Blakeney and his lady will be here presently, but they ain't a-goin' to stay — "

"Lady Blakeney?" queried Lord Antony, in some astonishment.

"Aye, my lord. Sir Percy's skipper was here just now. He says that my lady's brother is crossing over to France to-day in the DAY DREAM, which is Sir Percy's yacht, and Sir Percy and my lady will come with him as far as here to see the last of him. It don't put you out, do it, my lord?"

"No, no, it doesn't put me out, friend; nothing will put me out, unless that supper is not the very best which Miss Sally can cook, and which has ever been served in 'The Fisherman's Rest.'"

"You need have no fear of that, my lord," said Sally, who all this while had been busy setting the table for supper. And very gay and inviting it looked, with a large bunch of brilliantly coloured dahlias in the centre, and the bright pewter goblets and blue china about.

"How many shall I lay for, my lord?"

"Five places, pretty Sally, but let the supper be enough for ten at least — our friends will be tired, and, I hope, hungry. As for me, I vow I could demolish a baron of beef to-night."

"Here they are, I do believe," said Sally excitedly, as a distant clatter of horses and wheels could now be distinctly heard, drawing rapidly nearer.

There was a general commotion in the coffee-room. Everyone was curious to see my Lord Antony's swell friends from over the water. Miss Sally cast one or two quick glances at the little bit of mirror which hung on the wall, and worthy Mr. Jellyband bustled out in order to give the first welcome himself to his distinguished guests. Only the two strangers in the corner did not participate in the general excitement. They were calmly finishing their game of dominoes, and did not even look once towards the door.

"Straight ahead, Comtesse, the door on your right," said a pleasant voice outside.

"Aye! there they are, all right enough." said Lord Antony, joyfully; "off with you, my pretty Sally, and see how quick you can dish up the soup."

The door was thrown wide open, and, preceded by Mr. Jellyband, who was profuse in his bows and welcomes, a party of four — two ladies and two gentlemen — entered the coffee-room.

"Welcome! Welcome to old England!" said Lord Antony, effusively, as he came eagerly forward with both hands outstretched towards the newcomers.

"Ah, you are Lord Antony Dewhurst, I think," said one of the ladies, speaking with a strong foreign accent.

"At your service, Madame," he replied, as he ceremoniously kissed the hands of both the ladies, then turned to the men and shook them both warmly by the hand.

Sally was already helping the ladies to take off their traveling cloaks, and both turned, with a shiver, towards the brightly-blazing hearth.

There was a general movement among the company in the coffee-room. Sally had bustled off to her kitchen whilst Jellyband, still profuse with his respectful salutations, arranged one or two chairs around the fire. Mr. Hempseed, touching his forelock, was quietly vacating the seat in the hearth. Everyone was staring curiously, yet deferentially, at the foreigners.

"Ah, Messieurs! what can I say?" said the elder of the two ladies, as she stretched a pair of fine, aristocratic hands to the warmth of the blaze, and looked with unspeakable gratitude first at Lord Antony, then at one of the young men who had accompanied her party, and who was busy divesting himself of his heavy, caped coat.

"Only that you are glad to be in England, Comtesse," replied Lord Antony, "and that you have not suffered too much from your trying voyage."

"Indeed, indeed, we are glad to be in England," she said, while her eyes filled with tears, "and we have already forgotten all that we have suffered."

Her voice was musical and low, and there was a great deal of calm dignity and of many sufferings nobly endured marked in the handsome, aristocratic face, with its wealth of snowy-white hair dressed high above the forehead, after the fashion of the times.

"I hope my friend, Sir Andrew Ffoulkes, proved an entertaining travelling companion, madame?"

"Ah, indeed, Sir Andrew was kindness itself. How could my children and I ever show enough gratitude to you all, Messieurs?"

Her companion, a dainty, girlish figure, childlike and pathetic in its look of fatigue and of sorrow, had said nothing as yet, but her eyes, large, brown, and full of tears, looked up from the fire and sought those of Sir Andrew Ffoulkes, who had drawn near to the hearth and to her; then, as they met his, which were fixed with unconcealed admiration upon the sweet face before him, a thought of warmer colour rushed up to her pale cheeks.

"So this is England," she said, as she looked round with childlike curiosity at the great hearth, the oak rafters, and the yokels with their elaborate smocks and jovial, rubicund, British countenances.

"A bit of it, Mademoiselle," replied Sir Andrew, smiling, "but all of it, at your service."

The young girl blushed again, but this time a bright smile, fleet and sweet, illumined her dainty face. She said nothing, and Sir Andrew too was silent, yet those two young people understood one another, as young people have a way of doing all the world over, and have done since the world began.

"But, I say, supper!" here broke in Lord Antony's jovial voice, "supper, honest Jellyband. Where is that pretty wench of yours and the dish of soup? Zooks, man, while you stand there gaping at the ladies, they will faint with hunger."

"One moment! one moment, my lord," said Jellyband, as he threw open the door that led to the kitchen and shouted lustily: "Sally! Hey, Sally there, are ye ready, my girl?"

Sally was ready, and the next moment she appeared in the doorway carrying a gigantic tureen, from which rose a cloud of steam and an abundance of savoury odour.

"Odd's life, supper at last!" ejaculated Lord Antony, merrily, as he gallantly offered his arm to the Comtesse.

"May I have the honour?" he added ceremoniously, as he led her towards the supper table.

There was a general bustle in the coffee-room: Mr. Hempseed and most of the yokels and fisher-folk had gone to make way for "the quality," and to finish smoking their pipes elsewhere. Only the two strangers stayed on, quietly and unconcernedly playing their game of dominoes and sipping their wine; whilst at another table Harry Waite, who was fast losing his temper, watched pretty Sally bustling round the table.

She looked a very dainty picture of English rural life, and no wonder that the susceptible young Frenchman could scarce take his eyes off her pretty face. The Vicomte de Tournay was scarce nineteen, a beardless boy, on whom terrible tragedies which were being enacted in his own country had made but little impression. He was elegantly and even foppishly dressed, and once safely landed in England he was evidently ready to forget the horrors of the Revolution in the delights of English life.

"Pardi, if zis is England," he said as he continued to ogle Sally with marked satisfaction, "I am of it satisfied."

It would be impossible at this point to record the exact exclamation which escaped through Mr. Harry Waite's clenched teeth. Only respect for "the quality," and notably for my Lord Antony, kept his marked disapproval of the young foreigner in check.

"Nay, but this IS England, you abandoned young reprobate," interposed Lord Antony with a laugh, "and do not, I pray, bring your loose foreign ways into this most moral country."

Lord Antony had already sat down at the head of the table with the Comtesse on his right. Jellyband was bustling round, filling glasses and putting chairs straight. Sally waited, ready to hand round the soup. Mr. Harry Waite's friends had at last succeeded in taking him out of the room, for his temper was growing more and more violent under the Vicomte's obvious admiration for Sally.

"Suzanne," came in stern, commanding accents from the rigid Comtesse.

Suzanne blushed again; she had lost count of time and of place whilst she had stood beside the fire, allowing the handsome young Englishman's eyes to dwell upon her sweet face, and his hand, as if unconsciously, to rest upon hers. Her mother's voice brought her back to reality once more, and with a submissive "Yes, Mama," she took her place at the supper table.

CHAPTER IV
THE LEAGUE OF THE SCARLET PIMPERNEL

They all looked a merry, even a happy party, as they sat round the table; Sir Andrew Ffoulkes and Lord Antony Dewhurst, two typical good-looking, well-born and well-bred Englishmen of that year of grace 1792, and the aristocratic French comtesse with her two children, who had just escaped from such dire perils, and found a safe retreat at last on the shores of protecting England.

In the corner the two strangers had apparently finished their game; one of them arose, and standing with his back to the merry company at the table, he adjusted with much deliberation his large triple caped coat. As he did so, he gave one quick glance all around him. Everyone was busy laughing and chatting, and he murmured the words "All safe!": his companion then, with the alertness borne of long practice, slipped on to his knees in a moment, and the next had crept noiselessly under the oak bench. The stranger then, with a loud "Good-night," quietly walked out of the coffee-room.

Not one of those at the supper table had noticed this curious and silent manoeuvre, but when the stranger finally closed the door of the coffee-room behind him, they all instinctively sighed a sigh of relief.

"Alone, at last!" said Lord Antony, jovially.

Then the young Vicomte de Tournay rose, glass in hand, and with the graceful affection peculiar to the times, he raised it aloft, and said in broken English, —

"To His Majesty George Three of England. God bless him for his hospitality to us all, poor exiles from France."

"His Majesty the King!" echoed Lord Antony and Sir Andrew as they drank loyally to the toast.

"To His Majesty King Louis of France," added Sir Andrew, with solemnity. "May God protect him, and give him victory over his enemies."

Everyone rose and drank this toast in silence. The fate of the unfortunate King of France, then a prisoner of his own people, seemed to cast a gloom even over Mr. Jellyband's pleasant countenance.

"And to M. le Comte de Tournay de Basserive," said Lord Antony, merrily. "May we welcome him in England before many days are over."

"Ah, Monsieur," said the Comtesse, as with a slightly trembling hand she conveyed her glass to her lips, "I scarcely dare to hope."

But already Lord Antony had served out the soup, and for the next few moments all conversation ceased, while Jellyband and Sally handed round the plates and everyone began to eat.

"Faith, Madame!" said Lord Antony, after a while, "mine was no idle toast; seeing yourself, Mademoiselle Suzanne and my friend the Vicomte safely in England now, surely you must feel reasurred as to the fate of Monsieur le Comte."

"Ah, Monsieur," replied the Comtesse, with a heavy sigh, "I trust in God — I can but pray — and hope . . ."

"Aye, Madame!" here interposed Sir Andrew Ffoulkes, "trust in God by all means, but believe also a little in your English friends, who have sworn to bring the Count safely across the Channel, even as they have brought you to-day."

"Indeed, indeed, Monsieur," she replied, "I have the fullest confidence in you and your friends. Your fame, I assure you, has spread throughout the whole of France. The way some of my own friends have escaped from the clutches of that awful revolutionary tribunal was nothing short of a miracle — and all done by you and your friends — "

"We were but the hands, Madame la Comtesse . . ."

"But my husband, Monsieur," said the Comtesse, whilst unshed tears seemed to veil her voice, "he is in such deadly peril — I would never have left him, only . . . there were my children . . . I was torn between my duty to him, and to them. They refused to go without me . . . and you and your friends assured me so solemnly that my husband would be safe. But, oh! now that I am here — amongst you all — in this beautiful, free England — I think of him, flying for his life, hunted like a poor beast . . . in such peril . . . Ah! I should not have left him . . . I should not have left him! . . ."

The poor woman had completely broken down; fatigue, sorrow and emotion had overmastered her rigid, aristocratic bearing. She was crying gently to herself, whilst Suzanne ran up to her and tried to kiss away her tears.

Lord Antony and Sir Andrew had said nothing to interrupt the Comtesse whilst she was speaking. There was no doubt that they felt deeply for her; their very silence testified to that — but in every century, and ever since England has been what it is, an Englishman has always felt somewhat ashamed of his own emotion and of his own sympathy. And so the two young men said nothing, and busied themselves in trying to hide their feelings, only succeeding in looking immeasurably sheepish.

"As for me, Monsieur," said Suzanne, suddenly, as she looked through a wealth of brown curls across at Sir Andrew, "I trust you absolutely, and I KNOW that you will bring my dear father safely to England, just as you brought us to-day."

This was said with so much confidence, such unuttered hope and belief, that it seemed as if by magic to dry the mother's eyes, and to bring a smile upon everybody's lips.

"Nay! You shame me, Mademoiselle," replied Sir Andrew; "though my life is at your service, I have been but a humble tool in the hands of our great leader, who organised and effected your escape."

He had spoken with so much warmth and vehemence that Suzanne's eyes fastened upon him in undisguised wonder.

"Your leader, Monsieur?" said the Comtesse, eagerly. "Ah! of course, you must have a leader. And I did not think of that before! But tell me where is he? I must go to him at once, and I and my children must throw ourselves at his feet, and thank him for all that he has done for us."

"Alas, Madame!" said Lord Antony, "that is impossible."

"Impossible? — Why?"

"Because the Scarlet Pimpernel works in the dark, and his identity is only known under the solemn oath of secrecy to his immediate followers."

"The Scarlet Pimpernel?" said Suzanne, with a merry laugh. "Why! what a droll name! What is the Scarlet Pimpernel, Monsieur?"

She looked at Sir Andrew with eager curiosity. The young man's face had become almost transfigured. His eyes shone with enthusiasm; hero-worship, love, admiration for his leader seemed literally to glow upon his face. "The Scarlet Pimpernel, Mademoiselle," he said at last "is the name of a humble English wayside flower; but it is also the name chosen to hide the identity of the best and bravest man in all the world, so that he may better succeed in accomplishing the noble task he has set himself to do."

"Ah, yes," here interposed the young Vicomte, "I have heard speak of this Scarlet Pimpernel. A little flower — red? — yes! They say in Paris that every time a royalist escapes to England that devil, Foucquier-Tinville, the Public Prosecutor, receives a paper with that little flower designated in red upon it. . . . Yes?"

"Yes, that is so," assented Lord Antony.

"Then he will have received one such paper to-day?"

"Undoubtedly."

"Oh! I wonder what he will say!" said Suzanne, merrily. "I have heard that the picture of that little red flower is the only thing that frightens him."

"Faith, then," said Sir Andrew, "he will have many more opportunities of studying the shape of that small scarlet flower."

"Ah, monsieur," sighed the Comtesse, "it all sounds like a romance, and I cannot understand it all."

"Why should you try, Madame?"

"But, tell me, why should your leader — why should you all — spend your money and risk your lives — for it is your lives you risk, Messieurs, when you set foot in France — and all for us French men and women, who are nothing to you?"

"Sport, Madame la Comtesse, sport," asserted Lord Antony, with his jovial, loud and pleasant voice; "we are a nation of sportsmen, you know, and just now it is the fashion to pull the hare from between the teeth of the hound."

"Ah, no, no, not sport only, Monsieur . . . you have a more noble motive, I am sure for the good work you do."

"Faith, Madame, I would like you to find it then . . . as for me, I vow, I love the game, for this is the finest sport I have yet encountered. — Hair-breath escapes . . . the devil's own risks! — Tally ho! — and away we go!"

But the Comtesse shook her head, still incredulously. To her it seemed preposterous that these young men and their great leader, all of them rich, probably wellborn, and young, should for no other motive than sport, run the terrible risks, which she knew they were constantly doing. Their nationality, once they had set foot in France, would be no safeguard to them. Anyone found harbouring or assisting suspected royalists would be ruthlessly condemned and summarily executed, whatever his nationality might be. And this band of young Englishmen had, to her own knowledge, bearded the implacable and bloodthirsty tribunal of the Revolution, within the very walls of Paris itself, and had snatched away condemned victims, almost from the very foot of the guillotine. With a shudder, she recalled the events of the last few days, her escape from Paris with her two children, all three of them hidden beneath the hood of a rickety cart, and lying amidst a heap of turnips and cabbages, not daring to breathe, whilst the mob howled, "A la lanterne les aristos!" at the awful West Barricade.

It had all occurred in such a miraculous way; she and her husband had understood that they had been placed on the list of "suspected persons," which meant that their trial and death were but a matter of days — of hours, perhaps.

Then came the hope of salvation; the mysterious epistle, signed with the enigmatical scarlet device; the clear, peremptory directions; the parting from the Comte de Tournay, which had torn the poor wife's heart in two; the hope of reunion; the flight with her two children; the covered cart; that awful hag driving it, who looked like some horrible evil demon, with the ghastly trophy on her whip handle!

The Comtesse looked round at the quaint, old-fashioned English inn, the peace of this land of civil and religious liberty, and she closed her eyes to shut out the haunting vision of that West Barricade, and of the mob retreating panic-stricken when the old hag spoke of the plague.

Every moment under that cart she expected recognition, arrest, herself and her children tried and condemned, and these young Englishmen, under the guidance of their brave and mysterious leader, had risked their lives to save them all, as they had already saved scores of other innocent people.

And all only for sport? Impossible! Suzanne's eyes as she sought those of Sir Andrew plainly told him that she thought that HE at any rate rescued his fellowmen from terrible and unmerited death, through a higher and nobler motive than his friend would have her believe.

"How many are there in your brave league, Monsieur?" she asked timidly.

"Twenty all told, Mademoiselle," he replied, "one to command, and nineteen to obey. All of us Englishmen, and all pledged to the same cause — to obey our leader and to rescue the innocent."

"May God protect you all, Messieurs," said the Comtesse, fervently.

"He had done that so far, Madame."

"It is wonderful to me, wonderful! — That you should all be so brave, so devoted to your fellowmen — yet you are English! — and in France treachery is rife — all in the name of liberty and fraternity."

"The women even, in France, have been more bitter against us aristocrats than the men," said the Vicomte, with a sigh.

"Ah, yes," added the Comtesse, while a look of haughty disdain and intense bitterness shot through her melancholy eyes, "There was that woman, Marguerite St. Just for instance. She denounced the Marquis de St. Cyr and all his family to the awful tribunal of the Terror."

"Marguerite St. Just?" said Lord Antony, as he shot a quick and apprehensive glance across at Sir Andrew.

"Marguerite St. Just? — Surely . . ."

"Yes!" replied the Comtesse, "surely you know her. She was a leading actress of the Comedie Francaise, and she married an Englishman lately. You must know her — "

"Know her?" said Lord Antony. "Know Lady Blakeney — the most fashionable woman in London — the wife of the richest man in England? Of course, we all know Lady Blakeney."

"She was a school-fellow of mine at the convent in Paris," interposed Suzanne, "and we came over to England together to learn your language. I was very fond of Marguerite, and I cannot believe that she ever did anything so wicked."

"It certainly seems incredible," said Sir Andrew. "You say that she actually denounced the Marquis de St. Cyr? Why should she have done such a thing? Surely there must be some mistake — "

"No mistake is possible, Monsieur," rejoined the Comtesse, coldly. "Marguerite St. Just's brother is a noted republican. There was some talk of a family feud between him and my cousin, the Marquis de St. Cyr. The St. Justs are quite plebeian, and the republican government employs many spies. I assure you there is no mistake. . . . You had not heard this story?"

"Faith, Madame, I did hear some vague rumours of it, but in England no one would credit it. . . . Sir Percy Blakeney, her husband, is a very wealthy man, of high social position, the intimate friend of the Prince of Wales . . . and Lady Blakeney leads both fashion and society in London."

"That may be, Monsieur, and we shall, of course, lead a very quiet life in England, but I pray God that while I remain in this beautiful country, I may never meet Marguerite St. Just."

The proverbial wet-blanket seemed to have fallen over the merry little company gathered round the table. Suzanne looked sad and silent; Sir Andrew fidgeted uneasily with his fork, whilst the Comtesse, encased in the plate-armour of her aristocratic prejudices, sat, rigid and unbending, in her straight-backed chair. As for Lord Antony, he looked extremely uncomfortable, and glanced once or twice apprehensively towards Jellyband, who looked just as uncomfortable as himself.

"At what time do you expect Sir Percy and Lady Blakeney?" he contrived to whisper unobserved, to mine host.

"Any moment, my lord," whispered Jellyband in reply.

Even as he spoke, a distant clatter was heard of an approaching coach; louder and louder it grew, one or two shouts became distinguishable, then the rattle of horses' hoofs on the uneven cobble stones, and the next moment a stable boy had thrown open the coffee-room door and rushed in excitedly.

"Sir Percy Blakeney and my lady," he shouted at the top of his voice, "they're just arriving."

And with more shouting, jingling of harness, and iron hoofs upon the stones, a magnificent coach, drawn by four superb bays, had halted outside the porch of "The Fisherman's Rest."

CHAPTER V
MARGUERITE

In a moment the pleasant oak-raftered coffee-room of the inn became the scene of hopeless confusion and discomfort. At the first announcement made by the stable boy, Lord Antony, with a fashionable oath, had jumped up from his seat and was now giving many and confused directions to poor bewildered Jellyband, who seemed at his wits' end what to do.

"For goodness' sake, man," admonished his lordship, "try to keep Lady Blakeney talking outside for a moment while the ladies withdraw. Zounds!" he added, with another more emphatic oath, "this is most unfortunate."

"Quick Sally! the candles!" shouted Jellyband, as hopping about from one leg to another, he ran hither and thither, adding to the general discomfort of everybody.

The Comtesse, too, had risen to her feet: rigid and erect, trying to hide her excitement beneath more becoming SANG-FROID, she repeated mechanically, —

"I will not see her! — I will not see her!"

Outside, the excitement attendant upon the arrival of very important guests grew apace.

"Good-day, Sir Percy! — Good-day to your ladyship! Your servant, Sir Percy!" — was heard in one long, continued chorus, with alternate more feeble tones of — "Remember the poor blind man! of your charity, lady and gentleman!"

Then suddenly a singularly sweet voice was heard through all the din.

"Let the poor man be — and give him some supper at my expense."

The voice was low and musical, with a slight sing-song in it, and a faint SOUPCON of foreign intonation in the pronunciation of the consonants.

Everyone in the coffee-room heard it and paused instinctively, listening to it for a moment. Sally was holding the candles by the opposite door, which led to the bedrooms upstairs, and the Comtesse was in the act of beating a hasty retreat before that enemy who owned such a sweet musical voice; Suzanne reluctantly was preparing to follow her mother, while casting regretful glances towards the door, where she hoped still to see her dearly-beloved, erstwhile school-fellow.

Then Jellyband threw open the door, still stupidly and blindly hoping to avert the catastrophe, which he felt was in the air, and the same low, musical voice said, with a merry laugh and mock consternation, —

"B-r-r-r-r! I am as wet as a herring! DIEU! has anyone ever seen such a contemptible climate?"

"Suzanne, come with me at once — I wish it," said the Comtesse, peremptorily.

"Oh! Mama!" pleaded Suzanne.

"My lady . . . er . . . h'm! . . . my lady! . . ." came in feeble accents from Jellyband, who stood clumsily trying to bar the way.

"PARDIEU, my good man," said Lady Blakeney, with some impatience, "what are you standing in my way for, dancing about like a turkey with a sore foot? Let me get to the fire, I am perished with the cold."

And the next moment Lady Blakeney, gently pushing mine host on one side, had swept into the coffee-room.

There are many portraits and miniatures extant of Marguerite St. Just — Lady Blakeney as she was then — but it is doubtful if any of these really do her singular beauty justice. Tall, above the average, with magnificent presence and regal figure, it is small wonder that even the Comtesse paused for a moment in involuntary admiration before turning her back on so fascinating an apparition.

Marguerite Blakeney was then scarcely five-and-twenty, and her beauty was at its most dazzling stage. The large hat, with its undulating and waving plumes, threw a soft shadow across the classic brow with the aureole of auburn hair — free at the moment from any powder; the sweet, almost childlike mouth, the straight chiselled nose, round chin, and delicate throat, all seemed set off by the picturesque costume of the period. The rich blue velvet robe moulded in its every line the graceful contour of the figure, whilst one tiny hand held, with a dignity all its own, the tall stick adorned with a large bunch of ribbons which fashionable ladies of the period had taken to carrying recently.

With a quick glance all around the room, Marguerite Blakeney had taken stock of every one there. She nodded pleasantly to Sir Andrew Ffoulkes, whilst extending a hand to Lord Antony.

"Hello! my Lord Tony, why — what are YOU doing here in Dover?" she said merrily.

Then, without waiting for a reply, she turned and faced the Comtesse and Suzanne. Her whole face lighted up with additional brightness, as she stretched out both arms towards the young girl.

"Why! if that isn't my little Suzanne over there. PARDIEU, little citizeness, how came you to be in England? And Madame too?"

She went up effusive to them both, with not a single touch of embarrassment in her manner or in her smile. Lord Tony and Sir Andrew watched the little scene with eager apprehension. English though they were, they had often been in France, and had mixed sufficiently with the French to realise the unbending hauteur, the bitter hatred with which the old NOBLESSE of France viewed all those who had helped to contribute to their downfall. Armand St. Just, the brother of beautiful Lady Blakeney — though known to hold moderate and conciliatory views — was an ardent republican; his feud with the ancient family of St. Cyr — the rights and wrongs of which no outsider ever knew — had culminated in the downfall, the almost total extinction of the latter. In France, St. Just and his party had triumphed, and here in England, face to face with these three refugees driven from their country, flying for their lives, bereft of all which centuries of luxury had given them, there stood a fair scion of those same republican families which had hurled down a throne, and uprooted an aristocracy whose origin was lost in the dim and distant vista of bygone centuries.

She stood there before them, in all the unconscious insolence of beauty, and stretched out her dainty hand to them, as if she would, by that one act, bridge over the conflict and bloodshed of the past decade.

"Suzanne, I forbid you to speak to that woman," said the Comtesse, sternly, as she placed a restraining hand upon her daughter's arm.

She had spoken in English, so that all might hear and understand; the two young English gentlemen, as well as the common innkeeper and his daughter. The latter literally gasped with horror at this foreign insolence, this impudence before her ladyship — who was English, now that she was Sir Percy's wife, and a friend of the Princess of Wales to boot.

As for Lord Antony and Sir Andrew Ffoulkes, their very hearts seemed to stand still with horror at this gratuitous insult. One of them uttered an exclamation of appeal, the other one of warning, and instinctively both glanced hurriedly towards the door, whence a slow, drawly, not unpleasant voice had already been heard.

Alone among those present Marguerite Blakeney and the Comtesse de Tournay had remained seemingly unmoved. The latter, rigid, erect and defiant, with one hand still upon her daughter's arm, seemed the very personification of unbending pride. For the moment Marguerite's sweet face had become as white as the soft fichu which swathed her throat, and a very keen observer might have noted that the hand which held the tall, beribboned stick was clenched, and trembled somewhat.

But this was only momentary; the next instant the delicate eyebrows were raised slightly, the lips curved sarcastically upwards, the clear blue eyes looked straight at the rigid Comtesse, and with a slight shrug of the shoulders —

"Hoity-toity, citizeness," she said gaily, "what fly stings you, pray?"

"We are in England now, Madame," rejoined the Comtesse, coldly, "and I am at liberty to forbid my daughter to touch your hand in friendship. Come, Suzanne."

She beckoned to her daughter, and without another look at Marguerite Blakeney, but with a deep, old-fashioned curtsey to the two young men, she sailed majestically out of the room.

There was silence in the old inn parlour for a moment, as the rustle of the Comtesse's skirts died away down the passage. Marguerite, rigid as a statue followed with hard, set eyes the upright figure, as it disappeared through the doorway — but as little Suzanne, humble and obedient, was about to follow her mother, the hard, set expression suddenly vanished, and a wistful, almost pathetic and childlike look stole into Lady Blakeney's eyes.

Little Suzanne caught that look; the child's sweet nature went out to the beautiful woman, scarcely older than herself; filial obedience vanished before girlish sympathy; at the door she turned, ran back to Marguerite, and putting her arms round her, kissed her effusively; then only did she follow her mother, Sally bringing up the rear, with a final curtsey to my lady.

Suzanne's sweet and dainty impulse had relieved the unpleasant tension. Sir Andrew's eyes followed the pretty little figure, until it had quite disappeared, then they met Lady Blakeney's with unassumed merriment.

Marguerite, with dainty affection, had kissed her hand to the ladies, as they disappeared through the door, then a humorous smile began hovering round the corners of her mouth.

"So that's it, is it?" she said gaily. "La! Sir Andrew, did you ever see such an unpleasant person? I hope when I grow old I sha'n't look like that."

She gathered up her skirts and assuming a majestic gait, stalked towards the fireplace.

"Suzanne," she said, mimicking the Comtesse's voice, "I forbid you to speak to that woman!"

The laugh which accompanied this sally sounded perhaps a trifled forced and hard, but neither Sir Andrew nor Lord Tony were very keen observers. The mimicry was so perfect, the tone of the voice so accurately reproduced, that both the young men joined in a hearty cheerful "Bravo!"

"Ah! Lady Blakeney!" added Lord Tony, "how they must miss you at the Comedie Francaise, and how the Parisians must hate Sir Percy for having taken you away."

"Lud, man," rejoined Marguerite, with a shrug of her graceful shoulders, "'tis impossible to hate Sir Percy for anything; his witty sallies would disarm even Madame la Comtesse herself."

The young Vicomte, who had not elected to follow his mother in her dignified exit, now made a step forward, ready to champion the Comtesse should Lady Blakeney aim any further shafts at her. But before he could utter a preliminary word of protest, a pleasant though distinctly inane laugh, was heard from outside, and the next moment an unusually tall and very richly dressed figure appeared in the doorway.

CHAPTER VI

AN EXQUISITE OF '92

Sir Percy Blakeney, as the chronicles of the time inform us, was in this year of grace 1792, still a year or two on the right side of thirty. Tall, above the average, even for an Englishman, broad-shouldered and massively built, he would have been called unusually good-looking, but for a certain lazy expression in his deep-set blue eyes, and that perpetual inane laugh which seemed to disfigure his strong, clearly-cut mouth.

It was nearly a year ago now that Sir Percy Blakeney, Bart., one of the richest men in England, leader of all the fashions, and intimate friend of the Prince of Wales, had astonished fashionable society in London and Bath by bringing home, from one of his journeys abroad, a beautiful, fascinating, clever, French wife. He, the sleepiest, dullest, most British Britisher that had ever set a pretty woman yawning, had secured a brilliant matrimonial prize for which, as all chroniclers aver, there had been many competitors.

Marguerite St. Just had first made her DEBUT in artistic Parisian circles, at the very moment when the greatest social upheaval the world has ever known was taking place within its very walls. Scarcely eighteen, lavishly gifted with beauty and talent, chaperoned only by a young and devoted brother, she had soon gathered round her, in her charming apartment in the Rue Richelieu, a coterie which was as brilliant as it was exclusive — exclusive, that is to say, only from one point of view. Marguerite St. Just was from principle and by conviction a republican — equality of birth was her motto — inequality of fortune was in her eyes a mere untoward accident, but the only inequality she admitted was that of talent. "Money and titles may be hereditary," she would say, "but brains are not," and thus her charming salon was reserved for originality and intellect, for brilliance and wit, for clever men and talented women, and the entrance into it was soon looked upon in the world of intellect — which even in those days and in those troublous times found its pivot in Paris — as the seal to an artistic career.

Clever men, distinguished men, and even men of exalted station formed a perpetual and brilliant court round the fascinating young actress of the Comedie Francaise, and she glided through republican, revolutionary, bloodthirsty Paris like a shining comet with a trail behind her of all that was most distinguished, most interesting, in intellectual Europe.

Then the climax came. Some smiled indulgently and called it an artistic eccentricity, others looked upon it as a wise provision, in view of the many events which were crowding thick and fast in Paris just then, but to all, the real motive of that climax remained a puzzle and a mystery. Anyway, Marguerite St. Just married Sir Percy Blakeney one fine day, just like that, without any warning to her friends, without a SOIREE DE CONTRAT or DINER DE FIANCAILLES or other appurtenances of a fashionable French wedding.

How that stupid, dull Englishman ever came to be admitted within the intellectual circle which revolved round "the cleverest woman in Europe," as her friends unanimously called her, no one ventured to guess — golden key is said to open every door, asserted the more malignantly inclined.

Enough, she married him, and "the cleverest woman in Europe" had linked her fate to that "demmed idiot" Blakeney, and not even her most intimate friends could assign to this strange step any other motive than that of supreme eccentricity. Those friends who knew, laughed to scorn the idea that Marguerite St. Just had married a fool for the sake of the worldly advantages with which he might endow her. They knew, as a matter of fact, that Marguerite St. Just cared nothing about money, and still less about a title; moreover, there were at least half a dozen other men in the cosmopolitan world equally well-born, if not so wealthy as Blakeney, who would have been only too happy to give Marguerite St. Just any position she might choose to covet.

As for Sir Percy himself, he was universally voted to be totally unqualified for the onerous post he had taken upon himself. His chief qualifications for it seemed to consist in his blind adoration for her, his great wealth and the high favour in which he stood at the English court; but London society thought that, taking into consideration his own intellectual limitations, it would have been wiser on his part had he bestowed those worldly advantages upon a less brilliant and witty wife.

Although lately he had been so prominent a figure in fashionable English society, he had spent most of his early life abroad. His father, the late Sir Algernon Blakeney, had had the terrible misfortune of seeing an idolized young wife become hopelessly insane after two years of happy married life. Percy had just been born when the late Lady Blakeney fell prey to the terrible malady which in those days was looked upon as hopelessly incurable and nothing short of a curse of God upon the entire family. Sir Algernon took his afflicted young wife abroad, and there presumably Percy was educated, and grew up between an imbecile mother and a distracted father, until he attained his majority. The death of his parents following close upon one another left him a free man, and as Sir Algernon had led a forcibly simple and retired life, the large Blakeney fortune had increased tenfold.

Sir Percy Blakeney had travelled a great deal abroad, before he brought home his beautiful, young, French wife. The fashionable circles of the time were ready to receive them both with open arms; Sir Percy was rich, his wife was accomplished, the Prince of Wales took a very great liking to them both. Within six months they were the acknowledged leaders of fashion and of style. Sir Percy's coats were the talk of the town, his inanities were quoted, his foolish laugh copied by the gilded youth at Almack's or the Mall. Everyone knew that he was hopelessly stupid, but then that was scarcely to be wondered at, seeing that all the Blakeneys for generations had been notoriously dull, and that his mother died an imbecile.

Thus society accepted him, petted him, made much of him, since his horses were the finest in the country, his FETES and wines the most sought after. As for his marriage with "the cleverest woman in Europe," well! the inevitable came with sure and rapid footsteps. No one pitied him, since his fate was of his own making. There were plenty of young ladies in England, of high birth and good looks, who would have been quite willing to help him to spend the Blakeney fortune, whilst smiling indulgently at his inanities and his good-humoured foolishness. Moreover, Sir Percy got no pity, because he seemed to require none — he seemed very proud of his clever wife, and to care little that she took no pains to disguise that good-natured contempt which she evidently felt for him, and that she even amused herself by sharpening her ready wits at his expense.

But then Blakeney was really too stupid to notice the ridicule with which his wife covered him, and if his matrimonial relations with the fascinating Parisienne had not turned out all that his hopes and his dog-like devotion for her had pictured, society could never do more than vaguely guess at it.

In his beautiful house at Richmond he played second fiddle to his clever wife with imperturbable BONHOMIE; he lavished jewels and luxuries of all kinds upon her, which she took with inimitable grace, dispensing the hospitality of his superb mansion with the same graciousness with which she had welcomed the intellectual coterie of Paris.

Physically, Sir Percy Blakeney was undeniably handsome — always excepting the lazy, bored look which was habitual to him. He was always irreproachable dressed, and wore the exaggerated "Incroyable" fashions, which had just crept across from Paris to England, with the perfect good taste innate in an English gentleman. On this special afternoon in September, in spite of the long journey by coach, in spite of rain and mud, his coat set irreproachably across his fine shoulders, his hands looked almost femininely white, as they emerged through billowy frills of finest Mechline lace: the extravagantly short-waisted satin coat, wide-lapelled waistcoat, and tight-fitting striped breeches, set off his massive figure to perfection, and in repose one might have admired so fine a specimen of English manhood, until the foppish ways, the affected movements, the perpetual inane laugh, brought one's admiration of Sir Percy Blakeney to an abrupt close.

He had lolled into the old-fashioned inn parlour, shaking the wet off his fine overcoat; then putting up a gold-rimmed eye-glass to his lazy blue eye, he surveyed the company, upon whom an embarrassed silence had suddenly fallen.

"How do, Tony? How do, Ffoulkes?" he said, recognizing the two young men and shaking them by the hand. "Zounds, my dear fellow," he added, smothering a slight yawn, "did you ever see such a beastly day? Demmed climate this."

With a quaint little laugh, half of embarrassment and half of sarcasm, Marguerite had turned towards her husband, and was surveying him from head to foot, with an amused little twinkle in her merry blue eyes.

"La!" said Sir Percy, after a moment or two's silence, as no one offered any comment, "how sheepish you all look . . . What's up?"

"Oh, nothing, Sir Percy," replied Marguerite, with a certain amount of gaiety, which, however, sounded somewhat forced, "nothing to disturb your equanimity — only an insult to your wife."

The laugh which accompanied this remark was evidently intended to reassure Sir Percy as to the gravity of the incident. It apparently succeeded in that, for echoing the laugh, he rejoined placidly —

"La, m'dear! you don't say so. Begad! who was the bold man who dared to tackle you — eh?"

Lord Tony tried to interpose, but had no time to do so, for the young Vicomte had already quickly stepped forward.

"Monsieur," he said, prefixing his little speech with an elaborate bow, and speaking in broken English, "my mother, the Comtesse de Tournay de Basserive, has offenced Madame, who, I see, is your wife. I cannot ask your pardon for my mother; what she does is right in my eyes. But I am ready to offer you the usual reparation between men of honour."

The young man drew up his slim stature to its full height and looked very enthusiastic, very proud, and very hot as he gazed at six foot odd of gorgeousness, as represented by Sir Percy Blakeney, Bart.

"Lud, Sir Andrew," said Marguerite, with one of her merry infectious laughs, "look on that pretty picture — the English turkey and the French bantam."

The simile was quite perfect, and the English turkey looked down with complete bewilderment upon the dainty little French bantam, which hovered quite threateningly around him.

"La! sir," said Sir Percy at last, putting up his eye glass and surveying the young Frenchman with undisguised wonderment, "where, in the cuckoo's name, did you learn to speak English?"

"Monsieur!" protested the Vicomte, somewhat abashed at the way his warlike attitude had been taken by the ponderous-looking Englishman.

"I protest 'tis marvellous!" continued Sir Percy, imperturbably, "demmed marvellous! Don't you think so, Tony — eh? I vow I can't speak the French lingo like that. What?"

"Nay, I'll vouch for that!" rejoined Marguerite, "Sir Percy has a British accent you could cut with a knife."

"Monsieur," interposed the Vicomte earnestly, and in still more broken English, "I fear you have not understand. I offer you the only posseeble reparation among gentlemen."

"What the devil is that?" asked Sir Percy, blandly.

"My sword, Monsieur," replied the Vicomte, who, though still bewildered, was beginning to lose his temper.

"You are a sportsman, Lord Tony," said Marguerite, merrily; "ten to one on the little bantam."

But Sir Percy was staring sleepily at the Vicomte for a moment or two, through his partly closed heavy lids, then he smothered another yawn, stretched his long limbs, and turned leisurely away.

"Lud love you, sir," he muttered good-humouredly, "demmit, young man, what's the good of your sword to me?"

What the Vicomte thought and felt at that moment, when that long-limbed Englishman treated him with such marked insolence, might fill volumes of sound reflections. . . . What he said resolved itself into a single articulate word, for all the others were choked in his throat by his surging wrath —

"A duel, Monsieur," he stammered.

Once more Blakeney turned, and from his high altitude looked down on the choleric little man before him; but not even for a second did he seem to lose his own imperturbable good-humour. He laughed his own pleasant and inane laugh, and burying his slender, long hands into the capacious pockets of his overcoat, he said leisurely — "a bloodthirsty young ruffian, Do you want to make a hole in a law-abiding man? . . . As for me, sir, I never fight duels," he added, as he placidly sat down and stretched his long, lazy legs out before him. "Demmed uncomfortable things, duels, ain't they, Tony?"

Now the Vicomte had no doubt vaguely heard that in England the fashion of duelling amongst gentlemen had been surpressed by the law with a very stern hand; still to him, a Frenchman, whose notions of bravery and honour were based upon a code that had centuries of tradition to back it, the spectacle of a gentleman actually refusing to fight a duel was a little short of an enormity. In his mind he vaguely pondered whether he should strike that long-legged Englishman in the face and call him a coward, or whether such conduct in a lady's presence might be deemed ungentlemanly, when Marguerite happily interposed.

"I pray you, Lord Tony," she said in that gentle, sweet, musical voice of hers, "I pray you play the peacemaker. The child is bursting with rage, and," she added with a SOUPCON of dry sarcasm, "might do Sir Percy an injury." She laughed a mocking little laugh, which, however, did not in the least disturb her husband's placid equanimity. "The British turkey has had the day," she said. "Sir Percy would provoke all the saints in the calendar and keep his temper the while."

But already Blakeney, good-humoured as ever, had joined in the laugh against himself.

"Demmed smart that now, wasn't it?" he said, turning pleasantly to the Vicomte. "Clever woman my wife, sir. . . . You will find THAT out if you live long enough in England."

"Sir Percy is right, Vicomte," here interposed Lord Antony, laying a friendly hand on the young Frenchman's shoulder. "It would hardly be fitting that you should commence your career in England by provoking him to a duel."

For a moment longer the Vicomte hesitated, then with a slight shrug of the shoulders directed against the extraordinary code of honour prevailing in this fog-ridden island, he said with becoming dignity, —

"Ah, well! if Monsieur is satisfied, I have no griefs. You mi'lor', are our protector. If I have done wrong, I withdraw myself."

"Aye, do!" rejoined Blakeney, with a long sigh of satisfaction, "withdraw yourself over there. Demmed excitable little puppy," he added under his breath, "Faith, Ffoulkes, if that's a specimen of the goods you and your friends bring over from France, my advice to you is, drop 'em 'mid Channel, my friend, or I shall have to see old Pitt about it, get him to clap on a prohibitive tariff, and put you in the stocks an you smuggle."

"La, Sir Percy, your chivalry misguides you," said Marguerite, coquettishly, "you forget that you yourself have imported one bundle of goods from France."

Blakeney slowly rose to his feet, and, making a deep and elaborate bow before his wife, he said with consummate gallantry, —

"I had the pick of the market, Madame, and my taste is unerring."

"More so than your chivalry, I fear," she retorted sarcastically.

"Odd's life, m'dear! be reasonable! Do you think I am going to allow my body to be made a pincushion of, by every little frog-eater who don't like the shape of your nose?"

"Lud, Sir Percy!" laughed Lady Blakeney as she bobbed him a quaint and pretty curtsey, "you need not be afraid! 'Tis not the MEN who dislike the shape of my nose."

"Afraid be demmed! Do you impugn my bravery, Madame? I don't patronise the ring for nothing, do I, Tony? I've put up the fists with Red Sam before now, and — and he didn't get it all his own way either — "

"S'faith, Sir Percy," said Marguerite, with a long and merry laugh, that went echoing along the old oak rafters of the parlour, "I would I had seen you then . . . ha! ha! ha! ha! — you

must have looked a pretty picture . . . and . . . and to be afraid of a little French boy . . .
ha! ha! . . . ha! ha!"

"Ha! ha! ha! he! he! he!" echoed Sir Percy, good-humouredly. "La, Madame, you honour
me! Zooks! Ffoulkes, mark ye that! I have made my wife laugh! — The cleverest woman in
Europe! . . . Odd's fish, we must have a bowl on that!" and he tapped vigorously on the table
near him. "Hey! Jelly! Quick, man! Here, Jelly!"

Harmony was once more restored. Mr. Jellyband, with a mighty effort, recovered himself
from the many emotions he had experienced within the last half hour. "A bowl of punch, Jelly,
hot and strong, eh?" said Sir Percy. "The wits that have just made a clever woman laugh must
be whetted! Ha! ha! ha! Hasten, my good Jelly!"

"Nay, there is no time, Sir Percy," interposed Marguerite. "The skipper will be here directly
and my brother must get on board, or the DAY DREAM will miss the tide."

"Time, m'dear? There is plenty of time for any gentleman to get drunk and get on board
before the turn of the tide."

"I think, your ladyship," said Jellyband, respectfully, "that the young gentleman is coming
along now with Sir Percy's skipper."

"That's right," said Blakeney, "then Armand can join us in the merry bowl. Think you,
Tony," he added, turning towards the Vicomte, "that the jackanapes of yours will join us in a
glass? Tell him that we drink in token of reconciliation."

"In fact you are all such merry company," said Marguerite, "that I trust you will forgive me
if I bid my brother good-bye in another room."

It would have been bad form to protest. Both Lord Antony and Sir Andrew felt that Lady
Blakeney could not altogether be in tune with them at the moment. Her love for her brother,
Armand St. Just, was deep and touching in the extreme. He had just spent a few weeks with
her in her English home, and was going back to serve his country, at the moment when death
was the usual reward for the most enduring devotion.

Sir Percy also made no attempt to detain his wife. With that perfect, somewhat affected
gallantry which characterised his every movement, he opened the coffee-room door for her,
and made her the most approved and elaborate bow, which the fashion of the time dictated,
as she sailed out of the room without bestowing on him more than a passing, slightly contemptuous glance. Only Sir Andrew Ffoulkes, whose every thought since he had met Suzanne
de Tournay seemed keener, more gentle, more innately sympathetic, noted the curious look
of intense longing, of deep and hopeless passion, with which the inane and flippant Sir Percy
followed the retreating figure of his brilliant wife.

CHAPTER VII
THE SECRET ORCHARD

Once outside the noisy coffee-room, alone in the dimly-lighted passage, Marguerite Blakeney seemed to breathe more freely. She heaved a deep sigh, like one who had long been oppressed with the heavy weight of constant self-control, and she allowed a few tears to fall unheeded down her cheeks.

Outside the rain had ceased, and through the swiftly passing clouds, the pale rays of an after-storm sun shone upon the beautiful white coast of Kent and the quaint, irregular houses that clustered round the Admiralty Pier. Marguerite Blakeney stepped on to the porch and looked out to sea. Silhouetted against the ever-changing sky, a graceful schooner, with white sails set, was gently dancing in the breeze. The DAY DREAM it was, Sir Percy Blakeney's yacht, which was ready to take Armand St. Just back to France into the very midst of that seething, bloody Revolution which was overthrowing a monarchy, attacking a religion, destroying a society, in order to try and rebuild upon the ashes of tradition a new Utopia, of which a few men dreamed, but which none had the power to establish.

In the distance two figures were approaching "The Fisherman's Rest": one, an oldish man, with a curious fringe of grey hairs round a rotund and massive chin, and who walked with that peculiar rolling gait which invariably betrays the seafaring man: the other, a young, slight figure, neatly and becomingly dressed in a dark, many caped overcoat; he was clean-shaved, and his dark hair was taken well back over a clear and noble forehead.

"Armand!" said Marguerite Blakeney, as soon as she saw him approaching from the distance, and a happy smile shone on her sweet face, even through the tears.

A minute or two later brother and sister were locked in each other's arms, while the old skipper stood respectfully on one side.

"How much time have we got, Briggs?" asked Lady Blakeney, "before M. St. Just need go on board?"

"We ought to weigh anchor before half an hour, your ladyship," replied the old man, pulling at his grey forelock.

Linking her arm in his, Marguerite led her brother towards the cliffs.

"Half an hour," she said, looking wistfully out to sea, "half an hour more and you'll be far from me, Armand! Oh! I can't believe that you are going, dear! These last few days — whilst Percy has been away, and I've had you all to myself, have slipped by like a dream."

"I am not going far, sweet one," said the young man gently, "a narrow channel to cross — a few miles of road — I can soon come back."

"Nay, 'tis not the distance, Armand — but that awful Paris . . . just now . . ."

They had reached the edge of the cliff. The gentle sea-breeze blew Marguerite's hair about her face, and sent the ends of her soft lace fichu waving round her, like a white and supple snake. She tried to pierce the distance far away, beyond which lay the shores of France: that relentless and stern France which was exacting her pound of flesh, the blood-tax from the noblest of her sons.

"Our own beautiful country, Marguerite," said Armand, who seemed to have divined her thoughts.

"They are going too far, Armand," she said vehemently. "You are a republican, so am I . . . we have the same thoughts, the same enthusiasm for liberty and equality . . . but even YOU must think that they are going too far . . ."

"Hush! — " said Armand, instinctively, as he threw a quick, apprehensive glance around him.

"Ah! you see: you don't think yourself that it is safe even to speak of these things — here in England!" She clung to him suddenly with strong, almost motherly, passion: "Don't go, Armand!" she begged; "don't go back! What should I do if . . . if . . . if . . ."

Her voice was choked in sobs, her eyes, tender, blue and loving, gazed appealingly at the young man, who in his turn looked steadfastly into hers.

"You would in any case be my own brave sister," he said gently, "who would remember that, when France is in peril, it is not for her sons to turn their backs on her."

Even as he spoke, that sweet childlike smile crept back into her face, pathetic in the extreme, for it seemed drowned in tears.

"Oh! Armand!" she said quaintly, "I sometimes wish you had not so many lofty virtues. . . . I assure you little sins are far less dangerous and uncomfortable. But you WILL be prudent?" she added earnestly.

"As far as possible . . . I promise you."

"Remember, dear, I have only you . . . to . . . to care for me. . . ."

"Nay, sweet one, you have other interests now. Percy cares for you . . ."

A look of strange wistfulness crept into her eyes as she murmured, —

"He did . . . once . . ."

"But surely . . ."

"There, there, dear, don't distress yourself on my account. Percy is very good . . ."

"Nay!" he interrupted energetically, "I will distress myself on your account, my Margot. Listen, dear, I have not spoken of these things to you before; something always seemed to stop me when I wished to question you. But, somehow, I feel as if I could not go away and leave you now without asking you one question. . . . You need not answer it if you do not wish," he added, as he noted a sudden hard look, almost of apprehension, darting through her eyes.

"What is it?" she asked simply.

"Does Sir Percy Blakeney know that . . . I mean, does he know the part you played in the arrest of the Marquis de St. Cyr?"

She laughed — a mirthless, bitter, contemptuous laugh, which was like a jarring chord in the music of her voice.

"That I denounced the Marquis de St. Cyr, you mean, to the tribunal that ultimately sent him and all his family to the guillotine? Yes, he does know. . . . . I told him after I married him. . . ."

"You told him all the circumstances — which so completely exonerated you from any blame?"

"It was too late to talk of 'circumstances'; he heard the story from other sources; my confession came too tardily, it seems. I could no longer plead extenuating circumstances: I could not demean myself by trying to explain —"

"And?"

"And now I have the satisfaction, Armand, of knowing that the biggest fool in England has the most complete contempt for his wife."

She spoke with vehement bitterness this time, and Armand St. Just, who loved her so dearly, felt that he had placed a somewhat clumsy finger upon an aching wound.

"But Sir Percy loved you, Margot," he repeated gently.

"Loved me? — Well, Armand, I thought at one time that he did, or I should not have married him. I daresay," she added, speaking very rapidly, as if she were about to lay down a heavy burden, which had oppressed her for months, "I daresay that even you thought — as everybody else did — that I married Sir Percy because of his wealth — but I assure you, dear, that it was not so. He seemed to worship me with a curious intensity of concentrated passion, which went straight to my heart. I had never loved any one before, as you know, and I was four-and-twenty then — so I naturally thought that it was not in my nature to love. But it has always seemed to me that it MUST be HEAVENLY to be loved blindly, passionately, wholly . . . worshipped, in fact — and the very fact that Percy was slow and stupid was an attraction for me, as I thought he would love me all the more. A clever man would naturally have other interests, an ambitious man other hopes. . . . I thought that a fool would worship, and think of nothing else. And I was ready to respond, Armand; I would have allowed myself to be worshipped, and given infinite tenderness in return. . . ."

She sighed — and there was a world of disillusionment in that sigh. Armand St. Just had allowed her to speak on without interruption: he listened to her, whilst allowing his own thoughts to run riot. It was terrible to see a young and beautiful woman — a girl in all but name — still standing almost at the threshold of her life, yet bereft of hope, bereft of illusions, bereft of all those golden and fantastic dreams, which should have made her youth one long, perpetual holiday.

Yet perhaps — though he loved his sister dearly — perhaps he understood: he had studied men in many countries, men of all ages, men of every grade of social and intellectual status, and inwardly he understood what Marguerite had left unsaid. Granted that Percy Blakeney was dull-witted, but in his slow-going mind, there would still be room for that ineradicable pride of a descendant of a long line of English gentlemen. A Blakeney had died on Bosworth field, another had sacrificed life and fortune for the sake of a treacherous Stuart: and that same pride — foolish and prejudiced as the republican Armand would call it — must have been stung to the quick on hearing of the sin which lay at Lady Blakeney's door. She had been young, misguided, ill-advised perhaps. Armand knew that: her impulses and imprudence, knew it still better; but Blakeney was slow-witted, he would not listen to "circumstances," he only clung to facts, and these had shown him Lady Blakeney denouncing a fellow man to a tribunal that knew no pardon: and the contempt he would feel for the deed she had done, however unwittingly, would kill that same love in him, in which sympathy and intellectuality could never have a part.

Yet even now, his own sister puzzled him. Life and love have such strange vagaries. Could it be that with the waning of her husband's love, Marguerite's heart had awakened with love for him? Strange extremes meet in love's pathway: this woman, who had had half intellectual Europe at her feet, might perhaps have set her affections on a fool. Marguerite was gazing out towards the sunset. Armand could not see her face, but presently it seemed to him that something which glittered for a moment in the golden evening light, fell from her eyes onto her dainty fichu of lace.

But he could not broach that subject with her. He knew her strange, passionate nature so well, and knew that reserve which lurked behind her frank, open ways. They had always been together, these two, for their parents had died when Armand was still a youth, and Marguerite but a child. He, some eight years her senior, had watched over her until her marriage; had chaperoned her during those brilliant years spent in the flat of the Rue de Richelieu, and had seen her enter upon this new life of hers, here in England, with much sorrow and some foreboding.

This was his first visit to England since her marriage, and the few months of separation had already seemed to have built up a slight, thin partition between brother and sister; the same deep, intense love was still there, on both sides, but each now seemed to have a secret orchard, into which the other dared not penetrate.

There was much Armand St. Just could not tell his sister; the political aspect of the revolution in France was changing almost every day; she might not understand how his own views and sympathies might become modified, even as the excesses, committed by those who had been his friends, grew in horror and in intensity. And Marguerite could not speak to her brother about the secrets of her heart; she hardly understood them herself, she only knew that, in the midst of luxury, she felt lonely and unhappy.

And now Armand was going away; she feared for his safety, she longed for his presence. She would not spoil these last few sadly-sweet moments by speaking about herself. She led him gently along the cliffs, then down to the beach; their arms linked in one another's, they had still so much to say that lay just outside that secret orchard of theirs.

CHAPTER VIII
THE ACCREDITED AGENT

The afternoon was rapidly drawing to a close; and a long, chilly English summer's evening was throwing a misty pall over the green Kentish landscape.

The DAY DREAM had set sail, and Marguerite Blakeney stood alone on the edge of the cliff over an hour, watching those white sails, which bore so swiftly away from her the only being who really cared for her, whom she dared to love, whom she knew she could trust.

Some little distance away to her left the lights from the coffee-room of "The Fisherman's Rest" glittered yellow in the gathering mist; from time to time it seemed to her aching nerves as if she could catch from thence the sound of merry-making and of jovial talk, or even that perpetual, senseless laugh of her husband's, which grated continually upon her sensitive ears.

Sir Percy had had the delicacy to leave her severely alone. She supposed that, in his own stupid, good-natured way, he may have understood that she would wish to remain alone, while those white sails disappeared into the vague horizon, so many miles away. He, whose notions of propriety and decorum were supersensitive, had not suggested even that an attendant should remain within call. Marguerite was grateful to her husband for all this; she always tried to be grateful to him for his thoughtfulness, which was constant, and for his generosity, which really was boundless. She tried even at times to curb the sarcastic, bitter thoughts of him, which made her — in spite of herself — say cruel, insulting things, which she vaguely hoped would wound him.

Yes! she often wished to wound him, to make him feel that she too held him in contempt, that she too had forgotten that she had almost loved him. Loved that inane fop! whose thoughts seemed unable to soar beyond the tying of a cravat or the new cut of a coat. Bah! And yet! . . . vague memories, that were sweet and ardent and attuned to this calm summer's evening, came wafted back to her memory, on the invisible wings of the light sea-breeze: the tie when first he worshipped her; he seemed so devoted — a very slave — and there was a certain latent intensity in that love which had fascinated her.

Then suddenly that love, that devotion, which throughout his courtship she had looked upon as the slavish fidelity of a dog, seemed to vanish completely. Twenty-four hours after the simple little ceremony at old St. Roch, she had told him the story of how, inadvertently, she had spoken of certain matters connected with the Marquis de St. Cyr before some men — her friends — who had used this information against the unfortunate Marquis, and sent him and his family to the guillotine.

She hated the Marquis. Years ago, Armand, her dear brother, loved Angele de St. Cyr, but St. Just was a plebeian, and the Marquis full of the pride and arrogant prejudices of his caste. One day Armand, the respectful, timid lover, ventured on sending a small poem — enthusiastic, ardent, passionate — to the idol of his dreams. The next night he was waylaid just outside Paris by the valets of Marquis de St. Cyr, and ignominiously thrashed — thrashed like a dog within an inch of his life — because he had dared to raise his eyes to the daughter of the aristocrat. The incident was one which, in those days, some two years before the great Revolution, was of almost daily occurrence in France; incidents of that type, in fact, led to bloody reprisals, which a few years later sent most of those haughty heads to the guillotine.

Marguerite remembered it all: what her brother must have suffered in his manhood and his pride must have been appalling; what she suffered through him and with him she never attempted even to analyse.

Then the day of retribution came. St. Cyr and his kin had found their masters, in those same plebeians whom they had despised. Armand and Marguerite, both intellectual, thinking beings, adopted with the enthusiasm of their years the Utopian doctrines of the Revolution, while the Marquis de St. Cyr and his family fought inch by inch for the retention of those privileges which had placed them socially above their fellow-men. Marguerite, impulsive, thoughtless, not calculating the purport of her words, still smarting under the terrible insult her brother had suffered at the Marquis' hands, happened to hear — amongst her own coterie — that the St. Cyrs were in treasonable correspondence with Austria, hoping to obtain the Emperor's support to quell the growing revolution in their own country.

In those days one denunciation was sufficient: Marguerite's few thoughtless words anent the Marquis de St. Cyr bore fruit within twenty-four hours. He was arrested. His papers were searched: letters from the Austrian Emperor, promising to send troops against the Paris populace, were found in his desk. He was arraigned for treason against the nation, and sent to the guillotine, whilst his family, his wife and his sons, shared in this awful fate.

Marguerite, horrified at the terrible consequences of her own thoughtlessness, was powerless to save the Marquis: his own coterie, the leaders of the revolutionary movement, all proclaimed her as a heroine: and when she married Sir Percy Blakeney, she did not perhaps altogether realise how severely he would look upon the sin, which she had so inadvertently committed, and which still lay heavily upon her soul. She made full confession of it to her husband, trusting his blind love for her, her boundless power over him, to soon make him forget what might have sounded unpleasant to an English ear.

Certainly at the moment he seemed to take it very quietly; hardly, in fact, did he appear to understand the meaning of all she said; but what was more certain still, was that never after that could she detect the slightest sign of that love, which she once believed had been wholly hers. Now they had drifted quite apart, and Sir Percy seemed to have laid aside his love for her, as he would an ill-fitting glove. She tried to rouse him by sharpening her ready wit against his dull intellect; endeavouring to excite his jealousy, if she could not rouse his love; tried to goad him to self-assertion, but all in vain. He remained the same, always passive, drawling, sleepy, always courteous, invariably a gentleman: she had all that the world and a wealthy husband can give to a pretty woman, yet on this beautiful summer's evening, with the white sails of the DAY DREAM finally hidden by the evening shadows, she felt more lonely than that poor tramp who plodded his way wearily along the rugged cliffs.

With another heavy sigh, Marguerite Blakeney turned her back upon the sea and cliffs, and walked slowly back towards "The Fisherman's Rest." As she drew near, the sound of revelry, of gay, jovial laughter, grew louder and more distinct. She could distinguish Sir Andrew Ffoulkes' pleasant voice, Lord Tony's boisterous guffaws, her husband's occasional, drawly, sleepy comments; then realising the loneliness of the road and the fast gathering gloom round her, she quickened her steps . . . the next moment she perceived a stranger coming rapidly towards her. Marguerite did not look up: she was not the least nervous, and "The Fisherman's Rest" was now well within call.

The stranger paused when he saw Marguerite coming quickly towards him, and just as she was about to slip past him, he said very quietly:

"Citoyenne St. Just."

Marguerite uttered a little cry of astonishment, at thus hearing her own familiar maiden name uttered so close to her. She looked up at the stranger, and this time, with a cry of unfeigned pleasure, she put out both her hands effusively towards him.

"Chauvelin!" she exclaimed.

"Himself, citoyenne, at your service," said the stranger, gallantly kissing the tips of her fingers.

Marguerite said nothing for a moment or two, as she surveyed with obvious delight the not very prepossessing little figure before her. Chauvelin was then nearer forty than thirty — a clever, shrewd-looking personality, with a curious fox-like expression in the deep, sunken eyes. He was the same stranger who an hour or two previously had joined Mr. Jellyband in a friendly glass of wine.

"Chauvelin . . . my friend . . ." said Marguerite, with a pretty little sigh of satisfaction. "I am mightily pleased to see you."

No doubt poor Marguerite St. Just, lonely in the midst of her grandeur, and of her starchy friends, was happy to see a face that brought back memories of that happy time in Paris, when she reigned — a queen — over the intellectual coterie of the Rue de Richelieu. She did not notice the sarcastic little smile, however, that hovered round the thin lips of Chauvelin.

"But tell me," she added merrily, "what in the world, or whom in the world, are you doing here in England?"

"I might return the subtle compliment, fair lady," he said. "What of yourself?"

"Oh, I?" she said, with a shrug of the shoulders. "Je m'ennuie, mon ami, that is all."

They had reached the porch of "The Fisherman's Rest," but Marguerite seemed loth to go within. The evening air was lovely after the storm, and she had found a friend who exhaled the breath of Paris, who knew Armand well, who could talk of all the merry, brilliant friends whom she had left behind. So she lingered on under the pretty porch, while through the gaily-lighted dormer-window of the coffee-room sounds of laughter, of calls for "Sally" and for beer, of tapping of mugs, and clinking of dice, mingled with Sir Percy Blakeney's inane and mirthless laugh. Chauvelin stood beside her, his shrewd, pale, yellow eyes fixed on the pretty face, which looked so sweet and childlike in this soft English summer twilight.

"You surprise me, citoyenne," he said quietly, as he took a pinch of snuff.

"Do I now?" she retorted gaily. "Faith, my little Chauvelin, I should have thought that, with your penetration, you would have guessed that an atmosphere composed of fogs and virtues would never suit Marguerite St. Just."

"Dear me! is it as bad as that?" he asked, in mock consternation.

"Quite," she retorted, "and worse."

"Strange! Now, I thought that a pretty woman would have found English country life peculiarly attractive."

"Yes! so did I," she said with a sigh, "Pretty women," she added meditatively, "ought to have a good time in England, since all the pleasant things are forbidden them — the very things they do every day."

"Quite so!"

"You'll hardly believe it, my little Chauvelin," she said earnestly, "but I often pass a whole day — a whole day — without encountering a single temptation."

"No wonder," retorted Chauvelin, gallantly, "that the cleverest woman in Europe is troubled with ENNUI."

She laughed one of her melodious, rippling, childlike laughs.

"It must be pretty bad, mustn't it?" she asked archly, "or I should not have been so pleased to see you."

"And this within a year of a romantic love match . . . that's just the difficulty . . ."

"Ah! . . . that idyllic folly," said Chauvelin, with quiet sarcasm, "did not then survive the lapse of . . . weeks?"

"Idyllic follies never last, my little Chauvelin . . . They come upon us like the measles . . . and are as easily cured."

Chauvelin took another pinch of snuff: he seemed very much addicted to that pernicious habit, so prevalent in those days; perhaps, too, he found the taking of snuff a convenient veil for disguising the quick, shrewd glances with which he strove to read the very souls of those with whom he came in contact.

"No wonder," he repeated, with the same gallantry, "that the most active brain in Europe is troubled with ENNUI."

"I was in hopes that you had a prescription against the malady, my little Chauvelin."

"How can I hope to succeed in that which Sir Percy Blakeney has failed to accomplish?"

"Shall we leave Sir Percy out of the question for the present, my dear friend?" she said drily.

"Ah! my dear lady, pardon me, but that is just what we cannot very well do," said Chauvelin, whilst once again his eyes, keen as those of a fox on the alert, darted a quick glance at Marguerite. "I have a most perfect prescription against the worst form of ENNUI, which I would have been happy to submit to you, but — "

"But what?"

"There IS Sir Percy."

"What has he to do with it?"

"Quite a good deal, I am afraid. The prescription I would offer, fair lady, is called by a very plebeian name: Work!"

"Work?"

Chauvelin looked at Marguerite long and scrutinisingly. It seemed as if those keen, pale eyes of his were reading every one of her thoughts. They were alone together; the evening air was quite still, and their soft whispers were drowned in the noise which came from the coffee-room. Still, Chauvelin took a step or two from under the porch, looked quickly and keenly all round him, then seeing that indeed no one was within earshot, he once more came back close to Marguerite.

"Will you render France a small service, citoyenne?" he asked, with a sudden change of manner, which lent his thin, fox-like face a singular earnestness.

"La, man!" she replied flippantly, "how serious you look all of a sudden. . . . Indeed I do not know if I WOULD render France a small service — at any rate, it depends upon the kind of service she — or you — want."

"Have you ever heard of the Scarlet Pimpernel, Citoyenne St. Just?" asked Chauvelin, abruptly.

"Heard of the Scarlet Pimpernel?" she retorted with a long and merry laugh, "Faith man! we talk of nothing else. . . . We have hats 'a la Scarlet Pimpernel'; our horses are called 'Scarlet Pimpernel'; at the Prince of Wales' supper party the other night we had a 'souffle a la Scarlet Pimpernel.' . . . Lud!" she added gaily, "the other day I ordered at my milliner's a blue dress trimmed with green, and bless me, if she did not call that 'a la Scarlet Pimpernel.'"

Chauvelin had not moved while she prattled merrily along; he did not even attempt to stop her when her musical voice and her childlike laugh went echoing through the still evening air. But he remained serious and earnest whilst she laughed, and his voice, clear, incisive, and hard, was not raised above his breath as he said, —

"Then, as you have heard of that enigmatical personage, citoyenne, you must also have guessed, and know, that the man who hides his identity under that strange pseudonym, is the most bitter enemy of our republic, of France . . . of men like Armand St. Just."

"La!" she said, with a quaint little sigh, "I dare swear he is. . . . France has many bitter enemies these days."

"But you, citoyenne, are a daughter of France, and should be ready to help her in a moment of deadly peril."

"My brother Armand devotes his life to France," she retorted proudly; "as for me, I can do nothing . . . here in England. . . ."

"Yes, you . . ." he urged still more earnestly, whilst his thin fox-like face seemed suddenly to have grown impressive and full of dignity, "here, in England, citoyenne . . . you alone can help us. . . . Listen! — I have been sent over here by the Republican Government as its representative: I present my credentials to Mr. Pitt in London to-morrow. One of my duties here is to find out all about this League of the Scarlet Pimpernel, which has become a standing menace to France, since it is pledged to help our cursed aristocrats — traitors to their country, and enemies of the people — to escape from the just punishment which they deserve. You know as well as I do, citoyenne, that once they are over here, those French EMIGRES try to rouse public feeling against the Republic . . . They are ready to join issue with any enemy bold enough to attack France . . . Now, within the last month scores of these EMIGRES, some only suspected of treason, others actually condemned by the Tribunal of Public Safety, have succeeded in crossing the Channel. Their escape in each instance was planned, organized and effected by this society of young English jackanapes, headed by a man whose brain seems as resourceful as his identity is mysterious. All the most strenuous efforts on the part of my spies have failed to discover who he is; whilst the others are the hands, he is the head, who beneath this strange anonymity calmly works at the destruction of France. I mean to strike at that head, and for this I want your help — through him afterwards I can reach the rest of the gang: he is a young buck in English society, of that I feel sure. Find that man for me, citoyenne!" he urged, "find him for France."

Marguerite had listened to Chauvelin's impassioned speech without uttering a word, scarce making a movement, hardly daring to breathe. She had told him before that this mysterious hero of romance was the talk of the smart set to which she belonged; already, before this, her heart and her imagination had been stirred by the thought of the brave man, who, unknown to fame, had rescued hundreds of lives from a terrible, often an unmerciful fate. She had but little real sympathy with those haughty French aristocrats, insolent in their pride of caste, of whom the Comtesse de Tournay de Basserive was so typical an example; but republican and liberal-minded though she was from principle, she hated and loathed the methods which the young Republic had chosen for establishing itself. She had not been in Paris for some months; the horrors and bloodshed of the Reign of Terror, culminating in the September massacres, had only come across the Channel to her as a faint echo. Robespierre, Danton, Marat, she had not known in their new guise of bloody judiciaries, merciless wielders of the guillotine. Her very soul recoiled in horror from these excesses, to which she feared her brother Armand — moderate republican as he was — might become one day the holocaust.

Then, when first she heard of this band of young English enthusiasts, who, for sheer love of their fellowmen, dragged women and children, old and young men, from a horrible death, her heart had glowed with pride for them, and now, as Chauvelin spoke, her very soul went out to the gallant and mysterious leader of the reckless little band, who risked his life daily, who gave it freely and without ostentation, for the sake of humanity.

Her eyes were moist when Chauvelin had finished speaking, the lace at her bosom rose and fell with her quick, excited breathing; she no longer heard the noise of drinking from the inn, she did not heed her husband's voice or his inane laugh, her thoughts had gone wandering in search of the mysterious hero! Ah! there was a man she might have loved, had he come her way: everything in him appealed to her romantic imagination; his personality, his strength, his bravery, the loyalty of those who served under him in that same noble cause, and, above all, that anonymity which crowned him, as if with a halo of romantic glory.

"Find him for France, citoyenne!"

Chauvelin's voice close to her ear roused her from her dreams. The mysterious hero had vanished, and, not twenty yards away from her, a man was drinking and laughing, to whom she had sworn faith and loyalty.

"La! man," she said with a return of her assumed flippancy, "you are astonishing. Where in the world am I to look for him?"

"You go everywhere, citoyenne," whispered Chauvelin, insinuatingly, "Lady Blakeney is the pivot of social London, so I am told . . . you see everything, you HEAR everything."

"Easy, my friend," retorted Marguerite, drawing herself up to her full height and looking down, with a slight thought of contempt on the small, thin figure before her. "Easy! you seem to forget that there are six feet of Sir Percy Blakeney, and a long line of ancestors to stand between Lady Blakeney and such a thing as you propose."

"For the sake of France, citoyenne!" reiterated Chauvelin, earnestly.

"Tush, man, you talk nonsense anyway; for even if you did know who this Scarlet Pimpernel is, you could do nothing to him — an Englishman!"

"I'd take my chance of that," said Chauvelin, with a dry, rasping little laugh. "At any rate we could send him to the guillotine first to cool his ardour, then, when there is a diplomatic fuss about it, we can apologise — humbly — to the British Government, and, if necessary, pay compensation to the bereaved family."

"What you propose is horrible, Chauvelin," she said, drawing away from him as from some noisome insect. "Whoever the man may be, he is brave and noble, and never — do you hear me? — never would I lend a hand to such villainy."

"You prefer to be insulted by every French aristocrat who comes to this country?"

Chauvelin had taken sure aim when he shot this tiny shaft. Marguerite's fresh young cheeks became a touch more pale and she bit her under lip, for she would not let him see that the shaft had struck home.

"That is beside the question," she said at last with indifference. "I can defend myself, but I refuse to do any dirty work for you — or for France. You have other means at your disposal; you must use them, my friend."

And without another look at Chauvelin, Marguerite Blakeney turned her back on him and walked straight into the inn.

"That is not your last word, citoyenne," said Chauvelin, as a flood of light from the passage illumined her elegant, richly-clad figure, "we meet in London, I hope!"

"We meet in London," she said, speaking over her shoulder at him, "but that is my last word."

She threw open the coffee-room door and disappeared from his view, but he remained under the porch for a moment or two, taking a pinch of snuff. He had received a rebuke and a snub, but his shrewd, fox-like face looked neither abashed nor disappointed; on the contrary, a curious smile, half sarcastic and wholly satisfied, played around the corners of his thin lips.

CHAPTER IX
THE OUTRAGE

A beautiful starlit night had followed on the day of incessant rain: a cool, balmy, late summer's night, essentially English in its suggestion of moisture and scent of wet earth and dripping leaves.

The magnificent coach, drawn by four of the finest thoroughbreds in England, had driven off along the London road, with Sir Percy Blakeney on the box, holding the reins in his slender feminine hands, and beside him Lady Blakeney wrapped in costly furs. A fifty-mile drive on a starlit summer's night! Marguerite had hailed the notion of it with delight. . . . Sir Percy was an enthusiastic whip; his four thoroughbreds, which had been sent down to Dover a couple of days before, were just sufficiently fresh and restive to add zest to the expedition and Marguerite revelled in anticipation of the few hours of solitude, with the soft night breeze fanning her cheeks, her thoughts wandering, whither away? She knew from old experience that Sir Percy would speak little, if at all: he had often driven her on his beautiful coach for hours at night, from point to point, without making more than one or two casual remarks upon the weather or the state of the roads. He was very fond of driving by night, and she had very quickly adopted his fancy: as she sat next to him hour after hour, admiring the dexterous, certain way in which he handled the reins, she often wondered what went on in that slow-going head of his. He never told her, and she had never cared to ask.

At "The Fisherman's Rest" Mr. Jellyband was going the round, putting out the lights. His bar customers had all gone, but upstairs in the snug little bedrooms, Mr. Jellyband had quite a few important guests: the Comtesse de Tournay, with Suzannne, and the Vicomte, and there were two more bedrooms ready for Sir Andrew Ffoulkes and Lord Antony Dewhurst, if the two young men should elect to honour the ancient hostelry and stay the night.

For the moment these two young gallants were comfortably installed in the coffee-room, before the huge log-fire, which, in spite of the mildness of the evening, had been allowed to burn merrily.

"I say, Jelly, has everyone gone?" asked Lord Tony, as the worthy landlord still busied himself clearing away glasses and mugs.

"Everyone, as you see, my lord."

"And all your servants gone to bed?"

"All except the boy on duty in the bar, and," added Mr. Jellyband with a laugh, "I expect he'll be asleep afore long, the rascal."

"Then we can talk here undisturbed for half an hour?"

"At your service, my lord. . . . I'll leave your candles on the dresser . . . and your rooms are quite ready . . . I sleep at the top of the house myself, but if your lordship'll only call loudly enough, I daresay I shall hear."

"All right, Jelly . . . and . . . I say, put the lamp out — the fire'll give us all the light we need — and we don't want to attract the passer-by."

"Al ri', my lord."

Mr. Jellyband did as he was bid — he turned out the quaint old lamp that hung from the raftered ceiling and blew out all the candles.

"Let's have a bottle of wine, Jelly," suggested Sir Andrew.

"Al ri', sir!"

Jellyband went off to fetch the wine. The room now was quite dark, save for the circle of ruddy and fitful light formed by the brightly blazing logs in the hearth.

"Is that all, gentlemen?" asked Jellyband, as he returned with a bottle of wine and a couple of glasses, which he placed on the table.

"That'll do nicely, thanks, Jelly!" said Lord Tony.

"Good-night, my lord! Good-night, sir!"

"Good-night, Jelly!"

The two young men listened, whilst the heavy tread of Mr. Jellyband was heard echoing along the passage and staircase. Presently even that sound died out, and the whole of "The Fisherman's Rest" seemed wrapt in sleep, save the two young men drinking in silence beside the hearth.

For a while no sound was heard, even in the coffee-room, save the ticking of the old grandfather's clock and the crackling of the burning wood.

"All right again this time, Ffoulkes?" asked Lord Antony at last.

Sir Andrew had been dreaming evidently, gazing into the fire, and seeing therein, no doubt, a pretty, piquant face, with large brown eyes and a wealth of dark curls round a childish forehead.

"Yes!" he said, still musing, "all right!"

"No hitch?"

"None."

Lord Antony laughed pleasantly as he poured himself out another glass of wine.

"I need not ask, I suppose, whether you found the journey pleasant this time?"

"No, friend, you need not ask," replied Sir Andrew, gaily. "It was all right."

"Then here's to her very good health," said jovial Lord Tony. "She's a bonnie lass, though she IS a French one. And here's to your courtship — may it flourish and prosper exceedingly."

He drained his glass to the last drop, then joined his friend beside the hearth.

"Well! you'll be doing the journey next, Tony, I expect," said Sir Andrew, rousing himself from his meditations, "you and Hastings, certainly; and I hope you may have as pleasant a task as I had, and as charming a travelling companion. You have no idea, Tony. . . ."

"No! I haven't," interrupted his friend pleasantly, "but I'll take your word for it. And now," he added, whilst a sudden earnestness crept over his jovial young face, "how about business?" The two young men drew their chairs closer together, and instinctively, though they were alone, their voices sank to a whisper.

"I saw the Scarlet Pimpernel alone, for a few moments in Calais," said Sir Andrew, "a day or two ago. He crossed over to England two days before we did. He had escorted the party all the way from Paris, dressed — you'll never credit it! — as an old market woman, and driving — until they were safely out of the city — the covered cart, under which the Comtesse de Tournay, Mlle. Suzanne, and the Vicomte lay concealed among the turnips and cabbages. They, themselves, of course, never suspected who their driver was. He drove them right through a line of soldiery and a yelling mob, who were screaming, 'A bas les aristos!' But the market cart got through along with some others, and the Scarlet Pimpernel, in shawl, petticoat and hood, yelled 'A bas les aristos!' louder than anybody. Faith!" added the young man, as his eyes glowed with enthusiasm for the beloved leader, "that man's a marvel! His cheek is preposterous, I vow! — and that's what carries him through."

Lord Antony, whose vocabulary was more limited than that of his friend, could only find an oath or two with which to show his admiration for his leader.

"He wants you and Hastings to meet him at Calais," said Sir Andrew, more quietly, "on the 2nd of next month. Let me see! that will be next Wednesday."

"Yes."

"It is, of course, the case of the Comte de Tournay, this time; a dangerous task, for the Comte, whose escape from his chateau, after he had been declared a 'suspect' by the Committee of Public Safety, was a masterpiece of the Scarlet Pimpernel's ingenuity, is now under sentence of death. It will be rare sport to get HIM out of France, and you will have a narrow escape, if you get through at all. St. Just has actually gone to meet him — of course, no one suspects St. Just as yet; but after that . . . to get them both out of the country! I'faith, 'twill be a tough job, and tax even the ingenuity of our chief. I hope I may yet have orders to be of the party."

"Have you any special instructions for me?"

"Yes! rather more precise ones than usual. It appears that the Republican Government have sent an accredited agent over to England, a man named Chauvelin, who is said to be terribly bitter against our league, and determined to discover the identity of our leader, so that he may have him kidnapped, the next time he attempts to set foot in France. This Chauvelin has brought a whole army of spies with him, and until the chief has sampled the lot, he thinks we should meet as seldom as possible on the business of the league, and on no account should talk to each other in public places for a time. When he wants to speak to us, he will contrive to let us know."

The two young men were both bending over the fire for the blaze had died down, and only a red glow from the dying embers cast a lurid light on a narrow semicircle in front of the hearth. The rest of the room lay buried in complete gloom; Sir Andrew had taken a pocket-book from his pocket, and drawn therefrom a paper, which he unfolded, and together they tried to read it by the dim red firelight. So intent were they upon this, so wrapt up in the cause, the business they had so much at heart, so precious was this document which came from the very hand of their adored leader, that they had eyes and ears only for that. They lost count of the sounds around them, of the dropping of the crisp ash from the grate, of the monotonous ticking of the clock, of the soft, almost imperceptible rustle of something on the floor close beside them. A figure had emerged from under one of the benches; with snake-like, noiseless movements it crept closer and closer to the two young men, not breathing, only gliding along the floor, in the inky blackness of the room.

"You are to read these instructions and commit them to memory," said Sir Andrew, "then destroy them."

He was about to replace the letter-case into his pocket, when a tiny slip of paper fluttered from it and fell on to the floor. Lord Antony stooped and picked it up.

"What's that?" he asked.

"I don't know," replied Sir Andrew.

"It dropped out of your pocket just now. It certainly does not seem to be with the other paper."

"Strange! —I wonder when it got there? It is from the chief," he added, glancing at the paper.

Both stooped to try and decipher this last tiny scrap of paper on which a few words had been hastily scrawled, when suddenly a slight noise attracted their attention, which seemed to come from the passage beyond.

"What's that?" said both instinctively. Lord Antony crossed the room towards the door, which he threw open quickly and suddenly; at that very moment he received a stunning blow between the eyes, which threw him back violently into the room. Simultaneously the crouching, snake-like figure in the gloom had jumped up and hurled itself from behind upon the unsuspecting Sir Andrew, felling him to the ground.

All this occurred within the short space of two or three seconds, and before either Lord Antony or Sir Andrew had time or chance to utter a cry or to make the faintest struggle. They were each seized by two men, a muffler was quickly tied round the mouth of each, and they were pinioned to one another back to back, their arms, hands, and legs securely fastened.

One man had in the meanwhile quietly shut the door; he wore a mask and now stood motionless while the others completed their work.

"All safe, citoyen!" said one of the men, as he took a final survey of the bonds which secured the two young men.

"Good!" replied the man at the door; "now search their pockets and give me all the papers you find."

This was promptly and quietly done. The masked man having taken possession of all the papers, listened for a moment or two if there were any sound within "The Fisherman's Rest." Evidently satisfied that this dastardly outrage had remained unheard, he once more opened the door and pointed peremptorily down the passage. The four men lifted Sir Andrew and Lord Antony from the ground, and as quietly, as noiselessly as they had come, they bore the two pinioned young gallants out of the inn and along the Dover Road into the gloom beyond.

In the coffee-room the masked leader of this daring attempt was quickly glancing through the stolen papers.

"Not a bad day's work on the whole," he muttered, as he quietly took off his mask, and his pale, fox-like eyes glittered in the red glow of the fire. "Not a bad day's work."

He opened one or two letters from Sir Andrew Ffoulkes' pocket-book, noted the tiny scrap of paper which the two young men had only just had time to read; but one letter specially, signed Armand St. Just, seemed to give him strange satisfaction.

"Armand St. Just a traitor after all," he murmured. "Now, fair Marguerite Blakeney," he added viciously between his clenched teeth, "I think that you will help me to find the Scarlet Pimpernel."

CHAPTER X
IN THE OPERA BOX

It was one of the gala nights at Covent Garden Theatre, the first of the autumn season in this memorable year of grace 1792.

The house was packed, both in the smart orchestra boxes and in the pit, as well as in the more plebeian balconies and galleries above. Gluck's ORPHEUS made a strong appeal to the more intellectual portions of the house, whilst the fashionable women, the gaily-dressed and brilliant throng, spoke to the eye of those who cared but little for this "latest importation from Germany."

Selina Storace had been duly applauded after her grand ARIA by her numerous admirers; Benjamin Incledon, the acknowledged favourite of the ladies, had received special gracious recognition from the royal box; and now the curtain came down after the glorious finale to the second act, and the audience, which had hung spell-bound on the magic strains of the great maestro, seemed collectively to breathe a long sigh of satisfaction, previous to letting loose its hundreds of waggish and frivolous tongues. In the smart orchestra boxes many well-known faces were to be seen. Mr. Pitt, overweighted with cares of state, was finding brief relaxation in to-night's musical treat; the Prince of Wales, jovial, rotund, somewhat coarse and commonplace in appearance, moved about from box to box, spending brief quarters of an hour with those of his more intimate friends.

In Lord Grenville's box, too, a curious, interesting personality attracted everyone's attention; a thin, small figure with shrewd, sarcastic face and deep-set eyes, attentive to the music, keenly critical of the audience, dressed in immaculate black, with dark hair free from any powder. Lord Grenville — Foreign Secretary of State — paid him marked, though frigid deference.

Here and there, dotted about among distinctly English types of beauty, one or two foreign faces stood out in marked contrast: the haughty aristocratic cast of countenance of the many French royalist EMIGRES who, persecuted by the relentless, revolutionary faction of their country, had found a peaceful refuge in England. On these faces sorrow and care were deeply writ; the women especially paid but little heed, either to the music or to the brilliant audience; no doubt their thoughts were far away with husband, brother, son maybe, still in peril, or lately succumbed to a cruel fate.

Among these the Comtesse de Tournay de Basserive, but lately arrived from France, was a most conspicuous figure: dressed in deep, heavy black silk, with only a white lace kerchief to relieve the aspect of mourning about her person, she sat beside Lady Portarles, who was vainly trying by witty sallies and somewhat broad jokes, to bring a smile to the Comtesse's sad mouth. Behind her sat little Suzanne and the Vicomte, both silent and somewhat shy among so many strangers. Suzanne's eyes seemed wistful; when she first entered the crowded house, she had looked eagerly all around, scanning every face, scrutinised every box. Evidently the one face she wished to see was not there, for she settled herself quietly behind her mother, listened apathetically to the music, and took no further interest in the audience itself.

"Ah, Lord Grenville," said Lady Portarles, as following a discreet knock, the clever, interesting head of the Secretary of State appeared in the doorway of the box, "you could not arrive more A PROPOS. Here is Madame la Comtesse de Tournay positively dying to hear the latest news from France."

The distinguished diplomat had come forward and was shaking hands with the ladies.

"Alas!" he said sadly, "it is of the very worst. The massacres continue; Paris literally reeks with blood; and the guillotine claims a hundred victims a day."

Pale and tearful, the Comtesse was leaning back in her chair, listening horror-struck to this brief and graphic account of what went on in her own misguided country.

"Ah, monsieur!" she said in broken English, "it is dreadful to hear all that — and my poor husband still in that awful country. It is terrible for me to be sitting here, in a theatre, all safe and in peace, whilst he is in such peril."

"Lud, Madame!" said honest, bluff Lady Portarles, "your sitting in a convent won't make your husband safe, and you have your children to consider: they are too young to be dosed with anxiety and premature mourning."

The Comtesse smiled through her tears at the vehemence of her friend. Lady Portarles, whose voice and manner would not have misfitted a jockey, had a heart of gold, and hid the most genuine sympathy and most gentle kindliness, beneath the somewhat coarse manners affected by some ladies at that time.

"Besides which, Madame," added Lord Grenville, "did you not tell me yesterday that the League of the Scarlet Pimpernel had pledged their honour to bring M. le Comte safely across the Channel?"

"Ah, yes!" replied the Comtesse, "and that is my only hope. I saw Lord Hastings yesterday . . . he reassured me again."

"Then I am sure you need have no fear. What the league have sworn, that they surely will accomplish. Ah!" added the old diplomat with a sigh, "if I were but a few years younger . . ."

"La, man!" interrupted honest Lady Portarles, "you are still young enough to turn your back on that French scarecrow that sits enthroned in your box to-night."

"I wish I could . . . but your ladyship must remember that in serving our country we must put prejudices aside. M. Chauvelin is the accredited agent of his Government . . ."

"Odd's fish, man!" she retorted, "you don't call those bloodthirsty ruffians over there a government, do you?"

"It has not been thought advisable as yet," said the Minister, guardedly, "for England to break off diplomatic relations with France, and we cannot therefore refuse to receive with courtesy the agent she wishes to send to us."

"Diplomatic relations be demmed, my lord! That sly little fox over there is nothing but a spy, I'll warrant, and you'll find — an I'm much mistaken, that he'll concern himself little with such diplomacy, beyond trying to do mischief to royalist refugees — to our heroic Scarlet Pimpernel and to the members of that brave little league."

"I am sure," said the Comtesse, pursing up her thin lips, "that if this Chauvelin wishes to do us mischief, he will find a faithful ally in Lady Blakeney."

"Bless the woman!" ejaculated Lady Portarles, "did ever anyone see such perversity? My Lord Grenville, you have the gift of gab, will you please explain to Madame la Comtesse that she is acting like a fool. In your position here in England, Madame," she added, turning a wrathful and resolute face towards the Comtesse, "you cannot afford to put on the hoity-toity airs you French aristocrats are so fond of. Lady Blakeney may or may not be in sympathy with those Ruffians in France; she may or may not have had anything to do with the arrest and condemnation of St. Cyr, or whatever the man's name is, but she is the leader of fashion in this country; Sir Percy Blakeney has more money than any half-dozen other men put together, he is hand and glove with royalty, and your trying to snub Lady Blakeney will not harm her, but will make you look a fool. Isn't that so, my Lord?"

But what Lord Grenville thought of this matter, or to what reflections this comely tirade of Lady Portarles led the Comtesse de Tournay, remained unspoken, for the curtain had just risen on the third act of ORPHEUS, and admonishments to silence came from every part of the house.

Lord Grenville took a hasty farewell of the ladies and slipped back into his box, where M. Chauvelin had sat through this ENTR'ACTE, with his eternal snuff-box in his hand, and with his keen pale eyes intently fixed upon a box opposite him, where, with much frou-frou of silken skirts, much laughter and general stir of curiosity amongst the audience, Marguerite Blakeney had just entered, accompanied by her husband, and looking divinely pretty beneath the wealth of her golden, reddish curls, slightly besprinkled with powder, and tied back at the nape of her graceful neck with a gigantic black bow. Always dressed in the very latest vagary of fashion, Marguerite alone among the ladies that night had discarded the crossover fichu and broad-lapelled over-dress, which had been in fashion for the last two or three years. She wore the short-waisted classical-shaped gown, which so soon was to become the approved mode in every country in Europe. It suited her graceful, regal figure to perfection, composed as it was of shimmering stuff which seemed a mass of rich gold embroidery.

As she entered, she leant for a moment out of the box, taking stock of all those present whom she knew. Many bowed to her as she did so, and from the royal box there came also a quick and gracious salute.

Chauvelin watched her intently all through the commencement of the third act, as she sat enthralled with the music, her exquisite little hand toying with a small jewelled fan, her regal head, her throat, arms and neck covered with magnificent diamonds and rare gems, the gift of the adoring husband who sprawled leisurely by her side.

Marguerite was passionately fond of music. ORPHEUS charmed her to-night. The very joy of living was writ plainly upon the sweet young face, it sparkled out of the merry blue eyes and lit up the smile that lurked around the lips. She was after all but five-and-twenty, in the hey day of youth, the darling of a brilliant throng, adored, FETED, petted, cherished. Two days ago the DAY DREAM had returned from Calais, bringing her news that her idolised brother had safely landed, that he thought of her, and would be prudent for her sake.

What wonder for the moment, and listening to Gluck's impassioned strains, that she forgot her disillusionments, forgot her vanished love-dreams, forgot even the lazy, good-humoured nonentity who had made up for his lack of spiritual attainments by lavishing worldly advantages upon her.

He had stayed beside her in the box just as long as convention demanded, making way for His Royal Highness, and for the host of admirers who in a continued procession came to pay homage to the queen of fashion. Sir Percy had strolled away, to talk to more congenial friends probably. Marguerite did not even wonder whither he had gone — she cared so little; she had had a little court round her, composed of the JEUNESSE DOREE of London, and had just dismissed them all, wishing to be alone with Gluck for a brief while.

A discreet knock at the door roused her from her enjoyment.

"Come in," she said with some impatience, without turning to look at the intruder.

Chauvelin, waiting for his opportunity, noted that she was alone, and now, without pausing for that impatient "Come in," he quietly slipped into the box, and the next moment was standing behind Marguerite's chair.

"A word with you, citoyenne," he said quietly.

Marguerite turned quickly, in alarm, which was not altogether feigned.

"Lud, man! you frightened me," she said with a forced little laugh, "your presence is entirely inopportune. I want to listen to Gluck, and have no mind for talking."

"But this is my only opportunity," he said, as quietly, and without waiting for permission, he drew a chair close behind her — so close that he could whisper in her ear, without disturbing the audience, and without being seen, in the dark background of the box. "This is my only opportunity," he repeated, as she vouchsafed him no reply, "Lady Blakeney is always so surrounded, so FETED by her court, that a mere old friend has but very little chance."

"Faith, man!" she said impatiently, "you must seek for another opportunity then. I am going to Lord Grenville's ball to-night after the opera. So are you, probably. I'll give you five minutes then. . . ."

"Three minutes in the privacy of this box are quite sufficient for me," he rejoined placidly, "and I think that you will be wise to listen to me, Citoyenne St. Just."

Marguerite instinctively shivered. Chauvelin had not raised his voice above a whisper; he was now quietly taking a pinch of snuff, yet there was something in his attitude, something in those pale, foxy eyes, which seemed to freeze the blood in her veins, as would the sight of some deadly hitherto unguessed peril. "Is that a threat, citoyen?" she asked at last.

"Nay, fair lady," he said gallantly, "only an arrow shot into the air."

He paused a moment, like a cat which sees a mouse running heedlessly by, ready to spring, yet waiting with that feline sense of enjoyment of mischief about to be done. Then he said quietly —

"Your brother, St. Just, is in peril."

Not a muscle moved in the beautiful face before him. He could only see it in profile, for Marguerite seemed to be watching the stage intently, but Chauvelin was a keen observer; he noticed the sudden rigidity of the eyes, the hardening of the mouth, the sharp, almost paralysed tension of the beautiful, graceful figure.

"Lud, then," she said with affected merriment, "since 'tis one of your imaginary plots, you'd best go back to your own seat and leave me enjoy the music."

And with her hand she began to beat time nervously against the cushion of the box. Selina Storace was singing the "Che faro" to an audience that hung spellbound upon the prima donna's lips. Chauvelin did not move from his seat; he quietly watched that tiny nervous hand, the only indication that his shaft had indeed struck home.

"Well?" she said suddenly and irrelevantly, and with the same feigned unconcern.

"Well, citoyenne?" he rejoined placidly.

"About my brother?"

"I have news of him for you which, I think, will interest you, but first let me explain. . . . May I?"

The question was unnecessary. He felt, though Marguerite still held her head steadily averted from him, that her every nerve was strained to hear what he had to say.

"The other day, citoyenne," he said, "I asked for your help. . . . France needed it, and I thought I could rely on you, but you gave me your answer. . . . Since then the exigencies of my own affairs and your own social duties have kept up apart . . . although many things have happened. . . ."

"To the point, I pray you, citoyen," she said lightly; "the music is entrancing, and the audience will get impatient of your talk."

"One moment, citoyenne. The day on which I had the honour of meeting you at Dover, and less than an hour after I had your final answer, I obtained possession of some papers, which revealed another of those subtle schemes for the escape of a batch of French aristocrats — that traitor de Tournay amongst others — all organized by that arch-meddler, the Scarlet Pimpernel. Some of the threads, too, of this mysterious organization have come into my hands, but not all, and I want you — nay! you MUST help me to gather them together."

Marguerite seemed to have listened to him with marked impatience; she now shrugged her shoulders and said gaily —

"Bah! man. Have I not already told you that I care nought about your schemes or about the Scarlet Pimpernel. And had you not spoken about my brother . . ."

"A little patience, I entreat, citoyenne," he continued imperturbably. "Two gentlemen, Lord Antony Dewhurst and Sir Andrew Ffoulkes were at 'The Fisherman's Rest' at Dover that same night."

"I know. I saw them there."

"They were already known to my spies as members of that accursed league. It was Sir Andrew Ffoulkes who escorted the Comtesse de Tournay and her children across the Channel. When the two young men were alone, my spies forced their way into the coffee-room of the inn, gagged and pinioned the two gallants, seized their papers, and brought them to me."

In a moment she had guessed the danger. Papers? . . . Had Armand been imprudent? . . . The very thought struck her with nameless terror. Still she would not let this man see that she feared; she laughed gaily and lightly.

"Faith! and your impudence pases belief," she said merrily. "Robbery and violence! — in England! — in a crowded inn! Your men might have been caught in the act!"

"What if they had? They are children of France, and have been trained by your humble servant. Had they been caught they would have gone to jail, or even to the gallows, without a word of protest or indiscretion; at any rate it was well worth the risk. A crowded inn is safer for these little operations than you think, and my men have experience."

"Well? And those papers?" she asked carelessly.

"Unfortunately, though they have given me cognisance of certain names . . . certain movements . . . enough, I think, to thwart their projected COUP for the moment, it would only be for the moment, and still leaves me in ignorance of the identity of the Scarlet Pimpernel.

"La! my friend," she said, with the same assumed flippancy of manner, "then you are where you were before, aren't you? and you can let me enjoy the last strophe of the ARIA. Faith!" she added, ostentatiously smothering an imaginary yawn, "had you not spoken about my brother . . ."

"I am coming to him now, citoyenne. Among the papers there was a letter to Sir Andrew Ffoulkes, written by your brother, St. Just."

"Well? And?"

"That letter shows him to be not only in sympathy with the enemies of France, but actually a helper, if not a member, of the League of the Scarlet Pimpernel."

The blow had been struck at last. All along, Marguerite had been expecting it; she would not show fear, she was determined to seem unconcerned, flippant even. She wished, when the shock came, to be prepared for it, to have all her wits about her — those wits which had been nicknamed the keenest in Europe. Even now she did not flinch. She knew that Chauvelin had spoken the truth; the man was too earnest, too blindly devoted to the misguided cause he had at heart, too proud of his countrymen, of those makers of revolutions, to stoop to low, purposeless falsehoods.

That letter of Armand's — foolish, imprudent Armand — was in Chauvelin's hands. Marguerite knew that as if she had seen the letter with her own eyes; and Chauvelin would hold that letter for purposes of his own, until it suited him to destroy it or to make use of it against Armand. All that she knew, and yet she continued to laugh more gaily, more loudly than she had done before.

"La, man!" she said, speaking over her shoulder and looking him full and squarely in the face, "did I not say it was some imaginary plot. . . . Armand in league with that enigmatic Scarlet Pimpernel! . . . Armand busy helping those French aristocrats whom he despises! . . . Faith, the tale does infinite credit to your imagination!"

"Let me make my point clear, citoyenne," said Chauvelin, with the same unruffled calm, "I must assure you that St. Just is compromised beyond the slightest hope of pardon."

Inside the orchestra box all was silent for a moment or two. Marguerite sat, straight upright, rigid and inert, trying to think, trying to face the situation, to realise what had best be done.

In the house Storace had finished the ARIA, and was even now bowing in her classic garb, but in approved eighteenth-century fashion, to the enthusiastic audience, who cheered her to the echo.

"Chauvelin," said Marguerite Blakeney at last, quietly, and without that touch of bravado which had characterised her attitude all along, "Chauvelin, my friend, shall we try to understand one another. It seems that my wits have become rusty by contact with this damp climate. Now, tell me, you are very anxious to discover the identity of the Scarlet Pimpernel, isn't that so?"

"France's most bitter enemy, citoyenne . . . all the more dangerous, as he works in the dark."

"All the more noble, you mean. . . . Well! — and you would now force me to do some spying work for you in exchange for my brother Armand's safety? — Is that it?"

"Fie! two very ugly words, fair lady," protested Chauvelin, urbanely. "There can be no question of force, and the service which I would ask of you, in the name of France, could never be called by the shocking name of spying."

"At any rate, that is what it is called over here," she said drily. "That is your intention, is it not?"

"My intention is, that you yourself win the free pardon for Armand St. Just by doing me a small service."

"What is it?"

"Only watch for me to-night, Citoyenne St. Just," he said eagerly. "Listen: among the papers which were found about the person of Sir Andrew Ffoulkes there was a tiny note. See!" he added, taking a tiny scrap of paper from his pocket-book and handing it to her.

It was the same scrap of paper which, four days ago, the two young men had been in the act of reading, at the very moment when they were attacked by Chauvelin's minions. Marguerite took it mechanically and stooped to read it. There were only two lines, written in a distorted, evidently disguised, handwriting; she read them half aloud —

"'Remember we must not meet more often than is strictly necessary. You have all instructions for the 2nd. If you wish to speak to me again, I shall be at G.'s ball.'"

"What does it mean?" she asked.

"Look again, citoyenne, and you will understand."

"There is a device here in the corner, a small red flower . . ."

"Yes."

"The Scarlet Pimpernel," she said eagerly, "and G.'s ball means Grenville's ball. . . . He will be at my Lord Grenville's ball to-night."

"That is how I interpret the note, citoyenne," concluded Chauvelin, blandly. "Lord Antony Dewhurst and Sir Andrew Ffoulkes, after they were pinioned and searched by my spies, were carried by my orders to a lonely house in the Dover Road, which I had rented for the purpose: there they remained close prisoners until this morning. But having found this tiny scrap of paper, my intention was that they should be in London, in time to attend my Lord Grenville's ball. You see, do you not? that they must have a great deal to say to their chief . . . and thus they will have an opportunity of speaking to him to-night, just as he directed them to do. Therefore, this morning, those two young gallants found every bar and bolt open in that lonely house on the Dover Road, their jailers disappeared, and two good horses standing ready saddled and tethered in the yard. I have not seen them yet, but I think we may safely conclude that they did not draw rein until they reached London. Now you see how simple it all is, citoyenne!"

"It does seem simple, doesn't it?" she said, with a final bitter attempt at flippancy, "when you want to kill a chicken . . . you take hold of it . . . then you wring its neck . . . it's only the chicken who does not find it quite so simple. Now you hold a knife at my throat, and a hostage for my obedience. . . . You find it simple. . . . I don't."

"Nay, citoyenne, I offer you a chance of saving the brother you love from the consequences of his own folly."

Marguerite's face softened, her eyes at last grew moist, as she murmured, half to herself:

"The only being in the world who has loved me truly and constantly . . . But what do you want me to do, Chauvelin?" she said, with a world of despair in her tear-choked voice. "In my present position, it is well-nigh impossible!"

"Nay, citoyenne," he said drily and relentlessly, not heeding that despairing, childlike appeal, which might have melted a heart of stone, "as Lady Blakeney, no one suspects you, and with your help to-night I may — who knows? — succeed in finally establishing the identity of the Scarlet Pimpernel. . . . You are going to the ball anon. . . . Watch for me there, citoyenne, watch and listen. . . . You can tell me if you hear a chance word or whisper. . . . You can note everyone to whom Sir Andrew Ffoulkes or Lord Antony Dewhurst will speak. You are absolutely beyond suspicion now. The Scarlet Pimpernel will be at Lord Grenville's ball to-night. Find out who he is, and I will pledge the word of France that your brother shall be safe."

Chauvelin was putting the knife to her throat. Marguerite felt herself entangled in one of those webs, from which she could hope for no escape. A precious hostage was being held for her obedience: for she knew that this man would never make an empty threat. No doubt Armand was already signalled to the Committee of Public Safety as one of the "suspect"; he would not be allowed to leave France again, and would be ruthlessly struck, if she refused to obey Chauvelin. For a moment — woman-like — she still hoped to temporise. She held out her hand to this man, whom she now feared and hated.

"If I promise to help you in this matter, Chauvelin," she said pleasantly, "will you give me that letter of St. Just's?"

"If you render me useful service to-night, citoyenne," he replied with a sarcastic smile, "I will give you that letter . . . to-morrow."

"You do not trust me?"

"I trust you absolutely, dear lady, but St. Just's life is forfeit to his country . . . it rests with you to redeem it."

"I may be powerless to help you," she pleaded, "were I ever so willing."

"That would be terrible indeed," he said quietly, "for you . . . and for St. Just."

Marguerite shuddered. She felt that from this man she could expect no mercy. All-powerful, he held the beloved life in the hollow of his hand. She knew him too well not to know that, if he failed in gaining his own ends, he would be pitiless.

She felt cold in spite of the oppressive air of opera-house. The heart-appealing strains of the music seemed to reach her, as from a distant land. She drew her costly lace scarf up around her shoulders, and sat silently watching the brilliant scene, as if in a dream.

For a moment her thoughts wandered away from the loved one who was in danger, to that other man who also had a claim on her confidence and her affection. She felt lonely, frightened for Armand's sake; she longed to seek comfort and advice from someone who would know how to help and console. Sir Percy Blakeney had loved her once; he was her husband; why should she stand alone through this terrible ordeal? He had very little brains, it is true, but he had plenty of muscle: surely, if she provided the thought, and he the manly energy and pluck, together they could outwit the astute diplomatist, and save the hostage from his vengeful hands, without imperilling the life of the noble leader of that gallant little band of heroes. Sir Percy knew St. Just well — he seemed attached to him — she was sure that he could help.

Chauvelin was taking no further heed of her. He had said his cruel "Either — or — " and left her to decide. He, in his turn now, appeared to be absorbed in the sour-stirring melodies of ORPHEUS, and was beating time to the music with his sharp, ferret-like head.

A discreet rap at the door roused Marguerite from her thoughts. It was Sir Percy Blakeney, tall, sleepy, good-humoured, and wearing that half-shy, half-inane smile, which just now seemed to irritate her every nerve.

"Er . . . your chair is outside . . . m'dear," he said, with his most exasperating drawl, "I suppose you will want to go to that demmed ball. . . . Excuse me — er — Monsieur Chauvelin — I had not observed you. . . ."

He extended two slender, white fingers toward Chauvelin, who had risen when Sir Percy entered the box.

"Are you coming, m'dear?"

"Hush! Sh! Sh!" came in angry remonstrance from different parts of the house. "Demmed impudence," commented Sir Percy with a good-natured smile.

Marguerite sighed impatiently. Her last hope seemed suddenly to have vanished away. She wrapped her cloak round her and without looking at her husband:

"I am ready to go," she said, taking his arm. At the door of the box she turned and looked straight at Chauvelin, who, with his CHAPEAU-BRAS under his arm, and a curious smile round his thin lips, was preparing to follow the strangely ill-assorted couple.

"It is only AU REVOIR, Chauvelin," she said pleasantly, "we shall meet at my Lord Grenville's ball, anon."

And in her eyes the astute Frenchman, read, no doubt, something which caused him profound satisfaction, for, with a sarcastic smile, he took a delicate pinch of snuff, then, having dusted his dainty lace jabot, he rubbed his thin, bony hands contentedly together.

CHAPTER XI
LORD GRENVILLE'S BALL

The historic ball given by the then Secretary of State for Foreign Affairs — Lord Grenville — was the most brilliant function of the year. Though the autumn season had only just begun, everybody who was anybody had contrived to be in London in time to be present there, and to shine at this ball, to the best of his or her respective ability.

His Royal Highness the Prince of Wales had promised to be present. He was coming on presently from the opera. Lord Grenville himself had listened to the two first acts of OR-PHEUS, before preparing to receive his guests. At ten o'clock — an unusually late hour in those days — the grand rooms of the Foreign Office, exquisitely decorated with exotic palms and flowers, were filled to overflowing. One room had been set apart for dancing, and the dainty strains of the minuet made a soft accompaniment to the gay chatter, the merry laughter of the numerous and brilliant company.

In a smaller chamber, facing the top of the fine stairway, the distinguished host stood ready to receive his guests. Distinguished men, beautiful women, notabilities from every European country had already filed past him, had exchanged the elaborate bows and curtsies with him, which the extravagant fashion of the time demanded, and then, laughing and talking, had dispersed in the ball, reception, and card rooms beyond.

Not far from Lord Grenville's elbow, leaning against one of the console tables, Chauvelin, in his irreproachable black costume, was taking a quiet survey of the brilliant throng. He noted that Sir Percy and Lady Blakeney had not yet arrived, and his keen, pale eyes glanced quickly towards the door every time a new-comer appeared.

He stood somewhat isolated: the envoy of the Revolutionary Government of France was not likely to be very popular in England, at a time when the news of the awful September massacres, and of the Reign of Terror and Anarchy, had just begun to filtrate across the Channel.

In his official capacity he had been received courteously by his English colleagues: Mr. Pitt had shaken him by the hand; Lord Grenville had entertained him more than once; but the more intimate circles of London society ignored him altogether; the women openly turned their backs upon him; the men who held no official position refused to shake his hand.

But Chauvelin was not the man to trouble himself about these social amenities, which he called mere incidents in his diplomatic career. He was blindly enthusiastic for the revolutionary cause, he despised all social inequalities, and he had a burning love for his own country: these three sentiments made him supremely indifferent to the snubs he received in this fog-ridden, loyalist, old-fashioned England.

But, above all, Chauvelin had a purpose at heart. He firmly believed that the French aristocrat was the most bitter enemy of France; he would have wished to see every one of them annihilated: he was one of those who, during this awful Reign of Terror, had been the first to utter the historic and ferocious desire "that aristocrats might have but one head between them, so that it might be cut off with a single stroke of the guillotine." And thus he looked upon every French aristocrat, who had succeeded in escaping from France, as so much prey of which the guillotine had been unwarrantably cheated. There is no doubt that those royalist EMIGRES, once they had managed to cross the frontier, did their very best to stir up foreign indignation against France. Plots without end were hatched in England, in Belgium, in Holland, to try and induce some great power to send troops into revolutionary Paris, to free King Louis, and to summarily hang the bloodthirsty leaders of that monster republic.

Small wonder, therefore, that the romantic and mysterious personality of the Scarlet Pimpernel was a source of bitter hatred to Chauvelin. He and the few young jackanapes under his command, well furnished with money, armed with boundless daring, and acute cunning, had succeeded in rescuing hundreds of aristocrats from France. Nine-tenths of the EMIGRES, who were FETED at the English court, owed their safety to that man and to his league.

Chauvelin had sworn to his colleagues in Paris that he would discover the identity of that meddlesome Englishman, entice him over to France, and then . . . Chauvelin drew a deep breath of satisfaction at the very thought of seeing that enigmatic head falling under the knife of the guillotine, as easily as that of any other man.

Suddenly there was a great stir on the handsome staircase, all conversation stopped for a moment as the majordomo's voice outside announced, —

"His Royal Highness the Prince of Wales and suite, Sir Percy Blakeney, Lady Blakeney."

Lord Grenville went quickly to the door to receive his exalted guest.

The Prince of Wales, dressed in a magnificent court suit of salmon-coloured velvet richly embroidered with gold, entered with Marguerite Blakeney on his arm; and on his left Sir Percy, in gorgeous shimmering cream satin, cut in the extravagant "Incroyable" style, his fair hair free from powder, priceless lace at his neck and wrists, and the flat CHAPEAU-BRAS under his arm.

After the few conventional words of deferential greeting, Lord Grenville said to his royal guest, —

"Will your Highness permit me to introduce M. Chauvelin, the accredited agent of the French Government?"

Chauvelin, immediately the Prince entered, had stepped forward, expecting this introduction. He bowed very low, whilst the Prince returned his salute with a curt nod of the head.

"Monsieur," said His Royal Highness coldly, "we will try to forget the government that sent you, and look upon you merely as our guest — a private gentleman from France. As such you are welcome, Monsieur."

"Monseigneur," rejoined Chauvelin, bowing once again. "Madame," he added, bowing ceremoniously before Marguerite.

"Ah! my little Chauvelin!" she said with unconcerned gaiety, and extending her tiny hand to him. "Monsieur and I are old friends, your Royal Highness."

"Ah, then," said the Prince, this time very graciously, "you are doubly welcome, Monsieur."

"There is someone else I would crave permission to present to your Royal Highness," here interposed Lord Grenville.

"Ah! who is it?" asked the Prince.

"Madame la Comtesse de Tournay de Basserive and her family, who have but recently come from France."

"By all means! — They are among the lucky ones then!"

Lord Grenville turned in search of the Comtesse, who sat at the further end of the room.

"Lud love me!" whispered his Royal Highness to Marguerite, as soon as he had caught sight of the rigid figure of the old lady; "Lud love me! she looks very virtuous and very melancholy."

"Faith, your Royal Highness," she rejoined with a smile, "virtue is like precious odours, most fragrant when it is crushed."

"Virtue, alas!" sighed the Prince, "is mostly unbecoming to your charming sex, Madame."

"Madame la Comtesse de Tournay de Basserive," said Lord Grenville, introducing the lady.

"This is a pleasure, Madame; my royal father, as you know, is ever glad to welcome those of your compatriots whom France has driven from her shores."

"Your Royal Highness is ever gracious," replied the Comtesse with becoming dignity. Then, indicating her daughter, who stood timidly by her side: "My daughter Suzanne, Monseigneur," she said.

"Ah! charming! — charming!" said the Prince, "and now allow me, Comtesse, to introduce you, Lady Blakeney, who honours us with her friendship. You and she will have much to say to one another, I vow. Every compatriot of Lady Blakeney's is doubly welcome for her sake . . . her friends are our friends . . . her enemies, the enemies of England."

Marguerite's blue eyes had twinkled with merriment at this gracious speech from her exalted friend. The Comtesse de Tournay, who lately had so flagrantly insulted her, was here receiving a public lesson, at which Marguerite could not help but rejoice. But the Comtesse, for whom respect of royalty amounted almost to a religion, was too well-schooled in courtly etiquette to show the slightest sign of embarrassment, as the two ladies curtsied ceremoniously to one another.

"His Royal Highness is ever gracious, Madame," said Marguerite, demurely, and with a wealth of mischief in her twinkling blue eyes, "but there is no need for his kind of mediation. . . . Your amiable reception of me at our last meeting still dwells pleasantly in my memory."

"We poor exiles, Madame," rejoined the Comtesse, frigidly, "show our gratitude to England by devotion to the wishes of Monseigneur."

"Madame!" said Marguerite, with another ceremonious curtsey.

"Madame," responded the Comtesse with equal dignity.

The Prince in the meanwhile was saying a few gracious words to the young Vicomte.

"I am happy to know you, Monsieur le Vicomte," he said. "I knew your father well when he was ambassador in London."

"Ah, Monseigneur!" replied the Vicomte, "I was a leetle boy then . . . and now I owe the honour of this meeting to our protector, the Scarlet Pimpernel."

"Hush!" said the Prince, earnestly and quickly, as he indicated Chauvelin, who had stood a little on one side throughout the whole of this little scene, watching Marguerite and the Comtesse with an amused, sarcastic little smile around his thin lips.

"Nay, Monseigneur," he said now, as if in direct response to the Prince's challenge, "pray do not check this gentleman's display of gratitude; the name of that interesting red flower is well known to me — and to France."

The Prince looked at him keenly for a moment or two.

"Faith, then, Monsieur," he said, "perhaps you know more about our national hero than we do ourselves . . . perchance you know who he is. . . . See!" he added, turning to the groups round the room, "the ladies hang upon your lips . . . you would render yourself popular among the fair sex if you were to gratify their curiosity."

"Ah, Monseigneur," said Chauvelin, significantly, "rumour has it in France that your Highness could — an you would — give the truest account of that enigmatical wayside flower."

He looked quickly and keenly at Marguerite as he spoke; but she betrayed no emotion, and her eyes met his quite fearlessly.

"Nay, man," replied the Prince, "my lips are sealed! and the members of the league jealously guard the secret of their chief . . . so his fair adorers have to be content with worshipping a shadow. Here in England, Monsieur," he added, with wonderful charm and dignity, "we but name the Scarlet Pimpernel, and every fair cheek is suffused with a blush of enthusiasm. None have seen him save his faithful lieutenants. We know not if he be tall or short, fair or dark, handsome or ill-formed; but we know that he is the bravest gentleman in all the world, and we all feel a little proud, Monsieur, when we remember that he is an Englishman.

"Ah, Monsieur Chauvelin," added Marguerite, looking almost with defiance across at the placid, sphinx-like face of the Frenchman, "His Royal Highness should add that we ladies think of him as of a hero of old . . . we worship him . . . we wear his badge . . . we tremble for him when he is in danger, and exult with him in the hour of his victory."

Chauvelin did no more than bow placidly both to the Prince and to Marguerite; he felt that both speeches were intended — each in their way — to convey contempt or defiance. The pleasure-loving, idle Prince he despised: the beautiful woman, who in her golden hair wore a spray of small red flowers composed of rubies and diamonds — her he held in the hollow of his hand: he could afford to remain silent and to wait events.

A long, jovial, inane laugh broke the sudden silence which had fallen over everyone. "And we poor husbands," came in slow, affected accents from gorgeous Sir Percy, "we have to stand by . . . while they worship a demmed shadow."

Everyone laughed — the Prince more loudly than anyone. The tension of subdued excitement was relieved, and the next moment everyone was laughing and chatting merrily as the gay crowd broke up and dispersed in the adjoining rooms.

CHAPTER XII
THE SCRAP OF PAPER

Marguerite suffered intensely. Though she laughed and chatted, though she was more admired, more surrounded, more FETED than any woman there, she felt like one condemned to death, living her last day upon this earth.

Her nerves were in a state of painful tension, which had increased a hundredfold during that brief hour which she had spent in her husband's company, between the opera and the ball. The short ray of hope — that she might find in this good-natured, lazy individual a valuable friend and adviser — had vanished as quickly as it had come, the moment she found herself alone with him. The same feeling of good-humoured contempt which one feels for an animal or a faithful servant, made her turn away with a smile from the man who should have been her moral support in this heart-rending crisis through which she was passing: who should have been her cool-headed adviser, when feminine sympathy and sentiment tossed her hither and thither, between her love for her brother, who was far away and in mortal peril, and horror of the awful service which Chauvelin had exacted from her, in exchange for Armand's safety.

There he stood, the moral support, the cool-headed adviser, surrounded by a crowd of brainless, empty-headed young fops, who were even now repeating from mouth to mouth, and with every sign of the keenest enjoyment, a doggerel quatrain which he had just given forth. Everywhere the absurd, silly words met her: people seemed to have little else to speak about, even the Prince had asked her, with a little laugh, whether she appreciated her husband's latest poetic efforts.

"All done in the tying of a cravat," Sir Percy had declared to his clique of admirers.

> "We seek him here, we seek him there,
> Those Frenchies seek him everywhere.
> Is he in heaven? — Is he in hell?
> That demmed, elusive Pimpernel"

Sir Percy's BON MOT had gone the round of the brilliant reception-rooms. The Prince was enchanted. He vowed that life without Blakeney would be but a dreary desert. Then, taking him by the arm, had led him to the card-room, and engaged him in a long game of hazard.

Sir Percy, whose chief interest in most social gatherings seemed to centre round the card-table, usually allowed his wife to flirt, dance, to amuse or bore herself as much as she liked. And to-night, having delivered himself of his BON MOT, he had left Marguerite surrounded by a crowd of admirers of all ages, all anxious and willing to help her to forget that somewhere in the spacious reception rooms, there was a long, lazy being who had been fool enough to suppose that the cleverest woman in Europe would settle down to the prosaic bonds of English matrimony.

Her still overwrought nerves, her excitement and agitation, lent beautiful Marguerite Blakeney much additional charm: escorted by a veritable bevy of men of all ages and of most nationalities, she called forth many exclamations of admiration from everyone as she passed.

She would not allow herself any more time to think. Her early, somewhat Bohemian training had made her something of a fatalist. She felt that events would shape themselves, that the directing of them was not in her hands. From Chauvelin she knew that she could expect no mercy. He had set a price on Armand's head, and left it to her to pay or not, as she chose.

Later on in the evening she caught sight of Sir Andrew Ffoulkes and Lord Antony Dewhurst, who seemingly had just arrived. She noticed at once that Sir Andrew immediately made for little Suzanne de Tournay, and that the two young people soon managed to isolate themselves in one of the deep embrasures of the mullioned windows, there to carry on a long conversation, which seemed very earnest and very pleasant on both sides.

Both the young men looked a little haggard and anxious, but otherwise they were irreproachably dressed, and there was not the slightest sign, about their courtly demeanour, of the terrible catastrophe, which they must have felt hovering round them and round their chief.

That the League of the Scarlet Pimpernel had no intention of abandoning its cause, she had gathered through little Suzanne herself, who spoke openly of the assurance she and her mother had had that the Comte de Tournay would be rescued from France by the league, within the next few days. Vaguely she began to wonder, as she looked at the brilliant and fashionable in the gaily-lighted ball-room, which of these worldly men round her was the mysterious "Scarlet Pimpernel," who held the threads of such daring plots, and the fate of valuable lives in his hands.

A burning curiosity seized her to know him: although for months she had heard of him and had accepted his anonymity, as everyone else in society had done; but now she longed to know — quite impersonally, quite apart from Armand, and oh! quite apart from Chauvelin — only for her own sake, for the sake of the enthusiastic admiration she had always bestowed on his bravery and cunning.

He was at the ball, of course, somewhere, since Sir Andrew Ffoulkes and Lord Antony Dewhurst were here, evidently expecting to meet their chief — and perhaps to get a fresh MOT D'ORDRE from him.

Marguerite looked round at everyone, at the aristocratic high-typed Norman faces, the squarely-built, fair-haired Saxon, the more gentle, humorous caste of the Celt, wondering which of these betrayed the power, the energy, the cunning which had imposed its will and its leadership upon a number of high-born English gentlemen, among whom rumour asserted was His Royal Highness himself.

Sir Andrew Ffoulkes? Surely not, with his gentle blue eyes, which were looking so tenderly and longingly after little Suzanne, who was being led away from the pleasant TETE-A-TETE by her stern mother. Marguerite watched him across the room, as he finally turned away with a sigh, and seemed to stand, aimless and lonely, now that Suzanne's dainty little figure had disappeared in the crowd.

She watched him as he strolled towards the doorway, which led to a small boudoir beyond, then paused and leaned against the framework of it, looking still anxiously all round him.

Marguerite contrived for the moment to evade her present attentive cavalier, and she skirted the fashionable crowd, drawing nearer to the doorway, against which Sir Andrew was leaning. Why she wished to get closer to him, she could not have said: perhaps she was impelled by an all-powerful fatality, which so often seems to rule the destinies of men.

Suddenly she stopped: her very heart seemed to stand still, her eyes, large and excited, flashed for a moment towards that doorway, then as quickly were turned away again. Sir Andrew Ffoulkes was still in the same listless position by the door, but Marguerite had distinctly seen that Lord Hastings — a young buck, a friend of her husband's and one of the Prince's set — had, as he quickly brushed past him, slipped something into his hand.

For one moment longer — oh! it was the merest flash — Marguerite paused: the next she had, with admirably played unconcern, resumed her walk across the room — but this time more quickly towards that doorway whence Sir Andrew had now disappeared.

All this, from the moment that Marguerite had caught sight of Sir Andrew leaning against the doorway, until she followed him into the little boudoir beyond, had occurred in less than a minute. Fate is usually swift when she deals a blow.

Now Lady Blakeney had suddenly ceased to exist. It was Marguerite St. Just who was there only: Marguerite St. Just who had passed her childhood, her early youth, in the protecting arms of her brother Armand. She had forgotten everything else — her rank, her dignity, her secret enthusiasms — everything save that Armand stood in peril of his life, and that there, not twenty feet away from her, in the small boudoir which was quite deserted, in the very hands of Sir Andrew Ffoulkes, might be the talisman which would save her brother's life.

Barely another thirty seconds had elapsed between the moment when Lord Hastings slipped the mysterious "something" into Sir Andrew's hand, and the one when she, in her turn, reached the deserted boudoir. Sir Andrew was standing with his back to her and close to a table upon which stood a massive silver candelabra. A slip of paper was in his hand, and he was in the very act of perusing its contents.

Unperceived, her soft clinging robe making not the slightest sound upon the heavy carpet, not daring to breathe until she had accomplished her purpose, Marguerite slipped close behind him. . . . At that moment he looked round and saw her; she uttered a groan, passed her hand across her forehead, and murmured faintly:

"The heat in the room was terrible . . . I felt so faint . . . Ah! . . ."

She tottered almost as if she would fall, and Sir Andrew, quickly recovering himself, and crumpling in his hand the tiny note he had been reading, was only apparently, just in time to support her.

"You are ill, Lady Blakeney?" he asked with much concern, "Let me . . ."

"No, no, nothing — " she interrupted quickly. "A chair — quick."

She sank into a chair close to the table, and throwing back her head, closing her eyes.

"There!" she murmured, still faintly; "the giddiness is passing off. . . . Do not heed me, Sir Andrew; I assure you I already feel better."

At moments like these there is no doubt — and psychologists actually assert it — that there is in us a sense which has absolutely nothing to do with the other five: it is not that we see, it is not that we hear or touch, yet we seem to do all three at once. Marguerite sat there with her eyes apparently closed. Sir Andrew was immediately behind her, and on her right was the table with the five-armed candelabra upon it. Before her mental vision there was absolutely nothing but Armand's face. Armand, whose life was in the most imminent danger, and who seemed to be looking at her from a background upon which were dimly painted the seething crowd of Paris, the bare walls of the Tribunal of Public Safety, with Foucquier-Tinville, the Public Prosecutor, demanding Armand's life in the name of the people of France, and the lurid guillotine with its stained knife waiting for another victim . . . Armand! . . .

For one moment there was dead silence in the little boudoir. Beyond, from the brilliant ball-room, the sweet notes of the gavotte, the frou-frou of rich dresses, the talk and laughter of a large and merry crowd, came as a strange, weird accompaniment to the drama which was being enacted here. Sir Andrew had not uttered another word. Then it was that that extra sense became potent in Marguerite Blakeney. She could not see, for her two eyes were closed, she could not hear, for the noise from the ball-room drowned the soft rustle of that momentous scrap of paper; nevertheless she knew — as if she had both seen and heard — that Sir Andrew was even now holding the paper to the flame of one of the candles.

At the exact moment that it began to catch fire, she opened her eyes, raised her hand and, with two dainty fingers, had taken the burning scrap of paper from the young man's hand. Then she blew out the flame, and held the paper to her nostril with perfect unconcern.

"How thoughtful of you, Sir Andrew," she said gaily, "surely 'twas your grandmother who taught you that the smell of burnt paper was a sovereign remedy against giddiness."

She sighed with satisfaction, holding the paper tightly between her jewelled fingers; that talisman which perhaps would save her brother Armand's life. Sir Andrew was staring at her, too dazed for the moment to realize what had actually happened; he had been taken so completely by surprise, that he seemed quite unable to grasp the fact that the slip of paper, which she held in her dainty hand, was one perhaps on which the life of his comrade might depend.

Marguerite burst into a long, merry peal of laughter.

"Why do you stare at me like that?" she said playfully. "I assure you I feel much better; your remedy has proved most effectual. This room is most delightedly cool," she added, with the same perfect composure, "and the sound of the gavotte from the ball-room is fascinating and soothing."

She was prattling on in the most unconcerned and pleasant way, whilst Sir Andrew, in an agony of mind, was racking his brains as to the quickest method he could employ to get that bit of paper out of that beautiful woman's hand. Instinctively, vague and tumultuous thoughts rushed through his mind: he suddenly remembered her nationality, and worst of all, recollected that horrible tale anent the Marquis de St. Cyr, which in England no one had credited, for the sake of Sir Percy, as well as for her own.

"What? Still dreaming and staring?" she said, with a merry laugh, "you are most ungallant, Sir Andrew; and now I come to think of it, you seemed more startled than pleased when you saw me just now. I do believe, after all, that it was not concern for my health, nor yet a remedy taught you by your grandmother that caused you to burn this tiny scrap of paper. . . . I vow it must have been your lady love's last cruel epistle you were trying to destroy. Now confess!" she added, playfully holding up the scrap of paper, "does this contain her final CONGE, or a last appeal to kiss and make friends?"

"Whichever it is, Lady Blakeney," said Sir Andrew, who was gradually recovering his self-possession, "this little note is undoubtedly mine, and . . ." Not caring whether his action was one that would be styled ill-bred towards a lady, the young man had made a bold dash for the note; but Marguerite's thoughts flew quicker than his own; her actions under pressure of this intense excitement, were swifter and more sure. She was tall and strong; she took a quick step backwards and knocked over the small Sheraton table which was already top-heavy, and which fell down with a crash, together with the massive candelabra upon it.

She gave a quick cry of alarm:

"The candles, Sir Andrew — quick!"

There was not much damage done; one or two of the candles had blown out as the candelabra fell; others had merely sent some grease upon the valuable carpet; one had ignited the paper shade aver it. Sir Andrew quickly and dexterously put out the flames and replaced the candelabra upon the table; but this had taken him a few seconds to do, and those seconds had been all that Marguerite needed to cast a quick glance at the paper, and to note its contents — a dozen words in the same distorted handwriting she had seen before, and bearing the same device — a star-shaped flower drawn in red ink.

When Sir Andrew once more looked at her, he only saw upon her face alarm at the untoward accident and relief at its happy issue; whilst the tiny and momentous note had apparently fluttered to the ground. Eagerly the young man picked it up, and his face looked much relieved, as his fingers closed tightly over it.

"For shame, Sir Andrew," she said, shaking her head with a playful sigh, "making havoc in the heart of some impressionable duchess, whilst conquering the affections of my sweet little Suzanne. Well, well! I do believe it was Cupid himself who stood by you, and threatened the entire Foreign Office with destruction by fire, just on purpose to make me drop love's message, before it had been polluted by my indiscreet eyes. To think that, a moment longer, and I might have known the secrets of an erring duchess."

"You will forgive me, Lady Blakeney," said Sir Andrew, now as calm as she was herself, "if I resume the interesting occupation which you have interrupted?"

"By all means, Sir Andrew! How should I venture to thwart the love-god again? Perhaps he would mete out some terrible chastisement against my presumption. Burn your love-token, by all means!"

Sir Andrew had already twisted the paper into a long spill, and was once again holding it to the flame of the candle, which had remained alight. He did not notice the strange smile on the face of his fair VIS-A-VIS, so intent was he on the work of destruction; perhaps, had he done so, the look of relief would have faded from his face. He watched the fateful note, as it curled under the flame. Soon the last fragment fell on the floor, and he placed his heel upon the ashes.

"And now, Sir Andrew," said Marguerite Blakeney, with the pretty nonchalance peculiar to herself, and with the most winning of smiles, "will you venture to excite the jealousy of your fair lady by asking me to dance the minuet?"

CHAPTER XIII
EITHER — OR?

The few words which Marguerite Blakeney had managed to read on the half-scorched piece of paper, seemed literally to be the words of Fate. "Start myself tomorrow. . . ." This she had read quite distinctly; then came a blur caused by the smoke of the candle, which obliterated the next few words; but, right at the bottom, there was another sentence, like letters of fire, before her mental vision, "If you wish to speak to me again I shall be in the supper-room at one o'clock precisely." The whole was signed with the hastily-scrawled little device — a tiny star-shaped flower, which had become so familiar to her.

One o'clock precisely! It was now close upon eleven, the last minuet was being danced, with Sir Andrew Ffoulkes and beautiful Lady Blakeney leading the couples, through its delicate and intricate figures.

Close upon eleven! the hands of the handsome Louis XV. clock upon its ormolu bracket seemed to move along with maddening rapidity. Two hours more, and her fate and that of Armand would be sealed. In two hours she must make up her mind whether she will keep the knowledge so cunningly gained to herself, and leave her brother to his fate, or whether she will wilfully betray a brave man, whose life was devoted to his fellow-men, who was noble, generous, and above all, unsuspecting. It seemed a horrible thing to do. But then, there was Armand! Armand, too, was noble and brave, Armand, too, was unsuspecting. And Armand loved her, would have willingly trusted his life in her hands, and now, when she could save him from death, she hesitated. Oh! it was monstrous; her brother's kind, gentle face, so full of love for her, seemed to be looking reproachfully at her. "You might have saved me, Margot!" he seemed to say to her, "and you chose the life of a stranger, a man you do not know, whom you have never seen, and preferred that he should be safe, whilst you sent me to the guillotine!"

All these conflicting thoughts raged through Marguerite's brain, while, with a smile upon her lips, she glided through the graceful mazes of the minuet. She noted — with that acute sense of hers — that she had succeeded in completely allaying Sir Andrew's fears. Her self-control had been absolutely perfect — she was a finer actress at this moment, and throughout the whole of this minuet, than she had ever been upon the boards of the Comedie Francaise; but then, a beloved brother's life had not depended upon her histrionic powers.

She was too clever to overdo her part, and made no further allusions to the supposed BILLET DOUX, which had caused Sir Andrew Ffoulkes such an agonising five minutes. She watched his anxiety melting away under her sunny smile, and soon perceived that, whatever doubt may have crossed his mind at the moment, she had, by the time the last bars of the minuet had been played, succeeded in completely dispelling it; he never realised in what a fever of excitement she was, what effort it cost her to keep up a constant ripple of BANAL conversation.

When the minuet was over, she asked Sir Andrew to take her into the next room.

"I have promised to go down to supper with His Royal Highness," she said, "but before we part, tell me . . . am I forgiven?"

"Forgiven?"

"Yes! Confess, I gave you a fright just now. . . . But remember, I am not an English woman, and I do not look upon the exchanging of BILLET DOUX as a crime, and I vow I'll not tell my little Suzanne. But now, tell me, shall I welcome you at my water-party on Wednesday?"

"I am not sure, Lady Blakeney," he replied evasively. "I may have to leave London to-morrow."

"I would not do that, if I were you," she said earnestly; then seeing the anxious look reappearing in his eyes, she added gaily; "No one can throw a ball better than you can, Sir Andrew, we should so miss you on the bowling-green."

He had led her across the room, to one beyond, where already His Royal Highness was waiting for the beautiful Lady Blakeney.

"Madame, supper awaits us," said the Prince, offering his arm to Marguerite, "and I am full of hope. The goddess Fortune has frowned so persistently on me at hazard, that I look with confidence for the smiles of the goddess of Beauty."

"Your Highness has been unfortunate at the card tables?" asked Marguerite, as she took the Prince's arm.

"Aye! most unfortunate. Blakeney, not content with being the richest among my father's subjects, has also the most outrageous luck. By the way, where is that inimitable wit? I vow, Madam, that this life would be but a dreary desert without your smiles and his sallies."

Supper had been extremely gay. All those present declared that never had Lady Blakeney been more adorable, nor that "demmed idiot" Sir Percy more amusing.

His Royal Highness had laughed until the tears streamed down his cheeks at Blakeney's foolish yet funny repartees. His doggerel verse, "We seek him here, we seek him there," etc., was sung to the tune of "Ho! Merry Britons!" and to the accompaniment of glasses knocked loudly against the table. Lord Grenville, moreover, had a most perfect cook — some wags asserted that he was a scion of the old French NOBLESSE, who having lost his fortune, had come to seek it in the CUISINE of the Foreign Office.

Marguerite Blakeney was in her most brilliant mood, and surely not a soul in that crowded supper-room had even an inkling of the terrible struggle which was raging within her heart.

The clock was ticking so mercilessly on. It was long past midnight, and even the Prince of Wales was thinking of leaving the supper-table. Within the next half-hour the destinies of two brave men would be pitted against one another — the dearly-beloved brother and he, the unknown hero.

Marguerite had not tried to see Chauvelin during this last hour; she knew that his keen, fox-like eyes would terrify her at once, and incline the balance of her decision towards Armand. Whilst she did not see him, there still lingered in her heart of hearts a vague, undefined hope that "something" would occur, something big, enormous, epoch-making, which would shift from her young, weak shoulders this terrible burden of responsibility, of having to choose between two such cruel alternatives.

But the minutes ticked on with that dull monotony which they invariably seem to assume when our very nerves ache with their incessant ticking.

After supper, dancing was resumed. His Royal Highness had left, and there was general talk of departing among the older guests; the young were indefatigable and had started on a new gavotte, which would fill the next quarter of an hour.

Marguerite did not feel equal to another dance; there is a limit to the most enduring of self-control. Escorted by a Cabinet Minister, she had once more found her way to the tiny boudoir, still the most deserted among all the rooms. She knew that Chauvelin must be lying in wait for her somewhere, ready to seize the first possible opportunity for a TETE-A-TETE. His eyes had met hers for a moment after the 'fore-supper minuet, and she knew that the keen diplomat, with those searching pale eyes of his, had divined that her work was accomplished.

Fate had willed it so. Marguerite, torn by the most terrible conflict heart of woman can ever know, had resigned herself to its decrees. But Armand must be saved at any cost; he, first of all, for he was her brother, had been mother, father, friend to her ever since she, a tiny babe, had lost both her parents. To think of Armand dying a traitor's death on the guillotine was too horrible even to dwell upon — impossible in fact. That could never be, never. . . . As for the stranger, the hero . . . well! there, let Fate decide. Marguerite would redeem her brother's life at the hands of the relentless enemy, then let that cunning Scarlet Pimpernel extricate himself after that.

Perhaps — vaguely — Marguerite hoped that the daring plotter, who for so many months had baffled an army of spies, would still manage to evade Chauvelin and remain immune to the end.

She thought of all this, as she sat listening to the witty discourse of the Cabinet Minister, who, no doubt, felt that he had found in Lady Blakeney a most perfect listener. Suddenly she saw the keen, fox-like face of Chauvelin peeping through the curtained doorway.

"Lord Fancourt," she said to the Minister, "will you do me a service?"

"I am entirely at your ladyship's service," he replied gallantly.

"Will you see if my husband is still in the card-room? And if he is, will you tell him that I am very tired, and would be glad to go home soon."

The commands of a beautiful woman are binding on all mankind, even on Cabinet Ministers. Lord Fancourt prepared to obey instantly.

"I do not like to leave your ladyship alone," he said.

"Never fear. I shall be quite safe here — and, I think, undisturbed . . . but I am really tired. You know Sir Percy will drive back to Richmond. It is a long way, and we shall not — an we do not hurry — get home before daybreak."

Lord Fancourt had perforce to go.

The moment he had disappeared, Chauvelin slipped into the room, and the next instant stood calm and impassive by her side.

"You have news for me?" he said.

An icy mantle seemed to have suddenly settled round Marguerite's shoulders; though her cheeks glowed with fire, she felt chilled and numbed. Oh, Armand! will you ever know the terrible sacrifice of pride, of dignity, of womanliness a devoted sister is making for your sake?

"Nothing of importance," she said, staring mechanically before her, "but it might prove a clue. I contrived — no matter how — to detect Sir Andrew Ffoulkes in the very act of burning a paper at one of these candles, in this very room. That paper I succeeded in holding between my fingers for the space of two minutes, and to cast my eyes on it for that of ten seconds."

"Time enough to learn its contents?" asked Chauvelin, quietly.

She nodded. Then continued in the same even, mechanical tone of voice —

"In the corner of the paper there was the usual rough device of a small star-shaped flower. Above it I read two lines, everything else was scorched and blackened by the flame."

"And what were the two lines?"

Her throat seemed suddenly to have contracted. For an instant she felt that she could not speak the words, which might send a brave man to his death.

"It is lucky that the whole paper was not burned," added Chauvelin, with dry sarcasm, "for it might have fared ill with Armand St. Just. What were the two lines citoyenne?"

"One was, 'I start myself to-morrow,'" she said quietly, "the other — 'If you wish to speak to me, I shall be in the supper-room at one o'clock precisely.'"

Chauvelin looked up at the clock just above the mantelpiece.

"Then I have plenty of time," he said placidly.

"What are you going to do?" she asked.

She was pale as a statue, her hands were icy cold, her head and heart throbbed with the awful strain upon her nerves. Oh, this was cruel! cruel! What had she done to have deserved all this? Her choice was made: had she done a vile action or one that was sublime? The recording angel, who writes in the book of gold, alone could give an answer.

"What are you going to do?" she repeated mechanically.

"Oh, nothing for the present. After that it will depend."

"On what?"

"On whom I shall see in the supper-room at one o'clock precisely."

"You will see the Scarlet Pimpernel, of course. But you do not know him."

"No. But I shall presently."

"Sir Andrew will have warned him."

"I think not. When you parted from him after the minuet he stood and watched you, for a moment or two, with a look which gave me to understand that something had happened between you. It was only natural, was it not? that I should make a shrewd guess as to the nature of that 'something.' I thereupon engaged the young man in a long and animated conversation — we discussed Herr Gluck's singular success in London — until a lady claimed his arm for supper."

"Since then?"

"I did not lose sight of him through supper. When we all came upstairs again, Lady Portarles buttonholed him and started on the subject of pretty Mlle. Suzanne de Tournay. I knew he would not move until Lady Portarles had exhausted on the subject, which will not be for another quarter of an hour at least, and it is five minutes to one now."

He was preparing to go, and went up to the doorway where, drawing aside the curtain, he stood for a moment pointing out to Marguerite the distant figure of Sir Andrew Ffoulkes in close conversation with Lady Portarles.

"I think," he said, with a triumphant smile, "that I may safely expect to find the person I seek in the dining-room, fair lady."

"There may be more than one."

"Whoever is there, as the clock strikes one, will be shadowed by one of my men; of these, one, or perhaps two, or even three, will leave for France to-morrow. ONE of these will be the 'Scarlet Pimpernel.'"

"Yes? — And?"

"I also, fair lady, will leave for France to-morrow. The papers found at Dover upon the person of Sir Andrew Ffoulkes speak of the neighborhood of Calais, of an inn which I know well, called 'Le Chat Gris,' of a lonely place somewhere on the coast — the Pere Blanchard's hut — which I must endeavor to find. All these places are given as the point where this meddlesome Englishman has bidden the traitor de Tournay and others to meet his emissaries. But it seems that he has decided not to send his emissaries, that 'he will start himself to-morrow.' Now, one of these persons whom I shall see anon in the supper-room, will be journeying to Calais, and I shall follow that person, until I have tracked him to where those fugitive aristocrats await him; for that person, fair lady, will be the man whom I have sought for, for nearly a year, the man whose energies has outdone me, whose ingenuity has baffled me, whose audacity has set me wondering — yes! me! — who have seen a trick or two in my time — the mysterious and elusive Scarlet Pimpernel."

"And Armand?" she pleaded.

"Have I ever broken my word? I promise you that the day the Scarlet Pimpernel and I start for France, I will send you that imprudent letter of his by special courier. More than that, I will pledge you the word of France, that the day I lay hands on that meddlesome Englishman, St. Just will be here in England, safe in the arms of his charming sister."

And with a deep and elaborate bow and another look at the clock, Chauvelin glided out of the room.

It seemed to Marguerite that through all the noise, all the din of music, dancing, and laughter, she could hear his cat-like tread, gliding through the vast reception-rooms; that she could hear him go down the massive staircase, reach the dining-room and open the door. Fate HAD decided, had made her speak, had made her do a vile and abominable thing, for the sake of the brother she loved. She lay back in her chair, passive and still, seeing the figure of her relentless enemy ever present before her aching eyes.

When Chauvelin reached the supper-room it was quite deserted. It had that woebegone, forsaken, tawdry appearance, which reminds one so much of a ball-dress, the morning after.

Half-empty glasses littered the table, unfolded napkins lay about, the chairs — turned towards one another in groups of twos and threes — very close to one another — in the far corners of the room, which spoke of recent whispered flirtations, over cold game-pie and champagne; there were sets of three and four chairs, that recalled pleasant, animated discussions over the latest scandal; there were chairs straight up in a row that still looked starchy, critical, acid, like antiquated dowager; there were a few isolated, single chairs, close to the table, that spoke of gourmands intent on the most RECHERCHE dishes, and others overturned on the floor, that spoke volumes on the subject of my Lord Grenville's cellars.

It was a ghostlike replica, in fact, of that fashionable gathering upstairs; a ghost that haunts every house where balls and good suppers are given; a picture drawn with white chalk on grey cardboard, dull and colourless, now that the bright silk dresses and gorgeously embroidered coats were no longer there to fill in the foreground, and now that the candles flickered sleepily in their sockets.

Chauvelin smiled benignly, and rubbing his long, thin hands together, he looked round the deserted supper-room, whence even the last flunkey had retired in order to join his friends in the hall below. All was silence in the dimly-lighted room, whilst the sound of the gavotte, the hum of distant talk and laughter, and the rumble of an occasional coach outside, only seemed to reach this palace of the Sleeping Beauty as the murmur of some flitting spooks far away.

It all looked so peaceful, so luxurious, and so still, that the keenest observer — a veritable prophet — could never have guessed that, at this present moment, that deserted supper-room was nothing but a trap laid for the capture of the most cunning and audacious plotter those stirring times had ever seen.

Chauvelin pondered and tried to peer into the immediate future. What would this man be like, whom he and the leaders of the whole revolution had sworn to bring to his death? Everything about him was weird and mysterious; his personality, which he so cunningly concealed, the power he wielded over nineteen English gentlemen who seemed to obey his every command blindly and enthusiastically, the passionate love and submission he had roused in his little trained band, and, above all, his marvellous audacity, the boundless impudence which had caused him to beard his most implacable enemies, within the very walls of Paris.

No wonder that in France the SOBRIQUET of the mysterious Englishman roused in the people a superstitious shudder. Chauvelin himself as he gazed round the deserted room, where presently the weird hero would appear, felt a strange feeling of awe creeping all down his spine.

But his plans were well laid. He felt sure that the Scarlet Pimpernel had not been warned, and felt equally sure that Marguerite Blakeney had not played him false. If she had . . . a cruel look, that would have made her shudder, gleamed in Chauvelin's keen, pale eyes. If she had played him a trick, Armand St. Just would suffer the extreme penalty.

But no, no! of course she had not played him false!

Fortunately the supper-room was deserted: this would make Chauvelin's task all the easier, when presently that unsuspecting enigma would enter it alone. No one was here now save Chauvelin himself.

Stay! as he surveyed with a satisfied smile the solitude of the room, the cunning agent of the French Government became aware of the peaceful, monotonous breathing of some one of my Lord Grenville's guests, who, no doubt, had supped both wisely and well, and was enjoying a quiet sleep, away from the din of the dancing above.

Chauvelin looked round once more, and there in the corner of a sofa, in the dark angle of the room, his mouth open, his eyes shut, the sweet sounds of peaceful slumbers proceedings from his nostrils, reclined the gorgeously-apparelled, long-limbed husband of the cleverest woman in Europe.

Chauvelin looked at him as he lay there, placid, unconscious, at peace with all the world and himself, after the best of suppers, and a smile, that was almost one of pity, softened for a moment the hard lines of the Frenchman's face and the sarcastic twinkle of his pale eyes.

Evidently the slumberer, deep in dreamless sleep, would not interfere with Chauvelin's trap for catching that cunning Scarlet Pimpernel. Again he rubbed his hands together, and, following the example of Sir Percy Blakeney, he too, stretched himself out in the corner of another sofa, shut his eyes, opened his mouth, gave forth sounds of peaceful breathing, and . . . waited!

CHAPTER XV
DOUBT

Marguerite Blakeney had watched the slight sable-clad figure of Chauvelin, as he worked his way through the ball-room. Then perforce she had had to wait, while her nerves tingled with excitement.

Listlessly she sat in the small, still deserted boudoir, looking out through the curtained doorway on the dancing couples beyond: looking at them, yet seeing nothing, hearing the music, yet conscious of naught save a feeling of expectancy, of anxious, weary waiting.

Her mind conjured up before her the vision of what was, perhaps at this very moment, passing downstairs. The half-deserted dining-room, the fateful hour — Chauvelin on the watch! — then, precise to the moment, the entrance of a man, he, the Scarlet Pimpernel, the mysterious leader, who to Marguerite had become almost unreal, so strange, so weird was this hidden identity.

She wished she were in the supper-room, too, at this moment, watching him as he entered; she knew that her woman's penetration would at once recognise in the stranger's face — whoever he might be — that strong individuality which belongs to a leader of men — to a hero: to the mighty, high-soaring eagle, whose daring wings were becoming entangled in the ferret's trap.

Woman-like, she thought of him with unmixed sadness; the irony of that fate seemed so cruel which allowed the fearless lion to succumb to the gnawing of a rat! Ah! had Armand's life not been at stake! . . .

"Faith! your ladyship must have thought me very remiss," said a voice suddenly, close to her elbow. "I had a deal of difficulty in delivering your message, for I could not find Blakeney anywhere at first . . ."

Marguerite had forgotten all about her husband and her message to him; his very name, as spoken by Lord Fancourt, sounded strange and unfamiliar to her, so completely had she in the last five minutes lived her old life in the Rue de Richelieu again, with Armand always near her to love and protect her, to guard her from the many subtle intrigues which were forever raging in Paris in those days.

"I did find him at last," continued Lord Fancourt, "and gave him your message. He said that he would give orders at once for the horses to be put to."

"Ah!" she said, still very absently, "you found my husband, and gave him my message?"

"Yes; he was in the dining-room fast asleep. I could not manage to wake him up at first."

"Thank you very much," she said mechanically, trying to collect her thoughts.

"Will your ladyship honour me with the CONTREDANSE until your coach is ready?" asked Lord Fancourt.

"No, I thank you, my lord, but — and you will forgive me — I really am too tired, and the heat in the ball-room has become oppressive."

"The conservatory is deliciously cool; let me take you there, and then get you something. You seem ailing, Lady Blakeney."

"I am only very tired," she repeated wearily, as she allowed Lord Fancourt to lead her, where subdued lights and green plants lent coolness to the air. He got her a chair, into which she sank. This long interval of waiting was intolerable. Why did not Chauvelin come and tell her the result of his watch?

Lord Fancourt was very attentive. She scarcely heard what he said, and suddenly startled him by asking abruptly, —

"Lord Fancourt, did you perceive who was in the dining-room just now besides Sir Percy Blakeney?"

"Only the agent of the French government, M. Chauvelin, equally fast asleep in another corner," he said. "Why does your ladyship ask?"

"I know not . . . I . . . Did you notice the time when you were there?"

"It must have been about five or ten minutes past one. . . . I wonder what your ladyship is thinking about," he added, for evidently the fair lady's thoughts were very far away, and she had not been listening to his intellectual conversation.

But indeed her thoughts were not very far away: only one storey below, in this same house, in the dining-room where sat Chauvelin still on the watch. Had he failed? For one instant that possibility rose before as a hope — the hope that the Scarlet Pimpernel had been warned by Sir Andrew, and that Chauvelin's trap had failed to catch his bird; but that hope soon gave way to fear. Had he failed? But then — Armand!

Lord Fancourt had given up talking since he found that he had no listener. He wanted an opportunity for slipping away; for sitting opposite to a lady, however fair, who is evidently not heeding the most vigorous efforts made for her entertainment, is not exhilarating, even to a Cabinet Minister.

"Shall I find out if your ladyship's coach is ready," he said at last, tentatively.

"Oh, thank you . . . thank you . . . if you would be so kind . . . I fear I am but sorry company . . . but I am really tired . . . and, perhaps, would be best alone."

But Lord Fancourt went, and still Chauvelin did not come. Oh! what had happened? She felt Armand's fate trembling in the balance . . . she feared — now with a deadly fear that Chauvelin HAD failed, and that the mysterious Scarlet Pimpernel had proved elusive once more; then she knew that she need hope for no pity, no mercy, from him.

He had pronounced his "Either — or — " and nothing less would content him: he was very spiteful, and would affect the belief that she had wilfully misled him, and having failed to trap the eagle once again, his revengeful mind would be content with the humble prey — Armand!

Yet she had done her best; had strained every nerve for Armand's sake. She could not bear to think that all had failed. She could not sit still; she wanted to go and hear the worst at once; she wondered even that Chauvelin had not come yet, to vent his wrath and satire upon her.

Lord Grenville himself came presently to tell her that her coach was ready, and that Sir Percy was already waiting for her — ribbons in hand. Marguerite said "Farewell" to her distinguished host; many of her friends stopped her, as she crossed the rooms, to talk to her, and exchange pleasant AU REVOIRS.

The Minister only took final leave of beautiful Lady Blakeney on the top of the stairs; below, on the landing, a veritable army of gallant gentlemen were waiting to bid "Good-bye" to the queen of beauty and fashion, whilst outside, under the massive portico, Sir Percy's magnificent bays were impatient pawing the ground.

At the top of the stairs, just after she had taken final leave of her host, she suddenly saw Chauvelin; he was coming up the stairs slowly, and rubbing his thin hands very softly together.

There was a curious look on his mobile face, partly amused and wholly puzzled, as his keen eyes met Marguerite's they became strangely sarcastic.

"M. Chauvelin," she said, as he stopped on the top of the stairs, bowing elaborately before her, "my coach is outside; may I claim your arm?"

As gallant as ever, he offered her his arm and led her downstairs. The crowd was very great, some of the Minister's guests were departing, others were leaning against the banisters watching the throng as it filed up and down the wide staircase.

"Chauvelin," she said at last desperately, "I must know what has happened."

"What has happened, dear lady?" he said, with affected surprise. "Where? When?"

"You are torturing me, Chauvelin. I have helped you to-night . . . surely I have the right to know. What happened in the dining-room at one o'clock just now?"

She spoke in a whisper, trusting that in the general hubbub of the crowd her words would remain unheeded by all, save the man at her side.

"Quiet and peace reigned supreme, fair lady; at that hour I was asleep in one corner of one sofa and Sir Percy Blakeney in another."

"Nobody came into the room at all?"

"Nobody."

"Then we have failed, you and I?"

"Yes! we have failed — perhaps . . ."

"But Armand?" she pleaded.

"Ah! Armand St. Just's chances hang on a thread . . . pray heaven, dear lady, that that thread may not snap."

"Chauvelin, I worked for you, sincerely, earnestly . . . remember . . ."

"I remember my promise," he said quietly. "The day that the Scarlet Pimpernel and I meet on French soil, St. Just will be in the arms of his charming sister."

"Which means that a brave man's blood will be on my hands," she said, with a shudder.

"His blood, or that of your brother. Surely at the present moment you must hope, as I do, that the enigmatical Scarlet Pimpernel will start for Calais to-day — "

"I am only conscious of one hope, citoyen."

"And that is?"

"That Satan, your master, will have need of you elsewhere, before the sun rises to-day."

"You flatter me, citoyenne."

She had detained him for a while, mid-way down the stairs, trying to get at the thoughts which lay beyond that thin, fox-like mask. But Chauvelin remained urbane, sarcastic, mysterious; not a line betrayed to the poor, anxious woman whether she need fear or whether she dared to hope.

Downstairs on the landing she was soon surrounded. Lady Blakeney never stepped from any house into her coach, without an escort of fluttering human moths around the dazzling light of her beauty. But before she finally turned away from Chauvelin, she held out a tiny hand to him, with that pretty gesture of childish appeal which was essentially her own. "Give me some hope, my little Chauvelin," she pleaded.

With perfect gallantry he bowed over that tiny hand, which looked so dainty and white through the delicately transparent black lace mitten, and kissing the tips of the rosy fingers: —

"Pray heaven that the thread may not snap," he repeated, with his enigmatic smile.

And stepping aside, he allowed the moths to flutter more closely round the candle, and the brilliant throng of the JEUNESSE DOREE, eagerly attentive to Lady Blakeney's every movement, hid the keen, fox-like face from her view.

CHAPTER XVI
RICHMOND

A few minutes later she was sitting, wrapped in cozy furs, near Sir Percy Blakeney on the box-seat of his magnificent coach, and the four splendid bays had thundered down the quiet street.

The night was warm in spite of the gentle breeze which fanned Marguerite's burning cheeks. Soon London houses were left behind, and rattling over old Hammersmith Bridge, Sir Percy was driving his bays rapidly towards Richmond.

The river wound in and out in its pretty delicate curves, looking like a silver serpent beneath the glittering rays of the moon. Long shadows from overhanging trees spread occasional deep palls right across the road. The bays were rushing along at breakneck speed, held but slightly back by Sir Percy's strong, unerring hands.

These nightly drives after balls and suppers in London were a source of perpetual delight to Marguerite, and she appreciated her husband's eccentricity keenly, which caused him to adopt this mode of taking her home every night, to their beautiful home by the river, instead of living in a stuffy London house. He loved driving his spirited horses along the lonely, moonlit roads, and she loved to sit on the box-seat, with the soft air of an English late summer's night fanning her face after the hot atmosphere of a ball or supper-party. The drive was not a long one — less than an hour, sometimes, when the bays were very fresh, and Sir Percy gave them full rein.

To-night he seemed to have a very devil in his fingers, and the coach seemed to fly along the road, beside the river. As usual, he did not speak to her, but stared straight in front of him, the ribbons seeming to lie quite loosely in his slender, white hands. Marguerite looked at him tentatively once or twice; she could see his handsome profile, and one lazy eye, with its straight fine brow and drooping heavy lid.

The face in the moonlight looked singularly earnest, and recalled to Marguerite's aching heart those happy days of courtship, before he had become the lazy nincompoop, the effete fop, whose life seemed spent in card and supper rooms.

But now, in the moonlight, she could not catch the expression of the lazy blue eyes; she could only see the outline of the firm chin, the corner of the strong mouth, the well-cut massive shape of the forehead; truly, nature had meant well by Sir Percy; his faults must all be laid at the door of that poor, half-crazy mother, and of the distracted heart-broken father, neither of whom had cared for the young life which was sprouting up between them, and which, perhaps, their very carelessness was already beginning to wreck.

Marguerite suddenly felt intense sympathy for her husband. The moral crisis she had just gone through made her feel indulgent towards the faults, the delinquencies, of others.

How thoroughly a human being can be buffeted and overmastered by Fate, had been borne in upon her with appalling force. Had anyone told her a week ago that she would stoop to spy upon her friends, that she would betray a brave and unsuspecting man into the hands of a relentless enemy, she would have laughed the idea to scorn.

Yet she had done these things; anon, perhaps the death of that brave man would be at her door, just as two years ago the Marquis de St. Cyr had perished through a thoughtless words of hers; but in that case she was morally innocent — she had meant no serious harm — fate merely had stepped in. But this time she had done a thing that obviously was base, had done it deliberately, for a motive which, perhaps, high moralists would not even appreciate.

As she felt her husband's strong arm beside her, she also felt how much more he would dislike and despise her, if he knew of this night's work. Thus human beings judge of one another, with but little reason, and no charity. She despised her husband for his inanities and vulgar, unintellectual occupations; and he, she felt, would despise her still worse, because she had not been strong enough to do right for right's sake, and to sacrifice her brother to the dictates of her conscience.

Buried in her thoughts, Marguerite had found this hour in the breezy summer night all too brief; and it was with a feeling of keen disappointment, that she suddenly realised that the bays had turned into the massive gates of her beautiful English home.

Sir Percy Blakeney's house on the river has become a historic one: palatial in its dimensions, it stands in the midst of exquisitely laid-out gardens, with a picturesque terrace and frontage to the river. Built in Tudor days, the old red brick of the walls looks eminently picturesque in the midst of a bower of green, the beautiful lawn, with its old sun-dial, adding the true note of harmony to its foregrounds, and now, on this warm early autumn night, the leaves slightly turned to russets and gold, the old garden looked singularly poetic and peaceful in the moonlight.

With unerring precision, Sir Percy had brought the four bays to a standstill immediately in front of the fine Elizabethan entrance hall; in spite of the late hour, an army of grooms seemed to have emerged from the very ground, as the coach had thundered up, and were standing respectfully round.

Sir Percy jumped down quickly, then helped Marguerite to alight. She lingered outside a moment, whilst he gave a few orders to one of his men. She skirted the house, and stepped on to the lawn, looking out dreamily into the silvery landscape. Nature seemed exquisitely at peace, in comparison with the tumultuous emotions she had gone through: she could faintly hear the ripple of the river and the occasional soft and ghostlike fall of a dead leaf from a tree.

All else was quiet round her. She had heard the horses prancing as they were being led away to their distant stables, the hurrying of servant's feet as they had all gone within to rest: the house also was quite still. In two separate suites of apartments, just above the magnificent reception-rooms, lights were still burning, they were her rooms, and his, well divided from each other by the whole width of the house, as far apart as their own lives had become. Involuntarily she sighed — at that moment she could really not have told why.

She was suffering from unconquerable heartache. Deeply and achingly she was sorry for herself. Never had she felt so pitiably lonely, so bitterly in want of comfort and of sympathy. With another sigh she turned away from the river towards the house, vaguely wondering if, after such a night, she could ever find rest and sleep.

Suddenly, before she reached the terrace, she heard a firm step upon the crisp gravel, and the next moment her husband's figure emerged out of the shadow. He too, had skirted the house, and was wandering along the lawn, towards the river. He still wore his heavy driving coat with the numerous lapels and collars he himself had set in fashion, but he had thrown it well back, burying his hands as was his wont, in the deep pockets of his satin breeches: the gorgeous white costume he had worn at Lord Grenville's ball, with its jabot of priceless lace, looked strangely ghostly against the dark background of the house.

He apparently did not notice her, for, after a few moments pause, he presently turned back towards the house, and walked straight up to the terrace.

"Sir Percy!"

He already had one foot on the lowest of the terrace steps, but at her voice he started, and paused, then looked searchingly into the shadows whence she had called to him.

She came forward quickly into the moonlight, and, as soon as he saw her, he said, with that air of consummate gallantry he always wore when speaking to her, —

"At your service, Madame!" But his foot was still on the step, and in his whole attitude there was a remote suggestion, distinctly visible to her, that he wished to go, and had no desire for a midnight interview.

"The air is deliciously cool," she said, "the moonlight peaceful and poetic, and the garden inviting. Will you not stay in it awhile; the hour is not yet late, or is my company so distasteful to you, that you are in a hurry to rid yourself of it?"

"Nay, Madame," he rejoined placidly, "but 'tis on the other foot the shoe happens to be, and I'll warrant you'll find the midnight air more poetic without my company: no doubt the sooner I remove the obstruction the better your ladyship will like it."

He turned once more to go.

"I protest you mistake me, Sir Percy," she said hurriedly, and drawing a little closer to him; "the estrangement, which alas! has arisen between us, was none of my making, remember."

"Begad! you must pardon me there, Madame!" he protested coldly, "my memory was always of the shortest."

He looked her straight in the eyes, with that lazy nonchalance which had become second nature to him. She returned his gaze for a moment, then her eyes softened, as she came up quite close to him, to the foot of the terrace steps.

"Of the shortest, Sir Percy! Faith! how it must have altered! Was it three years ago or four that you saw me for one hour in Paris, on your way to the East? When you came back two years later you had not forgotten me."

She looked divinely pretty as she stood there in the moonlight, with the fur-cloak sliding off her beautiful shoulders, the gold embroidery on her dress shimmering around her, her childlike blue eyes turned up fully at him.

He stood for a moment, rigid and still, but for the clenching of his hand against the stone balustrade of the terrace.

"You desired my presence, Madame," he said frigidly. "I take it that it was not with the view to indulging in tender reminiscences."

His voice certainly was cold and uncompromising: his attitude before her, stiff and unbending. Womanly decorum would have suggested Marguerite should return coldness for coldness, and should sweep past him without another word, only with a curt nod of her head: but womanly instinct suggested that she should remain — that keen instinct, which makes a beautiful woman conscious of her powers long to bring to her knees the one man who pays her no homage. She stretched out her hand to him.

"Nay, Sir Percy, why not? the present is not so glorious but that I should not wish to dwell a little in the past."

He bent his tall figure, and taking hold of the extreme tip of the fingers which she still held out to him, he kissed them ceremoniously.

"I' faith, Madame," he said, "then you will pardon me, if my dull wits cannot accompany you there."

Once again he attempted to go, once more her voice, sweet, childlike, almost tender, called him back.

"Sir Percy."

"Your servant, Madame."

"Is it possible that love can die?" she said with sudden, unreasoning vehemence. "Methought that the passion which you once felt for me would outlast the span of human life. Is there nothing left of that love, Percy . . . which might help you . . . to bridge over that sad estrangement?"

His massive figure seemed, while she spoke thus to him, to stiffen still more, the strong mouth hardened, a look of relentless obstinacy crept into the habitually lazy blue eyes.

"With what object, I pray you, Madame?" he asked coldly.

"I do not understand you."

"Yet 'tis simple enough," he said with sudden bitterness, which seemed literally to surge through his words, though he was making visible efforts to suppress it, "I humbly put the question to you, for my slow wits are unable to grasp the cause of this, your ladyship's sudden new mood. Is it that you have the taste to renew the devilish sport which you played so successfully last year? Do you wish to see me once more a love-sick suppliant at your feet, so that you might again have the pleasure of kicking me aside, like a troublesome lap-dog?"

She had succeeded in rousing him for the moment: and again she looked straight at him, for it was thus she remembered him a year ago.

"Percy! I entreat you!" she whispered, "can we not bury the past?"

"Pardon me, Madame, but I understood you to say that your desire was to dwell in it."

"Nay! I spoke not of THAT past, Percy!" she said, while a tone of tenderness crept into her voice. "Rather did I speak of a time when you loved me still! and I . . . oh! I was vain and frivolous; your wealth and position allured me: I married you, hoping in my heart that your great love for me would beget in me a love for you . . . but, alas! . . ."

The moon had sunk low down behind a bank of clouds. In the east a soft grey light was beginning to chase away the heavy mantle of the night. He could only see her graceful outline now, the small queenly head, with its wealth of reddish golden curls, and the glittering gems forming the small, star-shaped, red flower which she wore as a diadem in her hair.

"Twenty-four hours after our marriage, Madame, the Marquis de St. Cyr and all his family perished on the guillotine, and the popular rumour reached me that it was the wife of Sir Percy Blakeney who helped to send them there."

"Nay! I myself told you the truth of that odious tale."

"Not till after it had been recounted to me by strangers, with all its horrible details."

"And you believed them then and there," she said with great vehemence, "without a proof or question — you believed that I, whom you vowed you loved more than life, whom you professed you worshipped, that *I* could do a thing so base as these STRANGERS chose to recount. You thought I meant to deceive you about it all — that I ought to have spoken before I married you: yet, had you listened, I would have told you that up to the very morning on which St. Cyr went to the guillotine, I was straining every nerve, using every influence I possessed, to save him and his family. But my pride sealed my lips, when your love seemed to perish, as if under the knife of that same guillotine. Yet I would have told you how I was duped! Aye! I, whom that same popular rumour had endowed with the sharpest wits in France! I was tricked into doing this thing, by men who knew how to play upon my love for an only brother, and my desire for revenge. Was it unnatural?"

Her voice became choked with tears. She paused for a moment or two, trying to regain some sort of composure. She looked appealingly at him, almost as if he were her judge. He had allowed her to speak on in her own vehement, impassioned way, offering no comment, no word of sympathy: and now, while she paused, trying to swallow down the hot tears that gushed to her eyes, he waited, impassive and still. The dim, grey light of early dawn seemed to make his tall form look taller and more rigid. The lazy, good-natured face looked strangely altered. Marguerite, excited, as she was, could see that the eyes were no longer languid, the mouth no longer good-humoured and inane. A curious look of intense passion seemed to glow from beneath his drooping lids, the mouth was tightly closed, the lips compressed, as if the will alone held that surging passion in check.

Marguerite Blakeney was, above all, a woman, with all a woman's fascinating foibles, all a woman's most lovable sins. She knew in a moment that for the past few months she had been mistaken: that this man who stood here before her, cold as a statue, when her musical voice struck upon his ear, loved her, as he had loved her a year ago: that his passion might have been dormant, but that it was there, as strong, as intense, as overwhelming, as when first her lips met his in one long, maddening kiss. Pride had kept him from her, and, woman-like, she meant to win back that conquest which had been hers before. Suddenly it seemed to her that the only happiness life could ever hold for her again would be in feeling that man's kiss once more upon her lips.

"Listen to the tale, Sir Percy," she said, and her voice was low, sweet, infinitely tender. "Armand was all in all to me! We had no parents, and brought one another up. He was my little father, and I, his tiny mother; we loved one another so. Then one day — do you mind me, Sir Percy? the Marquis de St. Cyr had my brother Armand thrashed — thrashed by his lacqueys — that brother whom I loved better than all the world! And his offence? That he, a plebeian, had dared to love the daughter of the aristocrat; for that he was waylaid and thrashed . . . thrashed like a dog within an inch of his life! Oh, how I suffered! his humiliation had eaten into my very soul! When the opportunity occurred, and I was able to take my revenge, I took it. But I only thought to bring that proud marquis to trouble and humiliation. He plotted with Austria against his own country. Chance gave me knowledge of this; I spoke of it, but I did not know — how could I guess? — they trapped and duped me. When I realised what I had done, it was too late."

"It is perhaps a little difficult, Madame," said Sir Percy, after a moment of silence between them, "to go back over the past. I have confessed to you that my memory is short, but the thought certainly lingered in my mind that, at the time of the Marquis' death, I entreated you for an explanation of those same noisome popular rumours. If that same memory does not, even now, play me a trick, I fancy that you refused me ALL explanation then, and demanded of my love a humiliating allegiance it was not prepared to give."

"I wished to test your love for me, and it did not bear the test. You used to tell me that you drew the very breath of life but for me, and for love of me."

"And to probe that love, you demanded that I should forfeit mine honour," he said, whilst gradually his impassiveness seemed to leave him, his rigidity to relax; "that I should accept without murmur or question, as a dumb and submissive slave, every action of my mistress. My heart overflowing with love and passion, I ASKED for no explanation — I WAITED for one, not doubting — only hoping. Had you spoken but one word, from you I would have accepted any explanation and believed it. But you left me without a word, beyond a bald confession of the actual horrible facts; proudly you returned to your brother's house, and left me alone . . . for weeks . . . not knowing, now, in whom to believe, since the shrine, which contained my one illusion, lay shattered to earth at my feet."

She need not complain now that he was cold and impassive; his very voice shook with an intensity of passion, which he was making superhuman efforts to keep in check.

"Aye! the madness of my pride!" she said sadly. "Hardly had I gone, already I had repented. But when I returned, I found you, oh, so altered! wearing already that mask of somnolent indifference which you have never laid aside until . . . until now."

She was so close to him that her soft, loose hair was wafted against his cheek; her eyes, glowing with tears, maddened him, the music in her voice sent fire through his veins. But he would not yield to the magic charm of this woman whom he had so deeply loved, and at whose hands his pride had suffered so bitterly. He closed his eyes to shut out the dainty vision of that sweet face, of that snow-white neck and graceful figure, round which the faint rosy light of dawn was just beginning to hover playfully.

"Nay, Madame, it is no mask," he said icily; "I swore to you . . . once, that my life was yours. For months now it has been your plaything . . . it has served its purpose."

But now she knew that the very coldness was a mask. The trouble, the sorrow she had gone through last night, suddenly came back into her mind, but no longer with bitterness, rather with a feeling that this man who loved her, would help her bear the burden.

"Sir Percy," she said impulsively, "Heaven knows you have been at pains to make the task, which I had set to myself, difficult to accomplish. You spoke of my mood just now; well! we will call it that, if you will. I wished to speak to you . . . because . . . because I was in trouble . . . and had need . . . of your sympathy."

"It is yours to command, Madame."

"How cold you are!" she sighed. "Faith! I can scarce believe that but a few months ago one tear in my eye had set you well-nigh crazy. Now I come to you . . . with a half-broken heart . . . and . . . and . . ."

"I pray you, Madame," he said, whilst his voice shook almost as much as hers, "in what way can I serve you?"

"Percy! — Armand is in deadly danger. A letter of his . . . rash, impetuous, as were all his actions, and written to Sir Andrew Ffoulkes, has fallen into the hands of a fanatic. Armand is hopelessly compromised . . . to-morrow, perhaps he will be arrested . . . after that the guillotine . . . unless . . . oh! it is horrible!" . . . she said, with a sudden wail of anguish, as all the events of the past night came rushing back to her mind, "horrible! . . . and you do not understand . . . you cannot . . . and I have no one to whom I can turn . . . for help . . . or even for sympathy . . ."

Tears now refused to be held back. All her trouble, her struggles, the awful uncertainty of Armand's fate overwhelmed her. She tottered, ready to fall, and leaning against the tone balustrade, she buried her face in her hands and sobbed bitterly.

At first mention of Armand St. Just's name and of the peril in which he stood, Sir Percy's face had become a shade more pale; and the look of determination and obstinacy appeared more marked than ever between his eyes. However, he said nothing for the moment, but watched her, as her delicate frame was shaken with sobs, watched her until unconsciously his face softened, and what looked almost like tears seemed to glisten in his eyes.

"And so," he said with bitter sarcasm, "the murderous dog of the revolution is turning upon the very hands that fed it? . . . Begad, Madame," he added very gently, as Marguerite continued to sob hysterically, "will you dry your tears? . . . I never could bear to see a pretty woman cry, and I . . ."

Instinctively, with sudden overmastering passion at the sight of her helplessness and of her grief, he stretched out his arms, and the next, would have seized her and held her to him, protected from every evil with his very life, his very heart's blood. . . . But pride had the better of it in this struggle once again; he restrained himself with a tremendous effort of will, and said coldly, though still very gently, —

"Will you not turn to me, Madame, and tell me in what way I may have the honour to serve you?"

She made a violent effort to control herself, and turning her tear-stained face to him, she once more held out her hand, which he kissed with the same punctilious gallantry; but Marguerite's fingers, this time, lingered in his hand for a second or two longer than was absolutely necessary, and this was because she had felt that his hand trembled perceptibly and was burning hot, whilst his lips felt as cold as marble.

"Can you do aught for Armand?" she said sweetly and simply. "You have so much influence at court . . . so many friends . . ."

"Nay, Madame, should you not seek the influence of your French friend, M. Chauvelin? His extends, if I mistake not, even as far as the Republican Government of France."

"I cannot ask him, Percy. . . . Oh! I wish I dared to tell you . . . but . . . but . . . he has put a price on my brother's head, which . . ."

She would have given worlds if she had felt the courage then to tell him everything . . . all she had done that night — how she had suffered and how her hand had been forced. But she dared not give way to that impulse . . . not now, when she was just beginning to feel that he still loved her, when she hoped that she could win him back. She dared not make another confession to him. After all, he might not understand; he might not sympathise with her struggles and temptation. His love still dormant might sleep the sleep of death.

Perhaps he divined what was passing in her mind. His whole attitude was one of intense longing — a veritable prayer for that confidence, which her foolish pride withheld from him. When she remained silent he sighed, and said with marked coldness —

"Faith, Madame, since it distresses you, we will not speak of it. . . . As for Armand, I pray you have no fear. I pledge you my word that he shall be safe. Now, have I your permission to go? The hour is getting late, and . . ."

"You will at least accept my gratitude?" she said, as she drew quite close to him, and speaking with real tenderness.

With a quick, almost involuntary effort he would have taken her then in his arms, for her eyes were swimming in tears, which he longed to kiss away; but she had lured him once, just like this, then cast him aside like an ill-fitting glove. He thought this was but a mood, a caprice, and he was too proud to lend himself to it once again.

"It is too soon, Madame!" he said quietly; "I have done nothing as yet. The hour is late, and you must be fatigued. Your women will be waiting for you upstairs."

He stood aside to allow her to pass. She sighed, a quick sigh of disappointment. His pride and her beauty had been in direct conflict, and his pride had remained the conqueror. Perhaps, after all, she had been deceived just now; what she took to be the light of love in his eyes might only have been the passion of pride or, who knows, of hatred instead of love. She stood looking at him for a moment or two longer. He was again as rigid, as impassive, as before. Pride had conquered, and he cared naught for her. The grey light of dawn was gradually yielding to the rosy light of the rising sun. Birds began to twitter; Nature awakened, smiling in happy response to the warmth of this glorious October morning. Only between these two hearts there lay a strong, impassable barrier, built up of pride on both sides, which neither of them cared to be the first to demolish.

He had bent his tall figure in a low ceremonious bow, as she finally, with another bitter little sigh, began to mount the terrace steps.

The long train of her gold-embroidered gown swept the dead leaves off the steps, making a faint harmonious sh — sh — sh as she glided up, with one hand resting on the balustrade, the rosy light of dawn making an aureole of gold round her hair, and causing the rubies on her head and arms to sparkle. She reached the tall glass doors which led into the house. Before entering, she paused once again to look at him, hoping against hope to see his arms stretched out to her, and to hear his voice calling her back. But he had not moved; his massive figure looked the very personification of unbending pride, of fierce obstinacy.

Hot tears again surged to her eyes, as she would not let him see them, she turned quickly within, and ran as fast as she could up to her own rooms.

Had she but turned back then, and looked out once more on to the rose-lit garden, she would have seen that which would have made her own sufferings seem but light and easy to bear — a strong man, overwhelmed with his own passion and his own despair. Pride had given way at last, obstinacy was gone: the will was powerless. He was but a man madly, blindly, passionately in love, and as soon as her light footsteps had died away within the house, he knelt down upon the terrace steps, and in the very madness of his love he kissed one by one the places where her small foot had trodden, and the stone balustrade there, where her tiny hand had rested last.

When Marguerite reached her room, she found her maid terribly anxious about her.

"Your ladyship will be so tired," said the poor woman, whose own eyes were half closed with sleep. "It is past five o'clock."

"Ah, yes, Louise, I daresay I shall be tired presently," said Marguerite, kindly; "but you are very tired now, so go to bed at once. I'll get into bed alone."

"But, my lady . . ."

"Now, don't argue, Louise, but go to bed. Give me a wrap, and leave me alone."

Louise was only too glad to obey. She took off her mistress's gorgeous ball-dress, and wrapped her up in a soft billowy gown.

"Does your ladyship wish for anything else?" she asked, when that was done.

"No, nothing more. Put out the lights as you go out."

"Yes, my lady. Good-night, my lady."

"Good-night, Louise."

When the maid was gone, Marguerite drew aside the curtains and threw open the windows. The garden and the river beyond were flooded with rosy light. Far away to the east, the rays of the rising sun had changed the rose into vivid gold. The lawn was deserted now, and Marguerite looked down upon the terrace where she had stood a few moments ago trying in vain to win back a man's love, which once had been so wholly hers.

It was strange that through all her troubles, all her anxiety for Armand, she was mostly conscious at the present moment of a keen and bitter heartache.

Her very limbs seemed to ache with longing for the love of a man who had spurned her, who had resisted her tenderness, remained cold to her appeals, and had not responded to the glow of passion, which had caused her to feel and hope that those happy olden days in Paris were not all dead and forgotten.

How strange it all was! She loved him still. And now that she looked back upon the last few months of misunderstandings and of loneliness, she realised that she had never ceased to love him; that deep down in her heart she had always vaguely felt that his foolish inanities, his empty laugh, his lazy nonchalance were nothing but a mask; that the real man, strong, passionate, wilful, was there still — the man she had loved, whose intensity had fascinated her, whose personality attracted her, since she always felt that behind his apparently slow wits there was a certain something, which he kept hidden from all the world, and most especially from her.

A woman's heart is such a complex problem — the owner thereof is often most incompetent to find the solution of this puzzle.

Did Marguerite Blakeney, "the cleverest woman in Europe," really love a fool? Was it love that she had felt for him a year ago when she married him? Was it love she felt for him now that she realised that he still loved her, but that he would not become her slave, her passionate, ardent lover once again? Nay! Marguerite herself could not have told that. Not at this moment at any rate; perhaps her pride had sealed her mind against a better understanding of her own heart. But this she did know — that she meant to capture that obstinate heart back again. That she would conquer once more . . . and then, that she would never lose him . . . . She would keep him, keep his love, deserve it, and cherish it; for this much was certain, that there was no longer any happiness possible for her without that one man's love.

Thus the most contradictory thoughts and emotions rushed madly through her mind. Absorbed in them, she had allowed time to slip by; perhaps, tired out with long excitement, she had actually closed her eyes and sunk into a troubled sleep, wherein quickly fleeting dreams seemed but the continuation of her anxious thoughts — when suddenly she was roused, from dream or meditation, by the noise of footsteps outside her door.

Nervously she jumped up and listened; the house itself was as still as ever; the footsteps had retreated. Through her wide-open window the brilliant rays of the morning sun were flooding her room with light. She looked up at the clock; it was half-past six — too early for any of the household to be already astir.

She certainly must have dropped asleep, quite unconsciously. The noise of the footsteps, also of hushed subdued voices had awakened her — what could they be?

Gently, on tip-toe, she crossed the room and opened the door to listen; not a sound — that peculiar stillness of the early morning when sleep with all mankind is at its heaviest. But the noise had made her nervous, and when, suddenly, at her feet, on the very doorstep, she saw something white lying there — a letter evidently — she hardly dared touch it. It seemed so ghostlike. It certainly was not there when she came upstairs; had Louise dropped it? or was some tantalising spook at play, showing her fairy letters where none existed?

At last she stooped to pick it up, and, amazed, puzzled beyond measure, she saw that the letter was addressed to herself in her husband's large, businesslike-looking hand. What could he have to say to her, in the middle of the night, which could not be put off until the morning?

She tore open the envelope and read: —

"A most unforeseen circumstance forces me to leave for the North immediately, so I beg your ladyship's pardon if I do not avail myself of the honour of bidding you good-bye. My business may keep me employed for about a week, so I shall not have the privilege of being present at your ladyship's water-party on Wednesday. I remain your ladyship's most humble and most obedient servant, PERCY BLAKENEY."

Marguerite must suddenly have been imbued with her husband's slowness of intellect, for she had perforce to read the few simple lines over and over again, before she could fully grasp their meaning.

She stood on the landing, turning over and over in her hand this curt and mysterious epistle, her mind a blank, her nerves strained with agitation and a presentiment she could not very well have explained.

Sir Percy owned considerable property in the North, certainly, and he had often before gone there alone and stayed away a week at a time; but it seemed so very strange that circumstances should have arisen between five and six o'clock in the morning that compelled him to start in this extreme hurry.

Vainly she tried to shake off an unaccustomed feeling of nervousness: she was trembling from head to foot. A wild, unconquerable desire seized her to see her husband again, at once, if only he had not already started.

Forgetting the fact that she was only very lightly clad in a morning wrap, and that her hair lay loosely about her shoulders, she flew down the stairs, right through the hall towards the front door.

It was as usual barred and bolted, for the indoor servants were not yet up; but her keen ears had detected the sound of voices and the pawing of a horse's hoof against the flag-stones.

With nervous, trembling fingers Marguerite undid the bolts one by one, bruising her hands, hurting her nails, for the locks were heavy and stiff. But she did not care; her whole frame shook with anxiety at the very thought that she might be too late; that he might have gone without her seeing him and bidding him "God-speed!"

At last, she had turned the key and thrown open the door. Her ears had not deceived her. A groom was standing close by holding a couple of horses; one of these was Sultan, Sir Percy's favourite and swiftest horse, saddled ready for a journey.

The next moment Sir Percy himself appeared round the further corner of the house and came quickly towards the horses. He had changed his gorgeous ball costume, but was as usual irreproachably and richly apparelled in a suit of fine cloth, with lace jabot and ruffles, high top-boots, and riding breeches.

Marguerite went forward a few steps. He looked up and saw her. A slight frown appeared between his eyes.

"You are going?" she said quickly and feverishly. "Whither?"

"As I have had the honour of informing your ladyship, urgent, most unexpected business calls me to the North this morning," he said, in his usual cold, drawly manner.

"But . . . your guests to-morrow . . ."

"I have prayed your ladyship to offer my humble excuses to His Royal Highness. You are such a perfect hostess, I do not think I shall be missed."

"But surely you might have waited for your journey . . . until after our water-party . . ." she said, still speaking quickly and nervously. "Surely this business is not so urgent . . . and you said nothing about it — just now."

"My business, as I had the honour to tell you, Madame, is as unexpected as it is urgent. . . . May I therefore crave your permission to go. . . . Can I do aught for you in town? . . . on my way back?"

"No . . . no . . . thanks . . . nothing . . . But you will be back soon?"

"Very soon."

"Before the end of the week?"

"I cannot say."

He was evidently trying to get away, whilst she was straining every nerve to keep him back for a moment or two.

"Percy," she said, "will you not tell me why you go to-day? Surely I, as your wife, have the right to know. You have NOT been called away to the North. I know it. There were no letters, no couriers from there before we left for the opera last night, and nothing was waiting for you when we returned from the ball. . . . You are NOT going to the North, I feel convinced. . . . There is some mystery . . . and . . ."

"Nay, there is no mystery, Madame," he replied, with a slight tone of impatience. "My business has to do with Armand . . . there! Now, have I your leave to depart?"

"With Armand? . . . But you will run no danger?"

"Danger? I? . . . Nay, Madame, your solicitude does me honour. As you say, I have some influence; my intention is to exert it before it be too late."

"Will you allow me to thank you at least?"

"Nay, Madame," he said coldly, "there is no need for that. My life is at your service, and I am already more than repaid."

"And mine will be at yours, Sir Percy, if you will but accept it, in exchange for what you do for Armand," she said, as, impulsively, she stretched out both her hands to him. "There! I will not detain you . . . my thoughts go with you . . . Farewell! . . ."

How lovely she looked in this morning sunlight, with her ardent hair streaming around her shoulders. He bowed very low and kissed her hand; she felt the burning kiss and her heart thrilled with joy and hope.

"You will come back?" she said tenderly.

"Very soon!" he replied, looking longingly into her blue eyes.

"And . . . you will remember? . . ." she asked as her eyes, in response to his look, gave him an infinity of promise.

"I will always remember, Madame, that you have honoured me by commanding my services."

The words were cold and formal, but they did not chill her this time. Her woman's heart had read his, beneath the impassive mask his pride still forced him to wear.

He bowed to her again, then begged her leave to depart. She stood on one side whilst he jumped on to Sultan's back, then, as he galloped out of the gates, she waved him a final "Adieu."

A bend in the road soon hid him from view; his confidential groom had some difficulty in keeping pace with him, for Sultan flew along in response to his master's excited mood. Marguerite, with a sigh that was almost a happy one, turned and went within. She went back to her room, for suddenly, like a tired child, she felt quite sleepy.

Her heart seemed all at once to be in complete peace, and, though it still ached with undefined longing, a vague and delicious hope soothed it as with a balm.

She felt no longer anxious about Armand. The man who had just ridden away, bent on helping her brother, inspired her with complete confidence in his strength and in his power. She marvelled at herself for having ever looked upon him as an inane fool; of course, THAT was a mask worn to hide the bitter wound she had dealt to his faith and to his love. His passion would have overmastered him, and he would not let her see how much he still cared and how deeply he suffered.

But now all would be well: she would crush her own pride, humble it before him, tell him everything, trust him in everything; and those happy days would come back, when they used to wander off together in the forests of Fontainebleau, when they spoke little — for he was always a silent man — but when she felt that against that strong heart she would always find rest and happiness.

The more she thought of the events of the past night, the less fear had she of Chauvelin and his schemes. He had failed to discover the identity of the Scarlet Pimpernel, of that she felt sure. Both Lord Fancourt and Chauvelin himself had assured her that no one had been in the dining-room at one o'clock except the Frenchman himself and Percy — Yes! — Percy! she might have asked him, had she thought of it! Anyway, she had no fears that the unknown and brave hero would fall in Chauvelin's trap; his death at any rate would not be at her door.

Armand certainly was still in danger, but Percy had pledged his word that Armand would be safe, and somehow, as Marguerite had seen him riding away, the possibility that he could fail in whatever he undertook never even remotely crossed her mind. When Armand was safely over in England she would not allow him to go back to France.

She felt almost happy now, and, drawing the curtains closely together again to shut out the piercing sun, she went to bed at last, laid her head upon the pillow, and, like a wearied child, soon fell into a peaceful and dreamless sleep.

CHAPTER XVIII
THE MYSTERIOUS DEVICE

The day was well advanced when Marguerite woke, refreshed by her long sleep. Louise had brought her some fresh milk and a dish of fruit, and she partook of this frugal breakfast with hearty appetite.

Thoughts crowded thick and fast in her mind as she munched her grapes; most of them went galloping away after the tall, erect figure of her husband, whom she had watched riding out of sight more than five hours ago.

In answer to her eager inquiries, Louise brought back the news that the groom had come home with Sultan, having left Sir Percy in London. The groom thought that his master was about to get on board his schooner, which was lying off just below London Bridge. Sir Percy had ridden thus far, had then met Briggs, the skipper of the DAY DREAM, and had sent the groom back to Richmond with Sultan and the empty saddle.

This news puzzled Marguerite more than ever. Where could Sir Percy be going just now in the DAY DREAM? On Armand's behalf, he had said. Well! Sir Percy had influential friends everywhere. Perhaps he was going to Greenwich, or . . . but Marguerite ceased to conjecture; all would be explained anon: he said that he would come back, and that he would remember. A long, idle day lay before Marguerite. She was expecting a visit of her old school-fellow, little Suzanne de Tournay. With all the merry mischief at her command, she had tendered her request for Suzanne's company to the Comtesse in the Presence of the Prince of Wales last night. His Royal Highness had loudly applauded the notion, and declared that he would give himself the pleasure of calling on the two ladies in the course of the afternoon. The Comtesse had not dared to refuse, and then and there was entrapped into a promise to send little Suzanne to spend a long and happy day at Richmond with her friend.

Marguerite expected her eagerly; she longed for a chat about old school-days with the child; she felt that she would prefer Suzanne's company to that of anyone else, and together they would roam through the fine old garden and rich deer park, or stroll along the river.

But Suzanne had not come yet, and Marguerite being dressed, prepared to go downstairs. She looked quite a girl this morning in her simple muslin frock, with a broad blue sash round her slim waist, and the dainty cross-over fichu into which, at her bosom, she had fastened a few late crimson roses.

She crossed the landing outside her own suite of apartments, and stood still for a moment at the head of the fine oak staircase, which led to the lower floor. On her left were her husband's apartments, a suite of rooms which she practically never entered.

They consisted of bedroom, dressing and reception room, and at the extreme end of the landing, of a small study, which, when Sir Percy did not use it, was always kept locked. His own special and confidential valet, Frank, had charge of this room. No one was ever allowed to go inside. My lady had never cared to do so, and the other servants, had, of course, not dared to break this hard-and-fast rule.

Marguerite had often, with that good-natured contempt which she had recently adopted towards her husband, chaffed him about this secrecy which surrounded his private study. Laughingly she had always declared that he strictly excluded all prying eyes from his sanctum for fear they should detect how very little "study" went on within its four walls: a comfortable arm-chair for Sir Percy's sweet slumbers was, no doubt, its most conspicuous piece of furniture.

Marguerite thought of all this on this bright October morning as she glanced along the corridor. Frank was evidently busy with his master's rooms, for most of the doors stood open, that of the study amongst the others.

A sudden burning, childish curiosity seized her to have a peep at Sir Percy's sanctum. This restriction, of course, did not apply to her, and Frank would, of course, not dare to oppose her. Still, she hoped that the valet would be busy in one of the other rooms, that she might have that one quick peep in secret, and unmolested.

Gently, on tip-toe, she crossed the landing and, like Blue Beard's wife, trembling half with excitement and wonder, she paused a moment on the threshold, strangely perturbed and irresolute.

The door was ajar, and she could not see anything within. She pushed it open tentatively: there was no sound: Frank was evidently not there, and she walked boldly in.

At once she was struck by the severe simplicity of everything around her: the dark and heavy hangings, the massive oak furniture, the one or two maps on the wall, in no way recalled to her mind the lazy man about town, the lover of race-courses, the dandified leader of fashion, that was the outward representation of Sir Percy Blakeney.

There was no sign here, at any rate, of hurried departure. Everything was in its place, not a scrap of paper littered the floor, not a cupboard or drawer was left open. The curtains were drawn aside, and through the open window the fresh morning air was streaming in.

Facing the window, and well into the centre of the room, stood a ponderous business-like desk, which looked as if it had seen much service. On the wall to the left of the desk, reaching almost from floor to ceiling, was a large full-length portrait of a woman, magnificently framed, exquisitely painted, and signed with the name of Boucher. It was Percy's mother.

Marguerite knew very little about her, except that she had died abroad, ailing in body as well as in mind, while Percy was still a lad. She must have been a very beautiful woman once, when Boucher painted her, and as Marguerite looked at the portrait, she could not but be struck by the extraordinary resemblance which must have existed between mother and son. There was the same low, square forehead, crowned with thick, fair hair, smooth and heavy; the same deep-set, somewhat lazy blue eyes beneath firmly marked, straight brows; and in those eyes there was the same intensity behind that apparent laziness, the same latent passion which used to light up Percy's face in the olden days before his marriage, and which Marguerite had again noted, last night at dawn, when she had come quite close to him, and had allowed a note of tenderness to creep into her voice.

Marguerite studied the portrait, for it interested her: after that she turned and looked again at the ponderous desk. It was covered with a mass of papers, all neatly tied and docketed, which looked like accounts and receipts arrayed with perfect method. It had never before struck Marguerite — nor had she, alas! found it worth while to inquire — as to how Sir Percy, whom all the world had credited with a total lack of brains, administered the vast fortune which his father had left him.

Since she had entered this neat, orderly room, she had been taken so much by surprise, that this obvious proof of her husband's strong business capacities did not cause her more than a passing thought of wonder. But it also strengthened her in the now certain knowledge that, with his worldly inanities, his foppish ways, and foolish talk, he was not only wearing a mask, but was playing a deliberate and studied part.

Marguerite wondered again. Why should he take all this trouble? Why should he — who was obviously a serious, earnest man — wish to appear before his fellow-men as an empty-headed nincompoop?

He may have wished to hide his love for a wife who held him in contempt . . . but surely such an object could have been gained at less sacrifice, and with far less trouble than constant incessant acting of an unnatural part.

She looked round her quite aimlessly now: she was horribly puzzled, and a nameless dread, before all this strange, unaccountable mystery, had begun to seize upon her. She felt cold and uncomfortable suddenly in this severe and dark room. There were no pictures on the wall, save the fine Boucher portrait, only a couple of maps, both of parts of France, one of the North coast and the other of the environs of Paris. What did Sir Percy want with those, she wondered.

Her head began to ache, she turned away from this strange Blue Beard's chamber, which she had entered, and which she did not understand. She did not wish Frank to find her here, and with a fast look round, she once more turned to the door. As she did so, her foot knocked against a small object, which had apparently been lying close to the desk, on the carpet, and which now went rolling, right across the room.

She stooped to pick it up. It was a solid gold ring, with a flat shield, on which was engraved a small device.

Marguerite turned it over in her fingers, and then studied the engraving on the shield. It represented a small star-shaped flower, of a shape she had seen so distinctly twice before: once at the opera, and once at Lord Grenville's ball.

CHAPTER XIX
THE SCARLET PIMPERNEL

At what particular moment the strange doubt first crept into Marguerite's mind, she could not herself have said. With the ring tightly clutched in her hand, she had run out of the room, down the stairs, and out into the garden, where, in complete seclusion, alone with the flowers, and the river and the birds, she could look again at the ring, and study that device more closely.

Stupidly, senselessly, now, sitting beneath the shade of an overhanging sycamore, she was looking at the plain gold shield, with the star-shaped little flower engraved upon it.

Bah! It was ridiculous! she was dreaming! her nerves were overwrought, and she saw signs and mysteries in the most trivial coincidences. Had not everybody about town recently made a point of affecting the device of that mysterious and heroic Scarlet Pimpernel?

Did she herself wear it embroidered on her gowns? set in gems and enamel in her hair? What was there strange in the fact that Sir Percy should have chosen to use the device as a seal-ring? He might easily have done that . . . yes . . . quite easily . . . and . . . besides . . . what connection could there be between her exquisite dandy of a husband, with his fine clothes and refined, lazy ways, and the daring plotter who rescued French victims from beneath the very eyes of the leaders of a bloodthirsty revolution?

Her thoughts were in a whirl — her mind a blank . . . She did not see anything that was going on around her, and was quite startled when a fresh young voice called to her across the garden.

"CHERIE! — CHERIE! where are you?" and little Suzanne, fresh as a rosebud, with eyes dancing with glee, and brown curls fluttering in the soft morning breeze, came running across the lawn.

"They told me you were in the garden," she went on prattling merrily, and throwing herself with a pretty, girlish impulse into Marguerite's arms, "so I ran out to give you a surprise. You did not expect me quite so soon, did you, my darling little Margot CHERIE?"

Marguerite, who had hastily concealed the ring in the folds of her kerchief, tried to respond gaily and unconcernedly to the young girl's impulsiveness.

"Indeed, sweet one," she said with a smile, "it is delightful to have you all to myself, and for a nice whole long day. . . . You won't be bored?"

"Oh! bored! Margot, how CAN you say such a wicked thing. Why! when we were in the dear old convent together, we were always happy when we were allowed to be alone together."

"And to talk secrets."

The two young girls had linked their arms in one another's and began wandering round the garden.

"Oh! how lovely your home is, Margot, darling," said little Suzanne, enthusiastically, "and how happy you must be!"

"Aye, indeed! I ought to be happy — oughtn't I, sweet one?" said Marguerite, with a wistful little sigh.

"How sadly you say it, CHERIE. . . . Ah, well, I suppose now that you are a married woman you won't care to talk secrets with me any longer. Oh! what lots and lots of secrets we used to have at school! Do you remember? — some we did not even confide to Sister Theresa of the Holy Angels — though she was such a dear."

"And now you have one all-important secret, eh, little one?" said Marguerite, merrily, "which you are forthwith going to confide in me. Nay, you need not blush, CHERIE." she added, as she saw Suzanne's pretty little face crimson with blushes. "Faith, there's naught to be ashamed of! He is a noble and true man, and one to be proud of as a lover, and . . . as a husband."

"Indeed, CHERIE, I am not ashamed," rejoined Suzanne, softly; "and it makes me very, very proud to hear you speak so well of him. I think maman will consent," she added thoughtfully, "and I shall be — oh! so happy — but, of course, nothing is to be thought of until papa is safe. . . ."

Marguerite started. Suzanne's father! the Comte de Tournay! — one of those whose life would be jeopardised if Chauvelin succeeded in establishing the identity of the Scarlet Pimpernel.

She had understood all along from the Comtesse, and also from one or two of the members of the league, that their mysterious leader had pledged his honour to bring the fugitive Comte de Tournay safely out of France. Whilst little Suzanne — unconscious of all — save her own all-important little secret, went prattling on, Marguerite's thoughts went back to the events of the past night.

Armand's peril, Chauvelin's threat, his cruel "Either — or — " which she had accepted.

And then her own work in the matter, which should have culminated at one o'clock in Lord Grenville's dining-room, when the relentless agent of the French Government would finally learn who was this mysterious Scarlet Pimpernel, who so openly defied an army of spies and placed himself so boldly, and for mere sport, on the side of the enemies of France.

Since then she had heard nothing from Chauvelin. She had concluded that he had failed, and yet, she had not felt anxious about Armand, because her husband had promised her that Armand would be safe.

But now, suddenly, as Suzanne prattled merrily along, an awful horror came upon her for what she had done. Chauvelin had told her nothing, it was true; but she remembered how sarcastic and evil he looked when she took final leave of him after the ball. Had he discovered something then? Had he already laid his plans for catching the daring plotter, red-handed, in France, and sending him to the guillotine without compunction or delay?

Marguerite turned sick with horror, and her hand convulsively clutched the ring in her dress.

"You are not listening, CHERIE," said Suzanne, reproachfully, as she paused in her long, highly interesting narrative.

"Yes, yes, darling — indeed I am," said Marguerite with an effort, forcing herself to smile. "I love to hear you talking . . . and your happiness makes me so very glad. . . . Have no fear, we will manage to propitiate maman. Sir Andrew Ffoulkes is a noble English gentleman; he has money and position, the Comtesse will not refuse her consent. . . . But . . . now, little one . . . tell me . . . what is the latest news about your father?"

"Oh!" said Suzanne with mad glee, "the best we could possibly hear. My Lord Hastings came to see maman early this morning. He said that all is now well with dear papa, and we may safely expect him here in England in less than four days."

"Yes," said Marguerite, whose glowing eyes were fastened on Suzanne's lips, as she continued merrily:

"Oh, we have no fear now! You don't know, CHERIE, that that great and noble Scarlet Pimpernel himself has gone to save papa. He has gone, CHERIE . . . actually gone . . ." added Suzanne excitedly, "he was in London this morning; he will be in Calais, perhaps, to-morrow . . . where he will meet papa . . . and then . . . and then . . ."

The blow had fallen. She had expected it all along, though she had tried for the last half-hour to delude herself and to cheat her fears. He had gone to Calais, had been in London this morning . . . he . . . the Scarlet Pimpernel . . . Percy Blakeney . . . her husband . . . whom she had betrayed last night to Chauvelin.

Percy . . . Percy . . . her husband . . . the Scarlet Pimpernel . . . Oh! how could she have been so blind? She understood it all now — all at once . . . that part he played — the mask he wore . . . in order to throw dust in everybody's eyes.

And all for the sheer sport and devilry of course! — saving men, women and children from death, as other men destroy and kill animals for the excitement, the love of the thing. The idle, rich man wanted some aim in life — he, and the few young bucks he enrolled under his banner, had amused themselves for months in risking their lives for the sake of an innocent few.

Perhaps he had meant to tell her when they were first married; and then the story of the Marquis de St. Cyr had come to his ears, and he had suddenly turned from her, thinking, no doubt, that she might someday betray him and his comrades, who had sworn to follow him;

and so he had tricked her, as he tricked all others, whilst hundreds now owed their lives to him, and many families owed him both life and happiness.

The mask of an inane fop had been a good one, and the part consummately well played. No wonder that Chauvelin's spies had failed to detect, in the apparently brainless nincompoop, the man whose reckless daring and resourceful ingenuity had baffled the keenest French spies, both in France and in England. Even last night when Chauvelin went to Lord Grenville's dining-room to seek that daring Scarlet Pimpernel, he only saw that inane Sir Percy Blakeney fast asleep in a corner of the sofa.

Had his astute mind guessed the secret, then? Here lay the whole awful, horrible, amazing puzzle. In betraying a nameless stranger to his fate in order to save her brother, had Marguerite Blakeney sent her husband to his death?

No! no! no! a thousand times no! Surely Fate could not deal a blow like that: Nature itself would rise in revolt: her hand, when it held that tiny scrap of paper last night, would have surely have been struck numb ere it committed a deed so appalling and so terrible.

"But what is it, CHERIE?" said little Suzanne, now genuinely alarmed, for Marguerite's colour had become dull and ashen. "Are you ill, Marguerite? What is it?"

"Nothing, nothing, child," she murmured, as in a dream. "Wait a moment . . . let me think . . . think! . . . You said . . . the Scarlet Pimpernel had gone today . . . ?"

"Marguerite, CHERIE, what is it? You frighten me. . . ."

"It is nothing, child, I tell you . . . nothing . . . I must be alone a minute — and — dear one . . . I may have to curtail our time together to-day. . . . I may have to go away — you'll understand?"

"I understand that something has happened, CHERIE, and that you want to be alone. I won't be a hindrance to you. Don't think of me. My maid, Lucile, has not yet gone . . . we will go back together . . . don't think of me."

She threw her arms impulsively round Marguerite. Child as she was, she felt the poignancy of her friend's grief, and with the infinite tact of her girlish tenderness, she did not try to pry into it, but was ready to efface herself.

She kissed Marguerite again and again, then walked sadly back across the lawn. Marguerite did not move, she remained there, thinking . . . wondering what was to be done.

Just as little Suzanne was about to mount the terrace steps, a groom came running round the house towards his mistress. He carried a sealed letter in his hand. Suzanne instinctively turned back; her heart told her that here perhaps was further ill news for her friend, and she felt that poor Margot was not in a fit state to bear any more.

The groom stood respectfully beside his mistress, then he handed her the sealed letter.

"What is that?" asked Marguerite.

"Just come by runner, my lady."

Marguerite took the letter mechanically, and turned it over in her trembling fingers.

"Who sent it?" she said.

"The runner said, my lady," replied the groom, "that his orders were to deliver this, and that your ladyship would understand from whom it came."

Marguerite tore open the envelope. Already her instinct told her what it contained, and her eyes only glanced at it mechanically.

It was a letter by Armand St. Just to Sir Andrew Ffoulkes — the letter which Chauvelin's spies had stolen at "The Fisherman's Rest," and which Chauvelin had held as a rod over her to enforce her obedience.

Now he had kept his word — he had sent her back St. Just's compromising letter . . . for he was on the track of the Scarlet Pimpernel.

Marguerite's senses reeled, her very soul seemed to be leaving her body; she tottered, and would have fallen but for Suzanne's arm round her waist. With superhuman effort she regained control over herself — there was yet much to be done.

"Bring that runner here to me," she said to the servant, with much calm. "He has not gone?"

"No, my lady."

The groom went, and Marguerite turned to Suzanne.

"And you, child, run within. Tell Lucile to get ready. I fear that I must send you home, child. And — stay, tell one of the maids to prepare a travelling dress and cloak for me."

Suzanne made no reply. She kissed Marguerite tenderly and obeyed without a word; the child was overawed by the terrible, nameless misery in her friend's face.

A minute later the groom returned, followed by the runner who had brought the letter.

"Who gave you this packet?" asked Marguerite.

"A gentleman, my lady," replied the man, "at 'The Rose and Thistle' inn opposite Charing Cross. He said you would understand."

"At 'The Rose and Thistle'? What was he doing?"

"He was waiting for the coach, your ladyship, which he had ordered."

"The coach?"

"Yes, my lady. A special coach he had ordered. I understood from his man that he was posting straight to Dover."

"That's enough. You may go." Then she turned to the groom: "My coach and the four swiftest horses in the stables, to be ready at once."

The groom and runner both went quickly off to obey. Marguerite remained standing for a moment on the lawn quite alone. Her graceful figure was as rigid as a statue, her eyes were fixed, her hands were tightly clasped across her breast; her lips moved as they murmured with pathetic heart-breaking persistence, —

"What's to be done? What's to be done? Where to find him? — Oh, God! grant me light."

But this was not the moment for remorse and despair. She had done — unwittingly — an awful and terrible thing — the very worst crime, in her eyes, that woman ever committed — she saw it in all its horror. Her very blindness in not having guessed her husband's secret seemed now to her another deadly sin. She ought to have known! she ought to have known!

How could she imagine that a man who could love with so much intensity as Percy Blakeney had loved her from the first — how could such a man be the brainless idiot he chose to appear? She, at least, ought to have known that he was wearing a mask, and having found that out, she should have torn it from his face, whenever they were alone together.

Her love for him had been paltry and weak, easily crushed by her own pride; and she, too, had worn a mask in assuming a contempt for him, whilst, as a matter of fact, she completely misunderstood him.

But there was no time now to go over the past. By her own blindness she had sinned; now she must repay, not by empty remorse, but by prompt and useful action.

Percy had started for Calais, utterly unconscious of the fact that his most relentless enemy was on his heels. He had set sail early that morning from London Bridge. Provided he had a favourable wind, he would no doubt be in France within twenty-four hours; no doubt he had reckoned on the wind and chosen this route.

Chauvelin, on the other hand, would post to Dover, charter a vessel there, and undoubtedly reach Calais much about the same time. Once in Calais, Percy would meet all those who were eagerly waiting for the noble and brave Scarlet Pimpernel, who had come to rescue them from horrible and unmerited death. With Chauvelin's eyes now fixed upon his every movement, Percy would thus not only be endangering his own life, but that of Suzanne's father, the old Comte de Tournay, and of those other fugitives who were waiting for him and trusting in him. There was also Armand, who had gone to meet de Tournay, secure in the knowledge that the Scarlet Pimpernel was watching over his safety.

All these lives and that of her husband, lay in Marguerite's hands; these she must save, if human pluck and ingenuity were equal to the task.

Unfortunately, she could not do all this quite alone. Once in Calais she would not know where to find her husband, whilst Chauvelin, in stealing the papers at Dover, had obtained the whole itinerary. Above every thing, she wished to warn Percy.

She knew enough about him by now to understand that he would never abandon those who trusted in him, that he would not turn his back from danger, and leave the Comte de Tournay to fall into the bloodthirsty hands that knew of no mercy. But if he were warned, he might form new plans, be more wary, more prudent. Unconsciously, he might fall into a cunning trap, but — once warned — he might yet succeed.

And if he failed — if indeed Fate, and Chauvelin, with all the resources at his command, proved too strong for the daring plotter after all — then at least she would be there by his side, to comfort, love and cherish, to cheat death perhaps at the last by making it seem sweet, if they died both together, locked in each other's arms, with the supreme happiness of knowing that passion had responded to passion, and that all misunderstandings were at an end.

Her whole body stiffened as with a great and firm resolution. This she meant to do, if God gave her wits and strength. Her eyes lost their fixed look; they glowed with inward fire at the thought of meeting him again so soon, in the very midst of most deadly perils; they sparkled with the joy of sharing these dangers with him — of helping him perhaps — of being with him at the last — if she failed.

The childlike sweet face had become hard and set, the curved mouth was closed tightly over her clenched teeth. She meant to do or die, with him and for his sake. A frown, which spoke of an iron will and unbending resolution, appeared between the two straight brows; already her plans were formed. She would go and find Sir Andrew Ffoulkes first; he was Percy's best friend, and Marguerite remembered, with a thrill, with what blind enthusiasm the young man always spoke of his mysterious leader.

He would help her where she needed help; her coach was ready. A change of raiment, and a farewell to little Suzanne, and she could be on her way.

Without haste, but without hesitation, she walked quietly into the house.

CHAPTER XX
THE FRIEND

Less than half an hour later, Marguerite, buried in thoughts, sat inside her coach, which was bearing her swiftly to London.

She had taken an affectionate farewell of little Suzanne, and seen the child safely started with her maid, and in her own coach, back to town. She had sent one courier with a respectful letter of excuse to His Royal Highness, begging for a postponement of the august visit on account of pressing and urgent business, and another on ahead to bespeak a fresh relay of horses at Faversham.

Then she had changed her muslin frock for a dark traveling costume and mantle, had provided herself with money — which her husband's lavishness always placed fully at her disposal — and had started on her way.

She did not attempt to delude herself with any vain and futile hopes; the safety of her brother Armand was to have been conditional on the imminent capture of the Scarlet Pimpernel. As Chauvelin had sent her back Armand's compromising letter, there was no doubt that he was quite satisfied in his own mind that Percy Blakeney was the man whose death he had sworn to bring about.

No! there was no room for any fond delusions! Percy, the husband whom she loved with all the ardour which her admiration for his bravery had kindled, was in immediate, deadly peril, through her hand. She had betrayed him to his enemy — unwittingly 'tis true — but she HAD betrayed him, and if Chauvelin succeeded in trapping him, who so far was unaware of his danger, then his death would be at her door. His death! when with her very heart's blood, she would have defended him and given willingly her life for his.

She had ordered her coach to drive her to the "Crown" inn; once there, she told her coachman to give the horses food and rest. Then she ordered a chair, and had herself carried to the house in Pall Mall where Sir Andrew Ffoulkes lived.

Among all Percy's friends who were enrolled under his daring banner, she felt that she would prefer to confide in Sir Andrew Ffoulkes. He had always been her friend, and now his love for little Suzanne had brought him closer to her still. Had he been away from home, gone on the mad errand with Percy, perhaps, then she would have called on Lord Hastings or Lord Tony — for she wanted the help of one of these young men, or she would indeed be powerless to save her husband.

Sir Andrew Ffoulkes, however, was at home, and his servant introduced her ladyship immediately. She went upstairs to the young man's comfortable bachelor's chambers, and was shown into a small, though luxuriously furnished, dining-room. A moment or two later Sir Andrew himself appeared.

He had evidently been much startled when he heard who his lady visitor was, for he looked anxiously — even suspiciously — at Marguerite, whilst performing the elaborate bows before her, which the rigid etiquette of the time demanded.

Marguerite had laid aside every vestige of nervousness; she was perfectly calm, and having returned the young man's elaborate salute, she began very calmly, —

"Sir Andrew, I have no desire to waste valuable time in much talk. You must take certain things I am going to tell you for granted. These will be of no importance. What is important is that your leader and comrade, the Scarlet Pimpernel . . . my husband . . . Percy Blakeney . . . is in deadly peril."

Had she the remotest doubt of the correctness of her deductions, she would have had them confirmed now, for Sir Andrew, completely taken by surprise, had grown very pale, and was quite incapable of making the slightest attempt at clever parrying.

"No matter how I know this, Sir Andrew," she continued quietly, "thank God that I do, and that perhaps it is not too late to save him. Unfortunately, I cannot do this quite alone, and therefore have come to you for help."

"Lady Blakeney," said the young man, trying to recover himself, "I . . ."

"Will you hear me first?" she interrupted. "This is how the matter stands. When the agent of the French Government stole your papers that night in Dover, he found amongst them certain plans, which you or your leader meant to carry out for the rescue of the Comte de Tournay and others. The Scarlet Pimpernel — Percy, my husband — has gone on this errand himself to-day. Chauvelin knows that the Scarlet Pimpernel and Percy Blakeney are one and the same person. He will follow him to Calais, and there will lay hands on him. You know as well as I do the fate that awaits him at the hands of the Revolutionary Government of France. No interference from England — from King George himself — would save him. Robespierre and his gang would see to it that the interference came too late. But not only that, the much-trusted leader will also have been unconsciously the means of revealing the hiding-place of the Comte de Tournay and of all those who, even now, are placing their hopes in him."

She had spoken quietly, dispassionately, and with firm, unbending resolution. Her purpose was to make that young man trust and help her, for she could do nothing without him.

"I do not understand," he repeated, trying to gain time, to think what was best to be done.

"Aye! but I think you do, Sir Andrew. You must know that I am speaking the truth. Look these facts straight in the face. Percy has sailed for Calais, I presume for some lonely part of the coast, and Chauvelin is on his track. HE has posted for Dover, and will cross the Channel probably to-night. What do you think will happen?"

The young man was silent.

"Percy will arrive at his destination: unconscious of being followed he will seek out de Tournay and the others — among these is Armand St. Just my brother — he will seek them out, one after another, probably, not knowing that the sharpest eyes in the world are watching his every movement. When he has thus unconsciously betrayed those who blindly trust in him, when nothing can be gained from him, and he is ready to come back to England, with those whom he has gone so bravely to save, the doors of the trap will close upon him, and he will be sent to end his noble life upon the guillotine."

Still Sir Andrew was silent.

"You do not trust me," she said passionately. "Oh God! cannot you see that I am in deadly earnest? Man, man," she added, while, with her tiny hands she seized the young man suddenly by the shoulders, forcing him to look straight at her, "tell me, do I look like that vilest thing on earth — a woman who would betray her own husband?"

"God forbid, Lady Blakeney," said the young man at last, "that I should attribute such evil motives to you, but . . ."

"But what? . . . tell me. . . . Quick, man! . . . the very seconds are precious!"

"Will you tell me," he asked resolutely, and looking searchingly into her blue eyes, "whose hand helped to guide M. Chauvelin to the knowledge which you say he possesses?"

"Mine," she said quietly, "I own it — I will not lie to you, for I wish you to trust me absolutely. But I had no idea — how COULD I have? — of the identity of the Scarlet Pimpernel . . . and my brother's safety was to be my prize if I succeeded."

"In helping Chauvelin to track the Scarlet Pimpernel?"

She nodded.

"It is no use telling you how he forced my hand. Armand is more than a brother to me, and . . . and . . . how COULD I guess? . . . But we waste time, Sir Andrew . . . every second is precious . . . in the name of God! . . . my husband is in peril . . . your friend! — your comrade! — Help me to save him."

Sir Andrew felt his position to be a very awkward one. The oath he had taken before his leader and comrade was one of obedience and secrecy; and yet the beautiful woman, who was asking him to trust her, was undoubtedly in earnest; his friend and leader was equally undoubtedly in imminent danger and . . .

"Lady Blakeney," he said at last, "God knows you have perplexed me, so that I do not know which way my duty lies. Tell me what you wish me to do. There are nineteen of us ready to lay down our lives for the Scarlet Pimpernel if he is in danger."

"There is no need for lives just now, my friend," she said drily; "my wits and four swift horses will serve the necessary purpose. But I must know where to find him. See," she added, while her eyes filled with tears, "I have humbled myself before you, I have owned my fault to you; shall I also confess my weakness? — My husband and I have been estranged, because he did not trust me, and because I was too blind to understand. You must confess that the bandage which he put over my eyes was a very thick one. Is it small wonder that I did not see through it? But last night, after I led him unwittingly into such deadly peril, it suddenly fell from my eyes. If you will not help me, Sir Andrew, I would still strive to save my husband. I would still exert every faculty I possess for his sake; but I might be powerless, for I might arrive too late, and nothing would be left for you but lifelong remorse, and . . . and . . . for me, a broken heart."

"But, Lady Blakeney," said the young man, touched by the gentle earnestness of this exquisitely beautiful woman, "do you know that what you propose doing is man's work? — you cannot possibly journey to Calais alone. You would be running the greatest possible risks to yourself, and your chances of finding your husband now — were I to direct you ever so carefully — are infinitely remote.

"Oh, I hope there are risks!" she murmured softly, "I hope there are dangers, too! — I have so much to atone for. But I fear you are mistaken. Chauvelin's eyes are fixed upon you all, he will scarce notice me. Quick, Sir Andrew! — the coach is ready, and there is not a moment to be lost. . . . I MUST get to him! I MUST!" she repeated with almost savage energy, "to warn him that that man is on his track. . . . Can't you see — can't you see, that I MUST get to him . . . even . . . even if it be too late to save him . . . at least . . . to be by his side . . . at the least."

"Faith, Madame, you must command me. Gladly would I or any of my comrades lay down our lives for your husband. If you WILL go yourself. . . ."

"Nay, friend, do you not see that I would go mad if I let you go without me?" She stretched out her hand to him. "You WILL trust me?"

"I await your orders," he said simply.

"Listen, then. My coach is ready to take me to Dover. Do you follow me, as swiftly as horses will take you. We meet at nightfall at 'The Fisherman's Rest.' Chauvelin would avoid it, as he is known there, and I think it would be the safest. I will gladly accept your escort to Calais . . . as you say, I might miss Sir Percy were you to direct me ever so carefully. We'll charter a schooner at Dover and cross over during the night. Disguised, if you will agree to it, as my lacquey, you will, I think, escape detection."

"I am entirely at your service, Madame," rejoined the young man earnestly. "I trust to God that you will sight the DAY DREAM before we reach Calais. With Chauvelin at his heels, every step the Scarlet Pimpernel takes on French soil is fraught with danger."

"God grant it, Sir Andrew. But now, farewell. We meet to-night at Dover! It will be a race between Chauvelin and me across the Channel to-night — and the prize — the life of the Scarlet Pimpernel."

He kissed her hand, and then escorted her to her chair. A quarter of an hour later she was back at the "Crown" inn, where her coach and horses were ready and waiting for her. The next moment they thundered along the London streets, and then straight on to the Dover road at maddening speed.

She had no time for despair now. She was up and doing and had no leisure to think. With Sir Andrew Ffoulkes as her companion and ally, hope had once again revived in her heart.

God would be merciful. He would not allow so appalling a crime to be committed, as the death of a brave man, through the hand of a woman who loved him, and worshipped him, and who would gladly have died for his sake.

Marguerite's thoughts flew back to him, the mysterious hero, whom she had always unconsciously loved, when his identity was still unknown to her. Laughingly, in the olden days, she used to call him the shadowy king of her heart, and now she had suddenly found that this enigmatic personality whom she had worshipped, and the man who loved her so passionately, were one and the same: what wonder that one or two happier visions began to force their way before her mind. She vaguely wondered what she would say to him when first they would stand face to face.

She had had so many anxieties, so much excitement during the past few hours, that she allowed herself the luxury of nursing these few more hopeful, brighter thoughts. Gradually the rumble of the coach wheels, with its incessant monotony, acted soothingly on her nerves: her eyes, aching with fatigue and many shed and unshed tears, closed involuntarily, and she fell into a troubled sleep.

It was late into the night when she at last reached "The Fisherman's Rest." She had done the whole journey in less than eight hours, thanks to innumerable changes of horses at the various coaching stations, for which she always paid lavishly, thus obtaining the very best and swiftest that could be had.

Her coachman, too, had been indefatigable; the promise of special and rich reward had no doubt helped to keep him up, and he had literally burned the ground beneath his mistress' coach wheels.

The arrival of Lady Blakeney in the middle of the night caused a considerable flutter at "The Fisherman's Rest." Sally jumped hastily out of bed, and Mr. Jellyband was at great pains how to make his important guest comfortable.

Both of these good folk were far too well drilled in the manners appertaining to innkeepers, to exhibit the slightest surprise at Lady Blakeney's arrival, alone, at this extraordinary hour. No doubt they thought all the more, but Marguerite was far too absorbed in the importance — the deadly earnestness — of her journey, to stop and ponder over trifles of that sort.

The coffee-room — the scene lately of the dastardly outrage on two English gentlemen — was quite deserted. Mr. Jellyband hastily relit the lamp, rekindled a cheerful bit of fire in the great hearth, and then wheeled a comfortable chair by it, into which Marguerite gratefully sank.

"Will your ladyship stay the night?" asked pretty Miss Sally, who was already busy laying a snow-white cloth on the table, preparatory to providing a simple supper for her ladyship.

"No! not the whole night," replied Marguerite. "At any rate, I shall not want any room but this, if I can have it to myself for an hour or two."

"It is at your ladyship's service," said honest Jellyband, whose rubicund face was set in its tightest folds, lest it should betray before "the quality" that boundless astonishment which the very worthy fellow had begun to feel.

"I shall be crossing over at the first turn of the tide," said Marguerite, "and in the first schooner I can get. But my coachman and men will stay the night, and probably several days longer, so I hope you will make them comfortable."

"Yes, my lady; I'll look after them. Shall Sally bring your ladyship some supper?"

"Yes, please. Put something cold on the table, and as soon as Sir Andrew Ffoulkes comes, show him in here."

"Yes, my lady."

Honest Jellyband's face now expressed distress in spite of himself. He had great regard for Sir Percy Blakeney, and did not like to see his lady running away with young Sir Andrew. Of course, it was no business of his, and Mr. Jellyband was no gossip. Still, in his heart, he recollected that her ladyship was after all only one of them "furriners"; what wonder that she was immoral like the rest of them?

"Don't sit up, honest Jellyband," continued Marguerite kindly, "nor you either, Mistress Sally. Sir Andrew may be late."

Jellyband was only too willing that Sally should go to bed. He was beginning not to like these goings-on at all. Still, Lady Blakeney would pay handsomely for the accommodation, and it certainly was no business of his.

Sally arranged a simple supper of cold meat, wine, and fruit on the table, then with a respectful curtsey, she retired, wondering in her little mind why her ladyship looked so serious, when she was about to elope with her gallant.

Then commenced a period of weary waiting for Marguerite. She knew that Sir Andrew — who would have to provide himself with clothes befitting a lacquey — could not possibly reach Dover for at least a couple of hours. He was a splendid horseman of course, and would make light in such an emergency of the seventy odd miles between London and Dover. He would, too, literally burn the ground beneath his horse's hoofs, but he might not always get very good remounts, and in any case, he could not have started from London until at least an hour after she did.

She had seen nothing of Chauvelin on the road. Her coachman, whom she questioned, had not seen anyone answering the description his mistress gave him of the wizened figure of the little Frenchman.

Evidently, therefore, he had been ahead of her all the time. She had not dared to question the people at the various inns, where they had stopped to change horses. She feared that Chauvelin had spies all along the route, who might overhear her questions, then outdistance her and warn her enemy of her approach.

Now she wondered at what inn he might be stopping, or whether he had had the good luck of chartering a vessel already, and was now himself on the way to France. That thought gripped her at the heart as with an iron vice. If indeed she should not be too late already!

The loneliness of the room overwhelmed her; everything within was so horribly still; the ticking of the grandfather's clock — dreadfully slow and measured — was the only sound which broke this awful loneliness.

Marguerite had need of all her energy, all her steadfastness of purpose, to keep up her courage through this weary midnight waiting.

Everyone else in the house but herself must have been asleep. She had heard Sally go upstairs. Mr. Jellyband had gone to see to her coachman and men, and then had returned and taken up a position under the porch outside, just where Marguerite had first met Chauvelin about a week ago. He evidently meant to wait up for Sir Andrew Ffoulkes, but was soon overcome by sweet slumbers, for presently — in addition to the slow ticking of the clock — Marguerite could hear the monotonous and dulcet tones of the worthy fellow's breathing.

For some time now, she had realised that the beautiful warm October's day, so happily begun, had turned into a rough and cold night. She had felt very chilly, and was glad of the cheerful blaze in the hearth: but gradually, as time wore on, the weather became more rough, and the sound of the great breakers against the Admiralty Pier, though some distance from the inn, came to her as the noise of muffled thunder.

The wind was becoming boisterous, rattling the leaded windows and the massive doors of the old-fashioned house: it shook the trees outside and roared down the vast chimney. Marguerite wondered if the wind would be favourable for her journey. She had no fear of the storm, and would have braved worse risks sooner than delay the crossing by an hour.

A sudden commotion outside roused her from her meditations. Evidently it was Sir Andrew Ffoulkes, just arrived in mad haste, for she heard his horse's hoofs thundering on the flag-stones outside, then Mr. Jellyband's sleepy, yet cheerful tones bidding him welcome.

For a moment, then, the awkwardness of her position struck Marguerite; alone at this hour, in a place where she was well known, and having made an assignation with a young cavalier equally well known, and who arrived in disguise! What food for gossip to those mischievously inclined.

The idea struck Marguerite chiefly from its humorous side: there was such quaint contrast between the seriousness of her errand, and the construction which would naturally be put on her actions by honest Mr. Jellyband, that, for the first time since many hours, a little smile began playing round the corners of her childlike mouth, and when, presently, Sir Andrew, almost unrecognisable in his lacquey-like garb, entered the coffee-room, she was able to greet him with quite a merry laugh.

"Faith! Monsieur, my lacquey," she said, "I am satisfied with your appearance!"

Mr. Jellyband had followed Sir Andrew, looking strangely perplexed. The young gallant's disguise had confirmed his worst suspicions. Without a smile upon his jovial face, he drew the cork from the bottle of wine, set the chairs ready, and prepared to wait.

"Thanks, honest friend," said Marguerite, who was still smiling at the thought of what the worthy fellow must be thinking at that very moment, "we shall require nothing more; and here's for all the trouble you have been put to on our account."

She handed two or three gold pieces to Jellyband, who took them respectfully, and with becoming gratitude.

"Stay, Lady Blakeney," interposed Sir Andrew, as Jellyband was about to retire, "I am afraid we shall require something more of my friend Jelly's hospitality. I am sorry to say we cannot cross over to-night."

"Not cross over to-night?" she repeated in amazement. "But we must, Sir Andrew, we must! There can be no question of cannot, and whatever it may cost, we must get a vessel to-night."

But the young man shook his head sadly.

"I am afraid it is not a question of cost, Lady Blakeney. There is a nasty storm blowing from France, the wind is dead against us, we cannot possibly sail until it has changed."

Marguerite became deadly pale. She had not foreseen this. Nature herself was playing her a horrible, cruel trick. Percy was in danger, and she could not go to him, because the wind happened to blow from the coast of France.

"But we must go! — we must!" she repeated with strange, persistent energy, "you know, we must go! — can't you find a way?"

"I have been down to the shore already," he said, "and had a talk to one or two skippers. It is quite impossible to set sail to-night, so every sailor assured me. No one," he added, looking significantly at Marguerite, "NO ONE could possibly put out of Dover to-night."

Marguerite at once understood what he meant. NO ONE included Chauvelin as well as herself. She nodded pleasantly to Jellyband.

"Well, then, I must resign myself," she said to him. "Have you a room for me?"

"Oh, yes, your ladyship. A nice, bright, airy room. I'll see to it at once. . . . And there is another one for Sir Andrew — both quite ready."

"That's brave now, mine honest Jelly," said Sir Andrew, gaily, and clapping his worth host vigorously on the back. "You unlock both those rooms, and leave our candles here on the dresser. I vow you are dead with sleep, and her ladyship must have some supper before she retires. There, have no fear, friend of the rueful countenance, her ladyship's visit, though at this unusual hour, is a great honour to thy house, and Sir Percy Blakeney will reward thee doubly, if thou seest well to her privacy and comfort."

Sir Andrew had no doubt guessed the many conflicting doubts and fears which raged in honest Jellyband's head; and, as he was a gallant gentleman, he tried by this brave hint to allay some of the worthy innkeeper's suspicions. He had the satisfaction of seeing that he had partially succeeded. Jellyband's rubicund countenance brightened somewhat, at the mention of Sir Percy's name.

"I'll go and see to it at once, sir," he said with alacrity, and with less frigidity in his manner. "Has her ladyship everything she wants for supper?"

"Everything, thanks, honest friend, and as I am famished and dead with fatigue, I pray you see to the rooms."

"Now tell me," she said eagerly, as soon as Jellyband had gone from the room, "tell me all your news."

"There is nothing else much to tell you, Lady Blakeney," replied the young man. "The storm makes it quite impossible for any vessel to put out of Dover this tide. But, what seems to you at first a terrible calamity is really a blessing in disguise. If we cannot cross over to France to-night, Chauvelin is in the same quandary."

"He may have left before the storm broke out."

"God grant he may," said Sir Andrew, merrily, "for very likely then he'll have been driven out of his course! Who knows? He may now even be lying at the bottom of the sea, for there is a furious storm raging, and it will fare ill with all small craft which happen to be out. But I fear me we cannot build our hopes upon the shipwreck of that cunning devil, and of all his murderous plans. The sailors I spoke to, all assured me that no schooner had put out of Dover for several hours: on the other hand, I ascertained that a stranger had arrived by coach this afternoon, and had, like myself, made some inquiries about crossing over to France.

"Then Chauvelin is still in Dover?"

"Undoubtedly. Shall I go waylay him and run my sword through him? That were indeed the quickest way out of the difficulty."

"Nay! Sir Andrew, do not jest! Alas! I have often since last night caught myself wishing for that fiend's death. But what you suggest is impossible! The laws of this country do not permit of murder! It is only in our beautiful France that wholesale slaughter is done lawfully, in the name of Liberty and of brotherly love."

Sir Andrew had persuaded her to sit down to the table, to partake of some supper and to drink a little wine. This enforced rest of at least twelve hours, until the next tide, was sure to be terribly difficult to bear in the state of intense excitement in which she was. Obedient in these small matters like a child, Marguerite tried to eat and drink.

Sir Andrew, with that profound sympathy born in all those who are in love, made her almost happy by talking to her about her husband. He recounted to her some of the daring escapes the brave Scarlet Pimpernel had contrived for the poor French fugitives, whom a relentless and bloody revolution was driving out of their country. He made her eyes glow with enthusiasm by telling her of his bravery, his ingenuity, his resourcefulness, when it meant snatching the lives of men, women, and even children from beneath the very edge of that murderous, ever-ready guillotine.

He even made her smile quite merrily by telling her of the Scarlet Pimpernel's quaint and many disguises, through which he had baffled the strictest watch set against him at the barricades of Paris. This last time, the escape of the Comtesse de Tournay and her children had been a veritable masterpiece — Blakeney disguised as a hideous old market-woman, in filthy cap and straggling grey locks, was a sight fit to make the gods laugh.

Marguerite laughed heartily as Sir Andrew tried to describe Blakeney's appearance, whose gravest difficulty always consisted in his great height, which in France made disguise doubly difficult.

Thus an hour wore on. There were many more to spend in enforced inactivity in Dover. Marguerite rose from the table with an impatient sigh. She looked forward with dread to the night in the bed upstairs, with terribly anxious thoughts to keep her company, and the howling of the storm to help chase sleep away.

She wondered where Percy was now. The DAY DREAM was a strong, well-built sea-going yacht. Sir Andrew had expressed the opinion that no doubt she had got in the lee of the wind before the storm broke out, or else perhaps had not ventured into the open at all, but was lying quietly at Gravesend.

Briggs was an expert skipper, and Sir Percy handled a schooner as well as any master mariner. There was no danger for them from the storm.

It was long past midnight when at last Marguerite retired to rest. As she had feared, sleep sedulously avoided her eyes. Her thoughts were of the blackest during these long, weary hours, whilst that incessant storm raged which was keeping her away from Percy. The sound of the distant breakers made her heart ache with melancholy. She was in the mood when the sea has a saddening effect upon the nerves. It is only when we are very happy, that we can bear to gaze merrily upon the vast and limitless expanse of water, rolling on and on with such persistent, irritating monotony, to the accompaniment of our thoughts, whether grave or gay. When they are gay, the waves echo their gaiety; but when they are sad, then every breaker, as it rolls, seems to bring additional sadness, and to speak to us of hopelessness and of the pettiness of all our joys.

CHAPTER XXII
CALAIS

The weariest nights, the longest days, sooner or later must perforce come to an end.

Marguerite had spent over fifteen hours in such acute mental torture as well-nigh drove her crazy. After a sleepless night, she rose early, wild with excitement, dying to start on her journey, terrified lest further obstacles lay in her way. She rose before anyone else in the house was astir, so frightened was she, lest she should miss the one golden opportunity of making a start.

When she came downstairs, she found Sir Andrew Ffoulkes sitting in the coffee-room. He had been out half an hour earlier, and had gone to the Admiralty Pier, only to find that neither the French packet nor any privately chartered vessel could put out of Dover yet. The storm was then at its fullest, and the tide was on the turn. If the wind did not abate or change, they would perforce have to wait another ten or twelve hours until the next tide, before a start could be made. And the storm had not abated, the wind had not changed, and the tide was rapidly drawing out.

Marguerite felt the sickness of despair when she heard this melancholy news. Only the most firm resolution kept her from totally breaking down, and thus adding to the young man's anxiety, which evidently had become very keen.

Though he tried to hide it, Marguerite could see that Sir Andrew was just as anxious as she was to reach his comrade and friend. This enforced inactivity was terrible to them both.

How they spent that wearisome day at Dover, Marguerite could never afterwards say. She was in terror of showing herself, lest Chauvelin's spies happened to be about, so she had a private sitting-room, and she and Sir Andrew sat there hour after hour, trying to take, at long intervals, some perfunctory meals, which little Sally would bring them, with nothing to do but to think, to conjecture, and only occasionally to hope.

The storm had abated just too late; the tide was by then too far out to allow a vessel to put off to sea. The wind had changed, and was settling down to a comfortable north-westerly breeze —a veritable godsend for a speedy passage across to France.

And there those two waited, wondering if the hour would ever come when they could finally make a start. There had been one happy interval in this long weary day, and that was when Sir Andrew went down once again to the pier, and presently came back to tell Marguerite that he had chartered a quick schooner, whose skipper was ready to put to sea the moment the tide was favourable.

From that moment the hours seemed less wearisome; there was less hopelessness in the waiting; and at last, at five o'clock in the afternoon, Marguerite, closely veiled and followed by Sir Andrew Ffoulkes, who, in the guise of her lacquey, was carrying a number of impedimenta, found her way down to the pier.

Once on board, the keen, fresh sea-air revived her, the breeze was just strong enough to nicely swell the sails of the FOAM CREST, as she cut her way merrily towards the open.

The sunset was glorious after the storm, and Marguerite, as she watched the white cliffs of Dover gradually disappearing from view, felt more at peace and once more almost hopeful.

Sir Andrew was full of kind attentions, and she felt how lucky she had been to have him by her side in this, her great trouble.

Gradually the grey coast of France began to emerge from the fast-gathering evening mists. One or two lights could be seen flickering, and the spires of several churches to rise out of the surrounding haze.

Half an hour later Marguerite had landed upon French shore. She was back in that country where at this very moment men slaughtered their fellow-creatures by the hundreds, and sent innocent women and children in thousands to the block.

The very aspect of the country and its people, even in this remote sea-coast town, spoke of that seething revolution, three hundred miles away, in beautiful Paris, now rendered hideous by the constant flow of the blood of her noblest sons, by the wailing of the widows, and the cries of fatherless children.

The men all wore red caps — in various stages of cleanliness — but all with the tricolor cockade pinned on the left-side. Marguerite noticed with a shudder that, instead of the laughing, merry countenance habitual to her own countrymen, their faces now invariably wore a look of sly distrust.

Every man nowadays was a spy upon his fellows: the most innocent word uttered in jest might at any time be brought up as a proof of aristocratic tendencies, or of treachery against the people. Even the women went about with a curious look of fear and of hate lurking in their brown eyes; and all watched Marguerite as she stepped on shore, followed by Sir Andrew, and murmured as she passed along: "SACRES ARISTOS!" or else "SACRES ANGLAIS!"

Otherwise their presence excited no further comment. Calais, even in those days, was in constant business communication with England, and English merchants were often seen on this coast. It was well known that in view of the heavy duties in England, a vast deal of French wines and brandies were smuggled across. This pleased the French BOURGEOIS immensely; he liked to see the English Government and the English king, both of whom he hated, cheated out of their revenues; and an English smuggler was always a welcome guest at the tumble-down taverns of Calais and Boulogne.

So, perhaps, as Sir Andrew gradually directed Marguerite through the tortuous streets of Calais, many of the population, who turned with an oath to look at the strangers clad in English fashion, thought that they were bent on purchasing dutiable articles for their own fog-ridden country, and gave them no more than a passing thought.

Marguerite, however, wondered how her husband's tall, massive figure could have passed through Calais unobserved: she marvelled what disguise he assumed to do his noble work, without exciting too much attention.

Without exchanging more than a few words, Sir Andrew was leading her right across the town, to the other side from that where they had landed, and the way towards Cap Gris Nez. The streets were narrow, tortuous, and mostly evil-smelling, with a mixture of stale fish and damp cellar odours. There had been heavy rain here during the storm last night, and sometimes Marguerite sank ankle-deep in the mud, for the roads were not lighted save by the occasional glimmer from a lamp inside a house.

But she did not heed any of these petty discomforts: "We may meet Blakeney at the 'Chat Gris,'" Sir Andrew had said, when they landed, and she was walking as if on a carpet of rose-leaves, for she was going to meet him almost at once.

At last they reached their destination. Sir Andrew evidently knew the road, for he had walked unerringly in the dark, and had not asked his way from anyone. It was too dark then for Marguerite to notice the outside aspect of this house. The "Chat Gris," as Sir Andrew had called it, was evidently a small wayside inn on the outskirts of Calais, and on the way to Gris Nez. It lay some little distance from the coast, for the sound of the sea seemed to come from afar.

Sir Andrew knocked at the door with the knob of his cane, and from within Marguerite heard a sort of grunt and the muttering of a number of oaths. Sir Andrew knocked again, this time more peremptorily: more oaths were heard, and then shuffling steps seemed to draw near the door. Presently this was thrown open, and Marguerite found herself on the threshold of the most dilapidated, most squalid room she had ever seen in all her life.

The paper, such as it was, was hanging from the walls in strips; there did not seem to be a single piece of furniture in the room that could, by the wildest stretch of imagination, be called "whole." Most of the chairs had broken backs, others had no seats to them, one corner of the table was propped up with a bundle of faggots, there where the fourth leg had been broken.

In one corner of the room there was a huge hearth, over which hung a stock-pot, with a not altogether unpalatable odour of hot soup emanating therefrom. On one side of the room, high up in the wall, there was a species of loft, before which hung a tattered blue-and-white checked curtain. A rickety set of steps led up to this loft.

On the great bare walls, with their colourless paper, all stained with varied filth, there were chalked up at intervals in great bold characters, the words: "Liberte — Egalite — Fraternite."

The whole of this sordid abode was dimly lighted by an evil-smelling oil-lamp, which hung from the rickety rafters of the ceiling. It all looked so horribly squalid, so dirty and uninviting, that Marguerite hardly dared to cross the threshold.

Sir Andrew, however, had stepped unhesitatingly forward.

"English travellers, citoyen!" he said boldly, and speaking in French.

The individual who had come to the door in response to Sir Andrew's knock, and who, presumably, was the owner of this squalid abode, was an elderly, heavily built peasant, dressed in a dirty blue blouse, heavy sabots, from which wisps of straw protruded all round, shabby blue trousers, and the inevitable red cap with the tricolour cockade, that proclaimed his momentary political views. He carried a short wooden pipe, from which the odour of rank tobacco emanated. He looked with some suspicion and a great deal of contempt at the two travellers, muttering "SACRRRES ANGLAIS!" and spat upon the ground to further show his independence of spirit, but, nevertheless, he stood aside to let them enter, no doubt well aware that these same SACCRES ANGLAIS always had well-filled purses.

"Oh, lud!" said Marguerite, as she advanced into the room, holding her handkerchief to her dainty nose, "what a dreadful hole! Are you sure this is the place?"

"Aye! 'tis the place, sure enough," replied the young man as, with his lace-edged, fashionable handkerchief, he dusted a chair for Marguerite to sit on; "but I vow I never saw a more villainous hole."

"Faith!" she said, looking round with some curiosity and a great deal of horror at the dilapidated walls, the broken chairs, the rickety table, "it certainly does not look inviting."

The landlord of the "Chat Gris" — by name, Brogard — had taken no further notice of his guests; he concluded that presently they would order supper, and in the meanwhile it was not for a free citizen to show deference, or even courtesy, to anyone, however smartly they might be dressed.

By the hearth sat a huddled-up figure clad, seemingly, mostly in rags: that figure was apparently a woman, although even that would have been hard to distinguish, except for the cap, which had once been white, and for what looked like the semblance of a petticoat. She was sitting mumbling to herself, and from time to time stirring the brew in her stock-pot.

"Hey, my friend!" said Sir Andrew at last, "we should like some supper. . . . The citoyenne there," he added, "is concocting some delicious soup, I'll warrant, and my mistress has not tasted food for several hours."

It took Brogard some few minutes to consider the question. A free citizen does not respond too readily to the wishes of those who happen to require something of him.

"SACRRRES ARISTOS!" he murmured, and once more spat upon the ground.

Then he went very slowly up to a dresser which stood in a corner of the room; from this he took an old pewter soup-tureen and slowly, and without a word, he handed it to his better-half, who, in the same silence, began filling the tureen with the soup out of her stock-pot.

Marguerite had watched all these preparations with absolute horror; were it not for the earnestness of her purpose, she would incontinently have fled from this abode of dirt and evil smells.

"Faith! our host and hostess are not cheerful people," said Sir Andrew, seeing the look of horror on Marguerite's face. "I would I could offer you a more hearty and more appetising meal . . . but I think you will find the soup eatable and the wine good; these people wallow in dirt, but live well as a rule."

"Nay! I pray you, Sir Andrew," she said gently, "be not anxious about me. My mind is scarce inclined to dwell on thoughts of supper."

Brogard was slowly pursuing his gruesome preparations; he had placed a couple of spoons, also two glasses on the table, both of which Sir Andrew took the precaution of wiping carefully.

Brogard had also produced a bottle of wine and some bread, and Marguerite made an effort to draw her chair to the table and to make some pretence at eating. Sir Andrew, as befitting his ROLE of lacquey, stood behind her chair.

"Nay, Madame, I pray you," he said, seeing that Marguerite seemed quite unable to eat, "I beg of you to try and swallow some food — remember you have need of all your strength."

The soup certainly was not bad; it smelt and tasted good. Marguerite might have enjoyed it, but for the horrible surroundings. She broke the bread, however, and drank some of the wine.

"Nay, Sir Andrew," she said, "I do not like to see you standing. You have need of food just as much as I have. This creature will only think that I am an eccentric Englishwoman eloping with her lacquey, if you'll sit down and partake of this semblance of supper beside me."

Indeed, Brogard having placed what was strictly necessary upon the table, seemed not to trouble himself any further about his guests. The Mere Brogard had quietly shuffled out of the room, and the man stood and lounged about, smoking his evil-smelling pipe, sometimes under Marguerite's very nose, as any free-born citizen who was anybody's equal should do.

"Confound the brute!" said Sir Andrew, with native British wrath, as Brogard leant up against the table, smoking and looking down superciliously at these two SACRRRES ANGLAIS.

"In Heaven's name, man," admonished Marguerite, hurriedly, seeing that Sir Andrew, with British-born instinct, was ominously clenching his fist, "remember that you are in France, and that in this year of grace this is the temper of the people."

"I'd like to scrag the brute!" muttered Sir Andrew, savagely.

He had taken Marguerite's advice and sat next to her at table, and they were both making noble efforts to deceive one another, by pretending to eat and drink.

"I pray you," said Marguerite, "keep the creature in a good temper, so that he may answer the questions we must put to him."

"I'll do my best, but, begad! I'd sooner scrag him than question him. Hey! my friend," he said pleasantly in French, and tapping Brogard lightly on the shoulder, "do you see many of our quality along these parts? Many English travellers, I mean?"

Brogard looked round at him, over his near shoulder, puffed away at his pipe for a moment or two as he was in no hurry, then muttered, —

"Heu! — sometimes!"

"Ah!" said Sir Andrew, carelessly, "English travellers always know where they can get good wine, eh! my friend? — Now, tell me, my lady was desiring to know if by any chance you happen to have seen a great friend of hers, an English gentleman, who often comes to Calais on business; he is tall, and recently was on his way to Paris — my lady hoped to have met him in Calais."

Marguerite tried not to look at Brogard, lest she should betray before him the burning anxiety with which she waited for his reply. But a free-born French citizen is never in any hurry to answer questions: Brogard took his time, then he said very slowly, —

"Tall Englishman? — To-day! — Yes."

"Yes, to-day," muttered Brogard, sullenly. Then he quietly took Sir Andrew's hat from a chair close by, put it on his own head, tugged at his dirty blouse, and generally tried to express in pantomime that the individual in question wore very fine clothes. "SACRRE ARISTO!" he muttered, "that tall Englishman!"

Marguerite could scarce repress a scream.

"It's Sir Percy right enough," she murmured, "and not even in disguise!"

She smiled, in the midst of all her anxiety and through her gathering tears, at the thought of "the ruling passion strong in death"; of Percy running into the wildest, maddest dangers, with the latest-cut coat upon his back, and the laces of his jabot unruffled.

"Oh! the foolhardiness of it!" she sighed. "Quick, Sir Andrew! ask the man when he went."

"Ah yes, my friend," said Sir Andrew, addressing Brogard, with the same assumption of carelessness, "my lord always wears beautiful clothes; the tall Englishman you saw, was certainly my lady's friend. And he has gone, you say?"

"He went . . . yes . . . but he's coming back . . . here — he ordered supper . . ."

Sir Andrew put his hand with a quick gesture of warning upon Marguerite's arm; it came none too soon, for the next moment her wild, mad joy would have betrayed her. He was safe

and well, was coming back here presently, she would see him in a few moments perhaps. . . .
Oh! the wildness of her joy seemed almost more than she could bear.

"Here!" she said to Brogard, who seemed suddenly to have been transformed in her eyes
into some heaven-born messenger of bliss. "Here! — did you say the English gentleman was
coming back here?"

The heaven-born messenger of bliss spat upon the floor, to express his contempt for all and
sundry ARISTOS, who chose to haunt the "Chat Gris."

"Heu!" he muttered, "he ordered supper — he will come back . . . SACRRE ANGLAIS!"
he added, by way of protest against all this fuss for a mere Englishman.

"But where is he now? — Do you know?" she asked eagerly, placing her dainty white hand
upon the dirty sleeve of his blue blouse.

"He went to get a horse and cart," said Brogard, laconically, as with a surly gesture, he shook
off from his arm that pretty hand which princes had been proud to kiss.

"At what time did he go?"

But Brogard had evidently had enough of these questionings. He did not think that it was
fitting for a citizen — who was the equal of anybody — to be thus catechised by these SACR-
RES ARISTOS, even though they were rich English ones. It was distinctly more fitting to
his newborn dignity to be as rude as possible; it was a sure sign of servility to meekly reply
to civil questions.

"I don't know," he said surlily. "I have said enough, VOYONS, LES ARISTOS! . . . He
came to-day. He ordered supper. He went out. — He'll come back. VOILA!"

And with this parting assertion of his rights as a citizen and a free man, to be as rude as he
well pleased, Brogard shuffled out of the room, banging the door after him.

CHAPTER XXIII
HOPE

"Faith, Madame!" said Sir Andrew, seeing that Marguerite seemed desirous to call her surly host back again, "I think we'd better leave him alone. We shall not get anything more out of him, and we might arouse his suspicions. One never knows what spies may be lurking around these God-forsaken places."

"What care I?" she replied lightly, "now I know that my husband is safe, and that I shall see him almost directly!"

"Hush!" he said in genuine alarm, for she had talked quite loudly, in the fulness of her glee, "the very walls have ears in France, these days."

He rose quickly from the table, and walked round the bare, squalid room, listening attentively at the door, through which Brogard has just disappeared, and whence only muttered oaths and shuffling footsteps could be heard. He also ran up the rickety steps that led to the attic, to assure himself that there were no spies of Chauvelin's about the place.

"Are we alone, Monsieur, my lacquey?" said Marguerite, gaily, as the young man once more sat down beside her. "May we talk?"

"As cautiously as possible!" he entreated.

"Faith, man! but you wear a glum face! As for me, I could dance with joy! Surely there is no longer any cause for fear. Our boat is on the beach, the FOAM CREST not two miles out at sea, and my husband will be here, under this very roof, within the next half hour perhaps. Sure! there is naught to hinder us. Chauvelin and his gang have not yet arrived."

"Nay, madam! that I fear we do not know."

"What do you mean?"

"He was at Dover at the same time that we were."

"Held up by the same storm, which kept us from starting."

"Exactly. But — I did not speak of it before, for I feared to alarm you — I saw him on the beach not five minutes before we embarked. At least, I swore to myself at the time that it was himself; he was disguised as a CURE, so that Satan, his own guardian, would scarce have known him. But I heard him then, bargaining for a vessel to take him swiftly to Calais; and he must have set sail less than an hour after we did."

Marguerite's face had quickly lost its look of joy. The terrible danger in which Percy stood, now that he was actually on French soil, became suddenly and horribly clear to her. Chauvelin was close upon his heels; here in Calais, the astute diplomatist was all-powerful; a word from him and Percy could be tracked and arrested and . . .

Every drop of blood seemed to freeze in her veins; not even during the moments of her wildest anguish in England had she so completely realised the imminence of the peril in which her husband stood. Chauvelin had sworn to bring the Scarlet Pimpernel to the guillotine, and now the daring plotter, whose anonymity hitherto had been his safeguard, stood revealed through her own hand, to his most bitter, most relentless enemy.

Chauvelin — when he waylaid Lord Tony and Sir Andrew Ffoulkes in the coffee-room of "The Fisherman's Rest" — had obtained possession of all the plans of this latest expedition. Armand St. Just, the Comte de Tournay and other fugitive royalists were to have met the Scarlet Pimpernel — or rather, as it had been originally arranged, two of his emissaries — on this day, the 2nd of October, at a place evidently known to the league, and vaguely alluded to as the "Pere Blanchard's hut."

Armand, whose connection with the Scarlet Pimpernel and disavowal of the brutal policy of the Reign of Terror was still unknown to his countryman, had left England a little more than a week ago, carrying with him the necessary instructions, which would enable him to meet the other fugitives and to convey them to this place of safety.

This much Marguerite had fully understood from the first, and Sir Andrew Ffoulkes had confirmed her surmises. She knew, too, that when Sir Percy realized that his own plans and his directions to his lieutenants had been stolen by Chauvelin, it was too late to communicate with Armand, or to send fresh instructions to the fugitives.

They would, of necessity, be at the appointed time and place, not knowing how grave was the danger which now awaited their brave rescuer.

Blakeney, who as usual had planned and organized the whole expedition, would not allow any of his younger comrades to run the risk of almost certain capture. Hence his hurried note to them at Lord Grenville's ball — "Start myself to-morrow — alone."

And now with his identity known to his most bitter enemy, his every step would be dogged, the moment he set foot in France. He would be tracked by Chauvelin's emissaries, followed until he reached that mysterious hut where the fugitives were waiting for him, and there the trap would be closed on him and on them.

There was but one hour — the hour's start which Marguerite and Sir Andrew had of their enemy — in which to warn Percy of the imminence of his danger, and to persuade him to give up the foolhardy expedition, which could only end in his own death.

But there WAS that one hour.

"Chauvelin knows of this inn, from the papers he stole," said Sir Andrew, earnestly, "and on landing will make straight for it."

"He has not landed yet," she said, "we have an hour's start on him, and Percy will be here directly. We shall be mid-Channel ere Chauvelin has realised that we have slipped through his fingers."

She spoke excitedly and eagerly, wishing to infuse into her young friend some of that buoyant hope which still clung to her heart. But he shook his head sadly.

"Silent again, Sir Andrew?" she said with some impatience. "Why do you shake your head and look so glum?"

"Faith, Madame," he replied, "'tis only because in making your rose-coloured plans, you are forgetting the most important factor."

"What in the world do you mean? — I am forgetting nothing. . . . What factor do you mean?" she added with more impatience.

"It stands six foot odd high," replied Sir Andrew, quietly, "and hath name Percy Blakeney."

"I don't understand," she murmured.

"Do you think that Blakeney would leave Calais without having accomplished what he set out to do?"

"You mean . . . ?"

"There's the old Comte de Tournay . . ."

"The Comte . . . ?" she murmured.

"And St. Just . . . and others . . ."

"My brother!" she said with a heart-broken sob of anguish. "Heaven help me, but I fear I had forgotten."

"Fugitives as they are, these men at this moment await with perfect confidence and unshaken faith the arrival of the Scarlet Pimpernel, who has pledged his honour to take them safely across the Channel."

Indeed, she had forgotten! With the sublime selfishness of a woman who loves with her whole heart, she had in the last twenty-four hours had no thought save for him. His precious, noble life, his danger — he, the loved one, the brave hero, he alone dwelt in her mind.

"My brother!" she murmured, as one by one the heavy tears gathered in her eyes, as memory came back to her of Armand, the companion and darling of her childhood, the man for whom she had committed the deadly sin, which had so hopelessly imperilled her brave husband's life.

"Sir Percy Blakeney would not be the trusted, honoured leader of a score of English gentlemen," said Sir Andrew, proudly, "if he abandoned those who placed their trust in him. As for breaking his word, the very thought is preposterous!"

There was silence for a moment or two. Marguerite had buried her face in her hands, and was letting the tears slowly trickle through her trembling fingers. The young man said nothing;

his heart ached for this beautiful woman in her awful grief. All along he had felt the terrible IMPASSE in which her own rash act had plunged them all. He knew his friend and leader so well, with his reckless daring, his mad bravery, his worship of his own word of honour. Sir Andrew knew that Blakeney would brave any danger, run the wildest risks sooner than break it, and with Chauvelin at his very heels, would make a final attempt, however desperate, to rescue those who trusted in him.

"Faith, Sir Andrew," said Marguerite at last, making brave efforts to dry her tears, "you are right, and I would not now shame myself by trying to dissuade him from doing his duty. As you say, I should plead in vain. God grant him strength and ability," she added fervently and resolutely, "to outwit his pursuers. He will not refuse to take you with him, perhaps, when he starts on his noble work; between you, you will have cunning as well as valour! God guard you both! In the meanwhile I think we should lose no time. I still believe that his safety depends upon his knowing that Chauvelin is on his track."

"Undoubtedly. He has wonderful resources at his command. As soon as he is aware of his danger he will exercise more caution: his ingenuity is a veritable miracle."

"Then, what say you to a voyage of reconnaissance in the village whilst I wait here against his coming! — You might come across Percy's track and thus save valuable time. If you find him, tell him to beware! — his bitterest enemy is on his heels!"

"But this is such a villainous hole for you to wait in."

"Nay, that I do not mind! — But you might ask our surly host if he could let me wait in another room, where I could be safer from the prying eyes of any chance traveller. Offer him some ready money, so that he should not fail to give me word the moment the tall Englishman returns."

She spoke quite calmly, even cheerfully now, thinking out her plans, ready for the worst if need be; she would show no more weakness, she would prove herself worthy of him, who was about to give his life for the sake of his fellow-men.

Sir Andrew obeyed her without further comment. Instinctively he felt that hers now was the stronger mind; he was willing to give himself over to her guidance, to become the hand, whilst she was the directing hand.

He went to the door of the inner room, through which Brogard and his wife had disappeared before, and knocked; as usual, he was answered by a salvo of muttered oaths.

"Hey! friend Brogard!" said the man peremptorily, "my lady friend would wish to rest here awhile. Could you give her the use of another room? She would wish to be alone."

He took some money out of his pocket, and allowed it to jingle significantly in his hand. Brogard had opened the door, and listened, with his usual surly apathy, to the young man's request. At the sight of the gold, however, his lazy attitude relaxed slightly; he took his pipe from his mouth and shuffled into the room.

He then pointed over his shoulder at the attic up in the wall.

"She can wait up there!" he said with a grunt. "It's comfortable, and I have no other room."

"Nothing could be better," said Marguerite in English; she at once realised the advantages such a position hidden from view would give her. "Give him the money, Sir Andrew; I shall be quite happy up there, and can see everything without being seen."

She nodded to Brogard, who condescended to go up to the attic, and to shake up the straw that lay on the floor.

"May I entreat you, madam, to do nothing rash," said Sir Andrew, as Marguerite prepared in her turn to ascend the rickety flight of steps. "Remember this place is infested with spies. Do not, I beg of you, reveal yourself to Sir Percy, unless you are absolutely certain that you are alone with him."

Even as he spoke, he felt how unnecessary was this caution: Marguerite was as calm, as clear-headed as any man. There was no fear of her doing anything that was rash.

"Nay," she said with a slight attempt at cheerfulness, "that I can faithfully promise you. I would not jeopardise my husband's life, nor yet his plans, by speaking to him before strangers.

Have no fear, I will watch my opportunity, and serve him in the manner I think he needs it most."

Brogard had come down the steps again, and Marguerite was ready to go up to her safe retreat.

"I dare not kiss your hand, madam," said Sir Andrew, as she began to mount the steps, "since I am your lacquey, but I pray you be of good cheer. If I do not come across Blakeney in half an hour, I shall return, expecting to find him here."

"Yes, that will be best. We can afford to wait for half an hour. Chauvelin cannot possibly be here before that. God grant that either you or I may have seen Percy by then. Good luck to you, friend! Have no fear for me."

Lightly she mounted the rickety wooden steps that led to the attic. Brogard was taking no further heed of her. She could make herself comfortable there or not as she chose. Sir Andrew watched her until she had reached the curtains across, and the young man noted that she was singularly well placed there, for seeing and hearing, whilst remaining unobserved.

He had paid Brogard well; the surly old innkeeper would have no object in betraying her. Then Sir Andrew prepared to go. At the door he turned once again and looked up at the loft. Through the ragged curtains Marguerite's sweet face was peeping down at him, and the young man rejoiced to see that it looked serene, and even gently smiling. With a final nod of farewell to her, he walked out into the night.

CHAPTER XXIV
THE DEATH-TRAP

The next quarter of an hour went by swiftly and noiselessly. In the room downstairs, Brogard had for a while busied himself with clearing the table, and re-arranging it for another guest.

It was because she watched these preparations that Marguerite found the time slipping by more pleasantly. It was for Percy that this semblance of supper was being got ready. Evidently Brogard had a certain amount of respect for the tall Englishman, as he seemed to take some trouble in making the place look a trifle less uninviting than it had done before.

He even produced, from some hidden recess in the old dresser, what actually looked like a table-cloth; and when he spread it out, and saw it was full of holes, he shook his head dubiously for a while, then was at much pains so to spread it over the table as to hide most of its blemishes.

Then he got out a serviette, also old and ragged, but possessing some measure of cleanliness, and with this he carefully wiped the glasses, spoons and plates, which he put on the table.

Marguerite could not help smiling to herself as she watched all these preparations, which Brogard accomplished to an accompaniment of muttered oaths. Clearly the great height and bulk of the Englishman, or perhaps the weight of his fist, had overawed this free-born citizen of France, or he would never have been at such trouble for any SACRRE ARISTO.

When the table was set — such as it was — Brogard surveyed it with evident satisfaction. He then dusted one of the chairs with the corner of his blouse, gave a stir to the stock-pot, threw a fresh bundle of faggots on to the fire, and slouched out of the room.

Marguerite was left alone with her reflections. She had spread her travelling cloak over the straw, and was sitting fairly comfortably, as the straw was fresh, and the evil odours from below came up to her only in a modified form.

But, momentarily, she was almost happy; happy because, when she peeped through the tattered curtains, she could see a rickety chair, a torn table-cloth, a glass, a plate and a spoon; that was all. But those mute and ugly things seemed to say to her that they were waiting for Percy; that soon, very soon, he would be here, that the squalid room being still empty, they would be alone together.

That thought was so heavenly, that Marguerite closed her eyes in order to shut out everything but that. In a few minutes she would be alone with him; she would run down the ladder, and let him see her; then he would take her in his arms, and she would let him see that, after that, she would gladly die for him, and with him, for earth could hold no greater happiness than that.

And then what would happen? She could not even remotely conjecture. She knew, of course, that Sir Andrew was right, that Percy would do everything he had set out to accomplish; that she — now she was here — could do nothing, beyond warning him to be cautious, since Chauvelin himself was on his track. After having cautioned him, she would perforce have to see him go off upon the terrible and daring mission; she could not even with a word or look, attempt to keep him back. She would have to obey, whatever he told her to do, even perhaps have to efface herself, and wait, in indescribable agony, whilst he, perhaps, went to his death.

But even that seemed less terrible to bear than the thought that he should never know how much she loved him — that at any rate would be spared her; the squalid room itself, which seemed to be waiting for him, told her that he would be here soon.

Suddenly her over-sensitive ears caught the sound of distant footsteps drawing near; her heart gave a wild leap of joy! Was it Percy at last? No! the step did not seem quite as long, nor quite as firm as his; she also thought that she could hear two distinct sets of footsteps. Yes! that was it! two men were coming this way. Two strangers perhaps, to get a drink, or . . .

But she had not time to conjecture, for presently there was a peremptory call at the door, and the next moment it was violently open from the outside, whilst a rough, commanding voice shouted, —

"Hey! Citoyen Brogard! Hola!"

Marguerite could not see the newcomers, but, through a hole in one of the curtains, she could observe one portion of the room below.

She heard Brogard's shuffling footsteps, as he came out of the inner room, muttering his usual string of oaths. On seeing the strangers, however, he paused in the middle of the room, well within range of Marguerite's vision, looked at them, with even more withering contempt than he had bestowed upon his former guests, and muttered, "SACRRREE SOUTANE!"

Marguerite's heart seemed all at once to stop beating; her eyes, large and dilated, had fastened on one of the newcomers, who, at this point, had taken a quick step forward towards Brogard. He was dressed in the soutane, broad-brimmed hat and buckled shoes habitual to the French CURE, but as he stood opposite the innkeeper, he threw open his soutane for a moment, displaying the tri-colour scarf of officialism, which sight immediately had the effect of transforming Brogard's attitude of contempt, into one of cringing obsequiousness.

It was the sight of this French CURE, which seemed to freeze the very blood in Marguerite's veins. She could not see his face, which was shaded by his broad-brimmed hat, but she recognized the thin, bony hands, the slight stoop, the whole gait of the man! It was Chauvelin!

The horror of the situation struck her as with a physical blow; the awful disappointment, the dread of what was to come, made her very senses reel, and she needed almost superhuman effort, not to fall senseless beneath it all.

"A plate of soup and a bottle of wine," said Chauvelin imperiously to Brogard, "then clear out of here — understand? I want to be alone."

Silently, and without any muttering this time, Brogard obeyed. Chauvelin sat down at the table, which had been prepared for the tall Englishman, and the innkeeper busied himself obsequiously round him, dishing up the soup and pouring out the wine. The man who had entered with Chauvelin and whom Marguerite could not see, stood waiting close by the door.

At a brusque sign from Chauvelin, Brogard had hurried back to the inner room, and the former now beckoned to the man who had accompanied him.

In him Marguerite at once recognised Desgas, Chauvelin's secretary and confidential factotum, whom she had often seen in Paris, in days gone by. He crossed the room, and for a moment or two listened attentively at the Brogards' door. "Not listening?" asked Chauvelin, curtly.

"No, citoyen."

For a moment Marguerite dreaded lest Chauvelin should order Desgas to search the place; what would happen if she were to be discovered, she hardly dared to imagine. Fortunately, however, Chauvelin seemed more impatient to talk to his secretary than afraid of spies, for he called Desgas quickly back to his side.

"The English schooner?" he asked.

"She was lost sight of at sundown, citoyen," replied Desgas, "but was then making west, towards Cap Gris Nez."

"Ah! — good! — " muttered Chauvelin, "and now, about Captain Jutley? — what did he say?"

"He assured me that all the orders you sent him last week have been implicitly obeyed. All the roads which converge to this place have been patrolled night and day ever since: and the beach and cliffs have been most rigorously searched and guarded."

"Does he know where this 'Pere Blanchard's' hut is?"

"No, citoyen, nobody seems to know of it by that name. There are any amount of fisherman's huts all along the course . . . but . . ."

"That'll do. Now about tonight?" interrupted Chauvelin, impatiently.

"The roads and the beach are patrolled as usual, citoyen, and Captain Jutley awaits further orders."

"Go back to him at once, then. Tell him to send reinforcements to the various patrols; and especially to those along the beach — you understand?"

Chauvelin spoke curtly and to the point, and every word he uttered struck at Marguerite's heart like the death-knell of her fondest hopes.

"The men," he continued, "are to keep the sharpest possible look-out for any stranger who may be walking, riding, or driving, along the road or the beach, more especially for a tall stranger, whom I need not describe further, as probably he will be disguised; but he cannot very well conceal his height, except by stooping. You understand?"

"Perfectly, citoyen," replied Desgas.

"As soon as any of the men have sighted a stranger, two of them are to keep him in view. The man who loses sight of the tall stranger, after he is once seen, will pay for his negligence with his life; but one man is to ride straight back here and report to me. Is that clear?"

"Absolutely clear, citoyen."

"Very well, then. Go and see Jutley at once. See the reinforcements start off for the patrol duty, then ask the captain to let you have a half-a-dozen more men and bring them here with you. You can be back in ten minutes. Go — "

Desgas saluted and went to the door.

As Marguerite, sick with horror, listened to Chauvelin's directions to his underling, the whole of the plan for the capture of the Scarlet Pimpernel became appallingly clear to her. Chauvelin wished that the fugitives should be left in false security waiting in their hidden retreat until Percy joined them. Then the daring plotter was to be surrounded and caught red-handed, in the very act of aiding and abetting royalists, who were traitors to the republic. Thus, if his capture were noised abroad, even the British Government could not legally protest in his favour; having plotted with the enemies of the French Government, France had the right to put him to death.

Escape for him and them would be impossible. All the roads patrolled and watched, the trap well set, the net, wide at present, but drawing together tighter and tighter, until it closed upon the daring plotter, whose superhuman cunning even could not rescue him from its meshes now.

Desgas was about to go, but Chauvelin once more called him back. Marguerite vaguely wondered what further devilish plans he could have formed, in order to entrap one brave man, alone, against two-score of others. She looked at him as he turned to speak to Desgas; she could just see his face beneath the broad-brimmed, CURES'S hat. There was at that moment so much deadly hatred, such fiendish malice in the thin face and pale, small eyes, that Marguerite's last hope died in her heart, for she felt that from this man she could expect no mercy.

"I had forgotten," repeated Chauvelin, with a weird chuckle, as he rubbed his bony, talon-like hands one against the other, with a gesture of fiendish satisfaction. "The tall stranger may show fight. In any case no shooting, remember, except as a last resort. I want that tall stranger alive . . . if possible."

He laughed, as Dante has told us that the devils laugh at the sight of the torture of the damned. Marguerite had thought that by now she had lived through the whole gamut of horror and anguish that human heart could bear; yet now, when Desgas left the house, and she remained alone in this lonely, squalid room, with that fiend for company, she felt as if all that she had suffered was nothing compared with this. He continued to laugh and chuckle to himself for awhile, rubbing his hands together in anticipation of his triumph.

His plans were well laid, and he might well triumph! Not a loophole was left, through which the bravest, the most cunning man might escape. Every road guarded, every corner watched, and in that lonely hut somewhere on the coast, a small band of fugitives waiting for their rescuer, and leading him to his death — nay! to worse than death. That fiend there, in a holy man's garb, was too much of a devil to allow a brave man to die the quick, sudden death of a soldier at the post of duty.

He, above all, longed to have the cunning enemy, who had so long baffled him, helpless in his power; he wished to gloat over him, to enjoy his downfall, to inflict upon him what moral and mental torture a deadly hatred alone can devise. The brave eagle, captured, and with noble wings clipped, was doomed to endure the gnawing of the rat. And she, his wife, who loved him, and who had brought him to this, could do nothing to help him.

Nothing, save to hope for death by his side, and for one brief moment in which to tell him that her love — whole, true and passionate — was entirely his.

Chauvelin was now sitting close to the table; he had taken off his hat, and Marguerite could just see the outline of his thin profile and pointed chin, as he bent over his meagre supper. He was evidently quite contented, and awaited events with perfect calm; he even seemed to enjoy Brogard's unsavoury fare. Marguerite wondered how so much hatred could lurk in one human being against another.

Suddenly, as she watched Chauvelin, a sound caught her ear, which turned her very heart to stone. And yet that sound was not calculated to inspire anyone with horror, for it was merely the cheerful sound of a gay, fresh voice singing lustily, "God save the King!"

Marguerite's breath stopped short; she seemed to feel her very life standing still momentarily whilst she listened to that voice and to that song. In the singer she had recognised her husband. Chauvelin, too, had heard it, for he darted a quick glance towards the door, then hurriedly took up his broad-brimmed hat and clapped it over his head.

The voice drew nearer; for one brief second the wild desire seized Marguerite to rush down the steps and fly across the room, to stop that song at any cost, to beg the cheerful singer to fly — fly for his life, before it be too late. She checked the impulse just in time. Chauvelin would stop her before she reached the door, and, moreover, she had no idea if he had any soldiers posted within his call. Her impetuous act might prove the death-signal of the man she would have died to save.

"Long to reign over us, God save the King!"

sang the voice more lustily than ever. The next moment the door was thrown open and there was dead silence for a second or so.

Marguerite could not see the door; she held her breath, trying to imagine what was happening.

Percy Blakeney on entering had, of course, at once caught sight of the CURE at the table; his hesitation lasted less than five seconds, the next moment, Marguerite saw his tall figure crossing the room, whilst he called in a loud, cheerful voice, —

"Hello, there! no one about? Where's that fool Brogard?"

He wore the magnificent coat and riding-suit which he had on when Marguerite last saw him at Richmond, so many hours ago. As usual, his get-up was absolutely irreproachable, the fine Mechlin lace at his neck and wrists were immaculate and white, his fair hair was carefully brushed, and he carried his eyeglass with his usual affected gesture. In fact, at this moment, Sir Percy Blakeney, Bart., might have been on his way to a garden-party at the Prince of Wales', instead of deliberately, cold-bloodedly running his head in a trap, set for him by his deadliest enemy.

He stood for a moment in the middle of the room, whilst Marguerite, absolutely paralysed with horror, seemed unable even to breathe.

Every moment she expected that Chauvelin would give a signal, that the place would fill with soldiers, that she would rush down and help Percy to sell his life dearly. As he stood there, suavely unconscious, she very nearly screamed out to him, —

"Fly, Percy! — 'tis your deadly enemy! — fly before it be too late!"

But she had not time even to do that, for the next moment Blakeney quietly walked to the table, and, jovially clapped the CURE on the back, said in his own drawly, affected way, —

"Odds's fish! . . . er . . . M. Chauvelin. . . . I vow I never thought of meeting you here."

Chauvelin, who had been in the very act of conveying soup to his mouth, fairly choked. His thin face became absolutely purple, and a violent fit of coughing saved this cunning representative of France from betraying the most boundless surprise he had ever experienced. There was no doubt that this bold move on the part of the enemy had been wholly unexpected, as far as he was concerned: and the daring impudence of it completely nonplussed him for the moment.

Obviously he had not taken the precaution of having the inn surrounded with soldiers. Blakeney had evidently guessed that much, and no doubt his resourceful brain had already formed some plan by which he could turn this unexpected interview to account.

Marguerite up in the loft had not moved. She had made a solemn promise to Sir Andrew not to speak to her husband before strangers, and she had sufficient self-control not to throw herself unreasoningly and impulsively across his plans. To sit still and watch these two men together was a terrible trial of fortitude. Marguerite had heard Chauvelin give the orders for the patrolling of all the roads. She knew that if Percy now left the "Chat Gris" — in whatever direction he happened to go — he could not go far without being sighted by some of Captain

Jutley's men on patrol. On the other hand, if he stayed, then Desgas would have time to come back with the dozen men Chauvelin had specially ordered.

The trap was closing in, and Marguerite could do nothing but watch and wonder. The two men looked such a strange contrast, and of the two it was Chauvelin who exhibited a slight touch of fear. Marguerite knew him well enough to guess what was passing in his mind. He had no fear for his own person, although he certainly was alone in a lonely inn with a man who was powerfully built, and who was daring and reckless beyond the bounds of probability. She knew that Chauvelin would willingly have braved perilous encounters for the sake of the cause he had at heart, but what he did fear was that this impudent Englishman would, by knocking him down, double his own chances of escape; his underlings might not succeed so well in capturing the Scarlet Pimpernel, when not directed by the cunning hand and the shrewd brain, which had deadly hate for an incentive.

Evidently, however, the representative of the French Government had nothing to fear for the moment, at the hands of his powerful adversary. Blakeney, with his most inane laugh and pleasant good-nature, was solemnly patting him on the back.

"I am so demmed sorry . . ." he was saying cheerfully, "so very sorry . . . I seem to have upset you . . . eating soup, too . . . nasty, awkward thing, soup . . . er . . . Begad! — a friend of mine died once . . . er . . . choked . . . just like you . . . with a spoonful of soup."

And he smiled shyly, good-humouredly, down at Chauvelin.

"Odd's life!" he continued, as soon as the latter had somewhat recovered himself, "beastly hole this . . . ain't it now? La! you don't mind?" he added, apologetically, as he sat down on a chair close to the table and drew the soup tureen towards him. "That fool Brogard seems to be asleep or something."

There was a second plate on the table, and he calmly helped himself to soup, then poured himself out a glass of wine.

For a moment Marguerite wondered what Chauvelin would do. His disguise was so good that perhaps he meant, on recovering himself, to deny his identity: but Chauvelin was too astute to make such an obviously false and childish move, and already he too had stretched out his hand and said pleasantly, —

"I am indeed charmed to see you Sir Percy. You must excuse me — h'm — I thought you the other side of the Channel. Sudden surprise almost took my breath away."

"La!" said Sir Percy, with a good-humoured grin, "it did that quite, didn't it — er — M. — er — Chaubertin?"

"Pardon me — Chauvelin."

"I beg pardon — a thousand times. Yes — Chauvelin of course. . . . Er . . . I never could cotton to foreign names. . . ."

He was calmly eating his soup, laughing with pleasant good-humour, as if he had come all the way to Calais for the express purpose of enjoying supper at this filthy inn, in the company of his arch-enemy.

For the moment Marguerite wondered why Percy did not knock the little Frenchman down then and there — and no doubt something of the sort must have darted through his mind, for every now and then his lazy eyes seemed to flash ominously, as they rested on the slight figure of Chauvelin, who had now quite recovered himself and was also calmly eating his soup.

But the keen brain, which had planned and carried through so many daring plots, was too far-seeing to take unnecessary risks. This place, after all, might be infested with spies; the innkeeper might be in Chauvelin's pay. One call on Chauvelin's part might bring twenty men about Blakeney's ears for aught he knew, and he might be caught and trapped before he could help, or, at least, warn the fugitives. This he would not risk; he meant to help the others, to get THEM safely away; for he had pledged his word to them, and his word he WOULD keep. And whilst he ate and chatted, he thought and planned, whilst, up in the loft, the poor, anxious woman racked her brain as to what she should do, and endured agonies of longing to rush down to him, yet not daring to move for fear of upsetting his plans.

"I didn't know," Blakeney was saying jovially, "that you . . . er . . . were in holy orders."

"I . . . er . . . hem . . ." stammered Chauvelin. The calm impudence of his antagonist had evidently thrown him off his usual balance.

"But, la! I should have known you anywhere," continued Sir Percy, placidly, as he poured himself out another glass of wine, "although the wig and hat have changed you a bit."

"Do you think so?"

"Lud! they alter a man so . . . but . . . begad! I hope you don't mind my having made the remark? . . . Demmed bad form making remarks. . . . I hope you don't mind?"

"No, no, not at all — hem! I hope Lady Blakeney is well," said Chauvelin, hurriedly changing the topic of conversation.

Blakeney, with much deliberation, finished his plate of soup, drank his glass of wine, and, momentarily, it seemed to Marguerite as if he glanced all round the room. "Quite well, thank you," he said at last, drily. There was a pause, during which Marguerite could watch these two antagonists who, evidently in their minds, were measuring themselves against one another. She could see Percy almost full face where he sat at the table not ten yards from where she herself was crouching, puzzled, not knowing what to do, or what she should think. She had quite controlled her impulse now of rushing down and disclosing herself to her husband. A man capable of acting a part, in the way he was doing at the present moment, did not need a woman's word to warn him to be cautious.

Marguerite indulged in the luxury, dear to every tender woman's heart, of looking at the man she loved. She looked through the tattered curtain, across at the handsome face of her husband, in whose lazy blue eyes, and behind whose inane smile, she could now so plainly see the strength, energy, and resourcefulness which had caused the Scarlet Pimpernel to be reverenced and trusted by his followers. "There are nineteen of us ready to lay down our lives for your husband, Lady Blakeney," Sir Andrew had said to her; and as she looked at the forehead, low, but square and broad, the eyes, blue, yet deep-set and intense, the whole aspect of the man, of indomitable energy, hiding, behind a perfectly acted comedy, his almost superhuman strength of will and marvellous ingenuity, she understood the fascination which he exercised over his followers, for had he not also cast his spells over her heart and her imagination?

Chauvelin, who was trying to conceal his impatience beneath his usual urbane manner, took a quick look at his watch. Desgas should not be long: another two or three minutes, and this impudent Englishman would be secure in the keeping of half a dozen of Captain Jutley's most trusted men.

"You are on your way to Paris, Sir Percy?" he asked carelessly.

"Odd's life, no," replied Blakeney, with a laugh. "Only as far as Lille — not Paris for me . . . beastly uncomfortable place Paris, just now . . . eh, Monsieur Chaubertin . . . beg pardon . . . Chauvelin!"

"Not for an English gentleman like yourself, Sir Percy," rejoined Chauvelin, sarcastically, "who takes no interest in the conflict that is raging there."

"La! you see it's no business of mine, and our demmed government is all on your side of the business. Old Pitt daren't say 'Bo' to a goose. You are in a hurry, sir," he added, as Chauvelin once again took out his watch; "an appointment, perhaps. . . . I pray you take no heed of me. . . . My time's my own."

He rose from the table and dragged a chair to the hearth. Once more Marguerite was terribly tempted to go to him, for time was getting on; Desgas might be back at any moment with his men. Percy did not know that and . . . oh! how horrible it all was — and how helpless she felt.

"I am in no hurry," continued Percy, pleasantly, "but, la! I don't want to spend any more time than I can help in this God-forsaken hole! But, begad! sir," he added, as Chauvelin had surreptitiously looked at his watch for the third time, "that watch of yours won't go any faster for all the looking you give it. You are expecting a friend, maybe?"

"Aye — a friend!"

"Not a lady — I trust, Monsieur l'Abbe," laughed Blakeney; "surely the holy church does not allow? . . . eh? . . . what! But, I say, come by the fire . . . it's getting demmed cold."

He kicked the fire with the heel of his boot, making the logs blaze in the old hearth. He seemed in no hurry to go, and apparently was quite unconscious of his immediate danger. He dragged another chair to the fire, and Chauvelin, whose impatience was by now quite beyond control, sat down beside the hearth, in such a way as to command a view of the door. Desgas had been gone nearly a quarter of an hour. It was quite plain to Marguerite's aching senses that as soon as he arrived, Chauvelin would abandon all his other plans with regard to the fugitives, and capture this impudent Scarlet Pimpernel at once.

"Hey, M. Chauvelin," the latter was saying airily, "tell me, I pray you, is your friend pretty? Demmed smart these little French women sometimes — what? But I protest I need not ask," he added, as he carelessly strode back towards the supper-table. "In matters of taste the Church has never been backward. . . . Eh?"

But Chauvelin was not listening. His every faculty was now concentrated on that door through which presently Desgas would enter. Marguerite's thoughts, too, were centered there, for her ears had suddenly caught, through the stillness of the night, the sound of numerous and measured treads some distance away.

It was Desgas and his men. Another three minutes and they would be here! Another three minutes and the awful thing would have occurred: the brave eagle would have fallen in the ferret's trap! She would have moved now and screamed, but she dared not; for whilst she heard the soldiers approaching, she was looking at Percy and watching his every movement. He was standing by the table whereon the remnants of the supper, plates, glasses, spoons, salt and pepper-pots were scattered pell-mell. His back was turned to Chauvelin and he was still prattling along in his own affected and inane way, but from his pocket he had taken his snuff-box, and quickly and suddenly he emptied the contents of the pepper-pot into it.

Then he again turned with an inane laugh to Chauvelin, —

"Eh? Did you speak, sir?"

Chauvelin had been too intent on listening to the sound of those approaching footsteps, to notice what his cunning adversary had been doing. He now pulled himself together, trying to look unconcerned in the very midst of his anticipated triumph. "No," he said presently, "that is — as you were saying, Sir Percy — ?"

"I was saying," said Blakeney, going up to Chauvelin, by the fire, "that the Jew in Piccadilly has sold me better snuff this time than I have ever tasted. Will you honour me, Monsieur l'Abbe?"

He stood close to Chauvelin in his own careless, DEBONNAIRE way, holding out his snuff-box to his arch-enemy.

Chauvelin, who, as he told Marguerite once, had seen a trick or two in his day, had never dreamed of this one. With one ear fixed on those fast-approaching footsteps, one eye turned to that door where Desgas and his men would presently appear, lulled into false security by the impudent Englishman's airy manner, he never even remotely guessed the trick which was being played upon him.

He took a pinch of snuff.

Only he, who has ever by accident sniffed vigorously a dose of pepper, can have the faintest conception of the hopeless condition in which such a sniff would reduce any human being.

Chauvelin felt as if his head would burst — sneeze after sneeze seemed nearly to choke him; he was blind, deaf, and dumb for the moment, and during that moment Blakeney quietly, without the slightest haste, took up his hat, took some money out of his pocket, which he left on the table, then calmly stalked out of the room!

CHAPTER XXVI
THE JEW

It took Marguerite some time to collect her scattered senses; the whole of this last short episode had taken place in less than a minute, and Desgas and the soldiers were still about two hundred yards away from the "Chat Gris."

When she realised what had happened, a curious mixture of joy and wonder filled her heart. It all was so neat, so ingenious. Chauvelin was still absolutely helpless, far more so than he could even have been under a blow from the fist, for now he could neither see, nor hear, nor speak, whilst his cunning adversary had quietly slipped through his fingers.

Blakeney was gone, obviously to try and join the fugitives at the Pere Blanchard's hut. For the moment, true, Chauvelin was helpless; for the moment the daring Scarlet Pimpernel had not been caught by Desgas and his men. But all the roads and the beach were patrolled. Every place was watched, and every stranger kept in sight. How far could Percy go, thus arrayed in his gorgeous clothes, without being sighted and followed? Now she blamed herself terribly for not having gone down to him sooner, and given him that word of warning and of love which, perhaps, after all, he needed. He could not know of the orders which Chauvelin had given for his capture, and even now, perhaps . . .

But before all these horrible thoughts had taken concrete form in her brain, she heard the grounding of arms outside, close to the door, and Desgas' voice shouting "Halt!" to his men.

Chauvelin had partially recovered; his sneezing had become less violent, and he had struggled to his feet. He managed to reach the door just as Desgas' knock was heard on the outside.

Chauvelin threw open the door, and before his secretary could say a word, he had managed to stammer between two sneezes —

"The tall stranger — quick! — did any of you see him?"

"Where, citoyen?" asked Desgas, in surprise.

"Here, man! through that door! not five minutes ago."

"We saw nothing, citoyen! The moon is not yet up, and . . ."

"And you are just five minutes too late, my friend," said Chauvelin, with concentrated fury.

"Citoyen . . . I . . ."

"You did what I ordered you to do," said Chauvelin, with impatience. "I know that, but you were a precious long time about it. Fortunately, there's not much harm done, or it had fared ill with you, Citoyen Desgas."

Desgas turned a little pale. There was so much rage and hatred in his superior's whole attitude.

"The tall stranger, citoyen — " he stammered.

"Was here, in this room, five minutes ago, having supper at that table. Damn his impudence! For obvious reasons, I dared not tackle him alone. Brogard is too big a fool, and that cursed Englishman appears to have the strength of a bullock, and so he slipped away under your very nose."

"He cannot go far without being sighted, citoyen."

"Ah?"

"Captain Jutley sent forty men as reinforcements for the patrol duty: twenty went down to the beach. He again assured me that the watch had been constant all day, and that no stranger could possibly get to the beach, or reach a boat, without being sighted."

"That's good. — Do the men know their work?"

"They have had very clear orders, citoyen: and I myself spoke to those who were about to start. They are to shadow — as secretly as possible — any stranger they may see, especially if he be tall, or stoop as if he would disguise his height."

"In no case to detain such a person, of course," said Chauvelin, eagerly. "That impudent Scarlet Pimpernel would slip through clumsy fingers. We must let him get to the Pere Blanchard's hut now; there surround and capture him."

"The men understand that, citoyen, and also that, as soon as a tall stranger has been sighted, he must be shadowed, whilst one man is to turn straight back and report to you."

"That is right," said Chauvelin, rubbing his hands, well pleased.

"I have further news for you, citoyen."

"What is it?"

"A tall Englishman had a long conversation about three-quarters of an hour ago with a Jew, Reuben by name, who lives not ten paces from here."

"Yes — and?" queried Chauvelin, impatiently.

"The conversation was all about a horse and cart, which the tall Englishman wished to hire, and which was to have been ready for him by eleven o'clock."

"It is past that now. Where does that Reuben live?"

"A few minutes' walk from this door."

"Send one of the men to find out if the stranger has driven off in Reuben's cart."

"Yes, citoyen."

Desgas went to give the necessary orders to one of the men. Not a word of this conversation between him and Chauvelin had escaped Marguerite, and every word they had spoken seemed to strike at her heart, with terrible hopelessness and dark foreboding.

She had come all this way, and with such high hopes and firm determination to help her husband, and so far she had been able to do nothing, but to watch, with a heart breaking with anguish, the meshes of the deadly net closing round the daring Scarlet Pimpernel.

He could not now advance many steps, without spying eyes to track and denounce him. Her own helplessness struck her with the terrible sense of utter disappointment. The possibility of being the slightest use to her husband had become almost NIL, and her only hope rested in being allowed to share his fate, whatever it might ultimately be.

For the moment, even her chance of ever seeing the man she loved again, had become a remote one. Still, she was determined to keep a close watch over his enemy, and a vague hope filled her heart, that whilst she kept Chauvelin in sight, Percy's fate might still be hanging in the balance.

Desgas left Chauvelin moodily pacing up and down the room, whilst he himself waited outside for the return of the man whom he had sent in search of Reuben. Thus several minutes went by. Chauvelin was evidently devoured with impatience. Apparently he trusted no one: this last trick played upon him by the daring Scarlet Pimpernel had made him suddenly doubtful of success, unless he himself was there to watch, direct and superintend the capture of this impudent Englishman.

About five minutes later, Desgas returned, followed by an elderly Jew, in a dirty, threadbare gaberdine, worn greasy across the shoulders. His red hair, which he wore after the fashion of the Polish Jews, with the corkscrew curls each side of his face, was plentifully sprinkled with grey — a general coating of grime, about his cheeks and his chin, gave him a peculiarly dirty and loathsome appearance. He had the habitual stoop, those of his race affected in mock humility in past centuries, before the dawn of equality and freedom in matters of faith, and he walked behind Desgas with the peculiar shuffling gait which has remained the characteristic of the Jew trader in continental Europe to this day.

Chauvelin, who had all the Frenchman's prejudice against the despised race, motioned to the fellow to keep at a respectful distance. The group of the three men were standing just underneath the hanging oil-lamp, and Marguerite had a clear view of them all.

"Is this the man?" asked Chauvelin.

"No, citoyen," replied Desgas, "Reuben could not be found, so presumably his cart has gone with the stranger; but this man here seems to know something, which he is willing to sell for a consideration."

"Ah!" said Chauvelin, turning away with disgust from the loathsome specimen of humanity before him.

The Jew, with characteristic patience, stood humbly on one side, leaning on the knotted staff, his greasy, broad-brimmed hat casting a deep shadow over his grimy face, waiting for the noble Excellency to deign to put some questions to him.

"The citoyen tells me," said Chauvelin peremptorily to him, "that you know something of my friend, the tall Englishman, whom I desire to meet . . . MORBLEU! keep your distance, man," he added hurriedly, as the Jew took a quick and eager step forward.

"Yes, your Excellency," replied the Jew, who spoke the language with that peculiar lisp which denotes Eastern origin, "I and Reuben Goldstein met a tall Englishman, on the road, close by here this evening."

"Did you speak to him?"

"He spoke to us, your Excellency. He wanted to know if he could hire a horse and cart to go down along the St. Martin road, to a place he wanted to reach to-night."

"What did you say?"

"I did not say anything," said the Jew in an injured tone, "Reuben Goldstein, that accursed traitor, that son of Belial . . ."

"Cut that short, man," interrupted Chauvelin, roughly, "and go on with your story."

"He took the words out of my mouth, your Excellency: when I was about to offer the wealthy Englishman my horse and cart, to take him wheresoever he chose, Reuben had already spoken, and offered his half-starved nag, and his broken-down cart."

"And what did the Englishman do?"

"He listened to Reuben Goldstein, your Excellency, and put his hand in his pocket then and there, and took out a handful of gold, which he showed to that descendant of Beelzebub, telling him that all that would be his, if the horse and cart were ready for him by eleven o'clock."

"And, of course, the horse and cart were ready?"

"Well! they were ready for him in a manner, so to speak, your Excellency. Reuben's nag was lame as usual; she refused to budge at first. It was only after a time and with plenty of kicks, that she at last could be made to move," said the Jew with a malicious chuckle.

"Then they started?"

"Yes, they started about five minutes ago. I was disgusted with that stranger's folly. An Englishman too! — He ought to have known Reuben's nag was not fit to drive."

"But if he had no choice?"

"No choice, your Excellency?" protested the Jew, in a rasping voice, "did I not repeat to him a dozen times, that my horse and cart would take him quicker, and more comfortably than Reuben's bag of bones. He would not listen. Reuben is such a liar, and has such insinuating ways. The stranger was deceived. If he was in a hurry, he would have had better value for his money by taking my cart."

"You have a horse and cart too, then?" asked Chauvelin, peremptorily.

"Aye! that I have, your Excellency, and if your Excellency wants to drive . . ."

"Do you happen to know which way my friend went in Reuben Goldstein's cart?"

Thoughtfully the Jew rubbed his dirty chin. Marguerite's heart was beating well-nigh to bursting. She had heard the peremptory question; she looked anxiously at the Jew, but could not read his face beneath the shadow of his broad-brimmed hat. Vaguely she felt somehow as if he held Percy's fate in his long dirty hands.

There was a long pause, whilst Chauvelin frowned impatiently at the stooping figure before him: at last the Jew slowly put his hand in his breast pocket, and drew out from its capacious depths a number of silver coins. He gazed at them thoughtfully, then remarked, in a quiet tone of voice, —

"This is what the tall stranger gave me, when he drove away with Reuben, for holding my tongue about him, and his doings."

Chauvelin shrugged his shoulders impatiently.

"How much is there there?" he asked.

"Twenty francs, your Excellency," replied the Jew, "and I have been an honest man all my life."

Chauvelin without further comment took a few pieces of gold out of his own pocket, and leaving them in the palm of his hand, he allowed them to jingle as he held them out towards the Jew.

"How many gold pieces are there in the palm of my hand?" he asked quietly.

Evidently he had no desire to terrorize the man, but to conciliate him, for his own purposes, for his manner was pleasant and suave. No doubt he feared that threats of the guillotine, and various other persuasive methods of that type, might addle the old man's brains, and that he would be more likely to be useful through greed of gain, than through terror of death.

The eyes of the Jew shot a quick, keen glance at the gold in his interlocutor's hand.

"At least five, I should say, your Excellency," he replied obsequiously.

"Enough, do you think, to loosen that honest tongue of yours?"

"What does your Excellency wish to know?"

"Whether your horse and cart can take me to where I can find my friend the tall stranger, who has driven off in Reuben Goldstein's cart?"

"My horse and cart can take your Honour there, where you please."

"To a place called the Pere Blanchard's hut?"

"Your Honour has guessed?" said the Jew in astonishment.

"You know the place? Which road leads to it?"

"The St. Martin Road, your Honour, then a footpath from there to the cliffs."

"You know the road?" repeated Chauvelin, roughly.

"Every stone, every blade of grass, your Honour," replied the Jew quietly.

Chauvelin without another word threw the five pieces of gold one by one before the Jew, who knelt down, and on his hands and knees struggled to collect them. One rolled away, and he had some trouble to get it, for it had lodged underneath the dresser. Chauvelin quietly waited while the old man scrambled on the floor, to find the piece of gold.

When the Jew was again on his feet, Chauvelin said, —

"How soon can your horse and cart be ready?"

"They are ready now, your Honour."

"Where?"

"Not ten meters from this door. Will your Excellency deign to look."

"I don't want to see it. How far can you drive me in it?"

"As far as the Pere Blanchard's hut, your Honour, and further than Reuben's nag took your friend. I am sure that, not two leagues from here, we shall come across that wily Reuben, his nag, his cart and the tall stranger all in a heap in the middle of the road."

"How far is the nearest village from here?"

"On the road which the Englishman took, Miquelon is the nearest village, not two leagues from here."

"There he could get fresh conveyance, if he wanted to go further?"

"He could — if he ever got so far."

"Can you?"

"Will your Excellency try?" said the Jew simply.

"That is my intention," said Chauvelin very quietly, "but remember, if you have deceived me, I shall tell off two of my most stalwart soldiers to give you such a beating, that your breath will perhaps leave your ugly body for ever. But if we find my friend the tall Englishman, either on the road or at the Pere Blanchard's hut, there will be ten more gold pieces for you. Do you accept the bargain?"

The Jew again thoughtfully rubbed his chin. He looked at the money in his hand, then at this stern interlocutor, and at Desgas, who had stood silently behind him all this while. After a moment's pause, he said deliberately, —

"I accept."

"Go and wait outside then," said Chauvelin, "and remember to stick to your bargain, or by Heaven, I will keep to mine."

With a final, most abject and cringing bow, the old Jew shuffled out of the room. Chauvelin seemed pleased with his interview, for he rubbed his hands together, with that usual gesture of his, of malignant satisfaction.

"My coat and boots," he said to Desgas at last.

Desgas went to the door, and apparently gave the necessary orders, for presently a soldier entered, carrying Chauvelin's coat, boots, and hat.

He took off his soutane, beneath which he was wearing close-fitting breeches and a cloth waistcoat, and began changing his attire.

"You, citoyen, in the meanwhile," he said to Desgas, "go back to Captain Jutley as fast as you can, and tell him to let you have another dozen men, and bring them with you along the St. Martin Road, where I daresay you will soon overtake the Jew's cart with myself in it. There will be hot work presently, if I mistake not, in the Pere Blanchard's hut. We shall corner our game there, I'll warrant, for this impudent Scarlet Pimpernel has had the audacity — or the stupidity, I hardly know which — to adhere to his original plans. He has gone to meet de Tournay, St. Just and the other traitors, which for the moment, I thought, perhaps, he did not intend to do. When we find them, there will be a band of desperate men at bay. Some of our men will, I presume, be put HORS DE COMBAT. These royalists are good swordsmen, and the Englishman is devilish cunning, and looks very powerful. Still, we shall be five against one at least. You can follow the cart closely with your men, all along the St. Martin Road, through Miquelon. The Englishman is ahead of us, and not likely to look behind him."

Whilst he gave these curt and concise orders, he had completed his change of attire. The priest's costume had been laid aside, and he was once more dressed in his usual dark, tight-fitting clothes. At last he took up his hat.

"I shall have an interesting prisoner to deliver into your hands," he said with a chuckle, as with unwonted familiarity he took Desgas' arm, and led him towards the door. "We won't kill him outright, eh, friend Desgas? The Pere Blanchard's hut is — an I mistake not — a lonely spot upon the beach, and our men will enjoy a bit of rough sport there with the wounded fox. Choose your men well, friend Desgas . . . of the sort who would enjoy that type of sport — eh? We must see that Scarlet Pimpernel wither a bit — what? — shrink and tremble, eh? . . . before we finally . . ." He made an expressive gesture, whilst he laughed a low, evil laugh, which filled Marguerite's soul with sickening horror.

"Choose your men well, Citoyen Desgas," he said once more, as he led his secretary finally out of the room.

Never for a moment did Marguerite Blakeney hesitate. The last sounds outside the "Chat Gris" had died away in the night. She had heard Desgas giving orders to his men, and then starting off towards the fort, to get a reinforcement of a dozen more men: six were not thought sufficient to capture the cunning Englishman, whose resourceful brain was even more dangerous than his valour and his strength.

Then a few minutes later, she heard the Jew's husky voice again, evidently shouting to his nag, then the rumble of wheels, and noise of a rickety cart bumping over the rough road.

Inside the inn, everything was still. Brogard and his wife, terrified of Chauvelin, had given no sign of life; they hoped to be forgotten, and at any rate to remain unperceived: Marguerite could not even hear their usual volleys of muttered oaths.

She waited a moment or two longer, then she quietly slipped down the broken stairs, wrapped her dark cloak closely round her and slipped out of the inn.

The night was fairly dark, sufficiently so at any rate to hide her dark figure from view, whilst her keen ears kept count of the sound of the cart going on ahead. She hoped by keeping well within the shadow of the ditches which lined the road, that she would not be seen by Desgas' men, when they approached, or by the patrols, which she concluded were still on duty.

Thus she started to do this, the last stage of her weary journey, alone, at night, and on foot. Nearly three leagues to Miquelon, and then on to the Pere Blanchard's hut, wherever that fatal spot might be, probably over rough roads: she cared not.

The Jew's nag could not get on very fast, and though she was wary with mental fatigue and nerve strain, she knew that she could easily keep up with it, on a hilly road, where the poor beast, who was sure to be half-starved, would have to be allowed long and frequent rests. The road lay some distance from the sea, bordered on either side by shrubs and stunted trees, sparsely covered with meagre foliage, all turning away from the North, with their branches looking in the semi-darkness, like stiff, ghostly hair, blown by a perpetual wind.

Fortunately, the moon showed no desire to peep between the clouds, and Marguerite hugging the edge of the road, and keeping close to the low line of shrubs, was fairly safe from view. Everything around her was so still: only from far, very far away, there came like a long soft moan, the sound of the distant sea.

The air was keen and full of brine; after that enforced period of inactivity, inside the evil-smelling, squalid inn, Marguerite would have enjoyed the sweet scent of this autumnal night, and the distant melancholy rumble of the autumnal night, and the distant melancholy rumble of the waves; she would have revelled in the calm and stillness of this lonely spot, a calm, broken only at intervals by the strident and mournful cry of some distant gull, and by the creaking of the wheels, some way down the road: she would have loved the cool atmosphere, the peaceful immensity of Nature, in this lonely part of the coast: but her heart was too full of cruel foreboding, of a great ache and longing for a being who had become infinitely dear to her.

Her feet slipped on the grassy bank, for she thought it safest not to walk near the centre of the road, and she found it difficult to keep up a sharp pace along the muddy incline. She even thought it best not to keep too near to the cart; everything was so still, that the rumble of the wheels could not fail to be a safe guide.

The loneliness was absolute. Already the few dim lights of Calais lay far behind, and on this road there was not a sign of human habitation, not even the hut of a fisherman or of a woodcutter anywhere near; far away on her right was the edge of the cliff, below it the rough beach, against which the incoming tide was dashing itself with its constant, distant murmur. And ahead the rumble of the wheels, bearing an implacable enemy to his triumph.

Marguerite wondered at what particular spot, on this lonely coast, Percy could be at this moment. Not very far surely, for he had had less than a quarter of an hour's start of Chauvelin. She wondered if he knew that in this cool, ocean-scented bit of France, there lurked many spies, all eager to sight his tall figure, to track him to where his unsuspecting friends waited for him, and then, to close the net over him and them.

Chauvelin, on ahead, jolted and jostled in the Jew's vehicle, was nursing comfortable thoughts. He rubbed his hands together, with content, as he thought of the web which he had woven, and through which that ubiquitous and daring Englishman could not hope to escape. As the time went on, and the old Jew drove him leisurely but surely along the dark road, he felt more and more eager for the grand finale of this exciting chase after the mysterious Scarlet Pimpernel. The capture of the audacious plotter would be the finest leaf in Citoyen Chauvelin's wreath of glory. Caught, red-handed, on the spot, in the very act of aiding and abetting the traitors against the Republic of France, the Englishman could claim no protection from his own country. Chauvelin had, in any case, fully made up his mind that all intervention should come too late.

Never for a moment did the slightest remorse enter his heart, as to the terrible position in which he had placed the unfortunate wife, who had unconsciously betrayed her husband. As a matter of fact, Chauvelin had ceased even to think of her: she had been a useful tool, that was all.

The Jew's lean nag did little more than walk. She was going along at a slow jog trot, and her driver had to give her long and frequent halts.

"Are we a long way yet from Miquelon?" asked Chauvelin from time to time.

"Not very far, your Honour," was the uniform placid reply.

"We have not yet come across your friend and mine, lying in a heap in the roadway," was Chauvelin's sarcastic comment.

"Patience, noble Excellency," rejoined the son of Moses, "they are ahead of us. I can see the imprint of the cart wheels, driven by that traitor, that son of the Amalekite."

"You are sure of the road?"

"As sure as I am of the presence of those ten gold pieces in the noble Excellency's pockets, which I trust will presently be mine."

"As soon as I have shaken hands with my friend the tall stranger, they will certainly be yours."

"Hark, what was that?" said the Jew suddenly.

Through the stillness, which had been absolute, there could now be heard distinctly the sound of horses' hoofs on the muddy road.

"They are soldiers," he added in an awed whisper.

"Stop a moment, I want to hear," said Chauvelin.

Marguerite had also heard the sound of galloping hoofs, coming towards the cart and towards herself. For some time she had been on the alert thinking that Desgas and his squad would soon overtake them, but these came from the opposite direction, presumably from Miquelon. The darkness lent her sufficient cover. She had perceived that the cart had stopped, and with utmost caution, treading noiselessly on the soft road, she crept a little nearer.

Her heart was beating fast, she was trembling in every limb; already she had guessed what news these mounted men would bring. "Every stranger on these roads or on the beach must be shadowed, especially if he be tall or stoops as if he would disguise his height; when sighted a mounted messenger must at once ride back and report." Those had been Chauvelin's orders. Had then the tall stranger been sighted, and was this the mounted messenger, come to bring the great news, that the hunted hare had run its head into the noose at last?

Marguerite, realizing that the cart had come to a standstill, managed to slip nearer to it in the darkness; she crept close up, hoping to get within earshot, to hear what the messenger had to say.

She heard the quick words of challenge —

"Liberte, Fraternite, Egalite!" then Chauvelin's quick query: —

"What news?"

Two men on horseback had halted beside the vehicle.

Marguerite could see them silhouetted against the midnight sky. She could hear their voices, and the snorting of their horses, and now, behind her, some little distance off, the regular and measured tread of a body of advancing men: Desgas and his soldiers.

There had been a long pause, during which, no doubt, Chauvelin satisfied the men as to his identity, for presently, questions and answers followed each other in quick succession.

"You have seen the stranger?" asked Chauvelin, eagerly.

"No, citoyen, we have seen no tall stranger; we came by the edge of the cliff."

"Then?"

"Less than a quarter of a league beyond Miquelon, we came across a rough construction of wood, which looked like the hut of a fisherman, where he might keep his tools and nets. When we first sighted it, it seemed to be empty, and, at first we thought that there was nothing suspicious about, until we saw some smoke issuing through an aperture at the side. I dismounted and crept close to it. It was then empty, but in one corner of the hut, there was a charcoal fire, and a couple of stools were also in the hut. I consulted with my comrades, and we decided that they should take cover with the horses, well out of sight, and that I should remain on the watch, which I did."

"Well! and did you see anything?"

"About half an hour later, I heard voices, citoyen, and presently, two men came along towards the edge of the cliff; they seemed to me to have come from the Lille Road. One was young, the other quite old. They were talking in a whisper, to one another, and I could not hear what they said." One was young, and the other quite old. Marguerite's aching heart almost stopped beating as she listened: was the young one Armand? — her brother? — and the old one de Tournay — were they the two fugitives who, unconsciously, were used as a decoy, to entrap their fearless and noble rescuer.

"The two men presently went into the hut," continued the soldier, whilst Marguerite's aching nerves seemed to catch the sound of Chauvelin's triumphant chuckle, "and I crept nearer to it then. The hut is very roughly built, and I caught snatches of their conversation."

"Yes? — Quick! — What did you hear?"

"The old man asked the young one if he were sure that was right place. 'Oh, yes,' he replied, 'tis the place sure enough,' and by the light of the charcoal fire he showed to his companion a paper, which he carried. 'Here is the plan,' he said, 'which he gave me before I left London. We were to adhere strictly to that plan, unless I had contrary orders, and I have had none. Here is the road we followed, see . . . here the fork . . . here we cut across the St. Martin Road . . . and here is the footpath which brought us to the edge of the cliff.' I must have made a slight noise then, for the young man came to the door of the hut, and peered anxiously all round him. When he again joined his companion, they whispered so low, that I could no longer hear them."

"Well? — and?" asked Chauvelin, impatiently.

"There were six of us altogether, patrolling that part of the beach, so we consulted together, and thought it best that four should remain behind and keep the hut in sight, and I and my comrade rode back at once to make report of what we had seen."

"You saw nothing of the tall stranger?"

"Nothing, citoyen."

"If your comrades see him, what would they do?"

"Not lose sight of him for a moment, and if he showed signs of escape, or any boat came in sight, they would close in on him, and, if necessary, they would shoot: the firing would bring the rest of the patrol to the spot. In any case they would not let the stranger go."

"Aye! but I did not want the stranger hurt — not just yet," murmured Chauvelin, savagely, "but there, you've done your best. The Fates grant that I may not be too late. . . ."

"We met half a dozen men just now, who have been patrolling this road for several hours."

"Well?"

"They have seen no stranger either." "Yet he is on ahead somewhere, in a cart or else . . . Here! there is not a moment to lose. How far is that hut from here?"

"About a couple of leagues, citoyen."

"You can find it again? — at once? — without hesitation?"

"I have absolutely no doubt, citoyen."

"The footpath, to the edge of the cliff? — Even in the dark?"

"It is not a dark night, citoyen, and I know I can find my way," repeated the soldier firmly.

"Fall in behind then. Let your comrade take both your horses back to Calais. You won't want them. Keep beside the cart, and direct the Jew to drive straight ahead; then stop him, within a quarter of a league of the footpath; see that he takes the most direct road."

Whilst Chauvelin spoke, Desgas and his men were fast approaching, and Marguerite could hear their footsteps within a hundred yards behind her now. She thought it unsafe to stay where she was, and unnecessary too, as she had heard enough. She seemed suddenly to have lost all faculty even for suffering: her heart, her nerves, her brain seemed to have become numb after all these hours of ceaseless anguish, culminating in this awful despair.

For now there was absolutely not the faintest hope. Within two short leagues of this spot, the fugitives were waiting for their brave deliverer. He was on his way, somewhere on this lonely road, and presently he would join them; then the well-laid trap would close, two dozen men, led by one whose hatred was as deadly as his cunning was malicious, would close round the small band of fugitives, and their daring leader. They would all be captured. Armand, according to Chauvelin's pledged word would be restored to her, but her husband, Percy, whom with every breath she drew she seemed to love and worship more and more, he would fall into the hands of a remorseless enemy, who had no pity for a brave heart, no admiration for the courage of a noble soul, who would show nothing but hatred for the cunning antagonist, who had baffled him so long.

She heard the soldier giving a few brief directions to the Jew, then she retired quickly to the edge of the road, and cowered behind some low shrubs, whilst Desgas and his men came up.

All fell in noiselessly behind the cart, and slowly they all started down the dark road. Marguerite waited until she reckoned that they were well outside the range of earshot, then, she too in the darkness, which suddenly seemed to have become more intense, crept noiselessly along.

CHAPTER XXVIII

THE PERE BLANCHARD'S HUT

As in a dream, Marguerite followed on; the web was drawing more and more tightly every moment round the beloved life, which had become dearer than all. To see her husband once again, to tell him how she had suffered, how much she had wronged, and how little understood him, had become now her only aim. She had abandoned all hope of saving him: she saw him gradually hemmed in on all sides, and, in despair, she gazed round her into the darkness, and wondered whence he would presently come, to fall into the death-trap which his relentless enemy had prepared for him.

The distant roar of the waves now made her shudder; the occasional dismal cry of an owl, or a sea-gull, filled her with unspeakable horror. She thought of the ravenous beasts — in human shape — who lay in wait for their prey, and destroyed them, as mercilessly as any hungry wolf, for the satisfaction of their own appetite of hate. Marguerite was not afraid of the darkness, she only feared that man, on ahead, who was sitting at the bottom of a rough wooden cart, nursing thoughts of vengeance, which would have made the very demons in hell chuckle with delight.

Her feet were sore. Her knees shook under her, from sheer bodily fatigue. For days now she had lived in a wild turmoil of excitement; she had not had a quiet rest for three nights; now, she had walked on a slippery road for nearly two hours, and yet her determination never swerved for a moment. She would see her husband, tell him all, and, if he was ready to forgive the crime, which she had committed in her blind ignorance, she would yet have the happiness of dying by his side.

She must have walked on almost in a trance, instinct alone keeping her up, and guiding her in the wake of the enemy, when suddenly her ears, attuned to the slightest sound, by that same blind instinct, told her that the cart had stopped, and that the soldiers had halted. They had come to their destination. No doubt on the right, somewhere close ahead, was the footpath that led to the edge of the cliff and to the hut.

Heedless of any risks, she crept up quite close up to where Chauvelin stood, surrounded by his little troop: he had descended from the cart, and was giving some orders to the men. These she wanted to hear: what little chance she yet had, of being useful to Percy, consisted in hearing absolutely every word of his enemy's plans.

The spot where all the party had halted must have lain some eight hundred meters from the coast; the sound of the sea came only very faintly, as from a distance. Chauvelin and Desgas, followed by the soldiers, had turned off sharply to the right of the road, apparently on to the footpath, which led to the cliffs. The Jew had remained on the road, with his cart and nag.

Marguerite, with infinite caution, and literally crawling on her hands and knees, had also turned off to the right: to accomplish this she had to creep through the rough, low shrubs, trying to make as little noise as possible as she went along, tearing her face and hands against the dry twigs, intent only upon hearing without being seen or heard. Fortunately — as is usual in this part of France — the footpath was bordered by a low rough hedge, beyond which was a dry ditch, filled with coarse grass. In this Marguerite managed to find shelter; she was quite hidden from view, yet could contrive to get within three yards of where Chauvelin stood, giving orders to his men.

"Now," he was saying in a low and peremptory whisper, "where is the Pere Blanchard's hut?"

"About eight hundred meters from here, along the footpath," said the soldier who had lately been directing the party, "and half-way down the cliff."

"Very good. You shall lead us. Before we begin to descend the cliff, you shall creep down to the hut, as noiselessly as possible, and ascertain if the traitor royalists are there? Do you understand?"

"I understand, citoyen."

"Now listen very attentively, all of you," continued Chauvelin, impressively, and addressing the soldiers collectively, "for after this we may not be able to exchange another word, so remember every syllable I utter, as if your very lives depended on your memory. Perhaps they do," he added drily.

"We listen, citoyen," said Desgas, "and a soldier of the Republic never forgets an order."

"You, who have crept up to the hut, will try to peep inside. If an Englishman is there with those traitors, a man who is tall above the average, or who stoops as if he would disguise his height, then give a sharp, quick whistle as a signal to your comrades. All of you," he added, once more speaking to the soldiers collectively, "then quickly surround and rush into the hut, and each seize one of the men there, before they have time to draw their firearms; if any of them struggle, shoot at their legs or arms, but on no account kill the tall man. Do you understand?"

"We understand, citoyen."

"The man who is tall above the average is probably also strong above the average; it will take four or five of you at least to overpower him."

There was a little pause, then Chauvelin continued, —

"If the royalist traitors are still alone, which is more than likely to be the case, then warn your comrades who are lying in wait there, and all of you creep and take cover behind the rocks and boulders round the hut, and wait there, in dead silence, until the tall Englishman arrives; then only rush the hut, when he is safely within its doors. But remember that you must be as silent as the wolf is at night, when he prowls around the pens. I do not wish those royalists to be on the alert — the firing of a pistol, a shriek or call on their part would be sufficient, perhaps, to warn the tall personage to keep clear of the cliffs, and of the hut, and," he added emphatically, "it is the tall Englishman whom it is your duty to capture tonight."

"You shall be implicitly obeyed, citoyen."

"Then get along as noiselessly as possible, and I will follow you."

"What about the Jew, citoyen?" asked Desgas, as silently like noiseless shadows, one by one the soldiers began to creep along the rough and narrow footpath.

"Ah, yes; I had forgotten about the Jew," said Chauvelin, and, turning towards the Jew, he called him peremptorily.

"Here, you . . . Aaron, Moses, Abraham, or whatever your confounded name may be," he said to the old man, who had quietly stood beside his lean nag, as far away from the soldiers as possible.

"Benjamin Rosenbaum, so it please your Honour," he replied humbly.

"It does not please me to hear your voice, but it does please me to give you certain orders, which you will find it wise to obey."

"So it please your Honour . . ."

"Hold your confounded tongue. You shall stay here, do you hear? with your horse and cart until our return. You are on no account to utter the faintest sound, or to even breathe louder than you can help; nor are you, on any consideration whatever, to leave your post, until I give you orders to do so. Do you understand?"

"But your Honour — " protested the Jew pitiably.

"There is no question of 'but' or of any argument," said Chauvelin, in a tone that made the timid old man tremble from head to foot. "If, when I return, I do not find you here, I most solemnly assure you that, wherever you may try to hide yourself, I can find you, and that punishment swift, sure and terrible, will sooner or later overtake you. Do you hear me?"

"But your Excellency . . ."

"I said, do you hear me?"

The soldiers had all crept away; the three men stood alone together in the dark and lonely road, with Marguerite there, behind the hedge, listening to Chauvelin's orders, as she would to her own death sentence.

"I heard your Honour," protested the Jew again, while he tried to draw nearer to Chauvelin, "and I swear by Abraham, Isaac and Jacob that I would obey your Honour most absolutely, and that I would not move from this place until your Honour once more deigned to shed the light of your countenance upon your humble servant; but remember, your Honour, I am a poor man; my nerves are not as strong as those of a young soldier. If midnight marauders should come prowling round this lonely road, I might scream or run in my fright! And is my life to be forfeit, is some terrible punishment to come on my poor old head for that which I cannot help?"

The Jew seemed in real distress; he was shaking from head to foot. Clearly he was not the man to be left by himself on this lonely road. The man spoke truly; he might unwittingly, in sheer terror, utter the shriek that might prove a warning to the wily Scarlet Pimpernel.

Chauvelin reflected for a moment.

"Will your horse and cart be safe alone, here, do you think?" he asked roughly.

"I fancy, citoyen," here interposed Desgas, "that they will be safer without that dirty, cowardly Jew than with him. There seems no doubt that, if he gets scared, he will either make a bolt of it, or shriek his head off."

"But what am I to do with the brute?"

"Will you send him back to Calais, citoyen?"

"No, for we shall want him to drive back the wounded presently," said Chauvelin, with grim significance.

There was a pause again — Desgas waiting for the decision of his chief, and the old Jew whining beside his nag.

"Well, you lazy, lumbering old coward," said Chauvelin at last, "you had better shuffle along behind us. Here, Citoyen Desgas, tie this handkerchief tightly round the fellow's mouth."

Chauvelin handed a scarf to Desgas, who solemnly began winding it round the Jew's mouth. Meekly Benjamin Rosenbaum allowed himself to be gagged; he, evidently, preferred this uncomfortable state to that of being left alone, on the dark St. Martin Road. Then the three men fell in line.

"Quick!" said Chauvelin, impatiently, "we have already wasted much valuable time."

And the firm footsteps of Chauvelin and Desgas, the shuffling gait of the old Jew, soon died away along the footpath.

Marguerite had not lost a single one of Chauvelin's words of command. Her every nerve was strained to completely grasp the situation first, then to make a final appeal to those wits which had so often been called the sharpest in Europe, and which alone might be of service now.

Certainly the situation was desperate enough; a tiny band of unsuspecting men, quietly awaiting the arrival of their rescuer, who was equally unconscious of the trap laid for them all. It seemed so horrible, this net, as it were drawn in a circle, at dead of night, on a lonely beach, round a few defenceless men, defenceless because they were tricked and unsuspecting; of these one was the husband she idolised, another the brother she loved. She vaguely wondered who the others were, who were also calmly waiting for the Scarlet Pimpernel, while death lurked behind every boulder of the cliffs.

For the moment she could do nothing but follow the soldiers and Chauvelin. She feared to lose her way, or she would have rushed forward and found that wooden hut, and perhaps been in time to warn the fugitives and their brave deliverer yet.

For a second, the thought flashed through her mind of uttering the piercing shrieks, which Chauvelin seemed to dread, as a possible warning to the Scarlet Pimpernel and his friends — in the wild hope that they would hear, and have yet time to escape before it was too late. But she did not know if her shrieks would reach the ears of the doomed men. Her effort might be premature, and she would never be allowed to make another. Her mouth would be securely gagged, like that of the Jew, and she, a helpless prisoner in the hands of Chauvelin's men.

Like a ghost she flitted noiselessly behind that hedge: she had taken her shoes off, and her stockings were by now torn off her feet. She felt neither soreness nor weariness; indomitable will to reach her husband in spite of adverse Fate, and of a cunning enemy, killed all sense of bodily pain within her, and rendered her instincts doubly acute.

She heard nothing save the soft and measured footsteps of Percy's enemies on in front; she saw nothing but — in her mind's eye — that wooden hut, and he, her husband, walking blindly to his doom.

Suddenly, those same keen instincts within her made her pause in her mad haste, and cower still further within the shadow of the hedge. The moon, which had proved a friend to her by remaining hidden behind a bank of clouds, now emerged in all the glory of an early autumn night, and in a moment flooded the weird and lonely landscape with a rush of brilliant light.

There, not two hundred metres ahead, was the edge of the cliff, and below, stretching far away to free and happy England, the sea rolled on smoothly and peaceably. Marguerite's gaze rested for an instant on the brilliant, silvery waters; and as she gazed, her heart, which had been numb with pain for all these hours, seemed to soften and distend, and her eyes filled with hot tears: not three miles away, with white sails set, a graceful schooner lay in wait.

Marguerite had guessed rather than recognized her. It was the DAY DREAM, Percy's favourite yacht, and all her crew of British sailors: her white sails, glistening in the moonlight, seemed to convey a message to Marguerite of joy and hope, which yet she feared could never be. She waited there, out at sea, waited for her master, like a beautiful white bird all ready to take flight, and he would never reach her, never see her smooth deck again, never gaze any more on the white cliffs of England, the land of liberty and of hope.

The sight of the schooner seemed to infuse into the poor, wearied woman the superhuman strength of despair. There was the edge of the cliff, and some way below was the hut, where presently, her husband would meet his death. But the moon was out: she could see her way now: she would see the hut from a distance, run to it, rouse them all, warn them at any rate to be prepared and to sell their lives dearly, rather than be caught like so many rats in a hole.

She stumbled on behind the hedge in the low, thick grass of the ditch. She must have run on very fast, and had outdistanced Chauvelin and Desgas, for presently she reached the edge of the cliff, and heard their footsteps distinctly behind her. But only a very few yards away, and now the moonlight was full upon her, her figure must have been distinctly silhouetted against the silvery background of the sea.

Only for a moment, though; the next she had cowered, like some animal doubled up within itself. She peeped down the great rugged cliffs — the descent would be easy enough, as they were not precipitous, and the great boulders afforded plenty of foothold. Suddenly, as she gazed, she saw at some little distance on her left, and about midway down the cliffs, a rough wooden construction, through the wall of which a tiny red light glimmered like a beacon. Her very heart seemed to stand still, the eagerness of joy was so great that it felt like an awful pain.

She could not gauge how distant the hut was, but without hesitation she began the steep descent, creeping from boulder to boulder, caring nothing for the enemy behind, or for the soldiers, who evidently had all taken cover since the tall Englishman had not yet appeared.

On she pressed, forgetting the deadly foe on her track, running, stumbling, foot-sore, half-dazed, but still on . . . When, suddenly, a crevice, or stone, or slippery bit of rock, threw her violently to the ground. She struggled again to her feet, and started running forward once more to give them that timely warning, to beg them to flee before he came, and to tell him to keep away — away from this death-trap — away from this awful doom. But now she realised that other steps, quicker than her own, were already close at her heels. The next instant a hand dragged at her skirt, and she was down on her knees again, whilst something was wound round her mouth to prevent her uttering a scream.

Bewildered, half frantic with the bitterness of disappointment, she looked round her help-lessly, and, bending down quite close to her, she saw through the mist, which seemed to gather round her, a pair of keen, malicious eyes, which appeared to her excited brain to have a weird, supernatural green light in them. She lay in the shadow of a great boulder; Chauvelin could not see her features, but he passed his thin, white fingers over her face.

"A woman!" he whispered, "by all the saints in the calendar."

"We cannot let her loose, that's certain," he muttered to himself. "I wonder now . . ."

Suddenly he paused, after a few moments of deadly silence, he gave forth a long, low, curious chuckle, while once again Marguerite felt, with a horrible shudder, his thin fingers wandering over her face.

"Dear me! dear me!" he whispered, with affected gallantry, "this is indeed a charming surprise," and Marguerite felt her resistless hand raised to Chauvelin's thin, mocking lips.

The situation was indeed grotesque, had it not been at the same time so fearfully tragic: the poor, weary woman, broken in spirit, and half frantic with the bitterness of her disappointment, receiving on her knees the BANAL gallantries of her deadly enemy.

Her senses were leaving her; half choked with the tight grip round her mouth, she had no strength to move or to utter the faintest sound. The excitement which all along had kept up her delicate body seemed at once to have subsided, and the feeling of blank despair to have completely paralyzed her brain and nerves.

Chauvelin must have given some directions, which she was too dazed to hear, for she felt herself lifted from off her feet: the bandage round her mouth was made more secure, and a pair of strong arms carried her towards that tiny, red light, on ahead, which she had looked upon as a beacon and the last faint glimmer of hope.

CHAPTER XXIX

TRAPPED

She did not know how long she was thus carried along, she had lost all notion of time and space, and for a few seconds tired nature, mercifully, deprived her of consciousness.

When she once more realised her state, she felt that she was placed with some degree of comfort upon a man's coat, with her back resting against a fragment of rock. The moon was hidden again behind some clouds, and the darkness seemed in comparison more intense. The sea was roaring some two hundred feet below her, and on looking all round she could no longer see any vestige of the tiny glimmer of red light.

That the end of the journey had been reached, she gathered from the fact that she heard rapid questions and answers spoken in a whisper quite close to her.

"There are four men in there, citoyen; they are sitting by the fire, and seem to be waiting quietly."

"The hour?"

"Nearly two o'clock."

"The tide?"

"Coming in quickly."

"The schooner?"

"Obviously an English one, lying some three kilometers out. But we cannot see her boat."

"Have the men taken cover?"

"Yes, citoyen."

"They will not blunder?"

"They will not stir until the tall Englishman comes, then they will surround and overpower the five men."

"Right. And the lady?"

"Still dazed, I fancy. She's close beside you, citoyen."

"And the Jew?"

"He's gagged, and his legs strapped together. He cannot move or scream."

"Good. Then have your gun ready, in case you want it. Get close to the hut and leave me to look after the lady."

Desgas evidently obeyed, for Marguerite heard him creeping away along the stony cliff, then she felt that a pair of warm, thin, talon-like hands took hold of both her own, and held them in a grip of steel.

"Before that handkerchief is removed from your pretty mouth, fair lady," whispered Chauvelin close to her ear, "I think it right to give you one small word of warning. What has procured me the honour of being followed across the Channel by so charming a companion, I cannot, of course, conceive, but, if I mistake it not, the purpose of this flattering attention is not one that would commend itself to my vanity and I think that I am right in surmising, moreover, that the first sound which your pretty lips would utter, as soon as the cruel gag is removed, would be one that would prove a warning to the cunning fox, which I have been at such pains to track to his lair."

He paused a moment, while the steel-like grasp seemed to tighten round her wrist; then he resumed in the same hurried whisper: —

"Inside that hut, if again I am not mistaken, your brother, Armand St. Just, waits with that traitor de Tournay, and two other men unknown to you, for the arrival of the mysterious rescuer, whose identity has for so long puzzled our Committee of Public Safety — the audacious Scarlet Pimpernel. No doubt if you scream, if there is a scuffle here, if shots are fired, it is more than likely that the same long legs that brought this scarlet enigma here, will as quickly take him to some place of safety. The purpose then, for which I have travelled all these miles, will remain unaccomplished. On the other hand it only rests with yourself that your brother — Armand — shall be free to go off with you to-night if you like, to England, or any other place of safety."

Marguerite could not utter a sound, as the handkerchief was would very tightly round her mouth, but Chauvelin was peering through the darkness very closely into her face; no doubt too her hand gave a responsive appeal to his last suggestion, for presently he continued: —

"What I want you to do to ensure Armand's safety is a very simple thing, dear lady."

"What is it?" Marguerite's hand seemed to convey to his, in response.

"To remain — on this spot, without uttering a sound, until I give you leave to speak. Ah! but I think you will obey," he added, with that funny dry chuckle of his as Marguerite's whole figure seemed to stiffen, in defiance of this order, "for let me tell you that if you scream, nay! if you utter one sound, or attempt to move from here, my men — there are thirty of them about — will seize St. Just, de Tournay, and their two friends, and shoot them here — by my orders — before your eyes."

Marguerite had listened to her implacable enemy's speech with ever-increasing terror. Numbed with physical pain, she yet had sufficient mental vitality in her to realize the full horror of this terrible "either — or" he was once more putting before her; "either — or" ten thousand times more appalling and horrible than the one he had suggested to her that fatal night at the ball.

This time it meant that she should keep still, and allow the husband she worshipped to walk unconsciously to his death, or that she should, by trying to give him a word of warning, which perhaps might even be unavailing, actually give the signal for her own brother's death, and that of three other unsuspecting men.

She could not see Chauvelin, but she could almost feel those keen, pale eyes of his fixed maliciously upon her helpless form, and his hurried, whispered words reached her ear, as the death-knell of her last faint, lingering hope.

"Nay, fair lady," he added urbanely, "you can have no interest in anyone save in St. Just, and all you need do for his safety is to remain where you are, and to keep silent. My men have strict orders to spare him in every way. As for that enigmatic Scarlet Pimpernel, what is he to you? Believe me, no warning from you could possibly save him. And now dear lady, let me remove this unpleasant coercion, which has been placed before your pretty mouth. You see I wish you to be perfectly free, in the choice which you are about to make."

Her thoughts in a whirl, her temples aching, her nerves paralyzed, her body numb with pain, Marguerite sat there, in the darkness which surrounded her as with a pall. From where she sat she could not see the sea, but she heard the incessant mournful murmur of the incoming tide, which spoke of her dead hopes, her lost love, the husband she had with her own hand betrayed, and sent to his death.

Chauvelin removed he handkerchief from her mouth. She certainly did not scream: at that moment, she had no strength to do anything but barely to hold herself upright, and to force herself to think.

Oh! think! think! think! of what she should do. The minutes flew on; in this awful stillness she could not tell how fast or how slowly; she heard nothing, she saw nothing: she did not feel the sweet-smelling autumn air, scented with the briny odour of the sea, she no longer heard the murmur of the waves, the occasional rattling of a pebble, as it rolled down some steep incline. More and more unreal did the whole situation seem. It was impossible that she, Marguerite Blakeney, the queen of London society, should actually be sitting here on this bit of lonely coast, in the middle of the night, side by side with a most bitter enemy; and oh! it was not possible that somewhere, not many hundred feet away perhaps, from where she stood, the being she had once despised, but who now, in every moment of this weird, dreamlike life, became more and more dear — it was not possible that HE was unconsciously, even now walking to his doom, whilst she did nothing to save him.

Why did she not with unearthly screams, that would re-echo from one end of the lonely beach to the other, send out a warning to him to desist, to retrace his steps, for death lurked here whilst he advanced? Once or twice the screams rose to her throat — as if by instinct: then, before her eyes there stood the awful alternative: her brother and those three men shot before her eyes, practically by her orders: she their murderer.

Oh! that fiend in human shape, next to her, knew human — female — nature well. He had played upon her feelings as a skilful musician plays upon an instrument. He had gauged her very thoughts to a nicety.

She could not give that signal — for she was weak, and she was a woman. How could she deliberately order Armand to be shot before her eyes, to have his dear blood upon her head, he dying perhaps with a curse on her, upon his lips. And little Suzanne's father, too! he, an old man; and the others! — oh! it was all too, too horrible.

Wait! wait! wait! how long? The early morning hours sped on, and yet it was not dawn: the sea continued its incessant mournful murmur, the autumnal breeze sighed gently in the night: the lonely beach was silent, even as the grave.

Suddenly from somewhere, not very far away, a cheerful, strong voice was heard singing "God save the King!"

CHAPTER XXX
THE SCHOONER

Marguerite's aching heart stood still. She felt, more than she heard, the men on the watch preparing for the fight. Her senses told her that each, with sword in hand, was crouching, ready for the spring.

The voice came nearer and nearer; in the vast immensity of these lonely cliffs, with the loud murmur of the sea below, it was impossible to say how near, or how far, nor yet from which direction came that cheerful singer, who sang to God to save his King, whilst he himself was in such deadly danger. Faint at first, the voice grew louder and louder; from time to time a small pebble detached itself apparently from beneath the firm tread of the singer, and went rolling down the rocky cliffs to the beach below.

Marguerite as she heard, felt that her very life was slipping away, as if when that voice drew nearer, when that singer became entrapped . . .

She distinctly heard the click of Desgas' gun close to her. . . .

No! no! no! no! Oh, God in heaven! this cannot be! let Armand's blood then be on her own head! let her be branded as his murderer! let even he, whom she loved, despise and loathe her for this, but God! oh God! save him at any cost!

With a wild shriek, she sprang to her feet, and darted round the rock, against which she had been cowering; she saw the little red gleam through the chinks of the hut; she ran up to it and fell against its wooden walls, which she began to hammer with clenched fists in an almost maniacal frenzy, while she shouted, —

"Armand! Armand! for God's sake fire! your leader is near! he is coming! he is betrayed! Armand! Armand! fire in Heaven's name!"

She was seized and thrown to the ground. She lay there moaning, bruised, not caring, but still half-sobbing, half-shrieking, —

"Percy, my husband, for God's sake fly! Armand! Armand! why don't you fire?"

"One of you stop that woman screaming," hissed Chauvelin, who hardly could refrain from striking her.

Something was thrown over her face; she could not breathe, and perforce she was silent.

The bold singer, too, had become silent, warned, no doubt, of his impending danger by Marguerite's frantic shrieks. The men had sprung to their feet, there was no need for further silence on their part; the very cliffs echoed the poor, heart-broken woman's screams.

Chauvelin, with a muttered oath, which boded no good to her, who had dared to upset his most cherished plans, had hastily shouted the word of command, —

"Into it, my men, and let no one escape from that hut alive!"

The moon had once more emerged from between the clouds: the darkness on the cliffs had gone, giving place once more to brilliant, silvery light. Some of the soldiers had rushed to the rough, wooden door of the hut, whilst one of them kept guard over Marguerite.

The door was partially open; one of the soldiers pushed it further, but within all was darkness, the charcoal fire only lighting with a dim, red light the furthest corner of the hut. The soldiers paused automatically at the door, like machines waiting for further orders.

Chauvelin, who was prepared for a violent onslaught from within, and for a vigorous resistance from the four fugitives, under cover of the darkness, was for the moment paralyzed with astonishment when he saw the soldiers standing there at attention, like sentries on guard, whilst not a sound proceeded from the hut.

Filled with strange, anxious foreboding, he, too, went to the door of the hut, and peering into the gloom, he asked quickly, —

"What is the meaning of this?"

"I think, citoyen, that there is no one there now," replied one of the soldiers imperturbably.

"You have not let those four men go?" thundered Chauvelin, menacingly. "I ordered you to let no man escape alive! — Quick, after them all of you! Quick, in every direction!"

The men, obedient as machines, rushed down the rocky incline towards the beach, some going off to right and left, as fast as their feet could carry them.

"You and your men will pay with your lives for this blunder, citoyen sergeant," said Chauvelin viciously to the sergeant who had been in charge of the men; "and you, too, citoyen," he added turning with a snarl to Desgas, "for disobeying my orders."

"You ordered us to wait, citoyen, until the tall Englishman arrived and joined the four men in the hut. No one came," said the sergeant sullenly.

"But I ordered you just now, when the woman screamed, to rush in and let no one escape."

"But, citoyen, the four men who were there before had been gone some time, I think . . ."

"You think? — You? . . ." said Chauvelin, almost choking with fury, "and you let them go . . ."

"You ordered us to wait, citoyen," protested the sergeant, "and to implicitly obey your commands on pain of death. We waited."

"I heard the men creep out of the hut, not many minutes after we took cover, and long before the woman screamed," he added, as Chauvelin seemed still quite speechless with rage.

"Hark!" said Desgas suddenly.

In the distance the sound of repeated firing was heard. Chauvelin tried to peer along the beach below, but as luck would have it, the fitful moon once more hid her light behind a bank of clouds, and he could see nothing.

"One of you go into the hut and strike a light," he stammered at last.

Stolidly the sergeant obeyed: he went up to the charcoal fire and lit the small lantern he carried in his belt; it was evident that the hut was quite empty.

"Which way did they go?" asked Chauvelin.

"I could not tell, citoyen," said the sergeant; "they went straight down the cliff first, then disappeared behind some boulders."

"Hush! what was that?"

All three men listened attentively. In the far, very far distance, could be heard faintly echoing and already dying away, the quick, sharp splash of half a dozen oars. Chauvelin took out his handkerchief and wiped the perspiration from his forehead.

"The schooner's boat!" was all he gasped.

Evidently Armand St. Just and his three companions had managed to creep along the side of the cliffs, whilst the men, like true soldiers of the well-drilled Republican army, had with blind obedience, and in fear of their own lives, implicitly obeyed Chauvelin's orders — to wait for the tall Englishman, who was the important capture.

They had no doubt reached one of the creeks which jut far out to sea on this coast at intervals; behind this, the boat of the DAY DREAM must have been on the lookout for them, and they were by now safely on board the British schooner.

As if to confirm this last supposition, the dull boom of a gun was heard from out at sea.

"The schooner, citoyen," said Desgas, quietly; "she's off."

It needed all Chauvelin's nerve and presence of mind not to give way to a useless and undignified access of rage. There was no doubt now, that once again, that accursed British head had completely outwitted him. How he had contrived to reach the hut, without being seen by one of the thirty soldiers who guarded the spot, was more than Chauvelin could conceive. That he had done so before the thirty men had arrived on the cliff was, of course, fairly clear, but how he had come over in Reuben Goldstein's cart, all the way from Calais, without being sighted by the various patrols on duty was impossible of explanation. It really seemed as if some potent Fate watched over that daring Scarlet Pimpernel, and his astute enemy almost felt a superstitious shudder pass through him, as he looked round at the towering cliffs, and the loneliness of this outlying coast.

But surely this was reality! and the year of grace 1792: there were no fairies and hobgoblins about. Chauvelin and his thirty men had all heard with their own ears that accursed voice singing "God save the King," fully twenty minutes AFTER they had all taken cover around the hut; by that time the four fugitives must have reached the creek, and got into the boat, and the nearest creek was more than a mile from the hut.

Where had that daring singer got to? Unless Satan himself had lent him wings, he could not have covered that mile on a rocky cliff in the space of two minutes; and only two minutes had elapsed between his song and the sound of the boat's oars away at sea. He must have remained behind, and was even now hiding somewhere about the cliffs; the patrols were still about, he would still be sighted, no doubt. Chauvelin felt hopeful once again.

One or two of the men, who had run after the fugitives, were now slowly working their way up the cliff: one of them reached Chauvelin's side, at the very moment that this hope arose in the astute diplomatist's heart.

"We were too late, citoyen," the soldier said, "we reached the beach just before the moon was hidden by that bank of clouds. The boat had undoubtedly been on the look-out behind that first creek, a mile off, but she had shoved off some time ago, when we got to the beach, and was already some way out to sea. We fired after her, but of course, it was no good. She was making straight and quickly for the schooner. We saw her very clearly in the moonlight."

"Yes," said Chauvelin, with eager impatience, "she had shoved off some time ago, you said, and the nearest creek is a mile further on."

"Yes, citoyen! I ran all the way, straight to the beach, though I guessed the boat would have waited somewhere near the creek, as the tide would reach there earliest. The boat must have shoved off some minutes before the woman began to scream."

"Bring the light in here!" he commanded eagerly, as he once more entered the hut.

The sergeant brought his lantern, and together the two men explored the little place: with a rapid glance Chauvelin noted its contents: the cauldron placed close under an aperture in the wall, and containing the last few dying embers of burned charcoal, a couple of stools, overturned as if in the haste of sudden departure, then the fisherman's tools and his nets lying in one corner, and beside them, something small and white.

"Pick that up," said Chauvelin to the sergeant, pointing to this white scrap, "and bring it to me."

It was a crumpled piece of paper, evidently forgotten there by the fugitives, in their hurry to get away. The sergeant, much awed by the citoyen's obvious rage and impatience, picked the paper up and handed it respectfully to Chauvelin.

"Read it, sergeant," said the latter curtly.

"It is almost illegible, citoyen . . . a fearful scrawl . . ."

"I ordered you to read it," repeated Chauvelin, viciously.

The sergeant, by the light of his lantern, began deciphering the few hastily scrawled words.

"I cannot quite reach you, without risking your lives and endangering the success of your rescue. When you receive this, wait two minutes, then creep out of the hut one by one, turn to your left sharply, and creep cautiously down the cliff; keep to the left all the time, till you reach the first rock, which you see jutting far out to sea — behind it in the creek the boat is on the look-out for you — give a long, sharp whistle — she will come up — get into her — my men will row you to the schooner, and thence to England and safety — once on board the DAY DREAM send the boat back for me, tell my men that I shall be at the creek, which is in a direct line opposite the 'Chat Gris' near Calais. They know it. I shall be there as soon as possible — they must wait for me at a safe distance out at sea, till they hear the usual signal. Do not delay — and obey these instructions implicitly."

"Then there is the signature, citoyen," added the sergeant, as he handed the paper back to Chauvelin.

But the latter had not waited an instant. One phrase of the momentous scrawl had caught his ear. "I shall be at the creek which is in a direct line opposite the 'Chat Gris' near Calais": that phrase might yet mean victory for him. "Which of you knows this coast well?" he shouted to his men who now one by one all returned from their fruitless run, and were all assembled once more round the hut.

"I do, citoyen," said one of them, "I was born in Calais, and know every stone of these cliffs."

"There is a creek in a direct line from the 'Chat Gris'?"

"There is, citoyen. I know it well."

"The Englishman is hoping to reach that creek. He does NOT know every stone of these cliffs, he may go there by the longest way round, and in any case he will proceed cautiously for fear of the patrols. At any rate, there is a chance to get him yet. A thousand francs to each man who gets to that creek before that long-legged Englishman."

"I know of a short cut across the cliffs," said the soldier, and with an enthusiastic shout, he rushed forward, followed closely by his comrades.

Within a few minutes their running footsteps had died away in the distance. Chauvelin listened to them for a moment; the promise of the reward was lending spurs to the soldiers of the Republic. The gleam of hate and anticipated triumph was once more apparent on his face.

Close to him Desgas still stood mute and impassive, waiting for further orders, whilst two soldiers were kneeling beside the prostrate form of Marguerite. Chauvelin gave his secretary a vicious look. His well-laid plan had failed, its sequel was problematical; there was still a great chance now that the Scarlet Pimpernel might yet escape, and Chauvelin, with that unreasoning fury, which sometimes assails a strong nature, was longing to vent his rage on somebody.

The soldiers were holding Marguerite pinioned to the ground, though, she, poor soul, was not making the faintest struggle. Overwrought nature had at last peremptorily asserted herself, and she lay there in a dead swoon: her eyes circled by deep purple lines, that told of long, sleepless nights, her hair matted and damp round her forehead, her lips parted in a sharp curve that spoke of physical pain.

The cleverest woman in Europe, the elegant and fashionable Lady Blakeney, who had dazzled London society with her beauty, her wit and her extravagances, presented a very pathetic picture of tired-out, suffering womanhood, which would have appealed to any, but the hard, vengeful heart of her baffled enemy.

"It is no use mounting guard over a woman who is half dead," he said spitefully to the soldiers, "when you have allowed five men who were very much alive to escape."

Obediently the soldiers rose to their feet.

"You'd better try and find that footpath again for me, and that broken-down cart we left on the road."

Then suddenly a bright idea seemed to strike him.

"Ah! by-the-bye! where is the Jew?"

"Close by here, citoyen," said Desgas; "I gagged him and tied his legs together as you commanded."

From the immediate vicinity, a plaintive moan reached Chauvelin's ears. He followed his secretary, who led the way to the other side of the hut, where, fallen into an absolute heap of dejection, with his legs tightly pinioned together and his mouth gagged, lay the unfortunate descendant of Israel.

His face in the silvery light of the moon looked positively ghastly with terror: his eyes were wide open and almost glassy, and his whole body was trembling, as if with ague, while a piteous wail escaped his bloodless lips. The rope which had originally been wound round his shoulders and arms had evidently given way, for it lay in a tangle about his body, but he seemed quite unconscious of this, for he had not made the slightest attempt to move from the place where Desgas had originally put him: like a terrified chicken which looks upon a line of white chalk, drawn on a table, as on a string which paralyzes its movements.

"Bring the cowardly brute here," commanded Chauvelin.

He certainly felt exceedingly vicious, and since he had no reasonable grounds for venting his ill-humour on the soldiers who had but too punctually obeyed his orders, he felt that the son of the despised race would prove an excellent butt. With true French contempt of the Jew, which has survived the lapse of centuries even to this day, he would not go too near him, but said with biting sarcasm, as the wretched old man was brought in full light of the moon by the two soldiers, —

"I suppose now, that being a Jew, you have a good memory for bargains?"

"Answer!" he again commanded, as the Jew with trembling lips seemed too frightened to speak.

"Yes, your Honour," stammered the poor wretch.

"You remember, then, the one you and I made together in Calais, when you undertook to overtake Reuben Goldstein, his nag and my friend the tall stranger? Eh?"

"B . . . b . . . but . . . your Honour . . ."

"There is no 'but.' I said, do you remember?"

"Y . . . y . . . y . . . yes . . . your Honour!"

"What was the bargain?"

There was dead silence. The unfortunate man looked round at the great cliffs, the moon above, the stolid faces of the soldiers, and even at the poor, prostate, inanimate woman close by, but said nothing.

"Will you speak?" thundered Chauvelin, menacingly.

He did try, poor wretch, but, obviously, he could not. There was no doubt, however, that he knew what to expect from the stern man before him.

"Your Honour . . ." he ventured imploringly.

"Since your terror seems to have paralyzed your tongue," said Chauvelin sarcastically, "I must needs refresh your memory. It was agreed between us, that if we overtook my friend the tall stranger, before he reached this place, you were to have ten pieces of gold."

A low moan escaped from the Jew's trembling lips.

"But," added Chauvelin, with slow emphasis, "if you deceived me in your promise, you were to have a sound beating, one that would teach you not to tell lies."

"I did not, your Honour; I swear it by Abraham . . ."

"And by all the other patriarchs, I know. Unfortunately, they are still in Hades, I believe, according to your creed, and cannot help you much in your present trouble. Now, you did not fulfil your share of the bargain, but I am ready to fulfil mine. Here," he added, turning to the soldiers, "the buckle-end of your two belts to this confounded Jew."

As the soldiers obediently unbuckled their heavy leather belts, the Jew set up a howl that surely would have been enough to bring all the patriarchs out of Hades and elsewhere, to defend their descendant from the brutality of this French official.

"I think I can rely on you, citoyen soldiers," laughed Chauvelin, maliciously, "to give this old liar the best and soundest beating he has ever experienced. But don't kill him," he added drily.

"We will obey, citoyen," replied the soldiers as imperturbably as ever.

He did not wait to see his orders carried out: he knew that he could trust these soldiers — who were still smarting under his rebuke — not to mince matters, when given a free hand to belabour a third party.

"When that lumbering coward has had his punishment," he said to Desgas, "the men can guide us as far as the cart, and one of them can drive us in it back to Calais. The Jew and the woman can look after each other," he added roughly, "until we can send somebody for them in the morning. They can't run away very far, in their present condition, and we cannot be troubled with them just now."

Chauvelin had not given up all hope. His men, he knew, were spurred on by the hope of the reward. That enigmatic and audacious Scarlet Pimpernel, alone and with thirty men at his heels, could not reasonably be expected to escape a second time.

But he felt less sure now: the Englishman's audacity had baffled him once, whilst the wooden-headed stupidity of the soldiers, and the interference of a woman had turned his hand, which held all the trumps, into a losing one. If Marguerite had not taken up his time, if the soldiers had had a grain of intelligence, if . . . it was a long "if," and Chauvelin stood for a moment quite still, and enrolled thirty odd people in one long, overwhelming anathema. Nature, poetic, silent, balmy, the bright moon, the calm, silvery sea spoke of beauty and of rest, and Chauvelin cursed nature, cursed man and woman, and above all, he cursed all long-legged, meddlesome British enigmas with one gigantic curse.

The howls of the Jew behind him, undergoing his punishment sent a balm through his heart, overburdened as it was with revengeful malice. He smiled. It eased his mind to think that some human being at least was, like himself, not altogether at peace with mankind.

He turned and took a last look at the lonely bit of coast, where stood the wooden hut, now bathed in moonlight, the scene of the greatest discomfiture ever experienced by a leading member of the Committee of Public Safety.

Against a rock, on a hard bed of stone, lay the unconscious figure of Marguerite Blakeney, while some few paces further on, the unfortunate Jew was receiving on his broad back the blows of two stout leather belts, wielded by the stolid arms of two sturdy soldiers of the Republic. The howls of Benjamin Rosenbaum were fit to make the dead rise from their graves. They must have wakened all the gulls from sleep, and made them look down with great interest at the doings of the lords of the creation.

"That will do," commanded Chauvelin, as the Jew's moans became more feeble, and the poor wretch seemed to have fainted away, "we don't want to kill him."

Obediently the soldiers buckled on their belts, one of them viciously kicking the Jew to one side.

"Leave him there," said Chauvelin, "and lead the way now quickly to the cart. I'll follow."

He walked up to where Marguerite lay, and looked down into her face. She had evidently recovered consciousness, and was making feeble efforts to raise herself. Her large, blue eyes were looking at the moonlit scene round her with a scared and terrified look; they rested with a mixture of horror and pity on the Jew, whose luckless fate and wild howls had been the first signs that struck her, with her returning senses; then she caught sight of Chauvelin, in his neat, dark clothes, which seemed hardly crumpled after the stirring events of the last few hours. He was smiling sarcastically, and his pale eyes peered down at her with a look of intense malice.

With mock gallantry, he stooped and raised her icy-cold hand to his lips, which sent a thrill of indescribable loathing through Marguerite's weary frame.

"I much regret, fair lady," he said in his most suave tones, "that circumstances, over which I have no control, compel me to leave you here for the moment. But I go away, secure in the knowledge that I do not leave you unprotected. Our friend Benjamin here, though a trifle the worse for wear at the present moment, will prove a gallant defender of your fair person, I have no doubt. At dawn I will send an escort for you; until then, I feel sure that you will find him devoted, though perhaps a trifle slow."

Marguerite only had the strength to turn her head away. Her heart was broken with cruel anguish. One awful thought had returned to her mind, together with gathering consciousness: "What had become of Percy? — What of Armand?"

She knew nothing of what had happened after she heard the cheerful song, "God save the King," which she believed to be the signal of death.

"I, myself," concluded Chauvelin, "must now very reluctantly leave you. AU REVOIR, fair lady. We meet, I hope, soon in London. Shall I see you at the Prince of Wales' garden party? — No? — Ah, well, AU REVOIR! — Remember me, I pray, to Sir Percy Blakeney."

And, with a last ironical smile and bow, he once more kissed her hand, and disappeared down the footpath in the wake of the soldiers, and followed by the imperturbable Desgas.

CHAPTER XXXI
THE ESCAPE

Marguerite listened — half-dazed as she was — to the fast-retreating, firm footsteps of the four men.

All nature was so still that she, lying with her ear close to the ground, could distinctly trace the sound of their tread, as they ultimately turned into the road, and presently the faint echo of the old cart-wheels, the halting gait of the lean nag, told her that her enemy was a quarter of a league away. How long she lay there she knew not. She had lost count of time; dreamily she looked up at the moonlit sky, and listened to the monotonous roll of the waves.

The invigorating scent of the sea was nectar to her wearied body, the immensity of the lonely cliffs was silent and dreamlike. Her brain only remained conscious of its ceaseless, its intolerable torture of uncertainty.

She did not know! —

She did not know whether Percy was even now, at this moment, in the hands of the soldiers of the Republic, enduring — as she had done herself — the gibes and jeers of his malicious enemy. She did not know, on the other hand, whether Armand's lifeless body did not lie there, in the hut, whilst Percy had escaped, only to hear that his wife's hands had guided the human bloodhounds to the murder of Armand and his friends.

The physical pain of utter weariness was so great, that she hoped confidently her tired body could rest here for ever, after all the turmoil, the passion, and the intrigues of the last few days — here, beneath that clear sky, within sound of the sea, and with this balmy autumn breeze whispering to her a last lullaby. All was so solitary, so silent, like unto dreamland. Even the last faint echo of the distant cart had long ago died away, afar.

Suddenly . . . a sound . . . the strangest, undoubtedly, that these lonely cliffs of France had ever heard, broke the silent solemnity of the shore.

So strange a sound was it that the gentle breeze ceased to murmur, the tiny pebbles to roll down the steep incline! So strange, that Marguerite, wearied, overwrought as she was, thought that the beneficial unconsciousness of the approach of death was playing her half-sleeping senses a weird and elusive trick.

It was the sound of a good, solid, absolutely British "Damn!"

The sea gulls in their nests awoke and looked round in astonishment; a distant and solitary owl set up a midnight hoot, the tall cliffs frowned down majestically at the strange, unheard-of sacrilege.

Marguerite did not trust her ears. Half-raising herself on her hands, she strained every sense to see or hear, to know the meaning of this very earthly sound.

All was still again for the space of a few seconds; the same silence once more fell upon the great and lonely vastness.

Then Marguerite, who had listened as in a trance, who felt she must be dreaming with that cool, magnetic moonlight overhead, heard again; and this time her heart stood still, her eyes large and dilated, looked round her, not daring to trust her other sense.

"Odd's life! but I wish those demmed fellows had not hit quite so hard!"

This time it was quite unmistakable, only one particular pair of essentially British lips could have uttered those words, in sleepy, drawly, affected tones.

"Damn!" repeated those same British lips, emphatically. "Zounds! but I'm as weak as a rat!"

In a moment Marguerite was on her feet.

Was she dreaming? Were those great, stony cliffs the gates of paradise? Was the fragrant breath of the breeze suddenly caused by the flutter of angels' wings, bringing tidings of unearthly joys to her, after all her suffering, or — faint and ill — was she the prey of delirium?

She listened again, and once again she heard the same very earthly sounds of good, honest British language, not the least akin to whisperings from paradise or flutter of angels' wings.

She looked round her eagerly at the tall cliffs, the lonely hut, the great stretch of rocky beach. Somewhere there, above or below her, behind a boulder or inside a crevice, but still hidden from her longing, feverish eyes, must be the owner of that voice, which once used to irritate her, but now would make her the happiest woman in Europe, if only she could locate it.

"Percy! Percy!" she shrieked hysterically, tortured between doubt and hope, "I am here! Come to me! Where are you? Percy! Percy! . . ."

"It's all very well calling me, m'dear!" said the same sleepy, drawly voice, "but odd's life, I cannot come to you: those demmed frog-eaters have trussed me like a goose on a spit, and I am weak as a mouse . . . I cannot get away."

And still Marguerite did not understand. She did not realise for at least another ten seconds whence came that voice, so drawly, so dear, but alas! with a strange accent of weakness and of suffering. There was no one within sight . . . except by that rock . . . Great God! . . . the Jew! . . . Was she mad or dreaming? . . .

His back was against the pale moonlight, he was half crouching, trying vainly to raise himself with his arms tightly pinioned. Marguerite ran up to him, took his head in both her hands . . . and look straight into a pair of blue eyes, good-natured, even a trifle amused — shining out of the weird and distorted mask of the Jew.

"Percy! . . . Percy! . . . my husband!" she gasped, faint with the fulness of her joy. "Thank God! Thank God!"

"La! m'dear," he rejoined good-humouredly, "we will both do that anon, an you think you can loosen these demmed ropes, and release me from my inelegant attitude."

She had no knife, her fingers were numb and weak, but she worked away with her teeth, while great welcome tears poured from her eyes, onto those poor, pinioned hands.

"Odd's life!" he said, when at last, after frantic efforts on her part, the ropes seemed at last to be giving way, "but I marvel whether it has ever happened before, that an English gentleman allowed himself to be licked by a demmed foreigner, and made no attempt to give as good as he got."

It was very obvious that he was exhausted from sheer physical pain, and when at last the rope gave way, he fell in a heap against the rock.

Marguerite looked helplessly round her.

"Oh! for a drop of water on this awful beach!" she cried in agony, seeing that he was ready to faint again.

"Nay, m'dear," he murmured with his good-humoured smile, "personally I should prefer a drop of good French brandy! an you'll dive in the pocket of this dirty old garment, you'll find my flask. . . . I am demmed if I can move."

When he had drunk some brandy, he forced Marguerite to do likewise.

"La! that's better now! Eh! little woman?" he said, with a sigh of satisfaction. "Heigh-ho! but this is a queer rig-up for Sir Percy Blakeney, Bart., to be found in by his lady, and no mistake. Begad!" he added, passing his hand over his chin, "I haven't been shaved for nearly twenty hours: I must look a disgusting object. As for these curls . . ."

And laughingly he took off the disfiguring wig and curls, and stretched out his long limbs, which were cramped from many hours' stooping. Then he bent forward and looked long and searchingly into his wife's blue eyes.

"Percy," she whispered, while a deep blush suffused her delicate cheeks and neck, "if you only knew . . ."

"I do know, dear . . . everything," he said with infinite gentleness.

"And can you ever forgive?"

"I have naught to forgive, sweetheart; your heroism, your devotion, which I, alas! so little deserved, have more than atoned for that unfortunate episode at the ball."

"Then you knew? . . ." she whispered, "all the time . . ."

"Yes!" he replied tenderly, "I knew . . . all the time. . . . But, begad! had I but known what a noble heart yours was, my Margot, I should have trusted you, as you deserved to be trusted, and you would not have had to undergo the terrible sufferings of the past few hours, in order to run after a husband, who has done so much that needs forgiveness."

They were sitting side by side, leaning up against a rock, and he had rested his aching head on her shoulder. She certainly now deserved the name of "the happiest woman in Europe."

"It is a case of the blind leading the lame, sweetheart, is it not?" he said with his good-natured smile of old. "Odd's life! but I do not know which are the more sore, my shoulders or your little feet."

He bent forward to kiss them, for they peeped out through her torn stockings, and bore pathetic witness to her endurance and devotion.

"But Armand . . ." she said with sudden terror and remorse, as in the midst of her happiness the image of the beloved brother, for whose sake she had so deeply sinned, rose now before her mind.

"Oh! have no fear for Armand, sweetheart," he said tenderly, "did I not pledge you my word that he should be safe? He with de Tournay and the others are even now on board the DAY DREAM."

"But how?" she gasped, "I do not understand."

"Yet, 'tis simple enough, m'dear," he said with that funny, half-shy, half-inane laugh of his, "you see! when I found that that brute Chauvelin meant to stick to me like a leech, I thought the best thing I could do, as I could not shake him off, was to take him along with me. I had to get to Armand and the others somehow, and all the roads were patrolled, and every one on the look-out for your humble servant. I knew that when I slipped through Chauvelin's fingers at the 'Chat Gris,' that he would lie in wait for me here, whichever way I took. I wanted to keep an eye on him and his doings, and a British head is as good as a French one any day."

Indeed it had proved to be infinitely better, and Marguerite's heart was filled with joy and marvel, as he continued to recount to her the daring manner in which he had snatched the fugitives away, right from under Chauvelin's very nose.

"Dressed as the dirty old Jew," he said gaily, "I knew I should not be recognized. I had met Reuben Goldstein in Calais earlier in the evening. For a few gold pieces he supplied me with this rig-out, and undertook to bury himself out of sight of everybody, whilst he lent me his cart and nag."

"But if Chauvelin had discovered you," she gasped excitedly, "your disguise was good . . . but he is so sharp."

"Odd's fish!" he rejoined quietly, "then certainly the game would have been up. I could but take the risk. I know human nature pretty well by now," he added, with a note of sadness in his cheery, young voice, "and I know these Frenchmen out and out. They so loathe a Jew, that they never come nearer than a couple of yards of him, and begad! I fancy that I contrived to make myself look about as loathsome an object as it is possible to conceive."

"Yes! — and then?" she asked eagerly.

"Zooks! — then I carried out my little plan: that is to say, at first I only determined to leave everything to chance, but when I heard Chauvelin giving his orders to the soldiers, I thought that Fate and I were going to work together after all. I reckoned on the blind obedience of the soldiers. Chauvelin had ordered them on pain of death not to stir until the tall Englishman came. Desgas had thrown me down in a heap quite close to the hut; the soldiers took no notice of the Jew, who had driven Citoyen Chauvelin to this spot. I managed to free my hands from the ropes, with which the brute had trussed me; I always carry pencil and paper with me wherever I go, and I hastily scrawled a few important instructions on a scrap of paper; then I looked about me. I crawled up to the hut, under the very noses of the soldiers, who lay under cover without stirring, just as Chauvelin had ordered them to do, then I dropped my little note into the hut through a chink in the wall, and waited. In this note I told the fugitives to walk noiselessly out of the hut, creep down the cliffs, keep to the left until they came to the first creek, to give a certain signal, when the boat of the DAY DREAM, which lay in wait not far out to sea, would pick them up. They obeyed implicitly, fortunately for them and for me. The soldiers who saw them were equally obedient to Chauvelin's orders. They did not stir! I waited for nearly half an hour; when I knew that the fugitives were safe I gave the signal, which caused so much stir."

And that was the whole story. It seemed so simple! and Marguerite could but marvel at the wonderful ingenuity, the boundless pluck and audacity which had evolved and helped to carry out this daring plan.

"But those brutes struck you!" she gasped in horror, at the bare recollection of the fearful indignity.

"Well! that could not be helped," he said gently, "whilst my little wife's fate was so uncertain, I had to remain here by her side. Odd's life!" he added merrily, "never fear! Chauvelin will lose nothing by waiting, I warrant! Wait till I get him back to England! — La! he shall pay for the thrashing he gave me with compound interest, I promise you."

Marguerite laughed. It was so good to be beside him, to hear his cheery voice, to watch that good-humoured twinkle in his blue eyes, as he stretched out his strong arms, in longing for that foe, and anticipation of his well-deserved punishment.

Suddenly, however, she started: the happy blush left her cheek, the light of joy died out of her eyes: she had heard a stealthy footfall overhead, and a stone had rolled down from the top of the cliffs right down to the beach below.

"What's that?" she whispered in horror and alarm.

"Oh! nothing, m'dear," he muttered with a pleasant laugh, "only a trifle you happened to have forgotten . . . my friend, Ffoulkes . . ."

"Sir Andrew!" she gasped.

Indeed, she had wholly forgotten the devoted friend and companion, who had trusted and stood by her during all these hours of anxiety and suffering. She remembered him now, tardily and with a pang of remorse.

"Aye! you had forgotten him, hadn't you, m'dear?" said Sir Percy merrily. "Fortunately, I met him, not far from the 'Chat Gris.' before I had that interesting supper party, with my friend Chauvelin. . . . Odd's life! but I have a score to settle with that young reprobate! — but in the meanwhile, I told him of a very long, very circuitous road which Chauvelin's men would never suspect, just about the time when we are ready for him, eh, little woman?"

"And he obeyed?" asked Marguerite, in utter astonishment.

"Without word or question. See, here he comes. He was not in the way when I did not want him, and now he arrives in the nick of time. Ah! he will make pretty little Suzanne a most admirable and methodical husband."

In the meanwhile Sir Andrew Ffoulkes had cautiously worked his way down the cliffs: he stopped once or twice, pausing to listen for whispered words, which would guide him to Blakeney's hiding-place.

"Blakeney!" he ventured to say at last cautiously, "Blakeney! are you there?"

The next moment he rounded the rock against which Sir Percy and Marguerite were leaning, and seeing the weird figure still clad in the Jew's long gaberdine, he paused in sudden, complete bewilderment.

But already Blakeney had struggled to his feet.

"Here I am, friend," he said with his funny, inane laugh, "all alive! though I do look a begad scarecrow in these demmed things."

"Zooks!" ejaculated Sir Andrew in boundless astonishment as he recognized his leader, "of all the . . ."

The young man had seen Marguerite, and happily checked the forcible language that rose to his lips, at sight of the exquisite Sir Percy in this weird and dirty garb.

"Yes!" said Blakeney, calmly, "of all the . . . hem! . . . My friend! — I have not yet had time to ask you what you were doing in France, when I ordered you to remain in London? Insubordination? What? Wait till my shoulders are less sore, and, by God, see the punishment you'll get."

"Odd's fish! I'll bear it," said Sir Andrew with a merry laugh, "seeing that you are alive to give it. . . . Would you have had me allow Lady Blakeney to do the journey alone? But, in the name of heaven, man, where did you get these extraordinary clothes?"

"Lud! they are a bit quaint, ain't they?" laughed Sir Percy, jovially, "But, odd's fish!" he added, with sudden earnestness and authority, "now you are here, Ffoulkes, we must lose no more time: that brute Chauvelin may send some one to look after us."

Marguerite was so happy, she could have stayed here for ever, hearing his voice, asking a hundred questions. But at mention of Chauvelin's name she started in quick alarm, afraid for the dear life she would have died to save.

"But how can we get back?" she gasped; "the roads are full of soldiers between here and Calais, and . . ."

"We are not going back to Calais, sweetheart," he said, "but just the other side of Gris Nez, not half a league from here. The boat of the DAY DREAM will meet us there."

"The boat of the DAY DREAM?"

"Yes!" he said, with a merry laugh; "another little trick of mine. I should have told you before that when I slipped that note into the hut, I also added another for Armand, which I directed him to leave behind, and which has sent Chauvelin and his men running full tilt back to the 'Chat Gris' after me; but the first little note contained my real instructions, including those to old Briggs. He had my orders to go out further to sea, and then towards the west. When well out of sight of Calais, he will send the galley to a little creek he and I know of, just beyond Gris Nez. The men will look out for me — we have a preconcerted signal, and we will all be safely aboard, whilst Chauvelin and his men solemnly sit and watch the creek which is 'just opposite the "Chat Gris."'"

"The other side of Gris Nez? But I . . . I cannot walk, Percy," she moaned helplessly as, trying to struggle to her tired feet, she found herself unable even to stand.

"I will carry you, dear," he said simply; "the blind leading the lame, you know."

Sir Andrew was ready, too, to help with the precious burden, but Sir Percy would not entrust his beloved to any arms but his own.

"When you and she are both safely on board the DAY DREAM," he said to his young comrade, "and I feel that Mlle. Suzanne's eyes will not greet me in England with reproachful looks, then it will be my turn to rest."

And his arms, still vigorous in spite of fatigue and suffering, closed round Marguerite's poor, weary body, and lifted her as gently as if she had been a feather.

Then, as Sir Andrew discreetly kept out of earshot, there were many things said, or rather whispered, which even the autumn breeze did not catch, for it had gone to rest.

All his fatigue was forgotten; his shoulders must have been very sore, for the soldiers had hit hard, but the man's muscles seemed made of steel, and his energy was almost supernatural. It was a weary tramp, half a league along the stony side of the cliffs, but never for a moment did his courage give way or his muscles yield to fatigue. On he tramped, with firm footstep, his vigorous arms encircling the precious burden, and . . . no doubt, as she lay, quiet and happy, at times lulled to momentary drowsiness, at others watching, through the slowly gathering morning light, the pleasant face with the lazy, drooping blue eyes, ever cheerful, ever illumined with a good-humoured smile, she whispered many things, which helped to shorten the weary road, and acted as a soothing balsam to his aching sinews.

The many-hued light of dawn was breaking in the east, when at last they reached the creek beyond Gris Nez. The galley lay in wait: in answer to a signal from Sir Percy, she drew near, and two sturdy British sailors had the honour of carrying my lady into the boat.

Half an hour later, they were on board the DAY DREAM. The crew, who of necessity were in their master's secrets, and who were devoted to him heart and soul, were not surprised to see him arriving in so extraordinary a disguise.

Armand St. Just and the other fugitives were eagerly awaiting the advent of their brave rescuer; he would not stay to hear the expressions of their gratitude, but found the way to his private cabin as quickly as he could, leaving Marguerite quite happy in the arms of her brother.

Everything on board the DAY DREAM was fitted with that exquisite luxury, so dear to Sir Percy Blakeney's heart, and by the time they all landed at Dover he had found time to get into some of the sumptuous clothes which he loved, and of which he always kept a supply on board his yacht.

The difficulty was to provide Marguerite with a pair of shoes, and great was the little middy's joy when my lady found that she could put foot on English shore in his best pair.

The rest is silence! — silence and joy for those who had endured so much suffering, yet found at last a great and lasting happiness.

But it is on record that at the brilliant wedding of Sir Andrew Ffoulkes, Bart., with Mlle. Suzanne de Tournay de Basserive, a function at which H. R. H. the Prince of Wales and all the ELITE of fashionable society were present, the most beautiful woman there was unquestionably Lady Blakeney, whilst the clothes of Sir Percy Blakeney were the talk of the JEUNESSE DOREE of London for many days.

It is also a fact that M. Chauvelin, the accredited agent of the French Republican Government, was not present at that or any other social function in London, after that memorable evening at Lord Grenville's ball.

9 788027 278695